I0735635

SILENT GUARDIAN

BOOKS 1 TO 3 IN BRANDON & MELODY'S STORY

SHANDI BOYES

Edited by
SWISH DESIGN & EDITING
Illustrated by
SSB COVERS & DESIGN

COPYRIGHT

Copyright © 2020 by Shandi Boyes

All rights reserved.

No part of this book may be reproduced in any form or by any electronic or mechanical means, including information storage and retrieval systems, without written permission from the author, except for the use of brief quotations in a book review.

Editing: Swish Design and Editing

Proofreading: Swish Design and Editing

Second Proof: Magnolia Author Services

Cover: SSB Covers and Design

Photograph: Lindee Robinson Photography

Model: Blake McKinney

DEDICATION

For those seeking courage,

You don't need to be the biggest dog to have the loudest bark. Just like you don't need to be the most vicious to have the toughest bite.

Be you, as there is no one fiercer than a person who knows their capabilities.

Shandi xx

PLAYLIST

You Said You'd Grow Old With Me - **Michael Schlute**

In Case You Didn't Know - **Boyce Avenue**

Supermarket Flowers - **Ed Sheehan**

No Matter What - **Calum Scott**

Memories - **Shawn Mendes**

Yesterdays Gone - **Angels Fall**

One Call Away - **Charlie Puth**

You can find Shandi's entire playlist here: https://open.spotify.com/playlist/0XfLHAaHPCuEtRGKIhko5X

ALSO BY SHANDI BOYES

Perception Series

Saving Noah (Noah & Emily)

Fighting Jacob (Jacob & Lola)

Taming Nick (Nick & Jenni)

Redeeming Slater (Slater and Kylie)

Saving Emily (Noah & Emily - Novella)

Wrapped Up with Rise Up (Perception Novella - should be read after the Bound Series)

Enigma

Enigma (Isaac & Isabelle #1)

Unraveling an Enigma (Isaac & Isabelle #2)

Enigma The Mystery Unmasked (Isaac & Isabelle #3)

Enigma: The Final Chapter (Isaac & Isabelle #4)

Beneath The Secrets (Hugo & Ava #1)

Beneath The Sheets (Hugo & Ava #2)

Spy Thy Neighbor (Hunter & Paige)

The Opposite Effect (Brax & Clara)

I Married a Mob Boss (Rico & Blaire)

Second Shot (Hawke & Gemma)

The Way We Are (Ryan & Savannah #1)

The Way We Were (Ryan & Savannah #2)

Sugar and Spice (Cormack & Harlow)

Lady In Waiting (Regan & Alex #1)

Man in Queue (Regan & Alex #2)

Couple on Hold(Regan & Alex #3)

Enigma: The Wedding (Isaac and Isabelle)

Silent Vigilante (Brandon and Melody #1)

Hushed Guardian (Brandon & Melody #2)

Quiet Protector (Brandon & Melody #3)

Enigma: An Isaac Retelling

Twisted Lies (Jae & CJ)

Bound Series

Chains (Marcus & Cleo #1)

Links(Marcus & Cleo #2)

Bound(Marcus & Cleo #3)

Restrain(Marcus & Cleo #4)

The Misfits

Russian Mob Chronicles

Nikolai: A Mafia Prince Romance (Nikolai & Justine #1)

Nikolai: Taking Back What's Mine (Nikolai & Justine #2)

Nikolai: What's Left of Me(Nikolai & Justine #3)

Nikolai: Mine to Protect(Nikolai & Justine #4)

Asher: My Russian Revenge (Asher & Zariah)

Nikolai: Through the Devil's Eyes(Nikolai & Justine #5)

Trey (Trey & K)

The Italian Cartel

Dimitri

Roxanne

Reign

Mafia Ties (Novella)

Maddox

Demi

Rocco

Clover

Smith

RomCom Standalones

Just Playin' (Elvis & Willow)

Ain't Happenin' (Lorenzo & Skylar)

The Drop Zone (Colby & Jamie)

Very Unlikely (Brand New Couple)

Short Stories - Newsletter Downloads

Christmas Trio (Wesley, Andrew & Mallory -- short story)

Falling For A Stranger (Short Story)

One Night Only Series

Hotshot Boss

Hotshot Neighbor

The Bobrov Bratva Series

Wicked Intentions (Katie & Ghost)

Sinful Intentions (April 25)

Devious Intentions (June 13)

WANT TO STAY IN TOUCH?

Facebook: facebook.com/authorshandi

Instagram: instagram.com/authorshandi

Email: authorshandi@gmail.com

Reader's Group: bit.ly/ShandiBookBabes

Website: authorshandi.com

Newsletter: https://www.subscribepage.com/AuthorShandi

SILENT VIGILANTE

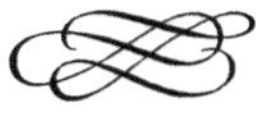

BRANDON

SIX YEARS OLD.

"Here. We can hide down here."

I flip over the bright pink ruffle skirt on Melody's Minnie Mouse bedspread before crawling under her bed. A cold breeze whistles through the cracks in the bendy floorboards, and it's dusty and dark, but I can keep Melody safe down here like I pinkie promised her dad two days after we met.

Melody had never lived in the country before. She came from one of those towns with big buildings that go all the way up into the sky. My horses scared her. My dogs scared her. Pretty much anything that moved scared her… except my mom and me. That's probably because we arrived to greet our new neighbors with freshly baked cookies. Only a silly person would be scared of peanut butter and chocolate chip cookies.

Melody isn't silly. She's really, *really* pretty.

Madden thinks so too.

I hate that my brother wants to be Melody's friend too, but Melody tells me I don't have to be mad. She thinks Madden is weird. He kind of is. For one, he doesn't like chocolate. Who doesn't like chocolate? I love chocolate. Do you?

When Melody joins me under her bed, I get a pain in my chest when I see how much water is in her eyes. They're so full, they are about to burst like our water balloons did earlier today when I filled them with too much water. I don't like it when Melody cries. It makes me sad.

After balancing my sweaty head on Melody's forehead, I cup my best friend's ears with my chubby hands. Mommy says Melody has doll's eyes because they're always twinkling. I think they're one of the things that make her pretty. They're as sparkly as the marbles digging in my hip and just as big.

I should've swapped sides with Melody, then she'd be better protected from the man chasing us down, and I wouldn't have a sore backside tomorrow. Marbles hurt. Not as much as Daddy's belt when Mommy goes to grandma's house, but they make some of the gloss in Melody's eyes jump into mine.

I won't cry, I'm too brave for that. Mr. Gregg tells me that very thing every time he sees me. I like his praise. He's so nice to me. When I look up at the stars stuck to the ceiling in my room, I wish for him to become my dad. He doesn't have much money, and he leaves his home for a long, *long* time to work, but he's still a good dad.

Melody's eyes shine with more wetness when the creak of the stairs in her family ranch vibrates through the gap in my fingers. According to my mom, I'm still carrying baby fat, so I should be able to block out the vibrations making Melody scared, but I'm not. I'm nose-bombing—*again.*

I'm still in trouble from pretending to be sick last week. Unlike two of my older brothers, Madden and Phoenix, I don't like going hunting with our dad. Watching Madden burn the wings off butterflies with a magnifying glass makes my tummy feel yucky, so I don't want to see what he does to the deer they catch. Just the thought has the peanut butter and jelly sandwiches Melody and I ate at lunch creeping up my food pipe.

Don't they know what they're doing is wrong? Melody and I

watched a special show with Melody's mommy one day that said even killing something as little as an ant can be catastrophic.

When you hurt something on purpose, you can cause a tornado. I don't want to cause a tornado, they make a lot of mess, so every time my dad packs up his big truck to go hunting, I pretend I'm sick. It makes him not like me, and he calls me names when Mommy isn't around, but I'm sure once he realizes I'm stopping our house from being demolished by a tornado, he'll love me again. Maybe.

Determined to show my dad I'm as brave as Mr. Gregg says, I wiggle closer to my very best friend in the world. Once Melody's heart is felt thumping against my chest, I calm the fear in her eyes as her daddy taught me. "One Mississippi. Two Mississippi. Three Mississippi…" By the time I reach five, Melody counts with me. She doesn't speak the words I do, but her lips mimic the movements mine make.

She's as brave as me. I just forget all the time because she's so pretty. You can't be brave and pretty at the same time.

I don't think.

"Six Mississippi. Seven—" I clutch my ears to stop Melody's screams from piercing my eardrums when her ankle is grabbed, and she's pulled out from beneath her bed. She holds her arms out for me to grab her, but I'm too slow. She's yanked away from me too quickly.

"No! Mellowy!" As I crawl out from beneath her bed, my heart makes a weird *boom-boom, boom-boom* noise. I can feel it in my throat. It's right where my roar-box sits, which I use a second later while charging for the man taking Melody away from me.

He wobbles more than you'd think when I push him in his stomach, and my leg barely touches his ankles when I try to swipe his feet out from beneath him, but he topples to the ground with a thud, making me leap into the air like a bullfrog.

I should be scared or crying in fear of the punishment I could face if my father finds out what I did, but I can't stop smiling about the praise Mr. Gregg bombards me with for taking him down. "Yes,

Brandon! Well done. You saved Melody just like you've been taught."

After placing a grinning Melody onto her feet, her daddy makes his way to me. He messes up my snow-white hair with his fingers before pulling me into his ginormous chest for a hug. "I'm so proud of you, Brandon." He tugs at the messy brown, green, and cream material of his pants before kneeling next to me, meeting me eye to eye. My father wears the same pants when he goes to work, but I've never seen his eyes shine as brightly as Mr. Gregg's when he signs to Melody and me, *"Remember, brave men and women always protect, honor, obey, serve—"*

"And eat cookies!" Melody and I sign in sync, giggling.

"Yes, cookies," Melody's dad responds both verbally and through sign language.

With an arm around each of our waists, he carries Melody and me down the stairs of her family ranch like we're the big bag he throws over his shoulder every time he goes to work. The *clomp, clomp, clomp* of his boots on the old stairwell makes my stomach rattle as much as my teeth. He's so big, every step he takes makes me feel like my bones are going to pop out of their skin.

When we enter the kitchen, my mouth salivates. Mrs. Gregg is removing peanut butter and chocolate chip cookies from the oven. They're my favorite, and the exact cookies Mrs. Gregg bakes for me every time I do Mr. Gregg's special drills.

Melody slaps a hand over her still misty eyes when Mr. Gregg plants a big sloppy kiss onto Mrs. Gregg's lips. She thinks it's gross when they kiss. I kind of like it.

Not them kissing… eww! They're really old, like nearly at the age of death, so I don't like watching them suck face like the kissing fish at the aquarium. My tummy gets a squidgy feeling wondering what Melody would do if I kissed her like her dad always kisses her mom. Will I get girl germs like my brothers say? And if I do, will those germs kill me?

I must be extra brave today because even with death being a

possibility, I lean across Mr. Gregg's huge and hard stomach to press my lips to Melody's cheek. I don't die, and she doesn't pull away, but I don't think cooties kill you when you kiss a girl.

I think their daddies do.

MELODY

TEN YEARS OLD.

I plop onto the soggy ground with a huff, annoyed, cold, and hungry. It doesn't take my best friend long to notice I've stopped running through the knee-high fields that border our family homes. He was holding my hand right up until the stage I decided to quit. I'm tired of the drills my father makes us do every weekend. I just want to watch movies and eat popcorn like a regular kid.

"Mellowy, what are you doing?"

The pain in my chest lessens at Brandon's purposeful incorrect signaling of my name. He's still learning his Ds, so he leaves them out while communicating with me via sign language. A bug made my mommy sick when I was growing in her tummy, so my ears didn't work when I was born. There's a special thingamabob the doctors can put on my ears, but since it costs a lot of money, I haven't got one yet. Daddy says I'll get one soon, but I'm not worried. Brandon can understand me, and that's all that matters.

Brandon taps my shoulder to return my focus to him before signing, *"We have to keep going. He is coming for us."*

"Let him come. I am tired." The slow movements of my hands reveal the honesty of my reply. I'm zonked.

Brandon shakes his head. *"We can't give up. Giving up isn't an option."* He bends down until his big hazel eyes meet mine. He had a growth spurt this year, but I'm still exactly an inch taller than him— not that he'll ever admit it. *"Just a little bit further, okay? I can see the fort we built last month just over there."*

My eyes stray in the direction he's pointing. Although I can see the fort made out of sticks, branches, and mesh camo material, I still want to stay put. This isn't normal. Mrs. Sprigs, my school guidance counselor, told me so, and if you take Brandon out of the equation, none of my friends think this is normal either.

I don't want bad men to hurt my mommy like they did five years ago, but I don't want to keep remembering either. The nightmares make me wake up in the middle of the night with soaked clothes. I don't know if my sheets are wet because I sweat so much while running away from the bad men chasing me, or if it's from the tears I cry when they catch me. If the wet patches that circle Brandon's shirt every time he wakes me from a nightmare are anything to go by, I think tears are to blame.

Before the bad men broke into my house, my daddy was a fun man. He taught me how to ride a bike and didn't care that the men in his barracks didn't like his bedazzled duffle bag. I made it for him, so he loved it.

He still uses the duffle bag I prettied up for him, but I haven't seen his real smile in a very long time. He gives us the fake one he gave Grandma whenever she visited. I know why he gave her his pretend smile. She was mean and a big 'O' word I can't pronounce much less sign. My mommy said it meant she thought she was better than my daddy. I think that makes my grandma a cow. No man is better than my daddy except perhaps Brandon. But he's not really a man. He's just a boy. A very handsome boy who pretends he's bigger than he is when we do our fathers' drills.

"Hop on my back. I will piggyback you," Brandon signs, smiling when he demonstrates the sign for piggyback.

My heart goes *bang, bang, bang* against my chest when he glances at me, waiting for my response. It does the same thing anytime his big, chubby cheeks turn the color of the roses my daddy buys my mommy. My mom says boys who blush are boys worth fighting for. I don't know what that means, but I think it might have something to do with the time I pushed Tania Rich off the swing because I didn't like the kissy faces she was giving Brandon. Brandon is my best friend, so he can't be her friend too, can he?

When Brandon's snow-white brow disappears into his hair, I sign, *"I am bigger than you, BJ. You can't carry me across a sloshy field."*

He pulls a face like I'm silly. *"Yes, I can. Hop on. I will show you."* He twists around until his back is facing me, then he gestures for me to climb aboard.

I tap his shoulder to gain his attention before asking, *"Are you sure?"*

I could walk, but I'm so interested in discovering how strong Brandon is that when he nods his head assuring me he's tough, I leap onto his back like a frog.

A grunt rumbles through his body before he magically stands to his feet and takes three hesitant steps forward. He can't see my face, but I make sure my hands are in front of his before signing, *"You are doing it, BJ!"*

I'm so proud of him, I want to plant a sloppy kiss onto his cheek like he did to mine years ago, but before I can, the man who made Brandon pinkie promise to protect me for eternity snatches me off his back.

BRANDON

SEVENTEEN YEARS OLD

"Yes, Brandon. Keep going."

Sweat glides down my cheeks as I move around the frayed boxing ring in the shed at the back of the Greggs' family ranch. Mr. Gregg and I have been working out for the past two hours. The first hour and a half was the standard workout we do three to four times a week when he's not deployed, but things were switched-up half an hour ago when Melody arrived home with a handful of her friends.

They're supposed to be catching the rays of an early spring on the field between the house and the shed, but I've noticed their eyes straying my way more times than not. Their attention has me prancing around the boxing ring in a manner my father would approve of.

Mr. Gregg… not so much.

I'm not showboating because I like Melody's friends' attention. It's because I love the way Melody's eyes slant the longer they ogle me.

The kiss we shared eleven years ago, that innocent, inconsequential cheek peck that made me feel like a hawk soaring above the highest mountain is the only kiss we've shared. I wouldn't necessarily say I've been friend-zoned by Melody—we're as flirty as we are friendly—but I sure as hell have been placed in the penalty box by her father.

He wants me to protect his daughter, not drool over her.

For years, I despised Mr. Gregg for his somewhat overbearing fathering. It was only when I learned the reason for his manic obsession did I understand his desire to protect his wife and daughter.

The Greggs didn't move out of the big smoke for no reason. It was because Mr. Gregg knew a lower population meant there'd be less chance of his family being tormented by psychopaths for the second time in their lives.

I've only seen home invasions in movies. Melody can't say the same thing. She was only five when it occurred, but the memories in her head are crystal clear. She remembers her mom's horrified expression when she was dragged away from her, the way her nails clawed the floorboards, and the tears that rolled down her father's cheeks when they shredded his wife's pajamas off her body with a knife.

My chest absorbed Melody's tears many times during her first ten years here. When she climbed into my window in the middle of the night with an ashen face and eyes full of moisture, I knew she wasn't crying in fear. Her tears were for her father, the loving goofball she lost when his unanswered pleas to the men attacking his wife forced him to become just as violent as them.

Three men entered the Gregg property that cold winter's night. Only one left breathing, and the punishment the courts served him was nothing compared to the life sentence Mr. Gregg is facing. His wife stands by his side, and his daughter loves him, but even a seventeen-year-old kid can see that the demons of his past still haunt him.

The man who hurt his family is now walking the streets, and there isn't anything Mr. Gregg can do about it. He didn't face a jail term twelve years ago because a jury of his peers believed he had acted in self-defense. That wouldn't be the case this time around if he once again takes justice into his own hands. He knows the law better than anyone because not only has he served and protected his country for the past twenty-two years, he married a super-smart woman.

Mrs. Gregg, or Wren as she advised me to call her, had a fancy office with floor-to-ceiling windows. She earned triple what her husband did in the military, and even with her being half the age of her associates, was a valued member of the New York justice system.

That all came crumbling down after their home invasion. Wren was forced to go against her colleagues who wanted her husband prosecuted for the death of two of the men who terrorized her, and it took selling their basement brownstone to fund the fight.

They won. Mr. Gregg walked away without a conviction, which meant he could keep his position in the military, but they were homeless, and although Mr. Gregg will never admit, too scared to remain living in the city.

I hate what happened to them and the tears Melody has shed during the many drills her father has forced her to endure the past decade, but I'm also grateful. If their world wasn't upended, mine might very well have never started.

My father is still a vicious-speaking, cold-blooded tyrant, but the sting of his scorns hasn't burned as they once did when the Greggs became a part of my life. They taught me the difference between right and wrong, and just because someone tells you something, doesn't mean it's true. Even my mom has taken their advice.

When my father told her we're moving to the city, she advised him that his way of thinking wasn't how a marriage worked, and any decisions that affected the family as a whole would be discussed, not ordered.

Her newfound backbone didn't go down well with my father. It has caused months of tension and more shouted words the past year than the previous three, but we're still here in Saugerties where we've lived since I was born.

And where I'm most likely to be buried when Mr. Gregg's right hook sends Tweety birds flying around my head. "Focus, Brandon. All it takes is a second of distraction to cause years of misery." When he swings at my head again, I bob in just enough time before jabbing at the pads covering his hands. "Better. Keeping going."

I'm not big like my brothers. If we were dogs, I'd be called the runt of the litter, but what I lack in height and muscle density, I make up for with speed and agility. I've got bumps in my midsection. I just keep them hidden with shirts. I don't see the need to show them off. Melody knows they're there, and she's the only one I'm out to impress.

Besides, I don't mind being the smaller guy in the room. The men Mr. Gregg has me constantly on the lookout for expect less from me. They aren't bothered when I watch them closely. More times than not, they encourage my gawks.

They probably think I'm gay. The thought makes me smile. If Mr. Gregg knew the thoughts I had about his daughter in the shower most mornings, I'm confident he'd be wishing the same thing.

Melody has always been pretty, but once she grew into her big marble eyes and tulip-shaped nose, my description of her assets quickly switched to gorgeous. Her hair is the same dirty blonde coloring it was when she was a child, but she brushes out her wild kinks every morning. We lost our baby fat around the same time, although my face is still a little rounder than hers. I can't say the same thing about our pecs. Much to Mr. Gregg's disgrace, it appears as if Melody's chubby cheeks lowered to her chest.

We stand at almost the same height, which Melody assures is a shit-ton taller than her mother, but nowhere near as gigantic as her father. My brothers think it's hilarious we're the same height. They'd never date a girl as tall or taller than them. I think it's convenient. Melody and I meet eye to eye. Nose to nose. *Lips to lips.*

I snap back to reality when my name cracks from Mr. Gregg's mouth like a whip. "Brandon, focus!"

His right tap to my ear raises more than my defenses. It also sends my frustration skyrocketing. "All right, fuck."

My right rib, left bicep, and every inch of my jaw gets punished for my cuss word. To ensure Mr. Gregg gets his point across about how much he dislikes cursing, he swipes my feet out from beneath me.

I hit the deck with a groan, my lungs as windless as Melody's gasp when she watches me go down. She's seen her dad lose his cool before, but it isn't usually at me. *"Daddy!"* While *tsking* him without hand signals, she joins us ringside. *"You need to calm down."*

Mr. Gregg rakes a hand over his sweaty military-style haircut before speaking slow and precise to ensure Melody can read his lips. "He needs to practice, not spend our sessions perusing your body like certain parts of it are on a menu. Protect, honor, obey, and serve. It isn't that hard."

Melody's friends giggle during the first half of Mr. Gregg's highly accurate statement. They believe my 'friendship' with Melody is pathetic, and I quote, 'A real man would've gotten the job done months ago,' but they quiet down during the last half of his statement.

No one knows what the Greggs went through years ago because despite their belief that they're important to Liam, Wren, and Melody, they're not. Excluding my family, I can't recall the Greggs having a single person over for dinner the past ten years. Even today's visitors are a rarity. They're only here because Mr. Gregg refused Melody's request to go to the 'beach' with her friends. It's prime camping season time, which means unknown guests in our town are at a pinnacle. Mr. Gregg doesn't trust anyone outside of his inner circle. Fortunately for me, I was invited inside that exclusive circle well over a decade ago.

After shushing her friends whose sniggers are felt as much as they're heard with a wicked sideways glare, Melody folds her arms under her chest, making the wooziness in my head ten times worse.

When her father fails to respond to the million questions I see in her eyes, she unfolds her hands and signs, *"He needs to be a kid, Dad. Not your vigilante."*

This isn't the first time she has called out her father's interest in me for what it is. Mr. Gregg cares for me, and his guidance hasn't seen me tiptoeing over the line many boys my age have, but I'm aware the instant his daughter's safety isn't my utmost priority, he'd drop me for another soldier waiting in the wings.

Since I don't want that to happen, I use years of training to my advantage.

After flipping up onto my feet, I stun Mr. Gregg with an open-handed punch to his sternum before knocking him onto the mat with a roundhouse kick to his head. The leverage I get off the ground ends Melody's friends snickering in an instant, not to mention me removing my shirt to place it under Mr. Gregg's head when my kick to his temple dazes him enough he stays down for the count.

BRANDON

"*Brandon James McGee!*"

As her face turns the color of a beetroot, Melody crawls through the crumbling ropes surrounding the ring. To an outsider, she seems upset. Luckily for me, I've been her best friend for over twelve years, so I know every one of her moods. Today's isn't fueled by anger. Don't get me wrong, she's concerned for her father, but she's also proud of me.

How do I know this? The ghost-like smile stretched across her face is a good indicator, but what she signs next most certainly keeps my worry at bay. "*Stop standing there with your rooster chest puffed out and go get some ice.*" She only calls someone a rooster when the person gloating is someone she likes. If she isn't a fan of theirs, she calls them a peacock.

With my house closer to the Greggs' shed than theirs, I nod before hot-footing it toward the barbwire fence that separates our properties. When the tread on the bottom of my sneakers fails to gain traction with the recently varnished floorboards on the back patio of my family home, I crash into the rusty steel material my family likes to call 'the drinks fridge.' I hit it with an almighty bang, but I doubt anyone heard my collision. It's hard to hear anything over the shouted voices coming from the living room.

I can't tell who my mom and dad are fighting about, but I guarantee it's about either Madden or Phoenix. Mom uses the word 'unacceptable' too many times in a row for it not to be about my older brothers. Phoenix's wildness calmed a little bit when he left for college. The same can't be said for Madden. Between a suspension for fighting last month and an arrest for underage drinking just this past weekend, he's been keeping my parents on their toes.

They've got enough issues on their plate right now, but Madden is too selfish to see that. He hasn't noticed that our father doesn't come home for the weekends anymore, and the only time he's here is when there's a mess to be cleaned.

Mom says it's because he's busy with work aspirations. I know it's more than that, and as much as this sucks to admit, I hope today's fight will extend my father's absence to indefinitely. Phoenix and Madden will never agree with me, but our lives would be a whole heap less complicated if our father wasn't a part of it. He isn't necessarily evil. He's just someone I hope never to become.

My hand freezes halfway between the ice bag in the freezer and the cloth I'm filling when my father's roar reaches my ears. "They're boys for crying out loud. Let them be!"

That's his excuse for everything.

They are boys which means they're more adventurous than girls.

You don't understand them, Barbara, because you've never been a boy.

You didn't seem to have any issues when I pursued you in the same manner.

And my mom replies with the same retort. "Just because they're boys doesn't give them the right to be bullies."

I recommence filling an old rag with ice when my dad shoots out the back screen door that leads to the patio a few seconds later. He runs his hand over his slicked-back hair before dragging it down his reddened face. The military uniform he paraded around in when I was a kid has been switched to an expensive-looking suit.

Although his shoes are still polished to perfection, they're no longer military-issued boots. They are a funky pair of leather loafers that cost more than my parents' first car.

My father's first twenty years in the military served him well. He used his connections to shift his skills from the battlefields to court chambers not long after my tenth birthday. Then, when he was no longer satisfied being a 'mere JAG officer,' he sought a much-higher position in a chain of command that could take him to the White House.

Shockingly, he's been given everything he has demanded.

Mrs. Gregg isn't as surprised as me. She said the sections my father works in are very male-orientated, and my father is seen as 'one of the boys.' Her husband is not. Along with an undying pledge to protect his wife and daughter, Mr. Gregg is a huge campaigner for women's rights. He believes in equality in both the home and workplace.

It's another thing he doesn't have in common with my father.

My mom attended the same college as Wren. She was studying law and had planned to use her degree to help those less fortunate. Her ideas went up in smoke when she bumped into my father one rainy afternoon twenty-three years ago. She stupidly believed military men had values higher than those out of uniform.

She learned otherwise only a few short months later.

Two months after their whirlwind relationship started, they wed in a low-key ceremony. Three days after they married, and on the day she discovered she was pregnant with Phoenix, my mom was encouraged to postpone her studies, so she'd have time for 'a more important role of wife and mother.' She agreed on the stipulation she'd finalize her degree once Phoenix was twelve months old.

That never happened. Madden was born only a month after Phoenix's first birthday, then Joey and I followed closely behind them.

My mom says she doesn't mind that her dreams were placed on the back-burner to become an at-home mom and wife, but I saw the disappointment in her eyes when my dad took it upon himself to borrow her dreams.

My father's step up from JAG officer to General adjourned his need to rule supreme in all aspects of his life for almost four years, but once the military couldn't satiate the craving any longer, he looked at America as a whole, aka, he shifted his focus to politics.

His run for Congress started at the District Attorney's Office a few years ago where he became an ADA. During his stint there, he chaired many charities, but it was my mom who did most of the heavy lifting. At my father's request, she signed on for way too many charity events than a woman raising four boys could handle. It put a toll on her time, and her relationship with her kids and marriage has suffered since—not that my father has noticed.

With one stepping stone out of the way, he's now vying for the top job. He wants to become the DA before using his connections there to help his bid for Congress. Mr. Gregg argues that a senator has more power than a congressman, but my dad is quick to disagree. He states it's the congressman who runs the state, so he must have more power than the Senate. Since politics have never been my thing, I tune out their debates as quickly as I try to ignore my father's attention when he notices me awkwardly standing at his side.

As his eyes glide down my half-naked form, the agitated expression on his face doubles. I'm not surprised. Disdain hardens his features every time we cross paths. Instead of appreciating that I haven't given him anywhere near as many gray hairs as my older brothers, he objectifies it. I don't know why. Perhaps it's because I never grew a love for hunting. Or maybe it's because I'm more like our mother than him. Whatever it is, we've never seen eye to eye, and it has nothing to do with the fact I don't stand as tall as him.

I'm saved from being scrutinized by him further when Madden's 1971 Pontiac GTO rockets down the driveway, producing a bloom of dust to follow its trail. He was gifted the rebuilt car on his birthday a little over eight weeks ago. I was pleased with my father's generosity—he's always been more stingy than lavish—but I was also pissed.

Mr. Gregg and I have been rebuilding a 1969 Charger Hellcat for years. It took us over three years to return the motor to its original condition, and for the past six months, we've worked on the interior and bodywork—which just happens to be the exact style and color to the car Madden was gifted.

It could be a coincidence, but just like I know there's more to my father's disinterest than my mom is letting on, I'm also skeptical Madden's car isn't almost identical to the one Mr. Gregg planned to gift me on my eighteenth birthday in four months for no reason. My father hates the relationship I have with the Greggs, so he's forever seeking a crack in the unbreakable foundation we've forged the past twelve years.

I work the rag full of ice from one hand to the other to hide their twitch when Madden parks his sleek ride an inch away from the back patio. He was only gifted his pride and joy two short months ago, yet it's already sporting a large graze down one side. It also doesn't look like it's seen a bucket and sponge since it was driven off the lot.

"I swear to God, Dad, it isn't as she's saying." While tucking his polo shirt into his ripped jeans, hoping a tidy appearance will hide his leering grin, Madden rounds the hood of his car. "You know what girls are like. As soon as the cinema security guard caught our little escapade, she pledges allegiance to sainthood."

After climbing the three stairs of the porch, Madden's blue eyes swing my way. He looks like he wants to say something about me lurking at the side, but our father steals his attention before he can. "She's the police chief's daughter, Madden."

"Exactly! That's my point." He slaps our father in the chest like he's one of his buddies. "She was all for it until the guard threatened to call her daddy, then the tears came out. I cross my heart..." he physically crosses his heart, "... that I only touched her *after* she begged me." His chest puffs high as arrogance beams from his eyes.

"I'm a star quarterback, for crying out loud, and I don't need to scare a high school senior into letting me touch her."

My eyes shoot to my dad when he growls under his breath, "The security officer noted in his report that you had your hand over her mouth."

Madden's scoff hides his snicker. "That's because her moans were going to get us busted." He stops, twists his smiling lips, then whispers, "They *got* us busted." When the anger lining Dad's face deepens, Madden tries another angel. "Call Racer. He organized our double date with Fable and Annie. He'll give you Fable's number. She's Annie's best friend, so she won't keep quiet if she thinks I hurt Annie."

This kills me to admit, but he has a good argument. Fable and Annie have been friends for as long as Melody and me. I can sure as hell tell you I'd have Melody's back before anyone's—even my brothers—so if Fable agrees with Madden's recollection of events, I don't see why our father won't.

When Dad jerks up his chin agreeing to investigate Madden's side of the story, Madden digs his Google Nexus One out of his pocket, doubling my jealousy. I still have an old flip phone with a cracked screen.

The wealthier my father becomes, the more generous he is, but only with the people he likes.

I'm not on that list.

After giving our father Racer's phone number, Madden stuffs his phone back into his pocket before shifting his focus to me. "Can you believe the lies girls come up with to remain pure in their daddies eyes?" Although he's asking a question, he doesn't give me a chance to answer him. "Kinda like her, hey?" He nudges his head to Melody, who's carefully slipping through the barbwire fence dividing our properties, so none of the skin her denim shorts and bikini top doesn't conceal is nipped. "I bet she's still running the we're-best-friends line to her dad, isn't she?" He rubs his hands together as his teeth graze his lower lip. "What's she like in bed? Phoenix swears the quiet ones are usually the wildest, so a deaf girl must be extra kinky."

I want to show him the ridges in my midsection aren't drawn on, but years of tactical response training ensures I don't respond to goading like most seventeen-year-old boys do. Besides, the sexual undertone in Madden's voice isn't anything for me to worry about. Even with my eyes narrowed into tiny slits, I can't miss the gag working up from Melody's stomach to her throat when she spots Madden's admired glare. She doesn't just think he's weird anymore, she thinks he's a creep, and I'm inclined to agree with her.

"Madden..." Melody signs in greeting before sidestepping him as if he's a fresh pile of dog shit. *"Don't worry about the ice. Dad is up and about."* Her smile makes my cheeks heat more than Madden's eyes being locked on her backside. Her teasing smirks have kept me awake many nights the past four years. *"Although I would not recommend coming over for an hour or two. He is demanding a second round."*

I bite my bottom lip with the hope it will slacken my smile. I don't want her thinking I liked hurting her father. It's the pride beaming from her eyes I'm eager to gobble up. We've been waiting over ten years for this day, so it's hard not to celebrate.

In any of the drills Mr. Gregg ran, it was always Melody and me against him. Although we came close a few times, today is the first time we can say we won without a smidge of doubt.

I stop grinning like an idiot when Melody signs, *"Mom is taking us to get milkshakes at Mary's Diner. Do you wanna come?"*

"Us?"

When she waves her hand at our right, I peer over at her friends waiting her return next to her old family sedan. The heat of their admiring gazes is felt from a distance, but since Madden is standing at my side, wiggling his fingers at them like he's a rock star and they're a bunch of horny groupies, I can't be confident they won't rag on me the entire time we're out.

Melody is great, I love spending time with her—especially the rare snippets of alone time we get—but the female half of her friends sure know how to make a guy feel the size of an ant. I'm relatively sure they're mocking is done in jest, but even the best jokes get stale when they're used on repeat.

My eyes drift back to Melody. *"I am good. I have got our bio-chem final to study for. I need to ace this test to guarantee my spot at Browns."*

I trained extensively in sign language twelve years ago. It was a struggle at the start, but now it seems like a walk in the park compared to the studying we've been doing the past four weeks. We're hoping to secure dual scholarships to the number one college in our state, which means we need above-average grades. We started our admissions process back in our sophomore year, so we'd have a jump on the students who usually begin their college search during their junior year. Melody wants to be a lawyer like her mother, and much to my father's disgrace, I'm hoping to study forensic science.

Our early-decision applications were approved at the commencement of our studies this year, but because it needed a binding commitment Melody's parents weren't able to commit to, we declined the agreement and applied for a scholarship instead. That was over ten months ago. We've yet to hear back from them. We've several rolling admissions lodged with other universities, but we have our fingers crossed our above-average grades will guarantee us a placement at Browns.

Melody's eyes drop to my lips when I say, *"Maybe once you finish your milkshake, you can come study with me?"*

"Okay. That sounds good. But I should warn you... I have not looked at my bio-chem notes in almost four weeks."

When she pulls an 'eek' face, I throw my head back and laugh. *"You better not let your mother hear that, or you can kiss your milkshake goodbye."*

She signs so fast, I almost miss what she says, *"I know. Why do you think I said it all the way over here?"*

Her hand shoots out to squeeze mine when I laugh again. It sends an electrical current shooting up my arm and has my pulse returning to what it was when I was prancing around the boxing ring. It's always like this with us—little touches that seem so much more than they are.

"Are you sure you don't want to come with us, BJ? I heard Mary has taken quite a liking to your dollop of peanut butter suggestion. It is more popular than she thought."

Mary, the owner of Mary's Café, almost castrated me last month when I asked her to add a dollop of peanut butter into my chocolate milkshake before whisking it. It took numerous reassurances that I'd clean up my mess if my experiment backfired before she succumbed to my plea.

My concoction wasn't just good, it was fucking delicious. Even Melody agreed, and she doesn't have a fascination with peanut butter like I do.

I love peanut butter. Not quite as much as the pleading look Melody is giving me, but it's an unhealthy relationship no matter how much I sugarcoat it.

Excitement tap dances through my veins when a brilliant idea pops into my head. *"While you hang out with your friends, I will get a head start on our study session. That way, we might be able to squeeze in a quick movie before your curfew tonight."*

Melody twists on the spot, hoping a touch of innocence will hide the wild child in her eyes dying to break free. With how opposing our personalities are, you wouldn't think our bond is as unbreakable as it is. *"Watching* 10 Things I Hate About You *for the hundredth time doesn't sound like a fun way to spend a Saturday night, BJ."*

I usually sign and speak at the same time to ensure everyone around us is included in our conversation, but since I have a set of ears listening that I don't want, I only sign my reply. Madden knows basic sign language but not enough to understand what I say to Melody. *"It will be if we do it snuggled under a blanket while drinking the frozen chocolate and peanut butter milkshakes you are going to bring back from Mary's."*

Although cautious as to why my lips didn't move, a zing of excitement still zaps through Melody's impressive eyes. It's amazing the safety net that comes with a little bit of coverage. We're a tad more touchy-feely friends when we're snuggled under a blanket. I can't really give our sneaky touches a base range, but I can tell you they're getting more adventurous as the years move on.

"Okay. I can do that." Melody soothes the fidgeting movements of her hands before adding, *"I will be back in around an hour."*

She looks like she wants to say more but settles for another squeeze of my hand before pivoting on her heels, dashing down the stairs, and jogging across the ground that will soon be dry because of the ghastly heat of summer instead of a freezing winter. We only have two temperature settings here in Saugerties. It's either boiling hot or freezing cold. There's no in-between.

Madden waits for Melody to slip in the front passenger seat of her family sedan before howling in hysterics. "Are you fucking kidding me? How long have you been aiming to tap that, yet you still haven't gotten past first base?" He slaps his knees as tears threaten to spill from his eyes. "Word to the wise, no matter what language she speaks, when a girl squeezes your hand, she wants you to squeeze her ass while riding her hard."

To ensure I can't misunderstand what he's saying, he gropes an invisible ass in front of him before jackknifing his hips on repeat. When he adds horse neighs into the mix, I dump the rag of ice into the freezer, then push off my feet with a shake of my head. "Things aren't like that with us. We're friends."

That hurt to say as much as Madden's ear-piercing laughter hurts my ears. I want to be more than Melody's friend. I just haven't worked out how to officially slide us from friends to lovers without risking our decade-long friendship. What if I'm reading the signs all wrong? And no, I'm not referring to the secret sign language code we made up when we were kids.

What if she only likes teasingly touching me because it's a secret? There's a lot of excitement attached to doing something you're not supposed to, and when you've been sheltered as much as Melody has, I'm certain it's even more appealing.

Madden follows me into our country style kitchen before asking a question he's asked a minimum of once a month for the past three years. "Are you gay?"

My heart rate jumps as high as my voice. "No!"

"Then what's the issue?" He props his hip onto the counter before plucking a handful of grapes out of the fruit bowl. For someone in the process of having a sexual assault case investigated by our father, he looks way too smug for my liking. His cockiness isn't unusual, but it's annoying as hell. "If you're not gay, and she's good to go, why haven't you fucked her yet? She was practically begging for you to do her on the porch."

The throb of my pulse is heard in my reply. "Because I respect her too much to disrespect her like that."

Madden's boisterous laugh awards me the glare of my father. I don't know why he's glaring at me, I'm not the one chuckling like a hyena, but no matter how far I step away from Madden with my hands held in the air, pleading innocence, our father's eyes remain rapt on me.

When subjected to undeserving anger, my mood gets sappy. "Do you need a reminder on what that call is about?" I motion our head to our father who's on the phone in the den. "If you had respected Annie, our father wouldn't be once again sporting his defense attorney cap."

"Whatever! I gave Annie what she wanted." He grabs at his crotch like he's about to star in a new hip-hop music video. "She's just disappointed she didn't get this." He steps up to me, chest to chest. "Just like you won't be craving kiddie milkshakes after Melody milks your dick of your spawn." He knocks me with his shoulder, ensuring I'm aware he noticed the pulse in my jaw before snickering. "You better hurry. If you wait too long, she'll move onto a guy who isn't nervous about giving her what she wants."

You have no clue how hard it is for me not to respond to the daring glint in his eyes. My fists are clenched at my side, and my nostrils are flaring, but Mr. Gregg's constant reassurance that bullying is the highest form of flattery keeps my hands at my side and my words in my throat.

Only those below you try and force you to stoop to their level.

Madden is my brother, so I'd like to believe if worse came to worst, he'd have my back as I'd have his, but none of that matters when it comes to Melody. I pledged to protect her before I even knew what the word meant.

I plan to keep my promise.

My intense stare-down with Madden ends when our father tosses his cell phone onto the dining room table on our right. After straightening his tie and suit jacket, he thrusts a hand at the stairwell. "Go to your room."

I return his stare, confident he's looking at the wrong son. When my stare doubles the pulse in his jaw, I splatter out, "Why am I being sent to my room? I didn't do anything wrong. Madden is the one—"

"Now, Brandon!" He steps up to me like Madden did, except he doesn't keep his hands balled at his side. He raises one high into the air, ensuring it has plenty of leverage if I dare to argue with him.

As hot breaths pump out of my nose, I march toward the stairwell. My stomps are extra firm with annoyance, but no amount of hullabaloo stops me from hearing Madden growl. "Fuck this. I'm out. If a few hours of being grounded in my room saves me from being lectured, I'll take it."

Our father's roar rumbles through my chest. "Sit down, Madden!" Things must be severe because he only ever uses our full names when we're in deep shit.

When I reach the landing in the middle of the L-shaped stairs, I crank my neck in just enough time to see my father forcefully shove Madden into a dining room chair. My Adam's apple bobs up and down in sync with Madden's when our father gets up right into Madden's face and snarls, "Because after what I just lost to keep your ass out of jail, you're sure as fuck going to get more than a lecture."

MELODY

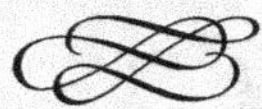

I glance at two of my friends in the back seat of my parents' station wagon when my mom pulls up to the curb in front of Mary's Café instead of parking in the dusty lot in the back. The apprehension on my face triples when she thrusts a bundle of notes at me across Carmen's chest before telling me she'll collect me after she finishes running some errands.

Excluding school, where either her or my dad drop me off and pick me up every *single* day, she's never left me alone. Our home invasion didn't just create cracks in my parents' marriage, it completely changed their outlook on life. They don't trust anyone—not even me—so I'm not just surprised by her decision today, I'm truly shocked.

Carmen snatches the bundle of notes I'm too stunned to accept before bumping me with her hip, demanding I scoot out of the relic dual bench-seat car before my mom changes her mind. Her bossy demeanor has us joining our friends on the footpath in a record-breaking two seconds, and even quicker than that, my mom pulls away from the curb.

While my friends count out my mom's generosity, which, in case you're wondering, is an impressive fifty-eight dollars, I watch my mom in her rearview mirror she's fiddling with while pulling into the steady flow of traffic.

Our eyes remain locked until the generous pitch of a rusty F150's roof steals them from my view. Her gaze is unsettling, and it sets off a kaleidoscope of butterflies in my stomach. It's not the same type of flutter I get when Brandon loads the DVD player with the corny romcoms we watch most weekends. It's ickier than that.

"*Come on, Mel,*" Carmen signs before pointing to her lips, so I can read the words she can't sign. "This is what freedom feels like. You're supposed to relish the loosening of the reigns, not rebel against it." She curls her arms around my shoulders, guides me into Mary's Café, then stops to stand in front of me. "You're eighteen next month. You're practically an adult. Live a little."

A smile tugs on my lips when the undeniable scent of peanut butter filters into my nose when I roll my eyes at Carmen's theatrics before walking into the main part of the café. Brandon should have patented his warped sense of taste. He would have made a killing from Mary's alone. It appears as if everyone here is giving his Peanut Choc Crunch Shake a try. I'm not a fan of peanut butter like Brandon, but I can admit the frozen version of his concoction is drool-worthy. That might have more to do with the fact we share the same spoon while eating, but it's still delicious, nonetheless.

By the time my friends have decided what flavored milkshake they'd like, twenty minutes has ticked by on the clock. I'm not necessarily counting down the minutes of freedom I have before I go back to the strict, no-leeway household I was raised in, but I'm curious as to how long my mom will be gone. Today is so out of character for her, I'm beginning to wonder if I'm dreaming.

I'm startled to within an inch of my life when a tattooed hand glides down my forearm. "Any tips for a novice milkshake mixer?" The fact the stranger speaks slowly reveals he knows I'm deaf. I'm not surprised. When you're the only deaf person at your school, word gets around. Also, I'm certain we've met previously, but his name is slipping my mind.

A smile full of praise raises my cheeks when I point to Brandon's concoction.

My guest twists his puffy lips while signing, *"Peanut butter and milk. I am not convinced."*

"You can sign?"

He smiles at the excitement on my face before jerking up his chin. *"My mom is deaf."*

"Sweet. Then you can trust me when I sign that that milkshake is the bomb."

My reply is a little dramatic, but it's fun interacting with people who can understand me—for a change. I don't see that being the case if it were an everyday occurrence, but since it's a rarity in my life, I'm going to treasure it. Although it won't be closer to what Carmen is suggesting behind the stranger's shoulder. She's air-humping him from a distance while pulling faces not suitable for public, but between those unladylike gestures, she's giving me clear live-it-up signs.

"All right." The stranger holds his hands out in front of himself like he's seconds from being arrested. *"I will take your signed oath."* After placing an order with the dairy clerk behind the counter, he shifts his blue eyes to me. *"What are you having?"*

I wave my hand through the air, shooing away his offer as if it's a fly. *"Thanks for the offer, but I am okay. I'm not just ordering for me. I am going to take an afternoon treat home for my friend."*

He slants his head to the side, his smile cocky. *"Do you live with this... friend?"* Even a sign language novice wouldn't have missed the disappointment in his unvoiced question. His facial expressions are very telling.

"Ah... no. He lives next door." I want to sign, *and he is more than a friend,* but since that isn't technically true, I keep that snippet of information to myself.

I've liked Brandon for years, but excluding the times his hands are hidden by a blanket, he doesn't touch me. Part of me thinks it's because he's trying to be respectful to my dad, but sometimes I worry that it's more than that. Perhaps he doesn't like me as much as I do him? My girlfriends assure me that isn't the case, but considering they think Brandon is below my league, they're not the best judges of character.

Although, I bet their opinion changed after watching Brandon take down my dad. When Suzie talked about him the entire twenty-minute drive to Mary's, she spoke so fast, I only caught parts of her gushing, and Racheal's nods of agreement were way too eager for my liking. I care for my friends, but Brandon is out-of-bounds for both their negative and positive praise. From my father's drills to creating our own secret language, it has always been us against the world, and I want to keep it that way.

The stranger returns my attention to him by clicking his fingers before signing, *"What would your neighbor like to eat?"*

My friends swarm closer like they did when Brandon removed his shirt as I reply to the stranger's gall with a touch of his cocky attitude. *"He is a growing man, so his choice in meals will most likely be out of price range."*

He doesn't even flinch at the snarky expression on my face. *"How about you let me be the judge of that?"*

"Okay." I peruse the menu board, acting as if I don't already know the most expensive item on the menu. I order it every time Madden is trying to act flashy in front of his friends by paying for everyone's meals. *"He will have the Wagyu beef burger with sweet potato fries and onion rings... if you can afford it."*

As the stranger chews on the silver ring in the corner of his bottom lip, his eyes rake my body. His prolonged stare is similar to the one Madden gave me earlier, just less creepy, although it does advise I'm treading in water way out of my depth.

I feel the vibrations of my friends hollers when the stranger asks, *"And you? What would you like to eat, duchess?"*

BRANDON

I catch a tennis ball in my hand when a knock sounds from my bedroom window. I've been bouncing it off the closet wall in my room for the past three hours. I'm bored out of my mind and should've filled the time studying, but the shouting that bellowed up the stairwell for the past two and a half hours had my mind on other things.

Since the floorboards in my house are better filled than Melody's were when she moved in twelve years ago, I couldn't hear much of the argument my parents had after Madden's lecture, but I'm confident in saying it wasn't the standard one they've had once a week for the past year.

This one had nothing to do with my dad's wish for us to move into the city, and everything to do with Madden's claims he didn't sexually assault Annie.

Fable agreed with Madden's recollection of events, but Annie's father wasn't buying it. Just like Mr. Gregg, he'd do anything to protect his daughter—even going against the man helming his campaign to be re-elected to his position.

I don't know what my father gave Mr. Langfield to weaken the

33

severity of Madden's fuck-up, but it must have been substantial because not only was Madden lectured for almost two hours, he was forced to hand over the keys to his pride and joy.

This frustrates me to admit, but with nothing but silence to occupy myself the past three hours, I looked a little deeper into what Madden said before our father ended our conversation. Not the gleam his eyes got when he underhandedly hinted he could give Melody want she wants if I wasn't up to the task, but his comment about girls squeezing your hand when they want you to squeeze their ass.

Whether under the blanket while we're watching a movie, when we were hiding out during one of her dad's many drills, and multiple times during our trips to school, Melody forever squeezes my hand. It's one of the touches we do even when we're in public, and it has me hopeful our slide from friends to lovers will be easier than predicated.

Even now, after crawling through the window I've just cranked open for her, Melody's hand shoots out to squeeze mine before she thrusts a grease-sodden bag into my chest. *"Sorry your burger and fries have gone cold. I ordered your stuff when I ordered mine, then we stayed longer than planned."* When guilt darts through her brown eyes, she shifts them to my empty desk. Her brows furrow in confusion before she signs, *"I thought you were going to get a head start on our studies while I was gone?"*

I love the disappointment on her face, but I'm also uneased. She's been gone for hours. *"And I thought you were only going for a milkshake?"* I jingle the bag in my hand. *"Late lunch or early dinner?"*

"Ah..."

She drops her hands to the fringed hem of her denim shorts. She placed a shirt over her bikini top, so she isn't feeling modest. She just doesn't want me to see her truth-bearing eyes, much less tell me what she's been up to.

Hiding her eyes from me is pointless. I don't need to see them to know she's keeping something from me. I can feel it in my bones.

Furthermore, physical training isn't the only training Mr. Gregg and I do. Psychology plays a major factor as well.

When the heat of my stare becomes too much for Melody to bear, she relents on her silent stance. *"We ran into some old school friends. They invited us to have an afternoon snack with them."*

Her eyes fall to my lips when I ask, "You ran into some guys who used to go to our school?" I purposely say 'guys,' hoping it will narrow down my list of suspects. When her chin dips, I ask, "Did your mother know them?"

"She wasn't there." She swivels on the spot like she always does when she's nervous. *"She had to run some errands, so she dropped us off at Mary's."*

"She left you alone?" My voice would have you convinced I didn't go through puberty years ago. That isn't the case. Even with having what Melody likes to call a babyface, I've been shaving since I was fourteen.

Melody peers at me as if she heard how ridiculously loud I shouted. *"She dropped me off with three friends at an overflowing café in the middle of the day."*

"That had men you didn't know inside. You know the rules, Melody. Your father has to screen anyone you come in contact with. Did you ask them for identification?"

"Jesus, BJ." She runs a hand down her face before taking a step back, hoping a little distance will hide her exaggerated eye-roll. *"They were seniors last year, which means they wouldn't have been much older than a toddler during the home invasion. So no, Captain Paranoid, I didn't request to view their photo ID before accepting their invitation to share their booth."*

Her reply reveals more than she intended. She disclosed her afternoon guests are older than us, and she was invited to eat with them, which means they are either unaware of Mr. Gregg's wish to keep his daughter away from strangers or they don't care about his rules.

"You should tell your dad. Give him a heads-up that strangers approached you—"

I choke on my words when Melody shakes her head. *"I am not doing that until you stop pretending this is about my safety."*

"This *is* about your safety," I both sign and shout.

As she splays her hands across her cocked hip, her face reddens with anger. It makes her appear years younger than her almost eighteen years, but it also makes her as cute as a button. She can't pull off an angry face any better than me. *"This has nothing to do with my safety, and you know it."* She steps closer to me, her nostrils broadening as she endeavors to cool the heat burning her cheeks. *"This is about you being jealous about something you have no right to be jealous over."*

I immaturely roll my eyes, pretending she didn't hit the nail on the head. I'm jealous, I can feel it clawing at my chest, but since Mr. Gregg swears jealousy is a sign of weakness, I'll never let her know that.

"You really should stop hanging out with Carmen. You sound more and more like her every day."

When I attempt to remove my bio-chem book out of my backpack, Melody snatches it out of my hand and tosses it onto my bed. *"I asked you to come with us, BJ. I invited you. You didn't want to come."*

Like all teenage boys backed into a corner, I come out swinging. *"Because I didn't want to hang out with your friends. They treat me like a lecher."*

Melody's angry growl enhances the frantic thrust of her chest. It's rising and falling as rapidly as mine and has me entranced in under a second, which almost has me missing her signing. *"That is funny, you didn't seem to mind their leering when you were prancing around the boxing ring like a ballerina."*

I swear steam nearly billows out of her ears when I mumble under my breath, "Who's jealous?" Even mumbling my reply doesn't stop her from lip-reading what I said.

Since her mouth is set into a firm, angry line, Melody's squeal rumbles more in her chest than my ears, but it's still felt, none-theless. *"You, Brandon James McGee, are impossible."*

After throwing her hands into the air like she just gave the performance of her life, she makes a beeline for the window she only crawled through mere minutes ago. I assume she's going to get her backpack so we can study, so you can imagine my surprise when she commences climbing through it.

I tap on her shoulder before asking, *"Where are you going? I thought we were going to study?"* I stop just before I mentioned the movie-date I set up in the corner of my room at the start of my banishment. *10 Things I Hate About You* is already loaded in the DVD player, but I don't want to appear desperate, even if I am.

Melody continues clambering out my window as if she didn't see the frantic movements of my hands.

I stomp down three times, shouting her name. *"Melody."*

Once she's on the other side of the window frame, she peers at me beneath lowered lashes for the quickest second. I put her brief glance to good use. *"Mellowy."*

That stops her in her tracks. It does every time. Although I had no issues signing her name when talking around her parents, I called her Mellowy as I couldn't pronounce my Ds—which I'm ashamed to admit lasted until I was ten. When her parents explained why they were laughing, Melody smiled the biggest grin I had ever seen. Ever since then, her nickname stuck. It's part of the special signing signals we developed not long after her eighth birthday.

"Come back inside and talk to me." When she remains standing firm, I beg, *"Please, Melody. I don't want us to fight. We have not had a single fight in over a decade. Don't make today of all days an exception. We had a win this afternoon. We should be celebrating."*

A familiar *boom-boom, boom-boom* sounds from my chest when she slowly paces my way. Her eyes are as wet now as they were during the many drills her father made her endure during her child-hood. She's just too brave to let them fall, and indisputably too pretty. Her courageousness the past twelve years has convinced me you can be both pretty and brave, and she's the prettiest of them all.

I'm about to tell her I'm sorry for reflecting my anguish onto her, but her confession stops me. *"Connor Eckhart asked for my number today. He was the most popular guy at our school, and he can also sign."*

I knew who Connor was before her glowing dossier. He's a friend of Madden's, which shows his low standards in friends, but I dislike him even more now. Furthermore, the admirable glint in Melody's eyes is way too bright for my liking. A guy like Connor doesn't deserve to be a casual acquaintance of Melody's, much less her friend. She's big-hearted and kind. Connor is not.

My back molars become friendly when Melody continues to confess, *"I was flattered. He had the attention of another four girls today alone, but he only asked for my number."*

This is proof she has no clue how beautiful she is. She catches the admired eye of many. She's just been taught to assess the motives behind the flattery. Usually, by the time they get close enough to notice her lashes are so long they touch her cheeks every time she blinks, they've lost interest. If Mr. Gregg didn't scare them away, Melody determines that they're not worthy to discover how her eyes can share a lifetime of secrets without her needing to speak. So, I'm not surprised Connor noticed her. Everyone notices her.

I just happened to notice her first.

The annoyance tainting my blood switches to excitement when Melody discloses, *"As giddy as I was about his attention, I didn't give him my number."* Her eyes dance between mine. They're glistening more with hope now than anger. *"Do you know why, BJ?"*

I want to say because a wannabee playboy doesn't deserve her, but since that would direct our conversation straight into the path of a tornado, so I shake my head instead.

I thought my less controversial response would ease the tension bristling between us, whereas all it does is douse the hope in

Melody's eyes. *"Then I guess this isn't your problem to solve. Is it, Brandon?"*

After a tight smile, she spins back around and recommences her descent down the old oak tree. This time, I let her go. Not because I'm a coward, but because I know she only ever calls me Brandon when she's really, *really* mad.

No matter how you communicate, talking when angry never serves you well because more times than not, insecurities are voiced before anything else. My solution for anger will always be silence. I'm sure it frustrates Melody, but I'd rather seek her forgiveness for my silence than words I can never take back.

BRANDON

The next morning, I'm about to gallop down the stairwell of my family home, but a partially open door halfway down the hallway stops me. This is the first time Joey's bedroom door has been open this early in months. Usually, it takes the sweet smell of French toast to get him out of bed before ten o'clock.

I suck in a big whiff of air through my nose to ensure the cold I had last week isn't still messing with my senses. Once I'm certain the air is free of anything remotely close to sugared-up eggs and toast and my nasal cavities are clear of germs, I pivot, climb the three stairs I just galloped down, then head for Joey's room to see if he needs help getting out of bed.

Joey has cardiomyopathy. It's a disease that affects his heart muscles. He's had it for a few years, but it has only slowed him down the prior twelve months. Lately, just getting out of bed causes him to become breathless, and his legs often swell to the point he looks like he skips arm day at the gym.

"Joey…" His door pops open another two inches when I rack my knuckles across the wood. "Are you decent? I don't want any more incidents recorded on your ledger."

Joey may be sick and essentially classed as an adult since he turned eighteen almost a year ago, but he's still very much a teenage boy. His antics are as adventurous as Madden and Phoenix's, they're just not as crude.

A grin tugs at my lips when Joey permits me to enter his room *after* the clunk of a magazine dropping to the floor to be shoved under his bed sounds through my ears. I'm doubtful he's reading one of those fancy-schmancy magazines our father purchases our mother with the hope it will glam her up before he commences his bid for Congress, and I'm just as confident despite its high price tag, there's barely anything inside it to read.

Joey flips the bird at me when I mutter under my breath, "Do you mark masturbation down on the movement activity sheet Dr. Giorgio makes you fill in?" Laughing, I flop onto the lower half of his bed not taken up by his long legs. Even with him only being a year older than me, he's four inches taller. "It will save her trying to work out the spikes in your pulse."

I nudge my head to the monitor next to his bed. Although my ribbing is returning his heart rate to a safe level, there's no missing the large valleys on the printout Dr. Giorgio doesn't need to physically assess to scrutinize. Joey's equipment is so advanced, it relays everything directly to his doctor's servers. "She might give you a bit of leeway if you say you were batting off to her."

"Does that work with Mr. Gregg?" I act stumped by his reply, but Joey knows me too well. Probably has something to do with the fact we're only eleven months apart. "Does he give you a bit of leeway when you tell him you choke the sausage over his daughter every single morning in the shower?"

"I don't choke the sausage every morning." I air quote my middle words. "I gently stroke it, too."

Joey smacks me up the side of the head with a pillow. For a teen whose fitness has faded to half of what it once was, he packs a lot of oomph in his hit. "You know you have issues when you can't even be aggressive while stroking one out. Newsflash, BJ, you're supposed to be pissed you're being forced to use your hand, not pleased."

I smile before lifting my chin, never a fan of arguing the truth.

"Once I'm out of this hellhole, you can be assured as fuck I won't be getting friendly with magazine cutouts. There will be pussy galore at the parties I'll host." He adjusts his position as his Adam's apple bobs up and down. "Consented pussy, of course."

"You heard that last night?" I nudge my head to his partially open door, acting as if our parents and Madden are filling the narrow gap.

Joey follows the direction of my gaze. "The almost two-hour straight lecture? Yeah, I heard that." He shifts his eyes back to me. They have a dash of mistrust in them. "What's your take on the matter?"

"I don't know, to be honest." A halfhearted shrug highlights my confusion. "From what I gathered through the floorboards, Fable agreed with Madden's recount of the event. But—"

"Some girls will say anything to be classed as one of the cool cats," Joey interrupts, much too wise for his almost nineteen years.

Although he's a little off the mark, I notch up my chin again. It isn't just girls who'll do anything to climb the popularity ladder. Boys are just as bad and don't get me started on grown men who should know better.

My eyes snap to Joey when he says, "Talking about girls, what was your argument with Melody about yesterday afternoon?"

"It was nothing." I slice my hand through the air like I didn't spend half my night evaluating every word she spoke. "It was just a misunderstanding."

"About you being jealous when you had no right to be jealous?" The morning sun bounces off his pearly white teeth when I snarl at him. "These walls are as thin as paper. How do you think I know about your daily shower routine?"

"'Cause you're a sicko who likes living precariously through your brothers?"

He physically gags. "If that were the case, I wouldn't have unfollowed Phoenix on Twitter. His tweets have no filter whatsoever."

I laugh, agreeing with him without words.

"Or…" he waits, building the suspense, "… shower antics aren't the only clue Melody has been your sole source of stroke material the past year. You've been hot for that girl for years. Why do you think Madden always riles you up about her?"

"Because he's an ass?"

"Or…" He pauses again. This time, it's twice the length of his last suspense-builder. "He's forcing you to face the truth before it's too late. You'll be leaving for college in a few months. That will create a new set of problems for you two."

My chest inflates with an unvoiced *ha!* "Madden isn't that nice. He doesn't care about anyone but himself."

Joey twists his lips that are a little bluer today than usual. "Normally, I'd agree with you, but he had some valid points yesterday." I'm about to rib him about becoming an old lady whose only joy in life is gossiping about other people, but he continues talking, stopping me. "Is it true? Did Melody squeeze your hand when she asked you to have milkshakes with her?" When I nod, he hits me with his pillow for the second time, causing a small bout of breathlessness to chop up his words. "You're an idiot, pipsqueak! That's a clear will-you-go-out-with-me sign for *anyone* between the age of twelve and forty-three."

"It is not," I scoff loudly.

His lips twitch as he prepares his rebuttal, but before he can, our mother joins the conversation, silencing us both. "It's true, BJ. It has been that way for centuries."

Her response piques my interest, but I'm more interested in discovering how long she's been standing outside of Joey's bedroom door. Did she just arrive? Or has she been listening in the entire time? If her red cheeks are anything to go by, I'd say the latter is more plausible.

With Joey not as shy as me, he interrogates our mom like he's destined to be a detective. "Did you hear *all* of our conversation or just the last half?"

"Umm…" She places a tray of breakfast onto Joey's bedside table before spinning around to face us. I swear my cheeks combust when she mumbles, "You've certainly reminded me of the importance of washing the linen every day."

"Mom…" I bury my head into my hands, too embarrassed to look up. "It's not true. I don't… *masturbate* in the shower." I stop just before I say, 'every day,' saving me some additional torture.

She rubs my arm all motherly like. "Brandon. Honey. It's fine. It's perfectly normal."

I don't know what's more concerning: my mother believing I have a fascination with stroking one out in the shower or her cradling me into her bosoms to comfort me. From the vomit creeping up my esophagus, I'm going to say it's a combination of both.

"But I do think the situation could be alleviated a little if you took both Madden and Joey's advice." She drops her glistening eyes to mine. "You've admired Melody since she fumbled down her stairs with a mouth full of toothpaste and her big doe eyes out in full force."

Although tempted to smack Joey's smirk into the next century, I don't refute our mother's statement because every single word she spoke was true.

Seeing a lack of argument in my eyes, my mom asks, "If you're hoping to be more than Melody's friend, why did you let her leave here yesterday believing you can't feel the chemistry between you two?"

After taking a mental note to check my room for surveillance devices, I reply, "She didn't ask about chemistry. She asked if I knew the reason she didn't give Connor her number."

Humor floods my mom's eyes, but she keeps her laughter contained. I can't say the same for Joey. He's laughing so hard, the spikes in the ECG printout are higher than they were when I entered his room.

"BJ. Honey. Brandon."

Three names? Jesus. Did I kill Madden yesterday as hoped and repress the memory?

"A girl only ever tells a guy she was hit on when it's to the guy she wants to hit on her."

Huh? Is she speaking English?

Recognizing that I'm struggling, Joey simplifies it for me as only a fellow teenager can. "Do you like Melody as more than a friend?"

After checking the coast is clear of the spying eyes of my enemies, I bob my chin.

"And she invited you to get milkshakes while squeezing your hand?" Mom asks, jumping back into the conversation.

I once again nod.

"Then, you're talking to the wrong blonde."

Joey nudges his head to his partially cracked open bedroom window. My heart launches into my throat when I spot Melody leading her horse, Socks, out of the barn on the edge of her property. Even being around animals most of her life and owning Socks for over five years, she's still scared shitless of horses, so I'm not only surprised she's taking him for a walk around the property lines alone, I'm also stunned to discover Socks is saddled-up.

While working through the oddity of Melody trying something new, the answer to her question yesterday smacks into me hard and fast. She didn't give Connor her number because she doesn't want to date him.

She wants to date me. *I think.*

Realizing there's only one way to prove my theory, I press a hurried kiss to my mom's cheek before hightailing out of Joey's room. Joey encourages the ludicrous thoughts in my head by wolf-whistling and catcalling like he's at one of his old football games.

I've galloped halfway down the stairs when I realize my bravery today might not end as rainbow-filled as I'm hoping. I doubt I'll get freshly baked cookies after this stunt. I may not even make it to this afternoon alive.

Lucky the reward will be worth the sacrifice.

"Hey, Mom…" When her head pops out of Joey's room, I take a moment to relish her huge grin before saying, "If Mr. Gregg kills me, can you and Joey go through my things? I don't want Madden or Phoenix in my room."

Instead of assessing why keeping two of my brothers out of my room is more detrimental than my safety, my mom nods. She's good like that. Forever liberal.

"Thanks, Mom. You're the best!"

She mumbles something in reply, but since my blood is pumping through my body as fast as my legs are thumping the glossed floorboards of the living room, I miss her response.

With my heart in my throat and my pulse sky-high, I charge through the kitchen, out the back patio, then across the land separating my family home from my best friend's. The smile on my face makes it seem as if I'm not about to place twelve years of friendship on the line because a teen much wiser than his years and my mom are hopeless romantics.

During the short trip, I tell myself on repeat that my conversation with my mom and Joey is the sole reason I'm taking a life-changing risk, but if I were honest, I'd admit snippets of Madden's conversation yesterday featured in my summary. He mentioned the squeezing hand thing long before Joey, and he saw the chemistry between Melody and me enough to believe we were more than friends, so I guess it's only fair he gets a tiny mention in the story I plan to tell my grandchildren one day.

The excitement slicking my skin with sweat tapers when I round the corner of the barn I saw Melody leading Socks from. My heart is still racing a million miles an hour. Its frantic pace just isn't compliments of exhilaration. It's galloping with jealousy. Hot, sick jealousy.

Melody isn't alone. She's with Connor—the motivator of our

first ever argument. He's showing Melody how to lead Socks around the round yard, having no clue she'd rather eat moldy pizza than place her hand within an inch of Socks' mouth. The fact Connor places Socks on his left shows he's familiar with horses, so Melody's safety isn't compromised, but I'm still opposed to the idea he's here.

Mr. Gregg doesn't let anyone get close to Melody—*anyone but me.*

Since the round yard is rarely used, grass has grown up the rusty steel material like a vine creeps up lattice, but unfortunately, it's nowhere near tall enough to hide the shocking event that occurs next. With the assistance of Connor, Melody attempts to mount Socks. It takes her three goes and a heap of encouragement from a man not worthy of her time, but Melody achieves something I've been working her toward for years without me.

That sucks.

I'm proud of her, and the beaming smile stretched across her face plays on my heartstrings, but it still guts me in a way I can't explain. I worked my ass off for years to gain her trust, however, it seems as if the only thing needed is a rigidly hard face and an un-wonky smile—two things I don't have.

With my heart rate sitting lower than it was only minutes ago, I spin on my heels and retake the route I just sprinted. My steps are nowhere near as fast as they were moments ago. I kick up more dirt than I tread.

Halfway back, I flip the bird at the person hackling me from the second-story window of my family house. Joey laughs off my voice-less threat as if it has no steam. "If you don't get your ass back there right now, I'm gonna get out of this bed and kick your ass back there."

"She's not alone," I reply to him, acting as if he can't see Melody and Connor from his window.

His bedroom is a little further back than mine, but he still has a prime view of the Greggs' round yard. The usually unsightly vista is the reason he suggested for Mr. Gregg to have a pool installed in its place. He thought the visual would be more entertaining if it included water and bikini-clad bodies. Since the many requests came from Joey, Mr. Gregg took his humor in stride. I honestly don't know how he would have responded if Madden had endorsed Joey's requests.

"She's with Connor."

Joey peers at me as if I'm an idiot. "Duh. But did you ever stop to wonder why she's grown a sudden interest in Socks... in the round yard of all places?"

I freeze halfway across the dewy ground, truly stumped. Melody loathes horses, but she absolutely hates spiders, which the round yard has a lot of this time of year.

After a couple of seconds of deliberation, I act as daft as I feel. "Isn't a round yard the ideal place to learn how to ride a horse?"

"Or..." If Joey pauses on me one more time today, a bad heart is going to be the least of his problems. "It's the perfect location to force a douche-canoe to admit he has feelings for her." He thrusts his hand at my bedroom window. It has a direct view of both the round yard and Melody's bedroom. I've taken advantage of the latter view multiple times the past two years. I swear Melody purposely teases me by keeping her curtains partially cracked open each evening. "You made out you weren't jealous yesterday. She's determined to prove you wrong."

"Seriously? That's ludicrous." Not as ridiculous as how high my hope is surging but stupid, nonetheless.

Although I'm not technically asking a question, Joey nods. "Look at her?" As I spin, he says, "She's not paying Connor an ounce of attention... because she's too busy peering at your bedroom window, waiting for you to spot them, and praying you'll respond how she's hoping."

He's right. Although I can see Melody as clear as day, she hasn't spotted my gawk because she's looking in the wrong direction.

When she's not retightening her grip on Socks' reins, her eyes are locked on my bedroom window.

As suspicions tighten the knot in my gut, I return my eyes to Joey. "How do you know what she's thinking? Were you a girl in a past life?" My jaw spasms when no amount of distance can hide the guilt in his eyes. "You set me up!" Since I'm not asking a question, it doesn't sound like one.

"No," he denies, shaking his head. "I helped Melody plot a ruse to force you out of your comfort zone."

I race toward the house, preparing to strangle him. Two feet from the patio, Joey's warning stops both my feet and my heart. "If you walk away now, you risk the chance of losing her for good."

I jump off the patio stairs before raising my head. "It isn't that simple, Joey. There's a whole heap of other shit sitting between us."

Nothing but agitated restlessness echoes in my tone. I care for Melody, so much so, letting her walk away from me yesterday was one of the hardest things I've ever done, but I did it so she'd know how far I'm willing to go for her. I'd hurt myself if it saves her from being hurt.

Never one to back down in a fight, Joey asks, "Like what, BJ? What's standing between you?"

"Mr. Gregg, for one."

My attitude takes a step back when he says, "And where is he now? Connor is practically coating his daughter in drool, yet he's nowhere to be found."

He has a valid point.

"He's also been aware of your fascination with Melody for years, but not once has he discouraged you against it." He twists his lips that are curved with both amusement and straightforwardness. "I haven't had a one-on-one with Mr. Gregg in years, but I don't think he'd ever shy away from telling someone if he doesn't like them or their ideas. The numerous debates he's had with our father the past decade is proof of this. If he has an issue with you dating his daughter, pipsqueak, you would know about it by now."

He has another good point, but I hate backing down. Backpedaling is for the weak. But what if Joey is right? If I lose Melody over this, I'll never forgive myself.

Realizing every tactical response is better handled in numbers, I return my focus to Joey and ask, "What should I do?"

His smile is extra blinding in the mid-morning sun, but it has nothing on the brightness of his golden locks. "Do exactly what you were planning to do two minutes ago. *Kiss. Her.*" His smile drops an inch. "You should probably help her off Socks first, though. He could make things awkward..." His words trail off as the color drains from his cheeks. I've never seen his face as white as it is now, and he hasn't been outside in over six months.

"Joey?" Goosebumps break across my skin when he falls away from his bedroom window with a groan. Even from this distance, I can see he's grabbing his chest. "Joey!"

I sprint into our house, my pulse as high as my panic. He's a jokester, but this is one thing he'd never joke about. He would never put our mother in a situation that would cause her additional stress. Unlike Phoenix and Madden, he isn't an asshole.

Despite almost barreling over my mom in the kitchen, I make it into Joey's room in a record-breaking six seconds. He's still clutching his chest, his eyes are closed, and his body is limp.

While taking in his lifeless form, I do what every teenage boy does when they're panicked.

I freak the fuck out.

"Mom!"

BRANDON

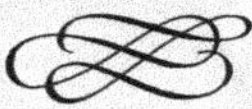

I leap out of the hard, plastic chair lining the visitors waiting room of the emergency department at our local hospital when Dr. Giorgio breaks through the clear flapping doors in the corridor. There's no blood on her smock like the stories Melody shared on the events after the Greggs' home invasion, and there are no police officers filling the room, but her face is as white as Joey's was when he collapsed, and her eyes are as drenched as mine.

My family watches her cross the room in silence. Since Joey's collapse was many hours ago, we're all here. Phoenix drove four hundred miles straight without stopping, Dad arrived at our ranch before the ambulance, and Madden rocked up three hours ago. We've spent a majority of the time pacing the corridor outside of the emergency triage room they raced Joey into. We only stopped when the security guard cited we were causing a fire hazard and requested for us to wait in the visitors waiting room.

I suck in my first breath in what feels like minutes when Dr. Giorgio dips her chin instead of shaking her head. No one wants a headshake. A head shake would've meant I was too slow getting to Joey. It would have meant he was dead.

"It's still touch and go," she advises us, her tone grim. "The medications we've been administering to him the past two years aren't working as they once did. The muscles around his heart are badly inflamed, causing an inadequate blood supply to be pumped to the rest of his body..." she bounces her eyes between my father and mother while saying, "... including his brain. That's the reason he collapsed today. His carotid arteries have been compromised. We've organized for stints to be placed in tomorrow afternoon, but they are only a temporary solution."

"Temporary?" my mom double-checks.

When Dr. Giorgio nods, my father seeks additional information. "What's a permanent solution? He can't keep living like this. He's barely been out of bed the past six months."

To an outsider, he seems like a caring, fretful father. Only those who know him best know the real reason for his questions. Just like no one wants a headshake when the doctor comes out to greet the family of a sick patient, no one who campaigns optimum strength and agility wants to admit they have a sick kid.

A majority of our family and almost all of Joey's friends are unaware he's sick. Our father hides his illness as well as he does his temper when members of the media try to rile a response out of him. He acts as if he's personally responsible for Joey's condition.

Joey jokes that he is. He said a faulty heart was his punishment for lining up for a heart when so many male members of our family before him skipped that line.

"What about a pacemaker, surely that's an option?" my father asks.

Dr. Giorgio steps closer to my parents. "We had considered a pacemaker, but it's too late for that now. The only thing capable of saving Joey is a heart transplant."

"A transplant?"

My mother falls back into her chair when Dr. Giorgio nods. "It truly is our only hope."

While Phoenix comforts our mother, Madden fills the silence of our father's gaped jaw. "Then how do we get one of those? Can you order it off Amazon? Have one shipped in from China? What do we need to do to get him a new heart?"

Although his timing is ill-mannered, Madden's first defense when he's grappling for a sense of normality is to joke around. Considering anger is his second go-to, I'd rather deal with his ignorance than his aggression.

"We'll place Joey on the organ donor registry, but I must be honest with you, the wait time could quite possibly be longer than the durability of Joey's heart."

Madden's switch flips in less than a nanosecond. Gone is the humor on his face, replaced with a man who looks like he wants to rip Dr. Giorgio's heart from her chest and give it to Joey. "What are you saying? Are you saying he could die before he gets a transplant?" When he gets right up into her face, I pull him away. "This is bullshit. He's barely lived. He's only eighteen years old!"

He shrugs out of my hold before storming out of the room, upending two chairs on his way. I watch his retreat until he disappears from view, then I switch my focus back to Dr. Giorgio. She's twice my age and a ton more sophisticated, but she's only ever had Joey's best interests at heart, so she doesn't deserve to be disrespected like that. "I'm sorry—"

"It's okay, Brandon. Don't apologize. It is a very trying time right now." She drifts her eyes between each member of my family before holding them on my mom's. "For all of us." She bends down until she's eye level with my mom. "I'll do everything I can for Joey. I promise you that."

My mother drags a balled tissue under her running nose before lifting her chin. "Thank you."

My brows stitch in confusion when Dr. Giorgio squeezes her hand before she stands to her feet, but since now isn't the time to decode anyone's body language, I shake off my confusion for a more appropriate time.

"I'll allow one visitor at a time to see Joey over the next hour, then we'll call it a night. It's important *everyone* gets some rest right now."

When my family sighs in collective agreement, Dr. Giorgio exits the room, leaving me with the task of proving to my father why it's more important for a mother to visit her son before his father.

It's a long, drawn-out forty minutes.

As I CLIMB the stairs of my family home, I rub at the tightness in the back of my neck. I have no clue what the time is, but if the rooster crowing in the background is any indication, I'd say it's a lot closer to dawn than dusk.

Since I spoke out against my dad's wish to see Joey first, I was the last of our family members to visit him, but it didn't take away from the experience. In all honesty, I'm kind of glad. Dad saved the best for last. Even Joey said that.

Since Joey was doped up on pain medication, he was in good spirits. He spent a majority of our twenty-minute chat encouraging me to fight for Melody as rigorously as he's planning to overcome his disease.

"Both are battles of the heart that could be lifesaving if done right," he said earlier.

What did I tell you? He's many years wiser than the date on his birth certificate.

My already sluggish speed slows even more when I notice my bedroom door is open. With privacy an extreme priority for me, I never leave my door open. Furthermore, I left my room at nine this morning, so why is my bedroom light on?

With my fists at the ready to cause damage, and my suspicion a smidge higher than my annoyance, I push open my bedroom door. My fists un-ball so quickly my knuckles pop in protest to their quick movements. Phoenix and Madden aren't snooping in my room, and neither are the men Mr. Gregg has me forever on the watch for. Melody is. I'd never mistake the crazy twists of her dirty-blonde hair when she lets it dry naturally after washing it, much less her extra-long legs.

After tapping on Melody's shoulder, startling her, I sign, *"You scared the shit out of me."*

A new type of fear takes hold when her eyes lift from my hands to my face. Tears are marking her cheeks, and her nose is raw from a tissue being dragged under it too often. This is the first time I've seen her cry in almost two years, and I truly hate it.

"Are you okay? What is going on? Where is your dad?" Both my words and the movements of my hands are full of uneased hesitation.

I stop peering at the Greggs' ranch through my bedroom window when I see Melody replying in the corner of my eye. *"He's asleep. I snuck out after reading your text messages."* She drags her hand under her nose, amplifying the redness highlighting the tip before continuing, *"I am so sorry, BJ. I was mad about our fight, so I shoved my phone into a drawer in my room. I only got your texts about Joey a little over an hour ago."*

She's one of a very rare few who know about Joey's condition. I had planned to tell her shortly after his diagnosis, but Joey beat me to it. He'd never cut his little brother's turf, but I'm reasonably sure he has a hidden fondness for Melody as well.

When I bridge the gap between us, Melody's tear-filled eyes bounce between mine, seeking any sign on Joey's condition. When my eyes fail to give her all the answers she's after, I fill in the gaps with words. "Despite whining about an uncomfortable mattress, he's in good spirits. Dr. Giorgio said he'll most likely have to stay admitted until they find him a new heart."

Fresh tears spill down Melody's cheek when she asks, *"He needs a heart transplant?"* It appears as if the world shifts from beneath her feet when I nod. *"Oh God. That isn't good."*

"It is okay. It is Joey. He will fight this," I sign with the utmost confidence.

As I wrap her up in a tight hug, the image of her with Connor this morning fades from my mind. It's pretty ridiculous at a time when my focus should've been on nothing but my family that Melody and Connor kept popping up in my head. They had left the round yard by the time Joey was placed into the back of an ambulance, and no matter how many times I texted Melody during the commute to the hospital, she never answered a single one.

Melody's heated breaths fan my chest when I tighten my grip around her waist. The thoughts in my head the past sixteen-plus hours weren't pleasant, and they most certainly didn't end like this, so you can be assured I'm going to relish the happy ending of this day instead of the gory way it started.

After taking a few moments to absorb the sentiment in the air, Melody pulls back and asks, *"How long is the organ donor list to get a heart?"*

I start my reply with a shrug. *"Dr. Giorgio didn't say, but she did agree with Joey's assumption that his odds are better here than in a big-city hospital."* When Melody peers at me with confused, moisture-filled eyes, I explain, *"There are more accidents and deaths per capita in any city compared to a country town, but that also means there are a lot of people on the organ donor list."* An unexpected giggle rips from Melody's throat when I add, *"There are also a shit ton of old geezers in our town dying for a chance to meet with Jesus. We have just got to hope one of them croaks it with a relatively healthy heart."*

"That isn't funny, BJ." She whacks me in the stomach before signing, *"Although I am kinda hoping it will come true."*

"Me, too," I admit.

Joey is my brother, but that isn't the only reason I'm hopeful. He's also a great person. Before his diagnosis, he excelled at school. He was both popular and polite, and he had the perfect amount of empathy and understanding. If anyone in our family is going to follow in our mother's footsteps, it will be Joey.

Melody and I stand huddled in the middle of my room for what feels like a lifetime but is more likely only a few minutes. We've never cuddled out in the open like this before. We hold hands and hug each other multiple times a day when her dad isn't looking, but Melody does that with her female friends too, so I've never looked into it as deeply as I am now.

This feels more complex than a standard friend hug. Not even a lack of life experience could have me mistaking our exchange as being fueled by sadness.

While recalling my conversation with Joey out of his bedroom window this morning, I peel Melody away from my chest before lowering my eyes to hers. They're as sad as they were when I entered my room, but that isn't the only spark brightening them. They're holding some of the fire they held yesterday afternoon when she asked me why she didn't give Connor her number, proving Joey is right. She wants me to fight for her.

"I know why you didn't give Connor your phone number—"

The rest of my reply clogs in my throat when Melody pulls away from me with an embarrassed huff. *"Please don't mention that now. We have more important things to worry about than my stupidity."*

I wait for her eyes to lock with my lips before saying, "No, we don't." I remove her hands from her inflamed face, hating when she hides from me. "This is important, too. We are important."

"We are?" When I nod, Melody's mouth falls open. *"I am deaf, but that didn't sound like a best friend 'we are' to me, BJ."*

A grin curls on my lips. I love her sass. *"That is because it wasn't. I want to be your best friend, Melody, but that isn't all I want to be."* I tuck a strand of her hair behind her ear before I continue my confession, *"I was jealous yesterday. I hated that Connor had your attention, and your friends most likely encouraged his pursuit."*

Her lack of response reveals I hit the nail on the head.

"But even if they did, I should have trusted you."

My heart patters out a funky tune when she dips her chin in agreement. *"Yes, you should have. I have never done anything to gain your mistrust, BJ. Not years ago, and not yesterday."*

As the knot in my stomach the past sixteen-plus hours untwists, I smile. My unusual peacocking causes Melody to shake her head in mock disgust, but instead of deflating my inflated chest with a stab to my ego, she pumps more air into the catastrophe.

"I didn't give Connor my number because I don't want to date him." I almost jig on the spot when she quickly adds on, *"I don't find him attractive. His nose is crooked thanks to too many bad tackles, and his breath reeked of energy drinks."* Something on her face shifts. It switches from the face of my best friend to the woman I plan to love for eternity. *"He is also too rugged looking for me. I like my men with softer edges..."* She drags her index finger down my round and embarrassingly inflamed cheek before tracking it across my quirked lips. *"... and perfectly wonky grins."* I give her my best crooked smile when her eyes lift from my mouth to my eyes. *"I want someone who will tell me I am brave even when I am sobbing, and who still thinks I am pretty when I am ugly crying."*

"You don't ugly cry." A small bout of laughter makes it hard for her to lip-read my next set of words. *"You just look like you are vying for the part of Rudolph in the Christmas play at church."*

Her miffed expression relaxes when I squeeze her hand with mine, then it completely disappears when I tug her two steps closer to me. *"Joey said you brought Connor over to make me jealous."* They weren't his exact words, but with the tension between us the highest it's ever been, I'm happy to summarize if it gets us to point A quicker. *"That you purposely used the round yard so I would see you with him. Is that true?"*

I realize courage comes in many forms when Melody dips her chin without the slightest pause for consideration. She doesn't need to lie to me because she knows no matter how bad the crime, I'll always forgive her.

"You wanted to make me jealous."

I'm not asking a question, but she nods anyway.

"Because you don't want to date Connor Eckhart."

She keeps nodding, her head bobbing up and down as frantically as the little vein in her neck.

"You want to date me."

It's a little harder for her to nod this time around. Not because she needs time to consider a response, but because she needs to be cautious that we don't knock heads since I'm narrowing my mouth down toward hers.

Our noses are touching, our lips are aligned, and for once in my life, the odds work in my favor. We're alone and not undertaking a drill, which means I'm about to kiss the girl I've loved for more than half my life without any interruptions.

The plea for me not to make her wait another eleven years fades from Melody's eyes when I press our lips together for the very first time. It sends a growling groan rolling up her throat before it's trapped in my mouth along with her relieved sigh. We've touched, cuddled, and fondled a little more than average friends do, but this is the first time our mouths have been attached, and it's even better than I imagined.

Her mouth is as soft, moist, and ten times tastier than predicated. It truly has me convinced she's perfect in every way—kind, beautiful, and scrumptious—a banquet I could easily become addicted to.

Our kiss starts out soft and delicate before the teasing movements of Melody's lips demand a more vigorous response. While relishing the little noises escaping from her throat, I kiss how I've forever dreamed to kiss her. It's one of those kisses that sends sparks shooting down my spine, hardens my cock, and has Melody moaning.

BRANDON

e've laughed, cried, and commiserated together the past twelve years, yet not once have I heard Melody moan like this. This isn't a moan of appreciation when the gooey insides of a freshly baked cookie hit her tastebuds, or the one she tries to keep on the down-low when our movie marathons get more adventure off-screen than on.

This is one of pure delight.

One of need.

"Please don't stop," Melody begs when I kiss the corner of her kiss-swollen lips before inching back. *"I have been waiting for this day for years, and it is even better than I expected, so I don't want you to stop."*

Nothing but pure smugness beams out of me when I reply, *"I am not going anywhere. I just need to close my bedroom door. Madden and Phoenix are home."* I don't need to say anymore. Melody is as untrusting of them as I am.

When I lodge a wooden chair under the door handle, the rise and fall of Melody's chest is heard more than seen. Even with my stomach being a bundle of nerves, I hate that's she nervous. She's never been uncomfortable with me before, and I'd hate for today to be the beginning of that.

"We don't have to do any more than we already have. I just value privacy—"

I stop signing when Melody raises her hands to the tiny pearl buttons on her shirt. While peering straight at me, she unclasps the first button before quickly moving onto the second one.

"Melody."

She signals for me to be quiet before her eyes reveal we're not doing anything she doesn't want to do.

When she unclips the third button, her breathing grows faster. If I believed her increased breaths were because of nerves, I'd stop this right now. But since I know her better than I know myself, I watch her like a hawk, incapable of tearing away my gaze. She's always been beautiful, but the confidence beaming out of her right now takes her beauty to an impossibly new high. There are no blankets hiding her and no shelter. She's open and exposed.

She undoes the fifth button on her shirt, then the sixth before lifting her eyes to mine. *"I don't just want to be your best friend either, BJ. I want to be your everything."*

Before I can tell her she already is, her blouse falls to the floor, and my eyes go wild.

"Melody..." I want to say more, but the image of her standing before me in a pair of boots, riding pants, and a bra is too much. I can't form words. I can barely breathe through the excitement clutching every inch of me much less speak.

After giving me time to take in how much her body has changed from the last time we played the I'll-show-you-mine-if-you-show-me-yours game, Melody signs, *"Your turn."*

Since I'm wearing a plain white shirt, it takes me not even two seconds to comply with her request. Usually, at this time of the morning, I'm cursing Mr. Gregg for his intensive training regime, but right here, right now, I'm thanking him.

Melody takes her time ogling the bumps that usually have me cramping up at all times of the night. I'm not as built as Connor, and I'm certainly nowhere near as tall, but the way Melody looks at me makes me feel like I'm a giant.

You have no idea how hard it is for me to keep my eyes on Melody's face when her hands creep down to the zipper in her pants. The hiss of the metal lowering sends a pleasurable zap through my body. It clusters in an area I'm certain will make the removal of my jeans extremely difficult. I'm as hard as a rock.

A few seconds later, my eyes drop to Melody's midsection. It isn't because I'm a pervert who couldn't hold back for a second longer, even if I can't. We lost eye contact from Melody bobbing down to undo the laces in her boots.

Once they're opened, removed, and lined up against my dresser, Melody finalizes tugging her pants down her thighs. She folds the rigid material into a neat pile before placing them onto the edge of my bed.

Although this morning is going above and beyond anything I could've ever anticipated, she must have had some inkling about how our proceeding would prevail because she's wearing matching undergarments. She only does that when she's afraid someone is going to see them, such as at summer camp. She hated the idea of being caught in mismatching underwear, so she made her mom purchase identical sets before every camp.

She didn't need to worry. I'd never let anyone see her in a compromising position, not to mention Mr. Gregg, who was the supervisor for every excursion and camp trip we attended.

While licking her lips, Melody's eyes drop to the crotch of my jeans. I don't look down, but I'm reasonably sure she can see the outline of my dick. It's so squashed against the zipper, I'm extra cautious not to nip my skin while lowering the flimsy mechanism keeping my erection contained.

After folding my jeans in a similar pattern to Melody's pair, I place them on top of her pants. Something so insignificant shouldn't seem like a big deal, but I really like seeing our clothes tangled together.

While moving back to stand across from Melody, I adjust my crotch, so the crest of my cock isn't peeking out of my boxer shorts. Melody's eyes are as wide as mine, and her skin appears just as sticky. We've stood across from each other like this before, but this time is starkly different. For one, even with my hands hiding my crotch, my erection can't be missed, and two, there's a heavy dose of sentiment in the air.

Joey's condition isn't the only thing about to have a major upswing today.

My life is as well.

"Don't," I plead when Melody pulls her arms behind her back, so she can fiddle with the clasps of her bra. I'm not asking her to stop because I don't want this to go any further. I want to remove her bra. It's been a fantasy of mine for years. *"Can I?"*

Melody watches the bob of my Adam's apple before lifting her chin. I feel like I'm floating on a cloud when I slowly bridge the gap between us. My room is a standard size room, but I shorten the length of my strides so that I have ample time to take in the stunning visual before me. Even if this is as far as we'll ever go, I'll die a happy man.

When I fail to unlatch her bra three times in a row, Melody's soundless giggles increases the heat on my cheeks. She steps back before advising the cause of my dilemma. *"The clasp is in the front."* Her chest balances against mine when she curls her hands around mine to assist me. Once it's removed, she peers at me with mischievous eyes. *"I think Mom bought this style on purpose. Only an ambidextrous could remove my bra without my knowledge."*

The mention of her mother should be awkward, but for some reason, it isn't. Her parents have featured in my thoughts a handful of times the past ten minutes, and although the many scenarios I've run through my head if her father finds out about this should have me stopping it immediately, they're not scary enough for me to believe the consequences of my actions will ever outweigh the gain.

Furthermore, we've been tiptoeing toward this for a decade, so I'm more than eager to skip another decade of torture.

"*Wait*," I plea when Melody's hands lower to the waistband of her hot pink panties. "*It is my turn.*"

My lips curl into my infamous lopsided grin when Melody nervously signs, "*But you don't have a bra.*"

"*I know, but we are going turn for turn, so it is only fair I go next.*"

Although I'm acting chivalrously, in reality, I'm dying for any excuse to step away from her. Our parents stopped bathing us together the instant Melody's breasts began developing. I've dreamed of seeing them uncovered ever since.

Melody doesn't take a page out of my book. With her politeness as long forgotten as our first fight, she stares at my crotch, gasping when my dick springs free from my boxer shorts. He's standing proud and tall, virally stretching up to my belly button. With my father in the military, I'm cut like many other brat kids, so nothing hides the glistening droplet at the tip Melody is eyeballing.

I'm stark naked, and Melody is still wearing panties, but when she circles her hand around my cock, I no longer care about our strip-tease game. The girl I've admired since we were five is stroking my dick. Now isn't the time to keep a tally on our game.

A thick groan shudders up my chest when Melody swipes her thumb over the crest of my cock to gather the droplet of pre-cum pooled there. She has touched my dick before, but it was always through clothes when we were snuggled under a blanket, and more times than not, it was made out as if it were an 'accidental' brush or grope. It has never been as direct and to the point as it is now.

The nervous fumble of Melody's strokes reveals she's not experienced in giving hand jobs. I don't mind. I love the way we're fumbling through this together almost as much as I love the way it only takes a few pumps for her confidence to soar. The gruff moans vibrating from my chest must be encouraging, not to mention the pre-cum her tugs produce. The head of my cock is glistening as much as Melody's mouth is salivating, and my balls are tucking in close to my body.

While her hot breaths cover my neck with tiny beads of condensation, Melody drags her hand from the base of my cock to the tip over and over again, only stopping when I beg her to. I need a minute to calm down before I make a fool of myself.

I should be ashamed at how quickly my excitement is building, especially since we're standing in the middle of my room like the novices we are, but you have no clue how good this feels. Her perfect combination of speed and firmness ensures not an ounce of unwanted friction is felt even without the addition of shower water.

When Melody peers at me with wide, apprehensive eyes, panicked as to why I stopped her, I blubber out the first excuse that pops into my head, *"It is your turn."*

"My turn—" A breathless moan freezes her hands when my fingertips flutter over the tiniest dip in her stomach, but I don't touch her until she adds verbal confirmation to the permission in her eyes. *"Please, BJ."*

I swear I've seen her sign those exact words a million times the past decade, but this is the first time they've been delivered with sheer desperation sparked in her eyes.

When my index finger sweeps the skin hidden by her panties, it dawns on me that I need to move our exchange to a better location. Melody's knees buckle so fiercely, I scoop her into my arms without considering where the throbbing rod projecting from my crotch will land. It jabs Melody in the ass, producing a combined moan and whimper from her mouth.

It's a sexy noise that switches our exchange from innocent to adulterous in under a second. Mouths collide, hands wander, and we land on my bed in a twisted, sexy mess.

I inch back so she can see my lips before saying, "Tell me if you want me to stop." When she silences my worry by pulling my mouth to hers by the back of my head, I spear my tongue between her lips. I kiss her hungrily like she could vanish at any moment—I'm certain this is a dream because it's too mind-hazing to be real.

I kiss her all over from the column of her neck to the sexy little indent of her belly button. Then I drop my lips even lower than that. When I stop my pursuit a mere inch from the damp crevice of her hot pink panties, Melody balances herself on her elbows before glancing down at me. *"If you stop now, BJ, I will never disclose where I reburied our time capsule."*

"You reburied our time capsule?"

"Yes," she signs before pushing my head closer to the area growing more heated with each ticking second. *"I didn't want you to find the love letter I wrote to you."*

Like I can get any thicker, my cock makes a quick liar out of me. Even Melody whimpers when it digs into her shin. Or is she moaning? They sound about the same.

"You wrote me a love letter?"

"Yes." As her thighs spread wider, the musky, mouthwatering scent surrounding me increases. *"I also told my mom you were allergic to peanuts because I hated when you gave her gaga eyes every time she made you your favorite cookies."*

"I didn't give her gaga eyes." I did, but since I'm an inch away from a pair of panties that no amount of darkness can hide their dampness, I don't need to admit that right now. *"If it makes you feel any better, I told Mr. Ferreter I would poison his apples like the witch did in Snow White if he kept pairing you with Jade Sierra."*

"Jade... the boy I did rubbish duty with for merit points?" When I nod, Melody laughs. I love that even with our sexual chemistry at an all-time high, we can still banter. *"That was in the third grade, BJ. What harm could he have done?"*

"Who cares that it was the third grade. I saw the way he looked at you." I playfully suck on the silky-smooth skin high on her inner thigh. *"He didn't volunteer to pick up trash for merit points."* I lick the section

of skin I marked before placing another bite a few spots higher. *"He was there for you."*

Melody's laughter vibrates down her body. It's barely noticed over the frantic shake of her thighs from my hot breaths fanning her barely concealed pussy. *"You are poorly mistaken, Mr. James. Jade is gay."*

"Now. He wasn't back then." I make my words extra breathy, ensuring her excitement remains higher than her wish to argue. Even though sign language should technically slow her down, she can talk underwater.

"He didn't flip a gay switch, BJ. He was born that way." Her knees curve inward when my fingers creep inside the waistband of her panties. She's always up for a debate, but I'm confident she's five seconds from waving the flag of defeat.

"He liked you, Melody. I would put money on it."

"Not as much as I liked you," she signs sneakily.

Her confirmation that she's liked me as long as I've been fascinated with her spikes my heart rate to an unsafe level, but I play it cool. *"You are just saying that because I have my fingers in your panties."*

Her reply is a unique mix of moans and hand gestures. *"Is that so?"*

"Uh-huh." It's the fight of her life to keep her eyes on me when I flutter the tips of my fingers over her wetness. My touch is super soft, but there's no doubting we're treading into foreign waters. *"Have you ever touched yourself here, Melody?"*

My dick throbs with want when she confesses, *"Yes. More than once."*

Loving her honesty, I push our friendship into a dark and temperamental zone. *"Did you think about me when you touched yourself?"*

I've never been overly confident. Some would even say I'm shy, but not an ounce of coyness is invading me now. I truly feel on top of the world—even more so when Melody hums out an agreeing moan.

"Will you touch yourself now? Then you can show me what you like."

I anticipate a stern no—we only kissed on the mouth for the first time twenty minutes ago—so you can imagine my shock when she briefly nods before skimming her right hand down her sweat-misted stomach.

When her panties hide the move she's trying to show me, I hook my thumbs into the waistband and guide them down her thighs. It feels like someone snaps an elastic band around my cock when the image of her thumb circling her clit swamps my vision.

I've never done anything like this before. I thought Mr. Patterson's graphic sex education videos two years ago were to blame for my lack of interest. Only now am I realizing that wasn't the case. It was because I didn't want to do this with anyone who wasn't named Melody. We've done *everything* together, so it's only right we cross this off our list together as well.

"Let me try." The pink hue stretched across Melody's chest deepens when I replace her thumb with mine. I press down on the little bud that appears to have its own pulse before swiveling it like she did. "Does that feel good?"

My eyes shoot to my bedroom door when Melody replies with a grunted moan. I don't know why I'm surprised to notice it's still closed. My parents have at least another two hours of arguing to do before they call it a night.

I've been impressed with Melody from the day we met, but she blows my fascination out of the water when she signs, *"It feels so good, BJ. Ten times better than the hundreds of dreams I have had since my fifteenth birthday party."*

Any leftover hang-ups wreaking havoc with my gut evaporate in an instant. Her fifteenth birthday was the first time we got friendly under a blanket. Our touches could barely be classified as feather-like, but since they were occurring at regions of our bodies we had previously not explored, it was an explosive encounter that was only dampened when Madden walked in on us. His presence kills even the most blistering mojo.

After toying with her clit for a little while longer, I tap my index finger on her belly button to gain the attention of her eyes. When I have them, I ask, *"Can I taste you?"*

If Madden had an inkling of what was occurring in my room right now, he'd tell me to man up and take charge, but since it's Melody's body I'm endeavoring to please, I'm more than happy to seek her permission on the many things I want to do to her. Or better yet, encourage her to lead the way.

With her eyes as blistering as the heat bouncing between us, Melody nods. She raises her backside off my bed to assist me in removing her panties before sweeping open her thighs so my shoulders can fit between them. I stare at her pussy for several long minutes, desperate to taste her, but too mesmerized seeing her laid out like this to rush. I take my time fondling, touching, and soaking it all in until the tension hissing and cracking between us becomes too much.

I peer up at Melody, needing an additional nod of approval before I can kiss her pussy as I did her mouth earlier. When she gives it to me, I pierce my tongue between her glistening folds before sliding it up to the aching bud that started this all. I moan an indescribable grunt when a taste I can't put into words bombards my tastebuds. It's a little musky and slightly tangy, but I understand why Phoenix says a pussy is addictive enough to kill for it.

We haven't even got to the main event yet, but I can confidently declare I'm going to be dependent on Melody's pussy for the rest of my life. It's my new favorite flavor.

I'm too busy eating Melody with hungry licks to take in the words she signs a few minutes later, but I'm reasonably sure they're something along the lines of, *"Yes, BJ. That feels sooo good."*

I tug, suck, and pull on her clit another four times before an intense shudder zaps through her body. She throws her head back to grunt into the cool air. I eat her like I'm an expert, confident I'm a professional when it comes to her happiness in every meaning of the word.

I swivel my tongue around her clit and drag it up her pussy for the next several minutes, only changing tactics when the desire to fill her with my body in some way overwhelms me.

Melody's pussy stops gripping at nothing when I fill the gap with my finger. The walls of her vagina clench around me as her moans send pre-cum dripping off the end of my cock. While imagining my finger is my cock, I pump it in and out of her to the rhythm her hips are rocking.

This kills me to admit, but Madden was right. Milkshakes and fondling under a blanket were child's play compared to this.

"More, BJ. Please," Melody signs a short time later.

I peer at her over her sweat-misted breasts. *"More?"*

I almost make a mess of myself when our eyes collide and hold. If I'm reading her as well as I believe I can, she isn't requesting an extra finger or additional swipes of my tongue. She wants me, or should I say, my dick.

"Are you sure? We don't need to do this. Tonight has gone way beyond anything I could have ever hoped for."

"I am sure." She gestures for me to climb up her body. When I do as requested, she cups my heated cheeks in her hands. I can't tell if she's shaking in fear or euphoria. I get an idea it may be both when she signs, *"Just go slow. This is going to hurt."*

"Mel—"

She cuts off my plea by issuing one of her own. *"Please, BJ. I don't want to do this with anyone else but you."*

When my eyes fail to announce a single smidge of the hesitation brewing in my gut, Melody scoots up the bed to the shoebox full of photographs hidden under my headboard. She knows there's a three-strip of condoms inside since she placed them in there.

I watch her with interest when she rips the first condom off the strip. She's smiling like she's pleased they're all still there. I don't know why. Even if I haven't been obsessed with her for over a decade, between school, training with Mr. Gregg, and being her best friend, I wouldn't have time to date, much less find a girl interesting enough to take it this far. I'm not Madden. I don't grade girls purely on the rumor they put out.

"Did you want to put it on, or would you like me to do it?" Melody signs while peering up at me with innocent yet sultry eyes.

"I will do it." More because I don't want to make a fool of myself than anything. If she puts her hands on me while I can still taste her on my tongue, I can't guarantee I'll have the ability to stop cum squirting out of my knob.

Melody smiles like she heard my private thoughts before her eyes lower to my dick. She watches me intently when I squeeze the tip before rolling the latex down my shaft as taught in sex ed.

"That was so much sexier than watching you do it on a banana." Her eyes snap up to my face when she feels the vibrations of my chuckle. *"What? It is true. Your dick isn't kinked like the banana."* She hits me with a frisky wink. *"But I bet it tastes just as good."*

And just like that, the uncomfortable friction in the air evaporates. It's once again my best friend and me playing a very raunchy game of doctors and nurses.

"Do you remember the position Mr. Patterson said is best for first-timers during sex ed?"

Melody's nose screws up. *"I do, but I would rather keep Mr. Patterson out of this for the time being. We can talk about adding bed partners once we are no longer virgins."*

She laughs at the playful squint of my eyes before moving off the bed so I can lay down. Our combined moan bounces around my room when she straddles my lap a few seconds later. My lips are still moistened with her arousal, and now so is my dick.

The image of her rising onto her knees to guide my erect dick between her legs is sensually overloading. It's not the general OMG-I-am-about-to-have-sex sensation hitting me. It is the OMG-I-am-about-to-have-sex-with-Melody-Gregg that has my brain fritzing, and don't get me started on the response of my dick, or this event will be over before it starts.

I loosen my grip on the bed sheet when Melody signs, *"BJ?"*

"Yeah."

She flashes me a smile I've only seen a handful of times. It's filled with beauty and gratitude. *"This will probably be a little bit easier if you help guide me."*

"Shit, yeah, sorry," I fumble verbally before fumbling physically. I almost strangle my dick when my nervous jabs poke it into her thigh and back entrance before it finally finds the hole it's meant to be penetrating. *"Is that okay?"* I mouth. My voice is brittle, but it has nothing to do with nerves. It's from the heat of her pussy scorching my cock.

"Yes." She swivels her hips before releasing the tight clench of her thighs so she can slowly sink down.

She makes it almost an inch before the pleasurable expression on her face switches to pain. *"We can stop. Just say the word."*

When she shakes her head, tears almost stream down her cheeks. I hate that I'm hurting her, but whether now or years down the road, she'll inevitably have to go through this pain, and I'd rather help her through it than pass the baton to another man. Just the thought of her with anyone but me clutches at my chest as firmly as her pussy strangles my dick.

As Melody's face tightens with pain, her pussy clamps more.

"Try not to think about the pain, Melody. Consider it a one-off discomfort that will soon go away."

"Okay." She weakens the grip of her thigh muscles again before taking another two inches. *"BJ..."*

"It's okay. You are okay," I assure her when the first lot of tears spring from her eyes. She wants to wipe them away, hating that they're making her look weak, but since she would have to remove her nails from my chest to do that, she leaves them where they fall. *"Can I touch you? It might help with the pain."*

Her tears topple onto my chest when she briskly nods. She's hurting so much right now, she can't sign, and I've barely taken a second to relish how good she feels wrapped around me. She's so tight, my dick is being more strangled than caressed, but it still feels awesome.

"I will make it feel better, Melody. I promise." She whimpers through an additional inch when I lean over to grab a bottle of lube out of my top drawer. I'd rather explain why I need lube than hurt her more than necessary. "This will help you slide down easier, okay?"

Not waiting for her to acknowledge she lip-read my reply, I squeeze a generous dollop of lube onto my index and middle finger before transferring it onto the section of my cock she's yet to take. Once I am confident I'm well lubed, I move my lube-glossed fingers to her clit. One twirl of the bud pulsating with both pain and excitement reminds her of the fun event we're endeavoring to undertake. It hurts now, but once we've carefully stepped her through this process, it will be more fun than painful.

I lock my eyes with her before saying, *"When you are ready, try sliding down a little more."* I circle her clit with three full rotations before she recommences her descent. *"Yes, nice and slow."*

My jaw tightens when she takes another three inches without extra tears. I don't see that lasting when we hit a barrier I'm certain is going to hurt. She's getting close to the base, which is the thickest part of my cock since it's being strangled by a rubber shorter than my dick. *Who needs a cock-ring when you have restroom vending machine condoms?*

After tapping on her thigh to gain her attention, I sign, *"Can you look at me for a second?"* When I get the full attention of her eyes that are brimming with wetness, I sign, *"I need to rock my hips up for just a second. It will hurt, but it should not last long, okay?"* I smile when she nods without pause for thought, loving her trust. She knows I'd never hurt her on purpose. *"Claw my chest, scream, and curse at me, and call me names if you need to, but please remember, I am doing this because I love you."*

She doesn't flinch at my use of the 'L' word. We've used it a handful of times the past year. It's never had this level of emotion attached to it, though. It's usually when she's really sleepy or super happy.

Fingers crossed tonight commences a new wave of affection.

After securing a grip on Melody's sweaty hip, I lock my eyes with hers, then swing my hips upward at a fast, virgin-stealing pace. Melody claws at my chest, and her eyes expose the silent screams ripping through her body, but the only movement her lips make is when she mouths what I said to her earlier, *"I love you."*

BRANDON

I wake up to waves of dirty-blonde hair fanned across my chest, a leg hooked around my waist, and a massive boner. My morning wood is nothing out of the ordinary. I'm a teenage boy—if I didn't wake with a boner, I'd be worried—but waking up with Melody in my arms is new. I wasn't sure it would happen after I broke us through the final barrier earlier this morning.

Melody shed more tears than I was hoping, and it took more than some additional lube to lessen the tears streaming down her face. After several long minutes of gentle penetration and dedicated attention to her clit, her tears stopped flowing, and the connection we've had since the day she galloped down the stairs of her ranch took over our exchange.

I didn't blow the first time we had sex. The idea of having sex with the girl of my dreams ensured my dick remained as virile as a man on Viagra, but I couldn't push past the barrier that I had to hurt her to get us to that stage.

Melody didn't seem to notice I didn't come. I removed the blood-smeared condom and dumped it into the trash before she could notice it was empty, then spent the next hour fussing over her.

That started a second avalanche of exploring. It was gentle and sweet, and that time I orgasmed like my cum was the only thing capable of dousing the heat blazing between us. It was brilliant, even better than the first time around.

It was also exhausting, hence Melody's near-comatose state.

The thump of my temples reveals we haven't been resting long, but with the sun peeking through the crack in my curtains, I have no other choice but to wake Melody. Usually, when she sneaks into my room in the middle of the night, she leaves not long before the sun is up. I can't see the time, but the high angle of the sun exposes it's very late in the morning.

I pull Melody's hair away from her face before tracking my index finger down her cheek. Her tears have dried, but the river cascade they careened down her cheeks is still noticeable.

With my lips pressed against her temple, I say, "Wake up, Melody. We need to get you home before your dad sends out a search party."

She can't hear the words I speak, but she can feel their vibrations against her skin. We discovered just how sensual that is for her in the wee hours of this morning when I growled her name into her pussy. It sent her freefalling into ecstasy in an instant.

It works just as well this time around. I've barely hummed her name for the second time when her eyes pop open. She drags them across my room, no longer holding our shirts we dumped on the floor last night before locking them on the window. *"Shit! What time is it?"*

While she slips out of my bed, grimacing through the touch of pain I'm sure most woman experience after losing their virginity, I shake my head. *"I don't know. My cell battery died at the hospital, and for some reason, I forgot to charge it."*

The morning wood I mentioned earlier throbs when she grazes her teeth over her kiss-swollen lips to hide her smile. Her response exposes the groove between her brow isn't there because she's regretting what we did earlier this morning. She's panicked about her father's reaction to her being out all night.

I'm freaked as well. So much so, I'm tempted to check my driver's license before walking Melody home to ensure my organ donor registration is up to date. If Mr. Gregg kills me, which is a very high possibility, the least I can do is make sure Joey gets a new heart.

As Melody tugs her riding pants up her legs, her brows cinch more. *"Did you clean your room while I slept?"*

"No. Why?" I join her in glancing around my room. Now that she's mentioned it, the shirts we left discarded on the floor are neatly folded on my desk, and the bin I placed the two used condoms in has been emptied. *"Oh shit."*

"Your mom was in here." Melody's head flops back so she can peer at the ceiling. *"How? You barricaded your door with a chair..."*

I stop watching her sign when the flush of a toilet sounds through my ears. I completely forgot about the Jack and Jill bathroom attached to my room because Joey's room is on the other side, and he's in the hospital.

Melody's wide eyes snap to mine when the heavy stomp of a pair of boots vibrates from outside my room. Like many other deaf people, her sense of touch and awareness of those surrounding her is greatly heightened, which means she knows as well as me that there's only one person in these parts getting around in boots.

After signing for her to remain calm, I scamper off my bed and race to my door. Melody's eyes bulge when she takes in my erect cock. Even with the possibility the boot-stomper is her dad, I'm sporting a boner. I could've thrown on some pants, but my family ranch was built many moons ago, so it has those old skeleton key locks that make perfect peepholes when you need to snoop.

A relieved sigh rolls up my windpipe when I spot Phoenix making his way down the stairs. Mom would've placed him in Joey's room as the loft, which was once his room, is being converted into a campaign office for my dad. It's full of corny posters of my dad smiling his slick, wonky-ass grin. That's the only feature I got from him—my wonky smile. It frustrated me when I was younger, but as I got older, I realized it could've been a lot worse. I could have been handed his personality.

"*It is Phoenix.*"

Melody looks relieved for all of two seconds before her panic returns. "*I doubt Phoenix would have gathered the laundry from your room.*" I smile when she flops onto my bed with a groan before dragging her boots over from the dresser. When she spots my grin, she signs, "*Why are you smiling, BJ? Your mom is going to hate me.*"

I brush off her worry with a wave of my hand. "*Why would she hate you? She loves you.*"

"*She won't when she discovers I popped her son's cherry.*" Her eyes pop out of her head. "*Twice.*"

I realize cockiness is contagious when my chest puffs high at her remark. Yesterday we were best friends precariously tiptoeing toward possible lovers. Today we're best friends who *are* lovers.

When Melody continues to fret, I join her next to my bed. "*Seriously, my mom is the least of our problems.*"

"*Don't remind me.*" She finishes doing up her laces before standing from the bed. "*I don't think you should walk me home today, BJ. If it is late enough for Phoenix to be awake, Dad would have awoken hours ago.*"

"*We need to tell him about us. He won't be happy if we keep this a secret from him.*" And neither will I. I waited years for this, so the last thing I want is to pretend it never happened.

"*I will, just not the morning... you know...*" she thrusts her hand between us as her cheeks redden like beetroots, "*... we did stuff.*"

I'm an ass for smiling, but I can't help it. Usually, I'm the blusher in our duo, so I love that we've switched things up again for the second time in less than twenty-four hours.

"*So, you will tell him about us?*"

Melody nods without pause for thought. "*Yes, of course, I will. I would just rather this cool down first."* She swivels her hand around her flushed face and loved-up eyes.

"Okay. I am fine with that." The gleam in her eyes doubles when I use her shirt to tug her closer to me. *"But can I kiss you before you leave? I don't think I can wait another ten years to do it again."*

Melody slaps my chest as her mouth falls open. *"You better not make me wait another ten years. That was pure torture."*

"I tried to lessen the gap." She slants her head, more in confusion than to ensure the aligning of our mouths doesn't render her incapable of reading my lips. "Do you remember the time we were hiding out in the barn for one of the nighttime drills?"

After a few seconds of deliberation, she nods. *"When we bumped heads?"* When I raise my chin, she asks, *"How old were we then? Thirteen?"*

"Twelve. I could not see a thing, but I was confident you were giving off kiss-me vibes, so I went for it." I rub my noggin. *"Ended up with a bulge on my head instead of in my pants."*

Melody throws her head back and laughs. *"I thought the same thing..."* Her nose screws up. *"The kiss-me vibes, not the bulging seams. That must have been why we knocked heads. We were both coming in for landing at the same time."*

"You wanted to kiss me back then?" Nothing but shock reflects from my eyes.

"Yes, BJ. God, yes. I have wanted to kiss you since the day you risked death to kiss my cheek in front of my father." Her eyes shine with happiness when the memory filters through her head. *"I tried a few times, but we were either interrupted, or Madden and Phoenix had me convinced I would get cooties."*

Even pissed about my brothers' interference, I laugh. *"They had me convinced of the same thing, too."* I step even closer to her, making us one. *"I guess we have the same cooties now, so it won't matter how often we kiss."*

"I guess we do."

She smiles up at me, her lips only sliding over her teeth when I arrow my mouth toward hers. I pull her closer with an arm around her back before sealing my mouth over hers. She opens up immediately for me, moaning when our tongues tangle.

This kiss proves our first kiss was merely a preview on how perfect they'll be if we keep practicing them. It's a deep, soul-encompassing embrace full of open rawness and compatibility, both sweet and sexy with plenty of tongue and even more passion. It turns what should be a simple embrace into something much more voracious. Just like last night, hands wander, teeth collide, and we land on the bed with a thud. Except this time, Melody groans in pain when my erection digs into the fly in her pants instead of moaning in pleasure.

"Sorry. Still sore?"

It kills her to do, but she jerks up her chin.

Before I can assure her I'm happy to wait until however long it takes for her to heal, a second wave of boot-stomping sounds up the hall. This one arrives with a shouted voice I'm all too familiar with. It's Melody's dad.

Fuck.

I dive up from my bed, only just unpinning Melody from it when her father barges through my reinforced door, the flimsy chair I lodged under the door handle no match for his big burly frame. He startles when he realizes I'm naked, but with his panic higher than his sorrow for bursting into my room unannounced, his expression remains neutral. "Get dressed. Melody is missing. I thought she took Socks for a walk, but I checked all the outbuildings, they're empty..." His words trail off when Melody shyly waves at him from the corner of my room.

Unlike me, she's dressed, but she doesn't need to be covering her private parts with her hands like me for her father to understand the motivation behind her disappearance. My room reeks of steamy sex, not to mention the lusty glint in Melody's wide eyes. Even a senile man would understand what was happening here.

"Daddy!" Years of boot-camp training ensures Melody wedges herself between her father and me before his fists can rain down on me, but no amount of endurance stops his scorn.

"She's seventeen!" he roars like I'm unaware her birthday is coming up next month. "But even if she wasn't, you're supposed to be protecting her. Not… not…"

He glares at me like he wants me to fill in the gaps. I keep my mouth shut. I'm not stupid. He'll kill me if I spell out what we did.

When my silence doubles the width of the vein in his neck, I stammer out, "I love her."

"No!" His one word is so violent, you'd swear he spoke ten dozen words. "You can't love *and* protect her. It isn't possible."

Melody cranks her neck back to read my lips when her father's words are spoken too fast for her to get the gist of what he's saying. "Yes, it is. You love Wren, and you protect her."

"Now. I didn't back then." His words physically shunt Melody. She didn't hear what he said, but the hurt in his voice was felt more than heard. "I failed because I became slack." His tone exposes he truly believes he's at fault for the maniacs who brutalized and tormented his family all those years ago. "She was hurt because of me." His wide, tormented eyes lower to his daughter, who looks very much like her mother. *"I won't let the same thing happen to you."*

When he grips the top of Melody's arm to drag her out of my room, Melody slings her head back my way. *"I am sorry,"* she mouths, her lips quivering.

"It is okay," I sign back. *"I love you."*

I only see her sign, *"I love,"* before she's yanked into the crowded corridor filled with the frozen bodies of most of my family.

When the back porch screen door slams shut a few seconds later, I rake my fingers through my hair. It exposes me to my brothers and mother who are stunned into silence in the hallway, but I don't care. Nothing will beat the embarrassment Melody is about to face when she's forced to explain to her mother why she was dragged out of my home at eleven in the morning, and I'm not going to mention the words her father shouts while bridging the gap between our properties.

82

BRANDON

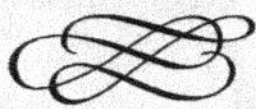

"What's the go?" Joey nudges his head to Mr. Gregg standing guard in the corner of the room. Although he's deep in conversation with my mother, his narrowed gaze is rapt on me. It's been that way all afternoon. He is pissed he's here, but no amount of muscle was going to stop Wren from visiting Joey before his operation this afternoon. Anywhere Wren goes, Mr. Gregg follows. Mercifully, that logic also applies to his daughter.

Melody sits on the younger generation side of Joey's hospital room, but she's kept her distance, untrusting that her dad won't restart the fight he didn't get to finish this morning. Her wet hair reveals she has showered and changed since I last saw her, but the hot water did little to remove the tearstains on her cheeks. They're even more vibrant than the ones her face was wearing this morning.

I'd give anything to block her ears and count to ten like I did when she was upset when we were kids, but my brother's hospital room when he's minutes from going into life-saving surgery isn't the right place, so instead, I continue stalking her from afar.

I'm reminded I failed to answer Joey's question when he says,

"The last time I saw Liam that pissed was when you kissed Melody's cheek." His heart monitor records his chuckle more than my ears. "You'd swear he had busted you checking her temperature with your pee-pee for the way he acted." I twist my lips in contempt about him calling my dick a 'pee-pee,' but Joey reads the expression on my face the wrong way. "Holy shit! Pipsqueak got his dick wet!"

"Shut up!" Faulty heart or not, I'm five seconds from suffocating him when his roared chuckles reach the parents' side of his room. "Nothing happened."

He slaps away the hand I'm trying to clamp over his mouth before saying more quietly, "Bullshit. You're the reason she's walking funny." When he notches his head to Melody, it's a fight to act nonchalant. My acting skills must be better this time around as Joey buys my ruse. "How bad is it?"

I exhale a big breath. "He dragged her out of my room after telling me I can't love and protect her at the same time." I tilt closer to his side to ensure we don't have any ears listening in. "I was naked, and it was clear what we were doing before he arrived."

"BJ... fuck." Joey looks like he wants to laugh, but instead, he drags his hand down his tired face. "You don't make things easy for yourself, do you?" When I shrug, he smiles. "What else did he say?"

"That she's seventeen—"

"She turns eighteen next month. Did you tell him that?"

I slant my head and arch a brow. "It wasn't really the time to point that out."

His smile lights up his face the way only medication can lately. "Good point. But what's stopping you now?"

I thrust my hand at his chest.

"Hey, don't use me as an excuse. You two have been tiptoeing toward this for months… if not years." He jerks up his chin, encouraging me to move closer. "What has Mom always told us? If anyone tells you that you can't do something, you prove them wrong by—"

"Doing it," we say in sync.

Joey nods. "Prove to him you can both love and protect his

daughter. Show him he's trained you well. He didn't raise you to cower away from a fight, BJ. He made you a machine."

It should be weird that he credits a man who isn't our father with raising me, but since it's Mr. Gregg, it isn't. He did raise me, and that's why I know Joey is right. Melody is young, but that didn't factor into the equation when Mr. Gregg forced her to relive her nightmares over and over again. Even if Melody wanted to forget what happened to her, her father wouldn't allow it. He wants her scared, so she'll be forever prepared.

It worked. Not just on Melody but me as well. I was gung-ho on *preparing* to protect her, I missed the one person capable of hurting her the most. Her father.

When Joey sees the determination on my face, he slaps his hand in mine before pulling me into his chest. "I'll see you on the other side."

I jerk up my chin, confident he has this, before shifting on my feet to face Melody. She pretends to continue acting interested in something my aunt is saying, but I can feel her eyes on me, burning me from the inside out. I can also feel the murderous glare of her father. His scold is life-threatening, but it won't stop me from sign-ing, *"Come grab a drink with me, Melody?"*

Melody stiffens for the quickest second before she briskly nods. When I fill the narrow gap between us, a commotion sounds from the corner of the room. It's most likely Mr. Gregg trying to inter-cept my play before I've called 'hut,' acutely unaware he has more than a defensive linesman to tackle to get to me. He has my family *and* his wife. I don't often get to play with a stacked team, but my family has been training for this day for years. Even Melody's mother saw it coming. It was only her father who's in denial of the inevitable.

After glancing back at Joey's room, noticing my mom and Wren are doing a majority of the heavy lifting to block Mr. Gregg's inter-cept, I devote my attention back to Melody. *"Are you okay?"* As she makes a beeline for the café at the entrance of the hospital, she jerks up her chin. *"Did you talk to your mom?"*

"Yeah." Gratitude fills her eyes when she smiles. *"She would have preferred for us to have waited until we were eighteen, but she said she understood."* She looks torn between rolling her eyes and gagging while adding, *"She was the same age when she lost her virginity to my dad. He is just cranky because he can't issue the same level of understanding. He was older than her, and he also wasn't a virgin."*

I'm aware Mr. Gregg is older than his wife, but I'm unsure by how many years. I doubt it's more than a handful. He has more gray hair than Wren, but that could be more compliments to hair dye than maturity.

I follow Melody to a drink fridge at the back of the café before asking, *"And how about you? How are you feeling?"*

She pulls down a diet coke before moving for the second fridge, aware I like my drinks fully sweetened. *"I am okay. Still a little sore, but nothing I can't handle."* She hands me a bottle of Mountain Dew before pulling five one-dollar bills from her pocket. *"What about you? Did you talk to your parents?"*

I smile at the fret on her face. *"Yes... well, my mom. We met Dad here. He stayed at a motel in town overnight."* She flashes me a sympathetic grin, cautious of the unease surrounding my family dynamic right now. *"My mom said similar things to your mom. That she would have preferred for us to wait, but she was glad we were sensible."*

"Oh. My. God." Melody slaps a hand over her face to hide her embarrassment. *"She emptied your bin, right?"*

I don't need to answer her, my grimace says it all, but I do anyway. *"Yeah. She also replaced the condoms in our box of photographs, so don't freak when there are more in there than you remembered."*

She whacks me in the gut like jealousy will never be an issue for us. I know she's lying. Just the way her eyes narrowed at her friends when they watched me prance around the boxing ring proves jealousy will pop up occasionally during our relationship, and I'm not going to mention the envious glare a man with a neck tattoo is giving Melody's butt. It has my jealousy skyrocketing, and Melody hasn't even noticed his gawk.

After paying for our drinks, Melody spins around to face me. Her face is wearing the same worried expression she had when she entered Joey's hospital room a little over an hour ago. *"I don't know how to get him past this, BJ. Mom said she would talk to him, but I don't see words removing the images from his head anytime soon."*

"It will be okay. He will come around." Her lips curve into a smile when I add, *"If not, we leave for Browns in four months."*

Melody groans before signing, *"If we get in."*

"We will get in. Think positive."

Nodding, she peers up at me with her big brown eyes out in full force. *"If Browns is our only option, can you wait that long?"*

Happiness beams out of her when I sign, *"I would wait an eternity for you."*

Sentiment is thick between us, but Melody acts as if she can't feel it. *"You are only saying that because you had your hand in my panties."*

I prepare my stomach for her hit when I jest, *"I had more than my hand in your panties."*

I'm about to kiss her cocky smile right off her face, but before I can, we're interrupted for the second time today. Thankfully, this time around, the interrupter is from the female half of Melody's parents. Wren waits for Melody to acknowledge her at the side before signing, *"Melody, it is time to go, honey. You have finals to study for."*

After gesturing to her mom she'll be a minute, Melody drifts her eyes back to me. They're not as panicked as they were only seconds ago. Our time together was short but very satisfying. *"Do you think my dad will let you over for a study session this afternoon?"*

Her lower lip drops into a pout when I mumble, *"I wish."* I twang on it before adding, *"But I will come over and talk to him after Joey is given the all-clear."*

Panic replaces some of the glee in her eyes. *"Do you think that is a good idea?"*

I shrug. *"It couldn't hurt, could it?"*

Hot air blows out of her nose as she signs, *"I guess not."* She returns her eyes to me. *"I will text you later?"*

When I jerk up my chin, she squeezes my hand before pivoting on her heels and stalking away. Once she's safely in the nook of her mother's arm, Wren farewells me with a friendly wave. Mr. Gregg's goodbye is nowhere near as pleasant. He narrows his eyes at me before shadowing his wife's exit.

I stand frozen in the middle of the café watching their exit, not moving until they're followed out of the hospital parking lot by a rusty F150 truck. Then I head back to Joey's room where I spend a majority of the next four hours working out what I plan to say to Mr. Gregg the instant Joey is out of recovery.

It's a conversation I was hoping never to have but will do anything to win.

BRANDON

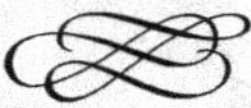

As gravel crunches under my feet, I raise my eyes to Melody's bedroom window. Her curtains are closed, but I know she's watching me. I can feel it in my bones. I yank one of my hands out of the pocket of my shorts, wave hello, then continue for the shed I hear classic Aerosmith music booming out of. Mr. Gregg is as straight as an arrow in all aspects of his life, except for his choice in music.

When he spots me rounding the corner, he peers up from the motor of his family station wagon for all of two seconds, grunts, then returns to tinkering with the motor. I was hoping to find him working on the Hellcat because that would've been an indication he's ready to forgive me. Regrettably, nothing is ever easy for me.

"What's the issue?" I ask, attempting to start our conversation we're both knowledgeable on. He didn't just teach me how to protect his daughter, he taught me many other things as well—motor rebuilding included.

I'm anticipating for him to continue giving me the cold shoulder, so you can imagine my surprise when he says, "Wren said it's making a shuddering noise."

I twist my lips. "Are you thinking it's the timing belt?"

"I checked that. It's good."

"Dirty fuel?"

He shakes his head. "I only ran a fuel cleaning agent through it last month. It coughed up the gunk within the first week."

Air blasts from my nose as I consider other possibilities. Although getting Wren's old station wagon back on the road isn't the reason for my visit, it made a perfect entrance for a long-overdue conversation.

When the spotlight hanging from the engine mount blows in a breeze, a possible reason for the shuddering noise is exposed. "She has a nail in her back tire."

"Huh?" Mr. Gregg pops his head up from the motor, only just clearing the hood to peer at the direction I'm pointing in.

Since his big frame is no longer shadowing the light, I spot three additional silver specks. "Actually, it looks like more than one."

He yanks down the spotlight like it's perfectly normal for a man to reach that high before shining it at the tire. "You're right. There are four in that section alone."

While he rotates the tire seeking additional nails, I say, "If they didn't puncture the valve, she wouldn't have noticed any difference in pressure. It would've just created a thud noise with the road surface."

He grunts in agreement. "Good pick-up." While muttering about useless teens having nothing better to do, he heads for a spare in the trunk.

He rolls it halfway to the damaged one before I blurt out the real reason for my visit. "I want permission to date your daughter." When hell-to-the-fucking-no flares through his eyes, I talk quicker. "I know I should've asked before it went as far as it did last night…" His growl has my gums flapping so fast I'm five seconds from take-off. "Can you at least admit you're lying to yourself if you say you never saw this coming?" The sternness in his eyes lessens when I add, "I've wanted this for years, Liam, and from what Melody said last night, so has she."

"She's seventeen, Brandon. She's not old enough to make life-altering decisions."

He glares at me when I give Joey's excuse a whirl. "She's eighteen next month."

After shoving the jack under the station wagon, he pumps up the car with the aggression he wishes he could pummel my face in with.

Since he's minus one dangerous weapon, I continue with my plea. "She's also very smart. Not just brain smart but street smart as well." When he huffs like he doesn't believe me, I ask, "You taught me to trust my instincts, so why aren't you giving Melody the same leeway?"

"This is different, Brandon. She's my daughter. My baby girl…" He curses under his breath when his voice cracks. "I don't want her to get hurt."

"I won't hurt her."

"It's not you I'm worried about!" With Hulk-inspired strength, he rips the damaged tire off Wren's car before replacing it with the spare. "If you are making gaga eyes at her, you're not monitoring the area. You're not watching her back. You're not doing *any* of the things I trained you to do."

"That's not true."

"It is, Brandon. You may not believe it now, but in the future, you'll discover I was right. But by then, it will be too late. Melody will already be hurting." I'm set to argue, but what he says next stuffs my words into the back of my throat. "They made me pick. They made me pick between Wren and Melody. They either raped my wife or my daughter. She was five, Brandon. Five!" He angrily brushes away a tear on his cheek. "Do you have any idea how much that question fucked with my head?"

I nod in full understanding. "But you stopped them. You fought back."

"Yes. But only *after* I had given them my answer. Only *after* I had broken my wife's heart."

Hearing the words he doesn't speak the loudest, I say, "Wren loves you, Liam. She's never stopped loving you."

He shakes his head, disagreeing with me. "You can't love someone who's incapable of loving themselves. It isn't possible." He stops screwing bolts onto the spare to lock his eyes with mine. "I appreciate you coming to me man to man as you should've months ago." I nod, admitting the wrongs I've done. "But I will not allow you to date my daughter. That wasn't what any of this was *ever* about." He gestures his hand between us. "I care for you, Brandon, and I tell everyone I know what a good kid you are, but I once again need to put my daughter first. Can you understand why I need to do that?"

I want to shake my head. I want to tell him in a month the decision will no longer be in his hands, but the raw pain in his eyes has me nodding my head instead.

Relief sparks through his eyes before he matches the bobs of my head. "I'll send Wren over later tonight to collect Melody's things."

His words are like a knife to the chest. "You can trust me with her. I won't hurt her."

My heart is already breaking, but he adds an additional crack when he replies, "No, I can't. I *trusted* you with her. I don't anymore."

The deafening buzz of an air-compressor steals my chance to reply. It's for the best. I truly don't know what to say. I had considered many scenarios in the hours Joey spent in recovery, but not even being trained to look for the negative in everything had me stumbling over this scenario.

My slow trudge to the dividing fences between our properties slows even more when I hear Melody's name being shouted by her mom. Even being scared shitless of all things that creep through uncut grass at night, Melody races across the overgrown paddock. Tears roll down her cheeks unchecked as she signs for me not to give up on her, for me to not to give up on *us*.

I'm about to push off my feet and meet her halfway, but before I can, her father arrives out of nowhere and curls his arms around her waist. She thrushes against him and claws her nails into his arm, but his hold is too strong. She has barely signed that she hates him when he drags her through the side door of their ranch.

Melody must break out of his hold not long after because, quicker than I can blink, she's peering down at me from the window of her bedroom. She's still crying, but now her tears are more in anger than fear. She wasn't lying when she told her dad she hated him. It was fueled by the same anger that burned her alive when she point-blank refused to do his drills anymore. It was shortly after her fifteenth birthday. She wanted to forget the nightmare of her past, but she couldn't do that with monthly real-life reminiscing. Her dad fought her all the way, but at the end of the day, Wren and Melody won.

They'll win this battle too. It might just take a few days longer than I'm hoping.

MELODY

"*W*ill *you please eat something?*" My dad replaces the untouched sandwich and unopened potato chips packet with a plate full of fried rice and satay chicken before pivoting around to face me. "*It has been three days, Melody. You need to eat, or you will end up sick.*"

While rolling my eyes, I shift onto my opposite hip, so I'm facing away from him. I haven't spoken to him since I told him I hated him. I'm so mad at him for taking away the only good thing in my life. I followed his rules, I did every one of his stupid drills, but instead of being rewarded for my dedication, I'm being punished for it.

Brandon has been a part of my life for so long, I genuinely feel hollow without him in it. We texted back and forth the night he braved my father alone, but we lost that branch of communication when my father discovered the reason behind my silence and confiscated my phone. Then he sent Brandon away this morning when he brought over our study notes for the bio-chem test we have later this week.

I know we're young, but it's hypocritical of my parents to preach sainthood when they didn't follow it. My mom wasn't a month out from being an adult when she slept with my dad. She had only just turned seventeen. At least Brandon is the same age as me. My father was twenty-one when he took my mother's virginity, so he should've known better.

I'd tell my dad he's a hypocrite if it wouldn't require me to communicate with him.

My flatlining pulse gets a massive spike when my father crouches down in front of me. *"We are going to visit Joey tomorrow."* Its unusual climb doesn't last long. It fades to barely a blip on the radar when he adds, *"Mr. McGee has assured me Brandon won't be there, so you can come with us if you would like."*

When I remain as still as a statue staring out in space, giving him no indication whatsoever I'm interested in his offer, he sighs before leaving my room. How do I know he sighed if I didn't see his lips move? I felt the vibration of his disappointment. It rattled right through my ribcage before belting my heart with painful slaps.

I flop onto my back when the pang of disappointment in my chest is overtaken by the hollow rumble of my hungry stomach. I'm starving, but since eating is the one thing my father can't control, I refuse to bow to the pleas of my stomach until my one demand is met. My father either lets me see Brandon, or I starve to death. The choice is his.

Curiosity overtakes my anger when a flash of light captures my attention a few minutes later. I'm not wearing anything reflective, so it isn't coming from me, and it's past nine o'clock, so it can't be from outside.

My inquisitiveness gets the better of me when it happens again. This flicker was quicker than the last one, but there's no doubting it isn't a natural event. Someone is purposely shining a light into my room.

My sludge-like steps from my bed double when I realize the light is coming from outside. It's projecting from an area I've glanced at more times than not the past three days. It's coming from Brandon's bedroom window.

When I hold up my hand to shelter my eyes from the bright light, I spot a shadowed figure in Brandon's window. Although white spots are dancing in front of my eyes, and Brandon is the size of a lady beetle, I'm confident he's smiling at me. I'd recognize that wonky grin anywhere.

It takes me a few seconds to work out why he places his hand in front of the flashlight longer sometimes than others, but when I do, my cheeks groan in protest to my smile. My father didn't just teach us how to physically survive an ambush, we learned many things—including Morse code.

After holding up my hand from Brandon to stop, I snatch a notepad and pen off my desk before hunting for the flashlight I hooked into my cupboard when I told my dad I wasn't doing his drills anymore. Fingers crossed the batteries are still good.

Once I've found my flashlight and tested its batteries, I return to the window. I almost give Brandon the signal to talk first, but the hurt in my chest has me sending him codes first. It takes me referencing old notes to recall the pattern needed to tell Brandon I miss him, but it was worthwhile when he replies that he misses me more.

We stare at each other across an overgrown field for several heart-healing minutes before Brandon commences his next lot of code. It only takes six letters for me to know what he's going to say.

Please eat.

Even through an ancient form of communication, I can feel his worry.

When I shake my head, he repeats his code again, but he adds an additional word at the end. *Please eat, Mellowy.*

His use of my nickname burns my eyes with tears, but they don't fall down my face. I'm too dehydrated and malnourished for that.

Please...

Brandon stops Morse coding when I briefly nod. I hate that I'm giving in, but since it's more for Brandon than my dad, it doesn't fill me with as much frustration as you'd suspect.

Brandon waits for me to consume one-third of my plate before responding to the question I asked before I commenced eating.

How did you know?

I've always been a talkative person, so the shortness of our conversation is annoying the shit out of me, but I'd rather it over continued nothingness.

Brandon's reply is shorter than my question but extremely anticipated.

Your mom.

When I put down the plate, his sequence of flashes beep closer together since he's so eager to get his message across.

More.

I shake my head.

Sick.

Even from a distance, I can see the panic on his face. I'm not feeling sick because I am unwell. It's because I haven't eaten in so long, my stomach needs time to adjust.

Since it would take all night to explain that to Brandon, I use an easier approach.

Full.

After nodding, advising he understands me, he switches on the light in his bedroom. Although there's a generous stretch of unused land between us, I'm certain he's signing that he loves me.

Smiling for the first time in days, I mimic his gesture, but I finalize my reply by blowing him a kiss. His smile beams brighter than the moon before his room suddenly plunges into blackness. I discover the reason for his quick departure when the waft of my bedroom door shooting open fans the fine hairs on my nape, and the clomp of my dad's boots vibrate beneath my bare feet.

He doesn't say anything about me being out of bed, or the fact I've eaten, but I don't need confirmation of his surprise to know about it. I felt his balk.

"Have you finished?" he asks, stopping at my side. He appears even larger than I remember since I'm sitting on the reading nook he built into my window, cuddling my knees with my arms.

I keep my arms wrapped around my legs, continuing the childish game he thrust us into with his unreasonableness.

My silence maims his heart more than usual. I feel it in my bones when he gathers my plate and exits my room. It adds cracks to my already fragile heart and has words of forgiveness sitting on the tip of my fingers, ready for release, but before I can, he turns around, locks his eyes with mine, then murmurs, "One day you'll understand why I did this, Melody."

His belief that he knows what's right for me refortifies the wall I commenced building between us two years ago, except now, it's stronger than it's ever been. This is no longer about a teenage girl wanting to spend her weekends like every other teen on the planet. This is about him having no clue who I really am, and how he could lose me forever if he doesn't learn that quickly.

BRANDON

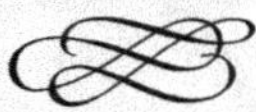

"What's the go? I haven't seen you home this often since…" Madden runs a hand over his military-style haircut before grunting, "*Ever.*"

His new 'do' is part restitution for his mishap last week. He's no longer attending college to earn a degree in fraternity partying. He's joining the military. My father accredits it with getting his life on track, so he's hoping it will do the same for Madden. I don't like his chances, but when you're grasping for straws, you take any option available.

I stop peering at Melody's house to lock my eyes with Madden. He's finally washing his Pontiac, albeit a little hesitantly. He's more watering it than giving it the scrub it needs. "Mr. Gregg has suspended our training until he gets back from deployment."

"He's going out again?" The hesitance in his tone is highly anticipated. I've never been a good liar.

"Not yet. He's just… *busy* until he does." Madden knows I'm lying, but since he cares about no one but himself, he returns to hosing his sleek ride. "Have you seen any movement over there today?" I haven't seen Melody since I convinced her to eat last night. I knew she'd rebel against her father's wish to keep us apart, but I had no clue she'd undertake a hunger strike. I was as panicked as her mother when she informed me Melody hadn't eaten in days.

Madden shakes his head. "Not since they left at ass-crack o'clock this morning."

"*They?* Melody went with them?"

I glance back over at Melody's house, suddenly aware as to why I haven't seen any movement from her room this afternoon. She wasn't at school, either, but that isn't surprising. The Greggs keep her home during finals, so she has plenty of time to study. I've been watching her room like a hawk the past three hours, only changing position because the lowering of the sun added a touch of coolness to the watch post in my room.

Before Madden can answer me, our mom comes barreling out of the house. She's wearing a frilly apron, which only covers her from the waist down, meaning she has a heap of flour on her shirt. She's been baking up a storm all day in preparation for the morning tea fundraiser my high school is having to help fund Joey's medical expenses. Since no one has the heart to tell them money isn't an issue for my family right now, my mom took it upon herself to supply all the baked goodies for them to sell. She'll then donate the money to a heart trust in Joey's name.

People assume we're still living a humble existence because my dad's salary has to stretch across four almost-adult children. They have no clue we still live here because it's our home. All the McGee children were born here. Our ranch is as important to our family as the matriarch of it—our mother.

"Mom?" Panic lodges in my throat when I spot the amount of gloss in her eyes. She's on the brink of sobbing.

Even Madden clicks on to her worry. "Ma? Are you okay? Is Joey okay?"

Her trance ends when Madden mentions Joey. "The hospital just called. They have a new heart for him."

"Huh?" I'm shocked, truly stumped. "Dr. Giorgio said it could take weeks if not months. How has it occurred so soon?"

My mom shrugs. "I don't know." She squeals before grabbing my cheeks and pressing a kiss to my forehead. "But this is exciting! Joey is going to be okay." After embracing Madden in the same manner, she hot-foots it inside. "Bring the car around while I call your father. Joey is being prepped for surgery as we speak."

WE TEAR out of the family driveway not even two minutes later. Mom is so excited, she dusted the flour off her shirt instead of replacing it with a clean one. A buzzing sensation is in the air. It has Phoenix, Madden, and our mother's smiles stretching from ear to ear, but I can't seem to produce half a smirk. I don't know why. There's just a twisted feeling in my stomach that has me more nauseated than excited.

I discover the reason for my unease a quarter of a mile away from my home. There's been an accident on the T-intersection at the end of our street. My mom has called it a hazardous crossing many times, but since it isn't a thoroughfare in a main town, nothing was done about it.

"Stop, stop, stop," I demand on repeat when the mangled wreckage surrounded by first responders and a fire truck registers as familiar. It's the Greggs' family station wagon. "Oh no, please," I beg to no one as I throw open the rear passenger door of my mom's sedan.

Ignoring my mom's plea for me to wait, I race toward the wreckage. It appears as if the station wagon was rammed by a large cattle truck. The driver's side is completely crumbled in, and the passenger side has been peeled open by the jaws of life.

"Were there any casualties?" I ask the first officer I stumble upon. He's wearing plain clothes, and an air of arrogance surrounds him. He must be higher up than his fellow officers.

It feels like the world crumbles beneath my feet when an officer manning the radio of a patrol vehicle shouts for the site to be placed into lockdown since two of the commuters were announced dead on arrival. "Forensics is being brought in."

"No!"

My panicked squeal gains me the attention of the man I attempted to speak to earlier. "Hey, kid, you can't be in here."

When he tries to guide me away from the wreckage, I shrug out of his hold. "That's my girlfriend's car. That's her family wagon. I need to know if she's okay."

I race for the crumbled vehicle, desperate for any signs of life. Strands of blood-smeared blonde hair stuck in a circular crack in the windscreen has me heaving, but I continue my mission, determined to unearth answers to the questions no one will give me.

Sick, twisted gloom overwhelms me when I discover Melody's cell phone on the floor of the wagon. It's coated with shards of glass and twisted metal, but there's no doubt it is her phone. Not only does it have our photo displayed on the cracked screen, it's a cell phone especially designed for deaf people. The flashing light that alerts her to messages is almost as big as my thumb.

"This is my girlfriend's phone. Does that mean she was in the wreckage?" I hold out Melody's phone to face the men circling me with grim, sorrow-filled expressions on their faces. "Was she taken to the hospital?" When they continue staring at me, not speaking a word, I shout, "Which hospital was she taken to? Where did you take her!" I push Phoenix off me when he curls his arm around my shoulders, then step closer to the men staring at me with pity. "I need to know. Please," I beg without shame, uncaring that the tears streaming down my face make me look weak. "Please tell me where she went. *Please.*"

My eyes shoot to my left when an older plain-clothes officer with arms as wide as my head says, "They took them to Mercer."

"Mercer?" I double-check, not wanting the thud of my pulse in my ears to mishear what he said. "On Macquarie and James?"

When the officer nods, Phoenix garbles, "That's Joey's hospital..." His face whitens as reality dawns. "Does that mean... is he..."

With his mouth not working, I take up its slack. "Joey isn't getting any random heart. He's getting a Gregg heart."

WITH MY HEAD a blurred mess of confusion, I don't recall any of our trip to the hospital, or the words my mom shouts when I rocket out of her car the instant she pulls into the parking lot. I hot-foot through the double automatic doors, race past the nurse on the emergency desk asking if I'm okay, and push through the flappy doors like I don't have a security guard on my tail. I know the layout of this hospital as well as I know every perfect imperfection on Melody's face, so I know the exact route to take to find out whose heart Joey is getting, and when I do find out, it shreds my heart to pieces.

The man being kept alive so his organs can be harvested is like a father to me. He taught me how to be brave, and love, and to fix car motors, but more than any of that, he taught me that his daughter is the most precious gift.

A fat, salty blob rolls down my cheek when my eyes shift to the right. There's another body under a white sheet in theater number two. It's small and petite, clear signs it belongs to a female.

"Let him go," Dr. Giorgio advises the security guard when I make my way into the operating room next to the one Mr. Gregg is in. She's one of the rare few who knows about my close kinship with the Greggs because I was visiting Melody when she tried to convince the Greggs to have cochlear implants inserted into Melody's inner ears.

Mr. Gregg refused her suggestion, and for the first time ever, he did it without signing. I told Melody what had happened the following morning. She was mad her dad wouldn't give Dr. Giorgio the time of day, but she also understood why he rejected her offer.

The Greggs never saw Melody's deafness as a disability. If anything, it makes her more unique. I agreed with them, so that was the last time a hearing implant was ever suggested.

Dr. Giorgio follows my solemn trek into the dead, silent space. Her hand raises to squeeze my shoulder when a sob breaks through the shudders wreaking havoc with my body. I don't know how I'm moving. I must be on auto-pilot mode.

A sigh expels from my mouth when I pull back the white sheet covering the patient's face. I'm ashamed to admit it's a sigh of relief. It isn't Melody on the cold steel table with her chest as still as a statue. It is her mom, Wren.

"Was anyone else brought in?" When Dr. Giorgio glances at me in confusion, I stutter out, "Melody. Was she brought in with them? She was in the car. I found her phone."

"No." She peers down at a clipboard in her hand to ensure she isn't mistaken before shaking her head. "First responders only advised us of two occupants in the car." Her brows furrow as her eyes speed-read the report in front of her. "The accident was called in by a TTY. The 911 operator cited in her report that the caller was female." Her heavy exhalation fans her cheeks with air. "She said her parents were in an accident." Her watering eyes lift to mine. "Oh God, she must have been there. Melody must have been in the car with them."

As she advises the security officer to send a patrol vehicle to the Greggs' family ranch, I race back out of the operating theater even faster than I stormed into them. I crash into my dad halfway down, knocking his cell phone and keys out of his hand.

"I need to borrow those." I snatch up the articles without waiting for permission before sprinting for the parking lot.

"Brandon!" Ignoring the wrath in my father's tone, I continue running. "Brandon, get back here!"

Like all pompous, arrogant men, my father parked in the disabled bay at the front of the hospital, halving my trek. I throw open the driver's side door of his sleek new Audi before sliding into the leather-trimmed seats. The engine cranking over almost drowns out my father's warning that he'll kill me if I get so much as a scratch on his car, but for good measure, I floor the gas to get my point across that I'm already dead on the inside.

With the main route to the Greggs' family ranch most likely closed so they can investigate the crash that killed two prominent members of our town, I take the back roads. My speed is excessive, ensuring my father's wish for me not to scratch his car isn't upheld. I take the corners too sharply, which causes bushy scrubs to drag along the pristine black paint, and we're not going to mention my miscalculation when I slide into the Greggs' dusty driveway. The rear end skids out, only righting itself when I wipe out the front gate.

I come to a stop next to a decked-out patrol car with mangled portions of the gate stuck under the back grill. Dispatch must have sent one of the officers from the crash scene to search for Melody, otherwise, how did he beat me here? I was driving speed limits beyond comprehension.

"Did you find her?" I ask the officer who broke protocol to tell me which hospital they had taken the Greggs.

He shakes his head, sending a dusting of dark hairs into his eyes. "No. I've searched the entire house. She's not in there."

"She has to be. She was taught to go home when she's in danger." I sidestep him before climbing the front porch stairs. I stomp on the ground three times, replicating the syllables of Melody's name. It's a way of shouting for her since she can't hear me.

After checking the coat closet, the walk-in pantry, and the storage nook under the stairwell, I take the stairs two at a time. I move toward the hidden closet in the far back corner of Mr. and Mrs. Gregg's bedroom before heading to Melody's room.

"Melo—" My three-stomp shout stops after two when the faintest sob trickles into my ears. It came from under Melody's bed, her once-favorite spot to hide when we did nighttime drills inside the house.

Flashbacks of when we were kids play through my head when I pull up the ruffled duvet around her bed and lay down on my side. There are no marbles in my pockets this time around, but I'm confident the pain when we eventually leave our hidey-hole will be much worse.

"*It is okay*," I sign to Melody when she scoots deeper into the far corner of the shadow she's hiding in. "*You are okay.*" Her eyes are wide and terrified, and the section of her chest I can see in the poor light reveals a smear of blood, but other than that, she appears relatively uninjured—physically. Emotionally is an entirely different story.

My hands shake when I lift them to cradle her ears. Her shallow breaths turn into long gasps when I balance my forehead on hers before counting to ten. "One Mississippi. Two Mississippi. Three—"

My words croak when Melody's lips mimic the movement of mine, "*Mississippi. Four Mississippi.*"

When we reach ten, one solemn tear glides down her cheek. That's never happened before. We never reached ten before her dad found us. It's a somber, terrifying thought that he'll haunt me for eternity, and Melody even longer than that.

BRANDON

"*I*s there anyone we can call? A grandparent? Aunt? Someone?" Melody's tear-drenched eyes stray from me to the detective I'm signing on behalf of before she shakes her head. "*Your family is the only family we have. I have not seen my grandparents in over a decade. I don't even know if my parents have...*" she stops for a second before correcting, "*... had brothers and sisters.*"

The detective who patiently waited over two hours for me to coerce Melody out from underneath her bed balances his mud-sodden shoe onto the back of the first responder she's being assessed by before leaning in close to her side. "While I run your information through the system, do you want to get a more thorough check-up at the hospital?"

Before I can relay what he said, Melody rapidly shakes her head, sending strands of blonde hair toppling into her ashen face. Even frightened, her lip-reading skills are notable. "*I am okay. I am not injured.*"

It turns out she wasn't in the car with her parents when they were hit. In the eerie quiet that forever bombards her, Melody felt the ripple of her parents' accident. She described it as feeling like an earthquake, but it shook her soul more than the earth. A normal teenager would've brushed off the vibrations. Melody knew better. She tunes into things differently than other people because she feels and senses sounds instead of hearing them.

She ran the entire quarter of a mile, barefoot, and was first on the scene at her parents' accident. The smear of blood on her chest was from her leaning over her mother's body to check if her father had a pulse. His door was too smashed in for her to check it any other way.

Not realizing her father had placed her confiscated phone into the glove compartment, she ran back home, informed 911 of their accident via the typewriter telephone her parents had installed years ago, then hid under her bed where she stayed for almost two hours before I found her.

The thought of her being alone and scared like that for so long truly guts me. I should've known she needed me earlier than I did. I should have pushed harder to settle the unease in my gut. I should have protected her from harm like I had promised her father all those years ago. But I failed. Again.

Nothing but hurt radiates from Melody's face when she says, *"I just want to have a shower and go to bed."*

"She can do that at my house." I point to my house that's barely seen in the blackness of the night. *"I live right next door."*

The detective shifts his eyes to me. They're full of kindness but still brimming with authority. "Son, I don't think that's a good idea. I sent an officer over there earlier. No one is home."

"Because they are at the hospital. They are..." I stop signing before I spill a secret I'm certain is going to hurt Melody more. *"She is my girlfriend. I won't hurt her."*

"Neither of you are eighteen, which means I can't legally sign her over to you." His kind eyes reveal he hates that he's being forced to follow protocol, but they also expose he won't be a pushover, either. "You will become a ward of the state until we can find a suitable caregiver for you."

"No," Melody gasps out at the same time I beg him to reconsider. *"There is no child services division in this region. She has lived here her entire life, you can't just ship her to another town."* When my pleas seem to be getting through to him, I up the ante. *"She just lost both her parents, can you just give her some compassion? Please."* I ensure I sign each word I speak, so Melody isn't left out of our conversation. She can read lips, but it's dark out, and I don't want to disadvantage her.

"I can't legally sign her over to you." The dip in the officer's tone reveals his wavering constraint. He's on the verge of giving in. I'm confident of that.

"What about my parents? Could you sign her over to them? My father is an ADA. Would he be a suitable candidate?" I ask through cotton-mouth.

As he slants his head to the side, his brow cocks. "Your father is Vincent McGee?"

"Yes," I respond for the first time ever with pride in my tone.

He cranks his head to Melody. "Is that true?"

I see a million thoughts filter through her eyes before she nods. She's confused as to why admirable and kind people like her parents are killed when men evil and vindictive like my father get to live.

Since I don't have an answer for her, I focus my attention back to the detective. *"Can you sign her care to my parents?"*

"Temporarily, I can..." I almost fist bump the air, but he continues talking, stopping me, *"... if you can get them here within the hour."*

I grit my teeth to hide my frustration. I don't know about you, but I'm fairly certain a heart transplant takes longer than three hours. However, since I'm just as confident Melody shouldn't be with anyone but me tonight, I yank my dad's cell phone out of my pocket, punch in his birthdate since he's too arrogant to have anyone's but his own, then dial my mother's number.

She answers two rings later, "Please tell me you found her?"

I twist away from Melody and the detective so I can speak to my mom in private. "I found her. She's a little rattled, but she's okay."

My mom sucks back in her relieved breath when I ask, "Is Joey getting Mr. Gregg's heart?"

"Yes," she answers through a sob. "Liam and Wren filled in a directed donation request when Joey was diagnosed. It ensured their donations were transplanted to specific recipients before anyone else. They had both Melody and you on the request as well." I hear the shuffling of her feet before she adds, "I know this is hard to understand right now, BJ, but this was what Liam wanted. In the event of his death, he wanted to help Joey."

"I understand that, but will Melody? This will hurt her, Mom."

Her snivels pick up as she replies, "I know, but we'll get her through this."

Her reply reminds me of the reason for my call. "The detective can't sign Melody over to me since I'm not eighteen. He needs a parental signature until he can find her a proper guardian." I lick my dry lips before forcing out the remainder of my request. "And he needs it within the hour."

I anticipate for her to tell me Joey is still in surgery, so she can't come, so you can imagine my shock when she murmurs, "Okay."

"Okay? You'll come?"

"Yes, I'll come. It's the least I can do for Melody." I overhear her tell my father she'll be back as soon as possible before the tapping of shoes on tiles sound down the line. She's racing away from my father as quickly as I did hours ago, ignoring his repeated demands for her to tell him where she's going.

"Mom?"

She doesn't answer me until the buzz of nighttime insects overtakes my father's burly roar. "Yes, BJ?"

"Please drive carefully."

<hr>

APPROXIMATELY THIRTY MINUTES LATER, I'm guiding a still shuddering Melody through the kitchen of my family ranch. Mom flicks on the lights for each inch of floorboard we travel, only stopping when she reaches the Jack and Jill bathroom between Joey's and my room.

When she places down two fresh towels and twists on the faucet, I nudge my head to the door. "Go."

Her eyes drop down to Melody before they pop back up to me. "No."

She's torn, which is understandable. She has one child in the middle of a very complicated surgery, and another, although not related to her by blood, mourning the loss of the person responsible for saving her child.

It's a terrible position for anyone to be in, so I try and ease her guilt. "It's okay. I can take care of her."

When my mom shakes her head again, Melody convinces her otherwise. *"Go be with Joey, Mrs. McGee. He needs you more than me right now."* When her watering eyes lift to me, they silently tell me she has everything she needs right here. They also reveal she knows whose heart Joey is being gifted.

"Are you sure, Melody?" my mom asks before cupping her tearstained cheek in her hand.

A small handful of tears fall from Melody's eyes when she nods. *"I am sure."*

Even with her assurance crystal clear, it still takes my mom another thirty seconds to leave the bathroom.

Melody's wish for us to be alone is exposed when the rumble of my mom's engine fades into the background. *"I told him I hated him. Those were the last words I spoke to him. My dad died thinking I hated him."*

"No, Melody." I crouch in front of the toilet she's sitting on to lift her downcast head so she can both see and feel my words. *"He knew you loved him."*

"That isn't what I told him." The heartbreak on her face increases with every syllable she signs.

"It doesn't matter what you told him. He knew. He always knew." Confident I can bring her around, I ask, *"How long have I loved you?"*

She glares at me like now isn't the time to discuss our relationship. It isn't, but since it's the only way I can convince her that her father knew she loved him, I'll take it.

"How long, Mellowy?"

More tears flow down her cheeks as she replies, *"For a long time."* A smile breaks through the cloud of sadness overwhelming her. *"Way before you could pronounce your Ds."*

I want to wrap her up in a protective hug before whispering in her ear that everything will be okay, but I can't, so instead, I continue communicating the only way we can. *"That is right. It has been that long... but when did I tell you I loved you?"*

The absolute pain in her eyes softens when she signs, *"Not that long ago."*

I clear away the tears sitting high on her cheeks before replying, *"Because I didn't need to tell you. You already knew. Just like your dad always knew. He knew, Melody. I swear to you, he knew."*

THREE DAYS LATER, I gallop down the stairs of my family's home to prepare Melody's breakfast before she wakes. Unlike the days before her family's accident, she's eating. It just isn't enough to give her the energy needed to get her out of bed. I'm hoping a fruit-boosted smoothie might encourage her to move our daily chats to the back porch.

We've communicated a lot the past three days, and Ms. Sprigs, our middle school guidance counselor and teacher for the deaf, dropped off some pamphlets on helping Melody through her grief. Everyone has been really great—even Phoenix and Madden. They've given Melody space, and Phoenix has been using the main bathroom, so Melody doesn't feel cramped.

The only person acting like Melody's entire life wasn't upended is my father. It took four hours of crying for Melody to collapse in exhaustion the night of her parents' accident, but my father's lecture about me needing to take responsibility for my actions couldn't wait until the following morning. Even with him having plenty of money in the bank, he wanted me to get a summer job to pay for the repairs to his Audi.

When I said, "Fine, whatever," he then demanded to know how long Melody was planning to stay like she had any other place to go. I was angry and so close to pummeling his scornful words back into his throat with my fists.

I would have if my mom didn't intervene. She told him the repairs to his car would be covered by insurance, and for what it lacked, she'd make up for, then she told him Melody could stay for a long as she wanted. He, on the other hand, was no longer welcome.

Although my mom gave him clear marching orders, it took almost an hour of arguing before my father stormed out like he always does. I haven't seen him since.

"Hey, Mom." I lean in to place a kiss on her cheek before moving to the fridge. "Any news on Joey?"

I'll be the first to admit I haven't done a good job of juggling my responsibilities lately. Between Melody's grief and Joey's heart surgery, it's been once clusterfuck after another, but my mom will never call me out on it.

"He's good. Keeping Dr. Giorgio on her toes. She said he'll be moved to the transplant wing later today. If Melody is up for it, perhaps you two can visit him later this week?"

I jerk up my chin, stumped of a better reply. I'm struggling to get Melody to leave my room, so I don't see her going into town anytime soon.

As I slice a fresh banana into the blender, my mom hesitatingly says, "Can I ask you something, BJ?"

"Uh-huh."

She waits for me to add strawberries, blueberries, and half a gallon of milk before replying, "We need to discuss Liam and Wren's funerals with Melody. Father Peters is coming over later today to discuss whether we should have a graveside funeral or one at the church."

"Graveside."

A motherly glint flares through my mother's eyes. "Are you sure that's what Melody wants, BJ?"

I nod without pause for thought. We haven't specifically discussed her parents' funeral, but I know her well enough to know she doesn't want to farewell her parents in an empty church. The Greggs didn't trust anyone, so there's barely anyone to attend their service. A large church service will just make it more uncomfortable for Melody. I want to ease her pain, not increase it.

"Okay." My mom rubs my arm that's still vibrating from the blender's furious buzzes. "I'll let Father Peters know."

"Thanks, Mom."

I stop pouring Melody's smoothie into a large glass when my mom says, "You should've added a dollop of peanut butter to the mix. I bet that would have given Melody the boost you're seeking." Fine lines crease in the corner of her eyes when she laughs at my pouty face. "Maybe next time?"

"Maybe," I agree, smiling for the first time in days.

BRANDON

*E*ight days after Melody's parents' accident, and three days following her first outing out of my room, Melody sits quietly next to two identical coffins. The large picture frames on top of the stark white coffins reveal whose funeral it is, but other than that, there's no indication of the drastic loss the world undertook only eight short days ago.

Melody's friends hover at the back of the half-dozen empty seats. They understand their friend is in pain, but they have no clue how to comfort her, so they stay away. My family fills the front row, and old teachers of Melody's and mine take up the second one.

That's it. Seventeen people to farewell two remarkable souls.

It's not fair. It truly isn't.

When Melody frees her hand from my grip so she can present her eulogy at the podium Father Peters has been manning the past twenty-five minutes, I stray my eyes to the procession of funeral cars, needing to distract myself from the moisture burning my eyes. There's only three—the hearse that brought Liam and Wren to their final resting place, my dad's Audi, and my mom's family sedan. My parents arrived separately, which isn't surprising considering no one has seen or heard from my father since my mother kicked him out. It's for the best. Right now, there's so much going on, no one can be selfish. My father isn't capable of doing that. He's only ever looked out for himself, so it's best for all involved that he stays away.

The woman Father Peters brought in to translate Melody's eulogy solemn tone fades away when I spot an old truck a few spots down from Madden's Pontiac. It's not a car I see often, but its rusty roof and paint-peeled body makes it stand out. I swear it's the same F150 that followed the Greggs' station wagon out of the hospital's parking lot almost two weeks ago.

My curiosity doubles when a flash of amber from inside the cab reveals someone is sitting inside. If they drove all the way out to Willow Meadows Lawn Cemetery to say their final goodbyes to Liam and Wren, why stay seated in their car? It's not like there isn't a spare seat closer to the service.

Unless they want to remain concealed?

I'm so immersed in discovering the truck owner's identity, I fail to notice Melody has finished her eulogy and has placed the roses she's been clutching the past thirty minutes onto her parents' coffins, which means it's now my turn.

I lay my roses on top of Melody's so quickly, it almost seems disrespectful. Luckily for me, everyone here knows I'd never disrespect the Greggs unless it were completely necessary.

"Can you watch Melody for a tick?"

Phoenix appears surprised I'm passing the protect-Melody baton onto him of all people, but he jerks up his chin, nonetheless. After telling Melody I'll be right back, I hot-foot it in the direction of the truck. My legs pump faster when the churns of the F150's motor breaks through the thud of the pulse in my ears. It chokes and splatters through poor quality fuel before it finally *vrooms* to life.

The owner, a man I'd guess to be in his early twenties, floors the gas pedal. Since there's only one way in and out of Willow Meadows Lawn Cemetery, he has no choice but to speed by me. I lunge for his truck, groaning when I crash into its big old driver's side mirror with enough force to smash the glass before I land on the ground with a thud. While working through the pain rocketing through my shoulder, I roll onto my stomach to take down the tags of the truck. With exhaust fumes covering a majority of his plate, I only get the last two numbers—73.

I watch the truck until it disappears through the gates of the cemetery before attempting to stand. Since my chase was concealed by large bur oak trees lining the cemetery roads, none of the mourners at Mr. and Mrs. Gregg's funeral witnessed my failure—thank God.

My shoulder is aching like a bitch, but it has nothing on the fury that tears through me when my father grips the lapels of my suit to shove me against the hearse. "What the hell are you doing, Brandon? Why would you chase down a random person like that?" When his tirade gains us the attention of the attendees of the funeral, he straightens the crinkles his grab caused my suit, then lowers the severity of his tone. "You could've gotten yourself killed."

"I know what I'm doing." *Not that you'd know that.* "And it also wasn't a random person. I've seen him before."

A shocked mask falls over my father's face. "When?"

I hate disclosing anything to him, but if it keeps him off my back, I'll tattle like a snitch. "At the hospital two weeks ago. He followed the Greggs when they left the parking lot."

He stills for two seconds, then he laughs—loudly. "I warned your mother this would happen. You're becoming as looney as him." He doesn't need to say Mr. Gregg's name for me to understand who he's talking about. I'm about to tell him I'd rather be over-obsessive about protecting my family than not caring at all, but he continues talking, stealing my words.

"You know his real name wasn't Liam Gregg, don't you?" I shake my head, incapable of speaking through the shock clutching my throat. "That's why the authorities haven't located any guardians for

Melody. There's no record of a Wren Gregg giving birth, much less her own birth records."

"Mr. Gregg most likely hid the information to protect his family." I'm throwing darts blindly at the board with the hope of a bullseye, but I've got to do something because my dad is like an attack dog when he's on the warpath. He doesn't back down for anything.

My father twists his lips. "Possibly… or perhaps he thought the government could read his mind through the internet, cell phone towers, and teller machines like every other whack job in this town."

I scoff before rolling my eyes. "Who's the looney? He worked for the government…" my words trail off when an all-too-familiar glint flares through my father's eyes. If we were playing poker, I'd fold because he's holding a straight flush.

"I worked in the military for over twenty years. It's clear as day in their records. They have no record of a Liam Gregg *ever* working for them."

His tone is flat and to the point, but I still don't believe him. "Your source is wrong. He was deployed for weeks on end. He wouldn't leave his family for no reason."

The knot my stomach has been twisted in all week tightens when my father says, "Maybe that's the reason he decided to end things the way he did."

End things? What's he saying?

It appears as if my father has mind-reading capabilities when he says, "There were no skid marks at the accident scene. The driver of the truck stated Liam failed to yield at the stop sign. The police are investigating the accident as a criminal act of negligence."

"No," I respond fiercely, shaking my head. "Mr. Gregg would *never* hurt his wife. He loved her."

My father's eyes stray to Melody, who's slowly making her way toward us before returning them to me. "Words damage people more than we realize… especially when you're unstable."

He untangles the twist in my tie, pats my chest with his open palm, then walks away. His I'm-the-perfect-father ruse is played to perfection. He's just acting around the wrong person. Melody sees straight through his scam. The way she sidesteps him to come straight to me is proof of this, not to mention how the sadness in her eyes can't hide the anger she's directing at him.

"Are you okay?" she asks, stopping to stand next to me.

I have a million thoughts in my head, but since this is the funeral of her parents, and we're leaning against the hearse responsible for bringing them to their final resting place, it can wait a few more days.

"Everything is fine. I just thought I knew the person in the truck."

When I wrap my arms around Melody's shoulders to guide her back to her parents' gravesites, her big brown eyes lift to mine. *"I thought the same thing."* I give her my best *'huh?'* face, which keeps her talking without additional prompting, *"The truck. I've seen it before."*

"At the hospital after visiting Joey?" The fast patter of my heart is heard in my tone.

Melody's brows furrow before she shakes her head. *"No. It was at Mary's when I went to get milkshakes with my girlfriends. It pulled in behind my mom's station wagon and followed her back out."* When she screws up her nose, fresh tears topple down her cheeks. *"Now that I think about it, that was the day she was really rattled. Remember how I told you she was acting weird?"*

I jerk up my chin. It wasn't a long conversation because it was smack bang in the middle of the two times we had sex. She told me how she felt like her mom was eager to get rid of her, and that she thought she looked scared when she held her gaze in the rearview mirror.

"Do you know if your mom told your dad about that day?"

She shrugs. *"I truly don't know. Things kind of blew up after that."* She stares into the distance as she licks her dry lips. *"Before I snuck out that night, I stumbled onto them talking in the kitchen. It was unusual for my mother to raise her voice, so I was surprised when her shouts vibrated my chest."*

"They would not have stayed mad at each other for long. They loved

each other too much to waste time fighting." Hating the sad expression on her face, I tug her under my shoulder and press my lips to her temple.

The tension strangling my heart slackens when she signs, *"Kind of like us, hey?"*

"Yes, exactly like us."

Mr. and Mrs. Gregg's wake is as subdued as their funeral. There's just one difference this time—a special guest has made an unexpected early trip home. The tubes from Joey's chest have been removed, and the staples from his collarbone to the end of his ribs have begun healing, but he's still as white as a ghost, and he's lost a bit of weight as well.

"Hey, pipsqueak." He messes my hair before pulling me into his chest for a halfhearted hug, then he strays his eyes to Melody standing next to the dining table laden with food. "How's our girl doing?"

Not a pang of jealousy hits me from him calling Melody 'our girl.' He's never been a threat to my friendship with Melody, and he won't be now that we're more than that.

"She's okay. She is strong."

"'Cause her daddy taught her to be." My lips lift into a smirk of agreement. "Do you think she's up for this?" When I drift my eyes to his, he waves his hand down his chest. "I debated coming, but Dr. Giorgio thought it would be good for us." The burn of moisture in his eyes is felt by mine. "I didn't want this, BJ. I was happy to wait."

"I know that, Joey, and so does Melody. She doesn't blame you for any of this. She's actually glad her parents' legacy gets to live on in some way." With that in mind, I stand from my chair before guiding Joey toward the dining table. He's a little weak on his feet. He shuffles more than walks.

I stomp my foot down three times, so I don't startle Melody

since I'm approaching her from behind before tapping her shoulder. She spins around, her mouth falling open when she spots Joey. She wraps him up into a firm hug before she remembers the staples in his chest aren't there for no reason.

"Oh my God, I am so sorry. Here, sit." She yanks out a dining chair from under the table and forcefully shoves Joey in it.

"Thanks," he signs with a chuckle, his one word breathy. *"I am sorry I didn't get to the service. We were given the runaround by the medical transportation company we hired."* When he says 'we,' his eyes drift to Dr. Giorgio standing in the corner of the living room, forever on alert when it comes to Joey's health.

"That is okay. You are here now." Because Joey isn't as knowledgeable in sign language as me, Melody talks to him slower than she does me. *"How are you feeling? Did the operation work?"*

Joey nods. *"Yeah, it went well."* I feel Melody's heart skip a beat when Joey asks, *"Do you want to listen?"*

Melody's tears wet my dress shirt when she dips her chin. *"Please."*

Smiling an apprehensive grin, Joey seizes Melody's hand in his before carefully placing it over his chest. Not even a nanosecond later, Melody's spare hand shoots up to clamp her mouth. Although tears are streaming down her cheeks, I know they are happy tears. The smile peeking out from behind her hand assures me of this, much less the faintest movement of her lips. *"Daddy."*

MELODY

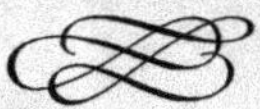

TWO MONTHS LATER.

y eyes pop up from the bright pink nail polish I'm painting on my toenails when the gust of a door bursting open flutters over my arms a mere second after three stomps vibrated my chest. When I spot Brandon standing in the doorway of my room, I smile at him. He's out of breath like he climbed the old stairs of his family ranch to reach me. That isn't the case. My room in the brand-spanking-new McGee residence is on the lower level. He's just panting because he's excited. It's a nice thing to see after months of turmoil. I haven't seen his face this lit-up since my eighteenth birthday. He was overjoyed that day because no matter what his father said, I'd never become a ward of the state.

I could've moved out on my own after my birthday; my trust fund is more than capable of funding a nice apartment in town and a few years of schooling, but Mrs. McGee was adamant her home was also my home.

That home now happens to be a sprawling mansion on the fringe of New York City.

I can't one hundred percent testify that Mrs. McGee finally relented to her husband's pleas to move closer to his office, because part of me still believes she only moved because she saw the pained expression on my face whenever I glanced over at my family ranch.

No matter how much I strived to build the courage, I couldn't bring myself to go there. The house looked like it always did, but it felt cold and empty from a distance, so I didn't want to test the theory up close. Home is where your heart is. My father's heart no longer lives in my family's ranch. It's Joey's chest, and he's right here in the room next to Brandon's.

Brandon has been my rock the past nine weeks. He held me when I cried and made me smile when I was confident I wouldn't be happy for years to come. He's been gentle when needed and stern to the point I wanted to kick his butt.

It's the stern moments I'll relish the most in the future because he only changed who he was for my benefit. I felt so much guilt at the start. I truly believed my dad died thinking I hated him. Brandon showed me otherwise. He taught me that words said in anger mean nothing unless they are attached to an action. It still hurts. Even now, while talking about it, I can feel tears pooling in my eyes. But it's getting better—slowly.

My lips lift against Brandon's hand when he cups my cheeks before placing a kiss to my temple. He must have seen the struggle in my eyes as he's perfected that move the past two months.

As his thumbs brush the shell of my ears like he's dying to cover them and count to ten, his eyes lower to mine. They're as gentle and kind as ever. *"You okay?"*

I nod, recalling his pledge about actions speaking louder than words. I stop bobbing my head when the logo on the envelopes he's holding register as familiar. It's the logo of Browns University, Brandon's and my university of choice. We had been accepted to study there before we had commenced our final year of high school but had to turn it down since my parents couldn't afford the excessive holding fee they requested.

We submitted again with the hope of a scholarship, but we never heard back from them. My dad believed we were being punished for turning down the first acceptance. Since I agreed with him, Brandon and I submitted a handful of applications to other universities, which were accepted, but we've been holding out on organizing living arrangements at our second pick, hopeful the admittance clerks at Browns would eventually forgive us.

Although I don't want to get my hopes up, any news from them is good news as far as I'm concerned. If they decline our applications, we'll move onto our next pick. If they approve it, this could be a game-changer for Brandon and me.

"Did you open it?"

Brandon plops his backside onto my bed before shaking his head. *"No. I wanted to wait for you."* He hands me the envelope with my name on it before lowering his eyes to the one he's clutching for dear life. *"Do you want to go first or shall I?"*

His eyes lock with mine when I reply, *"How about we do it at the same time?"*

When he nods, I get ready to pull on the open tab. I've barely slid my thumb under the flimsy cardboard when Brandon places his hand over mine. *"No matter what these applications say, nothing changes for us. We are still us, okay?"*

I nod in agreement without pause for thought. I waited over a decade for him to make his second move, so I'm more than capable of waiting another four years.

"Okay. On the count of three." He exhales his nerves with a big breath before saying, *"One Mississippi. Two Mississippi. Three—"*

The final Mississippi has barely left his mouth when I rip the tab across the envelope and tear out the single sheet of paper inside.

My eyes go crazy seeking any words along the lines of 'congratulations,' 'we're pleased to' or 'invited.'

All I find is a 'we regret to inform you…'

With my heart in my throat, I raise my eyes to Brandon. His cheeks are flushed, that's nothing out of the ordinary, he blushes all the time, but his smile sure is. It's one of pure exhilaration.

"You got in."

"Yes!" He nods his head in quick concession. *"I got in..."* The excitement on his face fades when he notices the glum expression on mine. I'm excited for him, but I'm also terrified about where we go from here. *"You didn't get in?"* When I shake my head, he snatches the paper out of my hand, certain I read the results wrong. *"You had to get in. You are smarter than me."*

"Clearly not." I give myself a stern warning to wipe the disappointment from my eyes. Brandon worked hard for this. He deserves both this and my praise. *"But you did. I'm so proud of you, BJ—"*

My hands freeze midair when he says, *"I will turn it down."* I watch him with my mouth hanging open when he stands from the bed, scrunches up his acceptance along with my rejection, dumps them into the bin under my desk, then spins around to face me. *"We will go to our second choice. It is a good school—"*

"It isn't Browns, BJ. It is the best school in the state."

He shrugs like it isn't a big deal he's giving up his dreams for me. *"I don't care. I am studying forensic science. I don't need to go to a $70,000 a year school for that."*

His attitude takes a step back when I reply, *"Brandon, you need to think about this."* I'm not overly angry at him, but I'm mad he can't put himself first for a change. For years, he did everything and anything my father asked of him. He did drills designed for men even though he was only a child, dangerous covert operations, and sat through psych exams for years, so if anyone deserves to sit back for just a tick and be selfish, it's him. *"I want you to go to Browns."*

He instantly shakes his head. *"No, Melody. We agreed to attend the same school when we convinced your parents not to homeschool you anymore."*

"That was in grade two, BJ. It wasn't meant to extend this far."

Ignoring his shaking head telling me nothing will change his mind no matter what I say, I dig out the applications with the 'acceptance' words I was seeking earlier. I rarely left Saugerties, so my geographical knowledge isn't the best, but I do recall Brandon jotting the distance of each approved application from Browns, so if a mid-degree transfer were ever approved, we wouldn't have far to travel.

Once I have my bearings right, I shift on my feet to face Brandon. *"I will go to Dartmore while you go to Browns. It is only an hour away. It is practically the same campus."*

His facial expression is worse than the one he was wearing when he crawled under my bed for the final time two months ago. *"An hour! That isn't close, Melody."*

"You are only saying that because you are used to having me right here. An hour is nothing for normal people." When his lips twitch, I hit him with a stern glare. *"If you say we are not normal, I will hurt you."*

My warning softens the harshness tainting his boyishly handsome face. *"If I say it while I have my hands down your pants, will that save me?"*

"No." It's the fight of my life not to squirm. Between grief, our move, and life in general, we haven't been intimate since the first night. It kind of makes me scared. Like I'll have to go through that horrendous virginity popping all over again.

I decide it will be worth the sacrifice when Brandon tugs me closer to him. He kisses my temple, my cheek, and my lips before inching back. *"We will go to Dartmore together like we planned."*

"When we were five."

"Six," he corrects.

My eyes snap to his. *"Still, kids too young to know what they were committing to."*

I feel a purr rumble in my chest when the prickles on his chin scratch my neck. He's gotten slack with shaving since summer break started. I don't mind. I like his whiskers.

"I want you to go to Browns, BJ..." I sign faster when he tries to interrupt me, *"... because who is to say they will accept you again when I hit them with a transfer request after transfer request after transfer request. You turned them down once and survived. That won't happen a third time."*

Brandon stops sneakily watching me from the crook of my neck to ask, *"You will apply for a transfer?"*

"Yes," I reply with utmost honesty. *"I won't stop until they get so annoyed seeing my name over and over again, they will approve my transfer just to shut me up."*

I see his brain ticking over a million miles an hour. *"So, our separation will only be temporary?"*

My lips purse. *"We are not separating. We are just attending different schools for the time being."* I sock him in the stomach. *"You can't get rid of me that easy. You are stuck with me for eternity."*

The sheer terror in his eyes completely evaporates when he says, *"I like the sound of that."*

"Not as much as I love the feel of this." I stroke him through his cargo shorts, switching his cock from semi-aroused to virally hard in an instant. *"Is your mom home?"*

Sprinkles of golden hair fall into his eyes when he shakes his head. *"She dropped me off, so I was saved a visit to my dad's office. His campaign flyers arrived with our letters."* Even with my hand on his crotch, his focus remains on my well-being. *"You should have come with us. Socks would have liked to have seen you."*

I huff. *"Socks doesn't care about anyone as long as he is getting fed."*

He doesn't argue with me. He never debates the truth.

"How was everything else?" I step him toward my twin bed while loosening the drawstrings on his shorts, acting like my heart is racing in excitement instead of mourning.

Brandon's hum vibrates my mouth before he adds words to his reply. *"It was good. The caretaker my dad hired is looking after the place."* A normal person would mistake his reply as meaning his family ranch. I know that isn't the case. He was referring to my family home because, to him, they're one in the same.

"And the crosses? Are they there?"

When I pull him onto my bed, he rolls us over until I'm straddling his lap. *"Yeah. They look good."* He tucks my hair behind my ear so it can't shelter my face before saying, *"Maybe one day you will come see them with me?"*

"Maybe..."

"Mel—"

"Shh," I interrupt. *"Not today. I don't want any more sadness today."*

He looks like he wants to argue, but the removal of my shirt stops him. Sex isn't the only thing we've refrained from the past two months. We haven't seen each other naked either. We share a house, but we still have separate rooms. It was at Mr. McGee's request more than Mrs. McGee's.

"BJ?"

Brandon watches me grind against his crotch three times before replying, *"Yeah?"*

"Do you still have lube in your drawer?" Need pulsates through my veins as I say, *"The one you swear you have not used in months."*

Smiling, he rolls his eyes. *"Joey is lying. I have not used it."*

I take a moment to relish the revitalizing zap roaring through my body before asking, *"Does that mean you still have it?"*

After slowing the movements of my hips, his teeth graze his bottom lip. *"Uh-huh. Should I go get it?"*

I look down at the man I've loved since he was a boy before nodding. The blush that creeps across his cheeks will keep my heart beating for months to come, much less his frantic dash into his room.

MELODY

FIVE MONTHS LATER.

randon and I stumbled into my dorm at Dartmore. Arms and legs go in all directions as we endeavor to strip each other's clothing before we reach my bed housing my latest rejection letter for Browns. I don't know what I did to the admissions officer from Browns in a previous life, but he obviously knows how to hold a grudge. Even with an article in the *New York Times* saying attendance was low for them this year, every request for a transfer I've made over the past five months has been denied.

My grades did slip a little at the end of my senior year due to my parents' death, but they're still remarkable. Brandon said that exact thing multiple times tonight when we attended one of his father's ritzy parties. It was brimming with people from all walks of life, including some law professors from Browns.

They assured Brandon that Mr. Darcy will come around eventually. I just hope it isn't by the time I graduate. I've missed Brandon so much our first three months at college, I mentally have to remind myself not to reflect my anguish to him. Brandon is loyal to a fault. He'd leave his studies at Browns in an instant if I told him our separation is breaking my heart.

I'm surrounded by thousands of people every day, but I've never felt more alone.

It's so lonely here, and it has nothing to do with the fact there are only two other deaf students at this university. Disability allowance cuts mean things like note-takers for the deaf comes out of the university's pocket, so a lot of universities are shying away from offering scholarships to people with hearing impairments. Most of the lecture theaters have hearing loops installed, but since I'm profoundly deaf, I can't use hearing aids. Cochlear implants are still a consideration, but since that's more than I'm willing to spend right now, I'll continue sitting at the front of the lecture halls to ensure I have a clear view of the lecturer's mouth, so I can read his lips.

I emerge from the dense cloud surrounding me when Brandon murmurs my name. He didn't sign it, but I felt the vibration on my chest.

"Sorry, I zoned out."

He tugs down on the cups of my strapless bra to expose my breasts to his more-than-avid eyes before saying, *"I was asking about your roommate. Have they mentioned when she will rock up yet?"*

If he wants me to answer him, he needs to stop sucking my nipple in his mouth. It feels too good to do anything but weave my fingers through his hair.

Brandon's lips raise against my chest before he releases my nipple from his mouth. *"Sorry. I forgot about your inability to communicate when my mouth is on you."*

"Brandon James McGee, is that cockiness beaming out of you? Say it isn't so."

He smiles at the jesting cock of my brow before placing a kiss on my left breast, my collarbone, my jaw, and then the little freckle behind my right ear. *"It is impossible for a man not to feel like a hero when he is invited into the bed of a beautiful woman every single weekend."*

I feel him grow heavier against my thigh when I reply, *"Then I guess it is okay to brag because not only are you bragging about me, you are also my superhero."*

"You are only saying that because I have my hand between your legs."

His laughter fans my face when I use a defense technique to flip him over, so I'm straddling his hips. *"Imagine what I will say now since your hand has been replaced with your dick?"*

Before he can reply, I seal my mouth over his. Our kiss is a hungry, all-consuming embrace, but it's also full of love and mutual understanding. Respect has always been a highly-valued commodity in our relationship, and I'm pleased to say it has remained that way even after we tiptoed from best friends to lovers.

I shiver into Brandon's mouth when his fingers brush down my dripping core. Although we attend different schools, distance hasn't stopped us from making up for the time we lost after my parents' accident. We go at it for hours every single weekend because each exchange strengthens our desire for each other.

After inching back, I sign. *"BJ... can we mix things up tonight? I want to try something new."*

His throat works hard to swallow. *"It isn't that pegging thing Carmen mentioned, is it?"*

The pure anguish on his face makes laughter bubble in my chest. *"No. Your butthole is safe..."* His smug expression is wiped away when I add, *"For now."*

Brandon isn't a fan of jokes in the bedroom, especially when they involve my friends telling me I should fuck him with a strap on since he is, I quote, "The bitch in our relationship."

They can't understand our dynamic because they're still chasing men who think waiting for them to fall asleep before sneaking out is how you treat a woman right.

When I slip off the bed and track to my makeshift kitchen in the corner of the room, Brandon props himself onto his elbows. His panicked expression as he watches me cross the room is hilarious. *"Stop fretting. I am pretty sure you are going to love this."*

A peculiar sensation rolls through me like liquid ecstasy when I bend down to remove his surprise from my backpack. I'm not wearing any panties, and since I refuse to bend with my knees when Brandon is around, he's given an uninterrupted view of my nether regions.

After hiding his gift behind my back, I lock my eyes with Brandon's cock. The pre-cum pooling at the top of his impressive manhood slides down the shaft when I pull out a super-large jar of peanut butter from behind my back. It's his favorite brand, but instead of the double-crunch version, I went for smooth. No one wants to chew during sex.

"You want to add peanut butter into our sex life?" I can't tell if Brandon is confused or amused. It could be a combination of both.

I shrug. *"Why not? It is your favorite flavor—"*

"No," he denies, cutting me off. *"You are my favorite flavor. Peanut butter comes in a very close second."*

Excitement burns my cheeks with heat. *"I wonder if your opinion will change if we mixed them?"*

He watches me with hot, hooded eyes when I twist open the lid, dip my index finger inside the sticky goodness, then pop it into my mouth. I'm not as in love with peanut butter as Brandon, but it sure does taste delicious when it elicits a prolonged moan from Brandon. I didn't hear his moan, but my pussy most certainly felt the amazing buzz it created.

Brandon is even harder now, and the goodness dripping from the crest of his cock pops an awesome idea into my head. While walking toward my bed, I circle a thin layer of peanut butter around my nipples and down my stomach, stopping just before the apex of my pussy.

When Brandon's hands shoot out to grab hold of his midnight snack, I slap them away. *"Nuh-uh. Where did your chivalry go? Women must always eat first."* It's harder to sign with mucky gunk on my hands, but I manage, somewhat.

After scooping a generous serving of peanut butter onto my index finger again, I set the jar down before pivoting around to face

Brandon. He falls onto his back with a cocky grin when I push on his shoulder with my spare hand. Once I have him flat on my bed, I draw the peanut butter over his skin like his body is a canvas and I'm Rembrandt.

A vibrating hum simpers through Brandon's body when I drag my tongue along my masterpiece, lapping up every drop of peanut butter off his silky-smooth skin. My lips raise against his taut skin when he mouths, *"I am never going to make a PBJ again without getting hard."*

The further my tongue travels down the bumps in his midsection, the higher his backside lifts from my bed. He doesn't work out as rigorously as he did when my father was in charge of his training, but he's maintained his strength and his delicious six-pack.

When I reach the thin patch of tight blond curls across his groin, Brandon's chest rises and falls as erratically as the pulse in between my legs. I'm dying to suck his impressively large cock into my mouth, but I can't help but tease him for a little.

"Mel..." He pulls a face like he's in pain when I creep back up his stomach. *"You can't do that to a guy. It isn't fair."*

"I missed a bit. No peanut butter can be left behind."

I lick and nib at the blob of nutty goodness I purposely left sitting on his right nipple before peering up at him with glistening, bliss-filled eyes. I'm an orphan with no known family members whatsoever, yet I feel like the luckiest girl alive when a pair of wide, lust-crammed eyes wink at me like I could tease him for five days straight, and he'd never get mad. I've suffered a lot of heartache in my short life, but there have been good points as well.

Brandon is by far the greatest.

Spotting the poignant expression on my face, Brandon flips me over like I did to him earlier. He does it gentler than I did because he'd rather take a knife to the heart than ever hurt me.

Although I feel a ball of muckiness sitting low in my stomach, I act annoyed at his interference in my game plan. *"Hey! This isn't your show, buddy."*

"You have eaten," he signs as his mouth lowers to my breasts coated in his favorite condiment. *"Now it is my turn."*

He pretends like he can't wait a second longer, but I know him better than that. He's keeping my head out of the dark, nothingness void it has tiptoed toward many times the past seven months. I'm happy, Brandon makes me incredibly happy, but sometimes I'm lonely too. My therapist says that's okay. Soaring highs can make the lows seem lower than they are, but she wants me to find a healthy balance between them.

I want that too. I just don't want to do it by lessening my crutch on Brandon as she's suggesting. She's judging our relationship by only seeing one side of the story. To an outsider, our dependency on each other could seem weird, but to us, it's perfectly normal.

My mind goes far from an empty void when Brandon's tongue reaches a section of my skin not sticky with peanut butter. He peers up at me staring down at him, patiently waiting for my wordless permission to devour me.

I give it to him without a smidge of hesitation, incapable of denying him. He's never been rough, in or out of the bedroom, but even if he wanted to be, I'd never stop him. If he needs to clutch my hair to get him through the greediness of my sucks when I am giving him head, I'm okay with that.

Just like I'm more than okay with this.

"Yes, BJ," I sign in my head when he drags the wetness of my slit up to my clit before he sucks my clit into his mouth.

As he entices my clit with quick, rapid-fire hits of his tongue, he slides two fingers inside of me. It's not as uncomfortable as the first time he fingerfucked me, but it still has a pang of pain attached to it. His fingers are still carrying some of his baby fat.

His skilled fingers plunge in and out of me as he draws my clit into his mouth with long, controlled sucks. The sensation is amazing. I'm quivering all over within a matter of seconds. College fucking shouldn't be like this. From the stories I've heard from my girlfriends, you're supposed to get drunk, fumble out of your clothes, then pray he gets it in before he comes.

That's never been the case with Brandon. Our make-out sessions last for ages, and he never comes before I do. I'm not even sure he came the first time we had sex. He was quick to dispose the blood-smeared condom that had me wanting to crawl into a hole and die, but I still noticed it was minus the liquid our second attempt had.

The night we stumbled into adulthood is long forgotten when a climax blindsides me. I usually feel the long, tingling build-up before exploding, but tonight's creeps up on me unaware. It doesn't weaken its brilliance, though. It's one of the strongest I've ever had.

As I grip the bed sheets, Brandon laps up the evidence of my arousal with teasingly long licks. He growls into my pussy, loving how quickly he sends me toppling into ecstasy before shifting his focus to the bundle of nerves throbbing with need.

With the sensation roaring through me still fresh, the quickest tug on my clit with his teeth sends me freefalling for the second time. I tremble violently, certain I won't survive another orgasm but desperate for another.

Brandon bites, kisses, and licks my sex before he peers up at me. "*More?*"

My hair sticks to my sweaty temples when I shake my head. "*Not yet. I can't.*"

Never one to take anything unwillingly, Brandon kisses my aching clit for the final time before crawling up my body. I don't know where his condom magically appears from, but he has it rolled down his shaft before the cleft of his cock gets anywhere near my drenched slit.

"*Do you want to swap positions?*"

I shake my head again. "*I don't think I can get my legs to move.*"

His smile nearly sends me falling into ecstasy again. "*All right. Then curl your legs around my hips, so you can slow my pumps if I get too excited.*"

Not waiting for me to answer, he guides my legs around his

sweaty waist. Missionary and cowgirl on top are our go-to positions. It has nothing to do with preference and everything to do with Brandon ensuring I only take as much of him as I can.

Once he has his cock lined up and at the ready, Brandon lowers his forehead to mine. *"Ready?"*

We breathe as one when my head dip sees him slowly notching inside of me. He takes it to the very base before slowly drawing it back out, his pace only quickening when I beg him for more. For each rock of his hips, he increases his pace. He plunges in and out of me on repeat, his speed gauged on the moans escaping from my throat.

I feel his cock throb when my thighs shake around him. I'm trembling, my skin both hot and cold. My pussy tugs at him, milking him, while also begging for him to come with me this time around. I love when he comes with me, his breaths heavy on my neck, and his cock fighting through the clenches of my pussy.

Brandon ignores the pleas of my pussy for him to focus on his own orgasm by concentrating all his attention on me. He adds a roll to his hips that has my eyes rolling into the back of my head before lowering his hand to the bud zapping like it could power a city.

I'm still recovering from my two earlier orgasms, so it takes him a little longer to ease my third one out of me. But he does it. He coerces me back into a state of deliriousness with a slow, body-ripping climax that takes everything from me.

I come silently, the intensity of my orgasm rendering me incapable of releasing the moan I feel vibrating in my chest. I'm incoherent, shaking, and heavy-limbed from the warmth spreading through me. It starts at the tips of my toes, then seeps to my pussy that Brandon is still tormenting with precisely timed strokes before it puddles in the orifice I was convinced would never thump again when I stumbled upon my parents' wreckage months ago.

I should've known better. Brandon was raised by my father to protect me, and that didn't just mean in the physical sense. He's keeping me emotionally stable as well, and it's time for me to return the favor.

BRANDON

THREE MONTHS LATER.

"*Mr. Darcy?*"

I follow a middle-aged man through the quad of Browns University. Although he personally knows every student on this campus, he's quite elusive. I've been chasing him for months.

"Mr. Darcy?" I try again when his speed increases so much, his hairpiece flaps in the breeze of his quick strides. "Ms. Melrose said you're the best person to speak to about a request for transfer."

When I reach him, he shoos me away as if I'm a nagging parent willing to do anything to get my kid into the number one school in the state. I'm willing to do anything. Melody just isn't my kid.

"You've denied my girlfriend's request for a transfer over a dozen times now, but you've not once given her a reason. All we want to know is why you keep refusing her application, so we can try and improve it."

His bushy brow shoots up high on his face. "This is an *education* facility, young man, not a place for you and your girlfriend to play house."

His response pisses me off, but I keep a cool head, recalling how intimidation is a form of flattery. "She doesn't want to play house.

She wants to study law. Browns has the best pre-law professors this side of the country."

Mr. Darcy tosses his suitcase into the back of his sleek new ride then holds down his toupee, so he doesn't lose it when he spins to face me. "Perhaps your girlfriend should consider a degree more suitable for her GPA."

"If law isn't suitable for a student with a 3.9 GPA, what would you suggest?"

That piques his interest. "She has a 3.9 GPA?" When I nod, he asks, "SATs?"

"Above average for both SAT and ACT. She even sat the graduate admission test for LSAT last month and passed."

He whistles, clearly impressed. "Not many seniors can pass that, so a freshman should be commended for the effort."

"She'll be a sophomore after summer break. That's how long she's been requesting a transfer." I sound pissed off. Justly so. Melody and I have lived separately for months now because this asshole couldn't see a gifted student if she were standing right in front of him. "She has organized to spend summer break as a personal paralegal at a law firm in the city. They've cited an interest in offering her an internship for additional credit if she can get into the right pre-law courses."

Mr. Darcy's pause reveals he doesn't like giving in, but his interests are too piqued for him to back down. "Where's she studying now?"

"She's spent her first year studying at Dartmore. It's about an hour from here." I nudge my head over my shoulder like he can see Melody's dorm from here.

He *ha's* out loud. "That's not a school. It's a slush fund for rich investors who collect tuition checks from trust fund babies without supplying them any education their parents are paying for."

"That's my point. That's why she needs to transfer her studies to Browns. She's smart, Mr. Darcy. She aces her tests, does extracurricular activities as required as part of her scholarship, and helps my mom with the many charities she chairs. She's perfect for Browns... you just need to give her a chance." I can already see I've won him over, but a little extra sweetener never hurt anyone. "My father has been a benefactor of Browns for years. When he eventually runs for Congress, I'm sure Browns will benefit even more from his contribution *if* they help out the girl he classes as family."

The sweat on the top of his brows is more noticeable when he slants his head. "You're Vincent McGee's son?"

For only the second time in my life, I admit who my father is without shame.

I expect my name-dropping to have Mr. Darcy slotting Melody in for an immediate admissions interview, so you can imagine my shock when our exchange switches from friendly to unpleasant in under a second.

"Unlike Dartmore, you can't buy a degree at Browns." I'm about to tell him Melody will work hard for her grades, but he continues talking, stopping me. "And I strongly suggest you encourage Melody to stop this farce immediately."

I stare at him in shock, confused as to how he knows Melody's name. I never mentioned it, and although she's been putting in a new request every time one is returned denied, there are thousands of students doing the exact same thing, so he couldn't have just plucked her name out of thin air.

"How do you know her name is Melody?"

When he attempts to brush me off as he did earlier, I press my hip to his driver's side door, fold my arms in front of my chest, then stare him down. I haven't grown much the past year, I'm still an inch or two under six foot, but for what I lack in size, I make up for in attitude, especially when I'm wearing my protective mask.

"I never told you her name, so how do you know it?"

Mr. Darcy acts as if I can't see his lips quivering. "You'll remove yourself from my car immediately, or I'll have you removed from the premises... *permanently.*"

There's no threat to his tone whatsoever, which can only

mean one thing—he isn't running the show around here. He went from collective to tightening a noose around his neck way too quickly to be a decision-maker. He'll turn on a dime. I guarantee it.

"Accept Melody's transfer application to Browns—"

His scowl cuts me off more than his sneered words. "I will not be strong-armed, young man."

I continue talking as if he never spoke. "Or I'll tell the board you accept payments from wealthy business associates to guarantee their child's placement at Browns."

His huff blows hot air onto my face. "They'd never believe such preposterous lies."

For once, he speaks the truth. He didn't look up and to the right like he's accessing his imagination, aka, inventing an answer, and the length of his blinks didn't extend. He's not even sweating more than he was when I approached him.

They're all clear signs he's telling the truth, so I try another angle. "Then I'll tell them you accept payments to refuse admittance to students who'd generally be accepted."

His eyes dart to the left as he blinks three times in a row. "That isn't true." He's lying. I'm so confident in my assumption, I'd put money on it. "I've never accepted money to alter *any* admission applications."

Now he's telling the truth. The white line on the top of his lip faded when he un-pinched them, and the pink hue on his cheeks quickly followed it.

Putting two and two together, I reach four. "Then what did you accept?"

While I scan his face, seeking hints of deception in his body language, he grabs my arm to yank me away from his shiny black sports car.

Sports. Car.

With the twitch in my jaw concealed by a smile, I say, "This is a flashy ride for an admissions officer." I whistle like he did earlier.

"What's the average salary of an admissions officer these days? Twenty-seven, twenty-eight thousand—"

"Thirty-three thousand," Mr. Darcy snaps, incapable of ignoring my underhanded goad at his poorly-paying profession.

I smirk like a smug prick. "Thirty-three thousand. Excuse me." I step back from his door, so I can get a better look at his sixty-thousand-dollar ride. Once I've got him sweating to the point I can smell his body odor, I mutter, "How does a thirty-three thousand dollar a year soon-to-be divorcee afford such a sleek ride? I bet your wife wants you to pay out the ass in spousal support, and she'll keep the family home, so how have you kept this little plaything off her divorce lawyer's radar?"

His Adam's apple bobs up and down, revealing I'm on the money. I hadn't researched him as Mr. Gregg urged me to do before approaching a target because up until ten minutes ago, I had no clue an admissions officer at Browns University was a threat to Melody.

I know better now.

I step back from his car. My smug grin only just hides my ticking jaw. "Have a pleasant evening, Mr. Darcy. I'm sure we'll talk again soon."

He watches me for a few seconds, shocked I'm seemingly letting him off scot-free. I'm not. I just need to dig a little deeper before presenting him the evidence that will have him granting Melody admission to Browns for study next year without a formal interview.

After blubbering out an incoherent reply, Mr. Darcy tosses open the driver's side door on his sleek ride, slides into the leather-trimmed seats, fires up the engine, then throws the gear stick into reverse. I maintain eye contact with him in the rearview mirror as he tears out of the lot, my eyes only dropping when I spot the only bumper sticker on the pimped-out BMW 7 Series.

McGee for Office

So, he knows of my father and supports him, but he backpedaled when I hinted he'd be owed a favor from him if he helped Melody. That makes no sense whatsoever. *Unless...*

Before I can work through half the confusion in my head, a deep voice at my left startles me. "How'd you know he's getting a divorce?"

When I pivot to face my inquirer, my brows fetter. The blond man with his shoulder propped against a tree appears around my age, if not a couple of years older, but he doesn't look like the academic type. He's a head taller than me, his shoulders are almost double mine, and he's smirking at my avid assessment of his body. Although I should categorize him as a threat, I'm not getting that vibe off him. He's not a comrade either but more a mutual associate.

"His wedding ring finger had a mark the width of a band. It had faded, but not enough to reveal his divorce was years ago." When he jerks up his chin, impressed, I test the limits of our developing alliance. I shared, so now it's his turn. "How long have you been standing there?"

When he pushes off his feet, I realize my assumption on his height was incorrect. He'd be a good head and a half taller than me —if not two. He could also be four to five years older than me. "Long enough." He scrubs at the bumfluff on his chin he wants me to believe is a beard. "Your body-reading skills are impressive. Who were you trained by?"

"I'm self-taught."

He laughs, calling me out as a liar without words. "Your skills are too advanced to be self-taught, and you don't give off the vibe of a psychology major, so I'll ask you again, who taught you?"

A smile tugs at my lips when he folds his thick arms in front of his chest. "The same man who taught me to ignore intimidation."

I dip my chin in farewell before spinning on my heels and stalking away. I make it halfway across the deserted lot when the stranger grumbles, "Because it's a form of flattery, am I right?"

When I crank my neck back to face him, he smiles a smug grin before nudging his to a large black truck. "Get in. The six-fifteen bus to Dartmore left ten minutes ago."

I walk toward his truck without the slightest quiver to my steps. You don't run when a threat approaches you head-on, you annihilate it. This man—I use the term lightly—knows too much about me to be a casual acquaintance, and I'm too curious to find out why to worry about a little bit of danger.

The blond-haired stranger waits for me to climb into the passenger seat of his truck before he jogs around the hood and slides into the driver's seat without using the side steps for a boost. Before tugging his seat belt across his large frame, he removes a semi-automatic pistol from his hip and stores it in the glove compartment.

His brand of gun is very telling. It's a four-chamber, nine-millimeter Sig Sauer P226, the weapon of choice for field agents in the Federal Bureau of Investigation. How do I know this? Mr. Gregg put me through intensive weaponry training as well.

The stranger's turn of the ignition key falters for a nanosecond when I ask, "Have you been with the Bureau for long? If the kiddy fluff on your chin is anything to go by, I'd say not."

The moon bounces of his white teeth when he smiles, but he remains as quiet as a church mouse.

Incapable of harnessing my curiosity, I slump lower in my seat before interrogating him like I'm wearing an invisible badge. "Your smooth ride would have most people believing you're a highly ranked agent, otherwise how could you afford a newly-plated truck? But you were hanging out at a local college, which means you can't be too far up the food chain, otherwise, why would they send you to investigate a college admissions scam?" He drums his fingers on the steering in beat to the song on the radio, acting unaffected by my interrogation until I say, "So that can only mean one thing. You're not here for Mr. Darcy. You're here for me."

His eyes stray from the road to me. "What could you possibly have of interest to me?" He's asking a question, but he doesn't give me time to answer him. He simply switches off the radio before slicing my attitude in half with a few well-crafted thoughts. "You're so punk-assed, you rocked up to an arena without first checking who was playing. Then, *after* donning a jersey for the team you *thought* was going to win, you switched your game plan from a plea to a con to an interrogation all within the first quarter."

"It worked. I stonewalled him."

His chuckle barrels around the cab of his truck. "You didn't do shit but make more work for me."

His laughter is nipped in the bud when I say, "So you were there for Mr. Darcy? What could he possibly have that you need?" I ask my question with the same mocking tone he used on me earlier. "Unless he's the little fish you're hoping will lead you to the big pond… then you might have a chance of gaining Daddy's stamp of approval."

I realize I hit the nail on the head when the skin under his eye flutters. He's twitching out, but instead of breaking under pressure, he muscles up. After stretching his long arm across the cab, he manually forces my head front and center. "Eyes on the road, punk, or you can get the fuck out of my truck and walk your ass to your girl's dorm."

Keeping his slip-up on the down-low, I mutter, "Don't blame me for calling it how I see it. I also don't recall asking for a ride."

We complete the rest of the trip in silence. I make good use of the time, although not all my focus is on the nameless giant seated next to me. Half is given to Mr. Darcy while the other quarter goes to my father. I don't believe it's a coincidence Mr. Darcy froze up right around the time I mentioned my father. There's more to this. I just need more than an hour to work out what it is, and the stranger's lead foot only gave me forty minutes.

When I spot Melody's dorm coming up on the right, I gather my backpack off the floor of the truck before requesting for the stranger to stop. "Here will be fine."

I don't want him knowing the exact dorm I'm going to, especially if he's investigating my father. Melody has been my girlfriend for almost a year, but the only ties she has with my family is that she was once our next-door neighbor. I'd like to keep it that way.

"Just pull into the front if you can't find a vacant spot," I advise when the stranger continues down the lane, acting ignorant to my demand for him to pull over.

"There's a spot right there," I garble out a few seconds later, my words strained through the anger clutching my throat. We're past Melody's dorm now. Only by a little, but enough to piss me off.

I clench and unclench my fists when his big black truck rolls past another six empty spaces before he eventually pulls to the curb at the very end of the block of dorms. I'm frustrated as fuck he has doubled my walk, but that annoyance has nothing on the fear that rains down on me when I take in the truck he's parked behind. It's as rusty and rundown as many other vehicles in this lot, but the last two digits of its tags send my pulse skyrocketing.

73.

With my heart in my throat, I throw open my door and race for the F150 like I did eleven months ago. When my sprint has me stumbling onto an empty cab, I drag my fingers through my hair. The lifting of my arms adds to the twisting of my stomach. The driver's side mirror is cracked like it was hit with force from a teenage boy lunging at it.

I almost hyperventilate while I add up the facts. This truck has been spotted around Melody too many times to be a coincidence.

When the blond FBI agent rounds the hood of the F150, a fatal flaw in my attempt to protect Melody as her father had is exposed. From this angle, the window of Melody's dorm is visible from the roadside. Because they angled the dormitories for better energy efficiency, over three dozen windows face the street, but I know the exact one that's Melody's. The curtains my mom made out of my old bedspread makes it stand out, not to mention the candle she lights for her parents every night.

My pupils dilate when a shadowed figure causes the candle's wick to flicker. Melody shouldn't be back from her Friday night study session yet. She doesn't get in until after seven. It's only six forty-five.

With my heart thudding out a familiar, *boom-boom, boom-boom* noise I haven't heard the past two years, I race for Melody's dorm, leaving my backpack in the unnamed FBI agent's truck. A professor shouts for me to slow down when I weave through a group of students gathered in the quad. Her demand is drowned out by the hum of excited chatter when I climb the front stairs of Melody's dormitory and toss open the front door.

I hear the thumps of my feet twice when they bounce off the bland white walls slowly closing in on me. Their hearty stomps follow me down the corridor on the first floor of Melody's dormitory building and into her room at the very end. Her father taught us to pick the room with the quickest exit point, but it must never be at the front of the property. This was the safest option out of the three rooms we had to pick from.

When I reach Melody's room, instead of knocking like I usually would, I rear back my shoe and kick the door handle. While charging into her room, I take a mental note to improve her security since her door buckled with only one kick.

I stomp my foot down three times, calling out Melody's name without using any words. Her room is dark, but I can sense someone's presence, and it isn't the tall blond man who followed my sprint from his truck.

"This is the police. Stay where you are until we've scoped the area."

I'm about to tell him that his words are useless to Melody since she's deaf, but I don't have time for that right now. My awareness of

Melody isn't as strong as it usually is, but that could be solely based on this being our first drill separately. For well over a decade, it was always her and me versus her dad.

My head snaps to the side when a creak shrieks through my ears. It sounded like someone tiptoeing across fading floorboards, which means the perpetrator is most likely in the bathroom.

I lift my chin when the stranger gestures for me to clear the bathroom while he searches the pitch-black room. He has his gun at the ready. I have my fists.

With my ears pitched for any signs of life, I creep toward the attached bathroom of Melody's dorm. My steps are fast enough to cross the room in less than a heartbeat but slow enough to be soundless to the person's shadow I can see underneath the door.

Dampness trickles over my skin when I lower the handle. I'm not sweating. It's steam from a shower, although I can hear no water running.

When I fling open the door with enough force the handle bursts through the drywall, my hearing gets damaged by a mangled squeal I'm very familiar with. Melody jumps away from the vanity so quickly, the laced-edge towel wrapped around her wet frame slips from her body.

"Jesus, BJ. You scared the shit out of me." She gathers up her towel before re-knotting it around her thrusting chest. *"What are you doing here so early? You are not supposed to arrive until seven."* Her facial expression has gone from panicked to pleased in less than a nanosecond.

Before I can answer her or gloat how ecstatic I am that even a year of us being together, she's still happy to see me, a male voice I assume belongs to the unnamed FBI agent shouts, "He's gone out the window."

"Seek shelter now," I demand to Melody before charging back into the main area of her dorm.

When I spot the back end of the agent darting into the hallway, I race for the only window in Melody's room. After diving through the gap left open by the perpetrator, I take off after him on foot. He could be one of many of the late teens to early twenty gentlemen surrounding me, but only one is heading for the parking lot west of the dormitories, so I'm confident I'm chasing the right man.

I reach the back of the F150 truck just as the dark-haired man dives into the driver's seat. Knowing I'll never make it to the cab before he takes off, I attempt to climb into the truck bed. I have one leg over the old-style fender when he takes the corner he was parked on too quickly not to dislodge me from his vehicle. Unlike the last time he got away from me, this time his plates are clean enough for me to see them in their entirety.

I'm not the only one taking notice. As the blond agent comes to a stop at my side, he shouts down his cell phone, "The perpetrator is driving a 1953 F150. He's going west on Albert. License Echo Delta Charlie—"

I miss the rest of his squawk. I can barely hear my pulse over the fire alarm sounding from Melody's dorm.

"Did you sound the fire alarm?" I ask the unnamed man. If he did, he's clearly an idiot. Mr. Gregg taught me to sound the alarm when I need a group of people to shield my exit, but if you're seeking someone, the last thing you want is a crowd.

"No," he replies, shaking his head. "I'm not that stupid."

Although my fitness isn't what it was twelve months ago, I push it to the absolute limit during my race back to Melody's dorm. The unnamed agent follows me stride for stride, only slowing when we reach the stream of people filing out the front exit.

"Seek her in the crowd," the stranger shouts, his words garbled by the furious pump of my legs since I'm still running. "The fire alarm will bring her out."

"No, it won't," I deny, my voice panicked. "She's not just deaf, she has also been taught not to fall for things like smoke and the flashing lights of unmarked cars. She'll stay hidden until I find her."

Smoke burns my lungs when I reach Melody's room. The curtains my mom made her are engulfed by a furious fire. Its flames lick the cracked paint shards on the wall, doubling the work of the fire extinguisher that's usually hanging halfway down the corridor.

"Aim the nozzle at the base of the fire, not the flames. It will stop it from spreading." The RA from Melody's dorm nods before following my instructions. He contains the fire remarkably quick, but my pulse is still at a heart-damaging high.

"Melody?" This stomp is harder than my previous one to ensure she can feel its vibration over the commotion outside of her dorm.

As the events of eleven months ago roll through my head, I check under her bed first. When I find it void of a living thing, I move to her closet. It's also empty.

I bang my foot down three times again before making my way to the bathroom I discovered Melody in earlier. Halfway there, in the corner of my eye, I spot the unnamed FBI officer signaling for local law enforcement officers to stand down. I was so honed-in on finding Melody, I didn't realize my hunt came with an audience.

"Melody, it is me, Brandon. Don't come out swinging, okay?" I sign to my reflection in the mirror, praying she's placed herself into a position she can see it.

A brittle creak breaks through the eerie silence when I push the bathroom door all the way open, but other than that, it's eerily quiet. Not even the thud of my pulse can be heard. With the shower curtain drawn all the way back, the vanity void of any storage underneath, and the door flush to the wall, a normal person would think the bathroom is empty.

I know that isn't the case. Melody's dad taught us to hide where no one would think to look—in plain sight but also hidden. The simpler the hiding spot, the less likely you'll be found, and we set up Melody's dorm to ensure she had numerous places to hide, such as the shower curtain that's so long, even when it's pulled over the tub, the massive bends in the thick material could conceal a body. It's also three inches longer than needed.

Before peeling open the almost black shower curtain, I stomp down another three times to assure her it's me. A heavy sigh escapes my mouth when the opening of the curtain reveals a huddled Melody hiding in the middle of it.

My first thought is to kiss her until her mouth soothes the panic burning me alive, but instead, I rest my forehead against hers and count to ten, bringing both our heart rates back to a safe, non-cardiac level before signing, *"Who scared who?"*

BRANDON

"What do you mean he'll most likely get off with a misdemeanor for evading police? He broke into my girlfriend's dormitory. Who knows what he would have done to her if we didn't arrive when we did."

Grayson, the blond FBI agent I met Friday night, sighs down the line like his week has been as long as mine. "Conspiracy to commit a crime is an offense *if* the DA believes there's sufficient evidence to corroborate the claim. The ADA doesn't believe that's the case this time around. He doesn't believe Crombie targeted Melody with the intent to harm her."

"You know that's a lie, Grayson. Who flees a scene unless they were planning to do something wrong?"

I rake my fingers through my hair, giving it an extra tug for good measure. I'm so fucking frustrated because no matter how many times I spell out the facts, no one listens to me. I'm just a kid who doesn't know what he's talking about. My father said that exact thing last week when the deans at Browns and Dartmore gave Melody and me permission to commence summer break early. I didn't tell them what had happened. I just shoved the report of Melody's dorm fire under their noses.

My annoyance gets a massive boost when Grayson says, "The ADA doesn't believe there's sufficient evidence for this case to go to court."

"Why? Because it might stain the stellar reputation of his peers?" My voice is smeared with repulsed sarcasm. I know who's attempting to run that branch of the Justice Department. He isn't an honorable man.

Just like me, Grayson refuses to back down when he's on the losing team. "Because this is a he-said-she-said case."

"That makes no sense. Crombie fled the scene—"

I step back in shock when Grayson interrupts, "Because he's claiming he cares for Melody too much to publicly expose her as an adulterous."

"What?" Surely, I heard him wrong. I'm completely and utterly confused.

Grayson increases his volume to ensure he's heard through the thud of my pulse in my ears. "Crombie is claiming he's known Melody since she was sixteen, and that they've been having an affair for the past two months."

"No," I reply without pause or consideration. "Melody isn't like that. She'd never sleep with another man." *She'd never break my heart like that.* "He's lying."

"The evidence doesn't look good, Brandon. That's why the ADA has to be cautious. Even you produced evidence that favored the accused's claims."

I scoff loudly. "What evidence? I haven't given them any evidence."

I hear a noise like Grayson dragging a hand over his kiddy-beard before he breathes out, "You told them about seeing Crombie's truck at Melody's parents' funeral, and how it followed the Greggs out of the hospital parking lot only a few days earlier."

"To prove he's stalking her! That had *nothing* to do with them possibly having an affair." I lower my burly tone when Melody murmurs in her sleep. She must feel the anger radiating out of me. While peering at her beautiful face, I say with utmost certainty, "Melody would never do what Crombie is saying. He's lying to save his tail, Grayson. We can't let him get away with this."

His sigh this time around sounds more tormented than his first. "I understand what you're saying, and I also agree with you, but even if Melody denies his claims until she's blue in the face, I don't see the DA agreeing to prosecute this case. It's a waste of their time. We would have had more chance of him facing time if we had prosecuted him for arson."

With my mind churning overtime, I ask, "Why would that make a difference?"

"Crombie has two prior convictions for arson. A third would've been an automatic felony. He could have faced twenty years behind bars."

The pieces of the puzzle fit together remarkably quick considering how late it is. "So why aren't they prosecuting him for the fire in Melody's dorm?"

Grayson pauses for a few seconds before muttering, "Because you bumped the candle into the curtain when you chased after Crombie."

"No, I *allegedly* bumped the candle into the curtain. Who's to say the fire hadn't already been lit before that?"

Grayson's huff reveals he knows where I'm going with this, but it doesn't indicate if he's for or against it. "You stated in your report that you dove through the window to chase down the attacker."

"I did… but not once did I say the curtain wasn't on fire."

"Was it?" Nothing but guarded inquisitiveness rings true in Grayson's deep tone.

My voice is calm and neutral when I reply, "I don't know. I wasn't in the right frame of mind at the time to take in the tiny flicker of a flame. It could have been."

"'Could have been' isn't a definitive answer, Brandon. I won't let you perjure yourself for a 'could have been.'"

"I'm not asking you to place me in the witness box. I'm asking you to do your job. Was the candle dusted for Crombie's prints? An arsonist is an arsonist, Grayson. Placing a lit flame in front of him would be the equivalent of cutting three lines of cocaine in front of an addict. He wouldn't have been able to resist himself." When he remains quiet, I gently coerce him over the ledge. "All we need is a fingerprint. If there's a fingerprint on the candle, we have the intent to commit a crime. That's all we need. *Intent.*"

I release the breath I'm holding in hope when Grayson mutters, "All right. I'll have the candle run through forensics." I stop fist-bumping the air when he murmurs, "But..." he pauses like Joey always does, "... if there's no print, you're going to spend your summers combing old case files of mine for spelling errors."

I smile, not the least bit concerned. "And if there is a print?"

My smile doubles when he grumbles, "You're going to spend your summers combing old case files." He didn't say for spelling errors, which can only mean one thing. He wants me on his team as much as I'm dying to become a member.

TWO WEEKS after the incident in Melody's dorm, David Alan Crombie was charged with intent to commit arson. Five weeks after that, he was found guilty by a jury of his peers for stalking, intent to cause bodily harm, and felony arson.

Three conclusive fingerprint matches were found on the candle from Melody's dorm. Along with the damning evidence, he was carrying a box of matches, and the fire forensic team believed the blaze spread quickly because an accelerant had been sprayed on Melody's curtains. The defense disputed that the chemical residue could've been placed there months earlier, but an empty bottle of hairspray in Crombie's truck had the jury siding in favor of the prosecution. It had the same chemical compound as the accelerant on the curtains.

The jury agreed with the ADA's claims that Crombie was stalking Melody's family because Mr. Gregg busted him attempting to set fire to an abandoned barn of a neighboring property and called the police. He blamed Mr. Gregg for his subsequent arrest and the loss of his sports scholarship. The gap between his previous stalking and this one was due to his nine-month sentence to a minimum-security prison.

Melody asked the ADA to seek any links between her parents' accident and Crombie's wish for revenge. Both the ADA and Grayson assured her they were not linked.

And that brings us to today, two months after Crombie was sentenced to ten years of hard time and six days out from Melody's admission interview at Browns. Her interview isn't being held by Mr. Darcy. Shockingly, he resigned from his position not long after our confrontation—right around the time my father endorsed him for a position in the District Attorney's Office in Miami. Coincidence? I highly doubt it. My father was endeavoring to keep Melody and me apart. I just need to find out why.

"Wear that one. It is perfect."

"Are you sure?" The hem of the designer dress Melody is trying on swishes around her luscious thighs when she nervously twists on the spot. *"It kind of feels too risqué for a professional lawyer."*

I screw my nose up. *"Why? Lawyers can be sexy. You sure will be."*

She does a face that reveals I did good with my compliment before spinning back around to face the mirror. She peers at herself for a few minutes before signing, *"I am still not convinced. Let me try on one more outfit."*

She giggles when I flop onto a studded daybed with a groan. I've been watching her try on interview-suitable outfits for almost three hours. The two hours before that was spent scouring for an outfit for her to wear to Joey's summer-break party tonight.

I'm so fucking bored, not that I'd ever tell Melody that. I love seeing her like this. The past few months have been good for her. She handled the anniversary of her parents' deaths with the grace and maturity a lot of almost nineteen-year-olds don't have, and she maintained her dignity when Crombie tried to pawn her off to the jury as being an adulterer.

They were as unbelieving of his story as me. Melody is beautiful, and she gains the eyes of men everywhere we go, but she's so pure and wholesome, nothing but virtue beamed out of her on the witness stand. Even if Crombie's fingerprints weren't found on the candle, I'm confident the jury would've still found him guilty. That's how convincing Melody's testimony was.

We've grown stronger than I could've ever imagined. I just wish it could have been done without so much interference. There has been so much drama in our lives since we became a couple, it feels like we've been doomed from the beginning.

I glance down at my phone when it vibrates, smiling when I notice it's a call from Grayson. He checks in every couple of days. I wouldn't say we're friends, but he's definitely a close confidant of mine.

After popping my head into Melody's dressing room to tell her I'll be back in a minute, I make my way outside of the dress boutique, swipe my finger across the screen of my new phone, then squash it to my ear.

Before I can greet Grayson, he says, "Tell her to buy the green one in the window, and then she can wear it again on St. Paddy's Day."

I scan the street quicker than usual, sighing in relief when I spot Grayson's black truck a few spots up from where I'm standing. I was getting worried he had installed a tracker on my phone. He'd never admit it, but he's sneaky like that. It's a known trait of rookie FBI agents willing to do anything to prove their worth.

"Can you spare a minute? I need to show you something."

When I spot Grayson's blue eyes in the side mirror of his truck, I jerk up my chin before lowering my phone from my ear. Since I told

Melody I'd be a few minutes, I don't bother popping back into the dress shop to tell her where I'm going. Excluding my father, there are no known threats to her at the moment, and she's also packing heat.

Don't come at me with your gun-toting gripes. It was Grayson's idea for Melody to get a gun, not mine. I wouldn't have objected, anyway. We're both extensively trained in good gun ownership. Melody just now *legally* carries.

When I pry open the passenger side door of Grayson's truck, he flips up the visor housing half a dozen pictures of his girlfriend. In all honesty, I don't know if the redhead is his girlfriend. I'm just assuming. He doesn't speak about her, but I've caught him a few times peering at her photographs, and the admiration in his eyes isn't one a brother would get for his sister, so they must be close. Perhaps they're best friends like Melody and I once were?

Recalling how much it sucked being in the friend zone, I say, "What's up? I didn't think you were coming back this way for a few months."

A smile curls my lips when Grayson speaks to me as if I'm an equal. "We had some new developments pop up, causing us to return east side earlier than planned." I don't know anyone in his team but him, but he says 'we' often when we've chatted.

My eyes lower to the first photograph in the stack he digs out of a manila folder. It's a six by ten-inch surveillance image of Mr. Gregg and a man I've never seen before.

"Do you know who this man is?"

Noticing he said 'man,' I keep the powerplay between us even. "Which man?"

The skin under his eyes twitches, but instead of reacting to my taunt, he points to the man standing across from Mr. Gregg. "This one. It was taken a few days before Mr. Gregg's accident. Things look heated."

His reply exposes more than he intended. Not only is this photograph proof he's been on this side of the country longer than he stated, it also reveals he knew who Melody was before he drove me to her dorm.

"I've never seen him before." When Grayson attempts to remove the photographs from my hand, I snatch them back. "This guy, however, I've seen him on the news." I push across the first picture until it exposes the man I'm referencing in the second printout. It shows Cormack McGregor walking into a rundown warehouse with a man around his age. "Wasn't he charged with rape earlier this year?"

"We're not interested in him."

Grayson glares at me when I ask, "Why? Keeping the streets free of rapists above your team's caliber, is it?"

I'm being sarcastic, but he doesn't hear it like that. "Yep. Something like that." He sounds frustrated, and it has my brain ticking overtime, but before I can sort through a single fact, Grayson says, "What about the guy with Cormack, have you seen him around?"

I take in the dark-haired, gray-eyed man with more diligence before shaking my head. "Is he of interest to your team?"

I hiss when Grayson's grab for the surveillance image gives me a papercut.

"That's what you get for being nosey."

I talk around my index finger popped in my mouth. "I'm not being nosey, I'm keeping an eye out for my girl. You have a surveillance image of her dad in a file full of criminals. Only an idiot wouldn't be cautious."

His eyes soften like he understands my plight. "You don't need to worry about Melody. She's good. I swear to you, we're not investigating her or her family."

Trust isn't something I easily give, but I trust Grayson. "Do you want me to show the photo to Melody? See if she knows who he is?"

"Would you mind?"

"Not at all." The relief on his face switches to annoyed when I add, "For a price." He doesn't say anything, but his silence speaks volumes. He's not happy I'm bartering, but he's willing to negotiate if it gets him what he needs. "Can you show me how to get past the security on my father's computer?"

His blond brow pops up. "You're still working that angle?"

"Yep. I don't care what anyone says. There's more to Melody's rejections from Browns than people are letting on, and I'm just as convinced my father was helming more than one campaign when our college applications were submitted."

Grayson waits a beat, his chest rising and falling in rhythm to mine. "If I show you the way in, will you let me follow your lead?"

Now it's my turn to pause. I want to find out what my dad's problem is, but do I really want the FBI involved in a family matter?

When I reach a decision, I lock my hazel eyes with Grayson's baby blues. "Who will you share your information with?"

"No one." He scratches his jaw, which is usually a sign of lying, but since it occurs while he says, "This is a personal matter," I'm suspicious he's lying to no one but himself.

"All right, but no external hacking. You'll have to get your information directly from the source. If you get me in, I'll let you snoop around a little." I grab the top photograph off the pile, slip out of his cab, and make my way back to the dress shop.

Aware I'm not taking no for an answer, Grayson shadows my walk. His boots click the floorboards faster when his arrival into the boutique gains him the admired eyes of three of its clients. He dips his grin in greeting, but not an ounce of interest flares through his eyes.

After checking that Melody is dressed, I gesture for Grayson to join us in the dressing cubicle. Melody's smile greatens when she spots him behind my shoulder. They've only met in passing, but they class each other as friends.

Grayson's eyes stray from the green dress Melody has chosen to me. "I told you she'd go for the green dress."

He smirks like a smug prick when I roll my eyes. *That isn't exactly how I remember it, but if it makes you feel better, we can pretend it is.*

Between reading Grayson's lips and my signed reply, Melody quickly catches the gist of our conversation. *"Don't pick on him. He has been tortured all morning."* Grayson looks a little unwell when she rakes her fingernails across my chest before cuddling into my side. Or is it envy? The cut features of his face make him a little hard to read. *"Everything okay?"* Even via American Sign Language I'm confident Melody's question would've been a whisper if she could talk.

I jerk up my chin. *"Yeah. Grayson's team is back in town to take a closer look at the Browns' admission scam."* Grayson chokes on his spit, but I continue talking as if he isn't about to blow my cover. I don't like lying to Melody, but I'd rather it over her believing any of the lies my father has been sporting about her the past fifteen months. He's still adamant Mr. Gregg was never in the military, and he tells anyone willing to listen. *"One of the agents stumbled onto a photo of interest during the investigation, so Grayson thought he would check if either of us knows who he is."*

"Okay." When she holds out her hand, requesting the photograph, I hesitate. She always clams up when anyone talks about her family. *"Where is it?"*

Sensing my hesitation, Grayson snatches the picture out of my hand, flattens out the crinkles of my grip, then hands it to Melody.

Our eyes snap to hers in sync when she gasps in a sharp breath. *"How long ago was this taken?"* Tears well in her eyes when she runs her index finger over her father's face. *"It looks like it was only taken yesterday."*

When Grayson attempts to answer her, I cut him off by slicing my hand through the air. She's not his informant right now. She's a daughter in mourning, so we must tread lightly.

I tap on Melody's shoulder to gain her attention before saying, *"It was a couple of months before our Browns' applications were returned."*

Melody is too smart to fall for my ruse. *"So around the time of his death?"* A tear rolls down her cheek when I nod. *"He looks angry."* Her giggle surprises Grayson as much as it does me. *"He always looked cranky."*

"He did," I agree, putting my life on the line to add to the happy memories in her head. I give her a few seconds to drink in every detail of her father's face before asking, *"Do you know the man he is talking to?"*

"Yes." Her agreement isn't a solid confirmation, and I find out why when she adds, *"He used to come to our house before the..."* She gives me a look like she doesn't want to spill family secrets in front of Grayson. *"I never saw him after that."* A concentration crinkle pops between her light brown brows when she signs, *"I called him uncle even though he wasn't my uncle. God... what was his name?"* She peers at the ceiling for so long, just as I'm certain she's never going to answer me, she signs, *"Henry. His name was Henry."*

My eyes shoot to Grayson when he mutters, *"Henry Gottle?"* He signs Henry's name as well as saying it. *"Was that his name?"*

While staring at him wondering how he knew the punchline of her joke long before she shared it, Melody responds, *"Yeah. I think so."* Melody nods with more confidence the longer she works Henry's name through her head.

"Thank you!" Grayson looks like he wants to plant a kiss on Melody's cheek, but instead, snatches the photograph from her hand and hot-foots it out of the dressing room. It's for the best as I'm five seconds from castrating him for his deceit, so who knows what I would have done if he put his lips on her.

"I will be back in a minute," I tell Melody before chasing Grayson down.

I find him on the sidewalk, talking erratically into his cell phone. Mr. Gregg's name is mentioned many times, and it sets my pulse skyrocketing.

Before I can consider the consequences of my actions, I slap Grayson's phone out of his hand, smash it with my shoe, unclip his gun from its holster, and press the barrel to the groove between his brows.

I assume that will keep Grayson still long enough so I can interrogate him.

I vastly underestimated him.

After doing a maneuver I only perfected twice under Mr. Gregg's watch, he regains control of his gun, then slams me into the concrete sidewalk. Without missing a beat, I swipe his feet out from beneath him, stun him with a jab to the kidney before scampering for his gun dumped on the sidewalk.

I'm within an inch of it when it's kicked out of my grasp by a pair of shiny black boots, and I'm knocked out by one of the biggest fists I've ever seen.

MELODY

After slipping into the passenger seat of Carmen's sedan, I peer back at Suzie and Racheal. We've kept in contact the past year, but this is the first time I've seen them in person since my parents' funeral. They're heading home for Joey's summer-break party, so they offered me to ride with them since Brandon up and vanished four hours ago.

I texted him nonstop when he left me stag at the dress shop. He didn't return my messages until an hour later. The lapse in time didn't improve his excuse. It was as pathetic as I'm feeling. He said he had something important to do and that he'd meet me at his family's ranch in a couple of hours.

I'm still fuming mad at him. Joey's venue of choice for his party already had me opposed to going, and now I have to arrive on the arm of a friend instead of my boyfriend. I understand Joey wanted privacy for what he assures will be the party of the century, but I haven't been home since the McGees moved to New York.

I also don't think Joey should be living it up as he is. I'm glad he's feeling better since his heart transplant, and that his life is relatively back to what it was before he got sick, but he was given a very precious gift not many people are privileged to get. Plus, I'm not going to mention the remarkable person who gave it to him, or the makeup I spent an hour prepping will slid down my face along with my tears.

Carmen drags her hand down my arm to gather my attention before saying, "If those tears are from Brandon, I'm about to whoop your ass." I give her a look that warns I'm not up for her I-hate-Brandon rant right now. It does little to weaken the resting bitch-face she generally wears. "What, Melody? You can't seriously be mad at me for looking out for you. He dumped you at a dress shop, then texts to say he'll meet you a few hours later. Who does that? Certainly not a boyfriend-of-the-year contestant."

"He said it was important."

Suzie taps my shoulder. "Important enough not to be here for you today, Mel?" She's usually the first to defend Brandon, so I'm stunned by obvious annoyance today. "It's your first time back at Saugerties in almost a year. He should be here supporting you."

"He does support me. He always has."

Carmen dry retching in the corner of my eye shifts my focus back to her. "Don't remind us of how long it's been, or I'll vomit." She's always believed my relationship with Brandon is gross because we were raised together, having no clue we've *never* seen each other as siblings. It's always been a much deeper connection than that. "You don't stumble onto your soulmate when you're five. That's just gross."

"How can you judge any relationship?" I fire back, annoyed. *"You have not even met a guy who can get you off yet, so you should not be judging anyone."*

I thought I was signing too fast for them to understand me, but Rachel proves me wrong when she says, "She has you there." Her shoulder touches her dark hair when she shrugs. "The last I heard, you drew Mal a map, and he still couldn't find your G-spot."

When Carmen and Suzie's laugh hums through my chest, I give Racheal my best *thank you* face.

She mouths, *"You are welcome,"* before leaning over the middle console to crank the radio up. When the thump of a familiar Top-Ten hit pulsates through the outdated speakers in the doors of Carmen's car, I forgot about Brandon and the possibly urgent situation he's in, and focused on ensuring my heart won't shred into a million pieces when we glide through a familiar T-intersection in a little over two hours.

THE HEARTBREAKING *THUD*, *thud*, *thud* of my heart lessens when Carmen pulls her VW Jetta into the dusty driveway of the McGees' family ranch. Since traffic was bad, we've arrived a little after dusk, meaning I only caught the quickest glimpse of the white crosses Brandon and his mom placed on the power pole near the T-intersection that claimed my parents' lives.

I also can't see my family home.

I'll brave it one day.

Today just isn't going to be that day.

"You okay?" Racheal asks, squeezing my hand.

I nod, hiding the panic flaring through me.

"If you need a breather, come find me."

Smiling, I nod again. I'd rather us all stay together, but considering I'm the only non-single member of our quartet, I don't see that being the case. Even with a majority of his teen years spent in a bed, Joey is rather popular. The McGee ranch is bursting with partygoers. They've spilled onto the lawn, and even a handful of people are gathered around the old oak tree I use to climb to reach Brandon's room.

The thought brings a smile to my face. My first in hours.

With most of Joey's guests being former students of my high school, the first two hours of his party goes remarkably fast. I talk to old peers, current ones, and a handful of girls who traveled over five hours to attend. They talked a bit too fast for me to understand, but from what I gathered, they were squabbling over who was going to occupy Joey's bed tonight.

Their fight settled when I joked that they'll most likely all end up in his bed at the same time. For some reason, my written suggestion interested them more than it disgusted them, which saw me seeking new people to converse with. I love Joey, but unlike Brandon, it's always been a big brother-little sister type of infatuation. I honestly feel a little ill even considering the possibility of it being more.

Talking about big brothers. *"Joey!"*

When I stomp out his name like Brandon always does mine, he spins around to face me so quickly, his drink spills over the rim of his glass and sloshes onto his Van shoes. *"You made it! Where's pipsqueak?"*

I shrug. *"Your guess is as good as mine."*

The women I was talking to earlier shoot daggers at me when Joey greets me by wrapping me up in a giant hug before spinning me around the room. Usually, I'd repel from any theatrics in public, I get enough eyes as it is, but since his actions put my ear within an inch of his chest, I drink it all in.

I can't hear my daddy's heart, but I can feel it, and I won't give that up for anything.

"Hey, none of that," Joey warns when he spots the tears in my eyes upon returning me to my feet. *"This is a celebration for both him and me."* He doesn't need to sign my father's name to know who he's talking about. The way he touches his chest anytime he remembers him ensures I can't be mistaken. *"I would not be here without him, Mel, and I will be forever grateful for that."*

"I know." I clasp my hands together when they shake so violently, my confirmation that I'm okay is barely legible.

"Are you drinking?"

I screw up my nose before shaking my head.

Joey smiles. *"Do you want a drink?"*

When I jerk up my chin, the tears in my eyes nearly tumble. *"I could be convinced if there is something enticing on the menu."*

The bass of music shuddering my toes weakens when Joey leads me into the kitchen. It's brimming with people, but the mood in here is more subdued than it was in the living room. I'm struggling with my emotions, but after a quick breather and perhaps a stiff drink, I'll be right as rain again.

While Joey moves to the fridge to gather a bottle of chilled soda water, I take in his fit frame. He's gained back the weight he lost when he was sick and added a few extra pounds. *"What is with the babyface? Are you trying to maintain your youth or accepting styling advice from Brandon?"*

Joey laughs before scrubbing a hand over his prickle-free chin. A wiry beard usually covers his cut jawline. *"I am trying something new. Do you like it?"*

When he drags his silky-smooth chin down my cheek, I ask, *"Are you trying to get me killed?"* He finishes topping up our vodka, soda, and lime concoction before straying his eyes in the direction I'm nudging my head. *"They were having quite the debate earlier."*

"Oh yeah... about what?" He pushes my drink to my side of the counter, knowing full well what they were arguing about, but praying I'll spell it out for him. He's shit out of luck. I can't make things easy for him.

He spits his drink in my face when I say, *"I told them you had crabs."*

"You didn't?"

Trained in both the art of deception and how to spot it, I give him my best *I'm sorry* face.

He buys it in a nanosecond. *"You little wench. I have been working on that outfit for months."* After bumping me with his hip, he locks his blue eyes with mine. *"You good?"* He doesn't say he's desperate to fix the damage I've caused to his player ways, but his eyes sure do.

"Yeah, I am good." I nudge my head at the scantily clad women for the second time. *"Go get them, Ace."*

With a playful wink, he slaps my backside before prowling toward the women no longer glowering at me. I wait for him to disappear back into the living room before taking my drink and me outside for a second breather. Since the earlier clouds have lifted, the moon bounces off the white wood trestles of the back porch of my family's ranch. The pain in my chest isn't as dense as I was anticipating. I actually smile while recalling how I tiptoed across the warped floorboards to escape to Brandon's house for an hour or two almost every night. The night of Joey's admission was the first time I had stayed the entire night.

As memories of my past make my heart thump with happiness, I dig my cell phone out of my pocket to text a well-used number. A ping of pain stabs me in the chest when I discover I don't have any reception. We're in the country, but anyone would swear we're in the middle of the Sahara for how bad the reception is out here.

When I pivot around to see if the reception is any better inside the house, I'm frightened to within an inch of my life. A partygoer I wasn't anticipating has his shoulder pressed against the thick tree trunk. His chin is covered with a thick beard, and his eyes are sunken and tired-looking.

"Madden," I greet him before sidestepping past him to climb the back patio steps, forever eager to get away from him.

This is terrible for me to admit since he's Brandon's brother, but I've always found him a little creepy. He hasn't done anything to me to make me uncomfortable. It's just the way he looks at me. There's not an ounce of respect or admiration in his slit eyes. More times than not, I feel like he's glaring at me with hate.

I stop on the second step when Madden taps my shoulder, requesting my attention. When I turn around, he asks, "Where's Brandon?"

His sign language capabilities are poor, so I keep my reply as simple as possible. *"I don't know. That is why I am trying to message him."*

His eyes drop to my phone that shows no signal before they lift back to my face. "You can use my phone."

I tap on the antenna signal on my screen that shows there's no reception before wordlessly thanking him for his offer.

My thanks freeze halfway when he says, "I have a satellite phone."

"Satellite?" I ask, certain I misread the movement of his lips. An error is understandable. It isn't often you hear of a first-year military officer being able to afford a satellite phone, and the number of times Madden runs his index finger under his nose makes it hard to read his lips.

"One of the perks of having a dad in a high position, I guess." He looks glum, which is also surprising. He's always been the apple of his daddy's eyes. Isn't that why he's following in his footsteps? "Here. Brandon's cell phone number is already loaded."

When I accept his phone, he removes my drink from my hand to save the barely consumed contents spilling onto his shiny new toy. *"Thanks."*

I pace deeper into the darkness for some privacy before hitting the message button. After typing out a quick "Pls call me" message, I stare down at the screen, begging for it to buzz.

As it did many times earlier today, my text message goes unanswered. This isn't like Brandon. He must either have his phone turned off or his battery has died. The latter seems more plausible for how often I texted it when he abandoned me at the dress shop.

"No luck?" Madden asks when I hand him back his phone.

I shake my head before accepting back my drink, needing something to soothe the dryness in my throat. After a big gulp, I confess, *"He said he would meet me here. I just didn't expect him to be so long."*

Either over our unusual small talk or sick of deciphering my replies, Madden mouths, "It could be worse. He could've left you to rot at Dartmore." Ignoring my stitched brows, he spins on his heels and stalks the stairs I attempted to walk only minutes ago.

After a few minutes of silent contemplation, I trace his steps. I'm not searching him down. I'm seeking the closest tap. Joey is known for mixing his drinks with more alcohol than soda water, but it shouldn't be hitting me this fiercely. I feel I've drunk half a gallon of vodka. When I bump into the island in the middle of the McGees' kitchen, Racheal's eyes lock with mine. She was talking to Douglas, the once wide receiver of our local football team.

"Are you all right?" she asks when she notices my clutch on the cabinets.

I brush off the worry mask slipping over her face with a quick nod. *"I am fine. Just zonked from a big day. I might go have a nap."*

"Okay, grandma." Even through the haze blurring my vision, I can tell her smile is apprehensive. "I'll come check on you in an hour or two."

"I am fine. Enjoy the party."

It's lucky I know the floorplan of the McGee ranch as well as I do, or my poor eyesight would have had me missing the balustrade of the stairwell. After guiding myself up the stairs, I enter the first room on the right. This is Brandon's childhood bedroom. It still has the twin bed we lost our virginity on pushed against the wall, and his desk is still housing the letters of acceptance we got while waiting for word from Browns.

Mrs. McGee was able to keep the ranch as a shrine because Mr. McGee decked their new house out with everything they could ever need. They basically just locked up and moved out—kind of similar to my family home, except there's no one to return back there but me.

Through both the pain of keeping my eyelids open and the memories keeping my happiness hostage, I dump my empty glass onto Brandon's desk, toe off my shoes, tug down my jeans, then slip between the sheets on Brandon's bed. A fond memory raises my cheeks when I recall the reason Brandon's bed is only made with a fitted and flat sheet. His mom turned his bedspread into curtains for me. I hate that Crombie set them alight. Just like this room is always featured in my dreams, so does Brandon's bedspread.

With my heart a twisted mess of confusion, and my eyelids the heaviest they've ever been, I fall asleep. I'm not a good judge of time, but I'd say I've barely napped for twenty minutes when a gust of air floats over my skin. Since the light I left on has been switched off, and Brandon's curtains are closed, I can't see who's approaching me, but I most certainly recognize his smell. The aftershave lotion Brandon's mom purchased to keep his skin baby smooth and fresh has always been a favorite scent of mine.

It's about time Brandon turned up. I've been waiting for ages. I whack him in the gut to reflect my anger when he slides between the sheets with me. I'm still mad at him, and I've been worried out of my mind.

When I roll onto my opposite hip to face him, I'm hammered by a horrendous dizzy spell. As my hands dart up to soothe the frantic thump of my temples, I bump away Brandon's hand attempting to caress my breasts. I want to tell him now isn't the time to appease my anger with sex, but my head is thumping too fiercely to form words.

I flop onto my back before snapping my eyes shut, praying some extra blackness will ease my thumping head. I've barely closed my eyes for two seconds when the weight of Brandon's body pins mine to the mattress. I don't know whether to giggle or scream when he buries his chin into my neck. It's minus the prickles it houses when he gets too lazy to shave over the summer, but I still can't handle it. I'm very ticklish around my neck and collarbone, especially when he's breathing as heavily as he is now.

"*No, BJ,*" I sign when his hand slithers down my bunched-up shirt to my underwear. It's still pitch black, but if his eyes aren't as blurry as mine, he may be able to see my demand. "*I don't feel good. Please stop.*"

My eyes pop open faster than a bullet leaving a gun when he roughly tugs my panties down my thighs, ignoring my many unvoiced demands for him to stop. Even if he can't see the words I'm speaking, my constant groaning would have to have his suspicions raised—surely. Usually, I never turn him down, so for me to deny him now should have alarms ringing in his head.

I frantically tap on his shoulder, demanding for him to stop when his manhood pokes and prods between my legs, but he acts ignorant to the signal I regularly use when requesting his attention. Fear overtakes my anger when my endeavor to kick him off me causes him to grip my thigh so painfully, I'm certain it will have a bruise in the morning.

The panic sinking me into a dark and lonely hole intensifies when he flips me onto my stomach before securing my hands behind my back, so I can't move or sign. I sign no on repeat in my head when he enters me with one quick thrust. He didn't request permission like he always does, and he doesn't wait for me to adjust to his girth before he drags himself all the way out before slamming back in.

That can only mean one thing. The person pinning me to the bed so fiercely I can't move isn't Brandon.

As tears trickle down my cheeks, I permit the grogginess clouding me to bury me beneath a hurt so strong, I don't think I'll ever survive it. For the next thirty or so seconds, I stare at the door of Brandon's childhood bedroom, my mind far away from the terrifying event overriding the many good ones I created in this very room. I only return from the terrifying nothingness when the brightness of a hallway light creeps across the floorboards and has me stumbling onto a pair of Van shoes exiting the room, and I fall into a deep, dark pit.

BRANDON

fter swishing spit around my mouth, I force down a swallow, praying it will send the vomit creeping up my throat back to my stomach. I'm only just waking up after being knocked out for who knows how long, so the last thing I want is for the people holding me captive to know I'm awake. It's amazing what you can unearth when people don't realize you're listening. That's why I love being the smaller guy in the room. They never see me as a threat.

Once the desire to be sick has lessened, I prick my ears. The shuffling of feet on a dirty concrete floor advises there are at least two other people in the warehouse-like space with me. I haven't lifted my head, but the echo of their words reveals the holding space is large and empty. It smells dusty, and a lack of street noise exposes it's set back from the hustle and bustle of the city. If it isn't a warehouse, my next guess would be a docking yard, but since there's no fishy odor, I'm doubtful.

My lips purse when I rotate my wrists and ankles without interference. I'm not bound, but my life is clearly in danger. The thick Russian accent that roars through my ears a few seconds later leaves no doubt of this. "We can't bring him into this, Grayson. There's such a thing as a conflict of interest."

"He's a good kid, and from what I've witnessed the past three months, he knows nothing about their operation."

I balance my chin closer to my chest when the scuffling of feet heads my way. My head looks like it's slumped to the side, but my new position allows me to see the man Grayson is arguing with. He's large, tall, bald, and clearly Russian. The tattooed flag on his thick bicep ensures I can't be mistaken, much less his accent when he spits out, "Trust isn't something I'm willing to give you right now."

Grayson appears devastated by his reply, but he doesn't back down. "You told me to push the envelope—"

"I said push it! Not set it on fire." The balding Russian thrust his hand at me. "You got into an altercation in broad daylight with a civilian."

"She knew who he was. Melody confirmed Henry Gottle was known to her family before their home invasion. That's the proof we've been seeking, Tobias."

Tobias backhands Grayson in the chest. "Proof? What proof? The only proof we have is that your obsession with this case is going to get you killed..." His words trail off when Grayson asks, "Like yours almost did with Isabelle?"

Tobias looks set to murder when he growls, "Leave her out of this. She has *nothing* to do with this."

Grayson shakes his head before folding his arms in front of his chest. "That's a lie. You told me to think outside of the box on this case because every time you look at Katie's photos, you see Isabelle." With Tobias unable to deny his claims, Grayson notches another nail into his coffin. "We got close at her sale. We've just got to try another angle."

I drop my eyes to the floor when Tobias's head bob causes him to spot my snooping stare. I can't see his smirk when I add to the bloody spit in the corner of my mouth to authenticate my ruse that

I'm still out cold, but I can feel it. He has one of those grins that burn right through you. It's as arrogant as it is heated.

"You're finally awake." He moves closer to the chair I'm slumped in. "Anyone would've sworn I had chloroformed you for how long you've been out." He spins around a rickety wooden chair, then straddles it backward. "Did you have pleasant dreams?"

When he lifts my head via my throbbing chin, I give him a blood-smeared grin. "It could've been better. It's not the best location for a catnap."

"It's better than a jail cell... where you *would* be waking if it weren't for Grayson." He nudges his head to Grayson, who's hanging at the back of the industrial-size warehouse. "You attacked a federal agent in front of witnesses. That's an instant jail term, kid."

I twist my lips, acting smug. "He swung at me first."

Tobias tosses a manila folder full of surveillance photographs onto the floor at my feet. "That isn't what these say."

I take in the play-by-play rundown of my exchange with Grayson before shrugging. "I don't care what they say. My lie detector test will say otherwise."

"Lie detector test?" Tobias sounds annoyed, but he also sounds curious.

I smile like I'm more arrogant than I am. "The lie detector test my lawyer will demand I sit when I say your team is only showing half the event." I gesture my head to Grayson. "He swung at me first. I swear he did, officer."

Tobias's tongue darts out to wet his bottom lip when I deliver my line as if it's the god honest truth. His silence makes Grayson laugh. He's either amused by my gall or thinks I'm stupid. It could be a combination of both. "I told you he was good."

My mask slips for the quickest second when Tobias says, "Liam trained him well."

I almost demand to be informed how he knows Mr. Gregg, but I keep my mouth shut, aware it would spoil my ruse.

"Ahh... you have quite the skills, kid. If only you were a few years older." After standing from his chair, Tobias shifts on his feet to face Grayson. "Drive him anywhere he needs to go." When Grayson smiles and rubs his hands together, Tobias grabs hold of his shirt to drag him to within an inch of his face. "And leave him there. He's not to be brought into this, you hear?"

TWENTY MINUTES LATER, Grayson pulls his truck onto a familiar state highway. We head north instead of south, the opposite direction from where he kidnapped me. He's following the route I had planned to take earlier tonight, the one that will take me to my family ranch. The fucker is taking me home.

After several long minutes of me glaring at him, Grayson finally succumbs to the heat of my wrath. "I saw your plans when I sent Melody a message so she wouldn't be worried about you. I didn't look at anything else in your phone, I swear." When I call him a liar while mumbling several other curse words under my breath, he adds, "I didn't even need to break through the lock code on your phone. I answered one of her many texts." His eyes stray from the road to me. "That's real stupid, by the way. You shouldn't have the reply button set up. Kind of leaves it open for infiltration without any hacking required."

"Not as stupid as believing any who work for the government are honorable."

"Hey. Low blow." I stop yanking my cell phone out of my pocket when he whispers, "Liam was one of the best."

I watch him through squinted eyelids for a few minutes, unsure if he's throwing out bait with the hope of reeling me back into his web of deception or being genuinely honest. It could be a bit of them both.

Although I'm dying to unearth more about Mr. Gregg's elusive past, at the moment, my focus needs to remain on Melody. Tobias wasn't lying when he said I had been out for a while. It's almost midnight.

After scrolling through numerous panicked messages from Melody, Grayson's reply, and a missed call and text message from the cell phone Madden uses while deployed, I punch out a reply to one of Melody's many texts.

Brandon: *I'm sorry if I scared you. I'm on my way now. With Grayson's lead foot, I should be there in around an hour. I love you, Mellowy.*

Grayson doesn't even attempt to hide the fact he's snooping. "What's the whole Mellowy thing about?"

I balance my phone on my thigh to ensure I don't miss any more of Melody's texts before straying my eyes to the scenery whizzing by the window. I'm too pissed at Grayson to strike up a conversation with him, but my gut is also twisted up in knots. Something feels wrong. Like my world is about to implode. I could blame it on the anger Melody is most likely going to project at me from leaving her at the dress boutique as I did, but this feels more than that.

It feels catastrophic.

———

When Grayson pulls his truck down a familiar driveway an hour and a half later, I'm not surprised to notice Joey's party is still in full swing. He said he was going to live it up when he got a new heart, and he's done precisely that. There are more scantily clad women than there are men, and the amount of empty liquor bottles spread across the front lawn and porch reveals the festivities have been enjoyed by those in attendance.

Grayson peers at me with shocked, wide eyes when I say, "Come on."

"You heard what Tobias said, Brandon. I can't bring you into this."

I arch my brow. "It's a little too late for that, don't you think? You lied when you said you weren't investigating me, then you kidnapped me, so the least you can do is keep your end of our agreement." When his face reflects his confusion, I say, "This place is like a relic. All my father's belongings are here... including his computer. He hasn't used it in almost two years, but he had his home office servers interlinked with his work ones long before we moved."

Nothing but pure shock resonates in Grayson's tone when he asks, "You're still going to let me follow your lead in?"

I jerk up my chin. "But only after you've helped me sort out things with my girl."

"All right." He slides out of the cab of his truck before hot-footing it to the other side. "Should I start with neck kisses or a foot rub?"

I shoot him a wry look. I'm tired, cranky as fuck, and my stomach won't quit churning. Now isn't the time for him to play dumb, or I'll show him how Mr. Gregg taught me to take down threats with more than words.

"Poor timing. I'm sorry." His last two words were harder for him to express than his first two.

Brushing off his cheeky grin as a consequence of having a cocky attitude, I climb the front stairs of the porch. I'm eager to get to Melody, but I'm also keen to see what my father is hiding on his computer. There are too many times his name has been linked to Mr. Gregg's for me to continue brushing it off as a coincidence. I'm done acting stupid. It's time to dig deeper into my father's past and work out exactly what his issue is. This is more than a dislike that I was raised by another man. It feels much more serious than that.

I'm worried Mr. Gregg was right. I've done a terrible job of protecting *and* loving his daughter. Instead of evaluating each threat as they arrived, I pushed them to the background of my mind, believing Melody's well-being was more important than her safety. It was stupid of me to do, and it needs to stop—starting now.

The first person I notice when I burst through the party-like atmosphere in the living room is Melody. She's slowly making her way down the stairs. Her hair is a mess, and she looks like she's been crying. I knew she'd have been panicked, but I had no clue she'd be sobbing about it.

When she spots my gawk, the absolute agony on her face intensifies. She gallops down the stairs, her fast pace hindered like she's had too much to drink.

I'm anticipating she will sling her arms around my neck and hug me tight, so you can imagine my surprise when she grunts while signing, *"Where were you?"* The absolute fury she releases when she slams her fist into my chest is easily audible over the boom box in the corner of the room. *"Where were you, BJ? Why were you not here!"*

The anger in her eyes utterly blindsides me. She isn't panicked or upset.

She's devastated.

"You said you would be here, Brandon. You promised you would always be here for me."

Her reply is like a punch to the gut. She hasn't called me Brandon since the time I came close to losing her.

Fretful she's about to pull away, I step closer to her. *"I am here. I have always been here."*

She yanks away from me when I attempt to cup her ears like I always do when she's panicked. Her brisk movement has her stumbling into one of the four dozen or more people witnessing our first fight as a couple.

Her face whitens even more when she spots her reflection in the mirror. She's as white as a ghost, her unnatural skin coloring amplifying the streams of mascara running down her face.

"Melody!" I shout, stomping down my foot when she pivots on her heels and pushes through the people swarming in close to get their daily dose of drama firsthand.

When I follow her through the packed kitchen and onto the isolated back porch, Grayson's feet thud along with mine. It's like we're once again hunting Melody's stalker, except this time, we're running for Melody instead of away from her.

I take the three steps of the back porch with one leap so I can get in front of Melody before begging for her to give me a chance to explain. *"Please give me the chance to explain. It isn't as it seems."* When she attempts to sidestep me, I get desperate. *"Please, Mellowy..."*

That stops her like it always does, but instead of appeasing her anguish, it doubles it.

"Don't call me that. I am not a child. I am also not as stupid as everyone thinks I am!"

The horror on her face truly guts me, but it has nothing on the gut-wrenching image I spot behind her left shoulder. "Joey!"

As my heart shatters beyond repair, I sprint toward the old oak tree Melody use to climb to sneak into my room when we were kids. When I reach Joey's still legs, I band my arms around his thighs, then hoist him as high as I can, praying a bit of leverage will loosen the grip of the noose around his neck.

"Help me!" I scream to anyone listening when the cool grass beneath my feet has them slipping out from beneath me.

Several people spin around to face me, including Melody, who appears seconds from collapse, but only one jumps into action. Grayson drags a stack of chairs off the back porch as if they're weightless, climbs on top of them, then scoots across the large branch the rope strangling Joey is flung around. It takes him ripping his switchblade knife through the rope three times before the weight of Joey's limp body falling into my arms causes my knees to buckle.

As I commence CPR on my brother whose lips are as blue as Grayson's eyes, mine stray to where Melody once stood, except she's no longer there. She's vanished. As invisible as the thin slither of hope I'm endeavoring to clutch.

MELODY

I step behind a tree when Brandon's head swings to the right before he slowly drags it to the left. He's seeking me amongst the crowd, aware I'm here for him but confused as to why I'm not filling the spare seat next to him.

It's been five days since Joey hung himself in the old oak tree situated between his and Brandon's childhood bedrooms.

Five days of recalling the smoothness of the chin that grazed my neck before I gave in to the dark pit attempting to swallow me whole.

Five days of remembering the stubble on Brandon's jaw when he finally arrived at the party as promised.

Five days of scrubbing my skin until it was red and blistering.

And five days of wondering if Joey killed himself because of what he had done.

The evidence is damning. It's right in front of me in black and white for the world to see, but no matter how many times I tell myself the nightmare is over, he can't hurt me again, I can't bring myself to believe it.

That's why I must leave this life behind because

You can't protect yourself from sadness without first protecting yourself from happiness.

—*Jonathon Safran Foer*

After casting a glance over the people filling the den, I turn my eyes to my mom. "Have you seen her?"

My mom's tear-filled eyes lift from the potato salad she's spooning into a dish that's so overloaded, several chunks of potato and egg sit on the glistening counter of the mega kitchen in the mansion her husband bought with money I'm certain isn't clean. Unlike my father, her life hasn't simply continued since Joey's death. She only crawled out of bed today to attend his funeral and cater his wake. Once it's all said and done, I'm reasonably sure she'll crawl straight back beneath the sheets. She's as lost as we all are. No one saw this coming.

My mom's voice is as faint as a whisper when she says, "Give her time, BJ. We're struggling, so I can imagine how hard this is for Melody."

"That's why she needs to let me in. We should be leaning on each other, not pulling away." I tighten my jaw when my words crack. "I saw her standing at the back of the group, but she acted like she couldn't see my request for her to join us."

A notion I hadn't considered enters my mind when my mom

says, "She's angry, BJ. Not at you but at the fact she lost her father all over again. Joey kept his memory alive. He kept everything..." I can't understand a thing she says through the gut-wrenching sob ripping from her throat. "She'll come back... we've just got to give her time."

"I don't know if I can. I'm struggling without her." That killed me to admit, but I am. I can't wrap my head around anything that has happened the last week. It feels like I hit the peak of the roller-coaster, and I've been screaming through a terrifying hairpin ever since. This isn't the life I signed up for, none of it is, but it would be a shit-ton easier to wade through the heartache if I had Melody at my side.

"BJ..." Realizing no amount of words will fix this, my mom wraps her arms around me and hugs me tight. Her tears wet my dress shirt, and they encourage mine to flow.

We stay huddled together in the middle of the kitchen for several long minutes, only breaking when my father reminds us that only the good die young. "Come on, Barb. Pull it together. We've got hungry guests waiting."

A little ray of sunshine breaks through the heartbreak clouding me when my mom signs for him to fuck off. Because he never took the time to learn how to communicate with Melody, he has no clue what her gesture means, and how impacting it is for me. Joey's death has floored us, but like all true heartache, we'll use the grief to come out the other side stronger. I just need Melody to give me the chance to assure her of this.

Annoyed about our silent but highly visible laughter, my dad grumbles under his breath before he returns to his 'waiting guests.' The swinging door separating the kitchen from the living areas of the house has barely stopped swinging when our voiceless laughter turns boisterous.

"He's such a moody old bastard. God, why couldn't I have seen it years ago?"

I bump my mom with my hip. "Because you had to wait for Joey and me to show up first."

A big inhalation lifts her chest. "That's true," she murmurs before squeezing my hand in hers. "You were both too wise for your age, and thankfully took after my side of the family."

She laughs at my agreeing nod before guilt for being happy smacks into her. It snaps her mouth shut and glosses her eyes with sadness instead of happiness. I'm feeling guilty too, but I'm aware she needs to smile as much as she needs to cry, so it doesn't affect me as diversely. Grief is a funny thing, and it has many stages. Laughter is one of them.

After several long seconds staring out at space, my mom's focus shifts back to feeding the two hundred plus people who traveled from near and far to bid farewell to Joey. Her ashen face whitens even more when she notices how much potato salad she has wasted. She's on the board of many charities endeavoring to feed the hungry children of the world, so she hates unnecessary wastage.

When she moves to the sink for a cloth, I enclose my hand over hers. "Leave it. I'll clean it up."

"Are you sure?" Her watering eyes bounce between mine when I nod. "You've always been a good boy, BJ. You and Joey were such good kids."

When her voice cracks during her last sentence, I pull her into my chest to hug her as tightly as she did to me only five minutes ago. "I won't stop until I find out what happened to him, Mom. I swear to you, I won't."

"Oh, honey, he committed suicide. There's nothing for you to find out."

The unmovable grief in her voice pricks my eyes with fresh tears. "I don't believe that, Mom, and neither do you. You know Joey wouldn't do this. He'd never hurt you like this."

She doesn't reply, but her silence speaks volumes. She knows as well as I do that there's more to this than we know. I've just got to stop putting my search on the backburner.

"Why don't you head up to bed? I'll get everyone fed, then come check on you once they've left."

Her eyes twinkle with thanks before she brushes her lips against my cheek. I hear her murmur how Joey and I were such good kids before she disappears down the long hallway that will take her to the master suite. Once she's out of eyesight, I gather up a bowl of potato salad and a bag of bread rolls then move into the den where Joey's wake is being held.

His true friends are huddled around the coffee table sharing jokes and looking lost. Our family members who never really knew him are keeping Phoenix occupied, and my father is in the corner of the room, smoking a cigar and drinking gin like his son didn't just end his life. He's mourning, the groove that hasn't smoothed between his brows the past five days reflect this, but he isn't mourning like a normal father would. He's not reminiscing or telling stories about when Joey was a kid as he wouldn't know any to share.

Instead, he talks about himself and his aspiration for Congress, then glares at me over his crystal glass when I slam down the bowl of potato salad onto the dining table before tossing the bread rolls into his chest. "Lunch is served!"

I can see in his eyes that he's dying to bite at the bait I'm throwing out, but since there are men in this room more influential than him, he keeps his frustration on the down-low. "I hope every-one's on the same liquid diet as me."

His fat, pompous friends laugh at his joke. I glare at him. He truly sickens me.

When Aunt Rhonda and Maree fill the pretentiously large twenty-seater dining table with the food I forgot, my father orders me out of the room without a word spilling from his lips. He doesn't care if I haven't eaten in days. He just wants me gone.

Happy to use his dismissal to my advantage, I make a beeline for the hallway that leads to my room, only altering the direction of my course when his undivided attention returns to his special guests.

After darting past the open doors of the den, I make a beeline for my father's office. I have the handle lowered halfway when the flush of a toilet across the hallway freezes my hand. I breathe out a sigh of relief when Madden exits the washroom a few seconds later. It's weird he's using the guest bathroom instead of the one in his room, but I guess a walk up a set of stairs is too much for someone as grief-stricken as him. He's so out of sorts, he shaved off the beard that took him a year to grow the night Joey died.

"Hey." He adds a head jerk to his greeting before joining me near our father's office. "What are you doing?"

I say the first thought that pops into my head. "Melody isn't answering my texts, so I'm going to call her dorm on the TTY phone Mom had installed for her when we moved in. You?"

He swipes his hand under his nose before shrugging. "Nothing. Just needed to get away for a bit."

"So, you went to the bathroom?"

He gives me a look that says he doesn't appreciate the snappiness of my tone. Twelve months ago, I wouldn't have cared about hurting his feelings. Now, five days after fruitlessly trying to resuscitate our dead brother, I care.

"Sorry. That was uncalled for." I slap his shoulder in a man-hug type of way before pulling him into my chest. "If you need me, reach out. I'll be right there."

"Yeah. Ah... thanks." He ends my half-hearted embrace as awkwardly as I started it before inching back. "Same to you."

Eager to take him up on his offer, I start my investigation five minutes earlier than planned. "Did you happen to see Melody or Joey Saturday night? Joey said he invited you to his party, but he didn't know if you'd be back from boot camp in time."

"Umm... no. I had only turned up when... you know... you were working on Joey." He gives off the signs that he's lying, but since it's a touchy subject, I give him a bit of leeway. I can't wipe the images from my head, and I wasn't watching it from afar like him.

"What about Melody?"

Madden scrubs at the stubble on his chin. Unlike the rest of the family, he didn't shave for Joey's funeral. "Why are you asking me about her whereabouts? She's your girlfriend, so shouldn't you know where she's at?"

"I'm not asking where she is now. I'm asking if you saw her at Joey's party." I lower the anger in my voice by just a smidge before saying, "She was upset Saturday night. I figured since you called me, maybe you knew what was wrong."

"Nah, I have no clue what her problem is. I was just reaching out, that's all. Seeing how you were." Now I know without a doubt he's lying. He doesn't care about anyone but himself, so there's no chance in hell he asked me to call him just to say hello. "If you ever find out what her issue is, give me a heads up. I'll back you up." He speaks his offer as if it were a person who upset Melody, not a thing or a reason.

"Yeah, thanks." I have no intention of accepting his offer, but if it gets him away from me quicker, I'm down with pretending I'm open to the idea.

Confident I'm falling for his helpful-big-brother ruse, he lifts his chin for the second time before joining Phoenix in the den. I slip into my father's office just as quietly. After switching on the antique lamp, I ruffle through the papers covering his old-style desk. When they appear to be nothing but endorsement sheets and campaign funding requests, I shift my focus to his laptop. It is password protected. The hint states it's a birthday. Naturally, I try my mother's birthdate first. When it comes back as incorrect, I try Phoenix's and then Madden's. Both fail.

Desperate, I give my father one last attempt to prove he loves all his children. That ends as disastrously as suspected. Neither mine nor Joey's dates of birth work. With the laptop warning, I have one final chance to input the correct code, I stray my eyes around my father's office, seeking any hints as to what his passcode would be.

I find several clues a few seconds later. They are a dozen crystal picture frames scattered amongst the law books on his shelves. They're all filled with photographs of one person. My father.

With my back molars grinding, I punch his birthdate into his laptop. I curse myself when it brings up the home screen a few seconds later. After closing down an acquisitions sheet for a Kirill Bobrov, I sign into his banking site. Mercifully, it doesn't require me to sign in because it's still logged in from an earlier access.

While flicking my eyes between the office door and the laptop's screen, I scroll through several deposits from idiots endorsing my father's run for office even this far out from the elections. The amounts reflected range from low three figures to some as high as six, notching toward seven digits.

One completely stops me. It isn't to Mr. Darcy as I was seeking, but the payee name is odd, considering my father drives an AUDI.

BMW Coastal Pty Ltd.

The sixty-three thousand, one hundred and seventy-eight-dollar transaction was right around the time Melody and I sent a second admission request to Browns. My application was granted. Hers was denied.

"I've got you now, you condescending prick," I mutter under my breath while hitting Control P to print out proof of my father's scheming ways.

The inkjet printer working overtime almost drowns the soundless buzz of my cell phone. I must have forgotten to turn the sound back on after Joey's funeral.

While digging my phone out of the pocket of my dress pants, praying it's a call from Melody, I recall the way she squirms when I talk against her skin. She can't hear the praise I bombard her with every time we make love, but she can sense the sentiment in the vibrations of my lips. It adds to our lovemaking and gives us another form of communication only we know.

My lips twist when I peer down at the screen. It isn't who I am hoping, but in a way, it kind of is. I'm not able to track down Melody's exact whereabouts, but a member of the Federal Bureau of Investigation sure does. I reached out to Grayson long before I sought advice from my father on tracking down a missing person. Although Grayson couldn't tell me where Melody was, he assured me she was safe and that he'd advise me if anything changed. My father told me anyone who hides from their responsibilities isn't worth finding. Excluding the three words I shouted at him ten minutes ago, I haven't spoken to him since then.

After sliding my finger across the screen of my phone, I squash it to my ear. I don't get to issue a greeting before Grayson says, "Planning a trip without me, punk?"

My eyes float over the screen of my father's laptop before they drift to the window. The standard cars are in the driveway, and the laptop is still open on the print screen. I can't see any signs of Grayson's watch.

"A trip?" I ask, feeling lost. I thought he meant his plan to follow my lead through my father's servers, but a lack of evidence has me moving away from that theory.

"I heard the Cali coast is nice this time of the year, but I'm not sure now is the right time for you to be taking a trip."

"What the hell are you talking about, Grayson? I'm not going to California."

My heart beats out a funky tune when he says, "Oh… so it's just your girl going? I had wondered when her printout said it was a one-way ticket."

I freeze, still lost but also panicked.

When the sound of a commercial aircraft hums through the phone, I clue onto Grayson's riddle. "You found Melody?" His murmur of agreement is soft but confirming. "At an airport?" When his agreeing hum keeps coming, I ask, "Which one?" I'm stunned. Justly so. Melody has never been on a plane, much less left the state, so why the hell is she going on an interstate trip without me?

"I can't tell you that. I could get into shit just for passing this info on."

"Please, Grayson. If I don't know where she is, I can't stop her from leaving." When my plea falls on deaf ears, I try another tactic. "I have information that could aid your team's investigation of my father."

I picture him scrubbing at the bumfluff on his chin when he asks, "Who said we're investigating your father?"

I scoff. "I'm not an idiot. I know he's one of the men you're chasing." Confident I'm about to reel in the little fish with the hope of a bigger catch, I snatch the bank documentation off the printer before snagging my dad's Audi keys from his top drawer. "If he isn't who you're after, I'm confident he's one of the many stones you'll need to turn over to get your man. I have possible information that could help you find Katie. Are you really willing to give that up for this, sharing information about a girl you swear you're not investigating?"

I'm once again blindly throwing darts at the board in the hope of a bulls-eye, but for once in my life, it pays off. "She's at Saugerties' domestic terminal." Grayson's reply comes with a whole heap of expletives and the honk of a horn that sounds like it's being battered by a fist.

I want to join him when my eyes stray to the clock on my father's desks. "Fuck. It's peak-hour traffic. It will take me over two hours to get there."

"Then you better hurry," Grayson replies, "Because her flight leaves in two hours and fifteen minutes."

I'm out the door before 'fifteen' leaves his mouth.

BRANDON

I abandon my father's car in one of the waiting bays just outside of the airport when the line to get into the domestic terminal parking lot stretches for as far as the eye can see. They can tow his car, I don't fucking care. This is much more important than a flashy chunk of metal.

Only while weaving dangerously through traffic the past one and a half hours did the entirety of Grayson's comment dawn on me. He said Melody purchased a one-way ticket to California. That means she doesn't intend to come back, that this isn't a breathe-and-recover break. She's leaving *permanently*.

I understand that she's upset, I get that she feels like she lost her father twice, but this won't fix anything. Running never fixes anything.

When I break through the throng of people all apparently leaving Saugerties at the same time, I check the flight boards to see which terminal flies to California. Once I discover it's from Terminal E, I exit the ticketing terminal as quickly as I entered it. Terminal E is down the other end of the runway.

I'm screamed at, called names, and almost get in a tussle when I push through the people waiting to go through security screening. I'm confident I'm seconds from being arrested when a TSA officer near an X-ray machine signals for me to step forward, so you can imagine my shock when he nudges his head to the right and tells me to run.

The reason for his assistance comes to light when the slant of his head exposes a pair of familiar blue eyes hidden under the brim of an official-looking hat. I didn't recognize Grayson straight away since he shaved off his kiddy beard.

"If you get arrested, I'm denying all knowledge of us ever meeting," Grayson shouts when I sprint through the X-ray machine before hightailing it to the right.

I'm out of breath, but I can't help but chuckle when a pompously arrogant voice announces over the loudspeaker that Nando's is offering free peri-peri chicken to the first one hundred travelers to arrive at their booth I just happen to be sprinting by. It creates a sea of people between me and the TSA officers chasing me down in less than a second.

Within a minute, I go from appearing like a fugitive evading arrest to an everyday traveler. It gives me a second to catch my breath, which I lose again when I spot Melody in a queue preparing to board her flight. I know she has spotted me like she did at Joey's funeral because she strayed her eyes to the ground to block out my words as only she can.

"Melody." The three stomps of my foot on the ground increases the shudders she's striving to ignore, but she keeps her head down, forcing me to shout her name again, and again, and again.

"Stop," she demands after spinning to face me. *"You need to go."*

I shake my head. *"I am not going anywhere until you tell me what the hell is going on."*

She goes with the same excuse every romance novel uses. *"I need time. We need time."*

When she steps forward to maintain her place in the queue, I snap. *"No. You don't get alone time when you are a couple. That isn't the way things work. The only place you get to run when you are scared is to me. You don't get to leave. That is how being a couple works."*

It feels like she stabs me in the chest with a big knife when she signs, *"Then maybe we should not be a couple anymore."*

When the man in front of her steps forward, I fill the gap, forcing Melody to face me head-on. *"Where is this coming from? I understand your upset about Joey—"*

"This isn't about Joey." My brows furrow when she looks up and to the right. *"This is about us needing some time apart. We are too dependent on each other. It isn't healthy."*

I both sign and shout my reply, *"You are lying. You looked up and to the right. That is a clear sign that you are lying."*

Her squeal only rumbles in her chest, but it's almost deafening. *"Don't read me. He didn't teach you everything he knew so you could use his skills against me."*

"Okay. Just don't cry. Please," I beg when the tears welling in her eyes threaten to spill. I've never seen her like this. Usually, she's controlled even when she's upset. A sense of normality isn't a vibe she's giving right now.

"Talk to me." When she steps forward to hand her boarding pass to the gate agent, I get desperate. *"Please, Mellowy."*

My nickname works as it usually does. *"I can't, BJ. I can't do this right now."*

"Then wait and let me come with you. Don't run." When she ignores my request, the anger and hurt that has festered inside of me the past five days spills over. *"Can you at least pretend you fucking care about me. My brother died, Melody, he fucking died, but you can't even give me a goddamn excuse as to why you are leaving me—"*

My rant ends in the worst way possible when she discloses, *"I slept with someone."*

"What?" I don't sign this reply. I can barely get my mouth to follow the commands of my brain, much less my hands. "You're lying. You're not telling the truth. You would never do that to me. You're not that type of person. I only just told the courts that a few months ago. This can't be true. It can't."

"It is. I slept with someone else. I cheated on you."

I stare at her, praying for her eyes to look up and to the right, for her to scratch her face, to sweat, to do something that will indicate she isn't telling the truth.

All I get in an apology. *"I am sorry. I never meant to hurt you."*

After squeezing my hand like she always did when we were kids, she accepts her scanned boarding pass from the ticket agent, spins on her heels, and walks away from me. She doesn't glance back to check I'm okay or mouth that she loves me. She just leaves me standing in the middle of the airport with a shattered heart and the determination to destroy anyone and everyone responsible for it.

Don't underestimate the power of a vigilante. He only shows you want he wants you to see, but he'll have you paying attention the instant his mask goes on.

To be continued in <u>Hushed Guardian</u>
Available NOW!

Facebook: facebook.com/authorshandi

Instagram: instagram.com/authorshandi

Email: authorshandi@gmail.com

Reader's Group: bit.ly/ShandiBookBabes

Website: authorshandi.com

Newsletter: https://www.subscribepage.com/AuthorShandi

If you enjoyed this book - please leave a review.

ACKNOWLEDGMENTS

We've reached another acknowledgement page, and once again I've run out of words. As always, thanks to my family, especially my husband who forever supports me. A special mention to all those crazy Enigma fans who have been dying for Brandon's story for years. I know this book hasn't fully explained him, but we've scratched the surface on unearthing why he's the lovable, grumpy, somewhat sly guy we've grown to love/hate.

Thank you to my mum, who knew from day one that Brandon's story was never going to fit into one book. To Nicki and Kaylene from Swish Editing & Design for sprucing up my messy work. Beth from Magnolia services for giving it a final once over to ensure it's super polished, and to the beta-readers who read the unedited copies and fill in the surveys to ensure I'm on the right track.

As I forever say, this isn't my story. I'm just sharing it, but it's nice to get advice along the way. It helps knowing you're hating the same person I'm hating.

If you're not, I've got something to fix.

Although I had planned on putting book 1 and 2 together, I truly feel like you need a pause to get the full effect of what has happened. Take some time to process it all, ask questions, and plot what you think happens next.

I will say, I don't think any of you will be prepared for what comes next. Brandon hasn't stopped surprising me since day one. Let's hope he'll surprise you too.

Talk soon.

Shandi xx

HUSHED GUARDIAN

BRANDON

SIX YEARS LATER...

"Our window is small. We need to be in and out in under ten minutes." Tobias, head operative of my unit, points out the most direct entrances of the Sicilian militant compound we're about to raid. Our objective is simple—seize the operation of an underage sex-trafficking ring with minimal casualties. "Martin, Copen, and Ellis will go in via the west entrance, Trace and Lloyd via the east, and Charlton and I will take the north."

Tobias spins back around to face the group of twelve heavily-armored men hanging off his every word. It's like this everywhere we go. From the moment I joined his team as a 'consultant' to repay the debt I owed when he kept my ass out of jail after the stunt Grayson and I pulled at the airport saw us being arrested for terrorism to right now, he's forever admired and respected.

Many men have come and gone from Tobias's team the past six years, but not once have they left on bad terms. Tobias is big, crude, and Russian, but he's also one of the most respected members of the Federal Bureau of Investigation.

He climbed the ranks quickly when he caught the eye of the Associate Deputy Director after a sting in Ravenshoe almost eighteen years ago. A Russian sanction was attempting to sink a foothold in the sleepy town where Tobias was once a detective.

There was no way in hell Tobias would *ever* let that happen.

I don't usually endorse rumors, but the story about how Tobias singlehandedly took down a consortium over ten years in the making is hard not to believe. The story was shared with me many times during the three years I worked as a 'consultant' for Tobias's team, over a dozen times during my six-month stint to become an official member of the Bureau, and more than a handful of times the past three years I've been a field agent, yet, the facts have never altered. Not once. They stayed exactly the same.

I can tell you from both experience on and off the job, that doesn't happen unless it's true. So, as the rumors have it, Tobias ran a Russian sanction out of his hometown for one reason and one reason only—his daughter, Isabelle.

The tales never included the reason why his daughter was the focus of his campaign, and her name was never mentioned in any of the write-ups he logged with the Bureau, but it must have been important. Even now, years after Grayson unknowingly disclosed Tobias's operations are solely chosen on if Tobias sees his daughter in the eyes of the children we're endeavoring to free from captivity, his team is still fighting the crusade he commenced over eighteen years ago.

Usually, operatives like his fold within six months. If they're not shut down completely due to a lack of resources, they're passed on to less-experienced agents whose funding would be sliced to a pittance of what's needed to bring down a massive cartel ring like the one we're endeavoring to seize today.

The only reason that hasn't happened is because despite Tobias's team not netting the primary player of an operation believed to be worth over 7.8 billion dollars, his team has notched up an impressive number of arrests since it was founded. They have disbanded more notorious crime syndicates the past six years than *all* the other divisions combined for the entirety of the Bureau's history.

Some say Tobias's unusual fondness for the man we're hunting is the reason he's failed to snag the number-one-wished-for-item on the FBI's hit list. Others say it's because Henry Gottle is always one step ahead of the authorities.

I'm somewhere in the middle.

It's clear Tobias's relationship with the mob boss of New York City blurs the line between corruption and righteousness, but Mr. Gregg taught me it's okay to cross lines when it comes to keeping your family safe. As long as you know how to find your way home, you can cross as many boundaries deemed necessary to uphold your pledge. You just eventually have to return to the right side of the law.

It was those infamous words ringing through my ears six years ago that kept my feet planted on the ground when Melody boarded her flight to California. They also had me looking at the bigger picture when Tobias explained exactly how long the piece of string I was endeavoring to unravel was.

At the start, my 'consultant' position with the Bureau involved scrubbing toilets, shredding files, polishing Tobias's boots, and any other mundane task he required me to do. Tobias milked it for all it was worth, and in all honesty, I hated him for it. My girlfriend had left me, my brother had supposedly killed himself, and my father won his bid to become the District Attorney of New York.

My life was shit, but Tobias never gave me time to dwell on it.

Grayson didn't fare much better than me. At Tobias's request, he was transferred to work under his father's division of the Bureau. It was a temporary, six-month rookie exchange, but to Grayson, it was more punishment than cleaning up after men who ate way too much fiber.

We were both in the shit—literally.

Grayson sucked it up, portrayed the ideal agent, and was returned to Tobias's team as a new man within four months.

It took a shit ton more effort for me to get on Tobias's good side.

Keeping my head down and my mouth shut added a handful of

murmured merits to Tobias's daily grunt regime, but it was only after he walked in on me packing up after his team at a firing range did he add sentences into the mix.

While Tobias's crew washed off the lead burning their skin from target practice, I coated mine in it. It had been over a year since I had held a gun, so I was more than eager to discharge a few rounds, and perhaps some of the anger I was still harboring over Joey's death and Melody's affair.

The fifteen bullets in the gun's magazine made the paper silhouette's head non-existent, and the one in the chamber ensured even if the target had survived fifteen kill shots to the head, he would have wished he was dead because I shot him right in the cock.

Thinking back now, it seems a little immature, but at the time, it felt fucking good to disperse some of the rage festering in my gut.

I looked into Melody's claims she had slept with someone the instant I was out of Tobias's idea of lock-up. I went through the belongings she had left in her room in my family's mansion, interviewed her friends, and I even sat through several of her lectures to see if anyone gave off any indication they were missing her as much as I was.

I found nothing, not a single shred of evidence to corroborate her claims. It was as if she hadn't lied until I went to supervise the removal of the old oak tree between Joey's childhood bedroom and mine.

As I sat at the window watching the arborist cut down the tree that had destroyed my family, I thought back to the many fond times I had looked at it. In particular, the last time Melody had climbed it.

For the first time in weeks, I smiled.

My happiness didn't last long.

With one set of memories instigating the wish for more, I dragged an old shoebox full of photographs from the headboard of my bed to my desk. The six-strip of condoms my mom had snuck inside the day after Melody and I had given each other our virginities had been reduced to five, and an empty package was sitting in the waste-bin under my desk.

I've never once in my life craved a violent, all-in rage as I did that afternoon. I wanted to demolish my room as the arborist was doing to the oak tree. I wanted to smash every piece of furniture I owned before dragging my mattress outside to set in on fire. I wanted my room to feel as bare and as hollow as I felt, and I was willing to lose everything to do it.

But instead of doing any of those things, I shoved the box of pictures under my arm, paid the tree chopper the exorbitant fee my father negotiated to have evidence of Joey's death removed from our lives as soon as possible, then left my family ranch without so much as a backward glance.

I've never been back since.

It was that afternoon that Tobias caught me expelling my rage on a defenseless paper target. I was in the process of reloading the Sig Sauer P226's magazine when Tobias said, "Liam always recruited the best officers, so how come he never mentioned you?"

Unaware his question was rhetorical, I replied, "The Bureau requires a degree. I was also too young."

Tobias smirked a smug grin before he turned away and mumbled, "I wasn't talking about the Bureau."

His reply stumped me for days. I was truly lost. It was only while pondering over a decade of stories did pieces of the puzzle start falling into place.

After a quick google search, I discovered the university Wren and my mother attended is one of the highest CIA recruited universities in the country. Mr. Gregg attended the same university as his wife four years prior. He possessed as bachelor's degree in political science that I can't find payment for, had a 3.4 GPA, was an American citizen, and his tax records for his senior year stated he was a military operative who hadn't left campus for more than a few days at a time.

It could have been a coincidence, but Tobias's lack of denial when I brought it up the following week all but confirmed my suspicions. Tobias is quick to tell you when you're wrong. His lectures last as long as my father's, and sometimes, he even goes as far as using a spreadsheet to show you exactly where you went wrong, so for him to keep quiet, I knew I was on the money.

Furthermore, despite what the movies portray, US-born employees recruited and trained to work as Intelligence Officers for the National Clandestine Service (CIA) are never referred to as 'agents.' They're called 'Operations Officers' or 'Case Officers' or some go by 'Officer' for short.

Tobias said 'Officer.' He doesn't fumble over his words, and he has never cracked under pressure, so to this day, I'm confident he didn't make his remark for no reason. Between cleaning urinals with a toothbrush, and making beds like I was an army cadet, I gave my theory a little more thought.

AKA—I snooped while Tobias and his team were sleeping.

Without Grayson's help, it took me eight weeks to unearth information that now would take me six minutes. The evidence wasn't damning, but it did add a stack of wood onto my claims that Mr. Gregg was an Operations Officer for the CIA.

He was either that or a mobster.

I prefer my earlier theory.

Just like Tobias's relationship with Henry Gottle gains criticism, so has links between the CIA and certain mafia syndicates. For decades, conspiracists have alleged connections between the CIA and organized crime. Rumors range from reputed members of the Chicago mob being killed days before government inquiries into the conspiracists' claims to CIA officers colluding with members of the Bureau to cause gang-related violence. If the head of one crime syndicate takes out another, who's going to mourn the loss?

Once again, I'm not a fan of rumors, especially ones that alter the more they're disclosed, but from the photograph Grayson shared with Melody and me in the dress shop years ago, to the many phone conversations between Henry Gottle and Mr. Gregg noted in confidential FBI records, I can conclusively say they knew one another. I just haven't deciphered how or why.

If Wren had been a defense attorney, their contact could have been brushed off as an acquaintance by association, but that isn't the case. The meeting Tobias's team intercepted between Mr. Gregg and Henry Gottle wasn't the only one they had in the weeks leading to Liam and Wren's death. They met a handful of times, including the night Melody said Crombie had tailed her mom from Mary's Diner.

My focus returns to the present when Tobias says, "James and Rogers will run communications while the rest of you enter via the south entrance."

No one blinks an eye at Tobias referring to me by my middle name because as far as anyone in this room is concerned, my name is Brandon James. I was born in Cleveland, Ohio, and my father isn't Vincent McGee, recently appointed Governor of New York. That would only make things awkward when rookie agents connected the dots. It's not every day a federal agent is on the team hunting down his father.

I've known since I was young that my father is an evil man. Years of service reveal I am right. The only thing is, just like many of his 'associates,' he's clever enough to keep himself out of jail. He hides bank records, keeps his hands clean by ensuring his name isn't associated with anything shady, and believes his position of Governor makes him untouchable.

I'm determined to prove him wrong.

He got away with admissions fraud by stating the car he purchased with campaign funds was for his campaign leader. That's how arrogant my father is. He doesn't believe the authorities are smart enough to realize Florida and New York aren't the same state, but because the Bureau would rather catch him for something bigger, they let his misdemeanor slide.

I won't let a second slip-up pass without prosecution. It will only be a matter of time before he stumbles, and when he does, I'll be there with my foot propped out, ready to aid in his fall.

As the agents check their weapons in preparation for the raid, Grayson scrubs at the beard that no longer looks like bumfluff while mumbling a curse word under his breath. He's pissed, wrongly believing he is being excluded from the sting because he's too close to the case to work it properly.

It's not true. He's one of the best field operatives in Tobias's team, but his hacking skills are even better than that. He is the equivalent of three black hatters, and with Tobias needing eyes and ears in every room of the fortified warehouse to ensure his team isn't walking into an ambush, he has to exclude Grayson from the raid.

Me, on the other hand, anticipated being seconded to comms. I fucked-up four years ago by letting my past affect my future. Tobias is a great team leader, but he can hold a grudge as well as he can down a bottle of vodka and not get a hangover.

My error almost got me kicked out of the Bureau before I was even an official agent. It brought me back onto the straight and narrow, but the hit it caused my personal life is still being felt. The incident took Melody from being the girl I once loved to a girl I no longer know.

While working my jaw side to side to keep my annoyance on the down-low, I slot into a chair behind a bank of monitors. Grayson has already logged into servers that should be unhackable, so I commence working on establishing a connection with the main compound.

Criminal associations like the one we're raiding tonight don't store their assets at their residences, they use offsite compounds and commercial properties. The more valuable the asset, the more guards to watch them. This site has three men walking the property line, four guarding the main entrance, and another two in a watchtower.

Once Grayson breaks through the firewall keeping him out of

the mainframe, I'm guessing there will be an additional dozen or so men inside. That's around the standard number of goons for this type of operation.

The web we're attempting to eradicate is massive. There are more than a dozen organizations sprouting off from it, and the list of suspects grows exponentially every day. Politicians, movie stars, drug lords, and a name I'm more than familiar with are only a handful of the men we're chasing. It's such a long process because this network wasn't built overnight. It has been operating longer than I've been born, and very rarely are the men helming the operations' cooperative with the authorities.

Today's sting will barely create a ripple to the empire as a whole, but it only takes one thread to loosen an entire web. That's the thread we're seeking today, and we will continue seeking until each member on our list of suspects has paid for their crimes, and men like my father realize no amount of power will save them from the law.

"Don't forget to check the sleeping quarters this time around. There are usually a few men down there every raid *testing* the merchandise." Grayson's jaw tightens at the way I snarl 'testing.' This operation isn't running drugs. They like underage women.

"Do you have a feed for the main residence?" Grayson asks, his tone curious.

I jerk up my chin. "Castro isn't going anywhere soon."

He gags when I point to Rimi Castro, suspected leader of a Sicilian crime syndicate currently based in New Mexico. He's in bed with three women. None of them are his wife, and I doubt any of them are over the age of twenty-one. He likes them young, but his buyers like them even younger than that.

"What's your total?"

Grayson ensures his live stream has every inch of the compound covered before moving for the infrared system to double-check his numbers. "Looks like twenty-three in total. Nine outside the compound, fourteen inside." He relays that to Tobias through the radio headsets the agents are wearing. They also have body cams and shoulder mics to stop any questions if our sting goes wrong.

Confident we have everything lined up, Tobias and the team climb into three blacked-out Escalades before testing communications. Once we give him the thumbs up, the operation starts. The two men in the tower are taken out first by a long-range sniper. One slumps into the wooden box they man eighteen hours straight while the larger of the two falls over the railing, landing smack bang between two guards manning the fence lines.

"Approach compromised. Sending message to Honey Pot. She's naked." I don't mean the female agent we placed undercover in this operation is *naked* naked. It means she's without backup and not carrying a weapon.

After switching my radio signal to a private channel, I say, "Infiltration negative. Target aware." She can't reply, but the quick *donk, donk* that sounds through my earpiece advises she heard me.

"Wait."

Leesa, our Honey Pot, freezes immediately, narrowly missing four men sprinting through the open command center she's tiptoeing toward. Usually, they wouldn't give a whore a second look, but since she isn't anywhere near the sleeping quarters at the back of the compound, their suspicions would rise as quickly as the sound of the AK-47s in the background of our feed.

"Move."

While Leesa races for the computer responsible for the digital locks on the cages in the basement, I stray my eyes back to Castro. He's still in bed entertaining his guests.

With my eyes back on the main monitor, and Leesa's displaying she needs a twelve-digit sequence for access, I say, "Input the code *exactly* how I state. One wrong key, and you'll be permanently locked out."

After peering up at the camera blinking in the corner of the room, she nods. She looks scared. I'm not surprised. It isn't every day a rookie agent goes undercover as a whore in a mafia syndicate.

Tobias had no choice but to pluck someone straight out of the academy. This job ages you very quickly. If he didn't wade through a long list of graduates, his team would have never made it this far.

Leesa made quite the impression on Castro's little brother, Paavo. He refused to share her with his men, and has been seen multiple times the past month in a jewelry store buying her gifts. It's been an almost seamless operation—almost too perfect.

"Are you ready?" I wait for Leesa to nod before relaying the string of text and numbers in front of me. "Delta, Juliet, three, hotel, bravo…" I stumble over my last word when I spot Castro moving out of frame in the corner of my eye. He's not adjusting girl number three's hips so he can fuck her from behind, he's throwing her off the bed. "Victor, kilo…"

While I continue reciting the passcode to Leesa, I ram my elbow into Grayson's rib. He's guiding agents through an almost pitch-black night, pointing out suspects lying in wait to kill them, while also remotely leading them through the warehouse, so they take the most direct route to the girls we're endeavoring to seize.

I've just finished relaying the last digit of the code to Leesa when Grayson's eyes stray to mine. When I point out Castro's movements, I stumble onto something much more sickening than him fucking three girls at once. He's speaking with someone, someone who can't possibly be in two places at once, much less on two different live feeds. Castro can't be liaising with Leesa at his residence while she's staring directly at me from his off-site compound. It isn't possible. *Unless…*

"Honey Pot has been compromised. I repeat, Honey Pot has been compromised. Pull back."

My warning comes too late. When Leesa places the last digit into the computer's mainframe, the cell doors in the basement pop open as predicted. They're just not filled with underage girls, they are brimming with Sicilian operatives eager to slaughter US government officials.

BRANDON

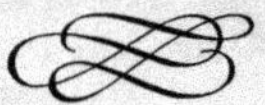

"Fuck, fuck, fuck, fuck, fuck!" Grayson screams before he switches his demands from the agents on the ground to the ones in the air. "We're being ambushed..."

While he calls in backup, my fingers fly wildly over my keyboard. Within minutes, I have the unhacked version of Castro's residence up on the main screen. I've tapped into a live feed via a satellite connection.

It doesn't improve the situation.

It makes it ten times worse.

Not a single soul can be seen via the infrared vision. It's as if his mansion that usually houses twenty-plus is a ghost town.

As I relay the information I've unearthed to Tobias, who's in the middle of an intense gun battle, Leesa peers up at the screen she was staring at earlier, smiles an evil grin, then kills the feed with a pistol she couldn't have unless she pried it out of the cold, dead hands of a fellow agent.

"Fuck this." I yank off my headset, throw open the drawer between Grayson's and my station, then remove my government-issued pistol. "She sent fellow agents to their deathbeds while smiling. She doesn't get to leave this compound alive unless it's in a pair of handcuffs."

Grayson doesn't utter a word, but I know he's on board with my plan. The removal of his gun assures me, much less his sprint to the weaponry cabinet to up the ante. "They were donning AK-47s. They're only distributed by one entity."

"The Russians?"

I'm not technically asking a question, but Grayson still lifts his chin. "We've had word syndicates were merging. Do you think this is the proof we've been looking for?" Don't mistake the length of his question as him not prioritizing his priorities correctly. While speaking, he loaded two Colt M4 Carbines, donned a bulletproof vest, and joined me in the remaining Escalade. "AK-47s are the Russians' weapon of choice. This is a Sicilian-run compound. Something is very wrong with this picture."

While I veer us through rose-colored deserts with snow-capped peaks in the background, Grayson takes down three men sneaking into the entrance of the compound within a second of them leaving their Ford Expedition. The bullet casings ting off the windshield before landing in my lap. The hairline cracks they cause to the windshield has nothing on the damage I instigate by t-boning a second vehicle.

As images of the visual Melody most likely experienced when she arrived at the scene of her parents' accident swarm my mind, I place a bullet between the eyes of the passenger in the Ford Expedition before adding one to the chest of the driver for good measure. He's clearly dead, but I'd rather be cautious than be played for a fool —again.

After taking in an overhead power line, the connection of the electricity box to the steel fence spanning the perimeter, and the hover of a helicopter overhead, Grayson and I move into the main hub of the compound. Situational awareness is one of the first things Tobias teaches his recruits. Being aware of what's going on around you is the only thing that increases your odds of living when you're amid an ambush.

Tear gas stings my eyes and irritates my upper respiratory tract, but the scene is one of many I've been a part of the past three years. Guns blaze, lives are lost, and it's all done without a sound seeping from my lips.

Calling out during a raid is one of the worst things you can do. It alerts the men you're targeting where you are and paints a bullseye on your back.

After creeping down the hallway I led Leesa down remotely earlier and killing an additional six Sicilian crime members on the way, I signal for Grayson to take the corridor on his left while I approach the main entrance.

Our enemies know we're coming. I can feel it in my bones, not to mention the brittle warning from a female voice a mere second before the barrel of my Colt M4 peeks out of the corner where I'm stationed. "If you come any closer, I'll kill him."

Every FBI agent handles this threat at one stage of their career. This is my fourth, although it feels different this time around. That might have more to do with the fact the person Leesa is holding hostage isn't just known to me, he took on the role of my mentor when Mr. Gregg passed away.

Leesa has her gun pointed at Tobias's head, proving my message about our Honey Pot being rogue wasn't received by Tobias. They must have infiltrated our communication servers as well as the mainframe because there's no way Tobias would have gotten within touching distance of Leesa if he'd known she was rogue.

He thought he was saving her, where in reality, he walked straight to his death.

This is one of the reasons Tobias's team is usually filled with male agents. He can't look at any female in distress without seeing his daughter. Normally, that type of conflict of interest would be discouraged by the hierarchies in the golden tower. In Tobias's case, it works in his favor. His impressive stats are solely because he can't separate his home life from his work life.

Even with no one in his team knowing why he's so protective of his daughter, we're very aware she comes before anything. We've never met her. I haven't even seen a photograph of her. That's how guarded Tobias is when it comes to Isabelle.

I stop scoping the area when Leesa sings, "Come out, come out, wherever you are."

My teeth grit when she fires at the shard of glass I was using to survey the area a few minutes later, annoyed by my lack of response. I'm not surprised she spotted my snoop, she was trained by the best. I'm just frustrated she's only using part of the skills Tobias taught her. His training goes beyond weaponry, tactical response, and combat drills. He coaches you to be a better person, and prepares you for the cruelness that generally comes with that. He taught me it's okay to forgive as long as I don't forget, and how dying with morals will forever outrank dying without them.

With that in mind, I press my trigger until it's halfway cocked, then chance a glance around the corner of the hidey-hole where I am staked out. I'm barely half an inch out when Leesa fires one shot at my head. She missed on purpose, but that isn't the point. The fact she thinks she can scare me irritates me more than the knife wound I spotted in Tobias's neck during my quick peek. The amount of blood pooling between his fingers reveals he was most likely stabbed in the carotid artery. If that's the case, he has one to three minutes before he bleeds out, and that's assuming he's only just been stabbed.

"Ahh… so there's a little bit of bad hiding in that boyish persona of yours." Leesa snickers with a laugh when I lodge three feet of air between the closest solid barrier and me.

I'm a sitting duck.

Well, so she thinks.

"Drop it."

I shake my head. "That might work in the movies, Leesa, but this is real life. The only way you're leaving this compound is by conceding or death."

She smiles before gesturing for the men I see hiding in the shadows to move forward. I'm not surprised to discover one of them is Paavo. His weapon of choice is more fitting than the men flanking him. He's holding a *lupara*, otherwise known as a sawn-off shotgun for English-speaking folks.

"Just shoot him and be done with it. I'm bored," Paavo whines like a child.

When Leesa hesitates for the quickest second, I use her delay to my advantage. Even the strongest couple crumbles when infidelity is placed on the line. My once-blossoming relationship with Melody is living proof of this. We haven't spoken in years.

Paavo balks exactly as planned when I murmur, "She can't. The memories we share are too strong for her to forget."

Like a child fighting for his favorite toy, Paavo falls into the trap I laid out for him. "What memories? What is he talking about?"

I steal Leesa's chance to reply by asking, "Does he know about the little freckle high on your thigh?" I have no clue about any of Leesa's freckles, but even someone with flawless skin has some sort of imperfection. However, men like Paavo don't seek them out like I do, so he is as blindsided by my comment as Leesa. "It sits just below the tattoo you got two weeks after your mother died of cancer."

This part of my comment is factual. Tobias ranks applicants on their academic accomplishments and word of their peers. I look at their pasts. Almost every single man and woman in the Bureau are there for a reason other than the wish to protect their country. They're either running, have run, or will run at some stage in their lives. Leesa fills more than one box. She's running from both her past and her present, and she'll be running in her future too. I guarantee it.

"Made you look like the ideal daughter, didn't it? But only you and I know the real reason you got that tattoo." When I peer down to her right thigh, Leesa's breaths become shallow and weak. "It wasn't in memory of your mother, it was a reminder of how you swore you'd never end up like her. That you'd be a moral and upstanding member of society. That you wouldn't be this." I throw a head nod to Paavo during my last statement. "You're a fraud, Leesa. You are *exactly* like your mother." A solemn tear rolls down her cheeks when I add, "A whore for sale no matter how low the bid."

With Leesa's eyes on me, wide and terrified, and Grayson in position, I make my move. Paavo is fired on first. I take him down with a direct hit to the heart while Grayson pops a bullet between the eyes of the two men flanking him. There's another six to be contained, but my focus must remain on one. Leesa.

Her finger hasn't moved for the trigger of the gun she's holding to Tobias's head, but that doesn't mean she's stable. The instant she realizes everything I just said to her is true, she'll go from calm to deranged in under a second.

An appreciation for perfect hearing pummels into me when Leesa's howling squeal overtakes the hiss of my bullet rotating through the air. This time next week, she'll be wishing I had aimed for her head. Instead, I ignore the pleas pumping out of her watering eyes and take a second shot at her right shoulder. It has her gun falling away from Tobias's temple before her finger gets anywhere near the trigger and has her spare hand shooting up to apply pressure to her wound.

She either applies pressure or bleeds out like Tobias is in the process of doing.

"We need a medic!" As bullets halo my head, I carefully lie Tobias onto the shell-case riddled floor. "Just hold on, all right? Help is on its way." After tearing a large swatch of material from my undershirt, I bunch it up then press it to Tobias's wound. The way it spurts at me when I switch his hands with mine reveals a vital artery has been severed. He's seconds from death. "We need a medic, now! He's not going to hold out for much longer."

"B-b J-j..." Excluding my mother, Tobias is the only one who has called me BJ the past six years. "I-I-I..."

I watch him through both the eyes of an agent and a mentee when he slithers his bloodstained hand to a little pocket in the front of his bulletproof vest. After pulling out a tiny slip of paper, he attempts to hand it to me. I can't take it. If I do, he'll bleed out even quicker than he is.

"Izzy. Izzy," he stutters out, tapping on the sheet of paper.

"Your daughter?" My daftness can be easily excused. He's not a fan of nicknames, so he's only ever called her Isabelle.

When confirmation flares through his eyes, I say, "It's okay. She'll be okay. I'll look after her." I peer over my shoulder to the members of Tobias's team not gunned down in a motherfucking shitstorm. There are more dead agents than militants. "Where's the medic!"

I return my focus to Tobias when he covers my warm hands with his dead-cold ones. "G-g-give her this." My brows furrow when he adds, "Make s-s-sure she knows."

When he shoves the slither of paper at me again, I snatch it out of his hand, dump it down the front of my bulletproof vest before screaming for the medic. Tobias convulsed through his last two pleas, and the cooling of his skin is all too familiar. It's as cold and as white as Joey's was when I attempted to resuscitate him.

The memories it bombards me with are sick and twisted. They have me responding in the way a deranged man would. Instead of pressing my hands down on a wound no longer pulsating since Tobias's chest is still and lifeless, I wrap them around my Sig Sauer P226, storm to Leesa cowering in the corner of the room, grip her chin, then ram the barrel of my gun between her teeth.

She doesn't recoil or flinch. She begs for me to kill her, to free her from the hell she's about to emerge in, to let her join Paavo on the other side.

I almost answer her pleas.

The only reason I don't is because Associate Deputy Director Agent Rogers tells me to stand down. He walks through the carnage being highlighted by the spotlights of helicopters hovering above, his shoulders high, his brows pinched.

From the stories Grayson shared, his father hasn't been on the field in years, so his arrival on the scene tonight announces that an ambush by a Sicilian criminal entity will seem like a walk in the park after the department heads are finished with Tobias's team. Heads are about to roll, so I may as well go down in a blaze of glory.

The guns of my comrades swing my way when I discharge three bullets into the brick wall Leesa's head is resting on. Her cheek will hold the scold of my bullet casings for years to come, but it will be nothing compared to the wound she inflicted on Tobias's daughter's heart.

BRANDON

My eyes lift from the inch by three-inch-long piece of paper in front of me to Grayson when he slumps into the chair next to me. He was the last of our team to be debriefed. The strain shows on his face. His father made him go last for a reason, and it's the sole reason I stayed here waiting for him. I know what it's like to be raised by an anal-retentive man who thinks the sun shines out of his ass, so the least I can do is lend Grayson an ear if he needs to vent.

"How'd you do?"

Grayson scrubs a hand over his recently clipped hair. "Four weeks. You?"

"Six months," I grind out through clenched teeth.

Grayson chokes on his spit. "You got a six-month suspension?" When I jerk up my chin, he coughs out, "How? I've been here all day. Other than tearing our team apart, the highest suspension was two weeks. So, why the fuck is yours twelve times that?"

I commence my reply with a shrug. "Supposedly loud noises, such as a gun firing close to someone's ear, does more than scare them."

Grayson is smarter than he looks. He reads my riddle in a way no one ever has—*no one since Melody.* "Could have been worse. I would have inched back the trigger when the gun was still in her mouth. She deserved to die after what she did."

In sync, our eyes stray to the room at the end of the hall. No one will admit it, but we know Tobias's body is in there being prepared for transport to his hometown of Tiburon.

I stare at the door for several sobering minutes before switching my focus back to Grayson. "Has anyone told his daughter?"

He shrugs. "I don't know. I was told I wasn't privy to that information." I didn't know you could hear a jaw tick until now. "Want to get out of here? Grab a beer or something? If I don't blow off some steam, I'm going to shoot someone… again."

I contemplate Grayson's offer for all of three seconds before shaking my head. As much as I don't want him shooting up the place, I failed to save Tobias, so the least I can do is make sure he makes it home. I did the same thing with Joey. I drove with him in the back of the ambulance from the ranch to the coroner's office in the city. If Tobias was being driven to his final resting place like Joey, today's trip would have been a lot longer than the two-hour one Joey and I took six years ago, but since he's being flown home, it will be around the same amount of time.

When Grayson stands to his feet, I copy him. "Reach out when you're back? Or better yet, come find me. They may have dismantled our team, but we'll always have each other's back." When I lift my chin, he slaps my shoulder twice before pulling me in for a man-hug. "And call your girl. This shit has gone on long enough."

Stealing my chance to reply, it's way too late to mend that bridge, he tousles my hair before spinning on his heels and stalking down the corridor. My lips curl into an ill-timed grin when his exit occurs with his middle fingers being projected at the office his father, and several executive members of the Bureau remain.

I stop watching his dramatic exit when my name is called. When I crank my neck, the agent in charge of Tobias's transportation asks if I'm ready to leave. Nodding, I slip the piece of paper Tobias handed me into the pocket of my trousers before following the agent's solemn walk.

As suspected, Tobias's body is in the room Grayson and I were staring at. He's covered by the same plain white sheet the first responders covered Joey with, but one of his arms isn't lifelessly flopped over the edge of the gurney. Thank God. I don't think I could have handled seeing that image for the third time in my life. The first was Mr. Gregg's.

"Is he going straight to a funeral home?"

The unnamed agent shakes his head. "A coroner from San Francisco will meet the transport team at Tiburon. Although he was killed on duty, we need the exact cause of death cited on his death certificate."

"His carotid artery was severed." Shock resonates in my tone. I'm not a medic, but the cause of Tobias's death is as obvious as the sun hanging in the sky.

The agent pulls an agreeing face. "I'm aware of that, but if we want Agent Fedora to spend the remainder of her life in jail, we need to ensure the defense can't come back with anything."

"What could they possibly come back with?" I'm shouting, and it's unacceptable, but I'm not as good at reeling in my anger as I was once. It takes practice, and I've had no one to practice on for a very long time.

My attitude takes a step back when the agent replies, "They could say his death was a result of a heart attack, not the stab wound to his throat. That he bled out quicker because of the blood-thinning medication he was on. Or they could even go as far as saying he died because the tumors in his lungs grew unmanageable, and his death just happened to correlate with the events of last night."

"He had lung cancer?" I sound shocked. Justly so. Despite being double the age of every man in his team, Tobias was the fittest. "Did his daughter know?"

The agent hangs a clipboard onto the end of Tobias's gurney

before moving to wash his hands in a stainless steel sink on our right. "His daughter?"

"Izzy…" I pause before correcting, "Isabelle."

He yanks two towelettes out of the dispenser next to the sink, dries his hands, then dumps the napkins into the bin. "There's no mention of a daughter in any of his files. Tobias was never married." He checks the clipboard again to ensure he's not missing anything before disclosing, "He moved his father into his property not long after he joined the Bureau. He passed away the beginning of last year."

"Then who's cited as his next of kin?"

He flips over two pages on the clipboard before lifting his eyes to me. "A detective in Ravenshoe. Regina W—"

"Wamba?" I interrupt. That was the only name other than Isabelle that Tobias mentioned on repeat. "He must not have updated his information because he has a daughter…" I stop when I realize I could be spilling secrets that aren't mine to share. If Tobias kept Isabelle's identity on the down-low, he did it for a reason, much like Mr. Gregg kept Melody's hidden. "Unless I was mistaken. Perhaps she was his girlfriend?" I pull on the collar of my shirt, acting as if I just dumped myself in a sticky situation. "Awkward."

"Indeed," the agent agrees, laughing.

When he commences pushing the gurney toward the exit at the back of the holding room, a Ziplock bag full of Tobias's personal belongings slides down the sheet. They're items that were found on Tobias and in the drawer he kept locked at headquarters. The information inside could be invaluable to someone seeking his true identity.

"Do you want me to hold them for you?" I offer, my voice friendly.

Once again, my smaller build and boyish features work in my favor. "That will be great. Thank you."

FOR THE TWO-HOUR flight from New Mexico to a small airstrip in Tiburon, I search for clues about Tobias's daughter in his belongings. Not a single shred of evidence about his private life is found. Not one. There are no pictures. No birthdates registered in his cell phone. Nothing. All I have is the sequence of numbers he handed me.

I've worked the numbers around multiple times to see if they're an anagram for a date of birth, an address, or case file number. Nothing has popped up. I'm truly stuck as to why Tobias used the last of his strength to hand me this sheet of paper, and I lose the chance to deliberate further when the cargo-like plane lands in Tiburon.

After slipping Tobias's piece of paper into the pocket of my trousers, I return his belongings to the foot of his gurney. The solemnness of his death hits me full force when I follow his gurney out of the back of the plane. There's no twelve-gun salute, no line of agents honoring his years of service. There's no one—not even his daughter.

My voice cracks when I ask the agent wheeling him out to stop. "Can you give us a minute?"

He looks a little surprised by my request, but he grants it, nonetheless.

Once it is just Tobias and me on a tarmac as empty as my life has been the past six years, I find his hand through the sheet, press my lips near his ear, then whisper, "I'll make sure Isabelle gets your message. I won't let you down." I calm the rattle of my vocal cords before continuing, "It was an honor working with you, Tobias."

After a final squeeze of his hand, I raise my right one to my temple to salute a man whose death should be more honorable than it is. Once again, this country has lost a true hero, and once again, they're none the wiser to their massive loss.

When my hand falls back to my side, the agent standing under the hangar returns to wheel Tobias into a waiting hearse. When the wheels of the gurney get stuck in the ramp, he gives it an extra push, sending Tobias's belongings toppling to the ground. Since I didn't zip it back up, the contents inside disperse in all directions.

"I'll get it," I assure the agent when he curses his supposed stupidity.

Because there aren't many items to gather, I have them collected rather quickly. It's only the impressive bounce of a first-edition copy of *War and Peace* by Leo Tolstoy I'm required to scamper for. It's lodged under the seat my backside kept warm the past two hours.

When I scoot across the checker-plate material of the plane's flooring, my heart rate increases. Tobias's book is open, and the sunlight coming in from outside reveals something I didn't notice earlier. There's a circular indent around one of the letters in the book. It appears to be written in Russian, but the symbol in the word resembles an 'H.' There are no other pen markings to make the gouge noticeable, just the solemn pressure of a pen nib, proving someone circled that exact letter.

With my back facing the agent, I fan through the remaining pages of Tobias's book. My already sky-high heart rate jumps up another notch when I discover several more indents scattered throughout the book. Just like the first one I noticed, the letter circled represents a letter in the English alphabet.

Since the agent's attention is fixated on guiding the wheels of Tobias's gurney down the ramp without additional incidents, he fails to notice me slipping Tobias's book into the breast pocket of my jacket.

His eyes only raise to mine when I hand him the Ziplock bag that's noticeably emptier than it was a few seconds ago. "Everything good?"

"Yep, everything is fine," I lie.

BRANDON

wenty minutes later, I've deciphered a majority of Tobias's hidden message. It appears to be an address in Tiburon. It's not the one cited on his FBI credentials. Although I'm confident I've decrypted his code correctly, a six-digit cryptology remains on the bottom of the long sequence of numbers. It's not a zip code or telephone number, and it doesn't appear to correspond with the code he hid in his book. It can't be a date of birth because the letters don't correspond with any months or dates when decoded.

I could spend an additional twenty minutes combing for clues, but with my inquisitiveness higher than my wish to spend more time at a morgue, I slip Tobias's book into my pocket, farewell the agent I traveled with the past three hours, then exit the coroner's office via the main entrance.

It takes a little longer to hail a taxi than I'm used to. This side of the country isn't as reliant on cabs as those on the east side. As my taxi weaves through the hilly landscape, I recall the last time I traveled these roads. I wasn't alone, and my company was an undoubtably attractive female.

When you put two moody, single, heartbroken people in a hotel room for the night, what outcome would you foresee? If it were for me to do my job without my moral compass being led astray, you still have a lot to learn about me.

I didn't go down the same destructive path Madden and Phoenix did after Joey's death, but I wasn't an upstanding member of society either. Honestly, if I didn't have Tobias and Grayson constantly riding my ass, I'd most likely be either living in the gutter or following in my father's footsteps.

Both outcomes are as bad as the other.

My 'altercation' with Olivia wasn't a hiccup I needed in my life, but at the end of the day, it was something that needed to happen. It got my head back into the game, and gave me the determination to ensure nothing like that ever happened again. Do I hate her for being the motive behind Melody and I not speaking for the past three years? In a way, somewhat. But in all honesty, I'm more pissed off at Melody than Olivia.

We separated because she cheated on me. Yet, I still reached out to her within a month of her leaving me to offer her my friendship, but the instant it appeared as if I was moving on, she cut me off cold turkey. The dozen or so text messages we exchanged each year before I sought her help didn't compare to how close we once were, but still, I thought she'd give me the chance to prove I didn't do what I was accused of.

She didn't.

She didn't give me the time of day.

Her silence is affecting me more than her. The last I heard she was dating some rich schmuck she met while interning at the DA's office in Los Angeles. They moved back to my side of the states when Melody commenced her final year of law at Browns. Part of her scholarship was to intern under a division my father was in charge of. I still can't believe that out of all the people in the world, she ended up working for the man who did everything in his power to keep her out of her university of choice.

To this day, I haven't unearthed the cause of my father's motive. Phoenix swears it's because he didn't want people to know his son was dating a 'disabled' person, but I believe it was more than that. My dad is a shallow, heartless man, but he keeps that side of himself hidden when he's running for office. Furthermore, Melody would have helped his campaign. Diversity is everything in politics.

I stop reminiscing about jaded memories when my cab comes to a stop at the front of a modest weather-clapped property perched over the Tiburon esplanade. It gives off the vibe of a family home, but it's a little unkempt like no one has a spare minute to run a lawn mower over the ankle-high grass or to trim the bushes hedging the fence line.

After digging a bundle of bills out of my pocket, I hand them to the driver of my cab. "Come back in around twenty minutes."

"For this amount of coin, I can wait." His eyes gleam as he stares down at the four twenty-dollar bills wrapped around a Benjamin Franklin. I'm on a modest third-year agent salary, but old family money reached my bank account not long after my twenty-first birthday. I rarely touch it, but for circumstances like this, I don't mind dipping into funds I hope never to need.

"I'd rather you circle the block and come back in twenty minutes." I don't know about you, but a taxi idling at the front of a property for twenty minutes would be highly suspicious, especially with how high gas prices are. "Actually, make it fifteen. I don't think this will take long."

"All right." After shoving the notes into the top pocket of his lint-riddled vest, the taxi driver pulls away from the curb.

While running my hand down the lapels of my suit to make sure none of his lint transferred to me, I commence walking down the cracked footpath. I'm halfway down when the front door of the residence creaks open. I don't know why, but I step behind a thick bush in desperate need of a trim, hiding from the woman I'd guess to be around twenty-two perhaps twenty-three bounding out of the door. If I were a person who still trusted my gut, I'd say because it isn't time for us to meet just yet.

"Wait! Please." She chases down the taxi I ordered away, her jog hindered by the mountain load of textbooks she's holding close to her chest.

When the driver seeks my gaze in the rearview mirror, I signal for him to stop. The unknown beauty with chestnut hair and a petite body smiles a blistering grin when the taxi's brakes squeal through the crisp morning air, doubling her attractiveness.

"Thank you so much. My uncle would have shot me if I missed another class."

She bundles her books into the back of the cab before slipping in behind them. She's halfway in when her head suddenly pops back out. My first thought is that she's spotted me hiding behind a bush at the front of her home, but the generous tilt of her jaw soon exposes my error. She's noticed the military cargo plane in the air—the same plane the Bureau chartered to deliver Tobias to his final resting place.

She watches it for several long seconds, her chocolate-brown eyes twinkling in the low hanging sun, her brows pinched. Only once it disappears behind a thick cloud does she fully enter the idling cab.

If she hadn't mentioned an uncle, I would have happily declared she is Tobias's daughter. Now I feel far from the scent. Excluding Isabelle, Tobias doesn't have any known living family members. His father passed away at the end of last year, his brother died decades ago, and his mother was never cited in any records.

Rumors circulated that Tobias's dedication to eradicate sex trafficking rings was because of his mother, but since those rumors were mostly based on speculation rather than facts, I brushed off the agent's comments.

Lies always travel further than the truth.

I learned that the hard way many times the past six years.

Once the taxi disappears into a gulley, I move out from the bush and make my way to the front door of the residence disclosed in Tobias's anagram. Even aware it most likely will go unanswered, I press in the doorbell. When its old-style buzz goes unheard, I jimmy the lock, or should I say, 'I *attempt* to jimmy the lock.' Tobias's security is tight, meaning I'll need more than a credit card and a bobby pin to gain access.

While observing the area for nosey neighbors, I slip down the side of the paint-peeled property. I whistle like I'm calling the family pet to get a treat to ensure no attack dogs are waiting in wake before climbing over the six-foot steel fence.

"Fuck it," I grumble to no one when my trousers snag a bent piece of wire. My descent saves my dick from being sliced, but my thigh isn't as lucky. It's now harnessing a nasty three-inch-long gash.

"Hello… is anyone home?"

It takes me a few seconds to remember why the hunt for my gun comes up empty. I had to hand it in at the commencement of my suspension. It's probably being logged into evidence as we speak, then Leesa will have more than bad-mentoring to argue when she pleads her case.

"My name is Brandon James. I'm an agent with the Federal Bureau of Investigation."

When my introduction falls on deaf ears, I test the back door to check if it's locked. It is, but the lace curtain on the window is thin enough I can see through to the kitchen. It's nothing out of the ordinary, the standard kitchen you find in many homes. Even the photographs on the fridge are the same. They show Tobias a good three decades or so ago with his arm wrapped around the shoulders of a much smaller and somewhat younger African American woman.

There are several pictures of them, but I'm more interested in the ones scattered between them. It's a timeline of events that leave no doubt that Tobias had a daughter. Even from a distance, I'm confident in declaring she was the woman who left here only minutes ago.

Isabelle looks around three or four in the first photograph up until a recent one that appears to be her first day of college. She's easily identifiable via her chocolate-brown eyes and button-shaped nose.

When I spot her in an image with a woman I swear I've seen before, I dig my cell phone out of my pocket. Because the fridge is on the far wall, and the picture is at the bottom of the stack, I can't get a good view of the stranger's face, but hopefully, the zoom on my phone will fix that.

After flattening the camera lens on the back of my phone against the glass, I wait for the familiar click to sound through my ears before dragging it back down. The quality is horrendous when I zoom in, but no amount of pixilation can detract from my belief that the woman photographed with Isabelle is Katarina Rouse, once lover of Henry Gottle, *the* mob boss of New York.

What the fuck?

Is this how Tobias and Henry met?

Is Katarina Isabelle's mother?

She has the same dark, wavy hair and petite features, but I'm still cautious. There are reports that Henry orders wakeup calls for any men stupid enough to date his ex, so there's no way he would have left Tobias breathing if he'd slept with Katarina. But what other reason would there be for Isabelle and Katarina to be photographed together? She's clearly young, and there are no additional pictures of them, but still, this is a development I never saw coming.

With my curiosity at a pinnacle, I check all access points of the house to gain unlawful entry. When my inspection of the multiple windows and doors fail to grant me entrance, I move toward a garage-type shed in the back corner of the property. It's daringly sitting on the edge of a cliff, appearing more hazardous than safe.

My lips twist when the sliding door opens with only the quickest pop of the mechanism. It has a silent alarm rigged into the tracks, but the wire cutters in my multi-combination pocketknife soon stop the speakers above my head alerting the neighborhood to an intruder.

The space inside is more appealing than its outside shell. It appears to be an office. A desk faces the Tiburon vista I mentioned earlier, but most of the space is gobbled up by shelves and shelves of files. They're four shelves deep and at least ten shelves long. The number of files here is nothing compared to the Bureau's field office in San Francisco, but it's impressive for a private file storage unit.

A smile tugs on my lips when I take in the paperwork scattered across the desk. For the most part, the drawings at the bottom of the stack appear to have been done by a child, and they're all signed Izzy, but the ones on top show an advancement in technique that comes with age. There are also a number of college papers, theses, and textbooks.

The evidence proves Isabelle was raised here, but why did Tobias hide her location?

"Why, Tobias? Why go to so much effort to hide your daughter's identity?"

While seeking answers to the many questions filtering through my head, I pace down the first line of shelves. When I drag my finger along the files, dust kicks up. It isn't the only thing spiking, though. So is my heart rate. The sequence of text written across the files is in the same configuration as the leftover code on the anagram Tobias gave me. A letter and two numbers followed by another letter and another two numbers.

After removing the sheet of paper from between the pages of Tobias's book, I head in the direction of the first letter on the code. I find the I's rather quickly, and even faster than that, I'm fanning through the files until I find the '09' section. My heart rate slows when I locate a file with the exact sequence of code I'm chasing. It's not overly thick, but the information inside is *nothing* like I was anticipating.

Isabelle isn't Tobias's daughter.

She was purchased on the black market when she was six.

I crash into the shelving when I take a step back, shocked about the next tidbit of information I unearth.

Isabelle isn't like the many other children stolen to be sold.

She has the blood of mafia royalty.

She's a Popov.

Vladimir Popov, Col Petretti, and Henry Gottle, Sr. are names commonly exploited during training at the academy. Excluding terrorist hub leaders and world diplomats we're not allowed to mention, the men stated above are three of the top ten most wanted by the Bureau. They all have mafia connections, they have all been in the game for decades, and they have over twelve billion dollars in assets funding their organizations.

The Popovs are only second to Gottle—not that Vladimir would ever agree with that. They're rivals. So much so, at one stage, rumors are Vladimir and Col joined forces with the hope of taking Henry down. Clearly, they failed, but it's said their union is the reason Henry branched out years ago.

Could that branch have extended to the CIA?

With my discovery giving me more questions than answers, I continue flicking through Isabelle's file. I discover the reason Tobias wanted me to know this information when I find an envelope at the very back of the file. It's addressed 'To the agent who watched me die.'

A set of instructions are printed on the back. They're brisk and to the point.

1. *Return the file to its rightful position.*
2. *Leave the envelope inside in a place Isabelle will find it.*
3. *Leave.*

That's it. Nothing more, nothing less.

Tobias was never known for a fondness of words.

My throat grows scratchy when I carefully pry open the envelope the instructions are printed on. The envelope inside is an inch shorter and half an inch narrower than the one casing it. It's pink in color and appears as if it was written quite a few years ago. The familiar handwritten font on the front is faded, and the edges are frayed. Even the greeting is as direct and forward as Tobias had always been.

To Isabelle

There are no other markings on the envelope, and it's sealed shut. A DNA test isn't needed to know Tobias sealed it, though. A hint of the aftershave he wore every day I knew him is lingering on the paper. It's embedded in almost every inch of this office, revealing he spent more time here when he was home than the main house, meaning I know the best place to leave Isabelle's envelope.

I've only just propped the envelope onto the desk scattered with drawings and old case files when the crunch of gravel under tires sounds through my ears. When I peer out the sliding door I jimmied open only twenty minutes ago, a curse word spills from my lips. Isabelle has slid out of the back of the cab. She's racing my way.

"I'll be just a minute, I promise."

When Isabelle yanks open the sliding door I thankfully remembered to close, I sink into the far corner of the dusty space. Her head slants to the side when her attempt to punch the security code into the box on the side wall is met with a faulty keypad. It's flashing an alert that the system has been disabled.

"Stupid piece of shit," Isabelle mumbles under her breath as her eyes stray to a section of the roof that looks only weeks away from succumbing to the weather damage coating it.

When she paces toward the desk where I placed her envelope, I disappear into the shadows of the shelving. She spots the envelope in an instant, and if the way her eyes water the longer they swing around the room is anything to go by, I'm confident she knows its significance.

I watch her in silence when she lifts the envelope off the table and presses it to her lips. Tears stream down her face when the scent I noted only seconds ago filters into her nose, but she keeps relatively calm… until her finger slides under the seal.

The longer she reads Tobias's handwritten letter, the more her face scrunches up.

A few seconds later, a gut-wrenching sob breaks through the hand she clamped over her mouth. When the absolute grief surging through her becomes too much to bear, Tobias's letter floats away from her body as she takes a stumbling step backward.

After crashing into the glass sliding door she rocketed through only thirty seconds ago, she slides down it until her backside meets the floor, and her cheek rests on her knee. She appears as if she wants to scream. I can see the hurt in her eyes, but she bites on her palm instead, keeping her grief hidden from the world like she's not allowed to show her pain.

The terror on Isabelle's face and the hollow nothingness in her eyes are almost identical to the expression Melody wore when I found her under the bed after her parents' accident. She just lost her entire world, and there's nothing I can do or say to prove any different.

I want to comfort her, the urge is somewhat overwhelming, but before I can, the taxi driver beeps, reminding Isabelle that even though her life may be falling apart, it's still business as usual for everyone else.

That's the most vexing part about grief. How quickly everyone else moves on. The same thing happened with Joey. His friends returned to their studies the week of his death, Madden was deployed a week after that, and our father didn't even last thirty-six hours before he went back to work. It was only Mom, Phoenix, and me who were left suffering. Phoenix turned to drugs and alcohol, I turned to vengeance, and our mother spent the next six months in bed.

Melody wouldn't have fared much better after her parents'

deaths if she weren't required to attend school for her finals. Since giving up was never an option for her, she couldn't stay in bed for months on end. In a way, it helped her move on from her grief, but I've often wondered if my push for her to live a normal, grief-free existence was the reason she cheated on me. People become complacent when they get bored. Perhaps that was what happened to Melody and me?

My thoughts shift back to the present when the cab driver's second beep leaps Isabelle into action. She drags the sleeve of her shirt over her wrist before using it to clear away the contents spilling from her nose. Once her face is clear of tears, she stands to her feet, sucks in three big breaths to dislodge the sob in her throat, then shouts at the taxi driver that she won't be a minute.

When she moves to the desk to grab a forensic science biology book from a stack of four, her steps are extra shaky. I think I'm in the clear when she heads for the sliding door, but just before she exits, she remembers about Tobias's letter.

I scamper back when her bob to scoop it up from the ground has her spotting my shoes under the shelving. I curse my stupidity a million times in my head before switching my profanities for excuses as to why she shouldn't call the police on me.

All my plans fly out the window when she murmurs the quickest, "Thank you for telling me."

She doesn't wait for me to acknowledge her praise or to tell her I'm sorry for her loss. She just spins on her heels and hot-foots it to the taxi idling halfway down her driveway.

I wait for the cab's engine to replicate the annoying buzz of a mosquito before moving out of my not-so-inconspicuous hidey-hole. The longer the playdown of Isabelle's grief rolls through my head, the more the image of her face is replaced with Melody's. They have a lot of similarities. Not in appearance—excluding their brown eyes, they're quite the opposite, actually—but they both did lose influential men in their lives without anyone knowing exactly how far their grief extends. There's just one notable difference. My family rallied around Melody. We propped her up when she had no one.

Isabelle doesn't have that same crutch.

Or should I say, didn't have?

She does now.

Tobias said I was to deliver his letter then walk away. He didn't specifically state how long it had to be between the stages of his instructions.

BRANDON

"You lucked out, man. From what I heard, Theresa is a witch." Zayne, a recently recruited agent at the Bureau, backhands my chest like he's talking to a fellow rookie. This is one of many reasons I hate having a boyish face. "Are you packing heat?" When I raise my brow, wondering what the hell he's on about, he snickers. "From what I heard in the academy, if you can keep up with Theresa in the bedroom, she'll keep you out of the trenches."

"I'm not sleeping with my superior officer." I know how bad the consequences are when you slip between the sheets with an informant, so I'm as sure as fuck not going down that path again. If they're in any way associated with the Bureau, my dick is staying in my pants. I don't care how attractive they are. "And I suggest you stop listening to rumors if you want to last longer than six months in the Bureau. As far as rookies are concerned, your chances of fucking anything went out the door the day you arrived at the academy."

Zayne keeps talking, but I've lost interest in our conversation. It isn't that he bores me, I just have a more appealing development occurring than to care what a wannabe hero has to say. Isabelle's old Buick just pulled into the lot of the Bureau's training field office in San Francisco. She looks good compared to the last time I saw her. The weight she lost in the four days from finding Tobias's envelope to his funeral has been put back on, and the hair she used as a shelter during proceedings is pulled up and away from her face.

Her attendance at Tobias's funeral went unnoticed by the assembly of FBI agents and bureaucratic hierarchies because she hid at the back like Melody did at Joey's funeral.

She had a good reason to hide.

I'm still struggling to work out Melody's objective.

A smile tugs at my lips when I notice the paperwork Isabelle is clutching. It's one of the half a dozen applications I slid through her mail slot the past six months. She finished her studies not long after Tobias's death, but she kind of drifted between nothingness ever since. It was clear she needed something to occupy her time other than her grief.

Her strength I've admired from afar the past six months had me confident she'd ignore my gentle push if she weren't ready. The fact she's here proves she is eager to move onto the next stage of her grief—the onward and upward stage—the one full of hope that the world couldn't be so cruel to the same person twice.

The one stage of grief I no longer believe in.

After personally delivering her application to the agent manning the reception desk as Tobias would have taught her, Isabelle pivots back around to face the exit. Our eyes nearly collide, but a picture on the side wall gains her attention before they lock and hold. It's a photograph of Tobias on the wall honoring fallen agents.

Just like the morning she found out about Tobias's death, pain fills her eyes, but there's also pride shining through. Tobias was her family, I've been her shelter for the past six months, and now the Bureau will be her savior, once I push her application through the right channels.

BRANDON

EIGHT MONTHS LATER…

"I'm not doing it, Grayson. The last time I stuck my neck out for you, your brother's girl walked out of the bathroom wrapped in a towel."

Grayson scoffs. "Exactly! She was in a towel. She wasn't naked."

I continue speaking as if he never did. "Then you used the files I found on her computer, which could have gotten your brother in a heap of shit. You know he's not speaking to his girl anymore, right? Regan moved back to some bumfuckville town months ago, and they haven't been in contact since."

"They've had contact," Grayson denies, his tone lowering. "It didn't go down well."

"Exactly!" I agree. "I'm not doing that again. If you want info from Alex, ask him for it."

Alex is Grayson's younger brother. He's also my supervisor. He is a deadly marksman like Grayson but with the arrogance of their father, which grew worse after he granted me access to his girlfriend's laptop. I forgot that any computer accessed by the FBI's mainframe automatically uploads the hard drive to the Bureau's

242

servers. By the time I had noticed my error, it was too late, they had everything.

"It's a bank record, BJ. I'm not asking you to take one up the ass for the team." Grayson's voice switches from stern to playful in under two seconds. "If I were, we would have gotten Theresa off everyone's back earlier than we did."

I shake my head as my stomach rolls. I should have taken Zayne's advice eight months ago. Theresa, my previous supervisor, was a nasty piece of work. She belittled agents who had years more experience than her and treated everyone as if they were disposable —even more so when they turned down her offer for a nightcap after a long working week.

I discovered that the hard way my first week under her command.

She was more than friendly when I reported for duty at precisely nine in the morning the first Monday of my shift. She showed me the ropes, pointed out the best places to grab a bite to eat between shifts, and even went as far as picking me up a coffee on her way to work Thursday morning.

It all went to shit when I turned down her offer for a 'friendly' drink after my Friday night shift. My polite rejection was quickly chased by a change in my roster. Instead of having the weekend off as predicted, I was required to conduct surveillance on a supposedly high-ranked target.

I was twelve hours into a sixteen-hour shift when I bumped into Alex for the first time. He 'accidentally' spilled my tenth cup of coffee onto my keyboard with the hope he could wipe his kiss with an associate of the target our division was investigating. I led him to believe that was what occurred, although it wasn't close to the truth.

As taught by Grayson, I back up every piece of equipment I use. It was for the best. Otherwise, we wouldn't have had any footage of the perp who had entered Regan's apartment to leave her a rather nasty threat. His exit was never recorded.

I had no clue how unfit I had become during my six-month

suspension until I ran the stairwell of Regan's apartment building when I spotted the perp's exit on the security camera we were tailing after Alex had entered. Mr. Gregg would have rolled in his grave if he'd seen how red-faced and out of breath I was. It was a quick reminder that this game is as physical as it is mind-fucking. I've visited the gym once a day since.

We caught the perp who entered Regan's apartment. It wasn't who we anticipated, but his arrest was the equivalent of stomping on an anthill. It's been one motherfucking tornado after another since then. Grayson's request for me to dig a little deeper into Isaac's—my team's target—connection with Henry Gottle had us stumbling onto information no one outside of Isaac's tight-knit team knew about.

The instant the information was sucked into the Bureau's main-frame, it spread like wildfire. There was no chance in hell I could contain it. It burned all the way to the hierarchies glaring down at us. Even my father caught wind of what was happening. Add those points to the fact it was the anniversary of Joey's death, and I was beginning to confuse Madden's sadistic ways as my own childhood.

I must have done something catastrophic in my life because not only did I get rip-roaring drunk and confess my sins to Alex in a sequence of text messages and voicemails, I used Bureau contacts to track down Melody's email address so I could reach out to her after years of silence.

It wasn't a polite, hey-I've-missed-you email.

I poured my fucking heart out.

Did I get an answer?

Nope.

I know she read it. I still have the delivery receipt sitting in my inbox.

You know all is said and done when words directly from your soul can't move the woman who cheated on you into possibly forgiving you.

With my past weighing down my emotions, I divert my attention back to my phone squished against my ear. "What type of bank record are you chasing?"

I can't see Grayson, but I can picture him rubbing his hands together while grinning a slick smile. He loves that I can't say no to him.

MY MOM HAS ALWAYS SAID 'strange things happen for the most peculiar reasons.' My reply was always, 'No shit, Sherlock, because peculiar and strange mean the same thing.'

Now I'm eating my words.

This can't be true, can it? That can't possibly be Tobias's daughter walking into a sub-branch of the Bureau at Ravenshoe—surely.

I heard Isabelle had graduated from the academy a few months back, but with Alex's work schedule worse than Theresa's, I've not had the chance to check what she's up to. I got her on the straight and narrow as Tobias and Grayson did for me, then I walked away according to Tobias's request. But this, this changes everything, doesn't it? She's walking into my life, not the other way around, so Tobias's wishes no longer count, right?

Right.

Then why the fuck does it feel wrong to act like I have no clue who she is when her pretty brown eyes drift my way? I'm quick to divert my eyes like I did when keeping an eye on her from afar the months following Tobias's death, but the academy didn't just double her receptiveness. Maturity did as well.

"Hello," Isabelle greets, stopping at my desk.

She sounds the same as I remember, so I rake my eyes down her body to ensure she still looks the same.

Awareness of her surroundings isn't the only thing that has matured.

So did her body.

Jesus.

I should *not* be looking at her as I am, but before I can remind myself that anyone associated with the Bureau is off-limits, not to mention she's the equivalent of Tobias's daughter, Alex's grumpy baritone booms across the room. "I need that document now, Brandon."

Eager to move before my sweaty top lip gives away the fact we've met previously, I find the flight manifest that reveals our target, Isaac Holt—suspected mob associate, businessman, and somewhat ladies' man—flew home commercially this weekend instead of utilizing one of his many private jets. That's so unlike him, Alex is convinced it's the beginning of the end for Isaac. I'm inclined to agree with him. Isaac hasn't made a single mistake since we've been watching him. Although a trip home in a commercial plane seems innocent enough, usually there's more to unplanned actions than there are intended ones.

Alex has barely snatched the document from my hand when Isabelle joins us in the middle of the bustling office. "Hi, I'm Isabelle Brahn, your new agent." Her hand thrust directed at Alex reveals she has recognized him but not me.

I'm okay with that.

The last thing I want is a stalker charge added to the thick file the Bureau already has on me.

"Michelle," Alex roars a few seconds later, startling Isabelle. "I thought I ordered a blonde?"

When Michelle, a mid-forties techie who's obsessed with the head of our division, magically appears at Alex's side, Alex returns his slit-gaze to Isabelle. If the narrowed squint of Isabelle's eyes is anything to go by, she didn't appreciate his gawk of her body as much as she did mine.

I'm okay with that as well.

"Does she look brunette to you?"

Michelle bats her lashes, pleased Alex seems to have noticed a flaw in Isabelle. Just like our target, Alex has a fascination with blondes. The only difference is Alex was only seen with one blonde whereas Isaac has been seen with many the past eight months. "Umm, yes, she does appear to be a brunette."

Her reply irritates Alex more. "In the past two months, have you *ever* seen him with a brunette?"

I'm confused by Alex's line of interrogation, and I'm not the only one. Isabelle is as stumped as me. "What does my hair color have to do with my placement?"

Alex replicates nothing of the man I once knew when he snarls, "Isaac Holt fucks blondes. You're a brunette." He's had a hard few months, but he's taking it out on the wrong person.

Fortunately, Isabelle seems more than capable of holding her own. "Excuse me," she growls on a hiss. "I wasn't brought here to sleep with Isaac Holt, I was brought here to help with your investigation."

My chance to slap her back and say 'attagirl' is lost when Alex rebuts, "You were brought here as eye candy."

Finally recognizing Alex's game plan, I say the first thing that pops into my head. "We could bleach her hair."

I'm not a fan of degrading women, Mr. Gregg ensured that would never be a strong point of mine, but if switching Isabelle's locks from chocolate brown to blonde keeps her in Ravenshoe long enough I can work out why I was pleased to see her before I was worried, I'm open to offering up some suggestions.

"Not happening," Isabelle says with a snarl.

Tell me one man over the age of sixteen whose eyes don't lower when a woman crosses her arms. You can't think of one, can you? So don't blame me when my eyes *instinctively* lower from Isabelle folding her arms under her chest.

I'm a guy.

It's been a while.

Cut me some slack.

Recognition that Alex skipped the etiquette side of supervisor training is exposed when he mutters at Isabelle, "Once you're in a dress and a pair of stilettos, Isaac won't care you're a brunette."

"Once you have a personality transplant and a plastic groin inserted, nobody will care you're a Ken doll," Isabelle fires back, proving she's as quick-witted as she is beautiful.

My ears rouse when Alex whispers to Isabelle, "I know who your uncle was. I know his reputation, but you need to learn your place. You were only brought here as a distraction for Isaac. He never lets anyone in, and you're supposed to be our way in."

Isabelle's reply is fast, but I only catch half of it since I'm out the door faster than a rocket.

"If you're this quick between the sheets, no wonder why I haven't seen you with a woman in years." Grayson chuckles down the line, believing I'm returning his call to update him on the bank records he's chasing for his continued search to find Katie Bryne, a girl he met once many moons ago. She was abducted from a town not too far from here.

Grayson's chuckles diminish when I ask, "How does Alex know Tobias?"

"Everyone knew Tobias. He was an integral part of the FBI."

He has a point, so I extend the perimeter of my scope. "How does Alex know about Tobias's daughter, Isabelle, and that she calls him her uncle?"

"He doesn't know Tobias referred to Isabelle as his daughter, but the uncle reference is standard. Her birth certificate had Tobias's brother, Abraham, cited as her father. Remember, we improved its authenticity the day you pushed her application through the correct channels? She wouldn't have gotten in the door with the identification she was handing over."

"Fuck, I forgot about that." Tobias was skilled at keeping people hidden, but his documentation wasn't the best at the end of his career, so you can imagine how poor it was twenty years ago. "Seeing Isabelle again threw me off. My head isn't screwed on right."

"Isabelle Brahn is in Ravenshoe?" Grayson sounds as shocked as I felt when she walked into HQ.

"Yes!" He can't see me, but I nod, nonetheless. "It looks like Alex brought her in as a Honey Pot for Isaac."

"Whoa. Are you fuckin' serious?" His voice is a cross between a laugh and groan. "I heard she was a knockout from a rookie who joined my team last month, but Leesa's stunt had all sups stepping back from using fresh recruits as Honey Pots. If they don't end up dead, their entire team could be debunked like ours was, so none are willing to risk it." He stops talking for a bit, the sound of him scratching his beard the only noise resonating down the line. "For Alex to go this far, he must be desperate. Maybe hold back and see how it plays out."

"I can't hold back."

A chair squeaks like Grayson is adjusting his position. He's more a sloucher than a shoulders-rolled-back, spine-straight type of guy. "Why, Brandon? Because you've transferred your hero complex from Melody to Isabelle?"

I make a *pfft* noise. "It has nothing to do with that." It does, but I sure as fuck don't want to be called out on it. Although I wouldn't necessarily say it's a hero complex. Seeing the lost blankness in Isabelle's eyes when she was grappling with Alex reminded me what it felt like to have no one on your side. It's an experience I wouldn't wish on my worst enemy, let alone an orphan who has nothing. "We're friends, that's all."

I picture Grayson's cell phone speaker being coated with spit when he blows a raspberry. "Friends like you were with Melody? Or the *friendship* you had with Olivia? You know how this will end, punk. It's not worth it, so step back now before you get burned for the second time."

BRANDON

TWO MONTHS LATER...

This sucks to admit, and never in a trillion years did I think I'd ever say this, but Grayson was right two months ago. The burn this time around is nothing compared to what I experienced when Melody left me, nor the event I'm endeavoring to forget five years ago, but my 'friendship' with Isabelle definitely has enough sting to it to cause a blister.

It's not my fault I can't step back. For years, I was programmed to protect, honor, obey, and serve. It isn't something I can easily switch off, especially when it comes to women. If I didn't step forward to help Isabelle, Alex's plan to make her the Honey Pot of his operation will end as disastrously as the sting that claimed Tobias's life. That isn't an unfavorable chance. It's a statistic. It just won't be Alex left reeling once all is said and done. That burden will be solely placed on Isabelle's shoulders.

Isabelle has not yet fallen for Alex's ruse, but she has failed to notice how he's inconspicuously placing her on Isaac's radar. Between sending her to gather coffees from a local baker at the exact time Isaac has been observed in the area by the surveillance crew following his every move, to granting her a weekend off so she can release some of the pent-up wildness in her eyes with the hope it will initiate the natural dominance that beams out of Isaac anytime Isabelle is in his vicinity, he's all but dangling her in front of Isaac, luring him to take a moral-eradicating bite.

Alex's ploys are older than the handbook they are taught from, but regretfully, Isabelle seems blind to his deception. She doesn't realize how far some men go to snare their targets because she was raised by a man who valued respect above anything.

As was I.

That's why I'm here at a dance club in desperate need of a fresh coat of paint and better clientele, ordering the largest cocktail on the menu, praying the wooziness it will cause Isabelle's head will have her failing to notice Isaac eyeballing her from the corner of the room.

Now I understand why Alex slipped pamphlets for this nightclub into the break room at HQ earlier this week. Isaac is known for spending his Friday nights scouting new business endeavors. Alex must have caught wind that Isaac would be here tonight.

I could let Alex know I'm onto his ruse, but just like Grayson and I have kept our connection on the down-low, I'm going to keep this set of cards close to my chest as well. A good agent never lets his unease be announced prematurely because it isn't about the hand you've been dealt but what you make of it that counts.

When I replace Isabelle's bottle of water with the mammoth cocktail I just purchased, her nose screws up, but before she can voice a single worry I see in her eyes, I say, "Who knows when we might get another day off?"

I throw back a double scotch on the rocks, grimacing when it burns my throat. I'm not a fan of hard liquor, but I figured it would make my ploy more authentic if I drank along with Isabelle and Harlow, Isabelle's friend. I nursed my first drink to make it seem like I've had four or five, but Isabelle is too close to brush-off the watery contents my earlier glass had.

"I forgot how much that burns." When Isabelle giggles, I

remember that twenty-six-years is a lot further away from the grave than how I generally perceive it. "Oh, do you think you can do better?" After signaling for the bunch of college kids swarming us to follow my lead, I say, "Chug, chug, chug."

Tobias's stubbornness burns through Isabelle's impressive eyes when she succumbs to peer pressure. She downs the cocktail minus the screwed-up nose my face had when I threw back my drink, then curtsies the patrons applauding her gall. Her smile at their praise slams me with guilt. Just like me, I doubt she's ever let go of the reins like this, but instead of encouraging her to enjoy her weekend off, I'm plowing her with drinks to end it earlier than necessary.

I wouldn't if it weren't for her own good.

With my brows waggling, I continue my mission without missing a beat. "Another?"

While shaking her head, the color drains from Isabelle's cheeks. Taking that as a signal it's time for us to go, I pivot around to place our glasses onto the bar before yanking my cell phone out of my pocket to call us a taxi. I've only had two glasses, but I don't want to risk it. I don't drink enough to challenge a DUI charge if I were suspected of driving over the limit.

I swear, I barely let Isabelle out of my sight for two seconds, yet she still vanishes. I know who has her. The stool at the end of the bar is noticeably empty, so my panic is nothing like you'd expect. I'm more pissed than anything.

After paying the bartender the exorbitant drink tab Isabelle, Harlow, and I amassed in almost two hours, I scope the area, seeking where Isaac has taken Isabelle. There's radio silence from the surveillance team stationed in the corner of the club, so I know he hasn't left. He must have sought somewhere private for them to chat.

An idea on their location is discovered when a middle-aged man with over-gelled hair rounds the corner of the washrooms. He's an ideal candidate for a manager of a sleazy nightclub, and if his grumble about arrogant fuckfaces is anything to go by, I'm reasonably sure he just had a run-in with Isaac.

Isaac is almost as arrogant as my father, which is saying something. My father's snootiness rose along with his bank balances and his age. The bank accounts the Bureau is aware of gives Isaac's haughtiness some credit, but he's only twenty-seven, so why the fuck does he act as if he runs this town?

My hope to conduct some private investigating is snagged when my soundless steps down the washroom corridor to the manager's office at the end is spotted by a man I'd never forget. David Crombie is frozen halfway out of the men's restroom. He's stacked on a bit of weight since the last time I sat across from him, but I'd never forget his lazy eye, the family crest tattooed on his neck, and let's not forget how his fingertips are always colored with ash thanks to his fascination with flames.

I curse myself for not carrying a weapon tonight when Crombie rams me into the wall before he bolts for the closest exit. I wouldn't have shot him, but a bullet wound isn't needed to take down weasels like him. Just drawing a gun would have had him hitting the deck, and then I wouldn't have been forced to chase him down by foot.

As I break through a group of five partygoers Crombie burst through only seconds ago, I lift the cuff of my dress shirt to my mouth. "Agent James, code six with suspicious suspect at Lakers' exit. Tailing him on foot."

My earpiece crackles before one of the agents in the surveillance van tailing Isaac's every move responds, "Copy. Do you require assistance?"

Before I can answer him, Crombie's sprint comes to a dead stop, compliments of a plain-clothed officer coat-hanging him. How do I know he's an officer if he is wearing everyday clothes? He has the walk of a law enforcement officer, not to mention the arrogance beaming out of him.

When Crombie hits the ground with a thud, the officer rolls him onto his stomach to frisk and handcuff him. I use the gap in time to update my crew. "Agent James, stand down. Suspect has been arrested."

I wait for the man on the end of my connection to advise he heard my reply before tugging my earpiece out of my ear. The less I look on the job, the easier my conversation with the officer arresting Crombie will go. I hope.

After quietly bridging the gap between us, I ask, "What are you arresting him for?"

The dark-haired officer wearing designer jeans and a buttoned-up shirt stands Crombie to his feet before mashing his face with the brickwork outside of the club. I take a step back when he swings his government-issued pistol my way. "Stand down. This is no business of yours."

"I'm a federal agent." When he glares at me like he isn't stupid, I roll my eyes. This is another reason I hate having a baby face. "I'm just moving for my credentials," I assure him when my hunt for my wallet has his index finger creeping toward the trigger of his gun.

After flashing him my photo ID and badge like a real-life movie star, I retake the step I took back when he drew his gun on me. "Let me guess, suspected of arson?"

The dark-haired officer cocks his brow. "Old case?"

I shake my head. "No. He was before I joined the Bureau." A grin tugs on my lips when Crombie's throat works hard to swallow at my confession that I work for the FBI. I'm not surprised he didn't miss my revelation. I increased the volume of my voice to ensure he couldn't miss it. "He was given twelve years a little over six years ago." I drop my eyes to Crombie's face squished against a wall of bricks. "So how'd you get out so early?"

"Good behavior." As unbelieving of his reply as I am, the unnamed officer yanks Crombie back before ramming him forward. The crack his face makes with the brickwork curls my lips into a smile. "All right, all right," he garbles through the blood pooling in the corner of his mouth. "I pleaded out."

He's either trained to deceive, or he is telling the truth. His eyes didn't shift to seek his imagination, and he's only sweating because of my pursuit. Still, I'm shocked. He would have had to give something good to get his sentence reduced so dramatically.

"What information could you have possibly offered to have your sentence sliced in half?"

Crombie looks set to squeal like a nark but loses the chance when we're surrounded by four black Lincoln Navigators. If the words shouted by the agents piling out of the vehicles hadn't swallowed up his words, I'm sure the helicopter hovering above our heads would have taken care of the injustice.

"We'll take things from here." A female agent with raven hair and pretty eyes thrusts an arrest warrant into the unnamed officer's chest before she attempts to secure the target.

I say attempt as the plain-clothed officer isn't having any of it. "This isn't an arrest warrant. I have conclusive evidence the suspect is responsible for a warehouse fire on the outskirts of town. That means he's mine."

"Stand down, Detective Carter," the female agent grumbles on a groan over the turf war that always occurs when the Bureau is involved in local cases. "Federal agents can make arrests for *any* offense committed in their presence or when they have reasonable grounds that the person they're arresting committed or is committing a felony in violation of US laws."

"The warehouse fire was a week ago. You didn't witness anything."

The detective's attitude takes a step back when the female agent snickers. "That's not what that dumpster says."

I almost fist bump the air when my neck cranks to the side in sync with Detective Carter to take in a burning dumpster. The evidence Crombie was attempting to discard was most likely ignited by a cigarette butt, but since Detective Carter can't conclusively say that, he has no choice but to hand Crombie over to the Bureau.

"This is strike three for Crombie. Felony arson. *Felony*." The female agent repeats her last word extra slow to ensure Detective Carter doesn't miss the words she didn't speak.

With his sneer hidden by a half-hearted grin, Detective Carter hands Crombie off to the female agent. He's pissed, but he's aware even in his hometown, he has no jurisdiction when it comes to federal cases.

I wait for Detective Carter to slide into the driver's seat of his unmarked cruiser to call in his movements before shifting on my feet to face the lead agent on Crombie's case. "Where are you taking him? We have a field office set up on the—"

"Good evening, Agent James. Enjoy the remainder of your week-end," she interrupts, dismissing me as if I'm not a fellow agent.

I don't back down as quickly as Detective Carter, especially when it comes to my past. "I have an interest in this case."

She walks Crombie to the first Lincoln, places him in the back seat, shuts the door, then pivots around to face me. "I'm aware of that. That's why I said good evening."

"But—"

"Good evening, Agent James." Her tone is the same ball-crushing one she used on Detective Carter, and once again, her unspoken words are the loudest of them all. If I don't back down, she'll have Alex breathing down my neck with a click of her fingers.

"Good evening, Agent…" I leave my reply open for her to fill in the blank.

She follows along nicely. "Russell."

"Good evening, Agent Russell." *I'm sure we'll meet again soon.*

BRANDON

SIX WEEKS LATER...

I wait for Isabelle to disappear into the hallway before dialing a frequently called number and squishing my cell phone to my ear. Isabelle has been a little cold with me the past six weeks. I don't know if she's angry because I plowed her with drinks in the hope of ending her weekend early, or if she's hoping a bit of distance will stop her from revealing she went home with Isaac Holt the night we visited a dance club a little over six weeks ago.

She got lucky that night. When news of another team in Raven-shoe circulated throughout comms, the men responsible for tracking Isaac missed Isabelle slipping into the back of Isaac's BMW X7 SUV. I was certain she'd been snared by Alex's trap, so you can imagine my surprise when I discovered my assumption was wrong.

Word to the wise, if you don't want your private life witnessed by anyone with medium to well-developed hacking skills, don't buy any electronic devices. Cell phones, laptops, smart TVs, hell, I can even hack into the electronic panel in your fridge if it means I can listen in on a conversation I'm not privy to.

While Harlow tapped away on her phone, oblivious to the undercover work I was doing on her friend, I hacked into the smart

TV in Isaac's penthouse on Hyde. I couldn't see anything since it was in the blacked-out living room, but once I paired it with the microphone in Isabelle's cell phone and bounced the image off Isaac's glass coffee table to the mirrored ceiling in his bedroom, I got the gist of what was happening.

It was a lot more subdued than I had anticipated.

I may have even laughed when Isabelle's snores filtered through the pods in my ears, confirming the cause of her slumped form on Isaac's bed.

She was fast asleep.

This is hard to admit, but I failed Isabelle that night. I should have continued with my surveillance to ensure she was safe, but with Crombie in the forefront of my mind, my focus shifted to the past instead of the present.

As it is now.

"Hey, any news on Crombie yet?" I ask Grayson when he finally answers my call after several rings.

He exhales a growling breath. A telltale sign he's pissed. "They're not letting anyone near him. I've been denied over two dozen times the past six weeks."

"They're?" I know who he's talking about. I just want him to spell it out to me.

"Agent Russell. She has him on such a tight lockdown, Crombie's movement sheets aren't being logged each day."

That spikes my interest. "Can we get her on protocol? If she's doing shady shit, we could loosen her grip a little."

He makes another frustrated growl. "Already been there. I even went as far as filing a formal complaint. I got the same answer I always do. I'm not—"

"Privy to that information," we say in sync.

A hum of agreement vibrates down the line. "What about you? Got anything to share?"

I shake my head before sinking low into my chair. "Nah, she's got nothing. I don't think she's seen Isaac since the night she went home with him." Grayson is running on the same theory as Alex. That Isaac is a pillow talker, so he has me keeping tabs on Isabelle more than Alex has me watching Isaac.

"Are you sure, Brandon? Is your gut telling you she has a clear conscience? Or evidence?"

"Both." I sound pissed. Justly so. I heard the words he didn't speak. He's as untrusting of my intuition as I am because he saw me get burned for it more than once.

"I don't mean to be a prick. I just need—"

"Me at my best. I get it," I interrupt, my voice not as surly as it was moments ago. "I'm not dropping the ball on this one, Grayson. Izzy is as straight as an arrow. I don't think she knows how to lie."

His heavy sigh whistles down the line. "I've heard you say that before, Brandon."

"I know you have, and I'm not saying you won't hear me say it again, but this is different. Izzy isn't playing me." I stop just before I say, *like Melody and Olivia.*

Grayson scrubbing at his beard sounds down the line. "All right. I'll take your word on it. I trust you, Brandon. We've had each other's back for too long for me not to. I just need you to remain cautious. This is bigger than Tobias realized. I don't want it taking us down like it did him."

"It won't," I pledge without the slightest quiver in my words. "We just have to concentrate on one man at a time."

My eyes stray to the massive criminal web we've been striving to dismantle for years. Grayson's team is hunting the top-dog on the list. Mine is targeting the lone solider at the bottom. No matter which one falls first, the outcome will be the same. One loose thread unravels an entire outfit.

I strongly believe that thread is Isaac Holt.

BRANDON

I close down the picture of Isabelle and Isaac kissing in his car in the front of a recently retired police officer's house when my name comes tumbling out of Isabelle's mouth in a purring moan. Their kiss happened weeks ago, and excluding her confronting him the morning after it occurred, it appeared to be the only contact they'd had. But I learned a hard and fast lesson on not trusting my instincts when Alex asked me to upload the images a fellow agent had obtained.

It sucked spilling details of my idiocy to Grayson for the second time in my career, but his reply had my objective teetering on an unstable cliff in an instant.

Grayson: *When the Honey Pot has been compromised, bring in the beekeeper. He'll get the bees back in order.*

Anyone outside of Tobias's inner circle would have been lost as to what his reply meant. I understood it in an instant, and I fucking hated it. I understand there's no 'I' in team, and that I swore an oath to defend the Constitution of the United States from all enemies, both foreign and domestic, but this was different. This was the woman Tobias referred to as his daughter. She was his family as I was once the Greggs'. I couldn't see how using Isabelle for the benefit of the Bureau was worth it—until Grayson found a link between someone in Isaac's team and the cattle truck that crashed into the Greggs' station wagon.

It was the most minute connection you could possibly imagine, but when you're clutching at straws, you have to investigate every last thread.

That's what I'm doing. I'm placing every thread under this spotlight. This is nothing against Tobias or Izzy, it's solely about the pledge I made to Mr. Gregg when I was five years old. A promise I'll uphold no matter what the cost. Even if Melody no longer wants my protection, she'll always have it because I'm a man who keeps his word.

My mind shifts back to the present when Isabelle props her backside onto my desk. Her lips are pursed, and she's batting her eyelashes. I watch her through suspicious eyes when she undoes the top button on her blouse, exposing the slightest peek of a rack every male agent in this office has admired many times the past few months.

"It's so hot today," she murmurs, fanning her cheeks with her hand.

"What do you want, Izzy?" I keep my tone as friendly as my smile. It isn't really a ruse. I genuinely like Isabelle. I just hate that she's keeping secrets from me. I've done nothing but help her, so why doesn't she trust me?

Isabelle's huff fans my cheeks. "What gave it away?"

I hit her with straight-up honesty. "The greeting was okay. It gained my attention, but you lost me when unbuttoning your shirt and saying it was hot today. You do realize summer is over, don't you, Isabelle?"

"Ha ha."

The disappointment on her face disappears when I playfully whimper about her returning her blouse to her pre-Brandon tease state.

Once everything is in order, I ask, "So, what brought you strutting over to my desk?"

"I wasn't strutting," she defends, her mouth falling open.

"You were strutting. The hips were swinging, and you had an extra spring in your step. Total strut."

Isabelle smiles at me. "I'm glad you took such *detailed* notes of my performance."

Her smile grows when I rub at the thump her whack to my bicep caused. For a girl, she has a lot of power behind her fists.

Our banter has me forgetting there's a man lodged between us— a man we're supposed to take down—however, Izzy is quick to remind me of my error. "I need a favor."

"Anything." I'm hoping my fast reply will assure her she can tell me anything.

What I'm not anticipating for her to say is, "I need access to a sealed file from the DA's office in New York."

"I can't, Izzy."

During the process of trying to keep her out of Alex's trap, I shared many stories of my life with her. Some incidents, like Melody cheating on me, then subsequently assisting me with a fraudulent charge I left out, but she's aware where things stand between us now. She knows Melody and I are not on speaking terms, so why the fuck is she asking me to do this?

The sexy-kitten look in Isabelle's eyes switches to a begging puppy when she pleads, "Please, Brandon, you know I wouldn't have asked you if it weren't important."

Her expressive eyes answer my unvoiced question more than her words. This isn't for the Bureau. It's for him—Isaac. The desperateness coating her skin is telling enough, much less the name on the file she's seeking. Hugo Marshall. That's the name she logged into the Bureau database the day following her sleepover at Isaac's apartment. She didn't make her discovery public knowledge, so she's either casting her own net with the hope of proving she's a valuable member of Alex's team, or she's out to prove not everyone with a tragic backstory is a bad person.

I'm hoping it's a bit of both.

Nothing but honesty rings in my tone when I say, "I haven't had any contact with her in years, Izzy. She'll probably hang up the instant she realizes who's calling."

As I scrub my hand down my face, Grayson's words ring on repeat in my ears.

We're not doing anything illegal.

Everything is above board.

You just need your gut to get on board with our plans.

Since I somewhat agree with him, I mutter, "I'll try, but I can't guarantee I'll be able to get the file for you."

Happiness beams out of Isabelle. "Thank you, Brandon, thank you."

When she slings her arms around my shoulders, I murmur a quick, "You're welcome," before striving to work out the last time I've held someone like this.

I'm ashamed to admit, it's been almost longer than my memory stretches.

When Isabelle inches back, I recall the reason I'm sticking my neck out for the third time in my life and put actions in place to make sure my head isn't chopped off this time around. "It will cost you, though." Her eager nod doubles when I add, "I need you to do a search on this lady..." but it packs up and leaves town when I say, "... and you have to go on a date with me."

Honey Pot, Honey Pot, Honey Pot, I murmur to myself when shock is the first thing that registers on Isabelle's face. The guilt in her eyes would have you convinced I asked a married woman to have an affair. It proves Isaac has his hooks in her more profoundly than I realized.

"One date, Izzy, that's all I'm asking."

She waits a beat before dipping her chin. "Okay, but it will have to be after I return. I'm going away with Harlow this weekend."

The sting her delay caused my ego slips away when a smile stretches across my face. I still got it—even though I'm reasonably sure I don't know what 'it' is anymore.

"Why don't you come to my apartment, and I'll cook dinner?"

I smile to hide my shock at Isabelle's offer. This was not a path I expected her to lead us down. "Sounds great."

She returns my smile before diverting her attention to the manila folder I handed her at the commencement of our exchange. While she peruses photographs of Megan Shroud, a woman Intelligence believes has a romantic connection with Isaac, I watch her for any tell-tale signs of a scorned woman.

She appears more unwell than jealous—even more so when she asks, "Who is this lady?"

I commence my lie with a shrug, "We don't know. We've noticed her a few times hanging around the nightclub the past several weeks. We believe she may be a *companion* of Isaac's." Isabelle folds the card she's been holding close to her chest when I add, "I haven't seen Isaac with a girlfriend the entire time he's been under surveillance, but this lady has been in the picture more regularly than his standard dates, so she may be someone significant in his life."

"All right." Isabelle hops off my desk with a grunt. "I'll see what I can find out about her."

While she heads for her desk, needing distance before I see the unease igniting in her eyes, I send Grayson a text.

Me: *The beekeeper has landed.*

His reply weakens the knot in my stomach but only by a little.

Grayson: *Never feel guilty about protecting your first love. I never have.*

Talking about first loves, here comes one phone call I never saw coming.

MELODY

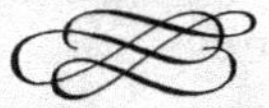

"*I* don't care if he has a baby face, Julian, he's a monster."

Julian, audiologist, wannabe defense attorney and my boyfriend, rests a box of noodles on his wash-board stomach when he slumps into my couch. He's making a mess, but since it gives him an excuse to take his shirt off, and hopefully spend the night, he's going for it. "How could someone that cute commit such horrendous crimes? It isn't possible."

I almost reply that you can't judge anyone on their moral upbringing, much less their looks, but the bright light of my TTY telephone in the corner of the room catches my eye.

No one uses that phone anymore.

No one except Brandon.

I shoo away Julian's nosey-nancying when he says, "Why do you still have that old thing, Mel? You don't need it anymore." I'm too busy scrambling to answer a phone call I swore I'd never answer again. I don't have time to hold his hand through the safety nets twenty-six-year-old women like me have a hard time giving up.

The last time I accepted a call from Brandon, a decade worth of memories was deleted from my mind in an instant. I had convinced myself for almost two years that Joey didn't do what he had done, that he was the lovable, sweet, brother-like teen I had remembered, and that my woozy head that night had me misconstruing what had actually happened.

Then Brandon called, and my entire world upended for the third time in my life.

His contact not only revealed how foolish I had been, it also proved that you can never judge someone's motives on their looks and upbringing. Some people are born to be evil. They can be taught to act differently, but the instant the protective cloak is removed, their true self comes out, and more times than not, it isn't pretty.

I didn't want to believe the reports Brandon forwarded me. I was certain every single word on the official documents were false. My thoughts only changed when Brandon didn't deny the claims. He had sex with an informant. He never denied that. The only thing he wanted to refute was the plaintiff's claim that she slept with him under duress. That she didn't believe she could safely turn down his advancement, so she had no option but to answer his every whim.

That hurt.

Seeing the name of the man I had loved, and still do love, written on the defendant's side of a sexual assault claim hurt. I can't put it any simpler than that.

Thinking back, I realize how immature it was of me to react to the news as I did, but in all honesty, could you say you would have responded differently if you'd been through what I had been through? I was raped in a house I had once called my home, by a man I had considered a brother. I wasn't in the right frame of mind to repress my thoughts and look at Brandon's case objectively.

I'm not even sure I am in the right mindset now. But I do know one thing, I swore I would handle things differently if given a chance again.

I'm going to keep my promise.

Brandon protected, loved, and cared for me after my parents

died, but the one time he needed me the most, I ran instead of explaining what had happened. I hid things from him and used my ability to pass a lie detector test with flying colors to my advantage. Then, when he needed me again, I failed him for the second time.

I refuse to do bad things in threes. It's time for the fear to end. I'm tired of living half a life because I'm constantly looking back at my past. I doubt Brandon's call will fully liberate me, but any step forward is a step in the right direction.

After counting to ten in my head, I hit the 'connect call' on my TTY phone. When the screen displays who's calling, my hand shoots up to cover my soundless sob from Julian. Brandon told the operator his name is BJ McGee. I haven't heard anyone refer to him by that name in years. Seeing it written across the screen is a whack to the gut, but it's a good whack.

I think.

When Julian spots my watering eyes from across the room, he offers me his support, but he does it from a distance. He knows about my past, and Brandon comes up more often than he'd like, but that's more to do with him being a major part of my childhood. I'm not doing it to be mean or to remind Julian I have loved before him. It's just hard to forget a massive chunk of your life when every decision you've ever made was based on that life.

I followed the plan Brandon and I made when we were kids to a 'T.'

I just did it without Brandon at my side as planned.

When the operator on the other end of the TTY phone advises another message is coming through, I drag my hands across my wet cheeks. The three-dash incoming message signal is worse than waiting for bar exam results to be released.

I'm tempted to call Brandon when his message comes through.

BJ McGee: *Melody, are you there?*

Even through a string of texts, I can feel his desperateness.

I'm partway through scrolling the contacts on my phone for his number when another message comes through.

BJ McGee: *I'm sorry for the late hour. I wouldn't have called unless it was urgent. I need a favor.*

I read the last four words of his message three times before another line of text erases it from my screen.

BJ McGee: *I've tried every other angle I could. I'm out of options.*

This set of messages is oddly similar to the ones he sent me years ago, and they make my heart a twisted mess of confusion.

BJ McGee: *I need your help, Melody. I promise this is the last thing I'll ever ask of you.*

That hurts more than I can explain. I was hoping his contact was a way of bridging the distance between us, but it appears as if it's going to instigate even more awkwardness.

BJ McGee: *Melody...*

After bracing my fingertips on the keyboard of the TTY phone, I stray my eyes to Julian. If he can't give me the courage to type a reply, no one will. His future is being held hostage by my past as much as mine, so he deserves input in this as well.

When he lowers his chin, encouraging me to reply, my fingers race across the keyboard.

Melody Gregg: *I'm here. What do you need?*

TWENTY MINUTES LATER, Julian joins me at my desk at the side of the living room.

"Are you okay?" He presses his lips to my temple before pinching the pleat in his trousers to lower himself to my level. It brings me in direct line with his shimmering baby blues. His gentle eyes were one of the first things I noticed about him, along with his ability to sign. "Is it anything I can help with?"

As I shake my head, my lips curl at his generous offer. Julian's family is extremely wealthy. Nothing is above their league, but Brandon isn't seeking anything of monetary value. He wants information. Information only I can give him.

When I explain that to Julian, he asks, "Do you want to give him the information he needs?"

I shrug. *"He's an FBI agent. I'm always willing to help one of my own."* He watches me with kind, understanding eyes, but his mouth remains shut. He knows I'm holding back the real reason I am hesitant. *"I just never thought this would be the norm for us. That he would only reach out to me when he needed something."*

Julian tracks his thumb over the vein throbbing in my wrist before he asks, "I thought you told him your friendship was over years ago?" He thinks holding my hand will stop me from signing my reply.

He's dead wrong.

I don't know how to express myself without American Sign Language, so it's my go-to anytime I'm feeling flustered.

I'm more than flustered today.

"I did say that, but it was said in the heat of the moment."

"And how is he to know that, Melody? I've seen you mad. It's scary."

The fake tremble of his last two words arches my lips higher. *"You haven't even scratched the surface of my mood swings yet—"*

He stops me mid-sentence by clasping my hands in his and raising them to his mouth. When he kisses the edge of my palms, the pain in my chest weakens. He has a way of healing me even when I don't realize I'm hurting.

"Give him the file, then come to bed." A sprinkling of light orange hair falls into his eyes when he slants his head to the side to hide his wickedly immoral grin. It's straight and perfect but filled with hidden cheekiness. The rumors about redheaded men being the spawns of rascal-like behaviors are true. "We have more important things to discuss than helping an old friend with a debunked case."

When Julian strays his vibrant blue eyes to the file I brought up to authenticate Brandon's claims the reports were buried deeper than a standard vehicular murder case, I follow the direction of his gaze. I still recall Marjorie Hawke's case. I hadn't commenced my studies in law school yet, but tell me one female who doesn't get misty-eyed when they hear of a pregnant lady being run down by a drunk driver, killing both her and her unborn child.

Up until twenty minutes ago, I never knew the outcome of Marjorie's case. I assumed the drunk driver was served a hefty punishment for his crime. I had no clue he was offered a plea bargain by the DA mere weeks before he disappeared. That DA happened to be Brandon's father, Vincent McGee.

The erroneous mishandling of Marjorie's case exposes why Brandon is interested in her file, but I'm still wary I am crossing a line by giving Brandon Marjorie's sealed file. They were locked in a vault so tight, I had to use the head of my department's credentials to find them. I wasn't given access to his passcodes for no reason. He trusts me with them, and I'm not willing to lose his trust to help an acquaintance, but since the person asking is Brandon, I don't know if I can say no.

After a few minutes of silent deliberation, I lock my eyes with Julian's before nudging my head to my bedroom. "Why don't you head up? I'll join you in a minute."

"I can wait." His swift reply hides his excitement at being invited to spend the night, and I won't mention how happy he is that I used my voice to express myself instead of my hands.

"It's okay. Head up. I won't be a minute."

"All right." When he tucks a strand of dirty-blonde hair behind my ear, I lean into his palm, seeking comfort for what I know will hurt me no matter how hard I try to brush it off as being nothing more than work. This is as personal as it gets for me. I'll never see Brandon as just an acquaintance. "Don't be too long."

When I nod, Julian presses a second kiss to my temple before standing from his crouched position and making his way to the staircase of my loft bedroom. My apartment is barely five hundred square feet in size, but the loft bedroom perched above the living area makes good use of the space. Apartments in New York don't come cheap, let alone ones close to the office. I'm only renting my apartment since most of my trust fund went toward having cochlear implants inserted into my ears a little over three years ago. They cost more per ear than four years of pre-law study. Were they worth it? I don't know yet. I never felt disadvantaged being deaf—*except that one time.*

I snap out of my dreary thoughts when the shower in the attached bathroom of my room switches on. My hearing isn't as good as a person born without profound hearing loss, and my voice is cringingly deep, but it's good enough for me to hear my raging heart as much as I can feel it. It is thumping so fast it's battering my ribs. Something so simple shouldn't make me so nervous, but it does.

After a stern warning on how my past has no right to affect my future, I divert my focus to the screen of my MacBook Pro. Although the file Brandon is chasing is directly in front of me, it's the scanned version every clue hunter hates. There are more redacted pages than text-filled ones.

With that in mind, I snag my keys off the desk before shouting Julian's name, cringing when my voice comes out sounding like a man's.

Due to the size of my loft and the fact Julian rarely showers with the door closed, he responds rather quickly. "Yeah?"

"I'm going to pop down to the office for a minute. I won't be long."

I'm reasonably sure he tells me to wait, but since I've already made up my mind, and I regularly use my poor hearing to my advantage, I continue for the door.

The doorman of my building greets me with a dip of his hat before his opening of the thick wooden door blasts the foyer with ghastly humid air. New York's weather is nothing like what I faced in California. It's more severe here with ice and snow every winter, and the humidity is atrocious. I've barely seen the sun past the skyscrapers the past year, and my California tan is paying for the controversy. I had quite the tan compliments to the lazy weekends I spent reading at Venice Beach.

That's where I met Julian. I wasn't on the prowl for a date. That wasn't something I had ever planned to do, but when you're wrangling a rude waiter unwilling to read the order I had written for her, sometimes you have to accept help from a stranger.

It would have been rude for me to reject Julian's request to dine with me after he jumped to my defense. He was charming, and the first guy I had spoken to in almost three years. One casual dinner turned into an afternoon movie date. Our friendly movie date extended to a thirteen-hour marathon text conversation where we organized to dine together again the following weekend.

There wasn't a great amount of sexual chemistry the first few months we knew one another. Julian was, and still is, gorgeous, but I wasn't looking for any type of relationship. It was just nice having someone to talk to.

Julian is an audiologist. His family has a range of hearing clinics on both the east and west side of the country. They specialize in hearing aids for the aged and cochlear implants for newborn babies. Since he grew up around people with hearing impediments, he learned ASL at a young age.

Around three months into our friendship, he made an appointment with me to meet with his father about having cochlear implants inserted. He was the first person since Dr. Giorgio to suggest them, and I wasn't a fan of the idea.

Julian's constant pushing for me to reconsider my objectives wedged a six-month gap into our friendship. We only reunited after I had a scare on the metro. A woman I had accidentally bumped into couldn't understand why I wouldn't verbally apologize for my mistake. She wanted an apology, and from what I gathered between the many thrusts of her hands in my face, she wanted it immediately.

I was so shaken by the incident, I broke down. I stopped

attending school. I failed to show up for lectures. I shut myself away from the world as I did the weeks following Joey's death.

Instead of my phone being blown up by Brandon offering his friendship, Julian reached out to me. He brought me food, held back my hair when I vomited through the panic attacks rendering me immobile, and promised nothing I could ever tell him would change his opinion of me.

I believed him.

I still do.

I told him everything—the home invasion when I was five, giving my virginity to Brandon, my parents' accident. I even told him a story I had never shared with anyone.

He didn't respond as I had predicted.

He held me until my tears dried, and the pain went away.

We've been together ever since.

My pace slows as good memories from my past slowly filter through my head. Julian is in a good chunk of them. Just remembering how he sounded like a duck the first time I heard him speak stretches a massive smile across my face. Then his smile when I said his name for the first time. Gosh—it was the stuff dreams are made out of. He's a true gentleman, so much so, I'm spinning on my heels before I'm even halfway to my office building.

My quick pivot has me crashing into a wall of hardness. As my hand shoots up to rub the sting in my nose, I throw my head back and laugh. I recognize the scent of the aftershave the man who bumped into me is wearing. I would never forget it.

"Julian. What are you doing? I thought you were taking a shower." I run my fingers through his hair that's darker than normal since it's soaking wet. "You're lucky it isn't winter, you would have caught pneumonia."

"You'd never be so lucky," he murmurs while tugging me closer to him by banding an arm around my back. When I peer up at him, confused, he adds, "To get rid of me so easily."

"I don't want to get rid of you."

"You don't, huh?" His last word garbles from me inching our mouths closer. "Do you want me to stick close by?"

"Of course, I do."

He nips on my lower lip before asking, "For how long?"

I glance straight into his eyes while replying, "Is eternity an option?"

I must not have answered him right because instead of awarding me the kiss I'm all but begging for, Julian steps back before curling his hand around mine. "In that case, I guess it's okay to show you this now instead of waiting for your birthday on Monday."

The suspicion on my face doubles when he commences jogging us through the almost isolated streets. New York rarely sleeps, but the late hour certainly doesn't impose any obstacles during our sprint to my office building.

I gasp out one of the urgent breaths I just sucked in when Julian secures a set of keys out of his pocket. I'm not stunned he owns a set of keys, his family has four hearing clinics in the upper east side alone. I'm shocked he has a key to a government building. I was lucky to be given access, and I work here.

"How did you get a key to my office building?" In my shocked state, I've reverted back to signing.

Julian remains as quiet as a church mouse. Not even the handing over of photo-ID to the guard standing firm at the elevator banks has a peep seeping from his lips.

"It was Mary-Anne, right? She has always had a soft spot for you."

For someone born deaf, Julian's silence shouldn't frustrate me as much as it does, but it does—very much so. I'm on the verge of stomping down my foot like an errant child just to force him to react. He hates when I act immature. That probably has more to do with him being ten years my senior. He loathes it when strangers notice our difference in age, much less people we know.

When the elevator dings on the floor my office is located on, Julian places his hand on the curve of my back to guide me down the hallway I've walked many times the past six months. The records section I was seeking earlier is in the opposite direction, but the thud of Julian's pulse thumping through my back has me keeping that snippet of information to myself.

"Julian…" Now I'm speechless—truly and utterly speechless.

Every inch of my office has been decorated with helium balloons, streamers, love hearts, and the ridiculous Pez collectibles I pointed out to him at the end of our first official date. He even got a Donald Duck one—his nickname since the day my cochlear implants were turned on.

"Happy birthday, Mel," Julian croons, moving to stand in front of me.

"Thank you, truly," I sign, incapable of both speaking and breathing. *"It's beautiful—"*

My hands freeze when Julian lowers himself onto one knee before producing a blue velvet box from the pocket of the trousers he threw on in haste. "I love you," he whispers when he spots the tears streaming down my face.

"I love you, too," I reply when I find my voice. Those are the only words Julian has never seen me sign. They were only ever signed to one man, and I can't bring myself to use them on another.

Speech is different, just like my relationship with Julian will be when I nod my head to the four words he speaks next. "Will you marry me?"

BRANDON

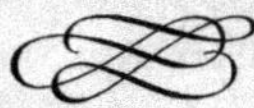

I stop pursuing the late edition of the *New York Times* online when Alex's grumble roars through my ears. "I don't give a fuck what the local authorities say, overrule them!" He bangs his phone on his desk three times before slamming it back against his ear. "They didn't log a flight plan. That makes them liable to an investigation."

He doesn't need to mention Isaac's name for me to know who he's talking about. The disdain in his voice replicates the contempt that scorched my throat when I read the new article about Melody's engagement to Julian McMahon. Because Julian's family are gazillionaires, news of their only son's engagement is supposedly page six news. The article was printed with a photograph from several months ago, but the timeline of events show Julian proposed a mere hour after I reached out to Melody.

Talk about being a schmuck. If proposing is the only trick you have up your sleeve to have your girlfriend forgetting the ghosts of her past, you've got issues.

Not as many as me, but still.

Fuck! It's been almost seven years, so why can't I let bygones be bygones. Melody has moved on—*clearly*—so why the fuck can't I?

Because you swore an oath to protect her until eternity long before you knew the meaning of the word.

Frustrated, I drag my arm along my desk, removing the contents on top in one quick sweep. Because the agents surrounding me are too busy inconspicuously watching Alex's rant from afar, they're none the wiser to my childish tantrum.

I'm not surprised. I'm not a threat to anyone except myself, don't you know?

With my teeth gritted, I bend down to gather up the files I was in the process of sorting. They're brimming with documents, bank records, and movement sheets that correspond with our target, Isaac Holt. But that isn't all the files I'm gathering. There's a thick manila folder I didn't notice earlier. It doesn't have the name of our target on the seal. It's the file I asked Melody to unlock for me.

As I scoop up the evidence that the old Melody is still hiding inside her somewhere, I scan my eyes across the office. This file is so confidential, it has more than one private stamp embossed on it. It even has a CIA seal.

Confident I'm not being eyeballed, I gather the file into my hand, hide it with my thick winter coat even though its extra humid today, then hightail it to the room every agent seeks when they want privacy—the supply room.

"Wʜᴀᴛ ᴅᴏ you mean you're not going to share the information you've unearthed with Isabelle?" Grayson questions down the line. His voice is as hoarse as mine, like he too has been sitting on a hard floor for over three hours, sorting through evidence on a massive injustice. "If she knows the type of men Isaac is hiding from prosecution, perhaps she won't be so eager to keep his secrets. He's harboring a rapist, Brandon. They're the worst of the worst."

"A rapist who gave testimony saying my brother was the ringleader of the gang rape of Gemma Calderon-Levesque."

"Hold on, what? Go back. What the fuck did I miss?" Grayson sounds as shocked as I felt when I read Hugo's testimony from a rape case five years ago. It happened when Madden, Gemma, and Hugo—a member of Isaac's security personnel—were deployed in Afghanistan. "Which brother are we talking about?"

"Madden." Considering I only spoke one word, it shouldn't have been as hard to express as it was. "Initial reports given to the JAG officer state Madden approached Gemma in the alleyway outside of a local bar. She was disorientated and dizzy, seemingly unaware of where she was. Madden said he tried to help her. Gemma's testimony didn't verify his version of events. She said Madden, along with an additional five officers, attacked her, and that Hugo stopped their assault."

"Jesus H Christ." I hear Grayson scrub at his beard. "Why would she change her testimony?"

"That's the thing, she didn't. She's always maintained her side of the story. She is adamant Hugo never assaulted her."

A chair creaking into place sounds down the line before Grayson asks, "Then why did he plead guilty to her rape?"

A shudder rolls through me when I recall the images attached to the file. They were when Gemma attempted to commit suicide. It was the night following my father slaughtering her in the witness box. He still had contacts in the military from his years of service, and they were more than happy to have a decorated defense attorney step in to help one of their own. Gemma was also an officer, but her name didn't have military distinction attached to it. Madden's did.

When I update Grayson on all aspects of my findings, he curses—loudly. "This is more fucked-up than my family shit. Jesus, punk." He takes a breather for a second before asking, "Is this the first time your father has stepped in like this?"

I almost nod before the faintest memory filters through my

head. "No. There was a similar incident when Madden was a sopho-more. It wasn't a gang rape, but he was accused of sexual assault by the police chief's daughter."

"What happened to those claims?"

I shrug. "I don't know. Madden had to hand over the keys to his Pontiac, and he joined the military, but I don't know what happened to…" I lose my train of thought for a moment. I usually have a knack for remembering names, but Madden's first victim is slipping my mind.

Victim… such an odd word for me to use if I believe Madden's recollection of events.

Clearly, I don't.

Ignoring my dead ass from sitting on a concrete floor for three hours straight, I stand to my feet before making my way out of the supply room. "If I forward you some info, could you work it through the pipelines on your end? It could be nothing, but it's rare for my father to place his hat into a ring he can't benefit from. This all occurred around the time he started his push for office. It could be one of those threads we've been seeking the past few years."

"Yeah, of course," Grayson replies without pause for thought. He knows the less my name is associated with the information I'm hunting, the better it will be for all involved. "Just prepare yourself, Brandon. When you're digging for shit, you immerse yourself in it."

"I can handle it."

I hear his smile through the phone. "I have no doubt. Send me what you have. I've got a few spare hours tonight, and from what I'm hearing, so do you."

Stealing my chance to question if he bugged my office, he disconnects our call.

I dump my cell phone onto my desk before logging into the official Bureau search engine. It only takes me a few minutes to remember the name of the girl who accused Madden of assaulting her in the middle of a movie date. I only had to search for the police chief in Saugerties the year Melody officially became my girlfriend.

I'll never forget that night. Not even years of grief have faded the memory I've worked on repeat the past seven years.

After forwarding Annie's details to Grayson, I dig a little deeper into Annie's father's bank records. Money has been my father's bribery tool for years. Ever since his inheritance from his great-grandfather's oil refinery hit his bank account, he bought respect more than he earned it.

I hit a dead-end in Mr. Langfield's bank records not even twenty minutes later. They ceased to exist five years ago. His family withdrew every penny they had a month after he was killed during a random traffic stop and left Saugerties for dust.

I'm about to commence a hunt for their whereabouts now, but before I can, a deep, moody voice scares the living daylights out of me. "What are you working on?"

"Ah..." I scratch my face, my ability to lie on demand long forgotten since I've rarely used the skill the past six years. "Just some stuff for another division. They wanted to see if there was any correlation between these bank records and Isaac's."

Alex purses his lips. He doesn't want to believe me, but he has no reason not to. "I need you to stop that for now and jump onto surveillance with Reid. Facial recognition picked up a positive match for Isaac at an airstrip near The Hamptons."

When I jerk up my chin, acknowledging I heard him, Alex balances his hip on my desk, announcing our conversation isn't over just yet. "Did you speak to Isabelle before she left?"

"Yeah, briefly. She unearthed the identity of the mysterious female in the yellow car outside of Isaac's nightclub." I don't know why I'm sugar-coating Isabelle's investigative skills. It's a habit I can't seem to let go of, much like my inability to remove Melody from my mind.

Alex scrubs at his jaw like Grayson always does. His is just minus the scruffy beard he had before he took a five-month hiatus from the Bureau. "Did she happen to mention where she was going this weekend?"

"Ah… not in full detail. She said she and Harlow were going away for the weekend." I'm not sugar-coating anything this time around. Isabelle either believed her weekend getaway was solely with Harlow or she's more skilled in lying than I once was. "Why are you asking? Is she in danger?"

"No," Alex denies with a shake of his head. "I just figured you were friends, that's all, so I'm trying to wrap my head around why you didn't get an invite to her weekend getaway."

He's a worse liar than Grayson, but I'm happy to lead him to believe he isn't. "Perhaps it's a girls-only weekend? I don't have the necessary equipment for an invite to one of those."

A side of Alex I haven't seen in months shines through when he ribs, "Are you sure about that, Brandon? After all the pussyfooting you've done the past few months, I'm beginning to wonder."

Smirking at my shocked expression, he returns to the glass box he calls an office, and I switch my investigation from Annie Langfield's whereabouts to Isabelle's. I can't change the past, but if I try to stay one step ahead of the future, I can hope it won't be nowhere near as painful.

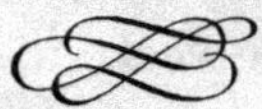

A grin tugs at my lips when the chime of a bakery bell dings into my ears. It's funny how the littlest things can cause the most joy. I had never considered what a bell sounded like. I always pictured the noise more than wondering about its happy little chime. It's a good ding to alert staff to customers just like loud and ear-hurting sirens are perfect for ambulances and fire trucks. I went from a world of silence to one that never stops humming. I guess that's why Julian understood my wish to move back to New York State. There are so many noises here I've never heard before, such as Mrs. McGee's voice when she waves for me to join her from the corner of the bakery. Her tone is as beautiful as her face, and her pitch is perfect.

"Hello."

She cries like I did the first time I heard someone speak, except this time, it's the other way around. She's hearing me talk for the first time.

"*Melody*," she signs my name as well as saying it. "You… oh… you're beautiful. Come here." When she wraps me up in a firm hug, my heart turns to mush. Her son hurt me, but Julian taught me it's okay to still love her. She didn't do anything wrong, and neither did Brandon. "I've missed you so much."

Once she pulls back, she gestures for me to sit. I hang my purse over the back of the wooden chair before sitting in the seat across from her. I smile in gratitude when she taps on my ankle with her foot to advise me the waiter is at my side, forgetting I can hear the faint patter of his feet, much less smell his deodorant.

After ordering a cup of coffee and a blueberry Danish, I divert my attention back to Mrs. McGee. My eyes automatically drop to her lips when she asks, "Is Julian going to be joining us?" Lipreading is an old habit I find hard to give up.

"Ahh, no. He said he would come next time. He didn't want you to feel uncomfortable." When she takes her time to respond to my reply, I sign. *I can sign if you would prefer. My voice is—"*

She encloses her hands over mine. "Your voice is beautiful. I'm sorry if I am appearing rude. I'm just stunned. I never thought this was possible."

"I didn't either. I was really opposed to the idea at one stage."

Mrs. McGee laughs. "Yes, you were. If I recall correctly, you didn't want the fantasy in your head ruined if you discovered we all had robot voices."

My laugh still sounds odd to me, but it springs tears into Mrs. McGee's eyes. "You should have seen my face when they switched on the devices. I was mortified my worst nightmare had come true."

Mrs. McGee laughs so hard, she covers her big beaming smile with a napkin coated with the crumbs of the muffin she was halfway through devouring before I joined her. Nerves made me over thirty minutes late. I'm glad she isn't mad I almost left her stag.

My smile sags when she asks, "Have you heard Brandon speak yet?"

When I shake my head, fresh tears twinkle in her eyes. "He called me last week, but it was on the TTY phone. I haven't told anyone I got cochlear implants. I don't know why." I do. I hate admitting I had a disability. I had never seen my deafness as a disability until I met Julian, and I don't want to now.

Mrs. McGee reminds me of the gorgeous soul she has when she asks, "You still have a TTY phone?" She sounds as shocked as Julian did when I ordered one to be installed in my loft. The speech side of my new skills was still in development, but I was far from needing a TTY phone. It was just something I couldn't give up straight away. "I thought that would have been the first thing you got rid of. With how advanced technology is, they're so clunky and outdated. Your beautiful face should be flashed across FaceTime for eternity."

"I had considered ditching my phone, but it's kind of like a safety net for me. It reminds me of home."

She nods, fully understanding what I mean as she too has many crutches she's not willing to let go of just yet.

"I heard you're moving back to the ranch. Is that true?"

Sadness crosses her face first, but it's quickly gobbled up by happiness. "Yes, I think it's time. There's nothing here for me anymore." She doesn't need to mention Mr. McGee's name for me to know who she's talking about. The tabloids make up for her lack of words, much less rumors of McGee's many affairs the past decade.

"For what it's worth, I'm sorry. Not just for what happened with Mr. McGee but with Joey as well." My teeth crunch when I almost lose the plot at the mention of Joey's name. It was easy to believe Julian when he said Mrs. McGee doesn't deserve the wrath of Joey's ill-judgment, but it's harder believing it is okay for me to still care for Joey.

"Don't apologize, Melody. I just wish you would have let Brandon be there for you as he was for me. I'm sure losing Joey hurt you as much as it did us."

"It did. It was just a… *different* type of grief."

Mrs. McGee curls her hand over mine. "Then why did you leave? I still, to this day, can't fathom why you stayed away for so long. I understand Joey represented your father—"

"It wasn't that. That isn't why I left."

"Then, what was it?" There's no malice in her tone whatsoever. She truly wants the best for me. I just don't know how I can be honest with her and not ruin the legacy of her son. She loves Joey, so much so, I could never burden her with the guilt and hurt I'm feeling. Joey killed himself because he couldn't live with what he had done. I don't want the woman I've seen as a mother blaming me for her son's death. I already blame myself, so there's no need to place the burden onto someone else's shoulders.

When I feel tears prickling in my eyes, I make an excuse to leave before they can fall. "I'm sorry. I forgot about an important meeting. I must go."

When I leap up to my feet, Mrs. McGee mimics my movements. "Melody, honey, what's wrong? I swear to you, nothing you could ever tell me would have me looking at you differently."

I want to believe her, but I can't as my secret isn't just about me. It's about her blood. "It's nothing. I'm fine. Give Brandon my best wishes."

I snatch up my purse before hightailing it out of the bakery. I barely make it halfway down the block when the hairs on my arms prickling to attention slows my brutal speed. After swinging my head to the left, I slowly drag it to the right. I stop holding my breath when I spot Julian standing at the corner of the bakery. He knew today was going to be hard for me, but instead of discouraging me against it, he positioned himself in an area where he could dispense soul-fixing hugs in an instant.

It makes me love him even more.

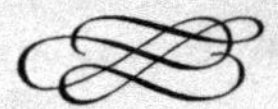

"Head in the game, punk. This is your punishment for scouring the pages of gossip magazines to keep up to date on your girl's life instead of being a part of it."

While riding the elevator to the floor of Isabelle's apartment, I respond to Grayson as if he's standing next to me instead of talking shit in my ear. "For one, how is a date with a gorgeous woman classified as a punishment? And two, I wasn't scouring the pages. I just happen to stumble upon an article about her upcoming engagement party."

"Bullshit. I don't even need to hack your phone to know you have her name on google alerts."

I use the elevator's ding announcing I've arrived at Isabelle's floor as an excuse to ignore Grayson snickering in my ear. I haven't stopped searching for news articles that include Melody's name since her engagement was announced two weeks ago, but I'm never going to admit that to Grayson. He has a memory like an elephant. He never forgets anything, and he forever uses my neuroses against me.

"Remind me again why you need to listen in on my dinner date with Izzy?"

I wait for Grayson to respond before rapping my knuckles on the white door of Isabelle's apartment. "Because she didn't request you to get the file she did for no reason. There are too many loose threads for us to brush this off as a coincidence."

He's right—again. Still fucking sucks, though.

With Alex breathing down my neck, I didn't put two and two together until much later than I care to admit. Annie's father was a police chief. He hadn't pulled over a rundown Mazda for a registration check in over two decades, so why the fuck did he do that the day he was killed?

If it wasn't the first time he had done something odd on the job, I would have brushed it off as a cop not being able to step away from the role when he isn't on the clock, but his name has popped up too many times the past two weeks to utilize that pathetic excuse.

Police Chief Langfield was the arresting officer cited on the non-doctored police file Isabelle requested. He was first on the scene when Marjorie Hawke, Hugo Marshall's baby sister, was mowed down by suspected mafia associate, Roberto Petretti. Even with Langfield witnessing the accident, his name wasn't on any of the official documents lodged with the court when Roberto was offered a plea bargain, nor was he brought forward as a witness.

If that isn't suspicious enough, he was killed on duty only five short weeks later.

It happened to be the same day Roberto disappeared off the face of the planet.

Coincidence? Unlikely.

"Either Tobias trained Isabelle better than he trained us, or Isaac opened up to our Honey Pot. It's the least he should have done after you revealed he's a cheating scumbag."

My jaw tightens as the memory of Isabelle's whitening face fills my head. Alex didn't have much luck tracking down Isaac's whereabouts the weekend Isabelle went away with Harlow, but it was obvious Isaac was with Isabelle. Not only did she attempt to resign the day after they returned, Isaac was seen walking with her to her door. It was a mere two hours before he was spotted on a date with a mysterious blonde. I showed the image of them kissing to Isabelle the following morning, hopeful it would get her back on the straight and narrow. It seems to have worked. Reid, Alex's head of surveillance, hasn't logged any activity between Isaac and Isabelle in weeks.

I'm drawn from my thoughts when Grayson says, "Whatever the reason, we need to record your conversations to ensure our asses are covered if the shit hits the fan."

"Recorded officially?"

"Fuck no," he replies, his voice almost a roar. "We'll let the Bureau know when they're—"

"Privy to know."

"Exactly," Grayson pushes out with a laugh.

He stops chuckling in my ear when Isabelle throws open the front door of her apartment as astounded by Isabelle's figure-hugging dress as me. Even with her not being on my radar doesn't stop me from dragging my eyes down her body. She has an extremely enticing form.

When my eyes land back on Isabelle's face, she greets me with a smile, acting oblivious to my gawk. "Brandon, hi. Come in."

As my eyes float over her impressive crash pad, a whistle sounds from my lips. "Wow, Isabelle, swanky residence."

She presses a hurried kiss to my cheek before guiding me into the foyer. Grayson makes gagging noises when I hand her a floral bouquet of irises and baby's breath. He can forget the morals his mother instilled in him the instant he left for university because it was only his mother reciting them to him. I wasn't so lucky. I didn't just have my mother reminding me about how to be a gentleman, I had Melody's mother as well.

"Thank you," Isabelle replies before offering to take my coat.

Once she has it hung in the coat closet, I follow her into her state-of-the-art kitchen.

Grayson mimics my earlier wolf-whistle when we enter the modest yet well-fitted space. "Is the dodgy camera you installed in your button this afternoon playing tricks on me, or are they high-end appliances I'm seeing?"

Since I can't reply to Grayson, I flick the microphone in the third button of my shirt to shut him up instead. People can have nice things without being suspected of criminal activity. I had to prove that before I was offered a position in Tobias's team. He was more suspicious of wealthy men than me.

Grayson laughs before the familiar creak of his office chair sounds through my ears. *Why am I not surprised he's still at work this late on a Saturday?*

My annoyance takes a back seat when a delicious scent filters through my nostrils. Years ago, I would have recognized the smell without a second whiff, however, since it's been a very long time since I've sampled these scents, I take a second undignified long sniff to authenticate the claims of my hungry tummy.

"It smells delicious in here." When I rub my stomach like a hungry gorilla, Isabelle giggles. "It smells just like my grandma's kitchen used to smell." My mouth salivates when I finally distinguish one of the scents. "Mariana meatballs?"

"Nah, dipshit. It's the smell of desperation."

Ignoring Grayson's swipe at my non-existent dating skills, I raise my index finger in the air. "Hold on." A smidge of hesitation crosses my features when I discover the cause for the extra grumble of my stomach. "Oh, for the love of God, please tell me that's homemade peanut butter and chocolate chip cookies?"

"They're due out of the oven any minute," Isabelle replies before she makes her way to the oven to check on two trays of baking cookies.

"She has good social awareness skills. Tobias taught her well,"

Grayson murmurs in my ear as shocked that she unearthed my favorite cookie flavor without asking me. "Now we just need to work out whose team she's on. Time to bring out the charm, big boy. Just try and do it without drooling on the camera. I'm smelling your spike in body temp all the way in New York. I don't need to witness the travesty firsthand."

I roll my eyes at Grayson's comment before joining Isabelle in the kitchen. When I attempt to snag a cookie from the tray she places onto the counter, she slaps away my hand. "They need to cool and harden." She pushes a memory of my mom to the forefront of my mind when she adds, "And you'll spoil your dinner if you eat them now."

My mom never let me eat cookies before dinner, and don't get me started on how much of a scrooge she was with the uncooked cookie dough. Fast hands were a much-needed skill in my child-hood, and I'm not just talking about the times Melody and I fooled around under a thick blanket.

Mistaking my reminiscing face as one of disappointment, Isabelle sets down a tray of still-warm cookies in front of me. Her eyes roll when she asks me if I'd like a glass of milk with my cookies is as cute as hell. It also explains Isaac's immediate interest in her. She's beautiful, but there's something in her eyes that brings out men's protective sides in an instant. It makes you desperate to keep her safe, even knowing you're too late. She's already been hurt.

I recognize that look anywhere. I saw it in Melody's eyes, and I was only five at the time. The second time it was just shy of her nineteenth birthday. It was when she galloped down the stairs of my family ranch demanding to know why I wasn't there for her. That was the last time I saw her up close. She kept her distance at Joey's funeral, and the angry blonde I wrangled at the airport wasn't the Melody I knew. She was a ghost of herself. Almost soulless.

My thoughts snap back to the present when Grayson reminds me that I haven't answered Isabelle's offer for a glass of milk.

"Yes, please." I cringe when I spray her counter with cookie crumbs. I either spoke with a mouth full of food or drifted off into my memories for another awkward thirty seconds. I went for the earlier. It didn't make it any less awkward, though.

Smiling at my apparent daftness, Isabelle moves to the fridge to secure a jug of milk. She fills a glass to the brim before inquiring, "Brandon, can I ask you something?"

I swallow down a cookie almost whole before jerking up my chin. "Anything."

The silent pledge I made to her months ago is still current. If she wants to flip the lid on everything right now by confessing she's romantically involved with Isaac, I'll help her through this because I remember what Mr. Gregg taught me. It's okay to tiptoe on the wrong side of the law as long as you find your way back. Isabelle is tiptoeing. She's just failed to pivot back around. Tonight, might be the end of that.

Grayson's balk isn't as soundless as mine when Isabelle finally asks her question, "Do you think Isaac Holt is a criminal?"

Although stunned she's commencing our 'date' by bringing up Isaac, I'm man enough to answer her question without the slightest bit of scorn in my tone. "His file—"

"Don't tell me what his file says, tell me what *you* think," she interrupts, her voice a cross between hopeful and panicked.

"Don't do it, Brandon. Don't fall into the trap. She's *not* your friend."

I ignore Grayson's advice by replying, "I don't know what to think." Because in all honesty, I don't. Isaac's case is trickier than the men I've previously investigated. His empire doesn't dabble in drugs, the prostitute conglomerate, or underage sex trafficking rings. Other than having Henry Gottle, Sr.'s number on speed dial, he seems like a legitimate businessman.

Does that mean he's undeserving of the Bureau's scrutiny? No, it doesn't. My father presents himself as an upstanding moral citizen as well, and he's as conniving as they come. Isaac is shady. That alone deserves scrutiny.

But I won't pass that knowledge onto a woman who could

possibly be sharing his bed. "But I will say one thing, I've been part of this investigation for nearly a year, and I've not yet stumbled on one shred of information that corroborates Alex's presumptions of Isaac."

A confused crinkle pops between Isabelle's brows. "Do you think he's hiding something?"

"Are we still talking about Isaac, or have we switched to Alex?"

Grayson's warning growl to keep his brother out of this almost drowns out Isabelle's reply, "Both."

"Everyone is hiding something, Isabelle." I lock my eyes with hers before breathing out, "Even you."

Like all women stuck in a situation they never anticipated, she doesn't refute my highly accurate recount of events. I don't necessarily believe she's lying to me, but she is definitely hiding secrets behind the massive barrier she forever places between us.

Perhaps this will help her lower them.

"Speaking of secrets, that file you requested has arrived."

When her eyes snap to mine, I nudge my head to my leather satchel hanging on one of her dining table chairs. I've taken out anything that links Hugo to a rape I'm not yet convinced he committed, but it has the basic information Isabelle is seeking.

"Can I?"

When I lift my chin for the second time, she smacks an overzealous peck onto my cheek. It causes Grayson to release a sequence of moans I'd give anything never to hear again.

His goading doesn't last long. My mention of his brother the second time tonight shuts him up rather quickly. "You have to promise Alex will never find—"

"Alex will never know," Isabelle interrupts, her eyes the most honest they've ever been. "I promise, Brandon."

"Once this is done and dusted, you better tell me what's the go with the two of them."

I peer at my reflection in the mirror of Isabelle's dining room before dropping my chin, approving Grayson's request without words.

When he hums out a similar agreement, I rib Isabelle with my elbow. "Come on, I'm dying."

I've scrutinized every single word in the report she's about to read more than once, but I'm anxious to observe her response. Will she look at the report through the eyes of an agent or a civilian? How she responds will guide how Grayson and I will handle our joint investigation from here on out.

After brushing away a tear sitting high on her cheek a few minutes later, Isabelle says, "That's incredibly sad, but it doesn't warrant the shroud of secrecy."

"No, but this does." I hand her a heavily redacted court document. It wasn't like this in the file Melody gave me, but I can't unlock all my secrets in one go, or this will end even more disastrously than a skeptic like me could have predicted.

Isabelle's silence reveals she's aware of the name on the police report she is perusing, but she keeps her cards close to her chest.

I do my best to change that. "Roberto didn't do any time behind bars, even with being arrested at the scene and recording a blood-alcohol level three times over the legal limit. His name was never reported in any news or press articles. He would have had to give the DA something substantial to get a plea that lenient."

"Or someone," Isabelle mutters, her voice surprisingly firm for how wet her eyes are.

I'm about to ask her if she has any idea about who that could be, but the tapping of keyboard keys stops me. Grayson only ever punishes his keys when he's pissed at someone attempting to undermine his hacking work.

I twist to face the kitchen before pointing out the saucepan hidden beneath a plume of black smoke. "Hey, Izzy. Is that supposed to be smoking like that?"

Isabelle's eyes bulge out of her head. "Shit. The Mariana sauce."

When she races to the kitchen to save our dinner, I devote my attention to Grayson. "What's going on?"

His words come out jarringly, compliments to how hard he's hitting the keys on his keyboard. "Someone is attempting to piggyback my feed."

"Which feed?"

He swears, tells them to back the fuck up before he answers my question, "The one in your button."

"They know I'm wired?" Panic resonates in my tone. I'll be kicked out of the Bureau if they discover I went to a fellow agent's house wired to the hilt. I'm not worried about the loss of salary, I have enough money in my bank account to keep me living comfortably for two lifetimes, but I'm worried about how I will occupy my time. The Bureau is all I have. Excluding my mother, I have no contact with the rest of my family. I'm pining over a girl who's going to marry a billionaire for fuck's sake. I'll have *nothing* if I'm kicked out. I don't even see Grayson hanging around if I can't help him with his quest to find Katie. It sucks, but it's the truth. I'll have nothing. *I have nothing.*

I suck in a relieved breath when Grayson responds, "No. They haven't gotten that far in yet. Fuckers. They're seeking any electronic devices in the area."

"Do you think it's Alex's team?"

Grayson starts his reply with a grunt. "No. I got tabs on him. He's nowhere near Izzy's apartment."

"You've got tabs on your brother?" When Isabelle pivots around to face me, my voice too loud for her to brush off as a weirdo who talks to himself, I point to a well-known gossip magazine on her entryway table. "Royals these days. Can't even have a conversation with your grannie without someone listening in."

"Or go on a fucking date. This is Isaac. It has his murky fingerprints all over it," Grayson hisses on a growl.

I wait for Isabelle to shift her focus back to scrounging up the sauce not burned to the bottom of the pan before twisting away from her and lowering my head to the microphone in my shirt. "How do you know it's Isaac? His hacker never leaves a trace."

"Exactly. That's why I know it's him." Grayson waits a beat before disclosing, "The timestamp is also very telling. The instant the guy sitting at the front of Isabelle's apartment ends his call, my surveillance is infiltrated." Another handful of keystrokes sound down the line before Grayson says, "He's in."

"He's in?" I move away from the mirror I'm standing in front of before lowering my hand to cover the camera I rigged into my shirt this morning.

"Not your feed, dipshit. I forced him into the camera in the hallway. When you leave Izzy's apartment, be sure to give Isaac a real show."

"A show?" I slowly float toward Isabelle when she requests for me to join her at the dining table where she's laid out the meal she prepared for us. "What kind of show?" When Grayson makes noises not suitable for a fellow agent to do to another agent, I whisper, "I'm not doing *that*. You know my thoughts on *that*."

"Jesus, Brandon. Are you sure your dick end has ever been wet? I'm not asking you to sleep with the girl. Just give me the chance to back trace the data. If you do something invigorating enough to gain Isaac's attention, I guarantee he'll watch it. All the sadistic ones do. When he watches it, most likely on repeat, I'll have a chance to follow his feed back to the source. It could lead us to his real residence."

His suggestion has many valid points—regrettably. Isabelle is under Isaac's skin enough to have his security team monitoring her twenty-four seven, so who's to say how he'll respond if he thinks he has competition.

"Can I at least enjoy my meal before I'm sent to slaughter?"

Isabelle returns to the dining room and gestures for me to take a seat at the same time Grayson replies, "Of course, because from what I've heard through the grapevine, this could be your last meal."

His laughter doubles when I grumble under my breath, "Shut the fuck up."

BRANDON

"Shut the fuck up, Grayson!" My roar is so loud, I hear it twice when it bounces off the brickwork in the alleyway siding Isabelle's apartment. "There was nothing wrong with my kiss. Isabelle said so herself." It's also been a while, but I sure as fuck am not disclosing that to Grayson.

Grayson told me to do something drastic to force Isaac to respond. I racked my brain for the two hours of our 'date' striving to think of something profoundly moving. I thought a kiss was the ideal solution. It would have been if I didn't have Grayson in my ear, egging me on. Have you ever tried to kiss someone with a thirty-three-year-old man catcalling and wolf-whistling in your ear? I got stage fright. Kill me.

Luckily for me, Isabelle was cool about my sudden desire to lock lips. She even jested about how she would have dragged me into her apartment if she didn't have a three-date rule. Did I believe her? Not really. I may have if she hadn't mentioned chasing an unattainable man. If that wasn't a flashing alarm alerting me to just how deep Isaac has crawled under her skin, I don't know what will.

While jabbing my finger into the key of my BMW, I tell Grayson to shut the fuck up for the third time. My ego is already blown to shit, I don't need his laughter.

"I'm not laughing at you, dipshit. I am terrified about how fucking hard I am. That was almost as good as porn for a saint like me. I have precum seeping into my pants and shit—" His chair popping into place drowns out his words. It's quickly chased by his fingers tapping the keys of his keyboard. "It fucking worked."

I yank open the driver's side door of my car and slide into the driver's seat. "Isaac is watching the feed?"

"No." Grayson's one word shoots out of his mouth so fast, it replicates the crack of a whip. "He's in Izzy's apartment."

My jaw quivers with annoyance more than excitement. "You rigged Isabelle's apartment?"

"No," he fires back again, his voice extra loud.

"Then how the fuck do you know Isaac is in her apartment?"

He jabs at his keyboard another three times before a voice I've heard on surveillance many times the past eight-plus months filters through the device in my ear. "No more men in your apartment, Isabelle."

"Your kiss with Isabelle got him so riled up, he had to pay her a visit," Grayson mutters, his voice husky with humored excitement.

As I crank my neck to watch the main entrance of Isabelle's apartment building, I ask, "How did you get the audio?" I've only just asked my question when the answer smacks into me. "I left my jacket in her coat closet." When Isaac bursts through the rotating doors of Isabelle's apartment a few seconds later, my lips curl into a grin. "And I'm going to need to get it."

"Yesss," Grayson replies with a hiss. "Play the fucker at his own game."

My steps back to Isabelle's apartment are nowhere near as weighed down as the ones I used when leaving it. They're extra springy and have me reaching Isabelle's front door in a record-breaking forty-eight seconds. Yes, I was counting.

"Play it cool, BJ," Grayson suggests, throwing me off my game with his unusual nickname. Usually, punk, dipshit, and dickface are his go-to terms of endearment. He must be cautious my overzealous knock has me walking into a trap like I did the night I babysat Olivia after Tobias informed her that her brother had gone missing. She was as miserable as me, and just as drunk. We stumbled into bed—once—and I'm still paying for it. "Be the charmer you were most of the night. Be the opposite of the man she's craving. She isn't seeking a hookup right now. She needs a friend."

"I *am* her friend," I mutter back just as Isabelle cracks open her door.

I'm taken back when I take in her red cheeks, water-brimming eyes, and cracked lips. I thought euphoria would be pumping out of her, not fear. "I… umm… forgot to get my coat. But you look busy, so I'll come back later."

"Where the fuck are you going?" Grayson asks at the same time Isabelle assures, "Brandon, it's fine. I'm not busy."

When she ushers me into the foyer of her home before moving to the coat closet to gather my jacket, Grayson reminds me to survey the area. "Is anything out of place?"

I shift on my feet to face the table we dined at. The glasses have been moved—mainly, my wine glass that's minus the lipstick print Izzy's has.

"He mentioned something about the glasses. Any chance you can offer to wash those at home for her? One of them could possibly have a print on it."

After jerking up my chin, I head for Isabelle's dining table. I'm barely a foot out of the entryway when Isabelle grumbles something under her breath before she curls her arm around my waist and forcefully evicts me from her apartment. "I'm sorry, Brandon, but I have to do something really important." She bumps me with her hip to dislodge me from her doorway before jabbing her key into the lock and twisting it into place.

The confusion on my face triples when Grayson coughs out,

"Nine o'clock." When I glance at the side wall of the hallway, he laughs. "Not your nine o'clock, dipshit. Nine o'clock on her neck."

"Jesus." I breathe out when I catch sight of what Grayson is on about. Even with her hair pulled over her shoulders, a massive love bite is peeking out of Isabelle's dark strands. It looks recent like it just happened, which I can testify to since it wasn't there the two hours we dined together.

We ride the elevator to the foyer of her building in silence, my voice only finding itself when Isabelle makes a beeline for a taxi idling at the curb. "I can give you a lift if you want?"

She doesn't give my offer any thought. After waving her hand through the air, she shouts, "I'll see you tomorrow."

The cab's door slamming shut gobbles up my reply.

I wait for her taxi to merge into a sea of traffic before sprinting for my car. After snatching a parking ticket off the windscreen, I toss my jacket onto the passenger seat, crank the ignition, throw the gearshift into reverse, then back out of the alleyway at a speed too dangerous for the number of people still on the sidewalk. I swear Ravenshoe is worse than New York when it comes to its residents' sleeping patterns. It doesn't matter what time it is, the streets are always littered with cars and foot traffic.

"Slow down, punk. I've grown too fond of you the past eight years to scrape your insides off the pavement."

I grin before firming the slant of my foot on the gas pedal. I've got nothing to lose, so I also have no fear.

"Take a left on Tracer. There's a collision on Clarence causing traffic to back up." Even though Grayson can't see me, I nod. "Remind me never to get in a car with you." He chuckles when the back end of my BMW slides out in the slippery conditions. "How do you know where she's going?"

"Do you remember Joey saying his zipper scar was proof he had a heart?"

I hear Grayson's cheeks rise into a smile before he says, "Yeah. It was around the time he said love bites were proof he had a girl."

"That's right." I shake my head as a good memory hidden by a vault load of bad ones breaks through the haze in my head. "I thought I'd give his theory a whirl."

Grayson laughs. "Your girl wasn't a fan?"

"Not. At. All. I swear she mentioned castration at one stage." I stop talking as my smile sags. "I thought it was because she didn't like the idea of being owned."

"That *was* what she meant, Brandon."

"You don't know that," I fire back. "She—"

"Made a mistake… *once.* One. Time. You've given Isabelle, a girl you barely know, chance after chance after chance, but you can't give the woman you grew up with the same leeway. That's shit, Brandon, utter and absolute shit."

Still incapable of arguing the truth, I keep my mouth shut. I don't know if it appeases Grayson's anger or doubles it, but I lose the chance to find out when I catch up to Isabelle's cab at the front of Isaac's nightclub. She throws a wad of cash at the driver before peeling out of the back seat. She looks as angry as Melody did when I marked her skin with a line of hickeys from the shell of her ear to her right rib.

"You're going to need to follow her inside if you want to hear their conversation. Isaac's goons scan his premises multiple times a day for listening devices." Grayson's tone reveals he's more pissed than happy about my silence.

I find a parking space at the very back of the lot. Once I have the engine shut down and my game face on, I exit my car. I barely make it two steps away when my approach of the back exit of The Dungeon is stopped by a face I've seen hanging on a wall more than in person.

Special Agent Phillipa Russell props her hip onto the rear quarter panel of my car before draping back her knee-length coat to display the badge on her hip, wordlessly announcing she's on the job.

"Do you regularly conduct surveillance on fellow officers, Agent

McGee?" She overemphasis my surname to ensure I can't miss it. "Or just the pretty ones?"

I play it cool even with my eyelid dying to twitch out. "Surveillance? I'm off the clock. I heard this place makes good margaritas. Thought I'd test the authenticity of the claim."

"Margaritas? *Right.*" She drags her eyes down my frozen frame, taking in my designer shirt, brand name jeans, and boots that cost more than most agents make in a month. "I heard you were more a whiskey type of man."

"Depends on the occasion. Tonight isn't really a whiskey kind of night." I scrub my hand across my jaw, curious as to why Grayson is noticeably quiet. Usually, I can't shut him up, but he hasn't even whistled in a breath since Agent Russell joined our duo. "Is that all, Agent Russell? I'd like to enjoy the remainder of my night off before I'm back on the field."

"Just one final thing." She clicks her fingers at a second agent I didn't notice lingering in the shadows until now. He hands her a single sheet of paper before once again becoming one with the late hour. "How'd you manage to tamper with evidence before you joined the Bureau?"

What the fuck is she on about? "I've never tampered with evidence." I can say that with the utmost honesty. I've conducted private investigations and hacked into files I shouldn't have access to, but I'd never meddle with evidence.

"Oh. Then how did Crombie's prints end up on a candle that was never logged into evidence?"

When Agent Russell slides the sheet of paper across the boot of my car, my eyes drop to it. It's as she states. The candle Crombie's prints were found on isn't in the evidence log she photographed. There's no mention of anything flammable. Not even the hairspray found in the cab of Crombie's truck.

"Fire accelerant was sprayed on Melody's curtains—"

"I'm not disputing that," Agent Russell interrupts, her tone surprisingly calm for how snappy mine is. "But that doesn't mean Crombie was the man responsible for it."

"He was found guilty by a jury of his peers! He was served a twelve-year sentence for his crime."

She steps closer to me, engulfing me with her honeysuckle smell. For how strong it is, I'd say it's in both her shampoo and body wash. "On fabricated evidence. The candle was never submitted to forensics, Brandon. There's no record it was ever dusted for prints, and not a single member of the forensic team from that case recalls seeing it."

I want to argue with her, I want to tell her to get her facts straight before spurting lies, but I'm too stumped to speak. She's not giving off the vibes of a liar. She isn't sweating like I am, and the only person I can hear scratching their face is Grayson in the earpiece in my ear.

"Choose your friends wisely, Brandon, because more times than not, they're looking out for no one but themselves." After lowering her eyes to the printout I'm strangling with a death-grip, Agent Russell says, "You can keep that. I have extra copies."

I watch her walk to a black Navigator with my fists opening and closing and my jaw tight. Once she's joined inside by the agent hiding in the shadows, they exit the parking lot as quickly as I entered it.

I wait all of two seconds for the dust of their tires to settle before projecting the rage tearing through me onto the trunk of my BMW. I just got painted as a rogue agent, and the man responsible for it is sitting on the other end of the wire in my ear as silent as a church mouse.

The blood on my knuckles drips onto my jeans when I rip off the camera button from my shirt and hold it out in front of myself. "Speak. Now." The tightness of my jaw doubles when the noise of Grayson scrubbing his beard sounds down the line. "If you fucking lie to me, Grayson, I'll tell Alex everything. Every. Thing."

"It didn't go down how she's saying—"

"Then how did it go down?" When my question is met with silence, I growl out his name. "Did you falsify evidence?"

After a beat, Grayson murmurs a simple, "Yes."

"Grayson... fuck! Why would you do that? Why fuck with evidence in a case that's a slam dunk?"

His voice bellows down my eardrums when he shouts, "Because it wasn't a slam dunk case. If I didn't forge his prints, Crombie would have walked. He would have gotten away with attempted murder." When I balk, physically shunted by his admission, he uses my silence to his advantage. "Crombie wasn't in Melody's apartment because he had a fascination with her curtains. He was there to finish the job a member of his association failed to complete."

"A job?" I'm shocked I can talk. My mind is reeling as it struggles to slot in all the pieces of the puzzle.

Mercifully, Grayson loves a good puzzle. "The Greggs' accident wasn't an accident. They were targeted."

"By who?"

I hear him swallow. "That's what Tobias and I were endeavoring to find out when I broke protocol to speak to you." He exhales a big breath before he continues, "Do you recall your father saying Liam didn't brake for the stop sign?"

I lift my chin since words are above me right now.

"That's because someone severed his brake lines. There was a trail of brake fluid from the front gate of his property to the intersection. Even if he'd pushed down on the brakes, they wouldn't have responded."

"Melody asked you specifically if there were any links between Crombie and her parents' accident. You told her there wasn't." Nothing but unbridled anger sizzles in my tone. I'm beyond pissed. All of this should have been admitted years ago.

"I had to follow protocol. Their accident was way above my paygrade."

My roar projects over the music bellowing out of Isaac's nightclub. "So you lied? You lied to the two people who trusted you to be honest!"

The whooshing noise sounding down the line has me picturing him nodding. "Yes."

I almost crush the micro camera in my hand when I squeeze down on it with all my might. Instead, I growl my frustration into the street. I'm pissed—beyond fucking outraged. I trusted Grayson because I thought he was the only person being honest with Melody and me.

I know better now.

"I'm done. You'll have to find Katie without my help."

As my hand moves to my ear, Grayson recites his last plea. "Brandon, you need to think about this. This is bigger than you realize. This is about more than Liam stumbling onto something he shouldn't have. Cutting me off now won't help anyone. We're so fucking close to finding out the truth—" His words are cut off when I rip the earpiece from my ear, throw it to the ground along with the camera button, then stomp on them.

Once I'm confident they're destroyed beyond repair, I toss open the door of my BMW and slide into the driver's seat. As I reverse out of the dusty lot at the speed of lightning, I demand Siri to bring up my call history. I throw my gearshift into first gear before tapping the screen on the dashboard. An operator at the Federal Bureau of Investigation answers my call two rings later.

"Brandon James, Agent 443567. I need you to patch me through to Agent Russell."

"Phillipa Russell from the New York Division of Internal Affairs or her father, Phillip, Acting Director of the Bureau?" the operator queries, doubling the knot twisted in my stomach.

MELODY

"Ms. Gregg, it's a pleasure to meet you," introduces a pretty brunette with a kind smile and bright, glistening eyes. "My name is Phillipa Russell. I'm an agent at the Federal Bureau of Investigation. Thank you for taking the time to meet with me today." She gestures her hand to a seat across from her and a male agent wearing a similar suit as hers, he just has a striped tie curled around his neck. "I asked Agent Moses to sit with us during your interview since he's familiar with ASL."

Phillipa's head slants to the side when I say, "I can talk." Her pale cheeks bloom with heat when I add, "I can also hear you."

"Oh… ah… okay." She straightens her suit jacket before screwing up her face. "I must apologize. Our reports state you were born deaf."

"I was. I had cochlear implants done three years ago. They made me not deaf." I almost laugh at the daftness of my reply, but the seriousness of the situation stops me from doing that. "Can you tell me what this is about? Your email was quite blasé, and when I called the number at the bottom of your message, the gentleman on the other end wasn't overly obliging, either."

She smiles to settle my unease. "It's a habit of the job. The less they know, the less—"

"Likely they'll find themselves in trouble." When surprise crosses her pretty features, I mutter, "My dad use to say that all the time."

Her eyes twinkle even more when she smiles. "Mine still does. Along with many more annoying odes." When she gestures for me to sit, I do. "Would you like me to excuse Agent Moses, so we can talk girl to girl?"

I hide the gurgle of my stomach with a cough. Why would we need to talk girl to girl? Female agents usually reserve that courtesy for victims of... *Oh, God, does she know my secret?*

Incapable of speaking, I shake my head, acting brainless to her reasoning behind us needing privacy.

The tight knot twisted in my stomach loosens when Phillipa says, "Okay," before she flips open the chunky file in front of her. It isn't full of witness statements from the attendees of Joey's summer party. It's evidence from my family's home invasion. "I know you were very young when this incident happened, but I'm hoping the steps your father took after it has kept it fresh in your mind."

She speaks as if she knows about the drills my father ran Brandon and me through every weekend he wasn't deployed.

When she requests permission to show me some photographs, I nod. "These were taken shortly after the incident. I don't want you to look at the objects the forensic team was focused on. I want you to look deeper. Take in the background of each photo."

I lick my dry lips before nodding again. "These are from the basement?"

"Yes," she agrees, nodding. "How did you know that?"

I point to a bike with pink tassels in the background. "My dad put the tassels on the day before the home invasion. I loved them so much, I wouldn't let him put the bike into the back shed. After a long-winded compromise, we agreed my bike could sleep in the basement for the night." I stop when I choke on my last three words.

The memory is a happy one, but it reveals how much my father changed only a few short hours later.

"That's good, Melody. What about the other images? Can you spot anything familiar in them?"

I half-heartedly shrug. "I think that was the table in the foyer. I didn't give it much attention when I was a kid. Dad always threw his keys on it."

Phillipa points to a line of picture frames on the table I just referenced. "And the photos on the table? Do you recognize those?"

As my lips curl, I smile. "Yes." My smile greatens when I recall my dad shoving them into the drawers of the table every time my grandma came over. My mother said she was so obnoxious, she criticized any photograph that didn't include her.

My eyes lift from the images to Phillipa when she asks, "How old were you in those pictures?"

My nose screws up. "Around three or four? I think."

"And these?" She pushes across a handful of photographs to reveal one of the stairwells in the old brownstone my parents sold to fund my father's legal fight. They have similar pictures to the one of the entrance table, but they're ten times the size. "I don't know. Around the same age, I guess."

"Is this not you?" Phillipa asks, tapping on an image of a baby in the far corner of the picture.

I shake my head. "No. That was a cousin of mine. I can't recall his name…" I stop talking when shock rockets through me. When my grandma passed away years ago, I thought that was the end of my family legacy. I completely forgot about the boy in the portrait at the bottom of the stairwell. "Do you know who he is?"

My wish to be a cooperative witness flies out the window when Phillipa's eyes shift upward and to the right before she shakes her head. She's lying, which doubles my hostility. "What is this about? This incident occurred over two decades ago. The people responsible for it are either abolishing their sins with God or rotting in jail."

Air whizzes out of Phillipa's nose as she discloses, "All the men responsible for terrorizing you and your mother that night are all abolishing their sins with God."

What's she saying? Is she underhandly telling me the third assailant is also dead?

When I fail to read the answers to my questions on her face, I straight up ask them. "How did the final assailant die?"

"We were hoping you'd be able to tell us that."

"How could I possibly know what happened to him?" I choke on my spit when she slides a familiar photograph over to my side of the desk. It was the one Brandon and Grayson showed me the day my life was upended for the third time. It's a picture of my father with Henry Gottle, Sr. I know who Henry is better now than I did back then. My position in the DA's office ensures I'm aware of the number one Mafia figure in the United States. "As I told one of your agents years ago, I don't know why my father met with Henry that day."

"But you do acknowledge you know who Henry is?"

I don't fall for her I'm-your-friend tone this time around. "Of course I do. I'm an Assistant District Attorney for the State of New York. If I didn't know who Henry was, I'd need a new profession." After standing from my chair, I run my sweaty hands down the front of my skirt. "Is that all? I have cases to prepare for."

Phillipa dips her chin, silently acknowledging she understands my frustration, but she's not willing to let me slip away just yet. "One last thing. Can you confirm if you've seen this tattoo before?"

My heart beats out a funky tune when she slides a blown-up photograph to my side of the desk. It doesn't show the face of the person she wants me to identify, just a tattoo of a family emblem.

"That tattoo belongs to the man prosecuted with setting my dorm on fire seven years ago. The last I heard, he was serving his twelve-year sentence at Wallen's Ridge State Prison."

My brows furrow when Phillipa slips away the blown-up image to reveal the original photograph below. The tattoo doesn't belong to the man charged with setting my dorm ablaze. It belongs to a man lying lifeless in a ditch with a single bullet wound to the forehead. He looks oddly similar to the man my mother sat across from when she testified at his trial for home invasion, deprivation of liberty, and attempted rape. The only man my father left breathing when he and two of his friends forced him to become as violent as they were being to my mother, and the date hidden in the far bottom corner of the photograph reveals he was killed the day of my parents' accident.

When my wide and uneasy eyes lock with Phillipa's, she mutters, "Do you think you could spare me a few minutes now?"

If our home invasion didn't change my father from a loving, caring man to a maniac obsessed with protecting my mother and me, I'd dip my chin without pause for thought. But since that isn't the case, I shake my head instead. "I'll be in contact once I've spoken to my lawyer."

I spin on my heels and stalk to the door, halting halfway when Phillipa says, "I'm not here to prosecute you, Melody. I'm here to warn you—"

I whip around so quick, my hair slaps my face. "Warn me about what? That the man who terrorized my mother for over an hour might come back from the grave and haunt me? That *that*..." I jerk my chin to the photograph of him lying lifeless in the gutter, "... was a much kinder punishment than he deserved? What exactly are you trying to warn me about, Agent Russell?"

"I'm here to warn you that vigilante justice isn't an appropriate action for anyone to take."

The heaving of my heart is heard in my shouted words, "*Alleged* vigilante justice. You're assuming my father killed a man. You have no proof of that."

"When did I once mention this was about your father?" Her almost black hair falls into her eyes when she shakes her head ever so gently. "I'm more concerned about who else unearthed this connection."

My heart falters when she places down a witness statement from my parents' accident with a blown-up copy of a driver's license of the man driving the cattle truck that struck my parents. Even with his cheeks a more natural color, I'm confident it's the same man lying lifeless in the ditch.

"Milo Bobrov was killed two hours after your parents' accident—"

I cut her off and talk through the bile burning my throat. "How can that be? Why wasn't he still in police custody? He mowed down my parents, for crying out loud! How could they not have held him for longer than an hour?" I'm yelling, and it's unacceptable, but when my mind is spiraling, anger seems to be my go-to way to express myself. I'm fuming mad because I asked several times if there was any link between my parents' death and Crombie's arrest. I was forever told there wasn't. It seems as if I wasn't the only person lying all those years ago. So was Grayson—*and perhaps Brandon.*

My attitude takes a step back when Phillipa replies, "I'm here seeking the same set of answers you are, Melody, but no one appears willing to ask the hard-hitting questions."

Her determination is inspiring, but I'm still cautious. Why after all this time is she interested in my parents' case? The prosecution of a deceased defendant is extremely rare. I've not heard of a single case since I commenced studying law over seven years ago. Unless I want to bring a civil suit against Bobrov, which I have no intention of doing, Agent Russell's investigation makes no sense whatsoever. *Unless...*

"What division of the Bureau did you say you were in again?"

The friendly mask Phillipa has been wearing the past twenty minutes slips away as her lips tug into an uneasy grin. "I didn't, but for whatever it matters, I'm part of a special task force that has a direct association with the IA Department."

"Internal Affairs," I say in full, ensuring she knows I'm not as silly as she seems to believe. "So, you're not here about my parents' deaths. You're here to take down one of your own for an *alleged* act of vigilantism."

She looks pleased more than annoyed by my reply. It's a known trait of any female when they realize the person they're attempting to railroad is just as smart, if not smarter, than them.

I push the photographs she placed down in front of me back to her side of the desk. "So much for comradery between peers."

"Two hours isn't enough time to protest the law and carry out your own agenda," Phillipa shouts, her voice rising to a level even my implants find distasteful.

Although I could retaliate with just as much malice, I keep a cool, collective head. "But it was certainly enough time for the officers on the scene to rule my parents' death as an accident. But you're not here to get justice for them or me, are you? You want the person responsible for freeing the world of a rodent nobody wanted. Why am I not surprised? Justice only occurs for those willing to fight for it."

When I immaturely roll my eyes before spinning on my heels and heading for the door, the real reason for Agent Russell's request for an interview is exposed. "You uncovered the connection yourself, Melody. You recognized Bobrov and Crombie's identical tattoos, so who's to say Brandon didn't also make the same connection?"

"Leave Brandon out of this. He had *nothing* to do with any of this."

"*Allegedly*," Agent Russell fires back, her smirk back to its previous smug appearance. "It's my job to prove what he did or didn't do." My stomach rolls when she slaps down a picture of a man hanging in a jail cell. I recognize his face in an instant. It's the man who set my dorm on fire years ago. "Two men killed years apart, and they both have one connection. You." She raises her eyes to mine, "Or should I say, you and Brandon?"

Years of legal studying ensures she can't rattle me. "A prisoner in *your* custody died on *your* watch, Agent Russell. If anyone should be interrogated, that person should be you." The image of Crombie hanging lifelessly bombards me with horrid, sick memories of Joey hanging from the old oak tree at the McGee's ranch, but I keep a rational head. "There are no defensive wounds on the defendant's hands, neck, or face. The noose is made from material similar to the jumpsuits prisoners are transported in, and even with your zoom capabilities being proven mighty effective today, it's obvious he's in a prison cell. Not even drug addicts like peeing in a lidless toilet." After pointing out each of my objectives on Crombie's photograph, I push it back to Phillipa's side of the desk before taking a big breath.

In my eagerness to talk, my words aren't as clear as I want. "If you came here hoping I'd help you pin a murder on an innocent man, you underestimated me. Even if I were still deaf, I still wouldn't have been stupid enough to fall for your tricks."

With my head held high, and my determination at a place I never thought it would be, I exit the room.

BRANDON

$\mathcal{I}$ drag my hand down my tired face when Grayson says, "I told you this was way bigger than us. It's as deep as it goes." For the first time in almost a year, he's standing across from me instead of tattling in my ear like he usually does.

We're conducting our meeting in the shadows of a shady back alley, hiding out like we're one of the many criminals we've put away the past seven-plus years. If we get caught with the files we have, we could very well end up behind bars with those men. They're not just sealed, they are a matter of national security, and the proof I've been seeking the past almost seven years.

Mr. Gregg didn't end things the way my father implied because of something hurtful Melody said. He was taken down by an organization the Bureau has been chasing for years. Because the hub of this entity is based on foreign soil, rumors are the Bureau had been working alongside the CIA to infiltrate it. As I've said before, I'm not a fan of rumors, but the information Grayson has shared with me the past hour is pretty damning.

I grip the file in my hand a little harder while asking, "Why is the CIA acting as if Liam's death was an accident? Why not come clean and say he was taken out by an organization he was investigating?"

Grayson shrugs. "I don't know. I figure that's why Tobias did some investigating under the radar. There's some murky shit going on here, Brandon."

As I shift my eyes to the photograph of a man believed to be the third assailant in the Greggs' home invasion, I ask, "Did Tobias have any leads on who killed this man?"

Grayson's shrug isn't as convincing this time around.

"Do you think his murder was payback for the Greggs' 'accident'?" I nudge my head to a photograph of a deceased body slumped in the gutter in a small town bordering Saugerties. When Grayson lifts his chin, I grind out, "That's why Crombie broke into Melody's dorm. He wanted to reinitiate their game of tit-for-tat. The only thing I can't work out is why there was such a big gap between incidents."

"They unearthed something no one knew previously." When I peer at him in shocked silence, he adds, "No one knew Melody was deaf."

"What does that have to do with anything?"

Grayson looks at me as if I'm an idiot. "Melody identified Henry Gottle, Sr. in the photo we showed her at the dress boutique. She mentioned she'd met him a handful of times before their home invasion. What if the men who organized the hit believed Melody had heard something she shouldn't have? I don't know about you, but if I discovered the only surviving witness to a massive conspiracy I was endeavoring to hide was deaf, I wouldn't be overly worried about tying up loose ends."

He has a point, but I still don't like it. "Something about this feels off. Melody attended school for months before Crombie found her."

"She attended school as Melody Gregg. I scoured over three decades of records seeking a home invasion or murder charge under that name when this case first popped up on Tobias's radar. I didn't find a single case with that surname attached to it."

"They didn't make that shit up, Grayson. I held Melody when she woke up screaming and drenched in sweat. You can't fake that kind of fear. The pain in her eyes… fuck. It still kills me now."

Grayson steps closer to me, his eyes comforting. "I'm not saying the home invasion didn't happen. I'm saying it occurred under a different name. The name those men…" his eyes drop to the massive file he handed me nearly an hour ago, "… knew. Liam kept them off Wren and Melody's scent for years, but somehow the thread unraveled." He locks his eyes with mine. They're more determined now than nurturing. "That's the thread we're hunting, Brandon, and I have a feeling it's hiding somewhere in these files."

Since I agree with him, I get started on my investigation. "How were Crombie and Bobrov related?"

Grayson makes a *'pfft'* noise. "Third cousins or some shit like that." He flips over the report I'm holding until he arrives at an image that looks like it was taken at a family reunion—if every member was part of the cartel. They're all holding guns, and they're standing in front of a massive shipment of drugs. "Crombie is the kid in the diaper. Bobrov is this guy at the back." He taps to a dark-haired man in the middle of the back row. "He was the older brother of Kirill Bobrov, once-Russian operative. Details on his movements are shady at best. Up until earlier this week, his last known citing was over two years ago in Kazan."

"Where was he seen last week?"

He hands me a second photograph. "Boarding a cargo ship in Portugal."

"Was Katie with him?"

My stomach drops when he points to a blur of fabric in the far right-hand corner of the picture. The height and size of the person hints to the fact it's a woman, much less Kirill's possessive clutch around her waist, but with most of her face covered, I doubt facial recognition picked up a positive match.

"Are you sure it's her?"

I don't mean to raise mistrust, but Grayson doesn't see it like that. "I'm sure," he grinds out before snatching the photograph out of my hand and devoting his focus back to Melody's case. "We've identified most people in this picture, but there are a handful of stragglers. They're usually dead—"

"I'm beyond accepting assumptions right now, Grayson. I need to know every man in this photo."

He takes my sooty attitude in stride better than he did my mistrust. "All right. I'll forward you the ones I have and get my crew onto the ones I don't."

I dip my chin in gratitude before handing him back the file. "Who do you have watching Melody?"

Grayson pulls a face like I don't know what I'm talking about. I'm more than aware he has a crew on Melody because he updated me on Agent Russell's visit to Melody's office last week before my guy did. Although Crombie was found hanging in his holding cell hours after his arrest, we must remain cautious. His 'death' could spark an entirely new war if anyone in his crew believes his death wasn't suicide.

Incapable of standing the heat in the kitchen, Grayson sings like a nark. "I put Malachi on her. He's a good kid. He'll make sure she's safe." I'm not worried about him calling Malachi a kid. Anyone under the age of twenty-six is classed as a kid to him. He's an old soul.

While licking my dry lips, I dig a business card out of my pocket. "Have Malachi make contact with my guy. I don't want them spooking each other."

He looks physically ill when he takes in the name of the private investigator I hired to protect Melody since I can't. It's not really my place anymore, but even if it was, I can't have Agent Russell thinking we still have contact with one another. That will add more flames to her fire that I killed a man to keep Melody safe. I would have, but I'd rather not be prosecuted for a crime I didn't commit.

"You hired a PI, Brandon? What the fuck is wrong with you?"

I whack Grayson in the gut before leaving the safety of our

hidey-hole. "Who should I have reached out to, Grayson? The Bureau who has IA so far up my ass, I'm not going to shit for a year? Or the CIA who's hiding the murder of one of their own?"

Grayson twists his lips. "They flew Crombie to New York on a private jet. Even if you had the capabilities to hire your own plane, there's no way they could fudge his time of death to make out you were in the same state as him, much less the same holding area."

"Agent Russell isn't implying I killed him. She's insinuating that I organized his death." As I pivot around to face him, my jaw gains a tick. "Kind of like I 'supposedly' arranged his incarceration years ago." I air quote one word in my statement, beyond pissed. I understand Agent Russell's objective, I too would be looking at me if the shoe was on the other foot, but that doesn't mean I can't be frustrated as well.

Grayson pulls on the collar of his shirt, suddenly hot. "You have a point." He joins me at the rear of my car, his strides apprehensive. "What about the local detective you mentioned a few weeks back? Do you trust him?"

I make an *iffy* face. "I don't know him well enough to trust him. Besides, my trust is at an all-time low right now."

Grayson holds his hands up and steps back, hearing the scorn I didn't articulate. He's still in my shit book—very much so. If he hadn't stuck his neck out to help me secure the files he did, we still wouldn't be talking. That's how annoyed I am that he kept all of this from me. I may have dropped the ball a handful of times back in the day, but once I proved my worth, he should have been honest.

Grayson watches me load the final box into the trunk of my BMW before asking, "What now?"

The tick of my jaw is heard in my reply, "We do exactly what Tobias taught us to do. Heads down—"

"Asses up," Grayson fills in with a smile. "Then, when no one is looking, we conduct our own investigations on the sly."

I smile for the first time in weeks. "Exactly."

Even though I'm still angry at him, I return his man-hug when he ups the ante on our usual chin-lift farewell by wrapping his arms around my back, although I'm tempted to strangle him when he mutters in my ear, "Call your girl. Now is as good a time as any."

I slap his back a little firmer than I usually do. "She's not my girl anymore." Before he can dispute my comment, I add, "And I've got a massive web to unravel first. I don't want to give her half-assed facts. She deserves to know the truth."

Incapable of denying my highly accurate statement, Grayson remains quiet, only speaking when I slip into the driver's seat of my car. "Reach out if you need me."

"Same to you." I don't know if he heard my comment or not. He disappeared into the darkness long before my eyes strayed to the side mirror.

MELODY

"**Y**ou can call him, you know?"

I stop peering down at the two-word text Brandon sent me a week ago to stray my eyes to Julian. He's supposed to be making beef stir-fry for dinner. All he's doing is making a mess. This is one of those times I hate his I-cook-you-clean rules.

After dumping my cell phone onto the coffee table, I join him in my compact kitchen. "And say what? I'm sorry your association with me when we were kids has you being accused of murder twice? Or that I'm not the cheating scumbag you think I am?"

His orange-tinged blond brow pops up high on his face. "You could say both, although I wouldn't recommend those exact words."

I bump him with my hip, steal an almond from the packet he's sprinkling into the almost-cooked mix, then spin around to sign, "*Smart-ass.*"

The almond gets stuck halfway down my throat when Julian says, "I saw that." He whacks my butt with a grubby wooden spoon. "Now I'll add even more nuts to the mix." After lowering my bottom lip into a pout, I pivot back around to face him. "Nu-huh." He

320

silently *tsks* me. "This is what happens when you lie. Your stir-fry gets extra nutty."

Ignoring the flutter of my heart as it recalls the last time I ate a nut-riddled dish, I say, "I wasn't lying. You *are* a smart-ass."

Since he can't deny the truth, he remains quiet.

After a few minutes of watching him in my kitchen like it's as natural as breathing to him, I ask, "Do you think he knows?"

Julian's eyes lift from the stir-fry with way too many nuts. "That they changed the ruling on your parents' accident?" When I jerk up my chin, he adds, "I'd say so. His name was mentioned a few times in the new reports." He places down his wooden spoon, lowers the gas flame from high to low, then props his hip onto the counter next to mine. "Have you decided what you want to do yet? You're well within your rights to sue."

"Sue who, exactly? The man who falsified the documents is dead." He was the police chief of my hometown. He died during a routine traffic stop a few months after my parents' accident.

"You could sue the state."

I sigh. "Then I would have to prove they were purposely negligent. It isn't as clear-cut as it seems." My teeth grit when my tone comes out harsher than I intended. Usually, we have these conversations about the incident that saw me moving across the country. Julian believes I should sue Joey's estate. It isn't about money, Julian has plenty of that. It's about giving a voice to a victim even if the accused is dead. Sometimes I agree with him, but it's only on very rare occasions.

Even now, years later, I still can't wrap my head around what happened with Joey. He was the equivalent of a big brother to me. I loved him—I still do in a sadistic, twisted way—so it's a struggle to understand what caused a massive change in his personality. It wasn't drugs. That was the first thing the coroner tested for. His blood-alcohol level was elevated, but it wasn't high enough to excuse a drastic shift in his persona. It truly seems as if it wasn't him in the room with me that night, and that my mind just made it all up.

If only I could forget about the evidence I hid in my room years ago. It abundantly proves something happened that night. I just can't prove it was Joey who hurt me without exposing my secret. My lunch date with Mrs. McGee weeks ago revealed she's doing better than she was seven years ago, but I don't think she'll ever be strong enough to warp her views on her son all because I want a dead man prosecuted. It makes me ill just thinking about what we'd be put through to see those charges transpire. And for what? To have my name on the victim's side of another report? It's not worth the heartache it could cause, and neither is suing the state for the belief they may have known my parents' death wasn't an accident.

I swallow to relieve my dry throat before returning my eyes to Julian. I kind of zone out when my mind shifts to the past. "In all honesty, I'd rather everything just go back to the way it was before we found out their accident wasn't an accident. The man who killed my parents is dead. His crew is debunked, and although I have my doubts, perhaps Crombie did end things the way he did as he felt guilty. It isn't the first time a convict has taken matters into his own hands, and I'm sure it won't be the last."

Julian looks prepared to enter a debate, but the wariness on my face must stop him. It's been an exhaustive few weeks. "I'll support your decision no matter what, Mel." He returns to stirring the stir-fry before nudging his head to my cell phone. "But I still think you should reply to Brandon's text. I'm not a lawyer—"

"You just wish you were," I interrupt, smiling to show him there's no malice in my tone. Julian is in the wrong profession. He loves political debates, conspiracy theories, and he devours murder mystery books like his life couldn't exist without them. He just happens to be an audiologist because that's what his father and grandfather were. I really wish he'd step outside the realm occasionally. He'd be a great politician or perhaps even a law enforcement officer.

When he spots my smile, Julian bumps me with his hip, his grin as playful as mine. "He put a lot of effort into the reports he submitted even with the likelihood of them ever seeing the light of day being low. That deserves a response."

"It does," I agree, nodding. If it weren't for Brandon, my parents' death would still be classified as an accident. He fought to have their deaths legally acknowledged, knowing it was what I wanted without needing to ask. "But aren't you worried, Julian?"

A sprinkling of orange hair falls in front of his eyes when he slants his head to eye me dubiously. "About?"

"One text could turn into a dozen. A dozen could turn into a hundred. A hundred could—" I yelp when he whips my thigh with the tea towel he had thrown over his shoulder, but I continue with my tease. "… turn into a thousand. Then, before you know it, we'll be best friends again."

He whips me another two times while muttering, "I can handle best friends." My heart turns a gooey mess when he bands his arm around my back to tug me in close to his fit body. "These, however, they will always be mine." He nips at my lower lip before giving it a friendly tug. After soothing the sting of his bite with a quick swipe of his tongue, he lifts his eyes to mine. "Won't they, Mel?"

For the quickest second, hesitation stirs my gut. Mercifully, I shut it down before Julian knows of its existence. It's a pity I can't wipe my guilt just as quickly. I hinted that we'd be together for eternity only months ago, so what's caused my sudden change of heart?

I can only think of one thing.

Brandon.

Up until a few weeks ago, he wasn't part of the equation. Although a two-worded text saying 'thank you' shouldn't cause such a massive upheaval to my life, it kind of did. We were inseparable for almost fourteen years. That's a big chunk of my life to pretend never happened, so not only did his two-worded text twist my stomach, it produced a foreign sound from my heart as well.

BRANDON

I've only just combed through the first box Grayson collected for me weeks ago in the boardroom at HQ when Isabelle bounces into the room. We've seen each other in passing the past couple of weeks, but our contact has been sporadic. My thoughts have been too focused on my past to add fuck-ups of the present into the mix.

It took longer than I would have liked, but I got justice for Mr. and Mrs. Gregg. The person responsible for their death can't face charges, but Melody knows the truth, and that's all that matters.

During the process, I also loosened the noose around my neck. Not only did I discover Crombie spilled details on his crew for a reduced sentence, I found out he was wanted for the arson of a building in New Hampshire that killed an 'associate's' wife and children. The target on his back was so visible, even if his death wasn't ruled a suicide, there were two dozen suspects closer to Crombie than me.

IA is still riding my ass, but not even someone determined to get out of her father's shadow could deny the evidence I produced. There will still be an inquiry into the fingerprints logged into evidence for Crombie's earlier conviction. I don't see it doing much. He was an arsonist, there's no denying that, so I'm confident in a matter of weeks, Agent Russell's valuable time will be focused on more important cases. Thank fuck. It's been a long few weeks.

I stop scrubbing at my tired eyes when Isabelle asks, "Hey, it's nearly ten o'clock, and we have the weekend off, so what are you doing hiding out in here?"

I smirk when the enthusiasm on her face drains to her shoes when I reply, "I no longer have the weekend off."

She takes in box after box after box of files before flipping the lid on the ones closest to her. "What are all these files?"

"They're your Uncle Tobias's records Alex had shipped here."

I'm not lying. Alex signed the shipment order. Grayson merely suggested he do it. I'm not necessarily interested in the files Tobias had on Isaac, more the men Isaac associated with back in the day. Many of the faces in the Bobrov crew group photograph were noted in the background of the surveillance images Tobias had of Isaac. Most were the standard bottom dwellers all mafia cartels have, but one was more noteworthy. Col Petretti.

He was the once leader of an Italian association based not too far from here. It all but debunked a few years ago when several high-up members of his association were served consecutive sentences for money laundering, tax fraud, loan racketeering, extortion, and gambling. The only man left standing was Col. Although that makes him an ideal candidate to slot in beneath someone powerful like Isaac Holt or Henry Gottle, no factual evidence alludes to this. Even certain they're linked in some way, I've yet to unearth their connection.

A curious crinkle pops between Isabelle's brows when I move to a stack in the far corner of the room. "These are your uncle's files from when he worked undercover in the Petretti family." I point to the smaller pile she's standing next to. "And these are his records on the Gottle family."

Shock is the first thing to register on her face. It's quickly chased by protectiveness, which is surprising since there have been no reports of her and Isaac uploaded for the past four weeks. "Isaac Holt doesn't have any business connections with either the Petretti or Gottle family."

I take my time deliberating what to say next. My trust isn't just low anymore, it's basically non-existent. "We already know Isaac is acquainted with Henry Gottle from the surveillance photo you got of Delilah Winterbottom months ago, but I agree, there has been no known association between Col Petretti and Isaac that would warrant me investigating them." It's just my desperateness to prove that they are linked that has me burning the candle at both ends, but since that isn't something I can share with the woman who could possibly be sharing Isaac's bed, I shunt the blame for my strong work ethic onto an unsuspecting target. "I can't find any connection between them, but Alex is adamant I have to spend my weekend rifling through these documents until I unearth Isaac's dark secrets."

Isabelle's interests are too piqued to pick up how my pitch accelerated during part of my reply. Alex wants me to compile these files into easy-to-read dot-point documents, but I volunteered for the job. I got justice for Liam and Wren, but I won't believe I've upheld the pledge I made to Mr. Gregg when I was five until I unearth the reason they were targeted to begin with. That has me digging through records almost as old as me.

"Do you believe Isaac's secrets are held within these boxes?" Isabelle's voice is a cross between worried and hopeful.

I play it cool even though my stomach is twisted up in knots. My intuition is telling me I'm about to stumble onto something great, but I am as distrusting of it as I am anything right now. "Maybe ask me again next month?"

My heart thumps against my ribcage when Isabelle asks, "Where do you want me to start?"

Is she offering to help me sort through these files with the hope of unearthing Isaac's secrets? Or does she already know them and praying she can veer me away from the truth?

I guess there's only one way to find out.

"It's fine, Izzy. Go and enjoy your weekend off."

When she slings her coat over a spare chair, I hide my surprise at her eagerness to dig in by rolling up the sleeves of my dress shirt.

I don't have a chance in hell of holding back my smile when she grumbles, "You're paying for the pizza, though."

HAVE you ever stepped back and thought *wow, I really fucked that up?* The first time I thought that was the night Melody left me. The second was when I was stopped by Agent Russell in the parking lot of Isaac's nightclub. And the third is now.

I was trained to evaluate every emotion that crossed someone's face, but for the past seven years, I've been so caught up gauging people's motives, I never truly stopped to see the person behind my in-depth evaluation. Mr. Gregg taught me how to lower the number of casualties of my mistakes, but I was never shown how to handle other people's errors.

Izzy is swimming in waters way out of her depth, but that doesn't mean she's set to drown. She probably has a better chance of surviving the treacherous waters than I do because she can assess situations without the emotional baggage I carry into every assessment.

Not once the past six hours has she denied Isaac has an association with Henry Gottle, Sr. She merely presented valid points on how their connection can be explained, such as why Isaac was photographed meeting with Henry's son, Henry, Jr., weeks ago.

Henry's ex-wife, Delilah Winterbottom, commenced working at Destiny Records, the record label owned by Isaac's business associate, Cormack McGregor, a month before Henry filed for divorce. Izzy believes Isaac did Henry the favor of getting Delilah out of his hair with the hope Henry would organize for his fighter, Jacob, to fight the current heavy-weight champion for this region,

Curtis Parker. Henry, Jr. is a fight promoter. He could have contacts Isaac needs.

Since Isabelle's conviction on the evidence was more plausible than fraudulent, I offer to write up a report on her findings and issue them to Alex before straying my eyes to the cause of my broken sleep the past month. "That's one mystery solved. Now, onto the much bigger one."

When Isabelle follows the direction of my gaze to the massive stack of Petretti files I'm itching to comb through, her eyes bulge when they float past the face of her watch. "Holy crap, it's close to two in the morning."

"I'm so sorry, Izzy. I didn't know it was that late. I hope I'm not keeping you from anything." My jaw tightens when I realize I'm once again judging her as I swore only minutes ago not to do.

She thankfully misses the snarky pitch of my tone. "Watching reruns of *Sex and the City* or unearthing the secrets of an enigma, I'll take what's behind curtain B, please, Roger."

I watch her in shocked awe when she laughs so hard, she snorts. She's embroiled in a huge mess, but she can still find the time to laugh. I could learn a thing or two from her. I've been so moody lately, I'm one grumpy gripe away from being mistaken for Alex.

When Isabelle catches my admired glance, she tugs up the sleeves of her shirt like she's suddenly overwhelmed with heat. "What?"

I could lie to her—again—but it's time to try a new approach. "You have a beautiful laugh, Izzy."

Heat treks across her cheeks as she whispers her thanks. Once the blemish on her face matches mine, she gathers a bunch of files from one of the boxes Grayson slipped between the less conspicuous ones and hands half of them to me.

"Holy fuck. I think I found a connection." I swallow my loud voice when my glance across the table has me stumbling onto a sleeping Isabelle. She was doing the funky head-bob thing everyone does when they commence falling asleep the past thirty minutes, but now her head has fully come to rest on the file she was highlighting.

While yanking my cell phone out of the pocket of my trousers, I make my way to Isabelle's side of the table. My ass is dead from sitting for almost over sixteen hours straight, and my legs have me walking like a robot since my knees refuse to bend, but I make it to her side of the table relatively unscathed.

I've just draped my jacket over her shoulders when Grayson answers my call. It's a little slow for him, but I give him some leeway considering it's barely five in the morning, and he's about to go undercover. He needs as much sleep as he can get. It's a rarity when you're undercover.

"Isaac was photographed entering an underground fighting circuit organized by Col Petretti," I confess, eager to get our conversation underway so he can go back to sleep. "In Col's circuit, all the fighters had owners... all *except* Isaac. Tobias cited in his files many times that Col refused for anyone to participate if they didn't have an owner. What if he allowed an exception that day because Isaac was his fighter?"

Grayson either yawns or makes an unsure murmur. "If that were the case, why weren't they photographed together more than once? Col is worse than Kirill. He's a gloater."

"True." Even though I only speak one word, nothing but annoyance is heard in my tone. "But I still think I'm onto something. In the group photo, CJ Petretti, Col's eldest son, is in the back right-hand corner of the image."

"Seriously?"

"Dead fucking serious."

I hear the ruffling of bedsheets before the tapping of feet stomping on wooden floorboards bellows down the line. I've never been to the underground hub Grayson runs in the basement of his family's B&B, but I've often wondered what it looks like. He has an entire setup down there, has since he stumbled onto Katie's file buried in a pile so deep, no one would have touched her case in years, if ever.

I twist away from Isabelle when Grayson asks, "Which guy?"

"See the kid in the diaper?"

"Crombie?" Grayson growls out, unimpressed at the snark in my tone.

"Yep. Now look two places up."

I picture Grayson's fists balling when the cracking of knuckles sounds down the line. "The kid would be four or five. There's no way facial recognition would have thrown back a match for that."

"Who said I used facial recognition?" When he growls, I talk faster. "Tobias was undercover in the Petretti crew two decades ago. He had many photos of their children." I place my phone on speaker before activating the camera app. After taking a photograph of a polaroid I found an hour ago, I send it via a secure email to Grayson.

I don't need to tell him to check his email. I hear the familiar ting before he curses. "The resemblance is uncanny. Still don't know why the fuck you're waking me up before the sparrows, though."

"It's a part of the web. Isaac, Henry, *and* Col. We need to add Col into the equation. That's probably where we went wrong. We're not looking at all the players. We're trying to sway the stack by knocking out the bottom prongs with the hope it'll have the hierarchies falling, but what if the answers we are seeking are from someone not in the stack?"

He scrubs at his jaw, a telltale sign he isn't one-hundred percent on board with my plan. "We could be wasting resources."

"Or..." I pause in a manner Joey would be proud of. "We just found the loose thread. You've had so much hassle tracking Kirill because he never leaves a stone unturned. This photo proves the Petrettis and the Bobrovs knew each other. That means Kirill forgot about Col." I choke out a laugh. "He's not the most stable right now.

A good push could have him crumbling. Are you really willing to bypass that for an hour or two of your time?"

Forever willing to push the boundaries when it comes to Katie's case, Grayson discloses, "I'll send one of my guys on the next available flight."

SOMEWHERE BETWEEN HIGHLIGHTING payments Col made to associations not in the United States over two decades ago to CJ Petretti's current whereabouts, I nodded off. Don't ask me exactly how long I've been sleeping, or why my cheek is more bruised than my ass as I won't be able to give you an honest answer. The thump in my head reveals I could do with another six or so hours of sleep, but the snatch of a file from beneath my cheek steals the chance.

As I rub the sleep from my eyes, Isabelle asks, "How many years ago was Col Petretti's son admitted to the hospital?" Her rumpled clothes expose she woke not long before me, and we won't mention the red ink mark on her cheek, or you'll be looking at her as if she's homeless like I am.

When she peers at me with wide, please-answer-me eyes, I mumble, "Umm, around six, seven years ago." I'm a little lost to where she's going with this. CJ's admittance could signify the commencement of him getting his life on the straight and narrow, but it has no link with Isaac, does it?

With CJ's hospital record in her hand, Isabelle moves for the stack of bank records she was working on before she dozed off. Her highlights correspond with the case we're meant to be investigating, not the one I'm hosting under the radar.

"Look." She thrusts the documents my way. "Isaac's hefty Monday morning cash deposits during his first two years at college ceased the weekend Col's son was admitted to the hospital. CJ's medical report indicates he was extensively covered in bruises, and he sustained multiple broken bones and fractures. Isaac was a fighter in the underground fight ring, just like his fighter, Jacob, is now. I'd put money on it that Isaac and CJ fought that weekend—"

My eyes lift from CJ's hospital records when Isabelle suddenly stops talking. I discover the reason for her gasping response when I spot Alex standing just inside the conference room door. *Has he been here the entire time? Or did I miss something in my half-asleep state?*

"How do you know Isaac was a fighter?" Alex asks Isabelle, stepping deeper into the room.

"Umm… I'm just assuming." Her chest rises and falls in rhythm to mine as she stammers out additional details. "It doesn't seem like an industry you'd get into unless you had some prior knowledge about it."

I watch Alex with unscrupulous eyes when he says, "Your investigative skills are starting to flourish, Isabelle. I'm very pleased with your dedication of late." He never gives a compliment, not even when it's earned, so there's something more going on here than he's exposing. I guarantee it.

I take a mental note to remind Grayson of our agreement to keep things between us when Alex discloses, "We recently discovered Isaac was indeed a fighter in an underground fighting ring during his years at college. That fighting ring's organizer was Col Petretti."

"Ah, hold on," I interrupt, more than happy to reveal to Alex that he's working on half-facts instead of full truths. "CJ's injuries weren't from a fight. That weekend he was involved in a car accident with his sister, Ophelia."

"What?" Isabelle blubbers out, her tone high.

I pass her the documents she handed me only minutes ago. "CJ and his younger sister, Ophelia, were involved in a fatal car accident six years ago."

Her hands shake as she speed-reads the hospital record that reveals CJ's injuries were extensive, but somewhat favorable compared to what happened to his sister. She didn't survive the carnage.

"Was anyone else in the car with them?" When Isabelle's eyes stray to mine, seeking an answer for her question in my eyes, I shake my head. "Did Ophelia survive the accident?"

She appears a little unstable on her feet when I once again shake my head. "Did you know Ophelia?" She's a year or two older than Isabelle, but that doesn't mean they didn't meet. They were both mafia princesses, so perhaps they met in passing.

"No. It's just incredibly sad, that's all." Isabelle scrubs her hand across her cheek on the exact area marked with red ink before nudging her head to the bathroom. "I'm going to go wash up."

Alex waits for her to disappear from view before shifting on his feet to face me. "Continue working that angle. I don't think it's a coincidence that Isaac's bank deposits ceased the exact week CJ was in an accident." When I lift my chin, he pivots on his heels and stalks away. He's halfway out the door before he mutters, "And the next time you update Grayson on matters pertaining to *my* case before me, I'll expect to see your resignation on my desk shortly after."

BRANDON

With Alex leaving the office not long after Isabelle, I grab my coat off the rack in the corner of the buzzing office before making my way outside. Usually, I'd slip an earpiece into my ear to keep Grayson updated on my whereabouts, but with my mistrust still paramount, I go without surveillance this time around.

Besides, an off-duty agent doesn't need surveillance when he's grabbing a bite to eat at a well-known Italian restaurant—even one named Petretti's.

AN ABUNDANCE of garlic and pureed potatoes filter into my nose when I walk through the single glass door of Petretti's. To someone outside of law enforcement, it appears to be a quintessential Italian family restaurant. It's only the armed men in each corner of the space, watching instead of eating, that gives away it's a shell for an Italian cartel. Many mafia operations have legitimate businesses. It makes it harder for the authorities to prove their wealth wasn't amassed illegally and gives them outlets to launder money and move merchandize without raising suspicion.

"Good morning, sir. A table for one?" The restaurant hostess's grin doubles when she drags her eyes down my body, seemingly oblivious to the fact I've been wearing the same trousers for two days now. I switched out my suit jacket for a more casual one and had a deodorant bath during my commute, but I'm reasonably sure not even the fragrant smelling air can hide the fact I'm in desperate need of a shower. Not that the hostess seems to mind. If we were in a cartoon, she'd have love hearts springing out of her eyes. "It's quiet. I could join you for a meal if you'd like?"

Her overzealous friendliness takes a step back when I flash her my credentials. "Agent Brandon James, I'm here to speak to Col."

"Col?" she queries, acting daft.

"Petretti." I point to the proprietor sign above the door. "Owner of this restaurant."

"Oh, Col." She overemphasizes his name with a nasally pitch that has my eardrums cringing. "He's not here."

Too tired to deal with her shit, I fan my jacket to display the gun on my hip before asking, "Do you know where I can find him?"

She looks a cross between wanting to jump my bones and gouge out my eyes while answering, "You should probably ask him." She jerks her head to the brute towering over me like I'm unaware he crept to my side of the room the instant Col's name left my mouth.

"Is he Col's keeper?"

"No," the stranger answers on her behalf. "I'm his exterminator."

When I turn around to face him, my throat works hard to swallow. He's a huge son of a bitch. "Oh. Okay. Good."

Since he won't get me any closer to Col than the bimbo in front of me, I daze him with a three-hit combination to his carotid artery. It's an old street fighting regime Mr. Gregg taught me when I didn't want to explain cracked and bloody knuckles to my father. Ninety percent of the time, it knocks them out. The other ten percent stuns them long enough for me to escape.

Hypothetically, this incident resides in the ninety-percent column, but since he isn't the only person I need to take down, his slump to the floor is quickly chased by me removing his gun from the waistband of his pants and pointing it and my gun at two of the three remaining security details. I subdue the third man by keeping my expression neutral and without panic. If he believes I have the skills to kill two of his associates before his bullet makes it halfway across the room, I'll come out of this alive. Considering the fact he didn't immediately fire at me, I have faith in my plan.

Our demented square standoff lasts for approximately thirty seconds before a deep voice at the side advises the men to stand down. Although his tone is enriched with the Italian heritage I'm seeking, it's not gruff enough to belong to Col. It's younger and more Americanized.

I discover why when I shift my eyes in the direction the voice came from. Dimitri Petretti, middle child of Col Petretti, is standing in the doorway of the kitchen. He has a tomato paste-stained napkin in his hand. Even with it only being an hour away from the lunch rush, the industrial-size kitchen is barren of any food bar a half-eaten serve of Malloreddus. Clearly, I'm not the only one who wakes early. Dimitri is eating lunch at a time most mobsters are waking for breakfast.

When the goons ignore Dimitri's English demand to leave, the wrath for their ignorance is recited in Italian. I'm not overly skilled in other languages, but I'm reasonably sure Dimitri's warning this time around came with a death sentence, because not only do the three men immediately lower their guns, they also assist the still-passed-out man off the floor before dragging him to the parking lot at the back of the restaurant.

Under Dimitri's watchful eyes, I remove the magazine from my borrowed gun, dump the ammo onto the floor, clean the barrel and the chamber with my shirt to remove my fingerprints, then place the dismantled weapon onto the hostess's podium.

Dimitri peers down at the gun, looks up at the frozen-in-fear blonde, then nudges his head to the parking lot his goons just raced through. "Go."

He doesn't need to tell her twice. She's out the door faster than a vulture on a dead carcass, and I'm crossing the room even faster than that.

Once were alone, Dimitri shifts his bright blue eyes to me. "You're an idiot showing up like this unannounced. You could have gotten yourself killed."

"By whom?" I ask Dimitri, following him into the kitchen. "By you? Or the man you're sheltering after sending every one of your siblings to their deaths?"

Growling, he shovels a generous serving of the Malloreddus on the stovetop into a bowl before gesturing for me to sit across from him. "I don't protect my father. You're well aware of that."

It kills me to do, but I dip my chin. Dimitri was turned by Tobias years ago. Don't misconstrue. He's still a gangster in every meaning of the word, he just works against his father instead of the authorities. I don't see that being the case once he takes over his father's reign, but for now, it works in the Bureau's favor.

"Have you been back long?" Dimitri was transferred to the international side of his father's operation a little over seven months ago. Although confident it was a short-term exchange, no one really knew if he'd ever return stateside again.

He places a bowl of tomatoey goodness in front of me. "I flew in early last month. The Bureau is unaware of my return." He slants his head to the side before viewing me through the eyes of a cold-blooded murderer. "I'd like to keep it that way."

Do you recall me telling you how it's okay to tiptoe on the wrong side of the law as long as you always find your way back? Today is one of those incidences. Mutual respect is a rare thing for an agent to have with a known mafia entity, but when the relationship is for the greater good, I'm not opposed to it.

"Your secret is safe with me, although I have a few questions I'd like to ask." Dimitri jerks up his chin before making his way to a stack of drawers at the side of the kitchen. His hand freezes halfway into a cutlery drawer when I ask, "Were you aware CJ was participating in your father's underground fighting circuit?"

He shoves the fork into my meal with aggression before replying, "I had a feeling a few months before I discovered it the hard way. CJ was a good fighter. He was also willing to do anything to get into our father's good graces, so I shouldn't have been surprised."

I don't point out the fact he always refers to CJ in past tense. He's done it for longer than I've known him even with CJ's disappearance years ago never being solved.

"Were you aware Isaac Holt fought under your father?"

I blow on a chunk of pasta to hide the crinkle in my top lip when he replies, "Who?" Dimitri is a dreadful liar. For a man set to become one of the most feared members of the Italian cartel, he needs to get less scrupulous eyes.

"Isaac Holt." I spoon a forkful of food into my mouth before digging out the photograph I stole from Isaac's file from my pocket. "This was obtained at an event your father organized."

Dimitri doesn't even glance at the evidence I'm presenting. "Isaac didn't fight for my father." He's still telling the truth—unfortunately. "Col wanted him to, but Isaac wasn't budging. We put steps in place to make it happen."

"We?" I almost choke on my food since I was so eager to ask the question I asked before swallowing.

Dimitri pours me a glass of water. I doubt he'd care if I died, but he'd rather not have the corpse of an FBI agent in his kitchen.

Once I've swallowed down half a glass, Dimitri expands on his confession. "We, as in Ophelia and me."

I put down my fork, too stunned to eat. "Your sister helped you, how *exactly*?" I need him to spell out the facts for me as I'm fucking lost.

Dimitri wipes at his lips with his stained napkin before placing his dirty bowl into the sink. "Our father wanted Ophelia to coerce Isaac into fighting for him—"

"So she dated him to deceive him?"

I almost feel sorry for Isaac, but Dimitri saves me from the farce. "No. Ophelia was never with him for that. She truly loved him." When he goes quiet, I wave my hand through the air, encouraging him to continue. He gives me his best you-make-me-sick face before continuing, "Ophelia wanted a way out—"

"Of?"

He glares at me, silently warning if I interrupt him one more time, our talk will be over. When I grumble out a half-hearted apology, he says, "She wanted out of the family. If you think my father was cruel to his sons, you should have seen how he treated his daughters. Monster is too kind of a word." The mood in the room drops dramatically fast. "We knew how desperate Col was to have Isaac fight under him. We were also aware of how good of a fighter Isaac was, so we plotted for them to meet, knowing Col would use Ophelia as a bargaining chip." He shakes his head as the tick in his jaw becomes noticeable. "We had no clue CJ was fighting for our father that night until it was too late."

You have no idea how hard it is for me to keep my surprise that Isabelle's assumption about Isaac and CJ fighting was correct on the down-low.

"They fought. CJ lost, and Ophelia went into a blackened rage." He snatches up my barely touched meal and throws it into the sink, chipping the dishware. "That was the night of their accident."

"Ophelia and CJ's?"

Dimitri lifts his chin. "CJ spent weeks in the hospital before he vanished, Ophelia was buried with only one member of her family in attendance..." his eyes reveal it was him, "... and I never told a soul about the ruse we attempted to pull. I'll take it to the grave." The sneer on his face reveals I will be taken to my grave if I share his secret.

He has no reason to fret. I'm sure he's already being bombarded with guilt over CJ being beaten so badly, not to mention his sister dying in a twisted wreck only hours later. I don't need to add to his grief. A shudder rolls down my spine just thinking about what CJ experienced that night. Liam and Wren's bodies had been removed from the wreckage before I arrived, and the scene still haunts me, so I can only imagine how much it still affects Melody to this day.

The letter I wrote last week but never sent feels less heavy in my pocket when Dimitri says, "What does this have to do with anything? I get your after Isaac, but the fight circuit you're talking about has been running for decades. The feds are well aware of its existence. They're not disbanding it for a reason."

"For intel," we say at the same time.

Dimitri nods. "So why are you bringing up old ghosts?"

It could be stupid of me to do, but his honesty today deserves some kind of acknowledgment, doesn't it?

"I'm seeking connections between Col, Isaac, Henry, and Kirill Bobrov."

He's quick to hide it, but I spotted the quickest flare of recognition dawn through his eyes when I said my last name. "Vladimir will be disappointed he didn't make the cut."

"He's still there," I reply, just not in a manner I wish to share. Keeping Isabelle's heritage hidden is as much on my shoulders as it is hers. "Have you heard of Kirill before?"

Dimitri hesitates for as long as I did when contemplating whether I should tell him the truth or not before saying, "It's been a while, but his name rings a bell. What's his kink?"

He classes underworld trades as kinks.

My shoulder touches my ear when I shrug. "Your guess would be as good as mine. We have an inkling perhaps he's in the sex trafficking trade, but we're only sitting on that theory because of one reason."

I stare at him like he's a mind reader when he says, "Katie Bryne?" When I lift my chin, stunned into silence, he curses under his breath. "I knew I had heard the name before."

When he gestures for me to join him in an office at the back of the kitchen, I pretend my tummy isn't grumbling. Excluding the two forkfuls I shoved in before Dimitri removed my meal, the only meal I have had the past two days was the pizza Isabelle and I shared last night.

Just before I enter the room, Dimitri fans his hand across my chest before arching his brow. Air whizzes out of my nose when I see the mistrust in his eyes. He reminds me so much of Grayson when he wolf-whistles about me raising my shirt in the air and spinning around to show him I'm not wired, then he completely fucks my outfit by removing every button from my shirt and coat with the quickest slice of a knife.

"Learned my lesson the hard way," he grumbles under his breath while dumping the buttons into a half-empty glass of whiskey on his desk. Once he takes a seat behind his big desk, he gestures for me to sit. "If word of this gets out to anyone outside of these walls, my guests will dine on freshly minced veal this evening." Veal is his way of calling me a contemptible bastard.

When I seal our agreement with a head bob, he pulls out a leather-bound document from a safe bolted to the floor under his desk. The beeps of the safe's electronic lock reveal his code is an eight-digit sequence, but Grayson and I have tried numerous times to unlock it remotely. We've yet to be successful.

Considering the thickness of the document, it should take Dimitri longer to find the page he's seeking. Since it happens remarkably quick, I'm confident in saying he has perused this page many times the past few years.

After pushing across a handful of legitimate business documents, he places the handwritten ledger down in front of me. "Katie Bryne..." he murmurs, dragging his index finger across her name in the ledger, "... was sold to K Bobrov for three hundred and eighty-five thousand dollars."

The evidence he's handing me is invaluable, but I'm a little lost. "The date shows her sale was a little under five years ago. Katie was abducted nine years ago."

Dimitri slaps the ledger shut before placing it back into the safe.

Once it's safely locked away, he slouches low in his chair before making a tee-pee with his fingers. He's willing to give me anything if it will help take down his father, but he doesn't want to get snared by the same lure.

"Tobias's arrangement is still in effect, Dimitri. You're immune from prosecution. Within reason, of course."

Leaning forward, he balances his elbows on his desk. "It's the men picking the reason that I'm wary of." He deliberates for a few more seconds before saying, "Hypothetically speaking, each sanction runs their operations differently. Some prefer underage girls, others prefer more mature ones. Then there are ones who aren't specifically looking for a whore. They want a wife, someone to raise children with, but they don't have the time to seek her in a crowd of millions, so they look to someone who can give them what they're seeking without additional training."

"Training?"

Dimitri licks his dry lips. "On being the ideal wife. They're taught how to cook, clean, raise children, and anything else their procurer wants of them. Some take months to learn their role. Others take years." His eyes drop to his safe. "Others never learn."

I don't know why, but I have a feeling his last comment wasn't referring to Katie. If I trusted my gut like I once did, I'd ask him about it, but since I don't, I thank him for his information by standing from my chair and giving him a tidbit of advice to even our exchange. "IRS is planning to raid this restaurant on the eighteenth. I suggest you do some in-house cleaning before then."

Not speaking another word, I exit Dimitri's office aware I broke a code but desperate enough for the truth not to care.

BRANDON

"*D*o the dates match?"

The thud of my feet through heavy foot traffic doesn't drown out Grayson's murmur of agreement. Dimitri's disclosure Saturday morning was more helpful to Grayson's personal campaign than my own, but one thread binds us all together, so any discoveries benefit us all.

Three days after Katie's sale, Tobias's team raided a Russian-strong sanction. Their operation was oddly similar to the one Dimitri mentioned. They imprisoned girls like the Sicilian operation we endeavored to dismantle when Tobias was killed, but they didn't rape and torture their captives. The more pure they were, the higher their selling price.

Don't get me wrong, the women who refused to follow orders at the drop of a hat were beaten into submission, and a handful were killed, but the head of that operation soon realized his virginal mail-order brides fetched double the price of his standard offerings. It meant the age of the girls taken got younger and younger as the years went on. They needed them to be pure in every sense of the word and young enough to be brainwashed into believing life as they knew it was over, which meant they typically sourced girls in the ten-to- thirteen-year age bracket.

Katie was a year, almost two older because she wasn't procured in the normal way. She was picked up by a rival associate before being subsequently sold to the Bobrovs. From my understanding, that was the first time the Bobrovs had paid for someone. They usually kidnapped them. I don't know if her uncommon purchase was the reason Kirill took an instant liking to her, but it's not often you can find sense in the madness of the underworld.

With Grayson's silence weighing heavily on my shoulders, I issue a plea I haven't given him in a very long time. "We'll find her, Grayson. It just takes time."

"Time I don't fucking have." He breathes heavily before saying, "I've got to go, BJ. I'll be in touch."

Not giving me the chance to reply, he disconnects our call. That's so unlike him. He usually hackles me about calling Melody, so for him to forget, he must have a lot on his mind.

Or perhaps he's sick of reminding you how much of a fuckhead you are?

Ignoring the highly-accurate voice in my head, I enter Harlow's bakery to grab a morning pick-me-up. Between Alex's demanding work ethic and my private investigations, I'm lucky to get three to four hours of sleep a night. I'm zonked.

My eyes float up from the ground when my arrival in the almost dead-quiet bakery is greeted by a friendly voice. "Oh, good, you've arrived. I was getting worried I'd need to make them fresh again."

I greet Harlow, the owner of Harlow's Scrumptious Bakery with a smile before joining her near the coffee machine. "Make what again?"

"The coffees." She cocks a brow before waving her hand over a dozen coffees in easy-to-carry cupholders. "Izzy usually picks them up by now, but I've not heard from her yet." She raises her begging eyes to mine. "You work with her, right? Could you take them for me? I really don't want them to go to waste. I can throw a handful of extra cookies in for you. Peanut butter and choc chip, right?" She takes a quick breather while moving to the section of the bakery where the cookies are stored. After stuffing half a dozen into a plain white paper bag, she stacks them on top of the coffees before handing them to me. "I really appreciate you doing this for me," she murmurs like I had a choice. "I don't want Izzy getting in trouble because her brains were banged out on the headboard if you know what I mean."

When she waggles her brows, the truth smacks into me. Izzy didn't spend her weekend knee-deep in old case files like me. She was being entertained by a man, and if the knot in my stomach is anything to go by, I know exactly which one.

Harlow stops busying herself with the coffee machine when I call her name. "If you see Izzy this morning, can you make out this was my idea?" When suspicion crosses her features, I quickly gabble out, "She got in the shit with the boss for a bad write-up she handed in on my behalf. I need to kiss ass to make it up to her."

"There are better ways to get back in someone's good graces than lying, Brandon," Harlow retorts, her tone low.

"I know." For the first time in years, my ability to lie on the spot shines brightly. "I'm just unsure what else I can do." When the sternness in her eyes lessens, I mutter, "I'm up for any pointers you're willing to give."

Her facial expression switches from wary to friendly in a nanosecond when she takes pity on my stupidly boyish face. "All right. I'm willing to help you out... *after* you've delivered the coffees."

Smiling, I lift my chin in thanks before making my way to the bakery door. The chime above the door has only just dinged when Harlow suggests for me to return with a notebook so I can jot down her 'dating tips.' Mercifully, the heavy flow of traffic that forever impedes the streets of Ravenshoe drowns out my disappointed groan.

I HAVE a new fondness for dictation when I leave Harlow's bakery for the second time today. She was as serious about the notepad as she was about me writing down every syllable she uttered. Years ago, I liked having boyishly handsome features that made me appear weak to my competitors. Now, I fucking hate it.

The past three hours was pure torture. I know as well as the next man that I have a lot to learn about the female species, but tell me one time you've crammed a lifetime of lessons into one three-hour study session. Melody is practically a genius, but even she would need more than three hours to digest everything Harlow just shared.

If it weren't for the little tidbits of Izzy's weekend she disclosed unknowingly, I would have pulled the gay card two hours ago. Alas, I've been more an agent than a man the past six years.

I climb the stairs to work off the dozen or so cookies Harlow fed me to keep me awake during her lecture. After dumping my leather satchel and notepad onto my desk, I make a beeline for the supply room where key members of the Bureau conduct strategy meetings to deliver the lunch Harlow made for Izzy.

I'm taken back when I discover Izzy with her back braced against the shelves. Her face is colorless, and she looks like she's been crying. I haven't dealt with a crying girl for years. I don't know if I have what's needed for this job, but I have no choice but to suck it up. Izzy spotted my approach the instant the door creaked open.

"I heard you had to work through your lunch break." I join her sitting on the floor before leaning in to bump my shoulder against hers like an A-grade fucking moron. I told you I'm not cut out for this shit.

She cleans away the blobs of mascara under her eyes while saying, "Yeah. I think Alex is more watchful than either of us perceived."

I delivered the coffees to our office as per Harlow's request.

Since Izzy was on deck, I gave them to her to distribute with the hope Alex would fail to notice she had arrived late. Either annoyed his coffee was stone-cold, or smarter than he looks, Alex took his annoyance out on Isabelle by demanding she work through lunch for her tardiness.

Once the mess is cleared from Izzy's face, I ask, "Why are you crying?"

She hands me a photograph that has scarcely chewed cookie dough racing up my food pipe. This is an image I anticipated seeing in Tobias's files at some stage, but it shouldn't be in the evidence Isabelle is scanning in the Bureau's mainframes.

My eyes snap to Izzy when she says, "Ophelia Whitney Petretti was only nineteen years old when the car she was driving was struck by a B-double truck that veered onto the wrong side of the road. She was killed on impact."

I swallow several times in a row to force down the bile scorching my throat before taking in the photograph Isabelle is convinced is Ophelia Petretti more diligently—brown hair, light brown eyes, and the tiniest heart-shaped mole on her neck. I've seen them all before, however, this woman's name isn't Ophelia. It's Olivia. *Isn't it?*

Isabelle must be mistaken. She's confusing a woman once under protective custody with Isaac's deceased girlfriend. A mishap is understandable. I almost had a coronary when I ran into a woman I was convinced was Olivia during my first consignment at Ravenshoe. The resemblance was uncanny, but thankfully, she was years too young to be Olivia.

That doesn't mean I didn't search her credentials to back up my claims. The stranger's name was Emily McIntosh. From the polite apology she gave when she bumped into me, I wondered if she had any clue on how closely tied her family is with the Italian cartel. Her father could have been as high as Col in the Petretti entity if Col's father had granted birthrights to the children his whores birthed. Since he refused to acknowledge Emily's father in his family hierarchy out of respect for his wife, Emily's grandmother refused to give their son his last name.

Although Emily is Dimitri's first cousin, I couldn't locate any evidence that they had met. They live one town apart but have starkly different lives. Emily's family lived close to the poverty lines when she was a child, but I'm confident in saying it was Dimitri who got the short end of the stick. He grew up thinking blood and gore were normal. I'm shocked he's as stable as he is.

A sob rumbling in Isabelle's chest returns my focus to the present, and has me stupidly saying the first thing that pops into my head. "I read the police report on her accident over the weekend. It's always sad when you hear of any life being taken too soon."

I'm not lying. I did read the report on Ophelia and CJ's accident. It just wasn't because I felt sorry for them. It was because the officer on the incident report was the same officer who was killed during a routine traffic stop years ago. He was another connection that proves how tightly woven the mafia entities are that we're chasing.

The crazy notions filtering through my head double when Isabelle hands me a second photograph. It's a picture of Isaac and Olivia together. It's time-stamped a few hours before the time cited in the traffic incident report of Ophelia's death.

"Isaac and Ophelia were a couple?" You have no idea how hard that question was for me to articulate. I worked it through my head a million times, and I still nearly said Olivia instead of Ophelia.

When Isabelle nods, I think with my rational head instead of the one spiraling out of control. "You have to tell Alex you've unearthed the connection between Isaac and Col Petretti. This will get you off coffee and filing duties in an instant."

Always end every hard truth with a joke is something my mom always suggests. It's supposed to smooth out any awkwardness before you leap into the bigger hitting stuff. I don't see it working quite as well for me this time around, but when you're drowning in shit, you take any life raft offered.

Eager to practice my swing, I leap up from the ground before spinning around to help Isabelle off the floor. The adrenaline surging through me has me yanking on her arm a little too sharply. Her chest slaps mine, producing an unexpected moan from her O-formed mouth.

Horrified by her body's response to our closeness, she takes a step back before straightening the crinkles in her blouse. Once she has everything in order, her eyes stray back to the copier only capable of scanning one page at a time. I felt sorry for Isabelle when Alex shunted this task on to her, but in a way, I also understood his objective. He has a compromised Honey Pot. That's a death sentence for some supervisors.

"I don't have time to type up a report on their relationship. This scanning will take me months as it is." When Isabelle shifts on her feet to face me, I wipe the riled expression off my face. "You spent your weekend going through Col's file. Eventually, you would have discovered these photos yourself." She gives me a pleading look, having no idea how much she's asking. "If you're willing to type up the report, I'll let Alex believe you discovered the photos."

"I don't want to take your credit, Izzy." It also isn't a conversation I want to have with Alex until I have all my ducks lined up in a row.

"You're not taking my credit, Brandon," Isabelle assures, stepping closer. "You're helping me out. I'm snowed under here." She waves her hand across the stacks of boxes she still has left to scan. In a normal office, a task like this would take a day or two at most. But since the copier here requires manual loading of each page, Izzy will be stuck in here for months. "This isn't even a small dent in the boxes left in the conference room."

I take a few minutes to deliberate on a response. In all honesty, my initial reply is hell-to-the-fucking-no, but a bit of pondering breaks a small ray of sunshine through the thick cloud hovering over my head. If I disclose the information Isabelle unearthed to Alex while revealing I could have a possible connection with our target's past, I won't have to include my discussion with Dimitri in our conversation. It's a win-win really. I get to keep an informant's identity undisclosed while ensuring the Bureau continues hunting the right man.

Relief floods Isabelle's eyes when I jerk up my chin, approving her suggestion for me to compile the report to present to Alex. "But you'll get the credit for finding the connection between Isaac and Col."

I leave the supply room like I have a rocket strapped to my back. I should go straight to my desk to commence drafting my report, but instead, I head to the roof for some privacy. And perhaps to assure myself I'm not going crazy.

When several long minutes of sucking in fresh air doesn't budge the elephant from my chest, I dig my cell phone out of my pocket and dial a number I rarely use.

"Petretti's Restaurant, are you making a reservation or placing an order?"

I swallow the lump in my throat before saying, "I wish to order the Peking duck. I heard the orange glaze is divine."

The hostess says nothing. She just patches me through to the private number I'm requesting. When Dimitri answers two rings later, I crack like a teen under pressure. "Can you send me a photo of your sister?"

"What?"

"I need a photo of your sister. A photo of Ophelia. The Bureau has some on file they believe are her. I want to double-check that they are her. They make fuck-ups all the time. This could be a fuck-up."

"All right. Calm down. Which contact?" Dimitri's tone reveals he's only doing this because of the heads-up I gave him about the IRS. If it were for any other reason, he would have hung up by now.

After sweeping the area to ensure it's free of nosy-parkers, I say, "The secure email server Grayson set up two years ago."

"The one you told me to only use in dire circumstances?"

"Yes!" I run my fingers through my hair when my voice ricochets off the rooftop. "This is an emergency. I need a photo as soon as possible."

Since nothing but sheer desperation is echoing in my tone, my phone pings two seconds later before Dimitri advises me to check my emails. I fumble so much I almost drop my phone when I lower it from my ear. Fear isn't something I readily feel, but I'm certain it's the cause of the shaking of my hands when I log into my email to download the image Dimitri attached to an email that will disappear within thirty seconds of me opening it.

After taking in the image Dimitri sent that unequivocally confirms my Olivia is Isaac's Ophelia, I squash my phone back against my ear. I'm tempted to smack it against my head another six times for good measure, but hold my punishment for a more appropriate time. "When did Ophelia die?"

"Six years ago—"

"Not the year. The *actual* date."

I know the answer I'm seeking. I read her death certificate three times this weekend and have the ability to retain anything I read, but my brain is nothing but puree right now. I'm stunned I can talk, even more so when Dimitri replies, "January 14th."

It reveals I have more than a minute connection with our target's past. It could completely fuck me over.

I bedded a mafia princess.

A mafia princess who had supposedly died nine months before we fooled around.

Fuck!

BRANDON

lex's head pops up from a family planning clinic brochure he's perusing when I knock on his office door. Since it's the same family clinic he requested me to hack into while on bereavement leave almost a year ago, I dither the reason for my visit for the umpteenth time the past four weeks. I understand the pain you experience when the woman you love leaves you, but I can only imagine how bad it feels to discover a receipt in her name at a clinic known for abortions.

I can't get over the fact Melody cheated on me, but the disbelieving gasp that left Alex's mouth when I confirmed an R. Myers had attended her appointment at Westminster Family Planning Clinic two months after they separated made me realize it could have been much worse. Melody destroyed us, but Regan destroyed something of Alex's he can never get back. That's a fierce burn for any man to digest.

When Alex arches his brow, prompting me that I'm the one interrupting him, not the other way around, I grind out the first excuse that pops into my head. "That report you wanted on Colt Enterprises has been uploaded to the Bureau's servers."

He slouches low into his chair. "Anything I need to be aware of?"

I shake my head before spinning on my heels and stalking back to my desk. Today isn't the first time I've tried to come clean about my connection with Ophelia Petretti. My first attempt was the morning after I discovered Olivia Wilde, once an informant for Tobias, is Ophelia Petretti, Isaac Holt's supposed 'deceased' girl-friend. Alex was adamant if it wouldn't grant him an arrest warrant for Isaac, he wasn't interested in anything I had to say.

He's always been a hard-ass, but it's grown substantially worse the morning he, Isabelle, and I had an unintended strategy meeting in the conference room at HQ. He has his sights set on one man, making him not only blind to how dangerous revenge is, but he also has no clue to the rift it's causing his team and family. I doubt he's even aware how deeply undercover Grayson went weeks ago. That's how far his head is up his own ass.

I've only just reached my desk when Alex whizzes by. "I'll be back in around an hour. Keep an eye on things for me until then." I glance behind my shoulder, certain he's talking to someone else.

When I fail to find anyone around me, I stray my eyes to his. "Me?"

"Keep playing the dumb card, Brandon. You have everyone here fooled." Alex shoves the pamphlet for the family planning clinic into his pocket before shifting on his feet to face me, placing on his jacket at the same time. "Except me." His words are projected at me, but his eyes reveal the real recipient of his scorn. He's doubting no one but himself right now. He's wearing the same look now he had last month when I told him Westminster didn't lodge electronic documentation on the procedures their patients have. "I want Isaac's movement sheets logged before I return."

Stealing my chance to say they're already uploaded, he leaves HQ. I slump into my chair before firing up my computer so I can sort through the information I was working on before my real job overtook my pretend one. There are so many threads Grayson and I are picking at, my head feels overloaded. It also feels empty. Don't ask me how you can have two contradicting responses. I'm just telling you how it is. My fuck-up with Olivia, sorry, correction, Ophelia, almost cost me my career before I joined the Bureau. However, it was nothing compared to what it cost me personally. She's the reason Melody and I haven't spoken in years.

I've always been pissed that Melody wouldn't give me the chance to explain myself, but when I sat down and truly looked at the facts, I understood her hesitation. The way Olivia tried to manipulate me should have disclosed her true entity long before Isabelle did, but I brushed off her nastiness as a consequence of grief.

Even to this date, details are sketchy, but one fact has never altered. I met Olivia the night her brother was abducted. Tobias needed the man assigned to Olivia's watch on the ground. Since I wasn't yet qualified for field service, I volunteered to babysit an alleged 'harmless' informant.

When Olivia was made aware of the reason for the change-up, she was clearly emotional. Since it was the anniversary of Joey's death, I wasn't fairing much better. We didn't react to the instant attraction we felt until after we'd consumed two bottles of wine with a greasy pizza and pasta combination.

The instant it was over, I knew I had fucked-up. It wasn't the fact I'd slept with an informant that had me instantly regretting my decision, it was the bitch-flip I seemingly turned on while fucking Olivia that had me backpedaling. We fucked, there's no doubt about that. It wasn't a sweet, let's-take-it-slow lovemaking session, but not at one stage did Olivia ask me to stop, slow down, or any of the other words you'd expect to hear when the other half of your fuck-fest isn't in it. She screamed for more, begged me to go harder, then initiated a second round the next morning when we woke in a groggy, twisted mess.

It was then that she mentioned how much trouble I could be in if I didn't do as asked. I stared at her, shocked as fuck at her gall. She wasn't just attempting to blackmail me into sleeping with her again, she wanted information she wasn't privy to. Hell, at the time, I wasn't even privileged to the files she wanted.

When I refused to bow to her demands, she said she'd say the event we undertook the night before wasn't mutually agreed upon. I told her to go ahead with her plans, aware intimidation was the highest form of flattery.

I assumed she'd back down.

I was dead fucking wrong.

She hung me out to dry, her deception only losing steam when she found another sucker to sink her claws into. The last I heard, they married within weeks of him being assigned to her case. Yep, you heard me right. He was a fellow agent. As far as I'm aware, he still works for the Bureau, although I don't know in what position or where. Tobias pulled me so far off Olivia's case. Up until four weeks ago, I hadn't heard her name in years, much less had an awareness of her real identity.

I wish I had paid more attention. Not only would it have saved Tobias months of grief, I wouldn't be feeling the scold of Olivia's burn years later. Fortunately for me, I got out after one sting. Her husband can't say the same thing.

My thoughts shift from the past to the present when a ding on my computer demands my attention. It's a ping announcing that one of the many names I logged into Ravenshoe Domestic Airport's servers months ago found a match. Although the visitor isn't one of the big hitters the Bureau has been chasing the past ten plus years, he's definitely of interest.

While grabbing my coat off the coat rack, I dial Alex's cell phone, cursing when I hear it vibrating on his desk. I could leave him a message stating Albert Sokolov, right-hand man to Russian mafia cartel leader, Vladimir Popov, has decided to pop into Ravenshoe for a visit, but I'd rather produce evidence along with my findings, so I head for the door before his voicemail greeting is halfway done.

"Michelle, if Alex returns before me, tell him to check his

emails." I set it up so any alerts are automatically forwarded to Alex's email.

Michelle gives me the same gaga face she always does Alex before nodding. "Shall I tell him where you're going?"

I consider a reply for all of two seconds before shaking my head. "No. I don't want him chewing me up and spitting me out for having an early lunch." I could tell her where I'm going, she's technically the same rank as me, but since Albert's visit skims along the line that separates my personal life from my work, I'm not so eager. If Albert is here for Isabelle, more than legalities could be at play.

"I'll keep it our little secret." Michelle's tone indicates she's hoping I'll pay my restitution with more than an iced mocha from Harlow's. She's shit out of luck. It's been a while since I've played sheet-twister, but I'm not *that* desperate. Even if she wasn't pushing forty, and agents aren't technically informants, it's still a no-go for me.

I take the stairs to the first level, mindful of Grayson's disclosure on Alex rigging common areas with hidden surveillance cameras, jog to my car parked on the corner, then slip into the driver's seat. When the engine fires to life, my mind drifts to fonder times. The Hellcat Mr. Gregg and I were rebuilding was a rust bucket when we started, but her engine always purred like a pussy cat. Although its purr was nothing on the one Melody made when my head was between her legs.

A lot of people assume deaf people can't moan or laugh. They're dead wrong. Our time between the sheets was when Melody was the most vocal. The only indication she had on how loud she was being was when her moans rumbled in her chest, so I did everything in my power to ensure she didn't have a moment to register the heartiness of her moans.

I shake my head when I catch sight of my arrogant grin in the rearview mirror. Anyone would swear she's under me now with how hard I'm smiling. It's the first time I've recalled us sleeping together without wondering who else has experienced her seductive moans, so I guess a little cockiness is okay.

After throwing the gearshift into first gear, I ask Siri to dial Grayson's private number. He answers a few seconds later, breathless and sounding sweaty. The fact he doesn't greet me by name reveals he's in a place he can't talk freely, much less his comment about me finally returning his call. We only spoke an hour ago when he once again tried to convince me I had no legal reason to disclose my one-night hook-up with Olivia to Alex. He went quiet when I asked about her resurrection from the dead. Even he's at a loss on what to do about that tidbit of information.

Recalling the reason for my call, I get back to the task at hand. "Albert Sokolov just landed in Ravenshoe."

"I'm aware. Your quote just came through," Grayson responds, still gasping. "I heard you're not local. How's Hopeton this time of the year? "

Hearing the words he can't speak, my tires lock up when I slam on the brakes. When I complete an illegal U-turn, horns honk, and the smell of burning rubber lingers in the air. "What's at Hopeton for him?"

"That's what I'm hoping you'll work out. It's a new fitting, so there's no reason for the sudden leak."

"Do you think it has anything to do with your placement?" He's undercover at the Bobrov camp. Kirill arrived stateside approximately four weeks ago. He can't enter US soil legally, so his method of transport was more modest than the private jets his competitors use, although I doubt he lived in shambles the past few weeks. "It seems suspicious the Popovs commenced sniffing around old Bobrov stomping grounds within weeks of Kirill's return to the States. Are they aware of his return?"

A door slides open before birds chirping in the distance overtakes a group of men talking in Russian. "I doubt that's the case. I tightened the connections. It didn't fix the leak. There's something more occurring here than a loose valve. If you can find out what that is, I might have a chance to stop wading through shitty waters every time I use the bathroom."

I'm not surprised about his underhanded comment that he's the shit-kicker of Bobrov's crew. He's blond-haired, blue-eyed, and has the worst Russian accent I've ever heard in my life. It's just his size, arrogant face, and cocky attitude that convinces criminals he's one of them. He also has no trouble pushing the boundaries undercover agents must use to prove they're far from law-abiding. Drugs, prostitution, dismemberment of body parts, you name it, Grayson has dabbled in it at one stage during his career. He took any steps necessary to get him closer to the man he's been chasing for almost a decade, and those steps walked him right into Kirill's crew.

"I'll pass on any information I find out."

He murmurs out an agreement before our lines go dead. It was a mere second after a female voice sang out a string of text more lyrical than the bluebirds in the distance. They hint more to Grayson's location than the cryptic messages he's sent me the past two weeks.

BRANDON

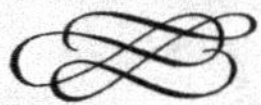

With traffic light and my foot heavy, I make it to Hopeton with ten minutes shaved off the usual commute time. I realize I'm not the only one with a lead foot when I spot Alex's old sedan parked a few spots down from Westminster Family Planning Clinic. Even if I didn't know his history with the location, the fact he took his car instead of the Navigator the Bureau assigned to him when he became supervisor of my division reveals he isn't on the job.

I slot my BMW into a parking spot three spaces back from Alex's car when he suddenly shoots out of the glass door of the clinic. My intuition could be leading me astray, but considering the bank of buildings across from the clinic are the first you stumble on when you enter Hopeton, I'm willing to give my intuition a little bit of leeway. Furthermore, Hopeton only has one entry and exit point, so this is the ideal place for me to commence my stakeout.

A wish to have an ability to plead to Melody over the phone smacks into me when Alex yanks his cell phone out of his pocket. I've spilled my guts electronically many times the past almost seven years. All but two were deleted before I hit send. The first one was the email Melody never acknowledged. The second was a text message I sent after reading the transcript from Agent Russell's interview with her. Even believing I'm no longer the boy she once knew, she defended me. That deserved some type of acknowledgment. Did she reply to that text? Yeah, she did. It was a simple 'you're welcome,' but it was better than the response I was anticipating.

I can't hear much of the message Alex leaves on Regan's voicemail, but his facial expression exposes how awkward he feels. For the first time since I've known him, his features aren't hardened with aggression. He almost seems remorseful, but before I can work out why he'd ever feel regret, a group of men entering a restaurant on my left captures my attention. The fact they enter the restaurant from the servers' entrance while wearing suits that cost more than I make per month exposes they're not Hopeton locals, much less the fact mobsters never travel anywhere without their favorite whores. The brunette in the skintight fluorescent pink dress being ushered in by a man with biceps bigger than my head is the equivalent of a neon sign. Her outfit screams, 'The mob is in town. Come get 'em if you dare.'

Never one to back down when dared, I slip out of my driver's seat. It occurs at the same time Alex glances up from his phone. Since his eyes are directed to the front of the restaurant, I make it across the double highway without him spotting me. My speed is so quick, my arm darts into the minute gap between the rapidly closing door left behind from the gang's entrance.

With my gun high, and my steps soundless, I quickly make my way down a corridor lined with tins of soups and other condiments I can't read since the labels are in Chinese. When I reach the end of the corridor, I'm confronted with a dead end. Since the sound of cutlery projects from my left, I head right. The scent of liquor and cigars grows the further I silently tiptoe down the isolated corridor. My cover is almost blown when a swinging door suddenly shoots open, but thankfully, not being the biggest guy in the room works to my advantage again today. By plastering my back to the wall, the waiter carrying a stack of dirty dishes on a black tray fails to notice me hiding behind the door.

I dash past the door, taking advantage of the gap of its swing. This restaurant won't be rated as a top server any time soon. The roof is stained with soot from the number of cigars its patrons smoke while waiting for below-par food. Think of an old western movie with dirt for floors and unbathed patrons. Now jump that image into the 21st century, and you'll have an idea of what I'm seeing.

I scan the area when a deep voice says, "Serve it to him raw. That will shut him up on it being overcooked."

Just before the owner of the voice bursts into the corridor, I pop out the lock of the manager's office at the end. There's nothing fancy about this office. A desk coated in papers that appear legitimate and a cracked leather chair take up most of the space, but it is the flooring I'm paying the most attention to. The desk was recently moved. The heavy indents in the carpet reveal this fact.

After failing to find any slits in the carpet that may indicate an in-floor safe, I raise my eyes to the ceiling. It's a relatively clean drop ceiling that a normal agent wouldn't look at twice. It's a pity for whoever dragged over the desk so it sits directly below the steel beam running down the middle of the room that I'm nothing close to ordinary.

With my eyes locked on the tiniest thread peeking out from one of the ceiling's panels, I screw a suppressor onto the barrel of my gun before adding an accessory every man about to crawl into a dark void loves. The dark material represents the fibers usually found in ski gear—more particularly, ski masks—revealing it's smart of me to weapon up.

I toe off my shoes before climbing onto the desk. My sock-covered feet slip on the highly varnished material, but they keep my approach silent to anyone who may be listening for it. After opening up the panel enough to check the coast is clear, I tuck my pistol into the back of my trousers before chin-lifting myself into the void. Upper-body strength was always a favorite workout of Mr. Gregg's, and days like today, I'm thankful for his dedication.

Once I'm through the tight opening, I scan the area. With nothing but blackness behind me, I head toward a sprinkling of light. If my bearings are correct, I'm moving toward the main hub of the restaurant.

A hum of chatter fills my ears a second before an Italian-rich voice says, "You need to change your aftershave. I could smell that shit long before you crawled through the vent."

When I flick on the torch mounted to my gun, Dimitri shelters his eyes with his hand. He's lying on his stomach, his shoulder a mere inch from a high caliber assault weapon. From my angle, I don't have the best vantage point to take in his target when he peers down the scope like a real-life sniper, but with the accents in the restaurant mainly featuring Russians, I reach a quick conclusion.

"You know I'm well within my right to shoot you, right?"

He makes a pfft noise. "If you wanted to shoot me, you would have done it the instant I turned my back to you." Even in the darkness of this hidey-hole, I can see the pegs of his teeth. "That's how most agents operate, isn't it?"

I take a moment to deliberate before housing my gun into the holster on my hip. If Dimitri was planning to kill Albert, he'd already be dead. The fact he's alive reveals Dimitri is here for the same reasons as me. He wants intel.

"Who's he meeting with?" I cringe through the cobwebs coating my suit jacket when I join Dimitri lying on a timber beam rats have made their home. "An old Russian sanction was here a few years back, but there's been no rumblings from their barracks in almost a decade."

"He's not meeting with a fellow Russian." Dimitri slants his head to the side before nudging his head to the scope of his weapon, permitting me to take in an unhindered view of proceedings.

"What the fuck?" I mumble to myself when my adjustment of the scope has me stumbling onto someone I never anticipated. Isaac Holt is being investigated because of suspected ties with the Mafia syndicates, but this is a plot twist I never saw coming. Is he aware he's commencing trade with the entity responsible for attempting to sell Isabelle into a sex trafficking ring when she was only a child?

If Tobias hadn't mortgaged his house to buy her, Isabelle's childhood would have been more damaging than being raised by a man with an inability to express himself. She most likely would have been dead before she reached double digits. No matter how well Isaac tries to brush off his business dealings with the Popovs, his actions today will negatively impact Isabelle. This will hurt her.

My throat becomes scratchy when I use Dimitri's generosity to survey the area. A bird's-eye-view of the space wouldn't increase my Yelp rating, but it does make me aware I'm not the only agent going rogue today. Alex is sitting at the bar, nursing a glass of amber-colored liquid. His Adam's apple bobs up and down as all good agents are taught, but I know he isn't drinking. He hasn't touched a drop of alcohol in years.

After inching back from the scope, I dig a handkerchief out of my pocket so I can scrub my fingerprints off a gun I'm sure the Bureau would love to log into evidence before angling my head toward Dimitri. "Unless you want to be stuck up here all night, or better yet, detained in a holding cell, I suggest you leave now. This place is about to be raided."

I've only worked with Alex on and off for a year, but I've known Grayson a lot longer than that. The Rogers all operate the same way —take down the foreigner before the native. Isaac will leave this restaurant believing his meeting with an underworld associate went unnoticed. Albert won't be so lucky.

A hint of smugness smacks into me when Dimitri immediately commences dismantling his customized M-4. I thought it would have taken more than my word to convince him to leave. Usually, some type of exchange of information occurs before he listens to anything a government official has to say. Not even Tobias had a knack for getting him to follow command when needed.

I discover the reason behind his eagerness when the zipper of his large black duffle bag is quickly chased by him handing me a single sheet of paper. "With the government eager to do some digging on my businesses, I commenced some of my own. Do you know who she's related to?"

When my eyes drop down to the paper he handed me, my throat works hard to swallow. He has a photograph of Isabelle. It isn't old and faded like the ones Tobias had of her in her file. This one was recently taken. How do I know this? Harlow is smiling in the background, most likely laughing at Isabelle's screwed-up nose from the bakery assistant cutting a generous serving of the pumpkin pie in front of her. Isabelle hates pumpkin.

"Ah… so you do know who she is," Dimitri says when my silence speaks volume. "If she is what this is about…" he nudges his head to the bullet hole in the wall he was using to line up his target, "… we're going to have issues. This isn't Russian territory—"

"She has nothing to do with this. I don't even know if Isaac is aware who her father is." My back molars crunch when I snap my mouth shut, pissed I unwillingly shared information I hadn't meant to give.

Dimitri laughs at my mortified expression. It isn't a pleasant we're-buddies laugh. It's as cold and vindictive as the man he was raised to be.

He slaps my shoulder harder than needed to ensure he gets his point across when he says, "Bring me everything you have in five days. *If* I find it satisfactory, I'll share some hard truths with you."

"And if it isn't?"

His evil grin says it all.

We won't be on the same team anymore.

We'll be enemies—mortal ones.

I wonder if his opinion would change if I disclosed his sister is alive. I could test the waters now, but sometimes the best secrets are revealed one tidbit at a time.

BRANDON

As suspected, Alex called in a tip to the authorities before Albert and his crew could re-board their private jet in Ravenshoe. In some ways, I was shocked he didn't arrest Albert himself, but in others, I'm not. For personal reasons, he wants Isaac no matter what the cost. He'd even go as far as handing over a high-up Russian cartel member to a local detective just for the chance of snagging his man.

Unbeknown to Isabelle, he's been working on an arrest warrant for Isaac the past four hours. It will depend on the judge whether his request is granted. His evidence is shady at best. Isaac did dine with a known Russian cartel member, but that isn't illegal. If having bad friends was a crime, all of Madden's would have been locked up years ago.

After I finished my report on the Greggs' murder, I put a little bit of focus into Hugo's concealed files—the real Hugo. Even with a majority of the court transcripts redacted to the point of being useless, for the first time in my life, I'm siding with the defense.

I don't know how any judge accepted Hugo's guilty verdict. The victim stated multiple times that he wasn't one of her attackers. A forensic scientist proved the finger-width bruises on Gemma's thighs were sustainably smaller than Hugo's fingers, and one of them even testified that the angle of the scratch wounds in Hugo's arm couldn't have been done during the assault. Still, the judge accepted Hugo's guilty plea, had him dishonorably discharged from the military, and exonerated Madden and three other defendants.

One was convicted of rape within twelve months of the judge's decision. Another committed suicide. According to Madden, that doesn't prove guilt. When I brought it up during a very one-sided conversation a few weeks ago, he used Joey's death as evidence. Not just for his fellow marine who killed himself, but on how people who appear stable can flip their personalities at a flick of a switch.

When I told him that isn't normal, he replied, "The only difference between psychotic and iconic is how they got what they wanted."

Nothing he said made any sense, but that's not unusual. He's had our father whispering in his ear the past seven years. That's enough to turn anyone insane.

I stop glancing at my clenched hands when Alex asks, "Is that the woman from the report you uploaded weeks ago?"

After joining him near the large tinted glass wall that stretches the entire length of HQ, I peer down at Megan Shroud. Talking about psychopaths, she's an A-grade lunatic. I lift my chin before giving Alex a brief rundown on Megan. He knows most of it from my report, so I keep my update brief.

"How long has she been sleeping in her car?"

I twist my lips. "She hasn't the past few weeks. She usually leaves not long after lock-up and is back bright and early the following morning...." My words trail off when, in the corner of my eye, I spot Detective Carter leading Albert into the conference room of HQ. Their slow track is being shadowed by Agent Russell. Seeing local law enforcement cooperating with Internal Affairs of the FBI isn't just shocking, it has my stomach twisted up in knots, but before I can ask Alex what the fuck he's playing at, I'm startled to within an inch of my life.

"What's going on?" Isabelle asks, stopping to stand next to me.

When her narrowed eyes dart between the agents laughing at Isaac's deranged once-lover scuffling with the head bouncer of Isaac's nightclub, I clue on to which disaster she's referencing. "Megan Shroud. She's brought out so much crazy today, even Alex is taking notice."

We've noted Megan outside of Isaac's club many times the past few months, but today is the first time she's gone full-blown skitzo like she is now. She's kicking and thrashing against the brute of a man who usually stands on the door of Isaac's dance club. She's tiny, but even the man who'd easily be six-foot-five is struggling to keep her contained.

When she breaks free from the bouncer's hold for the second time, Isabelle paces closer to the window. "Why isn't someone calling the police?" Her crackling voice exposes her worry. "She's clearly unstable and not just a threat to the public. She's a threat to herself." When no one jumps in to ease her worry, she strays her big brown eyes to Alex. "You need to call the police."

A flashback of Leesa's wide, panicked eyes in the minutes leading to her turning rogue whiz into my mind when Isabelle runs her hand down Alex's arm. It's clever to use her femininity to her advantage *if* she were using it on anyone but Alex. Just like me, he's immune to anyone who isn't his soulmate.

"Isaac made his bed, now he has to sleep in it."

While Alex frustrates the agents hovering around the window by lowering the blinds, Isabelle locks her eyes with mine. She stares at me, wordlessly begging for direction. I honestly don't know what to do or say. I don't want to encourage her to do one of the many dangerous things I see in her eyes, but I also don't want her to hang around here. Albert has been Vladimir's right-hand man for longer than Isabelle has been born. If they cross paths, he could recognize her.

When I shrug my shoulders, truly unsure about what to do, Isabelle makes a beeline to her desk. She removes her Bureau-issued pistol from her second drawer before scanning the room. Once she's confident she isn't being watched, she secures her revolver to her ankle. I wait for the hem of her pants to touch her shoes before nudging my head to the corridor, so we can have a private word. I have no clue what I'm planning to say, but I have to say something, don't I?

Isabelle agrees to my request but raises her finger in the air, requesting a minute. Although my curiosity is piqued, I make my way to the corridor, awarding her a trust I don't often give anymore.

Approximately thirty seconds later, Isabelle joins me in the corridor. She looks like she has something important to say, but I talk before she has the chance. "I'll follow her."

Her face screws up. "They'll know you're gone, Brandon. They won't notice me as I've spent the last four weeks in the supply room scanning documents. Nobody ever comes in there looking for me but you. Cover for me, and I'll owe you big time."

She has a point—regrettably.

I run a hand over my head while contemplating. If she's investigating Megan, she won't be here, exposed to a high-ranked man in her father's crew, but then she'd be thrust into Megan's line of sight. From the hospital records Isabelle unearthed on her months ago, there's no doubt Megan is unstable, but I doubt her crimes are worse than Albert's.

Believing an unhinged woman is the lesser of two evils, I dig my keys out of my pocket and place them into Isabelle's palm. "It's a blue BMW coupe half a block down."

She looks utterly shocked—so much so, she darts down the corridor without a word seeping from her lips. Just before she reaches the stairwell, she pivots around and races back my way. I'm taken aback when she slings her arms around my neck and hugs me tight. "Thank you, Brandon. I would have never made it this far without you."

I return her hug, both smug from her compliment and worried. "Be careful, Izzy."

After inching back, she nods, winks, and then sprints back down the corridor. I wait until she clears the first floor of stairs before re-entering the office. The buzz of Megan's antics is keeping the energy high. It's been like this most of the day. Tobias always said good agents have a knack for feeling change in the air. Great ones make it happen.

With that in mind, I make my way down the corridor I saw Detective Carter guiding Albert down only minutes ago. I'm not surprised to discover the conference room walls have been frosted. It's a pity for Agent Russell and Alex that Detective Carter has no trouble raising his voice to express his annoyance at the Bureau attempting to 'piss on his turf.'

"I brought him here as a mark of respect for your tip, not for you to gloat. If I want to hear a rooster crow, I'll visit a fucking farm."

I can't hear what Alex replies with, but I'm certain he's the one who's talking. His tone is too deep and low to be Agent Russell's.

Barely three seconds tick by before the conference door slings open, and Detective Carter steps out. "Two minutes and not a second longer."

His exit from the room is too quick for me to make out I wasn't spying. It's for the best. Detective Carter doesn't seem like the type to believe shit is chocolate. "You're the agent from the alleyway." Since he's not asking a question, it doesn't sound like one.

"I am." I fill the gap between us with three quick strides before holding out my hand in offering. "Brandon James."

He hesitates for a second before accepting my hand. "Brandon, as in Izzy Brahn's Brandon?"

My chest shouldn't swell at his assumption, but it does. Still, I try and downplay it. "A lot of people are called Brandon—"

"Not in this town, they're not." He takes in the bland walls like they're covered with family portraits while stepping closer to the main hub of the office. "Have you been here long? Prime commercial real estate like this hasn't been on the market in years, so you've either been here for a while, or you don't use the same channels as us regular folks."

I smirk, amused he thinks a friendly persona will have me slipping up. Local authorities are aware the FBI has a task force in Ravenshoe, but they have no clue who we're here for and exactly how long we plan to stay.

"I can see how this location can be popular for some, but it isn't up to my standards."

That gets a smile out of him, albeit reserved. "I thought this neighborhood would be right up your alley. Who doesn't want a big fancy nightclub straight across the street." He shifts on his feet to face me, his smirk smug since he knows who we're targeting without me needing to mention it. "Especially if you're a dancing type of guy."

"I'm not much of a dancer, either."

"No?" he fires back, his brows arching. "I wouldn't have guessed that. I've seen you at a handful of clubs."

My brows are dying to stitch, but I won't let them. The more impassive I act, the more Detective Carter's game plan will become exposed. "You don't have to be a dancer to enjoy a nightclub. More times than not, the view makes up for the annoying buzz in your ears the next three days."

He nods. "True." His lips twist as he struggles to hold back his smile. "*If* you're there for the female clientele."

His reply has me smirking like a smug prick. Our brief conversation exposes he saw me follow Isabelle to the Dungeon dance club weeks ago, but he has no clue about our kiss, which proves he's not watching Izzy. The only thing I need to work out is if he's targeting the same man our taskforce, is or is he playing devil's advocate.

I lose the chance to underhandly work it out of him when he taps on his watch, announcing the two minutes he gave Alex with

Albert is up, but his murmured comment when he heads back to the conference room door ensures I'll be keeping an eye on him. "Tell Dimitri I said hello."

I've only worked my jaw side to side twice when he guides a handcuffed and bloody Albert past me. I'm not shocked Albert was roughed-up by Alex, the Rogers are well known in the Bureau for their 'investigative tactics.' I'm just stunned he had the gall to do it in front of an IA agent. There's only one way in and out of the room. Agent Russell didn't leave.

I discover that Alex's tactic was successful when he hands me a crumbled piece of paper with a handwritten sequence of numbers on it. From the length of the digits, I'm going to assume it is a bank transaction. "I need to know anything this number could correspond to, and I needed it last week."

"Does this correspond with our target or the man who just left with a broken nose?" When he glances up from his bloody knuckles to me, his glare furious, I add, "If I know who to focus my search on, I'll have more chance of working out what these numbers correspond to. It could be anything."

Alex's trust appears as low as mine, but he still gives it to me. "I didn't have enough time to get more out of him, but I'd recommend adding both our target and Vladimir Popov into your search parameter."

BRANDON

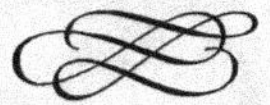

While climbing the stairs of my apartment building, I rub at a kink in my neck. If I had any doubt Isaac's many corporations weren't shady, I don't now. It took me over four hours to discover the sequence of numbers Alex handed me was a transfer of ninety-three hundred dollars from an offshore account of one of Isaac's many shell corporations to a casino in Las Vegas.

Whoever organized the wire transfer has a strong knowledge of cybercrime. Grayson taught me everything he knew. I've hacked into servers that are supposedly unhackable. Alas, even I'm struggling to work out exactly who the funds were transferred to. It probably doesn't help that I stopped my investigation partway through to help Isabelle write up a report on the evidence she located when she followed Megan to a Motel 6 on the edge of town.

Alex was as cocky as fuck when he told Isabelle he'd place two agents on Megan in the morning. He wasn't lying when he made his statement. That's how confident he is that his arrest warrant for Isaac will be issued overnight, freeing up a handful of his agents for less pressing matters like psychotic stalkers with a fascination for pop stars.

It turns out Megan isn't an ex-lover of Isaac's. From the evidence Isabelle unearthed, her eyes aren't set on a broody, enigmatic businessman. She wants his little brother—the playboy guitarist who's almost the polar opposite to his big brother. Nicholas Holt was put under the spotlight when the Bureau arrived in town. It didn't take the agents following him long to realize he had no clue about his brother's shady businesses. Other than sleeping-in until midday and playing lead guitar in his band, Rise Up, Nick occupied the rest of his time chasing a strawberry-blonde teenager lightyears out of his league.

Hey, don't judge. I'm just telling you what the reports said. They were taken by a rookie agent who seemingly had a crush on Nick's girl, so do with it as you may.

My hand drops from my neck to my chest when a shadowed figure moves into the light hanging above my apartment door. The lights in the hall were hardwired by the building supervisor, so I have no choice but to have my door lit up like a Christmas tree.

"Good evening, Agent Russell. A bit late for a house call, isn't it?"

She smiles at the snark in my tone instead of reacting negatively to it. "I heard Alex was a hard-ass. Wouldn't have believed it unless I had witnessed it for myself." Her tone is familiar, yet completely different to the ball-crusher one I handled when we first met. I guess since she believes I'm a cooperative witness, she has no reason to ride my ass anymore.

Don't misconstrue. I only told her what I wanted her to know, but, for the most part, it was honest. She knows how I joined the Bureau and why, she just doesn't know what keeps me here. No one knows that. Not even me.

When Agent Russell spots the heavy groove between my brows, her smile sags. "Could you spare a few minutes of your time? I bought food." She holds up a bag of Chinese, doubling my suspicion. Women don't feed you unless they want something. I fell for that trick with Olivia. I won't do it again.

"It's late. I'm sure anything you need to tell me can wait until the morning."

I freeze with my key halfway into the lock of my front door when she asks, "Even if it regards Melody?"

The tightness of my jaw is heard in my reply. "I doubt you have anything of interest to me."

"You haven't given me the chance to present my findings, so how can you say that?" Agent Russell fights back.

I finish shoving in my key, twist the lock, then push open my door. "Because there's nothing you could tell me about her that I don't already know."

"Once again, I beg to differ." To ensure I can't slam the door in her face, which I had no intention of doing, Agent Russell shoves her foot into the doorway. "I'm just going to leave this here in case you change your mind."

I eye her curiously when she places the bag of Chinese on my entryway table along with her business card and an almost flat FBI-sealed envelope. When she catches my curious gaze, her lips curl into a grin. "I already ate. Seeing a perp roughed up has always made me extra ravenous."

I throw my head back and laugh, stunning both Agent Russell and myself. She watches me in shocked awe like I did when I heard Isabelle giggle for the first time. It gives me a newfound appreciation as to why Isabelle acted like she was suddenly bombarded with hives. It's kind of creepy, and if I were honest, highly-craved. When you dig yourself out of the trenches every once in a while, even the most unsuitable suitor appears appealing. Don't get me wrong, Agent Russell is attractive, but not even a death wish would have me acting on any of the inane thoughts in my head.

"Call me when you're ready." The heavy stomp of her feet when she spins on her heels and gallops down the stairwell nearly drowns out what she says next, "I left my private cell number on the back of my card."

The heavily weighted door on the front of my apartment

building slams shut a few seconds later, then I make my way inside. I had planned to hit the shower before calling it a night, however, the scent of peanuts and marinated chicken alters the direction of my course. Agent Russell might work within the Internal Affairs division of the Bureau, but at the end of the day, we're on the same team. I'm also starving. That alone has me skipping the protocol I usually do to ensure my food hasn't been tainted.

After snagging up the bag of Chinese along with Agent Russell's business card and envelope, I make my way to my room to get changed. Once I'm donning a pair of gray sweatpants and a casual tee, I stack my pillows on top of one another before slipping between the sheets. Although I usually eat in the living room, with how heavy my eyelids are, I doubt I'll make it halfway through my meal before I fall asleep, so I'd rather eat in bed.

"Damn, she got the good stuff," I murmur to myself when I pry open the first container of Chinese. She purchased the most expensive items on the list, including abalone, which is a combination of shark fins, snails, and sea cucumbers.

With my nose screwed up, I dump the container of abalone onto my bedside table before digging into the combination fried rice and satay chicken. My grandfather's hard work may have lined his grandchildren's pockets with money, but that doesn't mean I'm a snob. Usually, two tablespoons of peanut butter get me through the night before I slather it on toast in the morning.

I'M three quarters the way through my meal, and almost comatose when my cell phone dings, announcing I have a text message. Considering the late hour, I'm confident it's Grayson, so you can imagine my surprise when I discover it's a text from an unknown number.

Unknown number: *What are you wearing?*

Assuming they have the wrong number, I reply.

Me: I think you have the wrong number.

Curious, I watch the three dots float across the screen instead of finishing my dinner.

Unknown number: Blond, five-eleven, 170ish pounds with a cute, although slightly wonky smile.

Cute?

Through twisted lips, I tap out my reply.

Me: Sounds about right. I still think you have the wrong number, though.

Unknown number: It's egotistical to think your smile is cute, BJ.

As I sit up straighter in my bed, my heart races. There's only one person young enough to be up this late who calls me BJ. She's in another state, engaged to another man. But that doesn't matter, right? We're texting, not organizing a hook-up. This is a perfectly acceptable form of communication for once best friends.

Now I just need my cock to get the memo. With the taste of peanuts on my lips, it's not recalling any of the years Melody and I were friends. It's remembering the time Melody obliterated my love of peanut butter by making it an obsession.

Ignoring the throbbing rod of flesh sitting heavy on my thigh, my fingers fly across the screen of my phone.

Me: It's only egotistical if it isn't untrue.

A grin curls my lips when Melody's reply pops up. She doesn't use any words. She just sends an eyeroll emoji.

I could let that be the end of our conversation, but with my brain a little mushy from a lack of sleep and way too many carbs, I tap out a reply.

Me: Do you still want to know what I'm wearing?

Good one, Brandon. Slot straight into creeper mode, you fucking creep.

I stop inwardly lecturing myself when Melody's reply sends my cock from semi-aroused to painfully thick in an instant.

Unknown number: I'd rather see for myself.

Before I can reprimand myself for not wearing underwear, the message screen on my phone is replaced by an incoming FaceTime request.

As my thumb hovers over the connect button, I scan my room. Don't ask me why. There's nothing in here but a giant bed, one I'm-so-fucking-alone-I-only-need-one-bedside-table and me in dowdy sweatpants that don't have a chance in hell of hiding my raging boner. I can see the outline of my cock, and I'm under a bedspread for crying out loud.

Panicked Melody's call is about to ring out, I hit the connect button. Well, that's the excuse I plan to use when this backfires in my face. After licking my dry lips, I raise my phone in front of myself like this is something I do often. The novelty of this type of communication is showcased in the worst way when I peer past the person taking up a majority of the screen to seek Melody behind Agent Russell's smiling face and dark locks.

When I fail to find any indication that Melody is anywhere in the vicinity, I stray my eyes back to the pair peering at me curiously. Agent Russell tries to play off my confusion with a playful taunt. "Sweats. Good choice. I was hoping you had changed into some-thing comfortable before digging in. A stretchy waistband is very much a requirement for all the food I purchased." When I remain staring at her like a fish out of water, she twists her lips. "Was it good?"

I do a weird head nod shake thingy. "It was okay. I didn't touch the abalone, though."

"Not a fan of shark?"

My nose screws up. "I don't mind the occasional serve of flake. It was the snails I was disinterested in."

With a laugh, Agent Russell sinks deeper into a padded material that resembles the headboard I couldn't be fucked buying for my bed since I never invite anyone into my room to see it before hugging an empty glass of wine into her chest. "I'm not a fan either, but the cook from the Chinese restaurant one block from your apartment assured me it was your favorite."

"You asked the cook at a Chinese restaurant that I've never dined at what my favorite dish was, and he told you the most expensive item on the menu. Hmm, makes sense." Her laugh is cute, but regretfully, it does little to ease my confusion. "Is there a reason for your call, Agent Russell?"

She rolls her eyes. "Will you please call me Phillipa? Every time I'm called Agent Russell, fellow agents shit their pants, assuming my father is on the prowl."

I can't help but smile at her comment. She slurred on a handful of her words, proving she wasted no time in opening a bottle of wine when she left here, but that isn't the reason I'm laughing. Her reply is the exact reason I legally changed my name to Brandon James.

When she fills her glass to the very brim with red wine, my brow quirks. "Long weekend?"

She blows a strand of dead straight hair out of her eyes before muttering, "You could say that." She takes a generous sip of her drink, amplifying the plumpness of her lips. "I was suspended earlier today."

"For?" The genuine shock in my tone can't be missed. It would take someone with balls of steel to put the daughter of the Director of the Bureau on leave.

An understanding hum vibrates from my chest when Phillipa breathes out, "Crombie. He died on my watch. I failed to find out why, so until the investigation is over, I'm on paid leave."

"Just because he died on your watch doesn't mean it was your fault." If that were the case, Melody's affair would be my fault. I told Mr. Gregg I wouldn't let her out of my sight for a minute. I didn't keep my promise.

Phillipa leans in close to the screen. "That's not what Melody said."

"She was defending me. She doesn't know any different." And neither do I, but I'll keep that snippet of information to myself.

The rustle of a deep sigh bellows down the line. "She had some good points, though. I was so gung-ho to place the burden onto someone else's shoulders, I went on a witch hunt." She drags her hand across her eyes that appear as tired as mine. "I didn't plan for our interview to take the route it did, I just got worked up. Her wit stunned me."

"If it makes you feel any better, her intelligence often catches people by surprise."

Phillipa's lips purse. "It doesn't, but thanks for trying." I discover the real reason for her reaching out when she says a few seconds later, "Talking about Melody, did you open the envelope I left with you?" She gags when I hold up the still-sealed document. "Have you never heard curiosity kills the cat?"

"It's lucky I'm not a cat then, isn't it?" She laughs again. I really wish she wouldn't as it's giving me the wrong idea. Not sexually. I'm just seeing her as more of a friend than a foe. "Do you want me to do the big reveal now or later?"

"Are we still talking about the envelope?" She slaps a hand over her eyes as her cheeks inflame with heat. "Oh my God. I'm so sorry. My college girlfriends always told me I got randy when I was drunk. I never believed them." She peers at me through her cracked fingers. "I do now."

My lips twitch, but I can't fathom a reply. I'm such a novice of dating, I had no clue what she meant until she mentioned getting randy while drunk. "I have rules—"

"Don't worry, so do I," she interrupts. "No fucking on the first date, and he has to be at least four inches taller than me. You're only three."

I don't know whether to laugh or cry, so I go with honesty instead. "I meant that I don't 'date' other agents."

"Oh..." The heat on her cheeks ignites. "There's that, too." She peers down at the envelope I'm clutching for dear life. "Will you please open that before I bury myself in a hole I'll never get out of?"

Nodding, I prop my phone onto the docking charger on my bedside table, rip open the seal, then yank out four surveillance photographs from inside. Confusion spirals through me when I take in the dirty-blonde hair, brown eyes, and cock-thickening body I was anticipating to see when I connected our call. Even for someone who hasn't been to New York in years, I recognize the landscape of the pictures. The bakery Melody is dining at was my mom's favorite anytime we traveled to the city to see my father at his campaign office.

After taking in each picture individually, I fan them across my bedspread so I can assess them as a whole. "She's beautiful."

"She sure is," Phillipa replies, making me realize I said my statement out loud.

I swivel my tongue around my mouth to loosen up my next set of words. "Is that her fiancé?" I'm reasonably sure the ginger-haired man in the third photograph is Julian McMahon, but I rarely paid him any attention when google alerts popped up for him. I was too busy scanning his images for Melody to pay him any attention.

Before Phillipa can confirm the man's identity, I make an inquiry about another. "Who's the guy in the suit?"

"Guy in a suit?" Even tipsy, Phillipa is a shit liar.

When she catches my glare, she rolls her eyes. "He's the reason I'm batting my eyelashes and wearing a push-up bra under my negligee. I need your help to identify him. We got partial DNA from a glass he left in the bakery, and a good set of prints, but other than that, we're walking around blind."

"Did you run his DNA through CODIS?"

She nods. "More than once. We never got a hit."

"Facial recognition?"

She glares at me like I'm stupid. "I've done everything. He has either never left New York or someone—"

"Is cleaning his steps?"

Air rustles down the line when she briskly nods. It comes to an immediate halt when I ask, "Do you think it could be the CIA?"

"Following Melody or covering his steps?"

I half-heartedly shrug. "Both."

Phillipa takes her time deliberating a response before saying, "Possibly."

She doesn't sound convinced until I disclose, "Melody's father worked for the CIA. The cover-up I cited in my reports to have his accident ruled a homicide was because the CIA didn't want to admit they'd failed one of their own—"

"*Allegedly*," Phillipa pushes out, breathlessly. "You need to choose your words wisely, BJ. You don't know who could be listening."

Although her reply was straight-up honest, it piques my interest more than it panics me. "Why do you call me BJ?"

When her eyes float up and to the right, I lift my phone off its charging dock in preparation to hit the end call button.

She unearths my plan of attack in less than a nanosecond. "I heard Melody call you BJ in the home videos from when you were kids. It kind of stuck."

"What home videos?" My mom shoved a camera in Melody's and my face many times when we were young, but not once do I recall being video recorded.

"Liam recorded some of your drills. He used them to strategize new plans of attack."

Although creepy, it does make sense. One thing doesn't, though. "Why would home videos of the Greggs be stored in the FBI database?"

I grow an appreciation for video chats when Phillipa's throat works hard to swallow. If we were communicating the old-fashioned way, I wouldn't have known she's rattled. "I didn't technically find them in the Bureau's records. I discovered them when I was working on another case." I wait and wait and wait for her to elaborate. Mercifully, she doesn't leave me hanging for long. "I was the agent assigned to Tobias's case. When hunting for evidence to help convict Leesa, I stumbled upon a first edition copy of *War and Peace* by—"

"Leo Tolstoy," I interrupt, smiling. I'm not surprised Tobias had more than one copy. No one can predict where they'll die, not even a man as smart as Tobias. "You found Tobias's anagram?"

"Yes," Phillipa confesses. "It didn't think much of it at the time, but once Leesa was convicted, it played on my mind for weeks on end."

"Did you decipher it?"

Even through a video lens, I can see her ego sparking in her eyes. "It took me almost a year since I didn't have a key to work with, but I got there in the end." I almost ask if she fully deciphered it, but she continues talking, saving me from spilling information that isn't mine to share. "There was a six-sequence code I couldn't work out. I thought it might have corresponded with one of the files in Tobias's home office, but when I looked for it, the file wasn't there."

My throat grows scratchy, but I hold back a relieving swallow. I'd hate for Phillipa to know I hid Isabelle's file in a place no one would expect to look.

My Adam's apple bobs up and down without thinking when she adds, "That's where I stumbled onto the Greggs' home videos."

"Tobias had a file on Melody?" I swear I sound like I haven't hit puberty yet. My voice is loud and cringeworthy.

"I'm assuming at one stage, but he doesn't anymore. Excluding the old reels I found buried beneath a pile of junk, none of the files dated the year of Melody's birth gave any indication they were associated with her."

"Did you check dates after their home invasion?"

Phillipa's brows pull together as she shakes her head. Her confusion is understandable. I only recognized Tobias's method of filing when I returned to remove Isabelle's file from its slot. The number didn't correspond with Isabelle's date of birth. It was the date Tobias purchased her.

"Where are you going?" Phillipa asks when I scoot across the bed.

"I'm feeling a little unwell. Perhaps some Tiburon sun will make me feel better."

"You can't go to Tiburon, Brandon. You just can't."

"Why not?" Forgetting that she can see everything I'm doing, I tug off my shirt before lowering my free hand to the waistband of my sweatpants.

My brain clicks back on when Phillipa chokes out, "You do realize your walk-in closet has a mirror, don't you?"

I inwardly curse when I spot the cause of the nervous tickle in her throat. Although my head is swamping most of the frame, the mirror behind me is in the far back corner, meaning she can see every inch of my naked backside, and we won't mention the bits dangling between my legs, or I may face a new set of charges.

After dumping my phone onto a shelf that's mercifully minus any mirrors, I pull on a pair of briefs then slide my feet into dark trousers. Once I'm dressed in my standard work gear, I discover the reason for Phillipa's silence. I accidentally muted her while endeavoring to save her from seeing my bits.

"Sorry, I muted you." I cringe down the line when her panicked rant about how I can't go to Tiburon roars through my speakers, startling the shit out of me. "What were you saying?"

"You can't go to Tiburon."

I exit my walk-in closet and take a left into the bathroom so I can scrub the fur off my teeth from eating too much satay. "We established that part of your debate. We've just yet to mosey over the reason why I can't go."

"Because your team is about to have a major breakthrough." The high pitch of her tone reveals she doesn't like giving me this information, but she understands she has to if she wants me to hear her side of the objective. "The arrest warrant has been approved. Isaac Holt is going to be arrested sometime tomorrow. Alex just has to finalize some stuff first."

"Like what?" I have a mammoth load of questions I'm dying to ask, but I went for the simpler one since my mouth is full of minty gunk.

Phillipa's reply is just as simple, "Stuff."

"Like?" When my question is met with silence, I try another approach. "Does it have anything to do with your visit to HQ today?" Since I've spat out my toothpaste, my question is crisp and precise.

She does a weird shrug. "A little."

Over the annoyance of two highly intelligent people incapable of having an intellectual conversation, I say, "Unless you can give me a good reason as to why I shouldn't go to Tiburon tonight, I'm catching the next available flight—"

"You're the union rep for the Ravenshoe chapter of the Bureau. You'll most likely be needed if Isaac's arrest has a carry-on effect to any members of your team."

Hearing what she doesn't say the loudest, I push, "Isabelle?"

Phillipa breathes in deeply before nodding.

"Could she face repercussions from Isaac's arrest?" I had wondered the same thing myself the instant Philippa disclosed Isaac's arrest warrant had been granted.

Nothing but remorse rings in Phillipa's tone when she says, "I can't tell you that, Brandon. The information is confidential—"

"You're on a suspension."

Her mouth falls open. "That doesn't mean I can flap my gums about another agent's case." She slaps her hand over her mouth instead of her eyes this time around. "Stupid, stupid wine." When I fail to hold in my chuckle about her childish rant, she lowers her hand from her face so it doesn't conceal her glare. "This is your fault. I've never had a dinner invitation rejected before. My ego was hit so bad it needed an immediate recovery mission."

"I didn't reject your invite because I don't find you attractive. It's because—"

"You prefer informants over agents, I get it," she interrupts, evening the playing field between us. It's a low blow but also effective.

"Ouch. You don't hold back, do you?"

Wetness fills Phillipa's eyes as a remorseful mask slips over her face. "I'm sorry. Trying to get out of a father's shadow can make some people really bitchy. By some people, I mean me. I'm some people." To show she didn't mean any harm by her comment, she explains how much trouble Isabelle could be in if anything Alex presented to her is true. "She won't just be suspended, Brandon. She could face charges."

"For what? Doing the job Alex recruited her for?"

"This goes way beyond that, and if you're honest with yourself, you'd agree with me."

I do, but it doesn't make it any easier to swallow.

"I need to go to Tiburon." Nothing against Isabelle. I assured Tobias I'd take care of her, but I made promises to the Greggs long before I knew the meaning of the word. "I could have a greater chance of identifying the man in the photos with Melody if I go to Tiburon. Then I can keep her safe as promised."

"I don't believe he wants to hurt Melody, Brandon. More times than not, he's protected her."

That piques my interest. "What do you mean he's protected her?"

Phillipa takes a huge gulp of her glass of wine before confessing, "Melody took a shortcut home down a side alley one day. She wasn't alone. The... *gent*..." she looks as uncomfortable calling him a gentleman as I feel knowing there's another man stepping up to the plate to protect Melody, "... stopped her from being followed."

I wash off my toothbrush, dump it in its holder, then make my way out of the attached bathroom. "Do you think he could have been hired by Melody's fiancé? He's not short of a penny. He could afford a security detail not afraid of a little rough-handling."

She apprehensibly squirms. "Possibly. I did look into the angle when I noticed the same guy in the background of the photos my surveillance team took, but I didn't get any solid leads."

"Did you ask Melody?"

"No." Guilt lines her face. "We're not really on speaking terms."

I lick my lips before putting out an offer that could benefit me as much as it could Phillipa. "Do you want me to reach out to her?"

She waits a beat before shaking her head. "Unless you want another IAs' agent looking at you with the same murky glasses I was wearing only weeks ago, I would suggest you hold out for a bit. There's a lot of shit going on right now." Although she doesn't exactly admit she was wrong accusing me of murder, her round-about way of saying she was loosened the weight on my chest.

Phillipa eyes me with apprehension slashed across her features when I ask, "Do you have any plans this weekend?"

"Is this whole push-up bra, unbrushed hair, and no makeup thing working for you?"

I laugh when she swivels her index finger around her scrubbed-clean face. "I wouldn't necessarily say it'll have you slotted into my dreams, but it does have me looking at you differently." She nods in agreement when I add, "It's amazing how much you can see someone when they're not hiding behind a title."

She returns my compliment by issuing one of her own. "Spell out your terms, Agent James. I'm listening."

"I won't go to Tiburon..." the excitement flaring through her eyes dims when I add, "... *if* you go on my behalf."

BRANDON

"Hurry the fuck up, Grayson. How long does this shit take?"

"Are you serious, punk? If it's so fucking easy, why didn't you hack in?" he replies, whispering.

While accepting a coffee from Isabelle, I smile like she didn't bust me requesting a fellow agent to hack into the Bureau's mainframe to interrupt surveillance at HQ. When she disappears to deliver the rest of the coffees to our teammates, I jump up from my seat and make my way to the corridor for some privacy.

"I can't keep ears out of a room I'm in, that's why I asked for your help, dipshit."

Grayson makes a *pfft* noise. "Whatever." A few seconds later, he coughs up the words I'm dying to hear. "I'm in…" I would have preferred for them not to be followed by, "… but directing the feed to another server is proving problematic."

After glancing down the hallway, ensuring our conversation isn't being overheard by anyone in my team, much less the IA agent approaching Isabelle near the coat rack, I squash my phone closer to my ear. "Can you terminate the feed altogether? Make it look like a glitch?"

"Maybe." Keys being frantically stroked sound down the line before Grayson says, "I think I can take it offline—"

"Think or can?"

He's most likely hiding out in a storage closet on the Bobrov compound, but it doesn't stop his frustrated growl vibrating down the line. He'd rather risk his cover being blown than lose the chance to announce how much I annoy him. "Either way, the interview you're hoping to be a part of is about to commence, so if you are planning to join it, move your ass, dickface."

The nerves in my gut are heard in my reply, "Get eyes and ears out of the room for me, Grayson. I don't just need them off Izzy, I need them off me as well."

"I'll do my best."

When he hits the end button, I switch off my phone, then make my way down the corridor buzzing with hyped activity. As Phillipa predicted, Internal Affairs was brought in within hours of Isaac's arrest Friday afternoon. Although they didn't immediately request to interview Isabelle, we all knew today's event was going to occur at some stage. Isabelle has a lot to answer for, but at the moment, IA agents are the only ones who can ask the hard-hitting questions without placing our entire division under the spotlight.

Unwanted scrutiny is the sole reason I stayed away from Isabelle the entire weekend. I can imagine how bad she's feeling after she was forced to arrest Isaac, but I'm surrounded by so much controversy right now, I have to thoroughly examine every step I take before taking it. It sucks, but it's also necessary.

The mood in the main hub of HQ is noticeably subdued. IA didn't just stir the pot by sending an interstate crew to investigate claims Isabelle aided and abetted a criminal by supplying Isaac with official government documents. They sent the ex-supervisor of this division—Theresa Veneto.

Phillipa broke protocol when she told me the charges IA was planning to pin on Isabelle, but considering she's currently on a flight back from Tiburon with a file I'm dying to get my hands on, her secret is safe with me. I won't let her be prosecuted for helping me any more than I won't let Isabelle be impeached because a scorned woman wants revenge. If Theresa has issues with how Alex took her down, she should be taking it out on him, not one of his rookie agents.

My teeth grit at my double standards. I've been striving for months to topple the Gottle entity by gunning for the bottom prong in his organization, so how is what Theresa is doing any different?

Realizing now isn't the time for a fucked-up riddle, I put on my game face. I make it to the conference room in just enough time. Theresa is seated across from Isabelle, but the recorder they brought with them hasn't been switched on.

Theresa's evil eyes snap up to mine when I knock on the glass door. She appears pissed by the interruption. Isabelle looks relieved. "As the union representative for this division, I need five minutes to talk to Ms. Brahn before her interview commences." I keep my tone neutral and strong, revealing I'm not seeking permission to speak with Isabelle. I'm telling them this is what's happening.

Theresa looks like she wants to chew me up and spit me out when she grinds out through clenched teeth, "Five minutes."

After gesturing for her male partner to leave the room before her, Theresa's eyes drift to mine. They're full of unvoiced warnings and skin-heating scorn. For a woman who has everything to lose, she doesn't act like it. Her gall would be impressive under different circumstances.

When the glass door of the conference room closes with Theresa and the unnamed agent on the other side, Isabelle's wide-with-panic eyes lock with mine. "Wha—"

"Be quiet, Izzy."

She's taken aback by the abruptness of my tone but brushes it off as a side-effect of a long week. "I—"

"Shut up, Isabelle." I mutter a curse word under my breath. I hadn't meant to take my frustration out on her. I'm annoyed by the blinking red light still flashing in the security camera mounted in the corner of the room, not her. I thought Grayson would have switched off the feed by now.

Like magic, two seconds later, the frustrating blip of red stops.

"What the hell?" Isabelle murmurs to herself as stunned as I am relieved.

Her shock grows when I advise her to follow the plan of attack Phillipa and I plotted late last night while FaceTiming and eating dinner. "I strongly advise you to plead the fifth—"

"I don't have anything to hide."

Usually, I'd welcome her determination, but now isn't the time for her to grow a backbone. "Please don't be stupid. They're here to charge you with conspiracy in aiding and abetting a criminal by supplying him with official government documents. If you don't plead the fifth, you're looking at over twenty years in jail."

"Why?" She looks incapable of sucking in an entire breath. "I've never given Is—"

"Shut up! I can't guarantee they don't have ears in here." I press my hands onto the white melamine tabletop before tilting closer to Isabelle. "Plead the fifth, then I'll do everything in my power to help you through this."

The plan Phillipa and I devised is risky, but the massive web I mentioned months ago grew tenfold over the weekend. It affects more people than we realized, including Isabelle. Her pleading the fifth won't stop Theresa's witch-hunt from occurring, but it will bide us some time to sort through the huge conspiracy that's been clouding my judgment the past umpteenth years.

Isabelle doesn't appear pleased with my suggestion. However, she lowers her chin, agreeing to do as I suggested. Her agreement eases the knot twisted in my stomach, grateful she trusts me enough to know I wouldn't push her to do this unless it was vital.

"I'll stay with you during your interview, but no matter what they say or do, continuously plead the fifth."

The color drains from her face as she once again nods.

Not long after that, Agent Theresa and her partner re-enter the room. "Your five minutes are up." Theresa arrogantly motions her head to the door, giving me my marching orders.

The haughty gleam in her eyes douses when I disclose, "Isabelle has requested a union representative be present during her interview."

Theresa's eyes snap to Isabelle's. "Is that correct, Isabelle?"

Isabelle's nod this time around is more affirmative than her previous two. "Yes, that's correct."

With her growl hidden by her frantic breaths, Theresa closes the door with force before moving toward a stack of chairs to gather me one. Once she rams it into my thigh, she joins her partner on the other side of the desk. When she ribs him with her elbow, her eagerness to conduct her interview is exposed, much less what she says next. "Are you in a relationship with Isaac Holt?"

Smugness swells my chest when Isabelle responds, "I plead the fifth."

As Theresa's brow shoots up high on her face, she wiggles her index finger in her ear. "Sorry, what did you say?"

"I plead the fifth amendment," Isabelle repeats, her tone higher and more confident than what it was seconds ago.

Never one to back down when sitting across from a woman as equally smart as her, Theresa switches tactics. "Are you in a *sexual* relationship with Isaac Holt?"

It's the fight of my life to hide my cringe when Isabelle says, "I plead the fifth." Her declaration this time around wasn't as confident, and Theresa is more than willing to use it to her advantage.

"Have you had physical contact with Isaac Holt since your placement commenced in this division of the FBI?"

"I plead the fifth."

There she is. Back stronger than ever.

When Theresa spots the smirk I'm unable to conceal, her eyes rocket to mine. "She's clever. A rookie agent knowing to plead the fifth. Who would have thought?"

My smirk grows, loving that she believes this plan was solely my idea. That means she has no clue not even agents from her department like her.

After returning her slit gaze to Isabelle, Theresa asks, "Are you planning to answer any of my questions, Ms. Brahn, or will you continue pleading the fifth amendment?"

Her partner chuckles when Isabelle parrots, "I plead the fifth." I realize I underestimated her as much as Theresa when she adds, "I choose not to answer your questions on the consideration that I may be unwillingly incriminating myself."

I'm tempted to wiggle my finger in my ear like Theresa did earlier when the feet of Theresa's chair scrape across the worn floorboards. After removing the sweat from her hands by dragging them down her stiff-as-a-board blouse, she gathers a manila folder from a briefcase cracked open on the edge of the boardroom-size desk. "You read a law book during your training… *impressive*." She uses Isabelle's seated position as an intimidation tactic by towering over her. "So, you're aware prostitution is illegal?"

"I'm well aware of that."

Even lost as to where Theresa is going with her investigation, I squeeze Isabelle's thigh, wordlessly advising her to stay on track. Theresa wants her to slip up. She won't do that if she continues pleading the fifth.

An indication on Theresa's game plan slams into me when she mutters, "Just because he didn't leave money on your bedside table when he was finished, doesn't make it any less of a crime."

She sets down a piece of paper in front of Isabelle. It appears to be a signed lease. Even from my side of the room, I can see the name scribbled across the owner section of the document. It's Isaac Holt, our target.

Fuck!

Isabelle clues on to Theresa's ruse as quickly as me. "I pay rent for my apartment in full every month." She ignores me squeezing her thigh to add, "The owner's details were not disclosed when my application was processed."

The relieved gasp I sucked in at her admission is quickly breathed out when Theresa replies, "I thought you might say that, so I dug a little deeper." She hands Isabelle a second piece of paper. It has a list of addresses with monthly figures jotted at the side. "The same two-bedroom apartments in your building rent for over three thousand dollars a month. You pay twelve hundred. That's not even half." She slants her head to the side as her lips tug into a rueful smirk. "Do you get a friends-with-benefits rate?"

Isabelle balls her hands into fists as she grinds out, "I plead the fifth."

Theresa continues to interrogate her with the fierceness of a shark. "Then, there's this." She slides a third piece of paper across the desk. "A charter for a private jet booked under Isaac Holt's name." I snatch the flight manifest out of Isabelle's hand before she has the chance to read it. "How romantic, most men don't take their mistresses on holidays with them," Theresa drones on.

"Isabelle's name isn't even on the manifest. That's explicit conjecture. Everything you've presented thus far is speculation." Over her attempts to ignore Isabelle's right to remain silent, I lock my eyes with Theresa's before sneering, "Isaac Holt owns over half of Ravenshoe, so it would be virtually impossible for Isabelle to rent anything in this town that didn't belong or have an association with him." I stand from my seat so fast, I knock it over. "This interview is over. If you speak to Isabelle again without a lawyer present, I won't hesitate to contact my father, who, in turn, will have a word with your superior officer."

I remove Isabelle from her seat with a tug on her arm before guiding her out of the conference room. I almost crack under pressure halfway down the corridor, but mercifully, Grayson's constant ribbing about Alex rigging HQ with motion-activated cameras stops me. There are only two places safe from his watchful eyes.

The washrooms, which I can't use since Agent Clarkston just burst through the doors like he does every morning when his laxative-laced coffee reaches his colon, and the supply room.

Supposedly, Alex always leaves one room free from surveillance. Grayson argues it's so he has a place to convene with his teammates in private. I believe it's in case a pretty blonde attorney pays him a visit in the middle of the night. Trust me when I say, he and Regan were fans of unusual hook-up locations when they were a couple.

Once we arrive in the supply room, I rake my fingers over my scalp while sucking in some big breaths. It's clear from Isabelle's fish-out-of-water response that she had no clue Isaac owns the apartment building she's living in, but I need to be sure as this is about more than Isabelle's job. It's way deeper than that.

"You didn't have a clue about any of that, did you?"

I don't know whether to laugh or cry when Isabelle shakes her head while saying, "I plead the fifth."

Is she maintaining her rights because she doesn't trust me, or does she use humor to reflect her anguish? I don't know her well enough to give a definitive answer. I know her, I just don't *know* know her if that makes any sense.

Even uneased, one thing is clear—she needs to be more cautious than she has been. "You need to be vigilant about anything you say or do over the next few days." When she nods without hesitation, I test her trust to the extreme. "Is Isaac Holt Mr. Unattainable?"

I watch her with uneased restlessness, knowing her answer but unsure if she trusts me enough to share her secret.

When she nods for the second time, I breathe out my relief that she trusts me. "Jesus, Isabelle. How long?"

Hesitation crosses her features first. It's quickly chased by honesty. "Officially, a little over a month." When the color drains from my cheeks, she rushes out, "But I met him before I knew he was being investigated." She lowers her girly squeal before revealing, "I'm petrified of flying." She takes a breather like just talking about her fear has made her scared. "I was working up the courage to enter the boarding area at the airport when my push off the railing had me crashing into Isaac." A smile replaces her frown. "Isaac took care of me. He iced the bump on my head before offering up a pain reliever for my throbbing head. I didn't think I'd see him again, so you can imagine my surprise when I was seated next to him for my flight to Ravenshoe. If that wasn't already shocking, it was a business-class seat."

Business class?

"You flew business class?" Nothing but shock registers on my face, even more so when Isabelle nods. Nothing against Tobias, but he left a good chunk of debt behind when he passed. He took out a thirty-year mortgage on his house to buy Isabelle. He still had a decade worth of payments left to make, and I'm not going to mention the funds he wasted on an apartment he never lived in, or you'll be looking at me as if I'm a rich schmuck when you discover I paid off his debt with some of the money my grandfather left me. I couldn't bring Tobias back, but I could make things a little easier for Isabelle as I wish I could have for Melody years earlier.

"Who paid for your flight?"

Isabelle glares at me like I'm stupid. "The Bureau."

I almost roll my eyes as if to say, *duh*. I might look young, but I'm not stupid.

"Did you request for your ticket to be upgraded to business class?" When she shakes her head, my suspicion grows. "Did Isaac have any way of knowing you were on his flight?" He's doing some shady shit right now that will impact Isabelle, so who's to say he wasn't back then?

Isabelle gets in half a head shake before her brows pull together. "Isaac collected my belongings from the floor, so he may have seen the boarding pass I had printed earlier that day, but it would have only been for the quickest second—" Her words stop when the supply room door rockets open.

Alex enters the room, killing our conversation in an instant. Although I trust him, it isn't enough to update him on the information Phillipa and I have unearthed the past three days. I haven't even told Grayson yet.

A tick impinges my jaw when Alex's eyes land on mine. They're as arrogant as his comment. "It's after eleven, and the report I requested first thing this morning is still not finalized, yet you have time for a chit-chat with Isabelle in the supply room. Perhaps I need to increase your workload?" The report he's requesting landed in his inbox before he arrived at the office this morning. This is just his way of telling me to piss off.

After diverting his focus to Isabelle, Alex says, "I need to see you in my office." Confident she'll jump when demanded, he pivots on his heels and stalks to the door, his brutal pace only slowing when Isabelle doesn't immediately jump to his command. "Now, Isabelle."

His clipped tone launches Isabelle into action. After straying her panicked eyes to mine, she races out of the room, falling in step with Alex's long strides within seconds. While she most likely will be placed on suspension, I dig my phone out of my pocket to call Grayson. When my call goes unanswered, I try Phillipa's number. Her plane was scheduled to land right around the time Isabelle's interview commenced.

"Hey, how'd you go?" she questions, not bothering to issue a greeting.

I rake my fingers through my hair for the second time, amplifying how badly in need of a trim it is. "Not good but better than expected."

I want to ask if she knew Isabelle was living in an apartment owned by Isaac, but I don't know if our trust circle extends that far yet. She has a file that could change my viewpoint on life in an instant, but until she places it into my hot little hands. My expectations must remain low, I've been burned in the past for issuing trust too quickly. I'd rather sidestep another scold.

"Have you just landed?"

A plane taking off almost drowns out her reply, "Yeah, I'm

sliding into the back of a cab as we speak. Where do you want to meet?"

My first thought is at HQ. However, if Phillipa bumps into Theresa, things could get mighty uncomfortable remarkably fast. "Can you come to my apartment? I have a heap of time off in lieu to take."

"All right." I could be wrong, but I swear a touch of excitement is dangling off Phillipa's vocal cords. "I should be there in around thirty. Will that work for you?"

"Thirty works. I'll see you in a bit."

"See you then."

When she disconnects our call, I slide my phone into my pocket before entering the hub of HQ. I'm not surprised to see Isabelle is packing her desk. An unpaid suspension is the Bureau's go-to punishment when an agent goes rogue. It's a penalty I've been handed twice in my almost five-year career.

Isabelle startles when I offer to walk her out. She was too busy returning Theresa's glare to notice my approach. After a final snarl, she devotes her attention to me. "I appreciate the offer, but I don't want you thrown under the bus with me."

I shoo away her worry as if it's a fly. "I don't care what they think. You're my friend, Izzy, and until proven guilty, which will never happen, I'll have your back." There's no doubt in my mind she's in a physical relationship with our target, but that doesn't mean she should be thrown in jail on false charges. The angle Theresa is working is weak at best, and I'm more than willing to show her just how pathetic it is.

Isabelle bumps me with her hip. "Thanks, Brandon."

Once she slides her pistol into her satchel and her phone into the pocket of her trousers, she shadows my solemn walk out of HQ. I kind of feel bad. If I had stopped jumping between our team's investigation and the numerous personal ones I'm undertaking, perhaps I could have avoided this. I kissed Isabelle with the hope Isaac would react. It worked, and I can't help but wonder just how effective it was. Jealousy is as potent as attraction when it's handed to the wrong person.

The constant drone of tires rolling over asphalt filters into my ears when we step onto the sidewalk at the front of HQ. Isabelle squints when the midday sun breaks through the handful of high-rise buildings surrounding us before she curls her arms around my neck.

"Thanks for your help," she whispers into my ear, her tone forlorn.

Understanding her struggle, I return her hug with just as much eagerness. "Fly under the radar, Izzy. Once I have any information, I'll bring it straight to you."

She sighs into my neck before inching back. "I will. And thank you again." Her lips tug into a grin before she says, "See you around?"

I nudge her with my hip as she did to me earlier. "You'll be back here filing before you know it."

My jest has the effect I'm aiming for. She doesn't smile a full-toothed grin, but it's pretty darn close. "Don't forget the coffees. God forbid Alex would have to fetch his own cup."

She takes in my laugh for a few seconds before spinning on her heels and sauntering down the sidewalk. I keep my eyes locked on her back until she disappears around the corner, then just as quickly, I race to my car, firing off an email to Alex about how I got a stomach bug on my way.

BRANDON

With traffic shit, Phillipa is waiting for me outside of my apartment block when I pull into the loading bay fifty-five minutes later. She leaps up from the three stairs that lead into my overpriced crash pad before walking my way. "You'll be towed within an hour if you park there."

"Pay a tow fee of one hundred dollars or an exorbitant parking garage fee that's almost three times that price." I twist my lips. "I'm willing to take a risk."

She laughs before rolling her eyes that are circled by dark rings. Even being on suspension hasn't seen her catching up on sleep the past three nights. We usually talk until around two in the morning, then we're back at it again before seven.

"Did you rewire the sliding door's alarm before you left?"

Phillipa shadows me into the foyer of my building before shaking her head.

"Why not? I don't know how things work for you IA agents, but you're supposed to leave things as you find them when you're out in the field."

My mouth gapes when she whacks me in the gut. Melody used

to do it all the time, but it seems odd coming from Phillipa. She seems too mature and anal about consequences to respond to a taunt with violence. "I didn't need to rewire the alarm because I didn't disarm it."

I gesture for her to enter the elevator car before me while asking, "Then how did you get in?"

She waits for me to push the button for my floor before disclosing, "I put in the passcode." When I peer at her in shocked awe, she frees me from being hooked by her awesomeness. "It's Isabelle's birthday."

"That's not right. I tried that combination when I reset it."

When the elevator arrives at my floor, Phillipa exits first, smiling. "Not her actual birthday. The day she was reborn." She pivots around to face me, her smile picking up. "The date referenced on the file that miraculously disappeared from Tobias's records."

"Who said there's a missing file?" I realize I need to up my lying game when her brow arches in suspicion.

Grumbling, I shove my key into the lock and twist. A wolf-whistle vibrates between Phillipa's O-formed mouth when she takes in the living area of my apartment. "Nice place. Have you lived here long?"

I toss my keys onto the entryway table before making my way to the kitchen. "Are you sure you don't work for Ravenshoe PD?"

She screws up her nose, my comment lost on her.

"Did you want something to drink?"

I hide my smile into the fridge when she replies, "Are you sure you want to walk down that path again, Agent James? You don't have a ten-mile safety barrier between us this time around."

The unconcealed sexual innuendo in her tone has my eyes darting between a bottle of water and an untouched bottle of wine. My deliberation barely lasts two seconds, but it still riddles me with guilt, which in turn, sours my mood. You can't cheat on someone if you aren't with them because they cheated on you.

Phillipa's mood slips as well as mine when she spots the bottle of water in my hand. "It's barely midday," I say, issuing her the first excuse that pops into my head. "Have you eaten? I could order in some food?"

"Does pretzels and a teeny tiny, practically-not-worth-swallowing glass of soda the airlines hand out during flights count as eating?"

Her snarky tone tugs a smile onto my face. "I'll order in. Anything in particular you want to eat?"

"I eat anything." She stops perusing the picture frames on my entryway table to stray her eyes to mine. "Except snails."

Her gag face is cute. Actually, she's cute in general. I've just never truly taken the time to look at her. Her hair is almost black and hangs to her petite waist. Her eyes are wide and almond-shaped, and both her name and skin-coloring allude to a Greek origin. She's tall for a girl, standing at approximately five-foot-nine, and she has a fit, slender frame she showcases with fitted pantsuits and shimmery blouses—a seemingly favorable outfit for female IA agents.

When Phillipa notices my gawk of her body, I drop my eyes to a drawer of pamphlets. If she weren't as receptive as she is, I would have gotten away with my wandering eyes. Unfortunately, anyone would swear she was put through the same drills as Melody and I when we were kids. "How come you didn't fight Ophelia's charges? You clearly didn't do what she said you did, so why didn't you deny her claims?"

I ruffle through the pamphlets, pretending I can't feel my heart rate picking up. "I did fight her claims—"

"No, you didn't. You allowed them to be pushed down your file when she found another sucker to do her dirty work, but you didn't have them expunged."

Part of Phillipa's comment refers to a file she put together today. It's a list of wire transfers between the Popovs and the Petrettis the past three decades. Not all of the Petrettis' transactions were issued from the east side of the country—their home turf. Some came from the west, and they were dated right around the time of a mafia princess's 'death,' and when a rookie FBI agent was assigned to a division far from her hometown.

We don't know if the transactions stopped because Ophelia's new marriage got her on the straight and narrow or because the transactions were switched to her married name. That's what we're endeavoring to work out today.

Ignoring Alex's message requesting a doctor's certificate for my absence, I bring up the Grubhub app to place an order for a plain cheese pizza and a double serving of tomato soup. While I do that, Phillipa removes two folders from her leather satchel. The first one is thick and bulging with papers, and the other one is barely the size of a few sheets of paper. Although it's small, I have no doubt the information inside will be mammoth. It isn't Melody's file, per se, more the Greggs' as a whole.

Just like Isabelle's record, it was coded to correspond with the date of the Greggs' home invasion. I don't know what's in their file yet. I asked Phillipa not to open it until she was in my presence. It could be nothing, but my gut isn't telling me that. It feels big, and it honestly has me twisted up in knots.

Once the order is placed, I dump my cell phone onto the kitchen counter before joining Phillipa in my dining room. She's using the six-seater table to sort the bank transactions into ten three-year piles. The number of transactions is impressive. It would have taken Tobias months to compile, but I can't take my eyes off the lonely file sitting at the end of the stack.

"Did you open it?"

Phillipa's eyes stray to mine before she shakes her head. She's either a good liar or she's telling the truth. "Although tempted, I didn't sneak a peek." She fights like hell to keep her expression neutral, but she loses her battle not even ten seconds later. "It's also sealed, so I didn't have much choice but to wait." She peers at me like a kid begging for a piece of candy. "Can we open it now?"

When I jerk up my chin, she snaps up the file and prepares to rip it open without a second thought like Melody did when our admissions applications were returned from Browns, but something stops her.

I realize what when she thrusts the light-weight file into my chest. "From what I saw in the videos I watched, you deserve to open this." I've never had an interest in twanging someone's lip until now.

After slipping my thumb under the seal, I lock my eyes with Phillipa's. "Will this stay between us?"

She nods without pause for thought, so I rip through the tape holding the file together. A handful of polaroid photographs slip out first. They're all of Melody. They must have been taken not long before she moved to Saugerties as she has the same length hair and huge doll eyes she had when she galloped down the stairs of her family ranch.

"How old is she in these?" Phillipa asks, gathering up the pictures.

I twist my lips. "Around four or five." I point to the one in the far left-hand side of her bunch. "Her mom had a similar photo sitting on her bedside table. She said it was from Melody's fourth birthday."

Phillipa lifts her chin as her eyes raise to mine. "What else is in there?"

I fan out the file to show her its empty.

"That's it? Just a bunch of polaroids?" she questions as she gathers up the final three photographs fanned across the table.

Our eyes snap down in sync when the crinkling of paper breaks through the silence teaming between us. When I notice the width and length of the thin slip of paper, I almost have a heart attack. It's identical in size to the one Tobias handed me moments before his death. Although it's folded, I can see it has a handwritten sequence of numbers across it. If I didn't know any better, I'd swear it's the same slip of paper.

It can't be, though, surely. Tobias had a morbid fascination with altering the lives of female mafia members, but the Greggs didn't hide Melody like Tobias hid Isabelle because she was sold like

Isabelle. Liam just wanted to keep her safe from the only man left living after their home invasion. He didn't buy her. He couldn't have. He didn't have the money.

Well, he did before he lost everything fighting charges of murder after his home invasion.

A home invasion no one can find any records of.

What if things aren't as exactly as Melody remembers them? What if her memories were muddled by a man trained in persuasive techniques?

The food I haven't eaten yet creeps up my food pipe when another disturbing notion bombards me.

What if I bedded more than one mafia princess?

To be continued in <u>Quiet Protector</u>
Or continue on to sample the first two *unedited* chapters.

Facebook: facebook.com/authorshandi

Instagram: instagram.com/authorshandi

Email: authorshandi@gmail.com

Reader's Group: bit.ly/ShandiBookBabes

Website: authorshandi.com

Newsletter: https://www.subscribepage.com/AuthorShandi

If you enjoyed this book - please leave a review.

QUIET PROTECTOR

MELODY

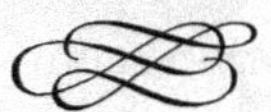

The mermaid tail of my dress swishes along wooden floorboards when I follow Julian through a packed ballroom. We received a last-minute invitation to the extravagance when I bumped into Mr. McGee last Thursday. He arrived at my office somewhat unexpectedly. It isn't unusual for government officials to do drop-in visits, but it's usually announced to the hierarchies before it occurs to ensure they're not left red-faced.

Mercifully, Leo, my boss, is always on the ball. He handled the Governor's visit without the slightest drop of sweat beading on his brow. Some would say his gall was compliments to years on the job. Others would say it's because he classes himself as an equal of Mr. McGee's. I say it's because he knew I wouldn't log out a classified file unless it were important.

Although I'll never have proof, I'm confident Marjorie Hawke's file was what Mr. McGee's visit was about. I followed the rules when Brandon requested her file. I logged its transfer into the database mainframe, doctored out anything deemed confidential, then couriered it to his branch at Ravenshoe via the private security firm our office generally uses. Protocol was followed, yet Mr. McGee believed additional scrutiny was needed.

When I pushed him on why such an insignificant case was being treated as if it held national secrets, I received an invitation to an event instead of a reason. Don't misconstrue my comment, I'm sure Marjorie's death was devastating for her husband and family, but for a governor to make a personal visit to the District Attorney's Office to demand an explanation seemed a little puerile to me.

Although unease was the first emotion I felt upon receiving Mr. McGee's invitation, inquisitiveness soon took over. I'm reasonably sure his agenda was to assert his importance, hoping it would have me falling into line, but I used his invitation with the hope of expanding both personal and work contacts.

Today's guest list is filled with the who's who of New York. The number of influential people in the one room has had Mr. McGee prancing around like a peacock all night. Despite all of that, for the most part, I've enjoyed myself. Julian is in his element. He's in awe of every person in the room, completely unaware they're eyeing him with an equal amount of admiration.

Money will never be an issue for Julian. His family has enough to last them decades into the future, but Julian doesn't see his family's success as his own. To him, he's just a humble audiologist. To people in this room, he's the billionaire mogul they're dying to sink their hooks into.

Perhaps that's why Mr. McGee invited us tonight? He loves showboating, so adding a recent Forbes 500 man onto his guest list seems like the smart thing to do. A politician is forever in campaign mode. I'm doubtful tonight is the first time Mr. McGee has approached a billionaire with the hope of a generous endorsement check. He's so unscrupulous, I wouldn't put it past him to approach the shady billionaires our office is frequently chasing for campaign funds. As long as their pockets are deep, he doesn't care who he rubs shoulders with.

I'm drawn from my thoughts when Julian stops in front of a

beautiful raven-haired woman with kind eyes and glossy red lips. "Katarina, I thought that was you." Julian places a kiss on Katarina's cheek before tugging me closer to the dynamic duo. Although there are twenty or more years between their ages, they have a unique spark. "This is my fiancée I was telling you about. Melody, please meet Katarina Rouse."

My heart pumps out an extra flutter when he mentions Katarina's surname. "You're on the board of Julian's charity. He talks about you all the time." I offer her my hand to shake, smitten to meet the woman Julian talks about often. Julian is extremely close to his mother, but she barely gets a mention when he gushes about the charity work Ms. Rouse does. "It's a pleasure to meet you."

"Hi." Katarina appears more shocked than me like I'm one of the big celebrities sending the paparazzi into a tailspin. I find out why she's eyeing me with star-filled eyes when she asks, "Have we met before?"

I twist my lips. "I don't think so." I run my hand down Julian's forearm. "I've wanted to volunteer with Julian, but life is hectic."

Katarina smiles. It's as adorable as her face, which isn't holding many wrinkles considering her age, which I'd guess to be mid to late fifties. I can only hope to have such a youthful face at her age. I want to say her smooth skin is compliments to Botox, but she doesn't have the overly-rigid face most Botox lovers do, so perhaps it's more good genes than a skilled dermatologist.

"Julian said you moved to New York to accept a position at the DA's Office. How are you finding it?" Katarina asks, appearing genuinely interested in my reply.

I pull a face. "It's good. Challenging but good." It usually takes me knowing someone for a good three to four months before I open up to them, but Katarina has the type of aura you can't help but be honest with her. She reminds me a lot of my mother. "There are more cases here than in the office I interned at in LA, but nowhere near as many staff, so it's taking me a little bit to adjust to the work-load. I'll get there... *eventually*."

Although I'm still treated as an intern by my colleagues, I'm quickly clueing in on how diverse each office is. Such as, it's not every day you'll be in the same room as a governor, a district attorney, three Federal Court judges, and a mafia kingpin. The latter has only just arrived, but he enters the room like a god, turning more than a few heads. Even I watch Henry Gottle, Sr. from afar, speechless and in awe. There's a natural arrogance to him that you can't help but be sucked in to.

Not sexually. Don't be uncultured, Henry is around the age of my father. It's the fact he presents as an extremely dark and dangerous man, but when you truly look at him, you get the sense he has a hidden nurturing side as well. He conceals it well with deadly blue eyes and a fiercely cut suit, but it's still there hiding in the dimples of his concealed smirk.

His hair is darker than a night's sky, and his skin looks like he spends his days lazing at the beach instead of amassing a vast amount of wealth from unscrupulous business adventures. His persona, even from a distance, could be described as mulish.

That is until his eyes swing my way.

I take a step back, surprised by the ownership in his heavy-hooded gaze. Unlike a handful of the women in the rape support group I commenced attending in the months following my confession to Julian, my assault didn't claim my innocence. If anything, it made me more naïve. But even someone with the purity of a saint couldn't miss the possessiveness in Henry's eyes as he makes his way across the room.

Even with the room filled with influential people, the crowd creates a pathway for him, knowing no amount of political backing will alter the facts. This state isn't run by men like Mr. McGee or Leo. It's owned by Henry.

I'm tempted to slap myself up the side of my head when the reasoning for Henry's across-the-room stare becomes apparent. He isn't parting the crowd like they're the Red Sea because he thinks I'm the most beautiful woman in the room, his eyes aren't even on me. They're on Katarina, who looks exactly how a woman should look when the man of her dreams spots her from across the room.

My brows stitch when Katarina presses a hurried kiss to Julian's cheek before she makes an excuse to leave. She's so flustered, nothing she says makes any sense, and we won't mention her unsteady footing as she darts for the exit, or you'll believe she's been downing as many cocktails as me.

I'm not drinking because I am as out of my league as Julian is in it. It's wondering if any other McGees would be at tonight's festivities. I've yet to spot Brandon in any of Mr. McGee's campaign photographs, but Phoenix and Madden occasionally pop up—Madden even more so the past six months since he announced he's running for office at the next election. He's starting at the Senate like his father did.

Thankfully, it appears as if Mr. McGee went stag tonight—*if* you exclude the three bug-eyed women who've been buzzing around him all evening. He's old enough to be their father, but they still fawn over him like he's a rock star and they're thirsty groupies.

It makes me sick.

I'm pulled from my thoughts for the second time tonight when my name is called from a voice I've never heard before. When I twist in the direction the thick, deep timbre came from, the caller of my name appears surprised I heard him as I am that he knows my name. We've met before, but that was an extremely long time ago, so why is he staring at me like a halo is circling my head.

"You heard me." Henry Gottle bridges the gap between us with three long strides. I'm tempted to bolt like Katarina did, but a weird sensation pinging through my veins keeps my feet planted on the ground. I also don't want to appear frightened in front of my colleagues because not only did Julian's grip on my hand tighten when Henry called my name, every set of eyes in the room honed in on me.

A silent gasp leaves my mouth when Henry cups my jaw in his palms. Because his hands are so big, his fingers weave through the hair I wore in tight curls with the hope it would hide the internal transmitters of the implants behind my ears. The difference in my pitch to people not born deaf already discloses I have cochlear implants, so they don't need additional proof. I'm not ashamed I was born deaf, I just hate when people assume it's a disability. It isn't, it's a uniqueness.

I can tell the exact moment Henry unearths the cause of my newfound hearing. His gasp is as silent as my earlier one, but I didn't need to hear it to know of its existence. It fanned my face with a pricy alcoholic scent.

"I can't believe you decided to get them done." Henry's words are only for my ears as are his eyes. "It's been years. Over two decades. Do you remember me?"

The hope in his eyes almost has me nodding, but the sweat from Julian's hand seeping into mine stops me. Since he's clutching my hand as possessively as Henry is holding my face, he's being roasted by the microscope of scrutiny right alongside me.

I won't have him subjected to a rumor-monger because my parents had a weird kinship with Henry many moons ago. For all we know, their meetings could have been business-related. But since this town loves gossip, and I can't shut them up by telling them to keep their eyes on their own paper, I lie as I was trained to do on cue.

"No, I don't, sorry." After stepping back, freeing myself from the fingers weaved through my hair and the hands warming my cheeks, I dip my chin in farewell. "But it was a pleasure meeting you. I hope you enjoy the festivities."

I hightail it to the exit as fast as my quivering legs will take me. Since Julian's hand is enclosed over mine, he falls into step rather quickly.

"What the hell was that?" Julian mutters when we break through the double doors of the ballroom guarded by secret service agents like the President is in attendance. "Do you know who that man is?" Although he's asking a question, he doesn't give me time to conjure a reply, much less articulate it. "He's Henry Gottle. *Henry. Gottle.*" He repeats his name slowly like I'm still deaf. "How do you know him, Mel? You've never mentioned him previously."

I move to the edge of the sidewalk to flag a cab. "I don't know him. He must have mistaken me for someone else."

"He said your name."

I roll my eyes like he's being ridiculous. He isn't, but when the chips aren't in my favor, I have a proven track record for acting immature. Brandon learned that the hard way seven years ago.

"There are plenty of people called Melody."

My eyes snap to Julian when he snickers. "And how many of them were born deaf?"

With my back up, I get snappy. "I don't know, Julian. How many? You're the one whose profession feeds off the 'disabled,' so your statistics would be better than mine."

All it takes is for our eyes to collide for the quickest second, and Julian's campaign to unravel the connection between Henry and me is set aside for comforting. He does the same thing any time we fight, and I'm ashamed to admit, I use his dislike of arguing anytime I'm overwhelmed with either fear or frustration, or sometimes both, such as tonight.

While joining me on the curb, Julian tugs off his swanky black tuxedo jacket. My heart warms as well as my body when he drapes the quality material over my shoulders, wrongly believing I'm shivering because of the late fall evening. I'm not scared. I am just disappointed about the idiot I've been portraying the past twenty minutes.

"Thank you," I whisper, pulling his coat in closer.

It smells like him, which is both comforting and exciting. He has a different scent than Brandon. His spicy aroma often reminds me of pumpkin spice lattes and freshly baked bread. Brandon's scent was woodsy and natural like it was plucked straight from nature. It was a smell I often craved before… you know.

I'm still lost as to why Joey smelled like Brandon the night of his summer party. We hung out only minutes earlier. The drinks he'd been downing before I arrived were clear on his breath, yet, I didn't detect an ounce of alcohol in the air when he slid into Brandon's bed. All I could smell was Brandon's aftershave. That's why I wrongly believed I was safe.

I guess Joey could have put it on to deceive me. In all honesty, that makes his switch in personality even more confronting. If he went to the effort to make himself appear to be Brandon, that means his assault was premeditated. That's so much worse than believing he had read my friendliness in the wrong manner. It breaks my heart believing he purposely set out to hurt me. We were close. He was my friend. I loved him even before he was given my daddy's heart, so why did he do what he did?

When tears prick in my eyes, I shift my head high and to the right to ensure Julian doesn't see the sheen threatening to spill down my cheeks. My sudden shift in visual has me stumbling onto Katarina being ushered into the backseat of a pimped-out SUV. Her protective detail isn't surprising. Not even Henry's suffocating presence stopped men eyeballing her with desire, however, the man guiding her into the four-wheel drive most certainly raises suspicion. I can't see his face, but not even his tall height, bald head, and massive biceps are behind the massive spike in my heart rate. It's his unique neck tattoo. I've seen it twice in my life. Both times it was on dead men.

BRANDON

My heart thuds against my chest as I stare down at a tiny slip of paper sitting solemnly on my dining room table. Half of me wants to snatch it up in an instant, whereas the other half wants to throw it into the fireplace with the hope the still-warm ash will ignite it as well as it set ablaze my panic. My fireplace usually gives my home a welcoming vibe, but all it's doing today is making the conditions extra muggy. I'm so hot, I am five seconds from ripping off my shirt, and we're tiptoeing toward December.

My eyes dart to Phillipa when she asks, "Shall I, or would you like the honor?"

I snatch up the paper, answering her question without words. Melody isn't technically mine anymore, but her safety is most certainly my responsibility, and I don't give a fuck if her fiancé believes otherwise.

My hands shake like I'm in the middle of a snowfield without gloves when I unfold the thin slip of paper. Even only being partially opened can't hide the single string of text scrawled across the middle. The handwritten black ink is similar to the script on the note Tobias handed me over a year ago, but it's a fourteen-digit number instead of the filing code I didn't want to discover.

I flop back my head and lock my eyes to the ceiling, relieved it's nothing close to the coding system Tobias used for his private files. Although I could swear on Joey's grave, I've seen a set of similar numbers before.

Mere days ago.

When recollection dawns on its familiarity, I head to my soft leather briefcase I dumped on the entryway table when I arrived home twenty minutes ago like I had a rocket strapped to my back. Phillipa watches me with wide, curious eyes when I tug out a similar-size scrap of paper from my briefcase. The handwriting is different, and this sequence of numbers was written with a blue pen, but the similarities between the numbers reveal a pattern, and it has my stomach twisted up in knots.

"For every check written, two check digits, a bank identifier, a branch identifier, and part of an account number is imprinted on the bottom. Is it the same with wire transfer payments?"

Phillipa looks lost to where I'm going, but she nods her head, nonetheless. "If they used the same bank and branch, you'd have similar digits on the transfer receipt, but the account number would be different." She gasps in a sharp breath when I place down the two sheets of paper side by side. "They're almost identical." Her eyes lift to mine. "Is that the number Alex pried out of Albert Thursday afternoon?" Her eyes widen when my chin balances on my chest. "But there are decades between transfers. The date on Albert's transfer reveals it only occurred this week. It was a down payment for something no amount of grappling had him disclosing, but the code on the Greggs' file is from twenty-two years ago."

The shock on her face slips away for annoyance when I mutter, "It isn't just legitimate businesses that have return customers, Phillipa."

Her face screws up. She appears utterly confused. "What do you mean? You need to spell it out for me, Brandon. I'm hormonal and five seconds from chewing off my arm in hunger, so my brain is beyond fried right now."

Trust isn't something I give easily, and tonight isn't any different. My next set of words don't just come out garbled, they're also brimming with distrust. "Did you make copies of the files I requested?" When Phillipa jerks up her chin, I ask, "Even Ophelia Petretti's?"

Her chest rises and falls four times before she pulls a third file out of her leather briefcase. This one is thicker than the Greggs' file. It's even bulgier than Isabelle's.

"Did you comb through it?" The instant I voice my question, I realize how stupid it was for me to ask. Phillipa's rant only minutes ago exposes she read Ophelia's file, otherwise, how would she know about Ophelia's bogus claims I used my position to instigate a sexual favor. "Did you find a wire transfer receipt inside?"

Phillipa's brows furrow before she shakes her head. "But that doesn't surprise you, does it? She wasn't sold, more removed from her situation, so her file wouldn't have a receipt for us to source similarities from."

With her honesty feeding my trust, I pace to an oil painting hanging above my fireplace. Phillipa groans when the removal of the painting from the wall reveals a hidden safe. "That's the first place thieves look."

My laugh comes out super breathy since I tried to hold it in. "That's the point. As soon as light is captured by the digital retina in the touchpad, an inbuilt camera commences recording. The footage is uploaded to both the security company's servers and is streamed live to my phone."

Phillipa joins me at the wall that divides my dining room from my living space. "There's a camera in there?" When I nod, she asks, "Where? That's got to be the world's smallest lens." After stepping back, she waves her hand across her body then strays her eyes to my phone that commenced streaming a live feed the instant the painting was inched away from the wall. "It's tiny but effective. I can see my crow's feet from here." She's clearly joking. Although she is a handful of years older than me, she doesn't look a day over twenty-five.

While Phillipa lady-boners over my state-of-the-art security system, I punch a six-digit code into the digital touchpad, push aside my personal weapon, bundles of emergency cash, and a shoebox full of photos and memorabilia I can't give up no matter how hard I try so I can grab a bright pink envelope from the very back. The greeting on the front of the envelope reveals it doesn't belong to me, much less the tiny slip of paper inside it.

I didn't buy Isabelle, but Tobias most certainly did, and he kept a record of his purchase.

I'm reasonably sure I won't eat for a week when I dig out the slip of paper from the envelope. The number sequence scrawled across it is a sixty percent match to the one Alex handed me. The only difference is the numbers that most likely correspond with the account the money was being withdrawn from. It abundantly proves Isaac is purchasing something significant from the Popovs. I just need to determine whether it's upstanding like the purchase Tobias made or something much more sinister.

MANY HOURS LATER, I fan a bedspread over Phillipa before heading to my room. We worked through both lunch and dinner, yet we've barely made a dent in the stack of wire transfer receipts Phillipa returned from Tiburon with. The angle Tobias was working is clear, each transfer appears to be an exchange of money between the Popovs, Bobrovs, and Petrettis. We just have no clue exactly what they purchased.

If it were children like Isabelle, this is worse than anyone could have imagined. Several of the receipts have the same transfer identity imprint as the wire transfer receipt in Isabelle's file, but without knowing the name of the child who could have been sold, we have no clue what their files are coded with.

We could scrounge through the thousands upon thousands of files in Tobias's personal collection, but that would take months.

We don't have months.

Phillipa disclosed Isaac's payment was a down payment. That means there's more to come. Furthermore, I can't live like this for months on end. I love cheese pizza and tomato soup, second only to peanut butter licked off Melody's skin, it's my favorite combination, but I barely touched it when it was delivered fresh. I didn't even reheat a slice when Phillipa's hungry stomach got the better of her four hours ago, meaning I'm once again going to bed with a tablespoon of peanut butter hanging out of my mouth.

It's the only thing that didn't make my stomach churn when placed within an inch of my nose. It had quite the opposite effect, actually. I told Melody I'd never make a peanut butter and jelly sandwich without getting hard. I should have said I'd never eat peanut butter again without testing the durability of the zipper in my pants. Just the smell of peanut butter mingling in the air gets me hard.

Eager to stop my zipper's nasty bite on my cock, I suck off the remainder of the peanut butter from the spoon, dump it and the jar of peanut butter onto my bedside table before making my way to my walk-in closet to change into something more suitable for sleeping.

When I catch sight of my white face, black-rimmed eyes, and cracked lips while standing in front of the full-length mirror, I'm tempted to snap a selfie and send it to Alex. He wouldn't need to demand a doctor's certificate if he could see what I'm seeing. The black rims circling my eyes give my skin a ghost-like appearance, and we won't mention my slouching shoulders, or we'll be here all night.

Once I'm dressed in a pair of sweatpants and a plain white shirt, I head to bed. My steps slow when I notice my iPhone screen is lit up with a text message. It's so late, Agent Phillipa crashed on me like Isabelle did weeks ago, but not nearly early enough for my mom to remind me that the best days begin when the sun is rising.

Curious, I check who the message is from before crawling into bed. I'm tired, but I can't take an ounce more curiosity.

My pulse spikes when I speed-read the message.

Unknown number: *Hey, BJ. Are you awake?*

I cross my room at the speed of lightning to check Phillipa is still asleep on the couch. Her faint snores are authentic, but she's the only female in a very long time who has called me BJ at this hour.

When I find Phillipa snuggled under my bedspread, I type out a reply to my mystery caller while pacing back to my semi-naked bed. I only have one blanket, and that's keeping Phillipa warm.

Me: *I am. Who's this?*

It feels like the planet circles the sun a million times while waiting for the three-dash message sequence to be replaced with a text.

For how long it takes, I expected more than a five-word response.

Unknown number: *It's Melody. Can we talk?*

As my eyes stray to my partially cracked opened door, my heart beats out a tune I haven't heard in years. Don't ask me why I'm checking if the coast is clear. Your guess on my weirdness of late would be as good as mine. I've barely felt myself the past seven years.

Me: *Okay.*

What? I'm on the verge of coronary failure, so it was either send a one-word text or collapse. I chose the one that wouldn't have the coroner snapping off my cock when he loads me into the back of his van. I have peanut butter on my lips, and the girl who turned my love into an obsession is asking if we can talk at three in the morning. A monster dick is understandable.

The situation in my pants grows worse when the message screen on my phone is replaced with an incoming FaceTime call. I tilt my head to the side to check Phillipa is still snoring before hitting the connect button. With my room bare of another place to sit, I rest my back on the wall my mattress is pushed up against before dragging across a second pillow to cover my crotch. I'm wearing sweatpants. The imprint of my dick is very noticeable.

Have you ever had a moment where you can neither speak nor move? That's what happens to me the instant my dodgy internet finally connects. Excluding the newspaper articles I regularly scanned for her pictures and the ones Phillipa gave me late last week, I haven't seen Melody's face in years. She's even more beautiful than I remembered. Her looks have matured, but just like her jump from adolescence to womanhood benefited her, so has the past seven years of adulthood.

From the way the screen of her phone illuminates her face, it's obvious she's sitting in a dark room. Not even the dingiest conditions could hide her gorgeous face, tulip-shaped nose, and bright brown eyes that are twinkling despite a small bout of wetness flooding them, though.

"*Hi, BJ*," Melody signs through watering eyes.

"*Hi.*" I want to say more, but I'm truly and utterly speechless. Usually, I speak while signing, but I can't even manage that this time around.

"*I am sorry for the late hour—*"

"*It is fine. I was awake,*" I interrupt. "*Are you okay?*"

The quick bob of her chin lowers my heart rate miraculously fast. "*I need a favor?*"

"*Anything,*" I reply without pause for thought. She helped me when I reached out to her a few months ago, so the least I can do is return the favor.

Who am I kidding? Even if she hadn't secured Marjorie's file for me, I still wouldn't have said no to her. I was trained to obey, protect, serve, and honor her. Years of silence didn't change that. It just taught me to ensure the person I'm helping is worthy of my assistance. Melody cheated on me, but Grayson is right. She made a mistake—*once*—so it's time to let bygones be bygones.

"What do you need?" Conscious not to wake Phillipa, I only sign my question instead of speaking it as well. Melody doesn't seem to mind. Just as much silence is resonating from her side of the conversation as mine. I can't even hear the annoying tick of the antique clock she keeps on her bedside table. It's one of those old wind-up styles. It ticked all damn night when I had sleepovers at her house when we were kids, so you can imagine how mortified I was when she packed it when we left for college.

Mercifully, Melody exhausted me to the point of being near-comatose the weekends we spent at her dorm, so it didn't keep me awake like it did in our youth.

The only good thing that could have come out of Melody's dorm fire was discovering that frustrating time contraption had been destroyed by flames. Alas, nothing ever comes easy for me. The damn thing survived with only a handful of scorch marks.

Although I can't testify that Melody packed her clock when she left for Cali all those years ago, but since its annoying tick couldn't be blamed for my lagging sleep schedule the following six months, I'd say she did.

After glancing up and to the left, Melody returns her eyes to mine. *"I was hoping you could help me identify someone."* When my head bobs, she continues, *"I only have a photo to go off. It is grainy, but I figured you would—"*

"Grainy is fine. Grainy works. Can you send it to me?"

Smiling, she nods. My phone dings two seconds later. This will make me sound like a sucker, but it takes me a good three seconds to log out of my FaceTime app to open up my messages. I don't want Melody to disappear again, even with this feeling more like a business call than a personal one.

I'm anticipating for the person in Melody's photo to match the man from Phillipa's surveillance images. I'm proven wrong when my eyes drink in a blurry image of a large bald man standing next to a dark four-wheel drive. His biceps are the size of bowling balls, and he is a good two heads taller than the raven-haired woman he's guiding into the back seat.

Once I'm confident I've taken in the photo with due diligence and wiped the riled expression from my face, I reopen my FaceTime screen. Melody is there, patiently waiting for me with her lower lip caught between her teeth. Even in the tense circumstances, the visual of her chewing on her lip sends blood rushing to my cock. She's always been undeniably beautiful, and tired, panicked eyes can't detract from that.

Recalling the reason for her uneasy gaze, I ask, *"Who is this man?"*

Melody's dirty blonde brow pops up high on her face. *"I was hoping you could tell me that. That is why I reached out."*

I scrub my hand along the scruff on my jaw, hoping it will conceal my lips when they respond to the smugness on her face. "Smart-ass."

Guilt for making light of the situation smacks into me when Melody's playful chew of her bottom lip turns lethal. She bites down hard as she fights with all her might to trap the sob I see in her eyes in her throat.

"I am sorry. It is late. I am being an ass."

She drags a hand across her wet cheeks before assuring me I have nothing to apologize about. *"It was not what you said. It was hear—"*

She stops signing when a male voice joins our voiceless conversation. "Mel, what are you doing hiding out in the living room? Come back to bed, baby. It's cold without you."

For the first time in my life, I dislike the taste of peanut butter in my mouth. It isn't just the guilty expression on Melody's face that has me regretting my dinner selection, it's the image of a man wearing nothing but a pair of sleeping pants in the top righthand corner of Melody's screen. The lamp behind him shows he's standing in front of a rumpled bed.

My eyes shoot back to Melody's face when I spot her signing in the corner of my eye. *"I have to go, BJ. Can I call you tomorrow?"*

With how hard sick, morbid jealousy is hitting me, I should say no, but for some fucked-up reason, I dip my chin instead.

My quick agreement returns the smile I was mesmerized by only seconds ago. *"Thanks, BJ."*

Melody stares directly at me for what feels like a lifetime before she disconnects our call. It takes me just as long to lower my phone from my face. Even with an immense amount of awkwardness fueling our exchange, it was so surreal, I'm beginning to wonder if I am napping on the couch with Phillipa.

The only reason I know I'm not is because Phillipa has her shoulder propped on the doorframe of my bedroom. Her brows are pulled together tightly, and her lips are pursed. "Do you often have wordless conversations in the middle of the night?"

I shake my head. "That was Melody."

"I kind of gathered that." Phillipa enters my room without waiting to be invited. "The sign language gave it away, and let's not forget *that*." She swallows harshly at the end of her sentence before dropping her eyes to the crotch of my pants—the *exposed* crotch of my pants since I knocked off the pillow somewhere between being astonished by Melody's call and blinded by jealousy. "What did she want?"

After covering the tent in my pants with a pillow, I arch a brow. "Do you really want to have this conversation now and in here, of all places?"

I stare at Phillipa with massive eyes when she touches her toes, twists her back, then does leg stretches like she's about to run a marathon. "I'm not as nimble as I was in my college days, but this old girl should still be up to the task." When she spots my whitening gills, she laughs. "I'm joking, BJ. Even if it's been a while, you don't have the equipment I need for an all-night romp-a-thon."

"Huh?"

Phillipa motions for me to scoot across the mattress. When I do as asked, she discloses, "I'm a lesbian."

"You're a lesbian?" I apologize to anyone within a five-mile radius of my apartment building. I can't help but shout. I've never been in the dating circuit, but I could have sworn she was giving me flirty kiss-me vibes earlier today.

Fuck, I'm in even more desperate need to get laid than I realized.

After slipping between the sheets of my bed, Phillipa slants her head to the side so she can peer at me with batting lashes. "I'm not a lesbian. But I'm more than happy to pretend I am if it saves my ass from spending another minute on your couch. Just because it's expensive doesn't mean it is habitable, BJ. I paid a fortune for a bonsai garden to fancy up my patio, and it died within two weeks."

Even though I shouldn't laugh, I can't help it. I'm so tired, deliriousness is the next logical step to full-blown craziness.

Phillipa waits for my chuckles to settle before nudging her head to my phone. "Are you going to show me what Melody sent you, or should I wait for you to fall asleep then hack into your phone?" When I give her a look as if to say, *I'd like to see you try*, the smugness on her face triples. "Melody's birthday, am I right?"

When she scoops up my phone, I snatch it out of her hand, grumbling about how I have a knack for picking up annoying strays. Once I have my message app open, I scroll down so Phillipa can't see I was unaware of Melody's private cell phone number until now, then pass her my phone.

"That's Kwan Turgenev. Why do you have a photo of him?"

The collision of our eyes is almost brutal. I'm desperate to find out how she identified the perp so quickly, and she's dying to know why I have a photograph of him.

Since Phillipa had a nap, her stability is more noticeable than mine. I dive over her legs without the teeniest bit of concern my male parts brush her shins on the way by. I need my laptop, and I left it on the dining table when I gathered the bedspread for Phillipa.

Phillipa's craziness jumps up a notch when I yank out a chair from beneath my dining table and take a seat in front of my laptop. "Whatcha doing?"

"Running a background search on Kwan Turgenev." I raise my eyes to hers. "Does his first name start with a K or Q?"

"K..." I stop typing Kwan's name into the search bar of the Bureau's mainframe when Phillipa adds, "But you won't find anything on him. He's a ghost. Has been for years."

With my lips twisted, I finalize typing his name, certain I have access to channels Phillipa doesn't know about.

TEN MINUTES LATER, I'm chewing on my tongue. There's not a single shred of evidence that a Kwan Turgenev exists, much less had an invitation to the campaign fundraiser I saw flyers for in the backdrop of the photograph Melody sent me.

"I told you he's a ghost." Phillipa slumps in the chair across from me before balancing her feet on part of the seat not taken up by her backside, so she can cradle her knees with her arms. Melody used to sit in the nook at her window the same way anytime she was tired. "It's been like that for years. Other than a handful of long-range surveillance photos a few years back, his file is empty. I'm shocked you have an image of him. I doubt you would if he noticed it was being taken."

Ignoring her underhanded comment that Kwan is dangerous, I ask, "Do you still have access to his surveillance photos?" Although the late hour could be playing havoc with my mind, I'm reasonably sure I've seen Kwan before. I just can't recall where.

Phillipa lowers her legs to the floor before she leans across the table to seize control of my laptop. "How long after a suspension does access to my Bureau email remain?"

I smirk a smug grin. "If you know the right people, your access will never expire."

BRANDON

*I*n a painfully quick thirty seconds, the images Phillipa mentioned are being uploaded to my laptop. I say 'painfully' as I wouldn't have minded flexing some hacking muscle tonight. If I have a reason to brag, my head might stop striving to work out what Melody has been up to in the eight hundred and thirty-six seconds since she ended our call. If the knot in my stomach is anything to go by, I won't eat for a week.

When the first image pops up on the screen, my brow arches. I've seen Kwan before, I'm certain of it. "How long ago were these photos taken?"

Phillipa's lips twist. "I'm not sure. Around seven or eight years ago." She swings her big, tired eyes my way. "Have you seen him before?"

I lift my chin. "Do we have any intel on how long ago he got his neck tattoo?" I stop just before I disclose his tattoo is the most telling sign that we've crossed paths before. It's a match to the family crest Crombie had tattooed on his neck, meaning Kwan has links with the debunked Bobrov crew. The only thing I can't work out is why he didn't have his tattoo in the images dating back to when the Bobrov crew was still current. It makes no sense. *Unless...*

Phillipa's eyes snap to mine when I garble out, "The Bobrov crew is reforming." She watches me cross the room with her mouth hanging open. "Kirill Bobrov arrived stateside a few weeks ago. Grayson is undercover in his crew." I show her the photo Grayson forwarded to my private email a few weeks ago. It shows Katie Bryne in the flesh standing directly in front of Grayson. She aged similarly to the composite sketch the Bureau funded years ago, but she doesn't look malnourished and scared. She's smiling in the picture, albeit apprehensively. "This could cause significant national security. Hence the CIA's interest."

"*Alleged* interest," Phillipa corrects while removing Katie's photograph from my grasp. "Does Grayson have direct conformation Kirill is stateside?"

I shake my head before arguing why that means nothing. "Kirill doesn't go anywhere without Katie. You thought I was obsessed with Melody enough to kill for her. There's no guessing with Kirill. He *has* killed for Katie. Many times."

Phillipa gives off a range of emotions during my comment. She nodded when I said she believed I was obsessed enough to kill for Melody, screwed up her face when I admitted Kirill has killed for Katie, then looked on the verge of vomiting when I added an unnumbered amount to my confirmation.

"Unless we have credible evidence Kirill is stateside, I can't take this to my father." She wobbles Katie's picture during the last half of her statement. "Get me proof, Brandon, and then I'll push for the privileges we swear we don't have."

"I'll get you proof, and I'll get it through him." When I nudge my head to my laptop to point out who I'm referencing, the peanut butter that raced up my food pipe when Melody's fiancé asked her to come back to bed coats my tongue. I knew I'd seen Kwan before, but it took me a few seconds to put the pieces together since it occurred the day my life was upended. He's as big and as thick as he was in Melody's photo, but the ones from Phillipa's secret files show how different someone can look with a head full of hair.

"He was on the scene of the Greggs' accident." Phillipa swallows as forcefully as me. "He broke protocol to tell me which hospital they went to." The width of my eyes doubles when another notion crashes into me. "He was at Melody's house looking for her when Dr. Giorgio disclosed she wasn't at the hospital."

As bile burns the back of my throat, I snatch my phone off the dining room table before scrolling through my recently called list. In my panic, it takes me a few seconds to recall why Melody's number isn't displayed. She had texted me before we FaceTimed.

Once I have the Messenger app open, I hit the number at the top of the screen before squashing my phone to my ear. Melody's phone rings and rings and rings and rings, only connecting when I've hung up and redialed for the fourth time.

"Where did you take the photo you sent me?"

I take a step back when a gruff male voice asks, "Who is this?" My panic had me forgetting Melody can't answer my call, so this must be Julian—her fiancé.

The idiocies keep coming when I reply, "It's Brandon. Is Melody there? I need to speak to her." *Of course, she's there. You were just talking to her, dipshit.*

"She's not available at the moment, Brandon." I don't miss the quickest hiss of disdain when Julian speaks my name. "Is it anything I can help you with?"

I'm about to demand him to put Melody on the phone, but the quickest flurry in the corner of my eye stops me. Phillipa is pushing across the four photos she took of Melody when scrutinizing her from afar. The ones with a man in the background that we've yet to identify.

I hear Julian gulp when I ask, "Do you have a security detail following Melody?"

"Melody's security is of utmost importance to me—"

"I'll take that as a yes." His silence speaks volumes. "How many?"

Phillipa silently begs for me to play good cop when my snippy tone wakes her from the dead, however, Julian doesn't seem to mind. What good, upstanding citizen would? I'm not attempting to mow his turf, I'm endeavoring to keep his fiancée safe. Only a narcissist would have an issue with that.

"At the moment, I have one man shadowing her, but her security detail consists of five men in total."

I choke on my spit. "Five? That's a bit obsessive, don't you think?"

He scoffs like I'm being outrageous. I'm not. I am pleased he's taking Melody's safety seriously. I just wish the burden wasn't on his shoulders. It was the job I was born to fill. "She had a bit of a scare a few years ago on the metro. I decided from then not to take any precautions."

"What type of incident?" I force through the fear clutching my throat.

Bare feet padding against wooden floorboards sound down the line as Julian replies, "She was assaulted. It's safe to say it rattled her."

I grip my phone so hard, I almost crack the screen. "She was assaulted?"

Julian must hear something in my voice I didn't mean to express. "Not like *that*. She wasn't hurt like *that*." I swear he whispers, 'this time,' but since my pulse is raging in my ears, I can't testify to that. "She bumped into a woman who wouldn't know class if it bit her in the ass. She spooked Melody into a nervous breakdown..."

He continues talking, but I don't hear what he says next. I'm too busy making my own assumptions. They all involve a guy in a sparkly gold cape galloping in to save the day. All men with money have a hero complex. Even without hearing the rest of Julian's story, I guarantee you they've been together since the day he rode in and saved Melody on his white horse. I'm not surprised, just disappointed. I thought Melody was too smart to fall in the category of a damsel in distress.

I tune back into Julian's dribble with barely a second to spare. "If this has anything to do with Melody's safety, I can assure you she's in safe hands."

"I'll be the judge of that. Your security is so lagging, they missed her exchange with a suspected Russian militant last week."

Julian doesn't take my snappy attitude in stride this time around. "Henry Gottle approached her, not the other way around, and we left shortly after. She was *never* in any danger."

Now I'm the one left gasping. "Henry Gottle approached Melody?" When an agreeing hum whistles down the line, I squeal like my nuts have never dropped, "When?"

"At the campaign function *your* father invited us to." Even a person with a hearing disability wouldn't have missed the disdain in Julian's tone when he mentioned my father.

I snap my fingers at Phillipa, demanding a pen and a piece of paper. She rustles up a notepad and a pen from her leather briefcase, acting as if her ears aren't pricked, eavesdropping on every word Julian and I share.

Once I have the pen and pad in my hand, I ask, more coolly this time, "Did you purchase anything at the function? A cocktail? Campaign pin? Anything at all you couldn't use cash for?"

I can't see Julian, but that doesn't mean I can't feel his shock at the swift change in our conversation. "I purchased a handful of cocktails. Why?"

"Can you recite me the receipt details?"

Julian scoffs. "It was a twenty thousand dollar a plate function. They don't hand out receipts for fifteen-dollar cocktails."

Someone without as many digits in their bank account as me would whistle at the impressive per-plate figure he quotes. However, I feel sick about it. The money doesn't go toward good, scrupulous causes. It funds corruption, political mongering, and keeps men like my father out of jail.

"What about your bank records?" I suggest in a hurry. "Even

minute payments have traceable transaction numbers associated with them."

Phillipa's face lights up when she clicks to the reason for my inquiry. I've suspected for years my father's campaigns for office were being funded illegally, but with the Bureau not responsible for that side of justice, I've never had the chance to prove my theory. Although a transaction number won't give me all the answers I'm seeking, it will show me where I should be directing my questions.

Julian is either scrubbing his chin or his tired eyes. I don't know him well enough to know his nervous traits. "Can this wait until the morning? I left my laptop at my penthouse, so I don't have access to my banking codes."

Disappointment should be the first thing I feel, but it most certainly isn't. "You don't live with Melody?"

Julian's sigh is more revealing than his next set of words. "No, I don't."

If he's worried I'm tempted to mow his lawn when he isn't home, he has no reason to fret. I know what it feels like to be cheated on, so I sure as hell won't put someone through the same thing even if I think he's a douche. Isabelle and Isaac weren't together when we kissed, so it technically didn't count, but I still felt like shit after it.

Julian fights for the top spot on the podium. "Melody and I are holding back on moving in together until after we wed. We think that will make it more special."

Confirmation of their upcoming nuptials is like a knife to the heart. It deflates my ballooned chest in an instant and has me more than eager to end our conversation. "Tell Melody I identified the man in the photo she sent me, and that I'll email her the details within the hour."

Julian's sigh this time around is ten times more devastating than his earlier bone. "She called you for help?" When I hum out an agreement, he asks, "Why didn't she ask me?"

Even though he can't see me, I shrug. "That's something you two need to work out."

After thanking him for his assistance, I disconnect our call then toss my cell phone onto the dining room table. I'm fucking wrecked, but I don't see me getting any sleep any time soon. The dots are starting to connect, so I can't shut down my mind now.

After a quick scrub of my eyes, wordlessly warning them to get with the program, I lock them with Phillipa. "He said Henry Gottle approached Melody at the fundraising gala."

Appreciation for her honesty buzzes through me when she replies, "I heard. I'm just unsure how that factors into the theories I've been mulling over the past few months. They were in a public place, and Henry isn't known for making mistakes, but I guess even the sturdiest man's knees would have buckled in that situation."

"Theories?" I query, shocked.

This is the first time I'm hearing about any theories.

Breathing out, Phillipa slips into the chair next to me while pondering on what to tell me. I assume she goes for honesty when she mutters, "The wire transfer receipt in Melody's file has you worried that she was sold, but what if she wasn't sold... more stolen? And the wire transfer receipt in her file was payment for an attempted recovery?"

When she spots nothing but confusion on my face, she digs into her briefcase for the umpteenth time the past sixteen-plus hours. "Do you remember how Tobias's fridge was covered with photos?" I jerk up my chin, my stomach too swishy to issue a worded reply. "I took a closer look when I was investigating Tobias's case." She slides the picture of Isabelle and Katarina I took a snapshot of with my cell phone across the table. "Do you know who they are?" I lift my chin again since words are still alluding me. "What about the child in the far back corner of this photo?"

My heart whacks out a funky tune when she hands me an almost identical picture. The child next to Katarina isn't Isabelle. Only half of her face is exposed since she's been removed part the way through the photograph being snapped, and she's barely a toddler, but I'm confident it's Melody. I'd recognize her face anywhere.

With my thrusting chest revealing that I'm clicking on to what she's implying, Phillipa opens the file she used when interviewing Melody at her office weeks ago. "There isn't a single photo of Melody before the age of four in *any* of her family snaps. She mentioned during our interview that her father hid her photos when her grandmother came to visit." My head bobs when I recall reading that on the transcripts Phillipa logged in the Bureau mainframe weeks ago. "Then, there's this." She pushes a blown-up photograph of a stairwell across the table. There are a dozen or so portraits lining the wall. "This is from the brownstone the Greggs owned before they moved to Saugerties."

Shock rains down on me. "How did you get this photo? I haven't unearthed any information about the Greggs before they arrived at Saugerties." *And believe me, I've been looking.*

Phillipa drags her teeth over her lower lip before murmuring, "I have my resources." After a quick swallow, she keeps my head in the game we're playing instead of the old one I continually slip into of late. "Once again, these photos show Melody at around the age of four or five... all except this one."

Confusion bombards me when she points to a portrait at the base of the stairs. "That's not Melody. The facial structure is wrong." I could be mistaken, but the child has boyish features.

"It isn't Melody," Phillipa discloses, putting me out of my misery. "It's Henry Gottle, IV."

"The fourth? As in Henry's son?" I'm taken aback when she nods. "That can't be right. Why would the Greggs have a portrait of Henry's son in their home?" Although I appear to be asking questions, I'm more summarizing than seeking answers. It's how I operate.

Phillipa doesn't realize that, though, "I don't know. I was hoping Melody would solve the riddle for me, but she appeared as shocked as you are now."

"Did you tell her this is Henry's son?" I point to the evidence I plan to authenticate the instant I catch my breath.

She shakes her head. "No. At the time, I didn't realize what I was stumbling toward." She slouches low into her chair as her brows pull together. "Come to think of it, I was put on suspension only hours after disclosing my findings to my supervisor."

I thought her late suspension for Crombie's death was weird but shrugged it off. She's the Director's daughter. That makes her virtually untouchable, but I guess this goes even higher than the head of the FBI. This extends all the way to the top rung of the ladder. It's just a criminal entity totem pole instead of the agency sworn to take them down.

"We have photographic evidence, a wire transfer receipt in a file relating to the Greggs, and knowledge Henry knows who Melody is. That's already damning, Brandon, but this… this is the icing on the cake."

The printout Phillipa hands me is badly water-damaged. Hardly any of the ink is legible, but it isn't needed to decipher what it is. It's the result of a hearing test conducted on a female child born the same month and year as Melody. The name the report is addressed to is smudged, but I can work out the last four letters— ttle.

That's not close to Gregg.

"I asked an audiologist to decipher the results for me," Phillipa discloses, her tone softening with sympathy. "He advises the child tested was born profoundly deaf."

"That doesn't mean anything. Two out of every thousand children born in the US have some type of hearing impediment." I slump into a seat, so I can cradle my throbbing head in my hands. My brain is so overloaded, it feels like it's about to seep out of my ears. "She also looks like her mother, Phillipa. Those genes can't be forced."

My head pops up from my hands when she asks, "What about her dad? Does she look like him?"

"What are you implying? Are you saying Liam isn't Melody's dad?"

Guilt fills her eyes when she replies, "I'm not implying anything. I'm just looking at the facts as they're presented to me."

"Facts can be wrong, Phillipa. Evidence can be wrong."

She glares at me as if I have a second head. "Evidence doesn't lie—"

"It does when it's put in the wrong hands!" I interrupt, shouting. "I'm not okay with this. This feels wrong. You didn't see Wren with Liam. She wouldn't have hurt him like you're suggesting. She loved him." *Kind of how Melody loved me before she cheated on me.*

"There's an easy way to untwist the knot in your stomach, Brandon." I realize I need to watch her more closely when she says, "Give me a strand of hair from her brush in your safe, and I'll run it through CODIS."

Even with my brain pounding my temples, I fiercely shake my head. "No. I'm not going to do that."

"It will give us answers."

"And it will have me breaking Melody's trust! I'm not doing it, Phillipa. I won't deceive her like—"

"She deceived you?"

My back molars smashed together. "Wow. You're full of low blows today, aren't you?" I pack up the files we were in the process of sorting before she fell asleep, stuff them into my briefcase in silent confirmation I'm the lead agent on this case since I'm not the one on suspension, then I make my way to my front door to open it for Phillipa. "It's late. We should reconvene in the morning."

Worry fills her face. "Brandon—"

"Good evening, Agent Russell." I feel like a bitch using her way of telling me to butt-out on her, but I'm too exhausted to play nice.

"I'm not your enemy, Brandon."

I lock my eyes with hers, so she can see the absolute truth in them when I reply, "And neither is Melody."

Hearing the determination in my tone, she stands to her feet to gather her belongings. Once she has everything in order, she joins me in the entryway of my apartment. "Call me once you've settled your emotions enough to look at the evidence through the eyes of an agent."

The anger burning my cheeks doubles when she presses her lips to the corner of my mouth before she saunters out of my apartment. I slam my door closed, clench my hands into fists, then soundlessly scream my frustration into the crisp morning air. I understand Phillipa's objective. I can see the evidence and comprehend how damning it looks, but she doesn't see the consequences as readily as I do. If any of this is true, it will destroy Melody's legacy of her father for the third time in her life.

I won't let that happen. Even if the universe has sent Melody another undeserved curveball, she won't be up at the home plate, swinging alone. I'll be right by her side as I was trained to be and how I *want* to be.

MELODY

Butterflies ignite in my stomach when the email Brandon promised in the wee hours of this morning drops into my inbox. I wanted to call him back after Julian disclosed he had called while I was in the shower, washing off the guilt on my face, but Julian said if the matter was urgent enough to contact someone at four in the morning, his private security firm should take care of it.

I don't know why, but I didn't want that to happen. The unnamed man's neck tattoo certainly set my nerves on edge, but it wasn't enough to seek professional assistance.

I know what you're thinking, *then why reach out to Brandon?* Brandon is different. He's not just an FBI agent. He's also my friend, so I feel he'd be more honest with me than anyone else.

Do I deserve his righteousness after lying to him?

Not at all, but I hope to still have it.

After scooting my chair in close to my desk, I click on Brandon's email. Excluding last night, we've only communicated via work contacts, so I had to wait until I arrived at the office to discover if he unearthed the identity of the man I snapped a photo of last weekend.

I'm not surprised to find a detailed dossier on the man in question attached to Brandon's email. His date of birth is missing from the report, but numerous surveillance images of him are attached to it.

I push away my double mocha latte when one of the images shows Kwan Turgenev wearing a white apron covered with blood. Although the butcher shop sign in the corner of the picture reveals the reason for his blood-smeared smocks, it's too early in the day to act nonchalant to that amount of blood.

I'm not a fan of blood. Haven't been since I arrived at my parents' accident barefoot and shrouded with panic.

My brows stitch when I commence reading the first sentence of the last paragraph in Brandon's email.

I have forwarded my findings onto Julian's security team, so they can keep watch for Kwan. I will update Grayson's and my guys by sunrise.

While wondering exactly how many men are watching my every move, my eyes drift to the time stamp on the email. It shows Brandon sent his email a little after five this morning. He must be exhausted. I'm dragging my feet, and I managed to get two solid hours after calling him. The first six were spent tossing and turning while pondering whether I should drag him into my messy life again. If I were a better person, I would have left him out of it.

Unfortunately, I'm only a shell of the woman I used to be.

Everyone thinks I have the ideal life—a dream job, an adorable fiancé who's stinking rich, and a face that doesn't require a heavy coat of makeup to be acceptable for public outings. They fail to recall I lost my parents a month before my eighteenth birthday, I have no known living family members, and even years later, I still attend support groups for victims of sexual assault because no matter how slow Julian is willing to go, I still don't think I'll ever be ready to take the next big step in our relationship.

In a way, I guess Julian's patience makes me lucky. He pledged he'd wait an eternity for me to be ready. He was just the second man to make that oath.

Brandon made it years before him.

This will sound stupid, and you probably won't believe me, but my concerns about people's opinions of me died a long time ago, so here we go. Julian and I haven't slept together. We've shared the same bed, fondled, kissed, and touched on every base before the home plate, but we haven't consummated our relationship as most modern-day couples do within the first few months.

Do you recall me saying how I couldn't get passed certain things after my assault? Intimacy is one of those neuroses. It isn't that I clammed up, my mind just wanders at the most inappropriate times, *then* I clam up.

When I admitted what was happening to my therapist, she suggested a period of abstinence so I could get to know Julian in a way intimacy doesn't allow. I needed to trust him not to hurt me. It was only supposed to be for six months, but when we noticed how less toxic our relationship was since we weren't forcing a sexual connection, it continued beyond that. We grew and matured as friends, and our love blossomed right along with it.

When it continued past the original six months, nothing was said. When it hit twelve months, I was certain Julian would bring it up, so you can imagine my surprise when it wasn't mentioned again until the big 'M' word was cited along with it.

Although neither of us are virgins, we like the idea of making our wedding night special, so we somewhat agreed to save that side of our relationship for the night we become husband and wife.

I know what you're thinking. I've panicked about the exact same thing multiple times the past two-plus years, but I truly don't believe Julian is cheating on me. For one, he isn't that sort of guy. He's sweet and kind and truly loves me enough to wait an eternity for me to reciprocate his love with intimacy as well as words.

He's good to me. Really, *really* good.

Riddled with guilt about my deceit, I return Brandon's email, thanking him for his assistance and assuring him I'll update him on anything Julian's security team finds out before forwarding Brandon's email onto Julian.

My computer has barely whooshed when my work phone commences ringing. I'm not surprised to see my incoming call is from Julian. He doesn't scour the wastelands of society to find hearing-impaired people anymore. He does a majority of his work from a huge skyscraper not too far from here, meaning he has plenty of time to plot a move into politics.

My lips curl into a smile when he issues the greeting he usually does when I get a head start on my day. "Good morning. I missed your snuggles this morning."

"Good morning, and I'm sorry. I was a little eager to get to work."

Julian is gorgeous, but that doesn't mean he isn't also smart. "To download Brandon's email?"

Even though he can't see me, I nod. "Yes. I'm sorry I didn't tell you about the photo and for contacting BJ behind your back."

His sigh makes me even more disappointed in myself. He only ever sighs when he's upset. "I'm not angry you reached out to Brandon. I just wish you would have kept me in the loop. I have men very capable of finding out *any* information you want, Mel. All you need to do is ask."

"I know, this is just different…" I pause to consider how I can explain that to Julian without hurting his feelings.

Mercifully, Julian knows me better than I give him credit for. "He's your past, so you can't help but run to him when it's a matter concerning your past."

He can't see me, but I nod my head, nonetheless.

My belief he has superpowers doubles when he adds, "But I'm your future, Mel, and anything happening to you right now is my responsibility."

"I know…" When he sighs, I add on more convincingly, "I do. I just didn't want you caught up in this mess."

"Your mess is my mess. I thought you understood that when you agreed to become my wife?"

"I did, and I still do." I almost roll my eyes at the dimness of my voice. I don't sound like a woman who graduated at the top of her class. No one feels smart when they're bringing up subjects that make them want to sob. "But these people killed my parents, Julian. They destroyed my life. I don't want to share how much that affected me with men who don't have the faintest clue what I've been through."

Julian's reply is both gut-wrenching and honest at the same time. "If that's the reason you sought Brandon's help, I still believe you reached out to the wrong person. I know *all* your secrets, Mel. Brandon doesn't." I wipe away the tears careening down my cheek from his statement when the high pitch of his personal assistant squawks down the line. "I have to go, but I'd like to talk more about this tonight."

"Okay."

"Mel…" He sounds truly devastated like he can hear the sob sitting in the back of my throat, begging to be released. "I'm not upset. I swear to you, I'm not. I just want to make sure you know I'm here for you, too. I've always been here for you."

I suck in a big breath. "I know. I'm just being silly. I'm fine."

"You're not fine. I can hear how upset you are in your voice." Julian cups his phone to tell his receptionist he's leaving for the day before focusing his attention back to me. "Go tell Leo you're not feeling well and that you need to go home."

I scoff like he's being ridiculous. "I can't leave, Julian. I just got here."

"You either tell Leo you aren't feeling well, or I'll demand he fire you."

I'd laugh if he didn't sound so serious. You don't realize the immense amount of pull money has until you're engaged to someone with a lot of it. Doors that were previously locked up like a vault have been swinging open for me lately—including my placement in this very office.

"If you get me fired, I'll eat ice cream until my ass becomes the size of a fridge."

I half-hiccup half-laugh when Julian replies, "Maybe then I'll finally have the chance to catch you." That there summed up our relationship with ten little words. Julian is forever chasing me. "Meet me outside your office in fifteen. I'm thinking it's a field trip kind of day."

The tears in my eyes burn away for happiness. Julian's adventurous day trips have taken us many places the past three years, they've just not landed us in the bedroom. I could see that changing today. His understanding has me opening up even more than his substantial wealth can. I just need to get the image of Brandon's matured yet still boyishly handsome face out of my head first.

BRANDON

Have you ever woken up feeling like you've swallowed an entire beach worth of sand? That's what replicates the dryness in my mouth when the shrill of a cell phone wakes me. Don't ask me what the time is, much less what day it is, as I wouldn't have the faintest clue. I must have nodded off a few hours ago with my mouth hanging open and my backside willing to accept the hardness of my couch just for the chance of a few hours of shut-eye.

Phillipa was right, my couch is as hard as a rock.

After blinking three times in a row to lube up my eyes, I glance down at my phone to see who's calling me. I'm hoping it's Melody, but I am not disappointed when I discover it's Isabelle.

"Miss me already?" I jest down the line, cringing when my voice comes out super groggy.

The sleep in my eyes scratches my eyeballs when my cheeks incline over Isabelle's playful reply, "I do… but I also need a favor."

"Another one." The chuckle that follows my witty comment exposes I haven't napped for long. I'm still on the cusp of insanity.

I sit up straighter when Isabelle discloses, "Megan Shroud was just seen leaving on a bus to New York. Can you please check if she purchased a one-way or a round-trip ticket?"

"Yeah, hold on." I drag my laptop across the coffee table before logging into the local bus company's web-hosting provider. I use the warrant my team was granted to track Isaac's movements as an excuse to access their servers. It only takes three strokes to unearth an answer to Isabelle's query. "It's a one-way ticket."

Isabelle's voice is sickly sweet when she asks, "Can you add Megan's name to the travel database? I want to know if she purchases a return ticket."

Papers crinkle under my backside when I add Megan's name to the alert field next to Isaac's. A heavy typing hand isn't responsible for my sudden wish to stand. It's the digits on the credit card Megan used to purchase her bus ticket. I've seen them before. Recently.

I stop ruffling through a pile of wire transfer receipts when Izzy mumbles, "Brandon?" Her tone is more questioning than her one word.

"Oh yeah, sorry, I was nodding," I force out, giving the first excuse that pops into my head.

Izzy giggles before replying, "Thanks, Brandon."

I exhale sharply when I find the document I'm chasing. The account number corresponds with a wire transfer that occurred almost thirty years ago. It's the first exact match I've found, and it wasn't anywhere I had considered looking. If it weren't for Isabelle, I would have never found it.

Happy for her to interrupt my naps anytime she likes, I say down the line, "Anytime, Izzy."

After bidding her farewell, I dive in for another twenty-plus-hour shift.

"I DON'T KNOW whether to be impressed by your gall or disappointed." When I crack open my apartment door, Phillipa saunters inside. "I figured you'd last a day at most. I hadn't factored a week into the equation…" Her words stop before she playfully swipes at her nose. "Have you showered since I left?"

I roll my eyes. "Yes… I just lost my deodorant somewhere in this mess."

By mess, I mean a huge web of conspiracy that stretches from my living room to the attached bathroom of the master suite. Although I'm working this angle for a completely different reason than Alex, he allowed me to work at home the past week with the hope I'd make a breakthrough on the sequence of numbers he handed me the afternoon before Isaac's arrest. I'm *this* close. I just have one final hurdle to jump first—hence my extend of the olive branch to Phillipa.

"This is crazy, Brandon," Phillipa mutters as she takes in the workflow of criminal activity covering every inch of my apartment walls. "Are you sure each wire transfer was for an individual purchase?"

I lift my chin. "It started well over three decades ago. From Christina Smite to Isaac's down payment last week, each wire transfer has been linked some way to the Popovs. A small pile of unmatched receipts remain, but for the most part, they correspond with sales that never went past the deposit stage."

Phillipa's pitch rises as quickly as her hope. "Did you find a match for Melody?"

My teeth grit, but I manage to push out a reply. It's short and to the point. "No."

When I pace to the stack of unmatched payments on my coffee table, Phillipa follows me. "The wire transfer identification digits in the Greggs' file revealed it came from the same bank and branch as the payment Isaac made last week, but the account numbers were different." I twist to face Phillipa. "Do you remember the massive payout the Petrettis were awarded when Col's wife was killed during a sting?"

She nods. "How could I forget it? It was the largest payment the state had seen. It certainly changed the way agents handle raids from thereon out."

I smirk, loving her eagerness even with this case being decades old. "Did you ever wonder where that money went?"

Phillipa shakes her head. "I was only a kid at the time so I didn't think much of it. Do you know what happened to it?"

Smiling, I hit her with the big stuff. "Most of it was squandered." Phillipa gags. She's not surprised nor shocked by my revelation. Col has never been good with money. "But a decent chunk of it was donated to a rival association."

"Col gave it away?" Her high tone reveals she thinks I'm full of shit. I wish I were.

"If I were to believe the paper trail, he donated to Vladimir's retirement fund a decade before he had reached retirement age," I disclose, gloating.

Phillipa looks as surprised as I did when Megan's bank records had me unlocking the very first match in the mail-order-bride conglomerate Dimitri hypothetically told me about weeks ago. If she hadn't used the same checking account her father utilized to purchase her mother, I'd still be picking at a massive ball of twine, seeking a thread.

Megan's mother, just like Isabelle, was sold when she was a child. She was just shy of her eighteenth birthday when Megan's father purchased her with the compensation payout he was awarded after a workplace injury. Her sale had me wondering why the payment was directed to the Popovs instead of the crew who specialized in those trades during their heydays.

It took several hours of trawling the dark web before I stumbled upon my answer. The Popovs have been running the ultimate pyramid scheme for the past forty-plus years. They find a lucrative product, mark it up by twenty-five percent, then sell it under their 'quality' brand. The training, sales, and shipment of goods all occur in-house. The Popovs just handle the currency side of things.

That's what happened with Megan's mother. She was groomed in a small town on the outskirts of Hopeton, sold at auction before being delivered to Carlyle Shroud, a once twenty-nine-year-old factory foreman.

He hasn't worked in almost thirty years after a stack of pallets fell on him, shattering multiple vertebrae in his back. Although he can still walk, the pain associated with his sloth-like steps deem him unemployable. Even with a perfectly groomed wife, I doubt he's enjoying life right now. His bank records the past decade show a majority of his support payments are spent on alcohol.

Although I feel sorry for Carlyle, his miserable existence is the thread Tobias was seeking for decades before his death. His lonesome fifty-eight-thousand-dollar payment twenty-nine years ago helped me link an incalculable number of wire transfers between the Petrettis, Castros, and Popovs the past three decades.

Three wire transfer receipts took me almost a week to work out. The one cited on the slip of paper found in the Greggs' file is included in that group. "All the unmatched wire transfers were for identical amounts. They were deposited in the Popovs' account within days of each other and dispersed at the same time, but no matter how deeply I scoured the records, I couldn't link the payments to the sales of property, guns, drugs, or people, leading me to believe they were for services."

"Services?" Phillipa jumps in, her brow cocking. "What possible services could the Popovs offer that they weren't already giving?"

I slap the wad of invoices in my hand against Henry Gottle, Sr.'s picture at the top of my criminal wish list. "The Petrettis, Popovs, and Castros were powerful, wealthy, and feared in their own right, but one man still reigned supreme. Henry Gottle."

The pieces click into place for Phillipa when I move to the far wall in my bedroom. "Henry had the biggest chunk of the pie, making him the ideal target if those beneath him decided to band together."

"Exactly." I point to a timeline of events that occurred the same weekend as the Greggs' home invasion, which happens to be exactly one month after the payments were distributed. "Going off the dates of the Greggs' home invasion, I discovered that several key members of the Gottle crew were hit consecutively one weekend. From the reports I found buried beneath a heap of bureaucratic tape, I unearthed that those targets were high-up associates of the Gottle cartel or direct relatives of Henry's. Details are sketchy, but it appears as if he lost five associates, two sisters, and a brother in one night." I twist to face Phillipa. "They also killed his mother during a failed attempt to force him to step down from his command. He lost almost his entire family within days of each other. There was only one brother unaccounted for. Rumors are that he was being sheltered by the CIA officer who had recruited him in his final year of college."

"Was?" Phillipa asks, her tone high.

"Was." I nudge my head to Mr. Gregg's profile picture tacked beside Henry's. When you see them side by side, some similarities are noticeable—most notably their strong facial structure. "Melody isn't Henry's daughter. She's his niece." I hand Phillipa a heavily redacted CIA file. "Two months before the birth of Henry's son, the Gottle compound was attacked in a similar fashion as the Greggs' home invasion years later. Henry's father was killed along with many members of their association. The men responsible believed they'd scare Henry into folding his operation. He was only seventeen and about to become a father, so the last thing he'd want is to enter a gangland war." I point to a picture of a young Katarina Rouse glancing down at her rounded stomach a baby-faced Henry is caressing. "Their plan backfired. Henry wanted revenge, he was just smart enough to know he couldn't place his family in the firing line to get it."

"So he gave them up instead," Phillipa fills in as an understanding glimmer ignites in her eyes.

I nod. "Except it wasn't just Katarina and his unborn son he removed from his memory. He wiped the entire slate clean. He moved Liam and his mother out of the family's brownstone in Manhattan, scaled down his crew to three men he trusted with the life of his only love and unborn son, then rebuilt his empire from the ground up."

"It worked." Phillipa arches a brow as shock floods her face. "A majority of his wealth was amassed in the five years following his father's death." Her throat works hard to swallow. "As was his death count."

What she's saying is true. I scoured the reports myself. Even with age not on his side, Henry won the war, but his victory came at a cost. "Katarina couldn't forget what he had done, and neither could Liam. They wanted nothing to do with Henry. Liam's opinion only changed when Melody was born, but their contact was still sporadic at best. Katarina still hasn't come around."

Phillipa stares at me in shock for several long seconds, only speaking when her inquisitiveness gets the better of her. "How did you unearth all of this so quickly? This is a year's worth of work, Brandon, and you did it in a week."

She scoffs when I say, "It isn't hard to unravel an entire outfit when you find a sturdy thread." I place the invoices onto my dining table before moving toward a third set of timelines. "Do you recall back in 2009 when the government was left reeling from a year-long intelligence failure that compromised its internet-based covert communication system?"

Her face reveals her confusion, but she answers my question, nonetheless. "I was in my third year of college, but I remember my father saying the compromise left CIA informants vulnerable to an attack."

I nod again, agreeing with her father's assessment. "Although a lot of effort was put forward to undo their error, intelligence sources revealed the damage was so severe, it would never be wholly undone. The exposure had already occurred. Even with CIA scrambling to secure their informants, they dropped like flies."

Phillipa's head slants as her brows join. "Do you think that glitch had something to do with the Greggs' accident? Although Liam wasn't an informant, he could have been before he was recruited."

I halfheartedly shrug before shaking my head, still uneased by my objective today. I'm usually the guy who coerces people off the ledge. I don't tiptoe them toward it. "I had considered that, but I couldn't work out why there was a stretch in timelines between his home invasion and their murders. So instead, I focused my efforts on the CIA's compromised system. I discovered this."

When I hand Phillipa Melody's birth certificate that undoubtedly proves her parents were named Liam and Wren, her eyes bulge out of her head. It isn't confirmation that Melody isn't Henry's daughter that has her shocked, it's the fact Liam used the last name of Gottle on Melody's birth certificate.

"Unlike me, Liam didn't change his name when he was recruited. He wasn't ashamed of it and had no issues discouraging people who believed he should have been. In some ways, it worked in his favor—"

"The Gottle name would have opened previously closed doors," Phillipa interrupts, smiling.

I lift my chin. "But regrettably, it also kept his family under the spotlight Henry tried to shelter them from almost a decade earlier." I exhale out a big breath before laying all my cards on the table. "I don't believe the donation Col made to the Popovs was out of the goodness of his heart. I believe it was his cut to fund the second attempted Gottle takedown." Phillipa looks shocked but remains as quiet as a church mouse. "The exact amount Col donated was transferred into a Russian operative's account precisely one month before the Greggs' home invasion. It was forwarded with two identical payment amounts… the Castros and Popovs share of the fee."

"If this is true, how are they still in operation? Henry's track record proves he doesn't sit on his hands when threatened. If he had an inkling to *any* of this, the FBI's wish list would have been sliced in half two decades ago."

"That's the issue. Henry doesn't know about anything I've unearthed." I stop before correcting myself. "Well, he didn't." Realizing I need to finish flipping one stone before moving onto a new one, I say, "When the takeover bid failed, the individual groups who orchestrated it folded rather quickly by pretending the Russian group they'd hired to do the hits had acted alone. Henry then responded with the notoriety he's famous for. He steamrolled them."

A vein in Phillipa's neck works overtime when I backhand two oddly familiar faces on a makeshift perp board. "The Russian entity hired to do the hit on the Gottles was the Bobrovs?" When I nod, she pushes out, "Are you sure, Brandon? This isn't child's play. We can't throw out an accusation like this without having the evidence to back it up."

"I have proof." She looks more panicked now than she did when I admitted to hacking CIA servers. "With Kirill's focus elsewhere…" I nudge my head to Katie's photo Grayson sent me weeks ago. "… cracks on the failed takedown bid only began surfacing eight years ago."

Phillipa's mouth drops open. "Right around the time Milo was released from prison."

"Correct." I flip open a file on a side table. "Mr. Gregg…" I pause, suddenly feeling odd referring to him by a name he wasn't born with. "Liam did disturb Crombie attempting to set fire to a barn on the outskirts of his property as stated. The only thing the reports failed to reveal was that he made a citizen's arrest before dropping him off at Saugerties PD. The officer who wrote up the report was—"

"Rory Langfield," Phillipa interrupts, reading the information from the incident report that has no claimant details jotted down. "With his trust low, Liam wouldn't have given his details to anyone, let alone to the Chief of Police." She takes a moment to absorb the information before locking her eyes with mine. "Do you think Rory recognized Liam?"

Nodding, I head to my laptop resting on the dining table before suggesting for Phillipa to take a seat. Once she does, I press play on a surveillance video of a dairy farm forty miles from Melody's family ranch. "The foreman had security installed after an insurance claim for an equipment shed blaze was denied because the assessor didn't believe the fire was sparked by the welders working on a neighboring milk shed. His report stated the fire was deliberately set."

"Crombie?" Phillipa intuits.

Her downcast lips shift into a smile when I jest, "Allegedly."

We watch the thirty-seven-second movie in silence. There's no sound, so we don't need to be quiet. I just want to see if Phillipa gasps the same way I did when I stumbled upon this footage.

She does, although it's more an annoyed groan than an angry gasp. "Langfield dropped Crombie off?"

"But wait, there's more." I point to the far corner of my monitor, steering her gaze to Milo Bobrov, who waits for Crombie to enter the residence before he joins Langfield at his car. "Milo was witnessed following the Greggs the very next weekend."

I don't disclose that I'm the sole witness of that statement. I don't know why. Perhaps because I've spilled a lot of information to a woman I hardly know. Or perhaps it's because I know Phillipa isn't being as sharing as I am. Whatever the reason, my purge still significantly lightened the weight on my shoulders.

"Do you recall me mentioning there was a possible link between Isaac Holt and the driver of the cattle truck that killed the Greggs?" When Phillipa nods, I toss a liquidation sale document to her side of the dining table. "Isaac purchased the dairy farm two weeks before the Greggs were murdered."

"What's your take on that?" Phillipa sounds more fretful for me than Isaac.

I give her a halfhearted shrug. "I wanted to believe he knew the type of business he was purchasing. Almost every employee at the farm had a criminal record as long as my arm."

"But?" Phillipa queries when she hears it hanging in the air.

"But... paperwork reveals Isaac terminated all employees with known cartel ties before handing over operations to one of his many feed-the-starving-children-of-the-world charity organizations. I plan to dig a little deeper into his tax records to see if the farm was purchased to launder funds for his illegitimate businesses, but I haven't had a chance to catch my breath just yet."

Phillipa folds her legs under her bottom before pursing her lips. "That's understandable. You looked wrecked." She laughs when I roll my eyes, then, not even five seconds later, she says, "This is all very impressive, and I'm stunned you squeezed a year's worth of work into a week, even if you skipped showering to do it. However, I'm still a little lost as to why you demanded my immediate attendance at your apartment. What does any of this have to do with me? I don't work cold cases."

She watches me with wide, panicked eyes when I cross the room to tug down David Crombie's mugshot taken the night he was found hanging in a prison cell. "He's your missing thread."

Phillipa touches her chest. "*My* missing thread?"

I leave her to stew for a few seconds before lifting my chin. "Milo had no clue Crombie was about to fuck him over as Rimi Castro had done to his brother years earlier."

"Whatever do you mean?"

Phillipa is a good actor, but I was trained to seek deceit in many forms.

"Not only did Crombie help Castro pin two murders on Milo, he drove him to his death as well."

Phillipa doesn't flinch because she knows every word I speak is true. I also have evidence. Footage from a gas station two miles from where Milo was found has footage of Crombie and Milo driving east. Ten minutes later, the same vehicle is seen heading west. It was minus its passenger that time around.

"Crombie was sentenced to twelve years. He was out in six. Before your team swooped in and plucked him from Detective Carter's grasp, he said he pleaded out. My guess is he threw Castro under the bus for a plea bargain. The Bobrovs weren't popular after the stunt they pulled on the Gottles, and although Crombie doesn't have their name, he has their blood." I slant my head, encouraging eye contact with Phillipa before muttering, "I'm just striving to work out what type of relationship he had with you."

BRANDON

When Phillipa scoffs as if I'm being ridiculous, I hit her with enough facts, even if she wanted to leave, she couldn't. "You've only worked for IA for the past eight months, and although you had proof an agent had forged evidence, you didn't need to come in as hard as you did to secure a witness. That means you wanted Crombie for more than taking down an agent suspected of tampering with evidence. You wanted to punish him for hanging you out to dry." The tears welling in her eyes would have most agents backing down. They don't work on me. Only one woman's tears have. They don't belong to a rogue agent. "What did he do, Phillipa? Give you false information? Turn you like Paavo turned Leesa?"

A tear almost rolls down her face when she rigorously shakes her head. "It was nothing like that?"

"Then what was it?" I fire back just as snappy.

I stare at her, silently warning her this is her *only* chance to come clean. If she continues with her I've-been-unfairly-suspended ruse she's been running the past week, I'll throw us both under the bus. I kept my searches hidden as much as possible, only scattering the teeniest bit of crumbs in case my plan folded, but I ensured Phillipa's name was scattered amongst the breadcrumbs with mine.

When my glare becomes too much for Phillipa to bear, she sighs. "Crombie was released early on the agreement he would be an informant for the Bureau. He had proof Castro encouraged Milo to seek revenge on the Greggs for the years he'd spent in prison. Having no idea that the Castros had paid for his participation that night, Milo fell for his ruse. An hour after the Greggs' accident, Castro requested for Crombie to bring Milo to an old mechanics shop once run by the Gottles. He thought he was there to collect the prize his brother had agreed to give him years earlier. Crombie stated Castro killed Milo before he'd fully exited the passenger seat of his truck. His blood was found in the tracking of the door. When Castro gave proof of his death to Henry, he was awarded a generous number of favors. They're invaluable to men in Henry's industry."

It's the fight of my life not to nod. The only reason I don't is because I do not want to give her any indication I'm agreeing with her.

"Crombie's evidence was credible, Brandon. We had DNA, photographic evidence, and a sworn statement from a witness."

"Then why didn't you put Castro away?" I ask, frustrated.

"Because the Bureau wanted more."

"They always want more," I shout as if the fucked-up system belongs solely on her shoulders. After a big breather, I ask more calmly, "How did Crombie know where the Greggs lived? Liam kept everything off the radar."

Phillipa shrugs. "I truly don't know. That information was never disclosed to me, and anytime I asked, our interviews were cut short."

I don't want to believe her, but I do. She isn't giving off any indication that she's lying. "What information *was* disclosed to you?"

She licks her dry lips before replying, "The sting in New Mexico was based on intelligence Crombie gave the head of my unit." Tears well in her eyes as she stares straight into mine. "I had no clue he was still working with Castro. If I had any inkling of how things would have transpired that night, I would have demanded that the raid be called off immediately, but I was just as blinded by the turn of events as your team was."

Genuine remorse fills her face, but some things still don't make sense. "How did Crombie know about the sting? Informants give us times, places, and locations. We don't share that information with them."

Anger burns me alive from the inside out when Phillipa scratches the back of her ear. If that isn't as obvious as a snitch asking to speak to the DA in private, I don't know what is.

After dropping her hand into her lap, Phillipa says, "Crombie didn't feel comfortable meeting in public."

Hearing the words she didn't speak, I ask, "So you held your meetings in hotel rooms?"

"Yes." The swiftness of her reply authenticates the honesty of it.

Too curious to hold back, I ask, "Did you sleep with him?"

Phillipa immediately shakes her head. "No. Our relationship wasn't like that."

I slant my head and arch my brow. "Relationship?"

She waves her hand around like a professor giving a lecture on ethics. "Studies have proven intimate relationships between under-cover agents and their informants are far more beneficial than casual relationships because intimacy involves a deep level of trust."

"You just said you didn't sleep with him."

Her hair slaps her face when her eyes rocket to mine. "I didn't. I flirted with him. I acted as if I was interested in having sex with him, but I didn't. I stroked his ego while doing my job! That's all I did."

Phillipa sounds honest, but I'm still wary. "Then how did he know about our sting?"

"I don't know! Even when I was undercover, I never discussed other ops around him. We barely talked, for crying out loud. He was one of those stare-at-you-from-across-the- room guys who thought adjusting his hardened crotch a hundred times a day was a turn-on." As she sucks in a sharp breath, the rattle of her vocal cords becomes more noticeable. "I had planned to ask him how he knew about the raid when his signature popped up at a warehouse fire in Ravenshoe, but I lost the chance when I discovered him hanging in his cell."

Although her face reflects her anger, there's also an immense amount of pain. Crombie's death isn't her fault, however, she's taking the blame for it.

"Do you believe Crombie killed himself?"

Her head shake isn't as quick as the one she gave me earlier, but it's still brimming with determined confirmation. "He was apologetic and remorseful, but I didn't see any indication he was suicidal. Cocky men like him don't commit suicide."

My thoughts drift to Joey for the quickest second. It isn't long enough to dispute Phillipa's claims that only the depressed end their lives, but it does award me a moment of clarity.

"If Castro killed Milo to garner favors from Henry, why didn't he wait for him to finish the job before killing him?"

Phillipa wipes her nose with her sleeve before leaning forward to grab her briefcase she dumped on my dining room table before my tour of the perp boards. "I don't have solid proof, but I'm beginning to suspect Henry is always one step ahead of his competitors because he has access to intel his enemies don't." When she pulls out a massive stack of paperwork, my eyes bug out. "You weren't the only one burning the candle at both ends the past week. My relationship with Crombie deserved scrutiny. It could have been perceived as immoral, but what I'm not okay with is being dumped into IA as punishment and being told to keep my mouth shut. That's not the way things work. You can't get answers if—"

"You don't ask questions."

She nods. "I've been asking questions for months, but since no one was willing to answer me, I went higher." She doesn't mention her father's name, but her face tells her story without additional words needing to be spoken.

When she dumps the massive file onto the table with a thud, a handful of photographs fall out. They're all of the same man—Kwan Turgenev.

"You were right. Kwan was on the scene at the Greggs' accident. He also took a witness statement after the death of Marjorie Hawke and her unborn son, and he was the first 'officer' on the scene when Police Chief Rory Langfield was gunned down." She slaps down photographs to each corresponding event. "He's also been a butcher, a chef, a pilot, and a marine."

My throat becomes scratchy. "A marine? So we have a file on him?"

Phillipa shakes her head. "No, we don't because he's a ghost."

I 'ha' out loud. "A ghost who enjoys having his photo taken."

"Not that type of ghost. He's a *ghost,* ghost." She speaks her last sentence super slow.

It takes me a few seconds to click on, but when I do, I'm left breathless. "He's a spy?"

"Allegedly," Phillipa responds, her mood picking up from what it was moments ago. Purging has that effect on you, especially when the person you're spilling your guts to believes you. "Crombie's sealed testimony was like unlocking a vault. He said Castro had jumped the gun when he killed Milo. He was so eager to claim his prize, he didn't authenticate Milo's story that all members of the Gregg family had been in the car when he plowed into them. He was at the Gottle compound when Henry received word from Kwan that Melody was alive."

My jaw twitches as it begs to drop open. "That's why he waited. It would have looked suspicious if Melody showed up dead hours after he claimed to have taken down the man responsible for the Greggs' murder."

Phillipa nods then sighs. "Believing justice had been served, Henry ordered that the scene be declared an accident. He'd risk another cartel war if his enemies discovered he had been hit unprepared." Air whizzes from her nose as she gently shakes her head. "He had no way of knowing every man on the scene that night would end up dead within the next two years. Castro had improved his game. Instead of making them straight-up murders, he covered them with a range of incidences—a boating accident, a drive-by shooting, a suicide—"

"Suicide? He made one of his murders look like a suicide?"

"Yeah…" She peers at me with unease before dropping her eyes to her file. "Crombie couldn't remember the exact date, but he told officials it was late May se—"

"Seven years ago? Fuck." I clench my fists so tightly, my nails dig into my palm. "My brother committed suicide seven years ago. He had blond hair like mine with a newly shaven chin. You couldn't mistake us as strangers. We had a lot of similar features." Moisture burns Phillipa's eyes when I lock my watering ones with hers. "I was on the scene of the Greggs' accident. Could they have mistaken Joey for me?"

"Don't make me answer that, Brandon. Please." Her demand is more telling than giving me a straight-up answer. "No matter what, we can't go back and change the past."

The brutal hammering of my heart is heard in my reply, "But I can prove Joey didn't kill himself. I can admit it was my fault."

Hair falls into Phillipa's eyes when she shakes her head with force. "It wasn't your fault—"

"They were supposed to kill me! I was the one they were targeting. How is this not my fault?"

I glare at her when she pulls a *duh* face. "I can think of a few things. Like you were just a kid. You trusted that not everyone had a black heart, and how about having no clue Liam was thrusting you into the middle of a mafia war when you were four!"

"Five, not that it matters. I would have signed up anyway." Nothing but honesty is heard in my reply. "You can't fault Liam for wanting to protect his family, Phillipa."

"Just like you can't fault Joey for doing the same thing." She lowers her voice a notch before my neighbors call in the feds, then locks her eyes with mine. "If any of this is true, if Joey was killed by Castro because he thought he was you, who's to say Joey didn't know that? Perhaps he was protecting you. You don't know what was going through his mind at that exact moment."

Her excuse is piss-poor, but when you're grasping at straws, you have to hold on tight. I want justice for Joey, and I'll get it, but only once I'm certain those still living won't fall on the same knife he did. "You said Castro was killing everyone on the scene, so why didn't he go after Kwan and Melody?"

My flipping stomach rolls through some extra churns when Phillipa slides a faded polaroid to my side of the table. It appears weathered, but to someone who didn't assess every perfect imperfection on Melody's face, they may believe the woman lying lifeless on a single bed in a dorm-like room was her. She has the same tulip-shaped nose, kinked hair when she lets it dry naturally, and the tiniest slither of silver above her right brow from her home invasion.

After sliding a second photo my way, Phillipa says, "The family crest tattooed on Milo and Crombie's neck are similar, but they're not identical."

I scoff at her, well aware she's wrong. "I went over their tattoos with a microscope. They're identical..." I eat my words when she reveals a third photo. This one has the lights switched off. "They had invisible ink embedded in them?"

Phillipa nods. "I asked a scientific photographer to take a look at the photo Melody sent you." I'm tempted to ask how she got a copy of an image on my phone, but the guilt in her eyes saves me wasting my breath. "Kwan's tattoo isn't real. It's as fake as his ties with the Bobrov entity." She hits me with photo after photo after photo that shows a timeline of Kwan's childhood. Katarina Rouse features in nearly every one of them. "Katarina adopted Kwan when he was ten. Unfortunately, it was years too late to save him from the lifestyle

Tobias removed Isabelle from. He was still grateful, though." Her next lot of images show Kwan with Henry. He's older, rougher, and ten times more deadly—especially in the last image where he appears to have a bullet hole between the eyes.

My lungs become breathless when the truth smacks into me. "Who faked their deaths?"

Phillipa shrugs. "We don't know. Crombie wouldn't say."

"Do you believe it was Henry?"

She glances over her shoulder to check we're still alone before nodding. "With the last two witnesses believed to have been contained and Kirill returning to Russia, things went dormant for years."

"Then Crombie's deal ruffled feathers."

Although I'm not asking a question, Phillipa answers me as if I am. "Yes. You weren't the only one suspicious about his early release. Henry started asking questions, and for some reason, his were answered more readily than mine."

"He also has a scary amount of access to government buildings in New York. Although Crombie wasn't technically a threat to Melody anymore, he was one of a rare few who knew Melody wasn't dead, so it makes sense for Henry to cut off that loose thread."

Phillipa remains as quiet as a church mouse, but I don't need her to speak to know she too believes Henry organized Crombie's death. Her eyes are very telling. The investigation of Crombie's death taught her the consequences of throwing someone into the deep end without first assessing all the evidence presented. She doesn't want to make the same mistake twice.

I use her silence to decompartmentalize all the information we've unearthed jointly and separately the past week. Although it appears obvious who I should be devoting my attention on, there are too many teams in game mode right now to solely focus on one. I can't change what happened to Joey, but I can stop the same thing happening to Melody.

If Melody is being sheltered under Henry's umbrella, she's virtually untouchable. An army of men couldn't protect her better than Henry's enemies knowing the consequences they'll face if they touch her, but I don't want to hand responsibility for her safety over to Henry. He may be related to her by blood, but Liam removed her and Wren from that environment for a reason. If he didn't believe Henry's reputation could keep them safe, why should I?

I shouldn't, and that's why I'm not going to.

Phillipa's chest stops showcasing her breaths when I say, "I need you to amend the transcript from your interview with Melody to include the photographic evidence you missed."

"What photographic evidence? I didn't take any." Her eyes pop open as the left side of her brain clicks on. "And aren't you concerned that will cause more conflict for Melody? As much as I love the Bureau and one hundred percent believe it does more good than bad, there's more going on here than we realize. What I had to give up to get access to these files is proof of that, not to mention being placed on suspension only hours after submitting my initial report." When I peer at her in confusion, uneased by the last half of her comment, she discloses, "My father only agreed to give me these files after I said I'd remain with IA for the rest of my career. If I'm chasing rogue agents, I'm not dodging bullets."

Her lips curve into a faint grin when I murmur, "Allegedly."

"Allegedly," Phillipa parrots as her smile picks up.

Her eyes float from her balled hands to my face when I ask, "Do you think his opinion would change if you took down the twelfth man on the FBI's most-wanted list?"

I smile when she replies, "Rimi Castro hasn't been seen since the foiled sting at his compound last year." An average agent wouldn't have known who I was referencing without first checking the FBI's database. Phillipa knew immediately, meaning she doesn't belong in IA for the next thirty-plus years. She should be on the field—with me.

"He could be tempted out of hibernation for the right reason."

The fact Phillipa doesn't jump in like she usually does, exposes her confusion. Hoping to ease it, I say, "Kirill Bobrov returned to the US stronger than he was when he left. He has amassed an impressive amount of wealth, grew his army by over a thousand men, and is wiser than he was seven years ago. That amount of growth gains him the admired eye of many, including his enemies."

When I hand Phillipa a flight manifest for a private charter from Taos, New Mexico to Fraser, Colorado, she reads between the lines. "Castro killed his brother, so why would Kirill side with him?"

I mentioned hearing bluebirds in the background of my call with Grayson two weeks ago when numerous attempts to reach him earlier this week failed to yield results. We pinpointed his last communication to be around the Colorado ranges, but we couldn't gain an exact location. Castro's operation has always been in the New Mexico region. The money his illegal activities pumped into the community means they'd be more than willing to shelter him and his men until the heat died down.

The flight manifest could be a coincidence, but I stopped believing in those a very long time ago. Furthermore, the Castros were utilizing Russian weapons during our raid, so I'm beginning to suspect Kirill's decision to return to the US wasn't made because he missed baseball. The Bobrovs and Castros are forming an alliance. I'm certain of it.

When Phillipa hands the manifest back to me, she arches her brow, reminding me I failed to answer her question. "We know Castro murdered Kirill's brother, but Kirill doesn't know that. Milo was killed on Gottle turf. Who's to say Castro didn't do that to play both Henry and Kirill?"

Her eyes bulge as her mouth falls open. "And Henry killing Crombie played right into Castro's hand. With Crombie dead, Castro thinks his secret is safe." The width of her pupils double. "Then, I logged a report full of misconceptions." She slaps herself on the forehead. "Stupid, stupid woman."

"Although I want to agree with you, your jump of the gun will help bring Castro out of hiding." She peers up at me with wide, uneased eyes when I say, "He's hunting Melody with decade-old photos. He'll have a better chance of finding her when you amend your report."

Phillipa's smirk matches mine when she mutters, "You want to slot an agent's photo in Melody's place?" When I jerk up my chin, smiling, she adds, "Do you have someone in mind?"

My grin doubles. "I do, and I think she'll be perfect for the role."

BRANDON

My stomach flips when I raise my hand to knock on Isabelle's apartment door. I'm not nervous because I don't have Grayson jabbering in my ear this time around to conceal my nerves, it's because Isabelle wasn't the agent I was referencing this morning. I was hoping Phillipa would fulfill the role, forgetting her earlier mention that she went undercover as Crombie's girlfriend with the hope of securing more information on Rimi Castro. Although she never directly met with Castro, he'd know who she is. He's as bad as Isaac about keeping tabs on any females in his crew's lives.

When Phillipa suggested bringing Isabelle into our ruse, I was dead set against it. She already has Theresa riding her ass, so the last thing I want to do is pull her into a shitstorm. Regretfully, after hours of consideration, we couldn't come up with another candidate. We can't trust anyone in Phillipa's team as it's clear she has a leak, and my connection to the failed Castro sting last year would have me yanked off this case the instant we disclosed our plans to the leader of my division.

That's why we've decided to go it alone. Phillipa's partner,

Arrow Moses, will be in charge of comms, and Phillipa and I will run recon. As much as I want to advise Isabelle of our plans, Phillipa talked me out of it. Until we can prove there are no links between Isaac and the Castros, we have to keep quiet because, for all we know, the down payment Isaac made to the Popovs last week could have been for anything, so we can't take any additional risks. Isabelle is an agent, she topped her classes, outranked every agent during marksmanship training, and is on suspension. Phillipa is right. She's the perfect choice.

I just need my stomach to get on board with our plans.

The jittery response of my stomach weakens when Isabelle swings open her apartment door. She's dressed casually like me and smiling brightly. I wait for her to stop soaking in my designer outfit before pulling out a bouquet of yellow roses from behind my back. I hadn't planned to arrive with anything when Phillipa and I stepped through our plan of attack, but the florist on the corner of Hyde called to me when I exited my vehicle. I've never officially dated, so I need all the help I can get to convince Isabelle to slip out of Isaac's grip for just a day.

"Brandon, you shouldn't have." Isabelle's eyes shine as brightly as the crystal vase the roses are in when she accepts them from my grasp.

"I thought they'd brighten your day."

I pat myself on the back when she leans in to place a kiss on my cheek, then I grimace when my cheeks inflame partway through her friendly gesture. I'm not aroused from her childish peck. I am being burned at the stake by Hugo, who's standing behind Isabelle's shoulder, glaring at me. I told Isabelle to fly under the radar. She can't do that and associate with a man whose movements have been as ghostly as Castro's the past five years.

My lips purse when Isabelle gives Hugo a warning look in the process of placing her gift onto the entryway table. She twists and turns the vase a handful of times before offering to take my jacket. Eager to establish whose side she's on, I join her in the coat closet.

The tight quarters increase Isabelle's florally scent while also doubling the odd heat bouncing between us. She must be struggling this week as her responses are usually cooler than they are.

"Isn't he Isaac's bodyguard?" I stumble over my last word. Even reading the transcripts from Hugo's court case hasn't unearthed who Hugo really is.

He's as enigmatic as Isaac.

Isabelle shrugs. "He isn't Isaac's bodyguard. He's more an *associate* of his." Smiling, she crosses the room before offering up an introduction. "Hugo, this is my *friend*, Brandon." I don't miss the way she emphasizes 'friend' any more than Hugo. "Brandon, this is my... *friend*, Hugo."

While smirking at Hugo's frustration about being placed on the same team as me, I join them in the middle of Isabelle's living room. "It's nice to meet you."

When I offer him my hand in greeting, Hugo accepts it, although hesitantly. "Pleasure." His ability to lie is as bad as his acting skills. He's not happy about my visit, not in the slightest, but for some reason, he doesn't believe he can express that to Isabelle, proving they're more work colleagues than friends.

That pleases me more than it should.

Nothing against Hugo, from what I've read, he was fucked over by my father as well as I was, but you can't excuse a lifetime of mistakes on one person. If you could, I would have stopped feeling guilt a long time ago.

My eyes stray to Isabelle when she mumbles, "When did I become Ms. Popular?"

Guilt floods her attractive features as quickly as amusement does when she catches Hugo's and my gawp. I don't know why Hugo is gawking at her. I'm staring because I am glad sleeping with the enemy hasn't changed her quirks. She was busted talking out loud many times her first six months on the job, but this is the first one I've heard since she was seen going home with Isaac.

Over our prolonged stares, Isabelle splays her hands across her cocked hip and arches a brow. "All right, spill, what are you two up to?"

It's the fight of my life not to roll my eyes like a child when Hugo mutters, "I've got nothing better to do with my time anymore, so I may as well hang out with you."

Although I'm confused by his statement, Isabelle has no trouble reciting it. As the guilt in her eyes augments, she shifts on her feet to face me. For a woman facing ten to twenty years for conspiracy in aiding and abetting a criminal by supplying him with official government documents, she looks remarkably smug.

Preferring to hold our conversation in private, I nudge my head to her apartment door. "I need to talk to you. In private."

Before Hugo can voice any of the disdain in his eyes, Isabelle clasps my hand in hers before making a beeline for the hallway. Hugo doesn't follow us, but I have my suspicions he's eager for some privacy. His eyes darted to a stack of boxes the instant Isabelle turned her back on him.

Once I'm confident I have my script in order, I raise my eyes to Isabelle's. "I need a favor."

I'm taken back when she answers, "Anything, Brandon."

I had hoped my friendship would be reciprocated one day, and today is as good a day as any. She didn't hesitate, not in the slightest, so it makes what I'm about to say ten times easier. "Thank you, Izzy."

What? Every man knows you always begin a negotiation with a compliment. Only once you've smothered them in gooey goodness do you hit them with the big stuff. "I need a date." When Isabelle balks, I talk faster. "My mom is chairman of a charity that holds an annual gala. I tried to get out of it, but she won't accept any of the excuses I'm giving." When her facial expression gives no indication she's sympathetic to my plea, I veer my ruse in a direction even I hadn't considered. "I don't want to go alone because Melody will be there." The uneased mask on Isabelle's face slips away in an instant, assuring me I'm on the right path. "I am so desperate for a date, I'm not below getting on my knees and begging. Please, Izzy. I'll do anything, anything at all if you'll fake liking me for one night."

The wish to find a shallow ditch to bury myself in weakens when Isabelle mutters, "I do like you, Brandon." Gratitude for charming, boyish features fills me when she adds, "So I'm sure it won't be hard pretending I'm your date for a night."

My cheeks groan in protest from their sudden movements when a blistering smile stretches across my face. "Thank you, Izzy, thank you."

My grin sags when she mutters, "You're welcome... but now, *I* need a favor."

Although hesitant, I agree to her request as quickly as she did mine. My favor comes with dangerous consequences, so it's only fair I give up just as much.

My heart beats out a thunderous tune when Isabelle discloses, "I've been looking a little deeper at Megan Shroud." I then realize I have no reason to panic when she garbles, "There are a lot of holes in her file I could fill in by driving out to her hometown to check things out." She licks her dry lips before adding, "The thing is, I don't have a car, so can I please borrow yours?"

I almost dip my chin, but the quickest idea pops into my head, stopping me. "It hasn't recovered from the last time you drove it." I wink and smile when she pouts. "But I'm more than happy to drive you there."

"Really?" She shouldn't be as stunned as she is. Not only will this give me a chance to look a little deeper into Carlyle Shroud's purchase twenty-nine years ago, but the guilt that's been eating me alive the past four hours may slacken.

"I still have nightmares from when you went to her hotel room alone. I refuse to make the same mistake twice." I'm not lying. Letting Isabelle go to Megan's hotel room alone was a stupid thing for me to do. I should have gone with her. Alas, I'm too nosy for my own good. "I have the weekend off, so why not go on an adventure?"

"Thank you, Brandon."

I squeeze her hand, assuring her that her gratitude isn't required. She's helping me more than I'm helping her. "You're welcome. I'd do anything for you." Cringing about the awkward wording of my thanks, I shift our conversation back onto mutual territory. "When were you wanting to head out?"

Isabelle twists on the spot, endeavoring to appear innocent. "I was hoping tomorrow morning?"

"Eager?" I ask through the lump in my throat.

She laughs, then nods. "There's something strange with her records."

I pull a face as if to say, *you have no idea.* When she spots it, she slaps my arm. "Too early?"

"Not at all," I assure with a laugh. "I'll pick you up around seven?"

Now she's the one cringing. She's clearly not a fan of mornings. "Seven works. I can do seven." I tell my cheeks to get with the fucking program when they burn from her childish peck. I know it's been a while, but still, blushing like a naïve virgin is fucked. "I'll see you tomorrow. Thanks again for this, Brandon."

After dragging her hand down my arm, Isabelle heads back into her apartment. While jabbing the call button on the elevator, I dig my cell phone out of my pocket. I almost call Phillipa while waiting for the elevator to arrive at Isabelle's floor but decide against it when a blinking red contraption at the end of the hall gains my attention.

My kiss with Isabelle weeks ago proves Isaac is watching her, but this watch feels different. It feels even murkier than a man with strong ties to the cartel. It feels like pure evil, and it has me saving my call until I'm in the safety of my car and many miles away from Isabelle's apartment building.

"I thought we agreed not to amend your report until the night before the gala?" I say when Phillipa answers my call, not bothering to issue a greeting. "I can't keep Isabelle safe from a distance."

"I haven't touched my report. I went to the gym, then recouped the calories at a bakery like I do every Friday afternoon. By continuing with our routines, we'll appear less suspicious," she quotes, snickering.

She's annoyed I wouldn't let her fill Grayson's shoes. I don't know why I refused her request. Perhaps because I'm a little uneased by Grayson's rare silence, or perhaps it's because I didn't want another witness to my horrendous dating skills.

"What's with the interrogation, BJ? Did you go off script?"

Yes. "No. Isabelle agreed to go to the gala with me."

The traffic noise heard through the Bluetooth speakers on my steering wheel is as noisy as the line of vehicles I'm weaving through. "Then what's the issue?" My hesitation annoys Phillipa as much as it does me. "If agreeing to remain in the graveyard the rest of my career isn't enough to gain your trust, BJ, I don't know what else I can do."

"I trust you." When nothing but silence resonates down the line, I reiterate, "I do, I just..." I've got nothing, so I go with honesty instead. "I spotted a surveillance van in the alleyway outside of Isabelle's apartment. It has government-issued tags."

"Did you jot them down?"

The high pitch of her tone switches to a giggle when I ask, "Do you know me at all?"

A car horn honks, and Phillipa curses before her noisy breaths overtake the revs of her motor. "Hit me with them." Seven seconds after I recite her the tags, she says, "The van belongs to the Bureau."

"Can you tell me who it's assigned to?"

The whooshing that sounds down the line has me picturing Phillipa shaking her head. "But I can probably get you a department..." Her words trail off to a groan. "It's someone from Internal Affairs." After a few seconds of silence, she adds, "Perhaps we should call this off? Wait until IA isn't hot on Isabelle's tail."

"We can't, Phillipa. The partial match of an account from the receipts Julian forwarded us is the only proof we have that Castro's crew is still in operation. Someone from his empire was at the same function Melody attended last week. If we wait too long, they'll find the real Melody before we direct them toward the fake one."

She sighs, unhappy with my statement but aware we don't have a choice. Phillipa's report put a price on Melody's head. Time isn't in our favor. "When I get back to my apartment, I'll update Julian's security team, so they know the threat is credible."

After humming out an agreement, I say, "While you do that, I'll pack an overnight bag."

With how quiet Phillipa is, I hear her brain ticking over. "You're going away?"

"Uh-huh."

"Now! Are you crazy? Our team consists of three people. We need *all* of them on the ground, conducting around-the-clock surveillance."

I'd laugh at the high pitch of her tone if she didn't sound so serious. "I'm not going on a weekend getaway. Isabelle wants to take a closer look at Megan Shroud."

"Shroud? As in Carlyle Shroud?" Nothing but unhinged excitement rings in Phillipa's tone. When I murmur in agreement, she gasps. "How is she linked with this?"

Phillipa whistles out a shocked breath when I give her a bullet-point update on Megan's obsession with Isaac's brother. "And this is why I'm convinced the world isn't flat. Life is a never-ending circle of unknown connections." With tiredness strangling my senses, my laugh comes out as more of a yawn. "Perhaps after you've packed, you might get some sleep." When I scoff, she whispers, "I can come prepare you a warm cup of milk and rub your tummy until you fall asleep if you'd like?" Don't take the childishness of her offer as being innocent. Her comment could have only been more insinuating if she had said it while naked.

Feeling playful, I mutter, "Phillipa?"

My cock twitches when she purrs, "Yes, BJ."

Her laughter roars above the pulse in my ears when a snippet of the old Brandon breaks through the dark cloud above my head. "Can I have some cookies with my milk?"

MELODY

When a shuffle sounds at the door, I peer up from the mountain-load of case files I've been sorting through the past few weeks. I have been in the reference library for hours, yet I've barely deciphered half the charge sheet in front of me. My mind is elsewhere, and I don't see that improving when I lock eyes with my caller. The Governor has popped in for another visit, except this time, he's minus his posse of advisors.

"Mr. McGee, good evening." My tone is lower than usual, somewhat skittish. I'm not a fan of my voice as it is, let alone speaking to a man who rarely stops glowering.

It's men like Mr. McGee who keep fear alive. Their insides are so evil even a deliriously handsome face can't hide it. For years, I believed the McGee children's personalities were evenly split between their mother and father. Brandon and Joey took after Mrs. McGee, and Phoenix and Madden adopted their father's traits.

My beliefs only changed the night of Joey's party.

Not wanting my mind to get sidetracked again, I ask Mr. McGee in a kind and professional voice, "Is there something I can help you with?"

He walks into the room, all regal-like. "I popped by your apartment. You weren't home. Clearly." His laugh makes me so uncomfortable I stand to give my flipping stomach room for its churns. "I figured you'd be here. Barbara put many hours into her studies before we wed. I often found her in the library." Even though they're in the process of separating, he speaks fondly of his wife while shuffling through the case files I'm working on. When his eyes lift to mine, I forcefully swallow. They're so hollow even with them being oddly familiar. "Will you continue working once you've wed?"

I nod without pause for thought. "Julian has no wish for me to stop. He knows how important this is to me."

"He sounds a lot like your father." He tosses down a file with more aggression than needed, ensuring I'm aware his dislike of my father is still apparent even years after his death. "I heard the ruling on his accident was altered. What are your thoughts on that?"

"Umm..." I'm truly lost for a reply. Mr. McGee isn't a caring man, so why is he pretending as if he is? "I'm not exactly sure what to think of it, to be honest. It's all rather new. I'm still trying to process it all."

A reason for his visit comes to light when he asks, "Are you planning to sue?" He's not worried about my well-being after discovering my parents were murdered by the man who brutalized them years earlier. He doesn't want a murky cloud placed over his state's head.

Yes, you heard me right. Vincent McGee believes he owns New York. He's wrong, but the last man to tell him that is buried in a cemetery next to his wife and my mother, so I'd rather not point it out when I'm alone with my attacker's father in a room that only has one exit. I'm not scared of Mr. McGee, I'm frightful of the children he raised.

With my mood hostile, my words get snappy. "I have no intention to sue, so you have no need to fret." I stack my files together before sliding them into my messenger bag. "What happened was unfortunate, but as far as I'm concerned, the matter has been attended to." I don't know who killed Milo Bobrov, and in all honesty, I don't care. Justice was swiftly served. I couldn't have asked for more than that. "If that's all, I'd like to get a head start on my weekend?"

I'm heading for the door before half my question leaves my mouth, my brisk strides only stopping when Mr. McGee's hand shoots out to seize my elbow. "Where do you think you're going? I've not yet finished speaking with you."

On instinct, I respond to his somewhat aggressive hold and statement with the same amount of edginess he used to deliver it. The breath that vacates Mr. McGee's lungs when I ram my elbow into his ribs fans my nape. When I lower my elbow ten or so inches, the remaining air in his lungs expels with numerous curse words. I saw him mutter them multiple times in my childhood, but the disdain they are delivered with this time around is nothing like I imagined. They're full of hate and disgust. Furthermore, I've been assaulted by a McGee once before. I refuse to let it happen again.

As I tear away from him, a scream peels from my throat. I bolt out of the Resources Office so fast anyone would swear I'm outrunning the Grim Reaper. Partway down, I crash into someone coming from the other end.

"Mel? What's going on? Why are you running?"

Although I recognize both the voice and the scent of the person gripping my shoulders, I break out of his hold with the determination I wish I had showcased seven years ago. I need fresh air, and no amount of reassurance that I'm safe can take that away from me.

"Mel? Melody?" Julian continues to shout until the fire alarm on the emergency door I burst through gobbles up most of his words. It's for the best because from the menace of his words, and the threat they arrive with, I don't think they were for me. He has his sights set on one man—the one I'm sprinting away from like my life is in danger.

I STOP TWISTING the hem of my skirt around my fingers when a pair of polished black dress shoes pop into my peripheral vision. I don't need to glance up to know who they belong to. The designer price tag is indicating enough, much less the reflection of his face gleaming in the shiny black material.

"Am I fired?"

Leo, my boss, plants his backside on the grimy step outside of our office building, acting as if his pricy suit isn't worth the coat hanger his dry cleaner hangs it on at the end of each week. The contents pooling in my nose almost spills when he hands me his embossed handkerchief. It's his compassion that makes him such a good DA. He understands what the victims have been through as he too is a victim. I don't know what he's been through, or how he overcame it, but I know he's been through something. Victims of crime have a way of recognizing each other. He saw the pain in my eyes as readily as I noticed his. I guess that could be the reason he went against protocol to hire me on the spot. I always thought it was because he's friends with Julian, but I'm doubtful now.

The sleeve of Leo's rolled-up dress shirt tickles my arm when he leans in close to my side to whisper, "Why would you be fired, Melody?"

I pull a *duh* face. "I hit the Governor."

Dark hair falls into Leo's eyes when he shakes his head. "You defended yourself when you were touched without permission. Much to Vincent McGee's disgrace, that isn't an offendable crime." His dark blue irises glisten in the streetlight when he slants his head to hide the curve of his lips. "If your second hit had been a little to the left, our conversation might have been starkly different."

Certain I'm reading the humor in his eyes right, I mumble, "I'll put more thought into my aim next time."

"I most certainly hope you do." When he stands to his feet, I attempt to hand him back his unused handkerchief. "Keep it. It'll do me great pleasure for Julian to find it in your underwear drawer."

He grazes his knee against my shoulder before signaling to

someone across the street. My heart leaps into my throat when I spot who curls out the back-passenger door of a heavily tinted SUV. Julian's knuckles are still red and swollen from when he roughed-up Mr. McGee, but the fury on his face when he was marched out of the DA's office in handcuffs is nothing like it once was. If anything, he looks panicked that I'll react negatively to his gallantry. I would have preferred to keep him out of my messy life, but I guess he knew what he signed up for when he asked me to become his wife.

When Julian stops in front of me, I slip my hand between his before raising my watering eyes. "I'm sor—"

"Shh." He pulls me into his chest before weaving his fingers through my hair. "I don't need your apologies, Mel. I just need to know you're okay. No woman should be required to handle Vincent alone, let alone one who's been through what you've been through." He whispers his last sentence only loud enough for me to hear.

"I'm okay." My words are muffled since he's holding me close, but I know he hears them as his racing heart calms within a nanosecond of them leaving my mouth. "But I'd really appreciate it if you could take me home. I need to shower."

Nodding, Julian inches back, secures my hand in his, then guides me toward his guarded, and most likely, bulletproof car. When he advises the driver to take us to my loft, I curl my unclutched hand over the balled one resting on his trousers. I don't know what was said between Mr. McGee and him, but it was clearly unpleasant. His jaw is ticking, and his blue irises are swamped by black pupils. I've never seen him so worked up.

"Can we stay at your place tonight? I don't want to go back to my loft." I didn't acknowledge it at the time, but shockwaves rained down on me when Mr. McGee said he had dropped by my apartment. Just the thought of our exchange taking place in my home has me breaking out in hives. I struggle being alone with Julian, so you can imagine how hard it is when your male guest shares the same blood as the man who raped you. "It's closer, and I'm really tired."

I'm lying. We can walk to my loft within five minutes at this time of the night. I just don't want to go there right now.

I also don't want to be alone.

"Of course." Julian hides his surprise at my request to spend the night at his penthouse for the first time with a high tone. "Shall we swing by your apartment and pick up some of your belongings first?"

I shake my head. "I have everything I need right here," I assure him while snuggling into his side. "Just take me home."

"Home," Julian repeats, smiling. "I like the sound of that."

BRANDON

*I*sabelle's eyes lower to the clipboard in her hand when Hugo asks, "Are you sure this is the address you're looking for?"

He pulls my BMW into the dusty driveway of the Shroud family ranch before swinging his eyes to Isabelle. How is he driving my car on the day Isabelle and I decided to travel to Megan's family home for some private investigative work? He took command of it when Isabelle shot out the tires of his Isaac-owned Audi hours ago.

I had noticed we were being tailed not long after we left Isabelle's apartment, but since I was too busy getting IA off Isabelle's ass, I failed to notice a second vehicle until we were on the freeway. I knew Isabelle's gall would be as high as she is tall—she was raised by a big, balding Russian with a short fuse—but I never anticipated for her to respond to the news we had a tail in the way she did. She approached the target as she was taught in the academy, then halted his wish to retreat when he failed to yield at her request.

I shouldn't have been relieved when we discovered the perp was Hugo but, for some reason, I was. I'm planning to toss Isabelle into shark-infested waters next weekend, so the more protection she has, the better it will be for all involved. I won't let Castro or anyone from his crew get to within an inch of Isabelle, but not even the most confident agents turn down a third set of eyes.

After double-checking the number hand-painted on a microwave at the front of the Shroud's family ranch, Isabelle nods. A stern mask slips over Hugo's face when he returns his foot to the gas pedal. He's barely driving five miles an hour, but dust still kicks up behind us. It doesn't look like these parts have seen a rain cloud for a few months.

It's as drought-affected as my mouth when a once-regal farmhouse comes into view. The steps are rickety, the porch is unloved, and it looks like no one has lived here in years. It has me wondering what my mother has endured the past two months. She moved back to our family ranch in Saugerties the day she filed for divorce from my father. I'm glad she has finally seen through his gleaming exterior, but I'm still not convinced the ranch is the best place for her. It's not just filled with haunted memories, no one has lived there in years. It's most likely in a state of disrepair.

My eyes float back to Hugo when he asks, "Whose house is this?"

When Isabelle seeks my advice on how to answer him, I shrug. If she's not comfortable being honest with him, it isn't my place to intervene. I'll go with anything she chooses.

After a few seconds of silent deliberation, Isabelle answers Hugo's question. "Megan Shroud."

I take a mental note to keep a closer eye on Hugo when air whizzes out of his nose. Has he heard of Megan before because she's stalking Isaac's brother? Or because Megan's father dabbled in the same industry Isaac is tiptoeing his empire toward?

A grin curls on my lips when Hugo foils Isabelle's attempt to exit the car when he pulls in front of the ranch. "Let us check it out first." He gestures his hand to me during his statement.

Although I commend Hugo's protectiveness, Isabelle has a point when she snarls. "I'm a federal agent, Hugo, I am *not* a child."

A chuckle steals the air from my lungs when Hugo snaps back,

"Yeah, and that's Freddy-fucking-Kruger's house. If Isaac finds out I let you go in there without me first scoping the premises, I won't be on his Christmas card list anymore. He gives very generous bonus checks in his Christmas cards."

An average man would believe he's merely doing the job he's paid to do. I'm far from average. He cares for Isabelle, but I am unsure if it's friendship based or because he lives his life in guilt from what happened to Gemma—the woman he was convicted of raping. It may be a bit of both.

Believing he has Isabelle subdued, Hugo exits the car. I quickly shadow him. We've barely creeped up the front stairs when the crank of a car door breaks through the silence teeming between us. Forever willing to test the boundaries, Isabelle has joined us on the porch.

Her gun is held high and without a quiver. She's assessing her surroundings as all good agents do, but Hugo still treats her as if she's a child. "Stay behind me."

Isabelle loses the chance to remind him that she's an agent when Hugo removes a gun from the back of his jeans. It isn't illegal to carry a concealed gun in this state, but I doubt Hugo has a permit. Even if his alias could have passed the background check, his weapon of choice is too high-powered to be licensed.

With silence paramount, my thoughts drift to the past. The wind whistling through the cracks of the floorboards reminds me of the Greggs' family ranch the year they moved in. It was rundown and old despite Liam having access to a bank account full of funds. I guess an eighty-three-thousand-dollar ranch paid for in cash is less conspicuous than a two-million-dollar penthouse. No one batted an eyelid when Carlyle Shroud spent fifty-eight thousand dollars in one afternoon at Hopeton thirty years ago, so would they care if a man funded a move to the country with tainted money. Money makes the world go around. Cash just slows its rotations.

My mind snaps back to the present when Hugo bumps me with his shoulder before nudging his head to the door, instructing for me to knock. Although stunned he's handing the reins to me, I do as requested. An odd sensation is filling the air, encouraging our joint operation.

The door swings open when I tap on the weather-damaged material. "I'm an FBI field agent, is anyone home?"

I hear Isabelle's swallow more than I see it when Hugo's eyes rocket my way. It's the fight of my life not to smile at the shock on his face. I had wondered if Isaac's security team had looked into me after my date with Isabelle months ago. Now I know without a doubt. I bet he didn't find anything. I'm as good at covering my tracks as my father is.

Endeavoring to keep my focus on the task at hand, I shift on my feet to face Isabelle. "Did you hear that?" When her brows scrunch, confused, I try another angle. "I *think* I heard someone yelling for help." Agents can't enter a property without a warrant *unless* it's to prevent an occupant inside from being seriously injured, hence my belief I hear someone shouting for help.

Hugo clicks onto my ruse quicker than Isabelle. "Yeah, I heard it, too. We should probably check on them."

Hugo puts his years in the military to good use when he silently signals for me to enter the residence before him. While he sweeps the lower left of the shambled conditions, I take the right. Isabelle is here with us, but the stench of rotten food scraps and the scattering of rats has her not as eager to lead our investigation. She'd rather hang toward the back.

Signs someone lives here is exposed when Isabelle switches on the tube lighting wired throughout the beamed roof. The smell alone should render this residence uninhabitable, much less the number of rodents. I've spotted five rats so far, and I've barely stepped into the living room. Carlyle clearly didn't get his money's worth with his groomed bride. This place is a pig-sty.

When Hugo signals for me to clear the lower level of the property while he and Izzy take the upper half, I nod, agreeing with him. I'd rather Isabelle stay with me, but I can't seek hidden clues if my every move is being watched. Carlyle purchased his wife at a live auction. They are invitation-only events, which means Carlyle most likely knew the men helming the operation. Although it was well before Isaac Holt's time, so Isabelle's attendance wouldn't cause a conflict of interest, the man believed to shelter Isaac's empire was most certainly in operation back then. Henry Gottle has been in this game since the day he took his first breath.

As the creaking of Isabelle and Hugo's steps sound through my ears, I move into the kitchen. The floor is coated with food scraps, giving the room an odd fermented smell.

My heart falls from my ribcage when Isabelle's squeal erupts into my ears. I dart for the stairwell, stomping halfway across the dirty living room before I realize the cause of her fright. Hugo's boot broke through the frail wooden steps, sprinkling the plastic-covered couches underneath with shards of wood.

While Hugo pulls his foot out of the big hole, I move closer to the sofas that look like they were purchased right around the time Megan's mother was bought. The plastic looks like it was placed on them to protect the floral material from being worn. Only a trained agent would know to look deeper into the reasoning. Why would you bother keeping a couch in new-like condition when you live in the equivalent of a pig-sty?

My brows pull together when the scent of dampness fills my nostrils at the removal of the first lot of plastic. We're heading toward winter, so the conditions aren't humid enough to cause the plastic to sweat. It appears as if the couches were cleaned but covered while still damp.

But why clean spotless couches? That doesn't make any sense. *Unless...*

I rip open the drawers in the entryway table before making my way into the kitchen. I don't have my equipment case with me, but even a novice can scan for bodily fluids with basic gear you'll find in any house. Although I don't recommend doing this if you enjoy vacationing. Semen shines the brightest because of its mix of chemicals, and it lasts the longest, so you'll generally find every bit of bedding in a standard hotel room will be coated in it. The amount will have you demanding to speak to the manager immediately.

When I find a roll of Scotch tape and a blue and purple marker, I push some rubbish from the kitchen counter to the floor so I can turn my iPhone into a UV light. After covering the flashlight in the back of my phone with a layer of Scotch tape, I color over it with the blue marker before adding a second layer of tape. Once the outer layer is filled in with the purple marker, abracadabra, I have a bodily-fluid detector.

With the sound of dripping water filling my ears, I wave my iPhone over the three-seater couch. As suspected, it has been scrubbed clean. Alas, unless you use a ton of bleach, semen, urine, sweat, and all those other nasty bodily fluids remain. The amount of semen on the three-seater couch isn't surprising considering it appears to have been purchased when Carlyle was in his late twenties, early thirties, but the other compound is shocking. I can't tell if it's urine or sweat, but considering it is mainly on the base of the couches, I'll go with the former.

With my fingerprints covered by the waistband of my shirt I tugged out of my trousers, I toss the removable seat covers off the couch to expose the sofa bed underneath. The damp smell I mentioned earlier doubles when I carefully fold out the bed. The mattress is the cause of the horrid smell filling my nostrils. It's stained—badly—enough to have me convinced the Shroud ranch doesn't have a downstairs bathroom.

Although disgusted about how some people live, ten minutes later, I've failed to stumble onto any evidence that will aid in my investigation of the Castros and Bobrovs. If I hadn't seen Megan's birth certificate, the mess would have me convinced Carlyle never had a wife, much less one trained to answer his every whim.

As I climb the stairwell, taking extra care not to fall through like Hugo did, I overhear Hugo telling Isabelle the master bedroom's closets are full of clothes, but the room is empty.

When the creak of warped floorboards announces my arrival, Isabelle's eyes swing my way. They are more questioning than her words could ever be. She's hoping I stumbled onto a vault of secrets. All I got was hives.

"Excluding a dozen rats, there's nothing down there but rubbish."

She looks as disappointed as me but knows a lack of evidence doesn't necessarily mean there isn't something shady going on. Carlyle's checks have been forwarded to this address for over two decades. His truck is parked at the front of his equipment shed. So where the hell is he?

As my heart beats out of funky tune, I follow the slant of Isabelle's head. There's one final room we've yet to search. It's at the very end of the hall.

Once Isabelle is safely behind us as she was when we entered the lower level of the property, Hugo curls his hand around the brass doorknob. After twisting it as far as it will go, he swings his eyes to me. "*One... two... three.*"

On three, he flings open the door for me to enter it. Bleach is the first thing to hit me. Shock closely chases it. This room is nothing like the ones downstairs. It's white, spotlessly clean, and reeks like someone showers in bleach.

"Holy shit," I mutter under my breath when I take in the room as a whole. Megan's medical records revealed that she's unhinged, but this is ridiculous. Every inch of her room is covered with cut-outs of Isaac's brother, Nicholas. Not even the ceiling is free of his face. For the most part, the collection seems to have been amassed through the gossip magazines that tail every move Nick's band makes, but there are a handful of images that deserve closer scrutiny. They couldn't have been taken by members of the paparazzi. They're in closed quarters—private quarters—such as childhood bedrooms.

I stop scanning the images for any pictures that don't include Nick when Isabelle asks, "Is this Jenni, Nick's fiancée?"

When she hands a photograph to Hugo which has Jenni's eyes gouged out and blood trailing down her legs, Hugo nods.

"Does Isaac have someone watching them?" Isabelle queries.

I hear the gurgles of my gut in Hugo's reply when he says, "He has Peters watching Nick from a distance, but I don't know about Jenni. His security team determined the threat pertained more to Nick than his fiancée."

"You need to get protection for Jenni," Isabelle says matter-of-factly before she shifts on her feet to face me. "What's the closest division associated with this district?"

My lips twitch, but I don't get a word out before Hugo jumps back into the conversation. "Don't call the authorities until Isaac's security team gets a look at this first. If you bring in the feds, this will get shut down quicker than Hunter turning down an offer to dance."

I'm torn when Isabelle wordlessly seeks my advice. Nothing here could hinder my personal investigation into the Bobrovs and Castros, but we entered the property under false pretenses. If there's a possibility that could have me sidelined for the next six to eight weeks, I'd rather not risk it. But I can't force Isabelle to tiptoe onto the wrong side of the law for me, can I? She already has IA riding her ass, so I can't dump more shit onto her pile because I have a private agenda.

The worry in Isabelle's eyes doubles when I place the burden of her decision back onto her shoulders. "It's up to you, Izzy. I'll go along with whatever you decide." I'm not lying. If she wants to call this in, I'll do it, but if she wants to conduct her own private investigation as I've been doing the past six weeks, who am I to judge her?

After a tense stretch of silence, Isabelle removes the sweat from her nape before digging out the cell phone Hugo handed her earlier. When she passes it to Hugo, I move to join her on the other side of the room. Although she's technically breaking protocol for Isaac, I want to offer her my support because this joint operation could benefit me as much as it does her. If Isaac views me as more of an ally than a foe, my chances of working out exactly what he's purchasing from the Popovs triples. Thus, not only giving me the opportunity to show Isabelle who he really is but also allowing me to do the job I'm paid to do without fear of repercussions.

It's a win/win for me.

The same can't be said for Isaac.

BRANDON

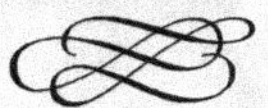

"Jesus, is she all right?"

Phillipa's battered breaths jingle down the line as she replies, "I believe so. A friend working that case said she seemed a little rattled at the time, but was more lucid when he arrived at Julian's penthouse to take her statement."

My body doesn't know which comment to react negatively to first—the fact Melody got into a tussle with my father or Phillipa's confirmation she stayed with Julian overnight. From the hours of surveillance videos I've trawled through the past few weeks, last night was the first time Melody would have been witnessed arriving at Julian's building by my private investigator. She usually sleeps at her loft apartment every night. Not always alone, but it was better than the thoughts entering my head now.

"Did your friend mention what spooked Melody? My father has always been a hard-ass, but Melody rarely responded to his riles. She usually left that bidding to her father."

I exhale deeply when the truth smacks into me. Her father can't fight her battles anymore. That task is now up to me, and if I had been fulfilling my position as promised, I wouldn't be hearing news about Melody's exchange with my father second-hand. With my head focused on Carlyle Shroud and his thirty-year-old purchase, I let my private investigator's email sit in my inbox unopened this morning. That's not acceptable, and I won't let it happen again.

"Better yet, can you forward me a copy of the police file—"

I swallow my words when Phillipa interrupts, "I would if either party was pressing charges. With both parties wishing not to pursue the matter further, there are no reports to forward."

"My father isn't pressing the matter?" Shock resonates in my tone. "I thought you said Julian hit him?"

"He did," Phillipa replies through a breathless chuckle. "Socked him right in the eye. From what I heard, his shiner took a makeup artist an hour to cover it for his conference this morning."

Something isn't right here. My father sues if the press so much as calls him an asshole. He's had tweets yanked and has been accused of suppressing freedom of speech on more than one occasion, so there's no way in hell he'd let a billionaire off scot-free without first fleecing him a few million. More is happening here than we realize.

"Did your police friend take notes of the incident?"

Phillipa hums out an agreeing noise. "I'd say so. They don't have information-retaining brains like agents do. Do you want them?"

"Please. Also…" I move to the notepad I scribbled a date on earlier. With my mind askew the past few days, I've started taking notes, so I don't forget all the little tidbits I keep setting aside when something more urgent comes up. Although this doesn't directly affect Melody, it's been playing on my mind all day. "Can you run a quick search for me? I'd do it, but the internet service here is rat shit. I'm shocked my call went through."

"Sure. Shoot." Approximately thirty-seconds after I give Phillipa Isabelle's flight number and date, she updates me on the credit card details used to bump her ticket up to business class.

Shock dangles on my vocal cords. "Alex Rogers? As in *the* Alex Rogers?"

"As in the sup of your division Alex Rogers."

"Are you sure, Phillipa? I'm sure Alex Rogers is a common name."

I eat my words for the second time tonight when she interrupts, "It was paid for with his Bureau credit card."

Fuck! "All right. I guess that's confirmation enough. Can you forward me the details?"

"I thought your service was shit?"

I groan. "It is, but I'm sure it's capable of downloading an email."

"If it's not, stand on your head and stick out your tongue. Perhaps the electrodes in your spit will improve the signal."

Even knowing everything she's saying is false, I can't help but ask, "What does standing on my head have to do with anything?"

"I've had a shit day. I need a laugh." My suspicion grows tenfold when Phillipa mumbles, "For a man with basically no ass, you certainly know how to fill in a pair of pants."

All sense of normality is lost when I notice the tiniest speck of red shining from the top of my laptop monitor. "You're spying on me. What if I were getting dressed?"

"I can only dream. Night, BJ." She disconnects our call before half of my growl rolls up my chest. I'm certain she still heard it, though, because not only is a red light still beaming from my laptop, the peaks and troughs of my microphone graph are rising and falling.

Seconds after I close down Phillipa's live feed of my room, my laptop dings, announcing I have a new email. Once again, prioritizing Melody above anything else, I print out Phillipa's email before scrolling to the one my private investigator sent me this morning. Although his dot-formatted update includes the incident Phillipa filled me in on, just like Phillipa, he's lost as to what caused Melody to flee her office building the way she did. He mentioned she was red-faced and on the verge of crying, but silent, which isn't surprising considering she can't talk.

I sink low in my chair as I consider what to do. I could FaceTime

Melody to make sure she's okay, but even Phillipa's confirmation that my ass fills in my trousers well doesn't have me convinced we wouldn't spend a majority of our conversation endeavoring to improve our connection. I could email her, but that feels impersonal, not to mention the fact it's the weekend, and I only have her work email. So, instead, I text her.

It's a basic, *I hope you are okay. Buzz me if you need me* text, but it lightens the load on my shoulders enough to shift my focus elsewhere for a second. It isn't to Isabelle or the fact Alex is more scrupulous than first perceived, it's to Grayson, and the vanishing act he's been conducting the past few weeks.

"Come on, Grayson, pick up," I mutter through the long shrill of my unanswered call.

Just when I think my call is about to be sent to his voicemail for the fourth time, it connects. "Hello?" I say down the line, stunned by the silence. Usually, you've got to grapple to issue a greeting before Grayson. "Grayson, are you there?"

I squash my phone in close to my ear when a faint voice whispers, "Grayson isn't here." It isn't the voice of a child, but it's weak and timid. "I haven't seen him in days."

"Katie?" I don't know what compelled me to say that, but I'm glad I couldn't hold back when the female on the other end of the line gasps in a shocked breath. "It's you, isn't it?" When she rushes out that she has to go, I breathe out even faster, "Is Grayson okay? That's all I need to know. You don't need to tell me anything else."

With silence teeming between us, nothing but the sounds of her tiny breaths resonate down the line for the next several seconds. They fill me with horrid thoughts that only clear when she mutters, "He's okay, but he needs to go. Kirill isn't happy."

"What do you mean? Why isn't Kirill happy—" My interrogation ends early when the creak of a door is quickly chased by a thick Russian voice. I can't hear exactly what the person says since Katie has the microphone muffled before a squeak pops from Katie's mouth, then our calls ends. I don't know if Katie disconnected it or if spotty service is responsible. Whatever the reason, I dial Grayson's number on repeat for the next eight minutes, only stopping when the cruel punches of my thumb on the screen has me accidentally connecting to an incoming call.

Since it's from an unknown number, I almost hang-up. Mercifully, Grayson's gravelly voice sounds down the line before I do. "Miss me, punk? Sorry I've been slack. I forgot how tiring wading through shit was."

"What the fuck, Grayson? You almost gave me a heart attack."

He laughs, having no clue I'm being truthful. I am on the verge of a coronary failure.

I have a million questions to ask, and even more scorns to deliver, but I lose the chance when Grayson says, "Kirill is on the move. Caught sight of a flight manifest in his office when I was running errands. He's heading to New York. The plane only has eight seats, so I don't see a war starting any time soon. Thought you'd be interested, though, considering I saw tickets for your dad's gig in the same pile of paperwork."

"What gig?"

"Hold up." I hear papers shuffle before he adds, "The Serena Scott Foundation. Your mom boards it, but from what I can see, your dad uses part of the funds to fatten up his campaign endeavors."

Is it wrong I'm not surprised to hear my dad rips off charity organizations? You can't do the devil's work if you're not willing to walk in his shoes.

"Is that why you gave Katie your cell? 'Cause Kirill is traveling light?"

"Uh-huh. Kirill's team constantly scans for bugs. I don't need to plant one on Katie if she's willing to cart my cell phone with her. I just need to trace my missing device on my laptop."

If we were more work acquaintances than friends, I would have mistaken the content in his voice for cockiness. "You've gained Katie's trust?"

Grayson's agreeing hum this time around is ten times more confident than his earlier one. "She's not gone yet, BJ. I can see the good in her eyes." Belief Katie is too far down the rabbit hole to be saved is the Bureau's main reason for treading lightly with her case. Stockholm syndrome usually kicks in within weeks. Katie has been with Kirill for seven years. A loss is anticipated, although Grayson will never believe that. "Hold up. Go back. How do you know Katie has my phone?"

"She answered my call. Said you need to go because Kirill isn't happy."

"She answered your call?" When I murmur in agreement, he swears. "Kirill has eyes on Katie everywhere. If she talked to you on the phone, that means Kirill knows what she said, for how long she said it, and exactly how she said it." He curses another three times in a row before he pushes out, "I've got to go."

"Do you want me to call in backup?"

"No!" Grayson shouts over the frantic tap of his feet. "I've got this. Just do me a favor."

"Anything," I reply without pause for thought.

I don't know whether to laugh or cry when he says, "Call your girl. This shit has gone on for long enough." We could be in the process of being probed by aliens, and he'd still find time to rib me about reaching out to Melody. He's done it for seven years now. I guess it's hard to give up familiarities.

When Grayson disconnects our call, I sit on the edge of my bed for a few minutes. The urge to call Melody is somewhat overwhelming, but it's late, and I'm fucking zonked. I wouldn't hesitate if she had returned my text. The fact she hasn't advises me she's either sleeping or wants to be left alone. Neither thought appeases my edginess, but instead of switching off for the night and starting fresh in the morning, I tiptoe toward something that could end as awkwardly as I start it.

Me: What are you wearing?

Phillipa answers my text a few seconds later.

Phillipa: I'd rather show you than explain.

I STOP CHUCKLING about something Phillipa says when the door of my hotel room shoots open. With the reception as bad as I anticipated, we switched from texting to a phone conversation around thirty minutes ago. I won't lie, it was a little awkward the first few minutes, but once we discovered we have more in common than just work, the conversation flowed more smoothly.

Although I don't see that still being the case when the barrel of Hugo's gun swings my way. "I'll call you back," I stammer into the phone, shocked at the fury on Hugo's face.

I doubt we'll ever be classed as friends, but I thought my understanding today when he requested to call in Isaac's security team before the Bureau would have given me some leniency in our clashing personalities. Clearly, my attempt to flirt with Phillipa wasn't the only foolish thing I've done today.

Hugo adjusts the scope of his aim when Isabelle places herself between us. With her chest balancing against his, she stares straight into his eyes. "I trust Brandon, he wouldn't do this. He is my friend. He's been helping me."

"What's going on?" I ask, completely lost. We ate dinner together only an hour ago. Hugo was fine then, so what the fuck flipped his switch?

"Why don't you tell us, *Blondie?*" Hugo spits out my nickname as if it burned his tongue during delivery.

When Isabelle pivots around to face me, flashing a warning look to Hugo on the way, the heat on her cheeks augments. She's embarrassed by Hugo's line of questioning, but her eyes are brimming with suspicion.

I discover the reason for her confusion when she divulges, "They found a listening device in my cell phone."

I soundlessly scoff, unsurprised. Theresa likes to play dirty.

I'm about to ask what Theresa's game plan has to do with me just as the truth smacks into me. "I didn't plant the bug. It wasn't me. Izzy, you know me, I've been helping you."

My eyes snap to Hugo when he growls, "You're the only one who's been with Izzy since I removed the last bug yesterday morning."

Before I can deny his accusation, Isabelle pipes up. "No, he wasn't." When she shifts on her feet to face Hugo, her strides are unstable. "Theresa Veneto and a male agent came to my apartment yesterday afternoon. She showed me photos of Col Petretti's right-hand man in a hospital bed. She said he was beaten the weekend Isaac and I went to Club 57. She was trying to coerce me into unwillingly incriminating Isaac."

My hand creeps for my revolver when a third male joins us. "That's bullshit. For one, if Isaac had tracked him down that night, he wouldn't have left him breathing. And two, Col would never file a police report on an assault, let alone have an FBI agent consider it. He would have swept it under the rug like he always does." A bearded man with sleeves full of tattoos walks into my room like he owns the place. He wordlessly suggests for Hugo to lower his gun by giving his shoulder a friendly squeeze before moving to stand in front of me. When I see nothing but aggression pumping out of him, it's the fight of my life not to smile. It doesn't matter how many notches you have on your belt, intimidation is always the best form of flattery. "Who are you?"

"Brandon James." When I offer him my hand to shake, my lips curl into a smirk. Just like my boyish face and wonky grin hide my smarts, so does his bearded face and tattooed body. I've just met my match. This bearded stranger just doesn't want to acknowledge it right now.

"What's your real name?" He folds his arms in front of his chest as the arrogance in his eyes doubles. "Because I searched Brandon James after your *date* with Izzy a couple of months ago, nothing came up."

"Just like your search on Izzy failed to yield any real results?" When shock registers on his face, a voice in my head whispers, *Checkmate, motherfucker.* "I buried Izzy's private life as much as I did mine." My eyes drift to Isabelle, who's watching me in shocked awe. "I knew they'd be looking." Nothing is private these days. Some men do background searches before exchanging numbers, and I'm not going to mention the lengths some women go to for a suitable match, or we'll be here all night.

With Isabelle's anxiety as high as her brow, her reply comes out in a squeak. "Isaac already knows."

"I'm not talking about Isaac. I'm talking about the Bureau." Realizing now is as good a time as any to update her on what I discovered earlier today, I move to the document I printed out before reading my private investigator's email. "You're not the only one who's been doing some research the past few days."

When I hand her proof that Alex is being as unscrupulous as Isaac, hopeful it will have her paying careful attention to everyone around her, she speed-reads the article. "The Bureau paid for me to fly business class?"

I shake my head. "Not the Bureau, Izzy. Alex signed off on it."

Isabelle's growl rumbles through my chest. "That son of a bitch. Why would he do that?"

I want to reply *because that's what all condescending, narcissistic men do*, but instead, I shrug. I'm standing across from two of Isaac's goons. Only an idiot would break cover now. Furthermore, this inches me one step closer to becoming a part of Isaac's team. Money can't buy this spot, but fake loyalty sure as fuck can.

BRANDON

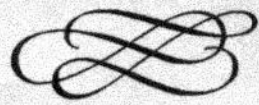

"Have you worked with Isaac long?"

Hunter slides open the back of his surveillance van before climbing in to gather the equipment needed to do a 3D scan of Megan's bedroom. Other than handing over the serial numbers of the listening devices found in Isabelle's apartment at Isaac's request last night, he hasn't spoken a word to me. He's not happy I'm here, but since he does whatever Isaac tells him to do, he's stuck with me.

"Want me to get a head start on logistics?" When I crack open one of his many laptops, Hunter slams down the screen, yanks it out of my grasp, then jerks his head to the open front door of the Shroud's family ranch, wordlessly telling me to fuck off. I could let him off easy, but where's the fun in that? "What processor are you using? Those things look chunky. You could cut down weight by—"

"They're chunky for a reason." I slant my head to hide my smile, stoked I forced him to talk. "Just like my foot... so it causes more damage when it's rammed up the asses of annoying fuckfaces who can't take the hint to fuck off when they're not wanted."

"Jeez. Did someone forget to eat their Wheaties this morning?"

He steps out of the van to meet me chest to chest. Since he's a good three to four inches taller than me, I have to look up to see his glare when he says, "I know what you're doing. I read your game plan from a mile out and followed the breadcrumbs you left while trying to conceal your tracks, so quit the fucking games and bow out of the fight before I tell Isabelle the real reason you changed your last name to James, Brandon McGee." The way he overemphasizes my last name makes me hate it even more. Not even my mom goes by it anymore, that's how bad the bile is anytime we're forced to use it.

Even with the horrid taste in my mouth thickening my tongue, I remember my objective. "I'm just trying to help."

I realize I've been swinging my bat the wrong way when Hunter snarls. "You're trying to get into Izzy's panties, which will never happen, so why not give up now and fuck off back to wherever you came from."

After slamming his van door shut, he makes a conscious effort to prove it's locked before he gallops up the rickety stairwell with a tripod and 3D camera thrust under his arm.

I take a quick breather to strategize my next move before following after him. I've only just gained Isaac's trust, so bowing out now isn't an option. I've got to up my game. Not just for me but Isabelle as well. She hung herself out to dry for me last night when she told Isaac she trusts me, so the least I can do is make sure she isn't falling for a guy set out to destroy her.

When my return to Megan's room has me stumbling onto Isaac taking a call in the hallway, I slow my strides before yanking my cell phone out of my pocket. Hoping to catch portions of his conversation, I dial my voicemail before leaving myself a message. The worst thing an agent can do when faking a call is not to dial a number. Trust me, you're guaranteed to get an unexpected call the instant you commence your ruse. It happened to Grayson more than twice when he was a rookie. Tobias never let him live it down.

I take on a second approach to my ruse when thoughts of

Tobias's training processes drift into my mind. He was often accused of having an unscrupulous friendship with Henry Gottle, yet I never judged him on it, so why am I not giving Isaac the same leeway? If he believes I'm his friend, and he's given me his trust, that has to be more beneficial than hiding in the shadows waiting for him to stumble, right?

Right.

This time, I dial a real number.

Phillipa answers quickly. "Good morning."

My brow cocks. "Morning? It's almost ten."

I hear her stretch in her yawn. "Cut me some slack. I had a late one, so I slept in."

Even with my chest swelling with smugness, I'm not taking any credit for the huskiness of her words. We talked until the wee hours of this morning, but that was more to drown out the noises I didn't want to hear two rooms over than anything else. We behaved—for the most part.

I can't say the same for Isabelle and Isaac. If I had any doubt they hadn't acted on the bristling chemistry that bounced between them last night, I don't anymore.

Disturbed by the waywardness of my thoughts the past week, I squish my phone closer to my ear before asking, "Can you give me the deets on Carlyle Shroud? Something fishy is still going on here, but it feels murkier than just a kidnap-for-sale arrangement."

"*Just* a kidnap-for-sale arrangement? Jesus, Brandon, you've been in the field too long. Time for desk duty."

I physically gag. "I'd rather die than work behind a desk. The months I spent at HQ between placements were bad enough."

Phillipa's laugh does weird things to my cock, but since I'm trying to pretend it isn't hardening in the middle of the day like a freak, I shift my focus elsewhere. "Did Grayson log movement sheets last night?"

"Yeah," Phillipa replies between keystrokes. "He also requested additional comms for the event he referenced last night."

"Was permission granted?"

I smile in gratitude when she says, "It was when I pushed through his request. You're right, BJ, sometimes flexing a bit of muscle does more good than bad." She breathes slowly out before asking, "Got a pen?"

I yank a notepad and pen from the breast pocket of my suit jacket before telling her to go ahead.

Once I have Carlyle's details jotted down, I thank Phillipa for her assistance before joining Isaac next to the only window in Megan's room. Pretending Phillipa's husky request for me to call her tonight wasn't laced with hidden innuendo, I lock my eyes with Isaac and say, "Boss… umm… Isaac."

My ruse is played to perfection. Not only does Isaac's chest rise so fast I'm confident I am moments away from having my eye gouged out by one of his peacock feathers, he reminds me were on an even playing field. "You can call me Isaac. I'm not your boss." It gains him my respect. A lesser man would have tried to play on my 'supposed' insecurities.

Isaac listens intently when I disclose, "I called in a favor with a girl I know. The owner of this property is Carlyle Shroud. He's fifty-eight years old and has been receiving disability checks since a workplace injury nearly two decades ago." Even with knowing everything I'm informing him by heart, I read it off my notepad. It makes it seem as if I am as unknowledgeable in this case as his crew, which keeps the playing field even as he strived to make it only seconds ago. "His disability checks have been deposited each month, but none of his bank accounts have been utilized in months, which is surprising. Carlyle is what you might call the local drunk. More than eighty percent of his support payments are spent at the liquor store in town."

"Does he have any vehicles registered in his name?" Isaac asks, curious.

Nodding, I flick through my notepad. "Yes, one. A black Dodge truck, license plate number 44W—"

My eyes float up from my notepad when Isaac interrupts, "2285?"

When I nod, his features flood with devastation before he yanks at the window we're standing next to. When it fails to budge from his frantic tugs, he smashes his elbow through the glass like he's a drug lord outrunning the DEA.

The urgency of his panic comes to light when he shouts out the window, "Where's Isabelle?"

Carlyle's only mode of transportation is parked at the front of his shed, and we're miles from the closest town.

That can only mean one thing.

He's still here.

When Isaac shouts for Hugo to "Get Isabelle," I follow his sprint down the warped stairs. They're not sturdy enough to take the weight of our frantic stomps, but we take the risk, preferring to fall through the rickety wood than have Isabelle reach the barn she's pacing toward before us.

During our sprint across the overgrown field, I call in backup. "My name is Brandon James. I'm an FBI field agent. My number is 443567. I need an ambulance and a police unit brought to 15634 Snow Mountain Road, Parkerville."

My stomach gurgles when I request a first responder, but I'd rather be safe than sorry. Carlyle purchased a woman on the black market. His stability has already been discredited and don't get me started on his daughter. People only go that crazy when they've been subjected to unimaginable things.

The churns of my stomach overtake the heaving of my lungs when I break through a partially cracked open barn door on Isaac's heel. The smell vaping off the rotting corpse hanging off the second story of the barn is inconceivable. I have an iron stomach, yet even it is struggling. Think of the worst smell you've ever imagined. Now triple it, and you're not even halfway there yet.

My neck cranks to the side when a pained sob tears through my ears. The expression on Isabelle's face when she buries her head into Hugo's pecs has me picturing what Melody's response would have been when she saw Joey hanging lifeless from the oak tree she climbed every week from the age of eight until almost eighteen.

Is that why she fled that night?

Was the image too much for her to bear?

I almost wanted to run that night, but since Joey's skin wasn't lifeless and unnatural like the man hanging from the beam, I tried to save him. My attempts were woeful, but at least I tried.

If only I could say the same thing about my relationship with Melody.

BRANDON

When Phillipa leans back in her bed, exposing more of the silk negligee she's wearing, I pretend not to notice the way the frilled lace edging grips at the generous swell of her breasts. She's drinking wine like she was the first time we Face-Timed, but she only just cracked open the bottle for our debrief.

I thought yesterday was a clusterfuck, but it had nothing on today. Isabelle is distraught after seeing her first dead body. I can't get Joey out of my head, and I'm stuck in this bumfuckville town for another night in case the agent brought in to investigate Carlyle's death wants to ask me any questions. I gave him my cell phone number and told him to call me any time, day or night, but like some 1950s black and white old-town sheriff movie, he doesn't like cell phones. He prefers face-to-face meetings.

"Who was called in?" Phillipa asks before taking another generous sip of her wine.

The bedding ripples around my backside when I scoot up the bed to rest my back on the headboard. I've seen the mess hotels like this one have on their sheets, so I refuse to slip between them—even when fully clothed. "Harvey Rose."

Phillipa's nose screws up. "I thought he retired?" When I pull a face as if to say, *he's well past retirement age*, she laughs. "I've heard he's a hard-ass. How'd you go about requesting to be kept in the loop on this case?"

Air whizzes out of my nose. "He said, I quote, 'Kid, we've got no time for mollycoddling around these parts. If you need a babysitter, I suggest you go back to the academy' unquote. But he came around... eventually."

Phillipa hears something in my words I didn't mean to express. "What did you give him?"

"Nothing." I roll my eyes like she can't see me. It doubles her glare. "I dropped some names that had him gasping like Marilyn Monroe was giving him head. No big deal."

Her mouth falls open. "You told him your father is Vincent McGee?"

I scoff. "What? No! Don't be ridiculous. I may have mentioned an Agent P. Russell," I mumble out my last sentence with a yawn. I'm tired, but that isn't the reason I yawned. I'm hoping it will have Phillipa missing my confession.

She doesn't—regretfully. "You used my name? Brandon! Shame on you."

Spit flies out of my mouth when I blow a raspberry. "I didn't use *your* name. I used your father's name."

Her eye roll is more sophisticated than mine. "Same thing. I'm named after him."

"But mercifully, you look nothing like him."

We both freeze, stunned by my compliment, but Phillipa isn't as willing to let it slide as I am. "Thank you for finally noticing, can't-take-a-hint McGee."

I love her playfulness. Her nickname, not so much. "Please don't call me that."

"Why not? It's your name, isn't it?"

I shake my head. "It's not my name. It's my father's name, and I hate it."

The jeering on her face is instantly replaced with sympathy. "Wanna talk about it?"

"Do you have five years?"

She leans in close to the screen before replying, "I could if you need me to."

Before I can register the shock of her offer, a text message pops up on my screen.

Melody: Hey BJ. Sorry for my late reply. I left my cell phone at the office. I'm okay. How are you?

Her message is as basic as the one I sent her, but the question at the end is practically an open invitation for a conversation.

Reading me with the knowledge not many people have, Phillipa asks, "What is it? Is it the case? Surely, they couldn't have gotten Carlyle's autopsy back this soon."

"It's not work." I lock my eyes with hers before adding, "It's Melody. I texted her last night. She only just replied. Said she left her phone at work."

"Oh… good." Phillipa's tone is more pleasant than her facial expression. She honestly looks like someone just ran over her cat. "I'll go. You should FaceTime her."

"You don't mind?"

She waves her hand through the air like she's shooing away a fly. "No, not at all. Have fun." She disconnects our chat before I have the chance to reply, and even quicker than that, I have my Messenger app open.

Me: Are you sure you're okay? The last time you were up this late was when you shook your way through a s'mores sugar-high.

I bunker down for another late night when the three dashes of an incoming message dart across the screen of my phone. My intuition is proven right when Melody's reply pops up two seconds later.

Melody: If I recall correctly, that was the night of my fifteenth birthday. Which means it wasn't a sugar-high keeping me awake...

"It was me," I whisper at the same time her next message arrives.

Melody: *It was you.*

UNSURE IF THE wetness seeping into my pants is because of the incalculable number of times Melody featured in my dreams last night, or the faulty pipes of the one-star motel I'm camped in, I slip my hand into my sweatpants. I'm hard and virile, my cock stretching well past the waistband of my boxers, but there's no sticky residue as I'm anticipating, so faulty pipes must be to blame.

I realize neither of my suggestions are right when icy-cold water is tossed over my bed. It shrivels my dick in an instant and has me scampering up the bed. After pushing my flopped hair out of my eyes, I stray them in the direction the water was flung from. A growl rumbles in my chest when I spot the condescending sneer of soon-to-be-retired Special Agent Harvey Rose.

"Up and at 'em, kid, you're gonna wanna see this." How he ever got through the academy with a lack of vocabulary shocks me. He could only be more hillbilly if he had a piece of straw stuck between his buck teeth. "And change your clothes. If your moans like the last twenty are anything to go by, I don't want you sitting in the cab of my truck in *those pants*." He stares at my no-longer extended crotch while snickering out, 'those pants.'

"Can you give me a minute?" I ask when he remains standing in the doorway of my attached bathroom, holding an empty bucket while smirking like a smug prick. "I can't really get dressed with you standing there staring at me, can I?"

"Can't get any worse, can it? You're lying on top of the bedding, stroking your dick through your pants. I've seen about all I can see."

His thick silver mustache wobbles when I growl, "I wasn't stroking myself. I was checking for wetness—"

"In your pants. Nuf said."

When he pushes off his feet to mosey out of the room like a real-life gunslinger, I stumble onto something more atrocious than a fellow agent breaking into my room to wake me as if I'm a prisoner of war. He got a piece of paper wet, a very important piece of paper.

"What the fuck? Do you have any idea what you have done? That's evidence you've ruined. You could be suspended for that." I climb out of my bed before carefully lifting the banking slip I swiped from Hunter's van yesterday when Isaac, Hunter, and Hugo were fussing over Isabelle. I felt like scum at the bottom of the shower in my motel room, but the recurring deposit placed into Hunter's account each month had my interests too piqued to leave the paper in his glove compartment. None of Isaac's many businesses have the trading name of the payee on Hunter's bank record, and the money appears to be coming from an offshore account. It could be a dead end, or it could be a gold mine, but it won't be anything if I can't stop the ink from smudging. "Grab me the hairdryer."

"The what?"

"The. Hair. Dryer." I speak my words super slow as if Harvey is hard of hearing. "It's under the vanity sink."

Harvey steps into the bathroom for a second before his big frame refills the doorway. That's how small the bathroom is. "This?" he asks, holding up the hairdryer with two fingers as if it's covered in cooties.

"Yes. Bring it to me."

When I click at him as if he's a dog, he pegs the hairdryer at my head before stalking to the door. "Come find me in my truck when you've finished fancying yourself up. If you're not out in ten, I'll leave you here." I'm about to tell him I'm fine with that, but his next set of words stop me, "And I'll pass your murder onto another agent."

I slant my head, my heart rate rising. "Murder?"

His lowriding ponytail swishes along his back when he cranks his neck back to face me. "Yep. Murder. That boy's feet were dangling above a shallow grave."

"You found a second body?"

Harvey doesn't answer me unless you count whistling as an agreeing sound.

"Is it a female?"

"Coroner is on her way, but I'd say so." He nudges his head to a truck that looks like it belongs on the top of a wreckage heap. "You coming or not?"

"I'm coming." After snapping a quick image of Hunter's bank record on my phone and forwarding it to Phillipa, I snag my shoes from the foot of my drenched bed and my jacket from the desk, then follow Harvey out of my motel room, acting ignorant to the droplets of water dripping off my trousers.

"CAUCASIAN FEMALE, early to mid-thirties. Multiple stab wounds to her chest. Several broken bones. Some have been fused over, though, so prolonged physical abuse is suspected."

Dr. Maude, a mid-fifties coroner from Parkerville, raises her gentle eyes to mine when I ask, "Did she have any children?"

She nods as her eyes soften more. "Yes. Multiple times."

I take a step back when she says 'multiple.' "More than once? Are you sure?"

"Uh-huh. She had both natural and caesarian births." She lifts a plain white sheet to show us a C-section scar. "Caesarian scars are still identifiable even on badly decomposed bodies, although hers are a little jagged, and the suturing for each one was horrendous."

"Indicating she most likely gave birth at home." Harvey jumps in as his eyes stray to a woman we believe is Rhianna Shroud, Carlyle Shroud's designer wife.

"It does look that way." Dr. Maude drags her glove-covered index finger along skin that doesn't really represent skin anymore. "Her sutures were an old military style. They were a running style instead of the favored continuous sutures most hospitals use. No staple marks were noted, either. Whoever stitched her up took no care. Her uterus is so poorly damaged, if she had survived her attack, she'd be infertile."

"Do her C-section scars give any indication on how long ago her children were born?" The weariness of my words reveals my tiredness. Harvey and I have spent the last five hours sitting on hard plastic chairs outside a morgue that would be lucky to see one to two patients a year, much less two murder victims. Mercifully, the lack of victims around these parts means Dr. Maude could get straight to work.

"Her scars are aged. I'd say most of her children were born twenty to thirty years ago. I'll have a more conclusive answer once I've finished my autopsy."

Nodding, I join Dr. Maude at the sink so she can wash her hands. "Is there any indication the victim's wounds could have been self-inflicted?" With Megan's mental instability beyond proven by multiple psychiatric hospital admissions the past ten years, I can't leave any stone unturned.

As Dr. Maude dries her hands, she purses her lips. "I had considered that at the start, multiple ligature marks and cuts were noted on her thighs and forearms, but the angle of the wounds indicate her attacker stood over her and thrust down." She demonstrates what she means on me. Her 'attack' replicates a poorly-scripted knife killing scene all B-grade horror movies have. "If the injuries were self-inflicted, the wounds would be straight with little to no angle manipulation." She demonstrates what she means by stabbing herself in the chest with an invisible knife. There's no downward thrusting, meaning the entrance wounds of the knife are straight.

"So, she was murdered?" Harvey asks, catching the gist of our theatrics.

"Yes." Dr. Maude nudges her head to Carlyle's body lying lifeless on a gurney. He's been deceased for so long, his head still sits at the odd angle the rope contorted it to. "As was he."

"Carlyle was also murdered?" Harvey asks, once again joining our conversation. I'm glad as I am so shocked, my words aren't working. "We believed Carlyle hung himself where he did because it was directly above the shallow grave of his wife."

Dr. Maude shakes her head before moving toward the early toxicology reports. "According to this, Carlyle had traces of tetrodotoxin in his stomach contents."

"Pufferfish is a delicacy in Japan, could incorrect preparation be the cause of his death?" I'm not a fan of fishy dishes, but I sampled pufferfish a few years ago when Phoenix dared me to. He was a risk-taker long before Joey died, but it grew substantially worse after his death.

Dr. Maude once again shakes her head. "That wasn't the only traces of poisoning we found in his stomach. It was as if someone googled the most poisonous foods and plants, and hit him with near-lethal combinations as often as possible."

With me needing a few seconds to decipher a possible reason for prolonging Carlyle's death, Harvey's years of service get a chance to shine. "If he were dead, the disability checks would have stopped coming. Keeping him alive, although sick, kept the money coming in."

"Quite possibly," Dr. Maude says through twisted lips. "I'll have a full workup to you by the end of the week. Perhaps sooner if you can supply me with a list of toxins to search."

Hearing Dr. Maude's request as readily as me, Harvey dips his chin in farewell before heading for the exit. I fall into step behind him a second later.

"Were any domestic disturbances reported at the Shroud property around the time of their deaths?" I ask Harvey while climbing into his truck. Yes, I said climb. His truck is one of those big-wheeled vehicles that short-asses like me need a step-ladder to enter.

Harvey shakes his head while firing up his truck. "I went back over three decades. No reports at all. Not surprising, though. They live too far out for neighbors to hear their screams."

With his honest comment gurgling the greasy egg and bacon

burger I scarfed down while waiting for Dr. Maude to do a preliminary autopsy on the female corpse found by the forensic team late last night, I keep my mouth shut during our drive back to the Shroud family ranch.

Even with the area being guarded by over a dozen members of the local sheriff's office, our silent descent down the long driveway is oddly eerie. The Bureau has stumbled onto many houses of horror since it was founded, but I have a feeling the Shroud ranch will top the cake on their previous cases.

After pulling in at the front of the property, Harvey locks his eyes with mine. "I'll start on the sheds while you go through the house. If Carlyle was moved from the house to the barn, some kind of help was needed. He wasn't a slim man by any means."

After lifting my chin, acknowledging his request without words, I hotfoot it up the front porch stairs. The agent side of me wants to head straight to the kitchen, certain the food scraps on the floor will have traces of the poisons Dr. Maude is chasing, but the right side of my head, the intuitive part, directs me to Megan's room instead. It's as sterile as a psychiatric hospital, making it the ideal place to store dangerous goods.

I dip my chin in greeting to a deputy at the door before snagging a pair of gloves out of the box at his side. CSI officers are still working the scene. They've removed a majority of the photographs from the walls, so now they're working on the ceiling.

With them occupied, I move for the room Isabelle, Hugo, and I discovered two days ago. It reeks of bleach and instigates horrid memories of seeing Mr. and Mrs. Gregg in the operating theaters years ago, but I keep moving, knowing my job will forever come first. And no, I'm not referencing my position in the Bureau.

"Has anything been removed from this room?" I ask a young techie who's digitally categorizing the space as Hunter did yesterday morning.

She peers up at me with her big almond-shaped eyes out in full force before shaking her head. If the width of her pupils is anything to go by, she's brand-spanking new to the job.

After nudging my head to the door, I ask, "Can you give me a minute? I work better in silence."

Her headshake switches to a nod as she stands to her feet. "I could probably do with a breather. This is a little creepy."

I purse my lips to hide my smile. Creepy is much too blasé of a word for what could possibly be going on here.

Once I'm alone, I stand in the middle of the all-white space before slowly pivoting around to take in each surface with due diligence. Most agents would move straight for the physically visible stuff before deepening their search. I prefer starting at the other end. When dealing with a deranged person, you must think outside of the box.

A few minutes later, my head slants to the side. A seam of drywall tape is running down one wall. It wouldn't have been visible if it weren't for the faintest portion of afternoon sun breaking through the storm clouds above my head.

"Can I borrow that?" I ask a male CSI officer who's holding a box cutter. Nick's photographs were glued to the wall, meaning they have to be sliced off the wall along with the drywall's plaster.

After handing me the cutter, the crime scene investigator joins me inside the room, halving its space with his broad shoulders. "What are you looking at?"

"Can you see the seam?" I outline the area I'm fixated on before twisting my torso back to face him. "All the drywall in this room is from a continuous sheet… except that one."

I can tell the exact moment he spots what I'm referencing as he purses his lips. "Do you want the pleasure, or shall I?"

"I'll cut while you photograph. If the amount of bleach in this room is anything to go by, and the fact we have missing children, we'll want to get everything on tape."

"All right." He grabs a video recorder off a kit just outside of the room before firing it up. The light on top of the recording device bounces off the stark white walls, blinding me, but mercifully, it also highlights the seam I'm about to slice through.

"Is that… *ugh*… the smell."

"At least it isn't a human corpse," I gabble through a gag while removing a mummified cat from the wall. It's so badly decomposed, I'm going to burn my nose hairs with bleach just with the hope it'll eradicate the smell from my nostrils.

I realize not all the smell is coming from the cat when I break away a large chunk of the drywall. There's a hand, a tiny one, and it's very much human.

While working my jaw side to side, hopeful its workover will hold back the bile scorching my throat, I move to the window Isaac broke with his elbow. After removing a thin piece of thread the CSI team has yet to discover and sliding it into my pocket, I shout down for Harvey.

When he pops his big head out of the wooden shed Carlyle's truck is parked in front of a few seconds later, I jerk up my chin. "You'll want to see this."

My brows inch together when he replies, "You first."

"I've got a body," I shout, stilling the deputies standing between us.

"So do I, kid," Harvey replies, "And more than one of them."

MELODY

I slant my head to the left before slowly dragging it to the right. Printing out the image Brandon sent me this morning hasn't improved its quality at all. I can tell it's a bank record, there's a familiar logo in the top left-hand corner, and some of the digits not covered by smeared ink could possibly be an account number, but without knowing every digit and what this document corresponds to, I'm running blind.

I would have more of an idea on what I'm seeking if Brandon had included text with his picture message. This soggy image is all I've got to work on. He gave me more information when he requested Marjorie Hawke's file.

There's a thought. I wonder if that corresponds with this?

Eager to check, I snag my loft keys off the coffee table, then dash into Julian's office. "I need to pop by my loft. Did you want me to pick up something for dinner on the way back?"

"You're going out… *alone?*" The shock in his voice is understandable. My backside has barely left the couch since my run-in with Mr. McGee two nights ago. Leo was adamant I was to take a few days off, and since Julian has a butler, a cook, and several housemaids, I haven't needed to lift a finger. Although Brandon's underhanded request for help isn't exactly heart-pumping stuff, it feels nice to be needed. Julian never needs anything, and if he does, he has a bucket load of staff at the ready, waiting to serve him.

When I nod, Julian asks, "Would you like me to come with you?"

"No, it's fine. You're snowed under. I should only be a few minutes." When a worried groove burrows between his brows, I nudge my head to the large Samoan man standing in the corner of the massive living room. "I'll take Tiny with me."

Tiny smiles a beaming grin when my nickname reaches his ears. Fetu isn't close to being tiny. He's thick, tall, and his face tattoos would have people double-guessing their approach before they've even considered it.

"If you're late, I'll wait up for you."

Julian's brow arches when I mutter, "I won't be late." He knows I barely turn up for anything on time, and let's not mention the fact he printed out Brandon's image for me, meaning he most likely knows what my trip home is about. I left a certified copy of Marjorie's file on my desk. "I'll be back soon."

When I spin on my heels, Julian calls my name. He waits for me to pop my head back into his gigantic office before he signs, *I love you.*

"I love you too," I reply with a smile.

When Fetu joins me outside of Julian's office, I hold my finger in the air, requesting a minute. The smell of freshly baked cookies streams through my nose when I dash into the kitchen. It's as large and as well-equipped as the rest of Julian's penthouse, but mercifully, it has a homey feel to it. That might have more to do with Julian's cook's fond fascination with dessert items.

Once I have three large walnut cookies stored in a white paper bag, I return to Fetu's side. "Hungry, miss?" he asks, holding out my coat for me.

"They're not for me."

When I press my finger to my lips, he nods. I don't want Julian knowing I'm sending meals out to the man Brandon has sitting outside of his penthouse. It isn't that I want to lie, I'm just unsure how Julian will feel about it. He's encouraging my friendship with Brandon as he believes it will be good for my state of mind, but he's also been distant the past few days.

Have you ever felt lonely even with someone sitting directly beside you? That's the only way I can explain Julian's distance of late. Part of me wonders if it has to do with his run-in with Vincent McGee. Although no formal charges were filed, their tussle was certainly picked up by the media. It thrust the story of Henry Gottle getting friendly with a woman half his age to the bottom of the stack.

It isn't what you're thinking. I'm confident Henry has plenty of young beauties at his beck and call. I'm just not one of them. The media didn't care about that, though. They saw the age-gap between Julian and me and assumed I have a thing for older men. In all honesty, the headlines made me ill. Julian is ten years my senior, but you wouldn't know it by looking at him. Henry Gottle is around the age my father would have been if he were still here.

Before I can let my thoughts run loose, I thrust my arms into the lightweight coat Fetu is holding out for me. "I'll drop these off while you grab the car, then I'll meet you out front."

"Yes, miss."

Fetu stops heading toward the underground parking garage when I call his name. "Will you please call me Melody? If you're willing to take a bullet for me, I'd say you've earned the honor to call me anything you like."

Dimples pop in his cheeks when they incline. "I can, thank you." My smile matches his when he adds, "You can also call me Tiny. It was what my mama called me."

My heart pains for him. If I had missed the 'was' part of his comment, I certainly couldn't ignore the grief in his eyes. He's lost his mother too. I guarantee it.

Embarrassed I caught his quick reflection of sorrow, he says, "I'll meet you out front."

Smiling to assure him he has no reason to be embarrassed, I nod. "I won't be a minute."

<hr>

COOL EVENING WINDS whip under my skirt when I exit the warmth of Julian's building a few seconds later. I tug my coat in close to my chest as I make a beeline for a car I'm stunned doesn't have a heap of parking infringement notices stuffed onto the windshield. Although I've never personally delivered the food as I am now, I know I'm heading for the right vehicle. It's the only one that hasn't budged like my ass the past couple of days. No matter what time of the day or night I check Julian's security feed, I see the same vehicle.

"Ma'am..." The driver greets apprehensively when I knock on his fogged window. He's younger than I thought he'd be. His dark hair is short at the sides but hangs loosely on top of his head. His eyes are blue, and his lips are plump despite being twisted with confusion. If I were single, his handsome features would certainly have my libido taking notice.

Once the stranger has his window wound down, I hand him the cookies I snagged from the cooling rack. "I'm heading back to my loft for an hour or two, so dinner will be a little late this evening. Figured these would tie you over until then."

"Oh..." He looks both confused and pleased. "Thank you. They smell great."

"Celeste is the best." I wave like an idiot before spinning around to face Julian's car rolling up the ramp of the underground parking garage. My eyes roll when I spot a man halfway down the ramp, snapping my picture. He can't get into the garage since it's guarded by security officers, but he's right at the gate, invading Julian's privacy as much as he can.

"Damn paparazzi," I mutter under my breath as I slip into the passenger seat next to Fetu.

Once my seat belt is latched into place, I drift my eyes to the side mirror. My brows furrow when the dark sedan parked at the front of Julian's apartment doesn't merge into traffic behind us. It stays in the loading bay, doubling not just my heart rate but my suspicions as well.

"You took brunch out to Brandon's PI yesterday, didn't you?"

Fetu's eyes stray from the road to me before he lifts his chin.

"What did he look like? Was he handsome? Big, brooding, somewhat the quiet type?"

He twists his lips as his cheeks whiten. "Not that I pay much attention to men, but if I did, I wouldn't categorize him as the handsome, moody type." He shrugs. "Perhaps it's just me. Maybe midfifties blond men don't tickle my fancy."

The humorous glint in Fetu's eyes dampens when I ask, "He's blond?"

When he lifts his chin for the second time, my stomach gurgles. If I didn't just hand freshly baked cookies to Brandon's private investigator, who did I hand them to?

BRANDON

"I'm an agent for the Federal Bureau of Investigation, how can that not outrank an apartment owner's 'request for privacy?'" I air quote the last half of my sentence, pissed as fuck.

The twists in Megan's case won't stop coming. Phillipa is speaking to me as more of a work colleague than a friend, and for some reason, Melody was photographed by my private investigator liaising with a man in a car with stolen plates. She's safe, and at her loft, but I'm juggling so many balls right now, I'm bound to drop one.

If that occurs because the head security officer at Isabelle's building won't let me up to see her, he'll be hit with the majority of my anger since he's responsible for it.

After exhaling a long, anger-relieving breath, I give it a final shot to have him seeing sense through the madness. "I'm not here to visit Mr. Holt. I'm here to see one of his tenants, and it's for a matter of utmost importance."

He keeps his tone calm and neutral when replying with the same crappy excuse he's been giving me the past ten minutes. "I'm sorry,

Mr. James, Mr. Holt's directive includes Ms. Brahn, so I can't let you up, no matter how urgent the matter."

Steam billows from my ears as my anger boils over, but before I can vent a smidge of my annoyance, a familiar voice sounds from over my shoulder. "Brandon!"

When I spot Isabelle darting my way, smiling, I twist back around to face the security officer responsible for the heat burning my cheeks. "Would you look at that? Ms. Brahn appears eager to see me. Perhaps you should pass that onto Mr. Holt the next time you see him. Or better yet, why don't you call him now, and I'll let him know if he had put as much effort into safeguarding his family as he does in controlling Ms. Brahn, his sister-in-law wouldn't have almost bled-out giving birth to his nephew." The last half of my comment is more a reflection of my failure to safeguard my family than Isaac's, but with my mood the lowest it's been in years, I've got to release some of it before I crack.

"I'll be sure to pass on your message, Mr. James. Have a pleasant afternoon." The security officer peers at Isabelle over my shoulder for the quickest second before he returns to the office his sidekicks absconded to when they begged their supervisor to back up their claim that Isabelle isn't allowed any visitors.

After a second exhale, I bridge the gap between Isabelle and me. As my shoes click against the gleaming marble tiles in the lobby of her building, I try to shake off my funk. The short length of my strides does me no good. You can hear the annoyance in my tone, much less feel it vibrating out of me when I snarl at Isabelle. "Are you aware no one can gain access to your floor without it first being approved by Isaac?"

Isabelle is quick to tuck it away, but I see shock dart through her eyes before she fully shuts it down. "No, I wasn't aware of that, but it does sound like something Isaac would do." She mumbles her last sentence under her breath.

"Not even an agent, for fuck's sake." I grit my teeth when my words come out with a roar. I'm annoyed and tired, but Isabelle doesn't deserve the wrath of my anger. She could have boarded the lets-hate-Brandon train back at Parkerville when Isaac arrived in the middle of the night. Instead, she told Isaac she trusts me as I do her.

Noticing the anger enveloping every inch of me is weakening, Isabelle asks, "What's going on, Brandon? You seem a bit stressed? Is it because I bailed on you at Parkerville? I'm sorry about that, I just wasn't—"

"Don't apologize, Izzy," I interrupt, "You have nothing to be sorry for."

When I spot the security officer I was tussling with earlier eyeballing our exchange, I guide Isabelle to a bank of chairs lining the lobby of her building. After planting my backside on a chair as I wish I could a bed, I scrub the back of my hand over my tired eyes. Have you ever been awake so long, you have a hard time separating reality from fiction? That's me right now. I've barely had more than three hours of sleep a night for over a week. I'm wrecked.

Isabelle plops into the chair next to me before bracing her knee against mine. "What's going on?"

With more knowledge than I have time, I push out, "Carlyle Shroud's death came back as a homicide."

Isabelle's throat works hard to swallow as her eyes widen. "But he was..." After a second swallow, she adds, "... *hanging.*"

"I know, but the coroner determined he died before then. They found poison in the food scraps in the kitchen. It looks like whoever killed him did it slowly in the hope it wouldn't be noticed by the authorities."

Isabelle looks like she can't take much more, but unfortunately, she doesn't have a choice. Even excluding Carlyle's purchase almost three decades ago, Harvey and I found links between the Shrouds, the Castros, and the man I know Isabelle is in a sexual relationship with.

Although I could pass on my findings to Alex, this investigation puts me one step closer to finding out what really happened to Joey.

Just the thought of getting closure on his death has me taking risks I'd usually steer well clear of.

"It gets worse…" After a quick swallow to relieve my parched throat, I disclose, "Megan Shroud is in Ravenshoe. She has been for the past week."

Isabelle's pupils dilate to the size of saucers. "How? We had protocols in place to ensure we knew her whereabouts."

"We did. Every database in the country was fixated on her. She must not have used public transportation or hired a car." The pitch of my tone reveals I'm as lost as her. If it wasn't for Phillipa sighting Megan during my drive back to Ravenshoe this afternoon, I wouldn't have known she was back. The system is failing, and it's failing badly.

With her head in agent mode, Isabelle asks, "Where is she?"

I nudge my head to the west, cringing when it amplifies the thump of my skull. "She's paying cash for a motel on the outskirts of town."

"Does Isaac know?"

Against my better judgment, I shake my head. "Not yet, but he soon will." When confusion distorts Isabelle's features, I do my best to settle it. "The hospital Nick's fiancée is staying at requested a police presence this afternoon. I hacked the hospital's mainframe. Jenni's blood workup showed she had a high dosage of Misoprostol in her system when she gave birth. It's an illegal abortion drug only sold on the black market."

Isaac failed to mention two nights ago that Jenni, his brother's fiancée, almost died giving birth. I don't know if it was an intentional lack of disclosure or if he was truly in the dark as Isabelle is portraying now.

"Do you believe Megan drugged her?"

I don't want to nod, but I must. If I want to keep Isabelle's trust, I have to give her no reason to doubt me. "The drug is found stateside in New York City. Small minority groups use it for terminations when they can't afford a doctor."

The prints on the vial found in Megan's workshop of horrors wasn't a match for neither Carlyle nor Rhianna, leading me to believe they belong to Megan. We're waiting for comparison prints from one of Megan's many psych-ward stays, but that will take a few days. They won't even disclose if a patient is admitted without sighting a warrant first.

My eyes float up from my hands when Isabelle garbles through big breaths, "Isaac will… he won't handle this, Brandon. He loves his brother."

While ignoring the buzz of my cell phone in my pocket, I say, "I know. That's why I haven't passed on any of the information to Hugo or Hunter yet. I wanted to get your opinion first." I lock my eyes with her, unsure of my next set of words, but confident they need to be expressed. "You're the only person I trust, Izzy—"

When she balks, I swallow the rest of my words. She isn't sickened by my comment. She's startled from being touched without warning. "I'm sorry, Ms. Brahn," says the security guard who denied my first request to see Isabelle. "But there's a gentleman by the name of Hugo requesting to be informed if you're in the lobby."

I'm anticipating for Isabelle to immediately jump to the command in the security officer's tone, so you can imagine my surprise when she swings her eyes my way to ask, "Do you have your car here?"

Suspicion heats my face, but I nod my head, nonetheless.

"I need one final favor."

"Anything, Izzy," I reply without pause for consideration.

It's a little late for me to act honorably. Phillipa attached Isabelle's picture to Melody's file hours before we knew the full extent of the case in Parkerville. We needed to ensure Castro's team had time to put measures into place since they're believed to be on the other side of the country, but by offering up my assistance, I'll feel less guilty. There's no need for culpability when the benefits of a friendship are being equally distributed between participants.

After exhaling a big breath, Isabelle returns her focus to the security officer. "Please inform Hugo that you have not seen me this afternoon."

She clamps her hand around mine before sprinting for the glass revolving door of her building. "We need to reach Megan before Isaac's team. She may talk to me. I'm less intimidating."

That was my exact thought when I asked Phillipa to head to Megan's hotel room after she unearthed her location by tracking her movements via the CTV cameras around Ravenshoe.

"I already have a friend on the way to her hotel—" My sentence is cut off by my cell phone buzzing in my pocket.

While digging it out, I hit the unlock button on my keys before gesturing for Isabelle to climb into the passenger seat. My heart beats in an unnatural rhythm when I see how many times Phillipa has attempted to call me the past twenty minutes. Since she didn't leave a voicemail, I open her unread message first.

Phillipa: Don't go to Megan's motel. She's dead.

When my eyes snap to Isabelle, instead of shocking her with the news of Megan's death, I'm the one left reeling. Isabelle is no longer climbing into the passenger seat of my car. She's being thrown to the ground by two officers double her weight and height.

When their knees landing in her back steals the air from her lungs as forcefully as it does mine, on instinct, I race to the other side of my car. I knock one officer off Isabelle with a stern punch to the face before grabbing a second officer in a sleeper hold. He's out in less than the time it takes for a third officer to attempt to subdue me by pressing his gun to my temple.

Rookie mistake.

It takes me five-seconds to disarm him before I set my sights on the fourth officer pinning Isabelle to the ground by his big, bulky frame. Even outnumbered, I hold my own for the next six or seven minutes, only lessening the severity of my attack when Isabelle is handcuffed and placed into the back of a marked cruiser by a female officer.

As much as I believe the officers are in the wrong, I can't hit a girl. I just can't. Furthermore, I'm stunned by the officer's disclosure that Isabelle is being arrested for the murder of Megan Shroud. Phillipa's message was only received fifteen minutes ago. That's nowhere near enough time to unearth a suspect, much less execute an arrest warrant.

"Get Isaac," is the last thing I hear Isabelle say before my feet are pulled out from beneath me, and I'm pinned to the grimy sidewalk by three officers climbing onto my back while a fourth aims a taser at the vein working overtime in my neck.

***

TEN MINUTES after arriving at Ravenshoe PD, and twenty minutes after being arrested, the rattle of a key being slotted into an old lock jingles into my ears. Believing it's an officer hoping to trick a confession out of me, I keep my eyes planted on my feet.

Inquisitiveness trickles through my veins when a gruff voice says, "For a man who swore an oath to defend the Constitution of the United States, you sure do get yourself in a lot of trouble."

My curiosity shifts to shock when the face in my head doesn't match the one peering back at me when I lift my head. From how rough his voice was, I thought Detective Carter was Harvey.

Even though I'm shocked, I'm too frustrated to hold back my retaliation. "Should you be quoting constitutional rights when you work in one of the most corrupt police departments I've ever come across?"

My anger loses some steam when Detective Carter doesn't attempt to refute my statement. He either knows every word I speak is true, or he believes his department has nothing to answer for. Both responses are unacceptable, but before I can tell him that, he nudges his head to the open cell door. "You're free to go."

"Who paid my bail?"

Detective Carter enters my cell, his swagger highly noticeable. "Who said anything about bail?" He straightens my crinkled dress shirt with more aggression than what's needed before lowering his eyes to my bruised knuckles. "Bail is only needed for criminals, don't you know?"

After returning his eyes to mine, he waves his hand across his body, wordlessly offering to show me the way out. Although my suspicions are still high, I gather my coat from the bench my ass went dead on within two minutes of sitting on it, then enter the hallway.

Prisoners gripe about favoritism when I shadow Detective Carter past three overcrowded holding cells. I do a quick scan of each cell to make sure Isabelle isn't in one of them, but within seconds, I realize Ravenshoe PD must separate their male and female lockups.

When our trip has us veering past the four officers I fought earlier, I tilt my wrists to ensure my cuffs sit low around my hands. Since I'm detained, the rigidness of the metal will make up for the restrictive range of my swings.

Confusion hits me for the second time when our walk past Ravenshoe PD's breakroom occurs without incident. I thought Detective Carter was walking me to my death. I had no clue he's actually showing me the way out until he stops me at the back-exit door to remove my cuffs.

Once he has the cuffs latched to his belt, he swings open the double-bolted door. "Have a wonderful night, Mr. James. We can only hope your short stay was a pleasant one."

The suspicion thickening my blood drops to a safe level when my glance out the door has me stumbling onto a blacked-out Navigator. Assuming Phillipa used her family name for the greater good, I gallop down the back stairs of Ravenshoe PD before sliding into the popped open back passenger door.

Confusion steamrolls into me when I fail to detect Phillipa's floral scent. This smell lingering in the air is spicy and masculine with the slightest hint of garlic.

Dimitri chuckles out a breathy laugh when I test the durability of his car's locks. "You'd have a better chance of shooting out the bulletproof windows than getting its lock mechanisms to budge. I paid out the eye to make this thing a tank, but the quality of the product was worth its exorbitant price tag."

After working my jaw side to side, I drag my eyes to Dimitri. "What do you want, Dimi—"

"Information."

His quick reply is more exposing than the shortness of it. I have something he needs—badly—and I plan to use that knowledge to my advantage. "That isn't how things work. We ask you for information. If we find it beneficial, we help you. That's what being an informant entails."

"*Informant?*" He scoffs out the word as if it's vomit. "I'm not an informant for the FBI. They work for me, not the other way around."

"That may have been how things worked with you and Tobias, but that won't fly with me."

Acting as if I never spoke, Dimitri hands me a sheet of paper. "Is this report accurate?"

My heart launches into my throat when I speed-read the document he handed me. It's a write-up on the mass burial site we found in the Shroud's equipment shed. The exact thing I had planned to interrogate him about. Although manufacturing and selling babies on the black market aren't the same thing as selling designer wives, it is when there's a common link. Rhianna Shroud was purchased from an association on the outskirts of Hopeton. The Petrettis have had a stronghold in Hopeton for over forty years. That can't be a coincidence.

"Where did you get this? This hasn't even been logged with the Bureau yet."

Even Harvey agreed that what we stumbled on is too big to be released publicly yet. If news of what we've discovered gets out, we'll have less chance of bringing the perps to justice. They'll go into sleeper-mode even quicker than the Castro crew did after our failed sting. Then once the heat dies down, they'll pop up in a new location, which will take authorities another decade or more to uncover.

My focus returns to Dimitri when he says, "Where I got this information isn't important. I just need to know if it's true?" A weird twinge is impeding his voice. It's possessive and somewhat manic, similar to the tone Grayson uses anytime he talks about Katie.

"Yes, it's true." I could have denied his claims, but my gut is telling me my honesty will be better rewarded. Furthermore, if the Petrettis are helming this operation, why would one of the top honchos be seeking information from me?

I nod when Dimitri asks, "Are all the victims female?" His jaw clenches as tightly as his fists. "What's the average age of the women found?"

"Preliminary findings state the victims are between the ages of thirteen to late twenties." I don't mention the toddler I found in the wall because as far as we can tell, her death isn't linked to the women buried outside. She wasn't of childbearing age, so she doesn't fit the profile Harvey is working.

My reply offers Dimitri little comfort. If anything, it agitates him more. "Had any of the victims recently given birth before their death?"

"We won't know that until the autopsies are completed."

"You would know!" Dimitri shouts, startling both the driver and me. "You'd know because she's eight months along…" He grits his teeth before correcting, "She *was* eight months along."

I learn how he and Tobias came into contact with each other when he hands me a photograph of a heavily pregnant woman with a gag in her mouth. Big splotchy tears are streaming down her cheeks as she stares past the newspaper someone is holding out in front of her. It's dated a little over two years ago.

Remorse stabs me in the chest when Dimitri mutters, "I paid the ransom they requested." I can't tell if it's anger filling in his face or overwhelming grief when he pauses to catch his breath but realize it could be a bit of both when he mutters, "They didn't uphold their side of our agreement."

I almost comment that paying a ransom is practically signing the kidnapped victim's death certificate, but I keep my mouth shut, knowing no amount of words will appease Dimitri right now. He wants justice, and he wants it no matter the cost.

"Was Tobias aware you paid the ransom?"

I'm not shocked when Dimitri shakes his head. Negotiations involving money are rarely recommended. "Tobias approached me a few days after the drop. He said there was a complication securing Audrey."

That's not good. Tobias only ever approached a target when things went wrong, but if that's the case here, why is Dimitri still searching for Audrey? He knows she's dead, doesn't he?

My inner monologue fades out when a disturbing thought enters my head. "You're not searching for Audrey. You're trying to find your child."

Dimitri's eyes almost turn black when they lock with mine. He stares straight at me for several long, heart-breaking seconds before he lifts his chin. "Tobias was supposed to get her out. He assured me she was safe, and that it would be only a matter of time before she was returned to me. Then..."

With words failing him, I take up the slack. "Tobias was killed during the Castro raid?"

Does that mean what I think it does? Was one of the many children seen on the surveillance images at Rimi Castro's compound Dimitri's child? If so, that's fucked. I struggle to keep a rational head when it comes to keeping adults safe, so I can't imagine what Dimitri is going through.

"When was your daughter last seen?"

I stop hunting for my notepad and pen in the breast pocket of my jacket when Dimitri says, "I didn't get you out of lockup to investigate my daughter's disappearance. I did it so you can continue with your ruse to force Castro out of hiding."

Although shocked by the extent of his knowledge, I won't be blackmailed. "You can't use the Bureau to get revenge on Castro."

Dimitri smiles a killer grin. "I'm not getting revenge on Castro. I'm going to kill him as he did my wife."

Wife? Fuck. That makes this ten times worse.

Although I understand his objective, I legally can't help him with this.

When I say that to Dimitri, the evilness of his smile flares through his eyes. "You'll do as I ask, or I'll release this to the hounds." He shows me a dot-point bulletin that looks like it was printed on an ancient printer. The wording is basic, but the prose of the message doesn't weaken the threat associated with it. If this consignment is activated, there will be a seven-figure payout placed on Melody's head.

Nothing but fury highlights my tone when I ask, "How do I know you haven't already released this?"

"She's still alive, isn't she? Living it up in a fancy penthouse apartment in New York City with her billionaire boyfriend." Partway through his reply, he plays a video on his cell phone that shows Melody exiting the building she was photographed leaving earlier today. "Even with a wrong set of photographs attached to her file, the real Melody wasn't hard to find."

Dimitri's words shift to a chuckle when I grip the lapels of his suit jacket to drag him to within an inch of my face. "If you hurt her—"

"You'll what? Kill me as I want to slay the man who murdered my wife. He cut our daughter out of her stomach, then left her to die! He treated her like fucking scum, so if I have to use your high school sweetheart as bait because your hero-complex wants to stop a war that started long before you joined the Bureau, I fucking will. I'll do anything it takes to gut Castro as he did me." After yanking himself out of my grip, he smooths out the crinkles my grab caused to his suit before raising his eyes to mine. "Do what needs to be done to get Castro out of hiding, then leave the rest up to me." He leans across my body to pop open my door. "And start here as he'll get your Honey Pot out of lockup even faster than your daddy's fancy title will."

Unease spins around me when my eyes drift in the direction Dimitri is facing. We're outside the office complex the Ravenshoe division the Bureau works out of, but Dimitri's focus isn't directed at the single glass entrance door of HQ. He's peering at Isaac's nightclub, which is directly across the street from the men and women endeavoring to take him down.

As I slide out of Dimitri's fortified ride, I consider my next step. I have a few options up my sleeve, but I take none of them when I pop my head back into the cab of Dimitri's ride and say, "If you do this, you'll be hunted as fiercely as you've been chasing Castro the past two years. What kind of life will that be for your daughter? Hasn't she been through enough? You're her father. You are supposed to protect her, not put her in more danger."

Confident my words will have a better chance of breaking through Dimitri's psyche than any amount of muscle, I inch back from his car, slam the door shut, then pivot on my heels. I have a million thoughts streaming through my head, but as much as this sucks to admit, one thing Dimitri said tonight was right. Isaac has more pull in this town than anyone. If he can't get Isabelle out of lockup, no one will.

Although my focus is elsewhere, and I still don't believe Isaac is being truthful with Isabelle, the least I can do is set the wheels in motion to get Isabelle released. Then, once she's out of danger, I'll sit down and work out how I can stop a cartel war from happening while also keeping Melody safe. It won't be easy, and in all honesty, I feel like I'm swimming in waters way out of my depth, but I didn't play nice for seven years for no reason. I have favors—many of them —and I'm about to cash them all in.

BRANDON

"*B*randon, what happened?"

I pull away from Phillipa just before her fingertips caress the red welts on my neck. I'm not embarrassed they're there, I just don't want to explain why I didn't respond to Isaac's anger with as much violence as he was instilling. I couldn't bring myself to use years of tactical training on a man who looked like I'd pulled the entire world out from beneath his feet.

I perused surveillance photos from Isaac's case for hours after Isabelle exposed Olivia Wilde was Ophelia Petretti's alias. Not once did Isaac's eyes hold the grief they did when he demanded to be updated on Isabelle's whereabouts, not even on the night he was informed of Ophelia's death. He cares for Isabelle. I'm just lost as to why he's keeping things from her. If he trusts her, why isn't he being honest with her?

"Did you reach out to Grayson?"

My head swings to the side when a gruff voice answers my question on Phillipa's behalf. "We did. He'll be here as soon as he can come up with a plan for his absence." Harvey smirks at my stunned expression before moving out of the shadow he was camped in. "Nice place you've got here, kid. Has me a little worried I'll wreck the décor when I stop you playing with your tackle... *again.*"

"Don't say a word," I warn to Phillipa when her brow pops up at Harvey's comment. "It was nothing close to what he's implying."

"Still, sounds juicy." She chuckles at the mortified expression crossing my face as she follows me into the foyer of my apartment.

A whistle rustles Harvey's mustache when he takes in the makeshift perp boards covering nearly every wall. "How long did you say you've been at this again?"

"A week," Phillipa pipes up, her tone laced with pride. "He swore he showered, but I'm skeptical." She taps the tip of her nose with her index finger three times before dodging the coffee table ornament I peg at her. It's a fake piece of fruit my mom thought would 'spruce up the place.'

I lock my eyes with Harvey. "Did Dr. Maude forward you a preliminary autopsy report on the toddler found in the wall?"

I hold my breath when Harvey jerks up his chin but remains quiet. We've only just met, but I can already say that isn't like him. He's worse than my mom after a couple of wine spritzers. He never shuts up.

"And?" I ask, pushing him along.

He swishes his tongue around his mouth to ease out his words. "She was around the age you guessed. Approximately twenty-two months old."

"Any indication on the time of death?" The increase in my blood pressure is heard in my question. If the date on the photograph Dimitri showed me is around the time his wife gave birth, the female corpse in the wall is the same age as his daughter.

"Rigor mortis—"

"Can alter depending on storage conditions and temperature. I'm aware of that. I just need to know whether her death was recent?"

The knot in my stomach untightens when Harvey discloses, "Doc is guessing her death took place over a decade ago."

"Who did you think she was?" Phillipa asks, reading the relief on my face as only one woman before her has.

Since I still feel one ball drop away from failure, I reply, "That's a story for another day." After plopping into one of the seats around my dining table, I drag over my laptop. "What can you tell me about Megan Shroud's death?"

I realize Harvey has been left in the lurch when he physically balks from my question.

Phillipa updates us at the same time. "A turf war is going on, but from what I gathered on the scene, there's no body."

"Then how were they granted an arrest warrant so quickly?" When Harvey's eyes snap to mine, I add, "An agent from my division was arrested for her murder. She's being held at Ravenshoe PD."

"Brandon was arrested with her," Phillipa fills in, unaware I wanted to keep that snippet of information between us.

Harvey folds his thick arms in front of his chest. "What were you arrested for?" When I remain quiet, his eyes drop to my bloody knuckles. "Ah. Tobias was right, Liam trained you well."

Not having the time nor the patience to be bombarded with another flurry of information, I jerk up my chin, agreeing with him, hopeful it will move us onto more pressing issues than old friendships.

Unfortunately, Harvey wouldn't recognize a giant pink elephant if it were standing right in front of him. "If your knuckles got friendly with the arresting officers, how are you sitting here now?" When my brow arches, his lips match the curve of their incline. "Ah, that's how it is, is it?" He spins a chair around, then straddles it backward. "We're going talk about that once this is all said and done, aren't we, kid?"

"I don't know, Agent Harvey, are we?" I reply, ensuring I answer his question by asking one of my own, effectively turning his interrogation hack back on him.

Phillipa's hand shoots up to clamp her mouth when Harvey slaps me up the back of the head. She's not squeaking in shock. She's struggling not to laugh. *Traitor.*

"Sorry," she garbles under her breath before joining us in being seated around the dining table. "Where do you want me to start?"

I scan the documents stretched from one end of my apartment to the other, truly unsure where to start first. They all interconnect in some way, so once again, we're hunting for a thread. We've just got over a dozen immaculately stitched outfits to sort through.

"I'll flick on the coffee pot," Phillipa says when she reads the expression on my face.

We're in for another all-nighter.

I WAKE up groggy and confused. The deafening drone of someone snoring like a freight train rolls through my ears as readily as the thump of my tired head. I don't need to look in the direction of my couch to know Harvey is responsible for the shudders of my apartment walls every time he exhales. The clam chowder he gobbled down without breathing last night fans my cheek with every loud exhale he does. I don't know how Phillipa is still sleeping. She's in my bed, and my apartment is a decent size, but still, Harvey's snores are loud enough to wake the dead.

It dawns on me that Harvey's need for a respirator isn't the cause of my sudden awakening. It's the buzz of my phone. It's vibrating against my desk, announcing I have a new text message.

My slit eyes snap open fully when I see who the message is from. Melody is texting me.

Melody: *Morning, BJ. I solved your riddle. Check your emails. Melody xx*

I stare at the double x's on the end of her message for far too long before logging out of my Messenger app to open my emails. Ignoring the three dozen notifications from my security firm, I click into Melody's email.

"Holy shit," I mutter to myself when I realize what I'm looking at. She deciphered the account number on the soggy printout I took a photo of yesterday morning. I must have accidentally text it to her instead of Phillipa, forgetting her number was at the top of the list since we texted until the wee hours of the morning.

I smile like a fucking lunatic, ecstatic Melody is part of our operation. It's only a small role, but its importance is undeniable. She trained just as hard as me when we were kids, and I've often wondered if she still uses her skills. Her email proves she still has what it takes. She not only unearthed the account holder's name, which just happens to be Isaac Holt, she linked his account to multiple other offshore accounts.

I send Melody's worksheet remotely to my printer before returning her email. I'm halfway through a gushing bout of praise when my phone dings, announcing I have another message. Hopeful it's Melody, I tap on the notification band at the top of my screen.

Although my message is from an unknown caller, I know who it belongs to. The tone of his message is very descriptive, not to mention the demand behind it.

Unknown number: *Should I follow your plan or make one of my own? If you're not here in thirty, the decision will be out of your hands.*

When an image of the Ravenshoe courthouse stairs being swarmed by media downloads onto my screen, I snag my jacket off the coatrack and hotfoot it out of my apartment.

With traffic light, I make it to the courthouse in half the time Dimitri demanded in his text. I've barely thrown my arms into my suit jacket when my gallop up the stairs is unexpectedly cut short by Alex.

"It was you, wasn't it?" Anger pumps out of him as readily as air whizzes out of his nose when he stops next to me. "I asked you to show me how to work her laptop, not steal information off her computer!"

My hands ball as I struggle not to scream my frustration into the street. Out of all the days in the year, today has to be the day Alex discovered I snooped on his Honey Pot's computer.

It was for the greater good, but I don't see Alex understanding that when he roars, "Regan thinks I stole information from her, that I used her to better my position."

"That was never my intention. I had no plans to use the information I found. I just forgot that anything uploaded to the Bureau's servers remains uploaded no matter how great your hacking skills are." Everything I'm saying is the truth. Once the Bureau is in, you can never get them back out.

Veins bulge in Alex's neck as spit flies out of his mouth. "You forgot? How can you fucking forget me instructing you to log out of her computer ten minutes before you did?" I could throw Grayson into the deep end with me, but I won't. He agreed to come out of undercover work to help me nab Castro, so I won't put him on bad terms with his brother.

After shoving a computer log printout sheet into my chest, Alex digs his cell phone out of his pocket. "If that isn't enough proof, how about this?"

Anger envelopes him when he spins his phone around to show me an image of Regan in a skimpy white towel. I've seen her like that before, but it was via a live stream, not a still shot. "You were watching her."

"No." I immediately deny, shaking my head. "I logged out the instant she entered the room."

"The instant she entered the room in *nothing* but a towel."

A lady dashing up the courthouse stairs yelps, startled by Alex's vicious roar. I understand why he's upset, but if he'd give me the chance to speak, I could explain it isn't anything like he's thinking. His anger isn't allowing him to see things clearly.

"What if she didn't have a towel on? What if she were naked?" He steps closer, his chest thrusting. "I brought you onto my team because I thought you were one of us… one of the good guys."

"I am—"

"No, you're fuckin' not," he interrupts, shouting. "You're just as rogue and corrupt as Theresa."

You know those balls I mentioned yesterday? The ones I was struggling to juggle? They've fallen, and their crash is brutal. "Who are you to talk? You slept with a target while undercover."

"Regan wasn't a target." Alex gets right up in my face, stealing every sense of normality I have. "She should have never been dragged into this fight. She's an innocent—"

"Just like Izzy?" I butt in, returning his glare. "Yet here she is, at your request, being pranced in front of Isaac like a little plaything *just* like Theresa forced you to do with Regan. There's only one difference… you stupidly fell in love."

I'm given a clear reminder that Alex is a Rogers when he pops his fist into my eye. It has the last of my balls falling to the ground while doubling the inane thoughts in my head, but before any of them can transpire, Reid, Alex's lacky, steps between us.

"Step back, Alex." He fists Alex's shirt before endeavoring to do the same to mine. I push him off me before he can. Wrongly assuming I'm stepping up to him, Alex comes at me again. "Step back!" Reid shouts for the second time. "He's not worth it." He glares at me like I'm a piece of dogshit he trod in before shifting his focus to Alex. "And you're not here for him, remember?"

I could laugh at their pathetic attempt to pin everything happening on me. Not once have I stepped over the line agents are forced to toe the past seven years. I was following direct orders.

Just not all of them were given by Alex.

"Nothing I did was outside of my role," I growl when my anger becomes too much for me to bear.

A festering pit of annoyance boils in my gut when Alex snarls, "A role you no longer hold."

I want to retaliate, a rebuttal is sitting on the tip of my tongue dying to be expelled, but I hold it back, aware that the relinquish-ment of my position from Alex's team could be a godsend if I play my cards right.

I won't be required to uphold the Constitution of the United States if I'm no longer an agent.

I'm free to do as I wish.

I can even side with mafia royalty if I want.

BRANDON

"And here I was thinking *The Forty-Year-Old Virgin* was based on fiction."

As I shoot daggers at Harvey, a familiar chuckle barrels out of Phillipa's cell phone resting on the bench stretched across one wall of a surveillance van. If I had known Grayson was hijacking the feed of the camera in the button of my shirt, I would have brushed up on my performance.

Ha! Who am I kidding?

My dating skills are as disastrous as my investigative skills of late.

"It wasn't that bad," Phillipa assures me as she runs her hand down my arm in comfort. "What?" she pushes out breathlessly when subjected to Harvey's cocked brow. "He was barely alone with the girl. No one likes performing in front of an audience."

"Ah—"

"Shut up, Grayson. All agents know undercover gangbangs are excluded from successful Honey Pot ruse tallies."

When Grayson laughs, my lips quirk in surprise. I'm not stunned by his lack of denial. I told you he's dabbled in many situations while undercover. It's the fact Phillipa is aware of his shady past. Is she keeping tabs on him as she does me, or have they talked more often than they've let on?

Realizing now isn't the time for an in-depth investigation into fellow agents' personal lives, I mutter, "I'll give it a shot when she returns from the harbor. Until then…" Even Grayson groans when I nudge my head to the stack of paperwork Harvey had couriered from Parkerville. He knows firsthand there's no such thing as a day off when you work for the divisions we do.

AFTER SLAPPING hands with Agent Moses, who's slotted into his new position of a doorman rather quickly, I ride the elevator to Regan's penthouse apartment. Isaac's security team removed the camera from the hallway of this apartment building not long after Regan moved back to Texas.

As I mosey down the corridor that's wider than most living rooms, I dip my chin in greeting to the undercover operative dusting a chandelier lamp partway down. Although our team is small, we set up an unprecedented around-the-clock watch for both Melody and Isabelle. Whether retired or current, agents came out of the woodwork when I commenced cashing in the favors I amassed as part of Tobias's crew. It was rare for Tobias's favors to be reciprocated, so his team was owed many at the time of his death.

"Calm those nerves, punk. You're not picking up your girl for the prom."

I hear Grayson's cheeks incline when I garble out, "Easy for you to say. You're not the one attempting to pick up a taken woman."

"True." His infamous chin-scrub any time his thoughts wander crackles down the wireless earpiece in my ear. "I much prefer the married ones."

While shaking my head, I tap on the microphone in my shirt to indicate for surveillance to commence before racking my knuckles on Regan's penthouse entrance door. When my knock is followed by a short stretch of silence, I whisper, "I thought you said no movements were recorded this morning?"

"They weren't. I'm looking at the sheets right now. People have come and gone, but neither Isabelle nor Regan were seen leaving. Call out. Maybe she's laying low?" My jaw tightens when Grayson adds, "Not surprising considering she's sleeping with the enemy."

"She's still an agent."

"A *compromised* agent," Grayson fires back, his tone unusually stern. "She'll get no sympathy from me."

After calling him a grumpy bastard under my breath, I give his suggestion a try. "Izzy, it's Brandon. Are you home?"

Although no voices project through the thick wooden door, I hear the scuffling of feet, then, a few seconds later, the door is pulled open.

"Damn... my brother had good taste."

Regan is gorgeous, but I can't look at her in the same light Alex and Grayson do. For one, Alex may kill me, and two, Regan is too fierce looking for me. She portrays a woman who'd rather whip me than snuggle with me. Melody and I experimented sexually our first year of college, but bondage never entered the equation.

I peer at Isabelle over Regan's shoulder when Regan removes my coat without speaking a word. Isabelle is giggling like she heard my inner monologue, but her chuckles are barely heard over Grayson's numerous lewd comments. I'm glad his last few months undercover didn't affect his ability to rile me, but I wish he'd pick a better time and location.

I can feel my cheeks heating, and it has nothing to do with Regan's thorough pat-down. If I didn't know any better, I'd swear she was the agent in the hall. I feel seconds from being told to bend over and unclench my butt cheeks so she can finalize her search of *all* the cavities in my body.

"Admit it, you're hard," Grayson mutters down the line, still laughing. "I am."

Fighting to hold back a gag, I dip my chin in thanks to Regan when she hangs my jacket in the entry closet. "Thank you."

"You're welcome. I'm glad it was as good for you as it was me..." When Grayson's words are stolen by a groan, I make a mental note to thank Phillipa for keeping him in line.

Just as Regan tells me, "It was my pleasure," Isabelle joins us in the foyer. The past twenty-four hours have been good for her. She looks like she got some sleep, and her eyes are glistening from I don't want to know what.

When she curls her arms around my shoulders to greet me with a hug, I whisper in her ear, "She scares me."

"Good one, punk. Bring out the frightened-boy act. It works on anyone with a vagina."

The annoyed expression on my face from Grayson's grading of my act can be excused for shock when Regan mutters, "I heard that." She saunters into a living area three times the size of mine before spinning back around to face Isabelle and me. "And you should be scared."

She snags a stack of paperwork off the coffee table before entering a hallway on our right, her brisk strides only slowing to do one final glance of my body.

My chin automatically lifts when Grayson's gravelly tone is switched for Phillipa's songful one. "She's onto you."

Although curious to discover what gave away my ruse, I don't have time to unravel the woman who has Alex twisted up in knots. The gala is two nights away. We're down to the wire.

Once I'm confident my expression is neutral, I shift on my feet to face Isabelle. "I hope you don't mind me popping in like this, Izzy, but I couldn't call you on your cell since Hunter smashed it, and I don't have any of Regan's contact details."

I realize we have more than Grayson, Phillipa, and Harvey listening in when a female voice from down the hall says, "I can give them to you. All you have to do is ask."

Laughing to hide her unease that she's forever being watched,

Isabelle guides me toward the living room, freeing up some privacy. "Sorry, she's a little…"

When she struggles to find the words to describe Regan's overbearing personality, I offer up a suggestion. "Like Isaac?"

Grimacing, she nods.

"She's got you played, punk. She's all but admitting she is sleeping with a target because she knows you won't do sweet-fuck-all about it, so why are you still hesitating? Let's get this done."

That's easy for Grayson to say. He's not the one standing across from the woman Tobias classed as a daughter with the hope of forcing her to become a Honey Pot against her knowledge. Although I'm skeptical she'll ever be in danger, it still feels like I'm using her.

After scrubbing my hand down my face, I test the boundaries of our friendship, hopeful our mutually respectful relationship will get Grayson off my back for a few hours. "I just wanted you to know I understand you not being able to come to the gala with me. With everything going on, you've got more pressing matters to handle than being my date for a night."

Shock is the first thing to register on Isabelle's face. It's closely followed by remorse. "The gala is this weekend?"

When I nod, she stomps her foot down.

"It's Friday night, but you don't have to come."

"I told you, she's as rogue as they come," Grayson mutters in disappointment when he spots the guilt on Isabelle's face not even the world's shonkiest camera could hide. "She's Leesa 2.0."

I'm about to step into phase two of my plan when assistance comes from the last person I expected. "You should go," Regan says, walking out from the hallway. "Having you out in public with another man will help make the jury believe you have no association with Isaac." A sugary smell similar to the one you get when you enter a bakery filters in the air when she reaches us. "It will also aid in your innocent plea. Only people with something to hide are concerned about prosecution."

"You don't think it will be distasteful for me to go to a fancy gala with a death hanging over my head?" Isabelle asks at the same time Grayson murmurs, "Smart and beautiful. Alex got lucky."

Regan shakes her head. "No. You knew of Megan from an FBI agent perspective, but you have no personal connection to her whatsoever. You don't mourn the death of a stranger." She looks like she's dying to bump her hip against Isabelle's, but since she's unsure if that's a normal thing for one woman to do to another, she adds a chirpy tone to her words instead. "And with you being out of Ravenshoe for a few nights, I won't have to check your room every ten minutes to make sure Isaac hasn't snuck in."

Have you ever felt like the odd man out? That's what I'm experiencing right now. Regan looks like she'd rather wrestle a tiger than continue with our conversation, and Isabelle is concentrating so hard, you'd swear I was asking her to divulge national secrets. And I'm just standing here like a dork, unsure if I'm coming or going. Even Grayson is quiet.

After what feels like an eternity, Isabelle locks her eyes with mine and asks, "What time are you picking me up?"

I almost fist bump the air, but since Regan is watching every expression crossing my face, I keep my euphoria on the down-low. "How does eight sound?"

Isabelle cringes like she didn't wake before the sparrows every day the past eight months. "Eight sounds great. I'll see you then."

"Great, see you then." Not thinking, I swoop in to plant a kiss on her cheek before pivoting on my feet and high-tailing it to the door.

"Don't forget your jacket, dipshit," Grayson reminds me, redirecting the course of my steps.

Once I have my coat in my hand and a good amount of distance between Regan's apartment door and the elevator car, I say, "Let phase two begin."

This one will be trickier than the one we just undertook. It isn't every day you endeavor to steer a mafia prince onto the right side of the law.

"This isn't what I meant by phase two," I mumble, shoving the printout Melody emailed me yesterday morning back into Grayson's hand.

Once the account number Melody unearthed was linked with the intel the Bureau's mainframe automatically uploaded from Regan's laptop when I helped Alex with a log-in issue, an avalanche of revelations were exposed. The down payment Isaac made to the Popovs two weeks ago was only a smidgen of the icing on the cake. Whatever he's buying is substantially more than a mail-order bride because its ticketed price came in at a little over 2.4 million dollars.

Although I'm curious to discover what Isaac is purchasing, I can't forget my exchange with Alex yesterday morning. "Your brother fired me *after* hitting me. I'm not on his team anymore."

"So a little misunderstanding means he doesn't deserve to know the man he's chasing is a criminal?" Grayson asks, glaring at me. "Those payments add up to over two million dollars—"

"I know what they add up to. I can count. Doesn't change my mindset, though." I'm pissed as fuck Alex retaliated with violence. I get he thinks I saw Regan in a compromising position, but if he had given me the chance to assure him that wasn't the case, he wouldn't have been so worked up.

"The Bureau has been hunting Isaac for years. You have proof his business matters aren't legit, but instead of manning-up because your ego got a little bruised, you're being a prissy punk-faced motherfucker who's acting like it's the first time he's been hit." As Grayson slumps onto my rock-hard designer couch, he grumbles, "Tobias would be rolling in his grave."

"Seriously, Grayson, you're going to bring Tobias into this?" When he fails to answer my question, I shout, "You're using the woman he classed as his daughter as a Honey Pot. He's already rolling."

"Hey, don't blame that shit on me. You suggested your ruse to

Phillipa long before you ran it by me. I merely agreed with Phillipa and Harvey that you should continue with your plan, so the guilt you're trying to place on my shoulders won't fly, dipshit. I've got nothing to answer for here."

Every word he speaks is true, but it doesn't make them any easier to swallow.

After scrubbing his hand along his jaw, Grayson tries another angle. "You've worked too fucking hard for too fucking long to let a misunderstanding take everything away from you." He holds out the scheduled wire transfer receipts that prove Isaac is making a significant purchase from the Popov entity before adding, "Give Alex this. Show him you aren't rogue like he thinks, then walk away. That's all you have to do."

Even with honesty being the strongest part of his statement, there's one part I can't sidestep. "You really do have tabs on your brother, don't you?"

I thought he was joking when he underhandedly mentioned it in the past, but his 'rogue' comment exposes that's a lie. I never mentioned Alex accusing me of being one of the bad guys. Although I had no reason to be embarrassed that Alex got one over me, I only told Grayson what I wanted him to know to save face. What man wants to admit they were hit and didn't retaliate? And let's not mention how it affected me emotionally. I've faced bad bumps in my life, and Alex's disrespect is now one of them.

I take a seat next to Grayson when he says, "Some murky shit is going on in his department, BJ. I don't want to believe it's Alex, but some evidence is hard to ignore."

"Like what?"

He hooks his ankle onto his opposite knee before twisting his torso to face me. "Do you recall me telling you about Addison and Isla, Dane's daughters?" When I lift my chin, he discloses, "Alex pretty much covers all their expenses... clothing, roof over their head, schooling."

"He feels guilty about what happened to Dane, so he's compensating for it with his daughters."

An agreeing hum leaves Grayson's mouth. "The thing is, the girls go to an upscale school. The admission fee alone costs more than what Alex clears in a year."

"Perhaps Dane's insurance is paying for it?"

He does a weird shrugging thing. "I had thought the same thing, so I dug a little deeper. Kristin's claim for insurance wasn't approved since his death was classified as a suicide."

Hearing something in his voice I'm unsure he meant to express, I ask, "Don't you believe Dane committed suicide?"

"I don't know. It's just not sitting right with me." His brows furrow when he lifts his head to peer at the ceiling. "He loved his girls, they were his world, so why would he leave them?"

His eyes drop back to mine when I say, "If your gut is telling you he didn't kill himself, dig deeper again, Grayson. I knew in my heart Joey didn't commit suicide, but instead of evaluating what really happened, I kept shifting my focus elsewhere."

"By elsewhere, you mean to Melody."

Unashamed, I dip my chin. "She needed me more, and I couldn't bring Joey back no matter what I did, so I had to pick my battles."

"You picked right, punk. There will be days you won't believe it, and times you'll think you royally fucked up, but you'll never regret protecting your first love." When I jerk up my chin, agreeing with him, he curls his arm around my shoulders, pulls me into his chest, then messes up my hair. "Now we just need to work on your shot-to-shit dating skills. My God, dickface, I doubt you'd know a girl was salivating to suck your dick even if she had it in her mouth."

"Whatever." I push him off me, faking annoyance. "You give me shit all the time about not dating, but not once have I seen you with anyone. Are you sure there isn't something you need to tell me, Grayson?"

He scoffs, then scoots off my couch, hating that the focus has been placed on him. He's happy to dish relationship advice, but he never listens to it.

When he snags the printout off the couch, I ask, "Where are you going?"

"This purchase isn't just detrimental to Alex's case. It affects the entire web we've been striving to unravel the past decade. I can't let news of its existence go unnoticed because Alex got a little hotheaded. He's had a rough year, too, BJ. Perhaps this might get him out of his funk?"

I agree with him, but it won't stop me from issuing a caution. "If you hand that to Alex, you'll break cover. No one from Kirill's team will believe you're in Ravenshoe scoping new compound locations if you meet with an FBI agent in a shady back alley."

"It's not like I've got much choice, do I..." His words trail off when I snatch the sheets of paper out of his hand.

The smug expression on his face, loving that he's forced me to jump to his command like a lap dog, clears away when I snarl. "If he hits me again, I'll retaliate."

My brisk strides to the door stop when Grayson shouts, "Wait up." After snagging his coat off one of the chairs around my dining table, he meets me in the entryway of my apartment. "If you think this will end in a tussle, you'll need backup."

His grin turns blinding when I mutter, "You're not backing me up. You're just coming to watch the show."

"Dating rule number one, always buy your date dinner before the entertainment begins... *especially* if there's a chance there will be an arrest at some stage during the night."

The ding of the elevator arriving at my floor gobbles up his laugh, not to mention my growl.

"MAYBE THE EXTRA funds for Dane's girls aren't coming from the direction you're looking? Perhaps Alex got himself a sugar mommy?"

I meant my comment in jest, but Grayson doesn't see it that way. His jaw is as tight as the expression on Regan's face when she flees the back of the surveillance van that spent the last twenty minutes rocking along with the thrusts of Alex's hips. It's two in the morning, so I doubt Alex realized his quickie with Regan would be witnessed by two agents. Well, one, since I'm technically not an agent anymore. As per Alex's demand, I emailed in my resignation earlier today. It scolded me more than I care to admit. The Bureau was my family, and now I have no one.

My thoughts return to the present when Grayson backhands my chest. "You better get a move on before we lose him again." We spent the past two hours trawling the streets of Ravenshoe to find him. Although Alex's response to believing I saw Regan naked should have placed her building on the top of our list, his undeniable dislike of our target had us visiting numerous nightclubs instead. It was a foolish mistake we'll be unlikely to make again. Time isn't on our side right now, so we can't waste a single second.

With that in mind, I crank open the driver's side door of my BMW. "Wish me luck."

The brutal slam of the surveillance van door we're parked a few spots up almost drowns out Grayson's reply, "You won't need it."

The undeniable scent of sex lingers in the air when I bridge the gap between Alex and me. When he pivots around, spotting my approach, the smell augments from the fiery heat blistering through him.

"Your resignation was forwarded to the head of our department this morning. As of five this evening, you were no longer an agent on my team."

When he attempts to skirt by me, I step into his path. "I stepped out of line."

Alex's shallow, painstaking chuckle booms through the crisp morning air. "You think? You not only risked my unit's investigation, you might even do time. Do you realize that? One word, and your entire fucking career will circle the drain." Shock registers on his features when I nod, but nothing can hold back his scorn. "If you don't want that, I suggest you take a step back."

"I wouldn't be here if it wasn't important."

When he steps up to me with his chest heaving, I maintain my ground, eager to show him I've been a vital part of his team. Yes, I've made mistakes. Yes, I've assisted other divisions with cases not linked with ours, and yes, I've placed personal investigations above Alex's, but not once did I put his investigation at risk by doing that. If anything, I halved his workload while doubling mine.

After a three-minute-long intense standoff, Alex snatches the document responsible for our late-night exchange out of my hand. It isn't the scheduled wire transfer receipts I had planned to show him. It's a flight manifest Grayson's team unearthed during our hunt for Alex. It's proof Isaac isn't just purchasing something from the Popovs, he's in cahoots with them, so much so, he lodged a flight plan to Vegas for later today.

Alex shoves the freshly printed document back into my chest before sidestepping me. "Isaac takes trips like this all the time. He has a comped room at Caesars."

He freezes mid-stride when I say, "Then why would he schedule the transfer of millions of dollars to an offshore account before his visit?" When he pivots back around to face me, his face giving nothing away, I dig a second piece of paper out of my pocket. "Over two hundred and fifty transactions verified to be distributed at the same time first thing tomorrow morning." I hand him the document with less aggression than the annoyance heating my blood. "He kept the transfer amounts under $10,000 so as not to raise suspicion."

Alex slants his head as his brow cocks. "Then how do you know about it?"

His suspicion is replaced with anger when I answer, "Once a device is introduced to the server, it's never forgotten."

"You used the intel you stole off Regan's laptop to unearth this?" His voice is a roar that ripples through the almost isolated streets.

He fists the paper in a firm hold when I nod. "But only because I'm trying to help you."

"You're helping me?" Spit flies out of his mouth when his words are delivered with a disbelieving huff. "Or are you helping yourself?"

While returning his glare, I tug on the collar of my shirt to soak up his spit on my neck.

I'm truly lost as to where Alex is going with this, but I get a better idea when he stands so close to me, our chests compete for space with every breath we take. "I'll hand it to you… you're smart, have a way with computers, and the looks to fly under the radar for as long as you have, but there's one skill you're lacking that will ensure other agents constantly step over you." He watches the bob of my Adam's apple before continuing, "You can't read people. You can't tell the difference between a friendly glance and a lusty one when a woman is asking you on a second date, or if she's sizing you up to see if you're a serial killer. Even when the painstakingly obvious is staring you in the face, you're too busy evaluating every-thing around it instead of the picture you should have been looking at the entire time."

When the fuck did this turn into a lecture about my dating life? Furthermore, who is he to give me advice? He doesn't know me. Nobody does.

My anger gets a second wind when Alex says, "You said on the courthouse stairs last week that the only difference between Isabelle and me was that I stupidly fell in love." His eyes bounce between mine as his lips curl. "You know that isn't true. Whether we agree with it or not, Isabelle loves Isaac."

I scoff and shake my head at the same time. "She doesn't know him—"

Before I can get out the rest of my sentence, Alex says, "I know, but neither do we. Not really. Isaac keeps everyone at arm's length, even those closest to him, so how can we trust anything we've read? We were trained from the get-go to devise our own opinions, but no one has done that in Isaac's case."

Is he saying what I think he is? Does he believe Isaac isn't the man his file portrays? If so, he needs to get his head checked because I just gave him proof Isaac isn't just lying to Isabelle, he's playing her for a fool.

My shock reaches an entirely new level when Alex says, "If you really care for Isabelle, help me help her."

"How?" I ask, confused and somewhat concerned I'm dreaming.

"The bugs in Isabelle's phone."

He knows about them?

"Do you have the serial numbers for them?"

I nod. They were one of the many tidbits of evidence Phillipa, Harvey, and I processed while Isabelle was being entertained on Isaac's yacht. No solid leads came from them. They were either privately purchased or not registered with the Bureau's mainframe. "They're no good. I ran them through our system twice. Nothing popped up."

"That's not what I asked, Brandon," Alex snaps, frustrated. "I have access to channels you can't access." A *pfft* noise vibrates my lips, but Alex pretends not to hear it. "The more people looking into Isabelle's case, the better off she'll be. I thought you cared for her, Brandon."

"I do," I admit, nodding. "Very much so." *Has the way I protected and looked out for her the past several months not proven that?*

The harshness tainting Alex's face softens when he requests, "Then give me what I need. It might not lessen the severity of your insubordination, but it will do more good than harm to Isabelle's case."

"Fine. I'll give them to you." Alex thinks my agreement is the end of our conversation. I have news for him. "On one condition."

"You're not in a position to make negotiations, Brandon."

His attitude takes a step back when I reply, "Neither are you.

Even if you *wrongly* believed I just arrived, you can't honestly believe I'm stupid enough not to smell the heady aroma of lust lingering in the air. You're in the wrong as much as I am, Alex. You're just too pigheaded to admit it."

The anger reddening his face is so convincing, even Grayson reacts to it. I hear the passenger side door of my car crack open before the faintest scuffle of a pair of boots trickles into my ears. Alex hasn't spotted his approach, though. His focus is too much on me to pay attention to anyone around us. "I am *not* rogue."

"Prove it. Release your bank records to the Bureau. Open the book you usually keep closed. Show them you're not so gung-ho on taking down Isaac, you're personally funding his demise." With his shock higher than his urge to pummel some sense into me, I side-step him before heading in the direction opposite the way Grayson is, ensuring I maintain his cover. "Once your bank records are uploaded, I'll forward you the serial numbers from the bugs in Isabelle's phone."

I make it halfway around the block before Grayson pulls my car up beside me. "That was risky, punk."

I slide into the passenger seat of my car. "You needed a way in."

"He may not come through. You pissed him the fuck off. I've never seen his face as red as it was when you walked away."

"He'll come through," I reply confidently, "He's too desperate not to." I know this because I too am willing to do anything for the woman I love. I'd even go as far as killing a man for her, so a little blackmail is barely a blip on the radar.

BRANDON

I never thought I'd miss Grayson's annoying snicker in my ear, but right here, right now, I'd give anything to have it. Our team is ready, Isabelle's extraction and departure from Ravenshoe occurred without incident, and Hugo—who I'm learning goes everywhere Isabelle goes—only wordlessly threatened me three times during our trip. Yet, one glance of Melody's back as she leads Socks down the property line, and I've forgotten my name, my age, and every detail of our operation I read three times the past twenty-four hours to ensure it was retained.

This is the first time I've seen Melody in the flesh in over seven years.

Seven.

Years.

Liam trained me well, but not even the world's most decorated gymnast could have prepared my stomach for the somersault of emotions that hit it when I spotted her. She isn't supposed to be here. She was witnessed by my private investigator entering her workplace this morning, so why is she here?

If I were a man who believed in coincidences, I'd say this is fate.

Since I'm more skeptical than a man swayed by influences outside of his power, I pretend my heart isn't racing a million miles an hour. Let me tell you, it's a fucking hard feat.

Even Isabelle notices my struggles. She squeezes my hand before giving me a reassuring smile. "You've got this."

Before I can respond, Hugo pulls my car in front of my family's ranch wooden garage, and an entirely new set of emotions takes hold of my senses. The oak tree my father had cut down within weeks of Joey's death has regrown. It's nowhere near the size it once was, and it is set back too far from my window to be used as an entrance, but it's still there, living and existing, unlike Joey.

When Hugo throws open the driver's side door of my car, familiar, homey smells add to the wetness pricking my eyes. I have a handful of bad memories here, but I also have a heap of good ones. The creek that runs through the back of the property is where Joey and I use to collect baby crayfish. Melody and I didn't just have a fort on her side of the fence, we also had one near the creek, and Liam taught us how to drive in a beat-up old Honda in the sloshy fields at the back of his paddock. It hurts coming here, but if I'm open to the idea, I think it could also be healing.

I wonder if that's why Melody is here too?

It wasn't just my life that crumbled here, so did hers.

A grin curls on my lips when Hugo protests to an aroma that instantly reminds me of home. "All I can smell is cow dung."

Isabelle's happiness is louder than mine. She has a reason to laugh. Hugo has plugged his nose like animal manure is more potent to his lungs than the pollution they suck in every day at Ravenshoe.

"Which bag is yours?" Isabelle eyes Hugo in confusion when he ruffles through the half-dozen bags she packed in search of mine. Her confusion is understandable. Only last night we discussed her staying at my family ranch. It isn't the glorious farmhouse it once was, but the contractors my mom hired are slowly restoring it to its former glory, so it's up to code for weekend visitors.

Besides, the wide-open spaces make it easier for the agents

staking the perimeter to keep watch. With the frosts of winter arriving early, the grass is dead and close to the ground. There's no place to hide—*except outbuildings like the one Melody just entered.*

My focus returns to Isabelle and Hugo when Isabelle says, "We need all the bags."

Hugo's slit gaze darts between Isabelle and me for several tedious seconds before they eventually settle on me. "Do you have a death wish?"

When I shake my head, hoping it will hide the curl of my lips, Hugo slants his head to Isabelle. "He doesn't have a death wish… so I guess we're staying at a hotel."

"Brandon's mom said it's fine for us to stay here."

"Oh, okay, since Brandon's mom said it's fine, I guess it's fine." Hugo's sarcastic tone reminds me of the tone Phoenix used anytime Joey pissed him off. "Where's the phone Isaac gave you in case of an emergency."

Isabelle takes a step back, disgusted by Hugo's request. "This isn't an emergency."

Their squabble gets interrupted by my mom squealing my name at the top of her lungs. "BJ!"

With her arms spread wide, she gallops down the front stairs of the porch, smiling a blinding grin. I won't lie, and I don't care if you call me a momma's boy, but my heart thuds extra hard when our eyes collide. The last time we were here at the same time, we were saying goodbye to someone we loved dearly. I also haven't seen her in almost three years. Life got busy, and in all honesty, I got slack.

That's done with now.

When my mom leaps into my arms, I spin her around and around and around like Joey always did. It floods my eyes with moisture, but her beautiful laugh ensures not a single droplet glides down my cheeks. They're the giggles of a woman finally on the road to recovery after a few hard years.

"Okay, enough spinning before I bring up the cookie dough I gobbled down before you could sniff it out."

My mom's smile doubles when I set her back onto her feet with a pout. I thought I could smell more than cow dung in the air. My mom has been baking, and my stomach is more than ready to make up for lost time.

After whacking me in the gut, intuiting what its hungry grumbles are about, Mom shifts her glistening baby blue irises to Isabelle and Hugo. They, along with my wonky grin, are the two features I didn't get off her. My hazel eyes are a recessive gene from my grandfather, and regretfully, my smile is one hundred percent accredited to my father, but other than that, I'm a male version of my mother.

"Isabelle! It's such a pleasure to finally meet you." I scrub a hand down my face when my mom wraps Isabelle up in a tight hug. "You're even more beautiful than Brandon described."

Don't misconstrue. Until you're a man of 'prime reproductive age' desperate to add names to a guest list that filled up over a year ago, you can't judge anything happening right now. I swore until I was blue in the face that there was nothing going on between Isabelle and me. Did my mother believe me? No, she didn't. She just did the weird coughing thingamabob she did the morning she tidied up my room after Melody and I slept together for the first time before telling me she'd keep my 'relationship' with Isabelle a secret.

If you haven't worked this out yet, my mom would make the worst spy.

The heat creeping across my cheeks jumps to Isabelle's when my mom inches back to assess every inch of her face. Its coloring has nothing on the red-hot fury that floods Hugo's eyes when my mom shouts, "Oh my goodness, my grandbabies are going to be beautiful."

I'm about to jump to my defense, but before I can, the quickest flurry of color in the corner of my eye stops me. Madden has his shoulder propped against the pole holding a new verandah up. His eyes are locked on Isabelle. They're brimming with the same interest they held anytime he gawked at Melody when we were kids, and have me moving away from preparing my defense to signing a guilty verdict in under two seconds.

"Mom, she hasn't even walked through the front door yet, so don't scare her away with baby talk."

Madden is a creep, but even creepers have standards. He won't mow his little brother's turf. That's against the bro-code Phoenix, Madden, Joey, and I swore never to break. Moseying in on another brother's girl was rule number one. Although Isabelle isn't my girl, something is telling me it's okay to lie this time around.

I suck in my first breath in what feels like minutes when Madden spins on his heels and walks away. I want to say it's because he remembered our bro-code as readily as me, but I'm doubtful that's the case. He only left after his eyes locked on Hugo. Not even the cockiest guy wants to stand across from the man he pinned a rape on.

With Hugo's glare icy enough to be felt, I rub my hands together before shifting on my feet to face him and Isabelle. As suspected, Hugo is eyeing me like he's mentally processing my death certificate.

Mercifully, Isabelle's stare isn't as dire. She's frustrated but not enough to deny my silent plea for her to follow along with my ruse. I understand that this puts her in an awkward predicament, but I'd rather have her tussling with Hugo than Madden, which is odd considering one of them is related to me by blood.

I lose the frigidness of Hugo's wrath when one much more disturbing steals his focus. My mom is staring at him. I'm not talking a hello-there-young-man stare, I am talking do-you-need-a-sugar-mommy stare. It churns my gut enough I'm certain I won't eat for a week.

"Ma'am," Hugo greets, as uncomfortable by her gawk as me.

A hope my mom hasn't completely fallen down the rabbit hole surfaces when she asks, "What squadron were you in?" I thought she was eyeing Hugo like he was her lunch. I had no clue she had noticed a tattoo on his forearm he has attempted to conceal with many.

Hugo tugs down the sleeves of his long-sleeve shirt while replying, "American Hornets, ma'am."

"Oh…" My mom looks as anxious as I was when I spotted Madden watching our exchange from the sidelines. "That's nice." After straying her wide eyes to Isabelle, she says, "How about we leave the boys to unpack the car while we freshen up?"

Not giving Isabelle the chance to reply, she grips Isabelle's hand in hers then hotfoots it up the front porch stairs. The screen door has barely swung closed when Hugo is up in my face. "What are you playing at, Blondie?"

"I'm not playing anything." I am, but since it has nothing to do with him, I'll keep him out of it. "My mom often gets the wrong idea."

Hugo scoffs, calling me out as a liar without words. "She wouldn't have gotten the wrong idea if you hadn't led her astray." When I drag one of Isabelle's suitcases out of the trunk, he snatches it out of my hand, shoves it back where it was, grabs mine, then tosses it onto the porch like he's taking out the trash. After slamming down my trunk with enough force my teeth feel the impact, he growls, "I don't need to unpack. We won't be here long."

Seconds after he traces the steps Isabelle and my mom took five minutes ago, Madden's car rockets out of the awning attached to the garage. The dust of a dry ground soon hides his flee, but no amount of mooing can conceal the thrashing he gives his engine. Madden doesn't respect anything, not even his pricy ride, because he doesn't know the meaning of the word.

After roaming my eyes over the Gregg family ranch for the quickest second, I follow Hugo's hasty retreat. I find him in the kitchen, towering over Isabelle like a tactical response strike is imminent, and his body is her shield.

When the scent of freshly baked cookies become too much for me to bear, I attempt to snag one off the cooling rack. I pout like a child when my mom slaps my hand away. "You'll spoil your dinner." Her tone reveals she's annoyed about something more than childish exploits. I'm given time to look into what is bothering her when Hugo requests to have a word with Isabelle in the hallway.

I wait for them to be out of earshot before saying, "Spill the beans, Ma. I haven't seen you this worked up since..." I stop just before I remind her of the time she walked in on her husband fucking his secretary. Like my father could get any more cliché, he took it to the max the year he won office.

After coating her hands with flour so the dough won't stick, Mom commences rolling the remaining cookie dough into balls. "Madden—"

"Just left," I interrupt, knowing her well enough to know she won't speak unfavorably about someone if they're close by. That's why my interests are too piqued to bookmark this as it seems more about Madden than an additional weekend guest she wasn't prepared for. I didn't know Hugo was coming with us until I arrived to collect Isabelle this morning. "Is Madden staying here?"

Mom shakes her head. "He came to collect some things for your father."

As anger trickles through my veins, I work my jaw side to side. "Is *he* the reason you're worked up?" The way I snarl 'he' ensures she knows who I'm talking about—my father. He's always the cause of my mother's dismay lately.

My annoyance takes a back seat when she says, "No. I haven't seen your father in months." Acting ignorant to the dough on her palm, she pats my hand, doubling the assurance in her eyes. When she spots my grimace from the tacky residue coating my hand, she pinches a dash of flour before sprinkling the tip of my nose like she did when I was a kid. It's supposed to help me grow. "It's good to have you back here, BJ. I know it's hard without Joey, but there are as many good memories here as there are bad."

"I know," I reply, stepping closer to her. "It's our home. It always has been. It always will be." When she nods, agreeing with me, I slant my head, so our eyes are better aligned. "Just like you'll always be my caring, kindhearted mother. Time and distance will never change that… and neither could anything you'd ever tell me. I'll always love you, Ma." *As I hope you will me when I tell you Joey's death is my fault.*

"Mom…" I push out breathlessly when a single tear rolls down her cheek. "What's going on?"

"It's nothing. I just—" She stops talking when the vibration of my cell phone overtakes the brittle crackle of her fragile voice. "Are you going to get that?" she asks when I dig my phone out of my pocket to silence Grayson's second call in a row.

"No. It can wait. You're more important."

She cups my cheek in a nurturing, loving way only a mother can. "Take your call, BJ. I'm not going anywhere, and neither is my news."

I don't want to hold-off a conversation years in the making, but my phone is hard to ignore when it immediately commences ringing again. Grayson agreed to adhere to strict radio silence while I was in Saugerties, so he wouldn't be reaching out unless it was urgent.

"Are you sure you don't mind?" Unease highlights my tone. I use to get so angry when my dad pushed my mother aside for work, yet I'm doing the same thing. I'd be pissed if my emotions weren't being swamped with unease.

The crippling weight on my chest slackens when not an ounce of disappointment is heard in my mom's tone when she replies, "I'm sure. Just promise me one thing."

"Anything," I answer without pause for thought.

Guilt rains down on me when she whispers, "Please be careful. My heart barely survived losing one son. I can't lose another."

I wrap her up in a firm hug before pressing my lips to the shell of her ear. "I'm not going anywhere. I promise you that."

Recognition on how hard my vow will be to keep smacks into me when I give my mom one final squeeze before connecting

Grayson's call and squishing my phone to my ear. "Dimitri moved before we could. We have reports of multiple casualties."

His words impact me like a punch to the stomach. I'm wholly and utterly shocked. "Dimitri agreed to wait. He fucking shook on it."

"He got desperate. Can't say I wouldn't have done the same thing if I were handed the news he was." He's right. Doesn't make it any easier to swallow, though. "We're preparing to move in. You coming?"

"How far out?"

Grayson releases a chuckle between frantic breaths. He sounds like he's running. "I've seen you drive. You could be here in ten."

"That close?"

My stomach gurgles when he replies, "It's practically in your back paddock." If Castro is that close, my plan to catfish him with Isabelle was a woeful waste of time. No one lives in this part of Saugerties anymore. It became a ghost town not long after my family moved to New York, so Castro didn't choose this location for no reason. He wanted privacy, and the many horrid reasons as to why he needs that privacy has me mentally suiting up for battle.

"Send me the deets."

"Will do," Grayson replies before disconnecting our call.

As I slide my phone back into my pocket, I pivot to face my mom, taking in Isabelle talking on the cell phone she refused to hand Hugo earlier. "I'm sorry—"

"Don't." Mom's stern glare cuts me off better than her snapped reply. She doesn't usually have the face to pull off snarky, but she's got it down pat today. "Go do what needs to be done, then get back here. We have a lot to talk about."

"All right. Thank you." I press my lips to her cheek before lowering my eyes to her keys resting on the kitchen counter.

Smiling, she rolls her eyes before agreeing to my request to borrow her car with the dip of her chin. My trunk is filled with Hugo and Isabelle's luggage. If the portions of their conversation I overheard while talking to my mom are anything to go by, they'll want their belongings when Hugo forces Isabelle to the hotel I'm confident Isaac booked for them.

"I won't get a scratch on it," I promise while snagging up the keys and hotfooting it to my mom's swanky new ride.

Much to my dad's dismay, she purchased a brand-new Genesis G80 with cash so she could drive herself to her divorce attorney's office. Its eighty-thousand-dollar price tag barely made a dent in my parents' joint bank account, but my father is still demanding for the value of the car to be taken out of my mom's side of the settlement before he'll sign their divorce papers. That's how cheap he is. He won't give up anything of value. Fortunately for all involved, he has no clue just how valuable my mother is.

EIGHT MINUTES LATER, my mom's car skids to a stop at the back of the surveillance van Grayson's motorbike is parked behind. "I thought you were waiting for me to arrive?" I say to Grayson when the sound of heavy combat fire booms into my ears.

"That's not us. It's a turf war we're about to break up, and we need to do it quickly. Word is CIA is honing in. If you want to speak with Castro before them, we need to move fast."

I accept the bulletproof vest he's holding out to me before joining him next to a table full of maps. With the CIA on their way, we have to storm the recently formed Castro compound via the front door. It's the quickest and safest entrance point.

"Shoot to kill is activated, but the less casualties, the better. We want Rimi Castro brought in alive." Grayson double taps his surveillance video. For a man who spent the last year and a half hiding, he looks dog-tired. "If you can show caution, use it, but if it's you or them, always place money on yourself. We good?"

When a collective hum of agreement vibrates through the

makeshift command center, Grayson claps his hands together two times. "Suit up, we're heading out in four."

"Where's Phillipa?" I ask Grayson while following him to a fleet of Escalades rigged with blinding spotlights and bulletproof windshields. My scan of the agents preparing to head into battle with me failed to locate a woman with eyes as dark as her raven locks.

Grayson shrugs before climbing into the passenger seat of the first Escalade. "I tried to reach her a few times. She hasn't gotten back to me." He unlocks the safety on his gun, slides it into the waistband of his pants before straying his eyes to me. "I can't hold out for her, BJ. If the CIA gets Castro before us, we'll never get the chance to talk to him."

Agreeing with him, I jog around to the driver's seat of the Escalade before sliding in behind the steering wheel. As adrenaline pumps through my veins, Grayson taps his out on the roof on our car. It's as if the past twenty-two months never occurred. We're once again on the field prepared to take down a syndicate with such fucked-up morals, they view women as nothing but babymakers.

"Ready for payback, punk?"

Smirking, I fire up the ignition, answering Grayson's question without words.

Thirty seconds later, we're rolling over untouched land with another thirty or so agents tailing us. The landscape is different than we faced in New Mexico, but the adrenaline high is exactly the same—as are the sound of bullets pinging off the windshield.

Grayson takes down two spotters on the gate before the tires of our Escalade ensure they remain down for the count. If a bullet between the eyes didn't kill them, five thousand pounds of steel will get the job done.

"Go, go, go," Grayson shouts at the agents piling out of the line of Escalades at the front of the eerily quiet farmhouse mansion. The silence is off-putting, especially considering the amount of gunfire I heard on arrival only minutes ago.

I lift my chin when Grayson signals for me to head left with half a dozen men while he climbs the front stairs. It's so quiet, I can hear the raging hearts of the agents behind me when we creep across floorboards in desperate need of repair. The scent of gun powder and blood is obvious, but no amount of deadly smells could prepare my eyes for what they stumble on when I push open the back-side door of the property.

The warped wooden floorboards of the basement are littered with dead bodies. Some have been shot, others have been knifed, and one is chained to a boiler heater. Although the dark-haired man has a large knife wound stretched from one side of his stomach to the other, his wide and terrified eyes are open and locked on me, begging for assistance.

He's suspected of killing my brother, so I should let him rot in hell, but I can't. Rimi Castro may be the only person capable of identifying the bodies found at the Shrouds' family ranch. Without him, the victims' families may never get the closure I'm hoping to give my family. That alone has me removing a switchblade knife out of my pocket to cut through the rope tying him to the boiler before lowering him to the ground.

After yanking off my bulletproof vest, I tug my shirt off, bundle it together, press it to the wound in Castro's stomach, then call in assistance. "We need a medic in the basement. Man with a stab wound to the stomach. No other survivors."

The crackle of a radio sounds through my ear before Grayson's deep voice gobbles it up. "Copy. Medic is coming down. His presence won't help anyone up here." He doesn't directly say he's facing the same body count I am, but his tone sure does.

When my eyes return to Castro, I notice his face is whiter than it was moments ago. The paleness of his cheeks has nothing to do with the amount of blood he has lost. It's because he's seeing a ghost, a man he was confident he ordered to be killed.

"What's the matter, Castro? You look like the Grim Reaper came to visit you." He chokes on the blood gurgling in his throat when I push down on his wound with more force than needed. "Or are you seeing a ghost?"

Before he can answer me, I discover the frantic thump of footsteps bellowing down the stairwell don't belong to the medically trained agents in our team. They're compliments of the CIA officers storming the basement, demanding for my men to place their weapons down.

"Lower your weapon," an agent requests of me for the second time, her voice oddly familiar even with it being tainted with remorse.

"If I do, he'll bleed out." I raise my eyes, drinking in black polished shoes, fitted trousers, a CIA emblazoned vest, and a pair of dark, stormy eyes. "Is that what you want, *Agent* Russell?" As my eyes narrow into tiny slits, I correct, "Or should I call you Officer Russell since CIA personnel aren't referred to as agents?"

BRANDON

"Is he going to survive?"

Phillipa's teeth crunch at the curtness of my tone, but she dips her chin, nonetheless.

"When can I see him?" When her eyes lift to the right, I snarl, "It's the least you can do. I brought you here. *Me.* I did all the leg work, so you can sure as fuck be guaranteed I won't sit back and watch you take credit for all the work *I* did." I bang my chest during my last 'I.'

Phillipa waits for the two dozen women and children found in the attic of the farmhouse to be guided past us before replying, "I have no intention of taking credit for your work, BJ." Her hair ruffles from my furious growl. She has no right to call me a nickname after she played me. "I wanted to tell you who I was. I sought permission. My supervisors wouldn't allow it."

"So you lied by making out you're one of the good ones." I freeze as well as Phillipa does, shocked by something I hadn't considered before. "How long have you been with the CIA?" When she pulls an I'm-not-going-to-break-cover face, I ask again, louder this time, "How long?"

After floating her eyes across the group of men and women watching us, the same men and women she deceived as well as me, she returns them to my face and whispers, "Thirteen years."

I take a step back, shocked. *She did just say thirteen years, didn't she?*

"How old are you?" That shouldn't be the focal point of my interrogation, but I'm too stunned to use the logical side of my brain.

"I'm thirty-five. I was recruited in my final year of college." Her voice softens when she adds, "Just like Liam."

"Did he recruit you?"

As regret fills her eyes, she shakes her head. "But he's the reason I went undercover in the Bureau. Conspiracy theorists for years have alleged CIA involvement with cartels. Liam's placement made them worse." An admired sparkle brightens her eyes. "But that doesn't mean he shied away from proving them wrong."

It's the fight of my life not to smile at her comment. The less likely someone was to believe him, the harder Liam worked to convert them to his way of thinking. The only person he couldn't persuade was my father.

"What Liam didn't know was that in the process of his investigation, he'd stumble onto some half-truths." She laughs when she spots the shocked expression on my face. "It's not exactly how you're picturing it, but there's always a handful of rotten apples in every barrel."

Everything she's saying is true, but I'm having a hard time processing it all. If killing an ant can cause a tornado, imagine what happens when the Acting Director of the Bureau discovers his daughter conducted a covert operation under his watch. The aftershocks will be felt for years to come, if not decades.

The only good thing that has come of her disclosure is the realization her hacking skills aren't better than mine. I couldn't for the life of me work out how she had photos of Melody before her family's home invasion. Excluding the pictures in the Greggs family ranch, I couldn't find any information on the Greggs before they moved to Saugerties. Only now am I realizing I didn't have access to the correct channels. That wasn't the case for Phillipa. The CIA is more upfront with their own.

Although I have a thousand questions in my head, one sounds louder than the rest. "Did Castro kill my brother?"

Phillipa scoops my hand into hers before raising her eyes to mine. "I don't know, but I promise I'll find out for you."

I shouldn't believe the honesty in her eyes. I should call her a liar before demanding access to Castro so I can pry the truth from him myself, but for some reason, I believe her.

Seeing the silent thanks in my eyes, Phillipa releases my hand before heading toward the armored SUV waiting for her next to our makeshift command center.

"One last thing," I ask before she slips into the front passenger seat of the car Harvey is commanding.

I was suspicious about how close they were for two strangers, but with my mind focused on more pressing matters, I played it off as two similar personalities having an instant kinship. It's a mistake I won't make again anytime soon. The CIA and the Bureau have worked together previously, but this is the first time a majority of the agents assigned to the joint operation have been left in the dark. I don't like it, and in all honesty, it's frustrating me more than Phillipa's deceit.

When Phillipa drops her chin, approving my request, I ask, "Why is the CIA interested in this case? Don't you usually handle overseas incidents?"

"Castro isn't a US citizen." She pauses for a second before adding, "We were also hoping he'd lead us to Kirill." Her straight-up honesty shocks me, but not as much as what she says next, "I believe we can still nab him without Castro's assistance. With your and Grayson's help, of course." When I don't voice a protest to her suggestion that we work together to bring down Kirill, she shyly waves before sliding into her awaiting chariot. "Enjoy your party, BJ. Perhaps if you've forgiven me by then, you'll save me a dance."

Party? What party?

Like he has a direct link to my psyche, Grayson arrives out of nowhere. "The shindig we're set to rock in around thirty or so minutes."

When he fans open five embossed gold tickets for the fundraising gala my mother chairs, I scoff. "Why would we still attend the gala? We got our man. The threat has been neutralized."

I choke on my spit when Grayson mutters, "For one, your girl will be there—" He doesn't get the chance to voice more points.

"Melody's going?" Think back to those pimple-faced boys who uncomfortably grabbed their crotches at random times of the day as they can't control their cocks. That's who my voice represents when I squeak out my question. "Is that why she was at her ranch this afternoon?"

While pursing his lips, Grayson waves the ticket back and forth, temptingly teasing me. "Only one person can answer your questions, punk. You've just got to decide if you're brave enough to ask them—" His words lodge into the back of his throat when I snatch one of the tickets out of his hand.

I already have a ticket with my name on it at home, but this one has VIP splashed across the front, meaning I'll have more chance of being in the same room as Melody and her gazillionaire fiancé.

I'm not planning to cause trouble for them. I just want to know why bundles of cash with serial numbers corresponding to the massive withdrawal Julian undertook last week was found in a safe in Castro's office.

TWENTY MINUTES LATER, I peer at my reflection in the foggy mirror of the Jack and Jill bathroom attached to my childhood room. I haven't showered in this room in almost eight years, yet everything is still in its place. My aftershave sits in the middle of the bottom shelf, my razor is just to its left, even my toothbrush and toothpaste are in the same spot. The only thing missing is my can of shaving cream, which is odd considering I barely needed it when I was a teen. My skin was as soft as a baby's bottom, so I didn't need to worry about unexpected nicks from the rough slide of my razor.

After dumping my rusted, hair-clogged razor into the bin under the vanity sink, I pull my electric razor out of my travel bag before quickly running it over my face, sprucing myself up. Once all the stray hairs are taken care of, I commence brushing my teeth. I'm usually one of those annoying brushers who leave the tap on while scrubbing. I can't do that tonight. Something is clogging the drain, slowing the water's escape.

I won't lie. My heart batters my ribcage when I pierce one of my mother's knitting needles through the backlog of water. I grew up with three older brothers. I found many gross things when unblocking a clogged sink.

Today's discovery isn't any better.

"That's fucking gross," I groan in disgust while transferring a condom from my sink to the bin, heaving. I can look at a dead body and not feel sick, but a used condom has my stomach somersaulting.

After dumping the offending product and the knitting needle into the bin, I scrub my hands like they're coated in cooties before entering my room to get dressed. I don't have time to dwell on how disgusting some men are. The gala has already started, meaning we're late.

Once I'm dressed in a tuxedo, brushed my wet hair, and thrown on a good dose of aftershave, I head to the room Isabelle has been getting ready in for the past several hours. Mom never had a daughter, so she used it as an excuse to keep Isabelle and Hugo occupied while I attended the raid. It's odd when you think about it—dangerous raid during the day, ritzy gala at night. At least I can't say my life is boring.

WOULD you think I am weird if I said I'm more nervous now than I was when I rolled a Ford Expedition over rose-colored deserts almost two years ago? Back then, I knew what I was heading to and knew both my target and my objective.

Here, I'm flying solo.

I once knew the girl I'm about to confront. I knew the way her eyelashes touched her cheeks when she blinked and how she signed super-fast when she was about to come. I knew her voice without her speaking a word and how she smiled any time she was nervous. I knew her better than I knew myself. But I don't know her anymore.

I don't want the fantasy in my head to end any more than I don't want our meeting to steal the only good memories I have of my childhood. I don't want to forget the person Melody once was.

I also don't want to see her with another man.

To know she loves him as she once did me may very well kill me. Our relationship will always be different. You never forget your first true love, but you can replace it. Replicate it. Strive for better. I haven't put the steps in place to do that, but it's clear Melody has. Although she was occasionally caught a little sad, she appeared happy in the surveillance images I've seen of her. Her sadness could have more to do with being an orphan than anything else. A part of her died when her parents did.

That's another thing that is bothering me. How do I tell Melody all the things I've unearthed about her father without possibly ruining her memories of him? Like every teen growing up, she thought her dad was a hard-assed tyrant who needed a personality transplant, but even when fighting him, I could see in her eyes how much she adored him.

Nothing I've discovered the past eight months paints Liam in a bad light, I just don't know how Melody will respond when she finds out she shares blood with one of the country's most notorious gangsters. She's an assistant district attorney. That would have to be a conflict of interest. I don't want her forced to give up a part of who she is because of the legacy she was born into. Her birthright wasn't her choice, and neither was mine.

I breathe out my nerves when Hugo pulls my car into the front of the hotel the gala is being held at. I'm shocked when Isabelle peels out of the car before popping her head back in as she did the morning she was released on bail. "Are you coming?"

What did I miss during my reminiscing?

As I slide across the seat to exit via the open back passenger door, Hugo grumbles for me to keep myself in check. He must be mistaking the fretful look on my face as envy as I've barely glanced Isabelle's way tonight. My mind is elsewhere.

Once Hugo pulls away from the curb, Isabelle curls her arm around my elbow. Her eyes are bright and filled with stars. I rarely attended these events as a kid, and they don't interest me much now, but I can understand how opulent it seems to Isabelle. She was raised by a big balding Russian who hid her from the world. I doubt she had many events to get dressed up for.

Halfway into the room full of socialites, rock stars, silver-screen darlings, and a group of pompous pricks who endorse my father's bid for Congress, the already frantic patter of my heart gains an extra beat. A long time ago, I would have immediately known the reason behind my spike in pulse. Now I have to be more cautious. I'd hate to make a fool of myself.

The mask I'm holding is crushed beyond repair when my eyes lock in on a silhouette of red across the room. The blonde beauty's hair is pinned off her face, and the tiny freckles that adorn her nose are covered with makeup, but I'd never forget the face of a woman who stands out in a crowded room. She's too beautiful to forget, and really, *really* pretty.

I'm reminded it isn't just Melody and me in the room when Isabelle leans into my side to whisper in my ear, "Is that Melody?"

I try to force some type of confirmation out of my mouth, but with my throat bone-dry from taking in the way Melody's ballgown hugs the curves of her body, I nod instead. I've never been good with words when it comes to Melody. I'm glad to see seven years didn't cure that neurosis.

The world fades out when Melody's head suddenly swings my way. Her eyes lock on mine in an instant, her lips curving. Her smile —fuck. Don't ask me to explain it. I couldn't possibly put into words how perfect it is. There's no slight wonkiness to her grin or apprehension weakening it. It's a blistering smile unlike any of the ones I've seen of her in print the past year.

"*Hi*," I inconspicuously sign, doubling the wetness in her eyes.

"*Hi*," Melody signs back at the same time Isabelle's elbow lands into my ribs. "Go say hello."

I glare at Isabelle like she's insane before shaking my head. I'm barely holding it together as it is, and Melody is on the other side of the room. There's no way I'm ready for a face-to-face confrontation. Furthermore, she isn't here alone. I asked Grayson to hack into the hotel's reservation software during the commute back to my family's ranch. It didn't have a Melody Gregg listed. Julian McMahon, though, was there. Regretfully.

My head shake has me stumbling onto another participant ready to board the talk-to-Melody train. Grayson is standing at the side of the ballroom, glaring at me. His designer jeans, fitted shirt, and fancy jacket should make him stick out like a sore thumb in a room full of men in tuxedos, but for some reason, he pulls it off. He fits in with the rock star family this gala was founded for.

When Grayson nudges his head to Melody for the fifth time while mouthing that I'm a soft cock, I give in to his rile.

"Wish me luck," I mumble under my breath before swooping down to place a peck on Isabelle's cheek.

After she gives my hand an encouraging squeeze, I weave through the hundreds of gala attendees separating Melody and me. My heart beats out a funky tune with every step I take, as does a vein in Melody's neck. She watches me cross the room, her lips parted in a smile, her eyes twinkling with moisture. She's alone which both annoys and appeases me. The main threat to her life is holed up in a hospital room guarded by enough CIA officers he could be mistaken as a national dignitary, but we must stay cautious. Until we can prove the Castros and Bobrovs aren't working together, alerts will remain high.

"Melody, hi." The tears in her eyes glide down her cheeks when I stop to stand in front of her. I don't know if it's from seeing me in the flesh for the first time in seven years, realizing we still stand at the same height, or how my voice cracked when I said her name during my greeting. If I weren't aware she's deaf, I would have gone with the latter. Alas, she can't hear me any more than I wish I could hear her say my name. *"What is wrong? Why are you crying?"*

I freeze like a statue when she responds, "Your voice... I can't... Oh, God, BJ." She didn't sign her response. She spoke it.

"Mel..." I can't speak. I'm too shocked and confident I am dreaming. "You can talk?" When she nods, I add, "And you can hear me?"

When she dips her chin for the second time, I cup her face, certain she's about to vanish. She was already the girl of my dreams before she could talk, so you can imagine how confident I am that I'm dreaming. Her voice is a little husky, but I'd say that's more to do with nerves than anything else. It matches the sweetness of her face while giving her still-girlish looks a touch of sophistication. It's perfect, and it will have me smiling long after I wake up.

As my fingers plait through the dirty blonde waves pinned off Melody's face, the reason for her newfound hearing is exposed. The faintest slither of coolness breaks through the heat teeming between us when my fingertips brace a speech processor behind her right ear.

"You got them done." My words are barely whispers and more a confirmation than a question, but Melody has no trouble picking them up.

After nodding, she places her hands over mine so she can gently float them over each processor. Once my fingertips have traced the processors and transmitters responsible for her hearing, she glides my hands down her ears and across her wet cheeks before stopping them within a millimeter of her lips. Our odd display of public affection has gained us many eyes, but not even being scrutinized by a million people could dampen the intensity brewing between us. It is as if we're in a room full of mute, tone-deaf people.

It's just us.

"Hi, BJ," Melody whispers a short time later, allowing me to feel the vibrations of her lips as she speaks my name for the second time. It's just as good as it was the first time around, if not better from the memories it floods my head with. I often murmured her name on sensitive regions of her body to enhance our sexual connections whenever we slept together. This seems innocent to anyone outside of our little bubble, but to me, it's just as provocative.

"Hi," I reply, still too shocked to articulate any of the millions of thoughts in my head. Only one will come through, which isn't surprising considering it's the most important of them all. "I've missed you."

"I've missed you, too," she replies as she throws her arms around my neck to hug me tight. "So very much."

MELODY

A blistering smile stretches across my face when Brandon mutters, "I'm sorry. I'm still having a hard time processing everything." He pinches himself for the third time the past ten minutes before he continues guiding us to the side of the room so we don't get trampled by the partygoers eager to enter the main part of the ballroom since the doors were recently opened for guests. "Are you sure I'm not dreaming?"

"If you were dreaming, wouldn't you have your hands down my pants by now?" My words flutter at the end, staggered by the heat creeping across Brandon's cheeks. He was a blusher when we were kids, but it seems to have grown worse as he progressed into adulthood.

The redness of his cheeks jumps onto mine when he replies, "Most likely. It's how most of my dreams end up."

When I slap his chest, the most beautiful noise in the world is exposed. His laugh… kill me now. I've never heard something so seductively enticing. I thought his voice was perfect when he called me a smart-ass all those weeks ago, but nothing compares to hearing it in real life. It's strong, clear, and mannish but with a smoothness that would have you nodding off like a baby if he read to you while holding you in his arms—that's, of course, if the book had a PG rating. If it wasn't, you'll be in for a very long and entertaining night.

"How long ago did you get the implants done? From the quality of your speech, I'm assuming it was a couple of years ago."

"Nearly three years," I reply, grateful he doesn't sound pissed. "I wanted to tell you when we were texting earlier this week, but I held back when a little birdie told me your name was on the guest list for this event." If the proud gleam in my eyes doesn't disclose to him who the little birdie was, I'm sure my quick wave to his mother gawking at us from afar will expose the truth. "I wanted to see your reaction firsthand." My teeth graze my bottom lip as I struggle to hold back my smile. "The wait was worth the torture. You looked a cross between wanting to chop off my head to make sure I wasn't a robot to fainting."

Brandon laughs again, still incapable of denying the truth. "I'm glad you waited. I don't think it would have had the same impact if it wasn't in person. Your voice…" I could kill him for his pause. It has me on tenterhooks and not in a good way. "It's beautiful, Melody. Kind of completes the package. Humble and sweet with the slightest twang you'd expect from a country girl living in the city."

"Thank you." My reply is pathetic, but what more can I say? Your praise means the world to me even though you're looking at me like you always have. I truly don't think he would have cared if I was still deaf. We had no trouble communicating when we were kids, and my deafness didn't create a barrier between us. If anything, it made us closer.

"Do you still know how to sign?"

My smile competes with the flashy chandeliers in the hotel bar when Brandon signs, *"It is like my love of peanut butter… everlasting."*

"Still? Jeez, BJ, you should extend your palette at some stage during adulthood. There is an entire menu of non-nutty dishes you are missing out on."

The earth shifts beneath my feet when he replies, *"Why? Lives end, but love does not. It never dies."* After tilting his head to hide the heat creeping across his cheeks, he asks, "What made you decide to get implants? You were pretty opposed to the idea when we were kids."

"People have changes of heart all the time." This is the first time I've wished I was still deaf. Then I wouldn't have heard Brandon's painful sigh. He's assuming I meant him. I wasn't, but that's a conversation for an entirely different day.

After slipping onto a bar stool recently vacated by a man with dark, stormy eyes and a well-fitted suit, I signal for the bartender. I need a drink or perhaps twenty. Warming my veins with alcohol may be the only way I can excuse the extra flutter in my pulse when Julian arrives. He's waiting on an important call and asked Fetu to accompany me to the gala, so I didn't have to show up stag. Fetu is keeping a safe yet amicable distance, acting as oblivious to Brandon's presence as Brandon is his.

"I'll just have water, thanks," Brandon says to the waiter after he jots down my order of an apple martini.

Curious as to why he isn't taking advantage of the free bar tab, I ask, "Are you on the job?"

His simple reply does weird things to my stomach. "Not officially."

When we were younger, he often said he was always on the job when it came to me, but I didn't think his pledge was in effect anymore, especially after how I ended things.

Certain it's too early in our reforming friendship to add a steaming pile of shit onto the stack, I shift my focus onto someone we both mutually admire and respect. "Have you been by the ranch? Your mom's contractors are making good headway on the restoration."

Brandon jerks up his chin, answering both my question and thanking the waiter for the bottle of water he sets in front of him. "I have. I arrived there earlier today." When he lifts and locks his eyes with mine, the butterflies in my stomach drop several inches lower. His beautiful eyes are a little greener today, which means they're being fired by love and devotion. His eyes are very telling. They're the gateway to his soul. "I saw you walking Socks around the property line."

"You did?" I don't know why the thought has me so misty-eyed, but there's no denying it. I'm on the verge of crying. "It wasn't a ploy this time around. I just wanted to take him for a final walk." I dap at the tears threatening to spill down my cheeks with a napkin, warning them to stay put before adding, "He's being rehomed later this month. I'm selling the ranch."

Brandon chokes on his spit. "You're selling the ranch?"

When I nod, a handful of rogue tears escape my eyes. "I'll never move back there, and even with it just being an old farmhouse, the costs to keep everything running is more than I can afford, so it's time to let it go."

I realize Brandon knows more about my personal life than I do his when he mutters under his breath, "I doubt it's outside the means of a gazillionaire."

Even though I hate how quickly our conversation is becoming heated, I can't harness my reply, "The ranch isn't Julian's responsibility. It's mine."

You have no idea how hard it was for me not to say 'ours.' Brandon was as much a part of the ranch as me. He's embedded in its bones, so I hate that I had to make this decision without him, but I didn't have a choice. If I want to be the strong, independent woman my parents raised me to be, I can't allow *any* man to pay my way—once best friends included. My loft is covered by my salary while the ranch's maintenance was paid for with my inheritance, but since that well dried up quicker than anticipated thanks to my cochlear implants, I have no other option but to sell.

My eyes snap to Brandon when he offers, "Let me help you." The brutal shake of my head lessens when he retorts with the same argument I internally battled only moments ago, "That place was a part of my childhood, Melody. I don't want to see it being demolished by some idiot who has no clue of its worth."

"Sentimental value can't enter the equation, BJ, or I'd never let her go," I blubber, quoting the words of the real estate agent I met earlier today.

"Good, then don't. Keep it."

Half of my martini spills on the countertop when I shout, "That's not an option." My voice was so loud, I startled the bartender so much he jumped.

Ignoring the bartender mopping up the mess with a napkin, Brandon asks, "Why? Because it reminds you of your past? Because you want to run from it as you did me seven years ago? Why do you have to sell it, Melody?"

"Because it reminds me of everything I lost. It reminds me of you and what he did to me." I take a quick breather before whispering, "What he did to us..." My haunted words trail off again when confusion crosses Brandon's face. An ordinary person would have excused my rant as anger at my father keeping us apart. Brandon isn't close to ordinary. When we were kids, he knew me better than I knew myself, which means he knows this goes way deeper than even he could comprehend. "I have to go."

When I snatch my clutch purse off the countertop, Brandon snatches my wrist just as fast. "No. I'm not letting you run this time." His eyes bounce between mine. They're as wet and brimming with the same amount of pain as mine. "Not until you tell me everything. And I mean *everything*, Melody." How he can express such pain and anger with only one word would usually be impressive. Today, it just hurts.

"I don't owe you anything, Brandon." I purposely use his real name, hopeful it will have him backing down.

It was foolish of me to do because all it does is get his back up. "You don't owe me? How don't you owe me? I gave up my entire life for you... my childhood, my teen years. I even gave you a good chunk of my adult life, yet you don't feel like you owe me an explanation for running out on me the week my brother died! That's shit, Melody. Absolute and utter shit."

"That's nothing compared to what he took from me! He broke me, BJ. He broke us!"

"*Who?* Who broke us?"

I slam my mouth shut, the pain in his eyes too much. He wants me to place the burden on someone else's shoulders, believing it will alleviate him of the heaviness on his, completely unaware it will make it ten times worse. My confession won't ease his pain. It will destroy him as it did me. For that alone, I'll take my secret to the grave.

"The keys for the Hellcat are in the glove compartment. You'll need to pick it up before the twelfth as appraisers are coming through to value everything. Old restored cars included."

"I don't want the Hellcat."

With our shouted words gaining us the attention of a handful of gala attendees, I resort to signing. It's my go-to when I'm stressed. "*Then what do you want, BJ? Help getting off charges? A file—*"

"*I want you...*" the stranglehold his three little signed words placed on my heart is quickly relieved when he finalizes his sentence, "*... to stop running. To tell the truth. To come clean on the real reason you cheated on me. What did I ever do to deserve that, Melody? What made you hate me so much you had to hurt me like that?*"

"I never hated you. I loved you." Tears roll down my cheeks as I sign words I've never signed to another man. "*I still love you. I will always love you.*"

Using his shock to my advantage, I spin on my heels, prepared to make my dash.

"Mellowy." Brandon stomps down my name as loudly as he shouts it, but before I can remind him he's not my protector anymore, much less the fact I'm not a child who melts over a silly nickname, he seizes my wrist, yanks me back, then seals his lips over mine.

His kiss is barely a peck, however, the damage it causes to my heart is catastrophic. It breaks the wall I built around it in an instant and has me acting recklessly.

Instead of acknowledging his embrace as a taken woman would, I take it from friendly to flirty by dragging my tongue along the seam of his lips. His growl sends liquid ecstasy rolling through my veins. His moans were hot and panty-wetting when I could only feel their vibrations, so imagine how unbelievable they are to hear them as well. It has me deepening our kiss in an instant, needing the fireworks sparking from the roots of my hair to the tips of my toes to be felt all over.

For how angry our embrace started, it should be filled with painful bites and cruel lashes of our tongues. Our kiss isn't anything close to that. It's a scorching embrace full of teasing nips and lingering touches. It fades the world from my mind as quickly as it drains the pain from my heart.

I'm not the only one caught unaware by our embrace. Brandon tugs me in closer before piercing his tongue between my wet lips. His growl is felt by both my heart and my pussy when he drags his tongue along the roof of my mouth, then I feel how turned on he is from my moans when our groins meet. He's thick and heavy against a part of my body that's only ever thrummed this way for him. His size is impressive considering how well-fitting his tuxedo is. I thought the nasty bite of his zipper would impact the size of his erection. It has to be digging in as every morsel of space in the crotch of his pants is being hogged by his cock.

Our kiss isn't a quick its-over-before-it-started embrace. It lasts for several long minutes, only weakened when a strange, yet somewhat familiar voice trickles through my ears. "He's gone. You're good now."

Brandon continues kissing me, acting ignorant to the man with tangy aftershave tapping on his shoulder. I want to ignore him too, but the quickest scan of piercing blue eyes, snow-white hair, and cut chin covered with thick, wiry hair ensures that will never happen.

The last time I stood across from these two men at the same time, my life had ended only minutes earlier.

"*Hi,*" Grayson signs, smiling to ward off the heat of my uneasy stare.

My eyes bounce between Grayson and Brandon like silver balls in a pinball machine when Brandon asks, "What's Henry doing here? He wasn't on the guest list."

Grayson's smile grows as he waits for Brandon to remove my spit from his lips. Once he has everything cleared away, he answers, "I don't know. We got reports on his whereabouts partway here. I wanted to tell you, but I also didn't want to ruin your mojo, so…" He locks his eyes with mine. They're twinkling with cheekiness. "You good, Melody? You look good."

Don't let his words fool you. He's not asking about my mental well-being. His focus is on nothing but the lust beaming from my eyes, and we're not going to mention the scent leeching from my pores, or Grayson will have you convinced he walked in on us fucking, which isn't the case, despite the silent pleas of my libido.

My eyes snap to Brandon's as quickly as Grayson's when Brandon asks, "Did Henry see her?" He doesn't need to say my name to know who he's referencing. His whole I-was-born-to-protect-Melody-Gregg persona is vibrating out of him. It used to feel suffocating when we were kids, and today isn't any different.

A topsy-turvy feeling hits my stomach when Grayson halfheartedly shrugs. "I doubt it. Your big noggin had her face pretty well covered."

Grayson stops playfully ribbing Brandon in the stomach when my lust-sluggish brain finally clues on to what's happening. "You kissed me to hide me?"

My lunch threatens to spill when Brandon's focus shifts to me. Even if he wanted to lie, it would do him no good. His eyes are too telling. They reveal his lie long before his mouth produces it.

"Why would you do that?" *And why did I stupidly fall for your trick?*

"You were hard." I thrust my hand at the crotch of his pants. "You still are."

Grayson's laughter is nipped in the bud when two suffocating auras steal the air from his lungs. I don't know who the man in the crisp black tuxedo is, but even in a room full of wealthy aristocrats, a man with a presence like Henry Gottle stands out.

When Brandon steps in front of me, butting his shoulder with Grayson's, I'm tempted to slap him out of my way before charging across the room. I've barely been at the gala for forty minutes, yet I already want to leave. Can you blame me? I returned the kiss of my first love because I thought he couldn't hold himself back for another second.

How foolish am I?

And let's not get me started on the guilt creeping through my veins. I only agreed to attend this stupid fundraiser because it was a great campaign starter for Julian's push for office, and what do I do within the first hour of arriving? Kiss another man in front of witnesses.

God, I'm not cut out for this life.

When Henry and the unknown gray-eyed man disappear under the hotel's awning, Grayson's naturally ingrained investigative instincts kick in. He moves to the far corner of the room to survey them from a close yet innocuous distance.

Brandon appears just as desperate to snoop, but since the sexual chemistry that forever crackles between us is quickly switching to unease, he maintains his command as my bodyguard, breaking my heart further.

"Why would you do that? Why kiss me to hide me?" My words are barely whispers since I had to force them through the pain clutching my throat, but I'm praying they'll reach Fetu's ears. If he realizes Brandon's kiss was a ploy to keep me safe, he may grant my plea for me to tell Julian about my stupidity before him. Julian should hear it from me since I'm the one who fucked up. "Despite his… *title*, Henry Gottle isn't a threat to me."

I'm not lying. Henry is a cruel, vindictive, cold-hearted murderer, but even those who want to take him down know his crimes are never undertaken on the innocent. Unlike the men who hope one day to be him, he's never been charged with rape, child molestation, sex trafficking, or any of those other horrendous crimes you usually associate with members of the cartel. If you were only to judge him by the stacks of papers in his file, some may say he's no different than my father. He protects the innocent by slaying the men hurting them. There are better ways he could go about it, but at the end of the day, not everyone can rely on the justice system.

My parents couldn't.

The tightness in Brandon's shoulders doubles when I demand him to answer my question by saying his name in a low, gravelly tone. I still loathe my developing voice, but I hate it even more when its pitched with sadness.

After a quick scan of the room, Brandon shifts on his feet to face me. "I'm not protecting you from Henry. I'm protecting you from the people who will hurt him by hurting you."

"What?" I'm wholly and truly lost. "Why would Henry be hurt if I were hurt? That doesn't make any sense..." My words clog in my throat when my run-in with Henry last month filters into my head. His eyes were more empathetic than you'd expect most mob bosses to have, particularly when he was cupping my cheeks in a loving, possessive way.

They had the same spark they have now when he spots me across the room. He's finished his chat with his friend, who's making his way back to the main section of the gala. He looks like he wants to approach me, but the fast fanning of Brandon's tuxedo jacket stops him. He's carrying, and the expression on his face assures Henry he'll have no hesitation using his weapon if it keeps him away from me.

Realizing I'm not worth a bullet wound, Henry dips his chin in farewell before he once again vanishes into the darkness of the night. I want to demand for Grayson to leave him alone when he's quick to follow Henry's retreat, but I lose the chance when Brandon pivots around to face me. He cups my cheeks as he did earlier, except this time, absolute awe isn't filling his eyes. Panic is.

"Are you okay?"

Although I'm still embarrassed I thought there was more behind his kiss than there was, and I'm overwhelmed with guilt, neither of those things are life-threatening, so I nod instead of shaking my head like I really want to. "I'm fine, just a little confused."

Brandon's thumbs swipe at my cheeks as he says, "That's understandable. We have a lot to discuss." As his eyes dance between mine, his tongue darts out to wet his lips. I can tell the exact moment he tastes my mouth on his. His nostrils flare as the faintest pink coloring creeps across his cheeks. I just have to hope his response isn't one full of remorse. His actions tonight are too contradictive for me to trust my intuition. It led me astray during our kiss. I won't let it happen again. "Is there somewhere we can have that discussion…" he steps closer to me, hiding both his face and the movement of his lips from Fetu. "… in private."

"Tiny is my… bodyguard." Since I'm embarrassed that I need a protective detail, it takes longer to express my last word. "Julian is adamant Tiny goes anywhere I go."

I assumed my comment would put Brandon on the defensive, so you can imagine my surprise when he keeps a cool, calm, and collected voice while asking, "What about when Julian is around? Does Tiny still hover like an annoying fly then?"

An ill-timed grin attempts to break across my face when Brandon's muttered words reach Fetu's ears. He glares at him, looking like he wants to snap him like a twig, but mercifully, he maintains his protective stance from afar.

Although half of me still wants to tell Brandon to go to hell, the other half is too inquisitive to know when to back away. "He's less intrusive when Julian is around, so perhaps we should take this back to my room. Julian is there waiting for a call."

I regret my decision in an instant when Brandon mutters, "Even gazillionaires have to wait for calls? Who would have known?"

"He's not a gazillionaire." I wait for the annoyance on Brandon's face to shift halfway to pleased before muttering, "But he's pretty damn close. He's off by a billion or two."

My comment was cruel and demoralizing, but one hundred percent necessary. It evened the playing field between us, ensuring both Brandon and my heart knows our kiss meant nothing. He was merely doing the job my father taught him to do, and once again, has me regretting my unusual upbringing.

As I turn toward Fetu to announce we are leaving, I spot the man I saw chatting with Henry earlier breaking through the hundreds of attendees of the gala. He's possessively clutching the waist of a pretty brunette as he makes a beeline for the hotel's valet parking bay. The worried expression on his face jumps onto mine when the woman he's sheltering swings her eyes to Brandon. It isn't the concern for him seen in her eyes that has my heart rate jumping, it's the nasty snarl of a second dark-haired man on her left. He isn't a fan of Brandon, which is surprising because most people love him. Furthermore, I swear I've seen him before, but I can't recall where exactly.

Before I can work through half my confusion, Brandon stacks a heap more into my head. Instead of acting like Fetu isn't in the room with us, he demands him to take me back to my room and not let me out until he says so.

"I beg your pardon," I snap back, yanking out of Fetu's hold. "I'm not a child. You can't banish me to my room because your date got carted out of here by another man."

My jealousy is unwarranted, but there's no forsaking it. It clutches at me as vehemently as Brandon signing, *"Seek shelter now."* He only ever signed those words when the situation was beyond his control, or he was scared. Today it appears to be a combination of them both.

"Please be careful." Since fear is strangling my senses, I sign my worry instead of verbalizing it.

Only once Brandon dips his chin, wordlessly agreeing to my request, do I allow Fetu to guide me toward the elevator banks. Every step I take is done with hesitation. I'm not just fearful Brandon is sprinting headfirst into danger, I'm petrified I am seconds from being in the same room as Julian again. Not even on my darkest days can I lie to him.

I don't see today being any different.

BRANDON

As soon as the elevator doors snap shut with Melody and the giant she calls Tiny on the inside, I make my way to Hugo standing on the footpath outside of the hotel. The veins in his neck pump as rapidly as his fists clench and unclench.

"What's going on? Why did Isaac drag Izzy out of here like her life was in danger?"

I swear to God, if I fucked up by chasing the wrong cartel entity, I'll hand in my gun and badge first thing tomorrow. All intel pointed the finger at the Castros. The only surviving member of that syndicate is fighting for his life in a hospital as locked down as Fort Knox is, so why the fuck did Isaac rush Isabelle out of here the way he did? I get he's a little possessive when it comes to her, but he agreed for her to spend the weekend at my family's ranch, so it isn't like her attendance at the gala was a surprise to him.

"Did it have anything to do with Henry Gottle's pop-in visit?"

That piques Hugo's interest. "Henry was here?"

I lift my chin. I could have left him in the dark, but his responses are telling me honesty will work better for me. "They were chatting outside just a few minutes ago."

Hugo works his jaw side to side before straying his eyes to mine. "Henry isn't a threat to Isabelle."

What's behind everyone's sudden belief a mafia kingpin is a saint? First, Melody, now Hugo. Henry isn't as bad as his predecessor, but still, he's far from saintly. You can't kill without punishment and anticipate a clear ride to heaven. It would take an ocean full of holy water to save that man, and that's if he wanted to be saved.

My rant ends when Hugo pivots on his heels and races back into the lobby of the hotel. "Go back to your *date*, Blondie. You're not needed."

If I were a man who didn't care about his responsibilities, I'd use his dismissal as an excuse to reignite my conversation with Melody. Since I'm not, I yank my cell phone out of my pocket to call Grayson while making a beeline for the security office in the corner of the foyer. I'm not going to lie, I am running uncomfortably. I was so fucking hard while kissing Melody, I was certain when she broke away, I was about to be arrested for indecent exposure. I could have sworn my dick had busted through the zipper in my pants because it wasn't just the tip feeling its nasty bite. It gnawed at my shaft as much as my teeth gnawed on Melody's lips.

Since we're being honest, I'll also admit that I'm shocked. I never in a million years would have imagined the outcome of my kiss. I spotted Henry purely by chance. Although his focus was elsewhere, not even men with supermodel wives on their arm couldn't help but drink in Melody when she floated by. She has a regal, old-Hollywood vibe going on tonight with pinned back hair, red-painted lips, and a dress that had my cock reacting long before the scrumptious taste of her mouth.

With time short, I had to think on the spot. I thought Melody would pull away in anger when I kissed her before reminding me she's engaged. She did no such thing. She deepened my embrace before wholly ruling it. Her kiss—our kiss—fuck me. It was the best we've had, and we had plenty worthy of the hottest romance books. It pulled me under and made me feel like I couldn't breathe, all the while making it seem as if my life didn't end along with Joey's seven years ago. It just paused for a little.

I ignore my once-again hardening cock when Grayson finally connects my call. "Please tell me you have eyes on Henry."

"Unfortunately not. His driver is as friendly with the gas pedal as you." Grayson's voice echoes when he asks, "Why? Did he do a loop around?"

I disconnect our call and slide my phone into my pocket when he breaks through the rotating doors of the hotel's lobby. "I haven't seen him, but Isaac just raced out of here with Izzy under his arm like a missile strike had been ordered."

Grayson slips his phone into the breast pocket of his jacket before twisting his lips. "Isaac wouldn't see Henry as a threat. They're more allies than enemies. Someone else must have a bee in his bonnet." He nudges his head to the security office I was racing to before he returned. "Wanna play good cop or bad cop?"

"How about we play give us want we want, or we'll have the feds use your hotel lobby as their haunt until your 'special' guests find another venue to host their 'meetings.'" I air quote my last word.

Grayson smiles a blinding grin. "That'll work." He curls his arm around my shoulders before spinning me to face the security office. "That kiss changed you, and I'm not just talking about the funky growth in your pants. I feel like I'm standing across from that baby-faced teen who put an admissions officer double his age on his ass with nothing but a few words. I like it. It's done you good." He feels my growl more than he hears it when he murmurs, "Let's just hope her fiancé doesn't put a tempting bounty on your head, or I might consider cashing it in."

NINETY MINUTES and one turf war later, we've identified the man Hugo spent the past hour and a half searching for. It isn't who I was anticipating. He's from neither the Castros' nor the Bobrovs' crews. He's a Popov, which means he's related to Isabelle by blood.

"What are you doing?" Grayson asks when I yank my cell phone out of my pocket.

While *tsking* his daftness, I swipe my finger across the screen of my phone. "I don't owe Isaac shit, but I sure as hell do Isabelle. She deserves to know her brother is on the lookout for her."

After snatching my cell phone out of my hand, Grayson shuts it down, then throws it on the desk we're camped behind. "Leave it."

"Leave it? That man is a killer. He wasn't here for no reason, and if it was for any of the derived thoughts in my head, she deserves to know she's in danger."

Grayson scrubs at his jaw before sinking low in his chair. "Are we still talking about Izzy?"

"Don't turn this onto me, Grayson. I'm too fucking tired to deal with another one of your mind twists."

He folds his arms in front of his chest while shaking his head. "I'm not playing mind games. I am being straight-up honest. Enrique isn't a threat to Isabelle any more than Henry is to Melody—"

"Just because they're family doesn't give them a free pass from scrutiny."

"Doesn't it..." he pauses in a way that would make Joey proud, "... 'cause it certainly seems to be the case with your family." He doesn't let me get over his first hit before he whacks me with another. "You know your dad is as shady as shit. Have you done anything about it?" Stealing my chance to reply that I'm waiting for enough evidence to have him jailed instead of getting a slap on the wrist, he asks, "And what about your brother? You know Hugo didn't rape that girl, but have you done anything to prove that? And Joey's death? That's still classified as a suicide."

My jaw tightens to the point it feels like it's about to crack when he adds, "And what about your girl? You tried and convicted her with the weakest evidence, even after seeing the devastation on her face the night she supposedly 'cheated' on you." He air quotes 'cheated' while gagging. "If you think that's normal, you're more fucked-up than I realized. Girls don't cheat on the loves of their lives then act defensive. They grovel. They beg. They don't race out of the house with tears streaming down their face and cracked, broken lips."

Even with it feeling like my heart is being ripped out of my chest, I can't hold back my retaliation. "Why say all this now? Why not call me on it when it was happening?"

Grayson sits up straight before flopping his head to the side. "And add more shit to your plate? You were barely holding on." He gets a sternness in his eyes I've never seen before. "Your fuck-up with Olivia was proof of that." He pushes back from the desk before standing to his full height. "Leave that alone." He nudges his head to an image of Isabelle and Enrique. "'Cause you've got enough of your own shit to handle."

After removing the old-style compact disc from the digital recorder, he exits the office, not speaking another word and leaving me in shambles.

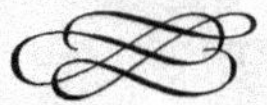

My eyes float up from my balled hands to Fetu when he enters the living room of the Presidential suite I'm not enjoying since numerous attempts to reach out to Julian have been thwarted. I've been back at our suite for almost two hours, yet I've not heard anything from neither Brandon nor Julian. I'm panicked out of my mind. Julian isn't known for disappearing acts, and Brandon usually finds me the instant the threat has passed.

"Anything?" I ask Fetu, hopeful Julian's security team knows of his whereabouts.

Fetu shakes his head. "I'm not surprised—" Before he can finish his sentence, the buzzer of the suite rattles my bones.

"Fingers crossed that's him." I race for the door before Fetu can. His legs are long, but the length of his strides have nothing on my determination.

The air in my lungs leaves in a hurry when I swing open the door. Not only is Brandon standing on the other side, so is Julian, although he isn't really standing. More leaning—*on Brandon.*

"Melly." Whiskey slaps me in the face when Julian stumbles my way. "I'b mizzed you, babe."

"Not quite as much as you missed the liquor bottle tonight." I catch him just before he falls, then Fetu backs up my staggered movements with his large frame. If he hadn't stood behind me, I'd be on my ass by now. That's how unstable Julian's sways are. "Did you drink any water tonight?"

Guilt crosses Brandon's face when Julian mumbles, "Water is for pussies… or pansies. What's the word again?"

"Either of them work." I grunt, struggling to keep him on his feet as I move him deeper into our suite. "Although I doubt that's true. Water is responsible." *Like you usually are.*

My heart does a weird flutter thingamabob when Brandon says, "Here, let me." He slides his arm around Julian's waist before pulling him back into his side as he was when I opened the door. "Which one is the master suite?"

"I'll take him."

Brandon shrugs off Fetu's offer like he's not dragging a man the same weight and height as him across a ballroom-size suite. "It's fine. I've got him." A faulty battery could be causing me to mishear things, but I swear Brandon adds, "It's the least I can do since his drunkenness is my fault."

After following Fetu into the master suite, Brandon flops Julian onto the mattress before dropping to his knees to remove his shoes. When Julian pats his head like he's a good puppy, the color drains from Brandon's cheeks. He isn't annoyed. He is feeling guilty.

"He's nice. I like him," Julian mumbles through hiccups. "You do, too, don't you, Melly?" I'm not a fan of his new nickname, however, I'd rather it over the pained look in his eyes when he drifts them my way. They're bloodshot and massively dilated, but they're still the same truth-bearing eyes I've grown to love the past three years, so I'm confident he knows I kissed Brandon. Just like I know it's tearing him up inside.

Hating how much I've hurt him, I join Brandon's mission to make him as comfortable as possible. "Let's get your jacket off. You'll get too hot if you sleep in it."

Every mumble of praise Julian bombards me with as I help him out of his tuxedo jacket before untethering his bowtie stabs my heart with pain. I deserve it. I deceived him when he's been nothing but faithful to me.

"Tell me you love me, Melly."

I accept the glass of water from Fetu and place it onto the bedside table before cupping Julian's cheek. "I do love you. I love you very much." I'm not lying. I do love him. I just don't deserve him. "We'll talk more in the morning, okay?" When he nods, I wipe away the tear rolling down my cheek before pulling the comforter up to cover him.

In faster than a heartbeat, I've switched off the light and partially closed his door, and even quicker than that, Brandon heads for the exit, his brisk strides only slowing when I whisper, "He knows we kissed, doesn't he?"

With his back facing me, and his shoulders low, Brandon nods.

"Did you tell him?" It's pathetic of me to try and shunt some of the blame onto a third party, but it seems to be my go-to party trick lately. I could use the excuse that a burden shared is a burden halved, but that isn't the case here. I'm just too weak to carry the load alone.

My father would be so disappointed.

When Brandon pivots around to face me, even Fetu feels the frustration radiating out of him. He places himself between us like Brandon is a threat to my safety. He isn't but only because his words are more damaging than his fists could ever be.

"Why would I tell him, Melody? So he could experience the pain I did seven years ago? I assumed you thought better of me. Clearly, I'm not the only one who had a major shift in personality when we merged into the real world."

After requesting for Fetu to leave and watching his hesitant exit, I devote all my attention to Brandon. This argument has been years in the making, and I'm reasonably sure it will be a doozy, so I'd rather it occur without witnesses. "You're not being fair."

"And neither are you," Brandon fires back, fighting the urge to shout. "Do you have any idea how hard that was for me to hear?" He thrusts his hand toward the room running water is sounding from. Julian must be hoping a hot shower will sober him up. "It killed me hearing it from him, but no, that's not enough punishment for you, Brandon. You kissed another man's girl, so you don't just get to hear him gush about how she's going to be his wife. You get to hear the woman you love tell another man she loves him. That's fucked, Melody. That is so fucked."

I barely get a second to get over the shock he still loves me when he confesses, "We had a great chat during our elevator ride. Julian was telling me all the things I had missed out on…" his nostrils flare as he growls, "… such as your wedding date being brought forward to next month."

When I balk but remain quiet, Brandon reads the truth from my eyes. It doubles the anger in his before it adds a frantic tick to his jaw. Julian and I were planning to get married next year, but Julian requested for us to bring the wedding forward earlier this week. I thought he meant by six or so months. I had no clue he wanted it so soon. Since I was still shocked at how complex my life has become the past few weeks, and feeling somewhat guilty about my recent contact with Brandon, I agreed to Julian's request.

My heart falls from my ribcage when Brandon asks, "Is every guest getting a last-minute invitation? Or did you just happen to lose mine as quickly as you fell out of love with me?"

"I didn't lie when I said I love you. You're a part of my life, BJ. You always will be."

Disbelief flashes through his eyes when he asks, "Then why did you move across the country without me? Why did you cheat on me?" Nothing but pain is heard in his voice when he mutters, "And why did you agree to marry him? That wasn't the plan, Melody. He was never in our plans."

"You don't know what it was like for me. I was alone. I didn't have anyone."

"Because you never gave me the chance to be there for you. You ran. You lied. You gave up on us—"

"For you!" I shout as devastation overwhelms me. "I did that for you."

"I didn't want it!" Brandon's roar shudders my heart out of my chest. "I didn't want any of that." He bangs his chest as he takes two steps closer to me. "I wanted you. I *always* wanted you." His eyes are as wet as mine when he says, "But the one time I *needed* you, you weren't there for me. You left... as I am now." After throwing open the suite door, he cranks his neck back my way. "Have a nice life, Melody. I hope he gives you everything I couldn't."

Confident I'll never see him again if I let him leave, I whisper, "You promised to protect me for eternity."

I realize I've lost him forever when he mutters, "That stopped being my job when you broke the vows we recited to each other eighteen years ago."

BRANDON

I swirl the dregs of a double shot of whiskey around the bottom of my glass. It's my sixth the past hour, a new record for me. I could have driven home, but I needed something to take the edge off. The location where my brother was murdered isn't the ideal spot for that to take place.

I also can't bring myself to leave. I don't know why. It could be because I don't want to drive back in the darkness of the night when the lie I told Melody gets the better of me. Or perhaps it's because my lie is already eating at me.

Whatever it is, I'm here, sitting in the hotel bar of the girl I'll never stop loving, drinking whiskey to fill the void in my chest where my heart once stood.

Hearing Melody tell Julian she loved him gutted me. It stung more than Julian's confession that they're getting married next month. Every report I had read on their upcoming nuptials said no date had been set, so you can imagine how hard the knock to my stomach was when I discovered it's only twenty-seven days away.

I should have told Julian he's too late. Melody is already married. We didn't have a celebrant, and we ate our Ring Pop wedding rings at our reception, but the vows we spoke certainly seemed real. I guess everything feels real to eight-year-olds who have no clue how fucked up adulthood can be.

It could be worse. Melody could have been walked down the aisle by her mother like Wren did for us that day. She thought it was 'cute' that we wanted our commitment ceremony witnessed by an adult. She even signed our fake marriage certificate. It's in our time capsule. The one Melody reburied so I wouldn't find the love letter she hid inside.

I stop reminiscing on all the places she could have buried it when a familiar voice jingles in my ears. Madden is making his way to the bar. His staggered walk is being followed by three of his friends. One I recognize even with the years not being kind to him. It's Connor Eckhart—the instigator of Melody's and my very first fight. He's looking a little haggard, kind of how I imagine Phoenix would have looked if he hadn't gotten off the drugs.

After ordering a round of drinks like he's one of the rock stars in the main area of the gala, Madden slings his eyes around the bar, seeking a vacant spot for him and his friends. I don't sink into the shadows. Madden's head is so far up his ass, he wouldn't recognize his own brother if he were standing directly in front of him, so my station in the corner of the room won't be noticed.

When my assumption is proven accurate, I throw down the last of my drink before requesting another. The bartender is generous with my refill. The fifty I threw in his tip jar when I arrived has served me well.

I switch from guzzling my drink to nursing it when the big gulp I take goes straight to my head. I'm not a heavy alcohol drinker, but even if I were, no amount of alcohol would have me missing the lady making her way to the counter. Even with her body covered in sweats and her wet hair hanging halfway down her back, I'd never forget the wild kinks her dirty blonde locks get when she lets it dry naturally, much less her gorgeous face.

It dawns on me that Melody isn't here to drown her sorrows

when the bartender hands her a leather wallet. It isn't the feminine type and considering this is the only bar in this hotel, I'm quick to realize who it belongs to.

After issuing her thanks to the bartender with a halfhearted smile, Melody spins on her heels, preparing to exit. Unlike Madden, she spots my stalk in an instant. Her lips part so she can suck in a shallow breath as her red-rimmed eyes prepare for another bout of crying. Our argument hurt her as much as it did me. I'm confident of that.

A single tear plops onto her cheek when I sign, *"I am sorry."*

She looks set to issue an apology of her own but loses the chance when Connor notices her standing at the bar. I'm shocked it took him so long to spot her. She's not dressed to the nines like the other women in the overly populated establishment, but she doesn't need a ritzy dress to be notable. She's captivating just as she is.

I can't see what Connor is signing to Melody, but her facial expression gives a clear indication she isn't interested in anything he's selling, and I won't mention the lewd gestures Madden and his two friends are making behind Melody's back, or it may tempt me to test the versatility of the weapon on my hip.

Just as I stand to my feet, over my pigheaded brother's lack of respect, Connor returns to his seat. His friends rally around him, acting as if Melody's rejection occurred in the middle of prom. I'm not surprised. Madden still acts like he's in high school when he gets a few drinks in him.

I think the worst is over, but not even two seconds later, I'm proven wrong. The color drains from Melody's face as her hand shoots up to clamp her mouth. As her chest thrusts like she can't suck in an entire breath, she cranks her neck back to peer at Madden and his friends. Her ghost-like stare ends their vulgarity in an instant. Even Madden seems taken aback—even more so when Melody upends his table, sending a jug of beer and six shots of Jägermeister spilling into his lap.

Even with a flipped table lodged between them, Melody is up in Madden's face in an instant. "You fucking pig!"

When she bangs on his chest with her fists, its hollow echoes launch me into action. No matter how hard she fights, she'll never drum any sense into a heartless man. It's not possible. I gave up on Madden six years ago for that very reason. Attempting to teach him morals is like flogging a dead horse. Utterly pointless.

"I thought it was him. I thought it was Joey!" Melody shouts as I band my arm around her waist to pull her back.

"It was him," Madden defends when I walk Melody toward the exit. "Don't try to pin that shit on me because you're running out of money."

Madden's reply agitates Melody more. She kicks and thrashes against me as she hurls abuse at Madden. She tells him she fucking hates him, and how she wishes it was him who was dead. She claws and screams and throws out threats as if they're grenades. Her rant only ends when my attempt to remove her from a volatile situation veers us past my mom. She freezes in an instant as the fury on her face switches to remorse.

"I'm sorry, so *so* sorry," she mutters to my mom on repeat, the anger gone from her voice. "I didn't know it wasn't him. I swear, I didn't know."

She repeats the same phrase another two times before the elevator doors closing gobbles up her words. I assumed a quiet, confined area would help get back her headspace, but it seems to do the opposite. The instant I jab the button for the Presidential suite, words fly out of Melody's mouth nonstop.

"I thought it was him. He was wearing his shoes. He had on your cologne." I place her onto her feet, fretful my clutch around her waist is hampering her breathing when she shudders through her last sentence. "He had no facial hair. None." It dawns on me how hard she's shaking when she runs her hand across my recently shaved jaw. "You had prickles. You didn't bother shaving when we weren't at school." She drops her hand, the wetness in her eyes doubling. "He must have shaved." She hiccups three times before adding devastatingly, "He wanted me to think he was Joey."

"Who wanted you to think they were Joey?"

She folds in two when Joey's name comes toppling out of my mouth. "Oh, Joey. I'm so sorry." Her apology is utterly gut-wrenching. It steals the air from my lungs as quickly as it does Melody's. She claws at her throat, begging for the strangling hold to lessen so she can secure a full breath.

"Breathe, Melody," I demand when her wheezy grapple for air has her face whitening to the point she looks seconds from passing out.

"I… thought… it was him," she squeaks between gasps.

"Don't worry about that now. Just breathe," I beg, panicked about how shallow her breathing is. With how frantic her chest thrusts with each breath she takes, her lungs shouldn't be working as hard as they are. "Take big breaths for me, Mellowy. Big, calming breaths."

When the elevator dings announcing our arrival at Melody's floor, the fret in my voice is replaced by someone I didn't anticipate. Julian is standing in the hallway dressed in a similar pair of sweats as Melody.

"Mel, what's going on?" The slight slur of his words reveals he's still drunk, but there's nothing like finding your fiancée in the midst of a panic attack to sober you up.

After pulling her out of the elevator car, Julian runs his eyes over every inch of Melody's face and body. The horrified expression on his face proves he loves her. He's just as devastated by the hollow look in her eyes as I am. It proves in an instant the money I found in Castro's safe wasn't for anything illegal. If it was, I'm certain it was to protect Melody.

Julian's eyes snap to mine when Melody croaks out, "I… can't… breathe."

Since he's lost on what to do, I move him out of my way before cupping my hands over Melody's ears. When I lower my forehead to balance against hers, then commence counting to ten, her nostrils mimic the flare of mine.

"Five Mississippi's. Six Mississippi's. Seven Mississippi's. Eight—"

Julian's whiskey-scented breath fans my cheek when Melody whispers, "Mississippi's. Nine Mississippi's. Ten Mississippi's."

"That's it, Mellowy. Big breaths. In and out. In and out."

As her eyes lower to lip-read my confirmation that she's okay and that I'll never let anything happen to her, sparks of the old Melody I once knew form in her eyes. She's fighting to claw her way out of the dark cloud attempting to swallow her whole, and I'm so fucking proud of her.

"Look at you. So brave and so—"

"Pretty," she says with me.

It's the worst time for me to smile, but I can't help it. "And so *damn* pretty," I correct.

Damn was on Wren's naughty list of words. I only found out about her dislike during Melody's and my mocked wedding. Supposedly, it's impolite to say damn during your vows.

My comment breaks through the dense cloud swarming Melody before it breaks her heart. "I'm so sorry, BJ. I didn't know. I thought it was Joey. This whole time I thought it was Joey."

Although skeptical she's fully out of the woods just yet, my curiosity is too strong to harness. "You thought who was Joey?"

I'm lost to what she means, but Julian isn't. "It wasn't Joey?"

Tears roll down Melody's cheeks when she answers Julian's question by shaking her head. "It was Madden."

"Madden… what does Madden have to do with this?"

I discover the reason for Melody's near breakdown when Julian snarls, "He raped her. All these years she thought it was Joey, but it wasn't, it was Madden." He drags a hand over his head like his confession is as shocking for him as it is for me. "How did you find out?"

Melody's focus isn't on Julian. I don't even know if she heard his question. She's staring straight at me, the truth in her eyes hitting me with blow after blow after blow.

My brother raped her.

He *raped* her.

"When?" I'm not authenticating her claims, I can see the truth in her eyes. I want to know the exact moment Liam's worry was founded.

I pledged to protect his daughter.

I swore an oath to keep her safe.

I fucked up.

Then I almost fold in two when Melody whispers, "Joey's summer party."

"The night you were upset because I wasn't there for you." I'm not asking questions. I am slotting the pieces of the puzzle together, one painful piece at a time. "That's why you left. He's the reason you left me." The whiskey in my gut gurgles when I'm hit by another revelation. "You didn't cheat. You said you had slept with someone because to you, it wasn't a lie."

Melody's voice is as low as my heart is sitting. "I knew you wouldn't let me leave unless I gave you a reason to hate me."

"Melody… *fuck.*" My fist breaks through the drywall at my side when the anger steamrolling into me becomes too much to bear. I failed her. Me. The man who pledged to keep her safe. That's unfor-givable.

As is Madden's crime.

"BJ, wait!" Melody shouts when I throw open the emergency fire exit door next to the elevator. "Let me go, Julian," she screams at him when he thwarts her attempts to follow my frantic gallop down the stairwell. "This has nothing to do with you. I need to be there for him!"

It's for the best he keeps her away. She knows I'm going to kill the man who hurt her. She doesn't need to witness it. Furthermore, I'm shocked she can look me in the eyes as it is. I don't want anything to taint that when I switch from a law-abiding citizen to a murderer.

By the time I've reached the foyer of the hotel, I'm sweating profusely, and my anger is at an all-time high. Everything now makes sense—Melody's decision to move across the country, her inability to say a proper goodbye to Joey, her response to Olivia's bogus claims I had abused my position to force her to sleep with me.

God, it must have killed Melody reading Olivia's witness statement. It would have made it seem as if Madden's assault is never-ending.

That's why I must end him, or Melody will never be at peace.

"Madden!" As I barge through the throng of people making their way from the ballroom the gala was held in to the hotel's entrance, I unharness my gun. I'm so worked up right now, I doubt I'll need it, but I'd rather be prepared.

"Madd—" My second shout clogs in my throat when I spot him under the awning of the hotel, waiting on the valet.

"You're dead," I mouth to him when he swings his head my way.

He thinks he is safe since he's standing next to our mother. He's dead fucking wrong. I'm out the door in an instant, the crowd no match for my determination.

Just as I break through the group of partygoers separating us, Madden darts down a side alley. I'm not surprised he's running. He's a coward. All cowards run.

I'm nipping at his heels before he's halfway down the piss-scented passageway, and even quicker than that, I toss him up against the brickwork. Once he's landed onto the stained concrete with a thud, I punish his ribs with my shoes.

"You raped my girlfriend, you fucking piece of shit!" Three good kicks have him coughing up blood and gains us an audience. I don't pay them any attention. There's no one in this alley but me and the piece of trash I'm about to exterminate. "Bet she wasn't your first victim, either, was she?"

With him gargling more than talking, I drag him to his feet before pinning him to the brickwork by his throat. My already dangerous heart rate skyrockets when he has the nerve to spit the blood in his mouth into my face. "Just because a bitch feels guilty after straying, doesn't mean she was raped."

Madden's lungs rattle when I yank him forward before throwing him back. The crack his head makes with the brickwork is lyrical gold to my ears, but his wheezy breaths steal every sense of normality I have. "She despised everything about you."

"Until she realized you couldn't give her what she wanted."

Thump, crack, motherfucking bang. I steal his words by breaking his ribs. "You wore my cologne. You shaved your beard." My grip on his throat tightens as I snarl through clenched teeth, "Why the fuck would you do any of those things if she wanted to be with you? You wouldn't have. That's why I know you raped her. You raped her like you did Annie and Gemma, and God knows how many other women. You're a fucking rapist!"

"Whoa, whoa, whoa, what the fuck, BJ," Madden stutters in panic when I remove my revolver from its harness to pinch the barrel with his temple. "You need to step the fuck back and remember blood always comes before water."

"You're not my family."

My eyes bounce between his as the world fades to nothing. I don't feel the begging eyes of my mother or hear her frantic gasps. It's just him and me. The lawbreaker and the vigilante. The rapist and the protector. Two men on the verge of death, but only one will go straight to hell. My journey will be slower, more painful, only occurring once I've fixed all the mistakes I've made.

Madden's will be now.

"You're a dead man."

I unclick the safety of my gun before inching back the trigger. Nothing is on my mind, not a single fucking thing. Liam was right. Sometimes the world doesn't need another hero.

They need a monster.

"Save a spot for our father in hell. I'm sure he'll be joining you there shortly because the men who hide rapists are just as evil as the ones committing the heinous acts."

My gun is cocked, the safety is off, but before I can send Madden to hell for his sins, I'm crash-tackled from the side. With Grayson putting all his weight behind his hit, we skid across the sidewalk before landing on the asphalt with a thud. Our impact with the rigid material shreds my pants, but it has nothing on the fury it bombards me with.

"Get the fuck off me!" I scream at Grayson, fighting to get out of his clutch.

He holds on tight, not relinquishing his grip in the slightest. "We'll get him, Brandon, but not like this. Not in front of your mother."

I continue to fight him, needing to end Madden's life before the pain tearing me in two ends mine. "He raped her, Grayson. He fucking raped her!"

His voice is lower than mine, more controlled. "I know, punk, I know. We'll get him. I promise you, he'll pay for what he's done. Just not like this. Not here. I won't have you locked up because of him. Melody needs you."

"He raped her." This confirmation doesn't come out as stern as my first since it's choked by a sob. "He fucking raped her. My Melody. He hurt my Melody."

As Grayson pins me to the ground as effectively as two plain-clothed officers do Madden to place cuffs on him, I break.

Not a little.

Not subtly.

I break wholly and without constraint.

MELODY

I shake my head when Julian jingles a decanter of whiskey from the bar in the living room of our suite my way. I'm still mad at him. He had no right to tell Brandon what he did, no right at all. He wasn't the one who was raped, so he doesn't get to choose who I share my secret with.

Furthermore, even in the midst of a terrifying panic attack, I couldn't miss the horrifying way he blurted out my news. Could you imagine how Brandon felt finding out his brother raped his girlfriend in his childhood home from the man she's planning to marry? That's a fucked-up set of circumstances. One I'd give anything to rewind and change.

I had only just gotten out of the shower when the receptionist from the hotel called to say Julian's wallet had been found in the bar downstairs. Julian offered to collect it when he overheard our call, but since the shower hadn't helped to unravel the massive knot in my stomach from my confrontation with Brandon, I thought a couple of minutes of fresh air would do me some good.

I also wanted to keep Julian away from alcohol since our room smelled like a distillery.

Part of me wants to say if I had known the outcome of my quick visit to the lobby, I would have asked Fetu to go down. The other half knows that's a lie. For years, I was convinced it was Joey who had raped me. I saw his shoes. I felt the smoothness of his chin. I was certain it was him.

I would still be convinced if Madden isn't as disgusting as he is abhorrent.

His comment was the weakest, most underhanded rile, but it flicked on the lightbulb in my head in an instant. He told Connor not to feel bad about my rejection because "Deaf girls aren't as vocal in bed as people make them out to be." I could have brushed off his comment as being a generalization of hearing-impaired females if he hadn't added, "Once I flipped her over and pinned her arms behind her back, she stopped fighting *and* moaning. Worst fuck I've ever had."

When my eyes rocketed to his, his face gave him away in less than a nanosecond. He wasn't just shocked I had heard what he said, he was panicked, aware Brandon wouldn't care that they share the same blood. No one is off-limits when it comes to protecting me.

My first response was anger. I was mad as hell to be standing across from the man who had raped me. Madden should count his lucky stars the closest weapon I had was his table.

Remorse only overtook my anger when my eyes collided with Mrs. McGee's as Brandon dragged me out of the bar. She wasn't upset I was making a spectacle of myself in front of important dignitaries I'm certain to cross at some stage in my career. She looked heartbroken like she knew my secret. But even worse than that was the guilt on her face. I don't know why she'd feel guilt. She hadn't done anything wrong. I was the one painting her deceased son as a rapist.

I'm drawn from my thoughts when the buzzer of the Presidential suite shudders my heart out of my chest. When my eyes stray to Julian, too nervous as to who could be visiting, he places down the whiskey decanter. "I'll get it."

My breathing stops, my eyes refuse to blink, and my heart doesn't beat when I follow Julian's solemn trek to the door. The low hang of his shoulders reveals the words I screamed at him when he thwarted my wish to follow Brandon's hasty retreat hurt him, but in all honesty, I won't apologize for them. I don't recall what I said, much less have had the time to decipher if they were honest or not. I've been too busy wearing a hole in the rug, pacing.

My heart falls from my ribcage when Julian swings open the door to display Brandon standing on the other side. Excluding some droplets of blood on the collar of his dress shirt, he appears relatively uninjured. It's the broken, lost boy I see in his eyes causing my stuttering response. He looks as defeated as I did when I peered at my reflection for the first time after my assault.

He's hurting—badly.

My heart breaks for him when he signs, *"I am so sorry—"*

"Don't," I sign back, stopping his unnecessary apology as quickly as I push off my feet.

"I failed, Melody. I did exactly what your father said I would do."

I push down his hands so he can't sign another stupid word before I throw my arms around his neck. His raging pulse vibrates my lips when I press them against the shell of his ear. *"You* didn't fail. *I* didn't fail. *Madden* did. This isn't our fault, BJ. We're not to blame for *anything* that happened."

He's set to argue, but I don't give him a chance. After inching back, I pull him into the entryway, kick the door closed, guide him to the couch, then crawl onto his lap. While comforting him how I should have after Joey's death, I tell him I'm sorry for how badly he's hurting and that I wasn't there for him when I should have been.

I can't tell if he believes me or not, his emotions are a little hard for me to read, but I don't give up. I'll stay in his arms until either the sun breaks through the curtains or my words break through the wall Brandon has erected between us.

My father always said the only time you fail is when you stop trying.

I stopped trying years ago.

That needs to end, and it will end with Brandon.

AS MY EYES slowly flutter open, I discover the reason the softness of cashmere is gracing my skin. Someone laid a blanket over Brandon and me. It must have occurred sometime after three this morning because the last time I glanced at my watch, it was only a few minutes away.

I won't lie. The six or so hours before exhaustion overcame me were some of the toughest in my life. I couldn't free Brandon from the torment eating him alive without hurting him. It was a cruel and twisted time, but it was also healing.

Not just for Brandon but me as well.

Although I cried more than I talked, it took the same amount of words for Brandon to comfort me. The sound of his heart thudding against my ear. The warmth of his hand running down my back. Even the way his five o'clock shadow tickled the tip of my nose when fatigue slowly overtook me was oddly soothing.

For the first time in years, I'm waking up minus the tired headache I usually have. I'm shocked I got any sleep. Brandon and I are still in the weird, pretzel-like cuddle we fell asleep in. It's not the most comfortable position to rest in, however, a soul doesn't need pristine conditions to heal. It just needs love.

That's probably why I'm minus a thumping skull.

My soul finally feels whole again.

Brandon lets out a grumble when I untangle myself from him, but mercifully, he remains asleep. He didn't get as many hours as me. The dark shadows under his eyes are proof of this, not to mention I heard him murmur my name when I startled myself a little after four this morning.

After a stretch to loosen my tight muscles, I cover Brandon with the blanket draped over us before making my way to the kitchen at the back of the living room. Julian usually has a coffee waiting for me on the bedside table any time I wake, so today I'm not just missing the groggy smile he normally delivers it with, I'm in desperate need of a sharp shot of caffeine.

My sluggish steps slow even more when I notice a suitcase sitting neatly outside the master suite doors. It's Julian's suitcase, and mine aren't stacked next to them like they generally are.

"Julian…" I murmur before pushing open the partially open door of his suite. The healing my heart did overnight is shoved back a step when his eyes float up from his hands to me. He's dressed in a powerhouse-ready suit, and he's clean-shaven, but his usually alluring gaze is lost and broken. "Are you going somewhere?"

The daftness of my question can be easily excused. He's like Brandon. He only shaves when required.

A lump lodges in my throat when I realize what Julian was eyeballing when I entered. He has our matching wedding bands out of their boxes. He brought them with us so he could have them engraved by a jeweler down the street from our hotel. With everything that happened yesterday, we've yet to get them done.

After placing the rings onto a handwritten letter, Julian stands to his feet. He sways slightly like he's still drunk, even though I'm confident he isn't. His eyes are too alert to belong to a drunken man. "I'm going home."

"Okay," I push out, confused as to why he's ending our trip early. We still have another two nights booked and paid for. "Give me a few minutes to get my things in order, then I'll request for Fetu to bring the car around."

I stop heading for the walk-in closet when he murmurs, "I'm not returning to New York. I'm going home. Back to California."

"Oh… why?" My daftness is justified. Excluding last night, we've had an almost perfect relationship. "If it was what I said last night—"

"It wasn't anything you said." As he struggles not to respond to the tears welling in my eyes, he rakes his fingers through his ginger locks. He hates when I cry. "Do you remember when we watched *The Notebook?*"

Salty blobs almost fall from my eyes when I nod. "Much to your dislike." That was the movie we watched when we went to the cinema as friends for the first time.

Julian smiles. It isn't his full smile, but I'll still take it. "At the end of the movie, you said something that didn't resonate with me until last night. You said it wouldn't have mattered who Allie ended up with because no matter what, Noah would always be her number one." He licks his dry lips before continuing. "It didn't make any sense to me. If Allie and Noah weren't together, how could he possibly still be her number one." His breathless chuckle is more pained than in glee. "Then, I saw you with Brandon, and I knew exactly what you meant. When you were panicked, I couldn't settle you. Brandon could. When you run in fear, you run away from me as well. When Brandon ran, you wanted to run into the fire with him."

Finally clueing in on where he's taking our conversation, I say, "That doesn't mean I don't love you, Julian. I do. I love you."

"I know," he replies, his voice cracking. "And I love you too… but I'll always be your number two."

Tears topple down my cheeks when I shake my head, trying to deny a truth I've always known. "No, you won't."

"Yes, I will," Julian immediately fires back. "When I placed a blanket over you and Brandon last night, I realized I deserve to have someone who'll sleep sitting up to comfort me. I deserve to have someone who looks at me how you look at Brandon. I deserve to be someone's number one, too."

"You do," I agree, nodding. "You deserve the world."

I'm not lying. Julian is the perfect man. He just isn't Brandon. Brandon was my first love, the man I loved before he was a man. I don't see anyone *ever* being able to compete with that, but that doesn't mean I also can't feel guilt.

"I'm sorry, Julian. For the years wasted, for the pain. I never meant to hurt you."

"No." He bands his arms around me before pulling me in close to his fit body. "This isn't on you, Mel. You never promised me anything you couldn't give me." He wipes away the tears streaming down my face before raising my chin to a position it doesn't deserve to be in. "In all honesty, I just didn't realize what I was missing out on until this weekend." His smile shouldn't be as comforting as it is, especially considering the circumstances, but for some strange reason, it is. "My campaign is probably a little long in the tooth, but I want to be selfish for just a moment."

Aware his comment has nothing to do with his political dreams, I assure him, "Love isn't selfish, Julian. Wanting to be loved unconditionally isn't selfish." I wipe under my nose with the sleeve of my shirt before squashing my ear to his chest. "It hurts thinking about you with anyone else, but the pain won't be as bad if it gives you the happily ever after you deserve. I'm sorry that person couldn't be me, Julian. I truly never meant to hurt you."

He doesn't reply. He doesn't need to. The extra flutter his heart got during my apology tells me everything I need to know. He is also sorry things didn't work out between us, but he's optimistic our relationship was a necessary path we had to take to make us better people.

I wholeheartedly agree with him. I wouldn't be the woman I am now if I had never met Julian. For that alone, I'll forever adore him.

We stay huddled together in the middle of Julian's room until the buzz of the Presidential suite doorbell rings through my ears. It adds an extra thump to Julian's heart, whereas it floods my eyes with fresh tears.

"That will be Fetu. He's driving me to the airport." After pressing his lips to my temple, Julian moves to the bed to gather the last of his belongings. "This is for Brandon." He folds the handwritten letter into quarters before handing it to me. "If he doesn't follow this exactly, I'll be back to kick his ass as I'm still kind of wishing I had done last night when he kissed you."

"Julian—" He pushes his finger to my lips, stopping my apology before it's close to being delivered.

Nothing but honesty rings in his tone when he says, "It felt like a million knives were being stabbed into my chest, but it was the sign I had been seeking the past nine months." Salty blobs slip down my face when he cups my cheeks so he can press his lips to my forehead. "I'll never regret us, Mel. You'll always have a place in my story. It just won't be the number one spot." I nod, deserving the flip his comment hit my stomach with. "Stay in touch."

"I will," I reply, shadowing him to the foyer. Although I can't see Brandon, I know he's awake. I can feel his eyes on me. He's keeping his distance because even a blind man would be able to see the tension bristling between Julian and me. It isn't an uneasy feeling, more sentimental than anything. "Will you tell your mom I said hello?"

Julian smiles a true grin. "I will… but I think she'd rather hear it from you."

"Okay." I suck in a big breath, relieved the end of our relationship doesn't mean I lose him altogether. I care for his mother, so losing her as well would have doubled the blow. "Thank you."

Julian dips his chin before handing his suitcase to Fetu and shadowing him to the idling elevator. Confident all is said and done, I commence closing the door, only stopping when Julian calls my name. "Yeah?"

Fresh tears burn my ears when he says, "Don't let that son of a bitch get away with what he did to you. You fight him until the end."

"I will." Even looking like a wreck, nothing can take away from the determination on my face.

"Good girl," Julian murmurs before he enters the elevator car on Fetu's heel.

Just before the doors close, I sign something I should have never withheld from him. "*I love you.*"

His smile eases the pain stretched across my chest before his reply utterly alleviates it. *"I love you too. I will never stop."*

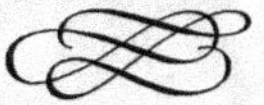

"How is she holding up?"

As my eyes stray from Melody, who's being led into the interview room at Saugerties PD, to Grayson, I prop my ankle onto my opposite knee, praying it will stop their nervous bobs. "She's doing okay considering. For years, she thought justice had been served. She had no clue the sick fuck was still walking the streets assaulting other women."

Grayson's jaw tightens at my last sentence, but since he can't deny my underhanded claim that Madden is a serial rapist, he shifts his focus elsewhere. "And your mom?"

The knot in my stomach tightens as I recall the expression on my mother's face when Madden was placed into the back of a police cruiser three days ago. She was pleased he was alive but devastated at the same time. She knows her children, so even with Madden denying all claims he raped Melody, she knows what he did to her. She was already struggling to work out how to tell me Joey's death wasn't suicide, so this really knocked her for a loop.

Contractors working on the house found surveillance cameras planted around the ranch in inconspicuous places. From the scope of the equipment and where they were planted, it was clear who had placed them there—Mr. Gregg.

Although the evidence was damning, the leading hand refused to let my mom watch the footage imbedded on a micro USB stick he found in one of the devices. He told her what had happened, then advised her to call the police.

She did precisely that two hours before Madden arrived at the ranch late last week. When he took the evidence the builder had given her, he told her our father would take care of it.

The USB hasn't been seen since.

When Grayson brushes his knee against mine, prompting me to answer his question, I give honesty a whirl for the first time the past three days, "She's faring better than expected, but she's still struggling. She believes Melody and has essentially banished Madden from her life, but she's blaming herself for his actions like she didn't raise him right or something."

"You can't fix fucked," Grayson mutters with a sigh.

"Right?"

After lifting his chin, Grayson scrubs at the wiry beard covering his jaw. "And what about you, punk? How have you been coping the past few days?"

This question is harder to answer than his first two. I truly don't know how I'm functioning. I'm moving, eating, and talking, but I still feel hollow on the inside. This isn't a standard second-chance romance story. I don't get to ride in on a white horse and save the day. I'm too late. Melody has already been hurt just like her father said she'd be.

Grayson reads me in a way not many people can. "You're taking all the right steps. You got her here, she's pressing charges. Now you need to let the system do the heavy lifting while you take care of you and your girl."

"What if they fail her like I did?" I ask, expressing the real reason I can't shake my depressing funk. "What happens then?"

Grayson scoots to the edge of his chair before slanting his head so he's facing me front on. "We do what we've always done. We get justice for the innocent." He slaps my shoulder two times before giving it a gentle squeeze. "Don't let *him* beat you down with his mind games, Brandon."

His sneer when he says 'him' reveals who he's referencing. He's not talking about Madden. His focus is on my father, the man Madden cited as his defense attorney when he was arrested for rape for the second time in his pathetic twenty-nine years.

As luck would have it, the judge at his preliminary hearing was Annie's grandfather. Annie was the first person to accuse Madden of sexual assault. Although no charges were filed for her assault, Judge Pearce took an instant disliking to Madden. He refused his request for bail before he dismissed my charge of battery under the guise it was self-defense.

"If he defeats you, he defeats her." Grayson nudges his head in the direction Melody just went. "You don't want that, do you?"

"No," I answer without pause for thought. "He's going down with Madden."

"Good. Then let's do that." He drops his eyes to the outline of my cell phone in my pocket. "Give me your phone. I've got some stuff I need you to take a look at."

"I can't work right now, Grayson. My focus has gone to shit." Although I'm saying no, I still dig my phone out of my pocket and hand it to him.

"You won't need to concentrate for this." He unlocks my phone without asking for the passcode before logging into the Bureau's mainframe. "Have you got access to a laptop at your fancy hotel?" When I shake my head, he snags his frumpy old leather suitcase from the ground. "This one is as old as shit, but it'll get the job done."

When I crack open the screen, it requests a passcode. "It's locked."

"You know how your passwords are *always* Melody's birthday."

He laughs a breathless chuckle when I rib him with my elbow. "Tobias's were Isabelle's."

I twist my lips, not surprised by his reply, but shocked about one thing. "Why do you have Tobias's laptop?"

Grayson's smile isn't one I've seen before. "Not even the sharpest minds retain the sweetest memories correctly." He nudges his head to the laptop. "That's full of them." I only just catch my phone when he tosses it back my way. "I put the file's deets in your notes. If you can, I'd like your thoughts by tonight."

"Tonight? Fuckin' hell, Grayson. I just said I'm not up for any work."

Ignoring me, he stands to his feet. "Do you love your girl, punk?"

The tightness of my jaw is heard in my reply. "If you need to ask, I clearly did a shit job of showing it back in the day."

"Not then. Now. Do you love your girl now as you did back then?"

Grayson looks shocked when I shake my head. He has no reason to fret. "I love her more. She's so brave, Grayson. So fucking strong." I give my tired eyes a quick scrub before continuing, "But it's not the time to show her that. Julian only broke off their engagement three days ago. Her heart is broken, so it isn't right for me to pretend she is not hurting." I also don't think I am up to the task. I'm not myself. Not in the slightest.

My eyes float up from my clenched fists when Grayson asks, "So friends can't help friends when they're hurting? Friends can't admit when they were wrong and underhandedly beg for forgiveness?"

Even knowing part of his comment resonates with his guilt over what happened to Melody, I won't call him out on it—today. He didn't technically knock me out the night Melody was raped, that was Tobias, but even if he had, what happened wasn't his fault. It wasn't even mine. It was Madden's. It's just going to take me more than three days to realize that.

Taking my silence as an inability to formulate a comeback to his question, Grayson jumps back into our conversation. "If you can't tell her how you feel, be her friend then. If that involves getting hot and heavy under a blanket while watching corny 90s movies, so be it. That's what friends do, right?"

I shake my head while grumbling, "I'm never getting drunk with you again. Your lips are looser than your vagina."

"*Va-gin-a*," he parrots, talking like Jackie Chan when he attempts to impersonate Chris Rock.

After knocking his foot against mine, he heads for the door. "Call me when you need me."

"Don't you mean *if?*"

He cranks his neck back to face me, smiling. "Nah, punk. I said 'when' for a reason." He drops his eyes to the pocket of my jeans. "And read that damn letter before you put it through the wash."

I don't argue that I've read Julian's letter.

I'm not a fan of lying.

"WHAT?" I ask Melody when her eyes float to mine for the fourth time the past two minutes. She came out of her meeting with the lead prosecutor from Saugerties with a spring in her step and a smile I was certain I wouldn't see for months.

I keep forgetting she's had seven years to handle the emotions bombarding me, so she's got a better grasp on things than I do. I should feed off her positivity, but with every unexpected smile reminding me about how many I missed because of my brother, it's a little difficult.

Nichole Aimes, ADA for this division of the New York District Attorney's Office, is confident Madden will face time for his crime. The evidence Grayson gathered from both Melody's ranch and mine is pretty condemning. Melody kept the clothes she was wearing when she was assaulted, and both the condom found in the sink in my bathroom and my bottle of cologne have trace matters that match Madden.

The urge to beat the living shit out of someone slammed into me hard and fast when Melody testified that the condom must have split as the underwear she hid in her childhood bedroom had semen residue in them. There was enough DNA to make it seem as if Madden didn't use protection.

My anger only subsided when I realized why Melody kept the evidence. If she truly believed Joey had raped her, she wouldn't have kept proof of his assault. He was dead, so justice would have never been sought. She preserved the evidence because she knew deep down inside that Joey would have never hurt her like that. He loved her like a sister and was as protective of her as I am.

Phillipa is still seeking answers on what truly happened to Joey the night of his death. She emailed me an update the morning following Castro's arrest, but with everything going on, I've not had the chance to sit down and digest it all. I haven't even had the time to ask Melody if she knew Julian had paid Rimi Castro 1.5 million dollars in cash for a pre-kidnap ransom.

With photographic evidence of Melody's movements and a threatening letter, Julian paid the amount requested, utterly oblivious that his eagerness to protect Melody placed her in more danger. If you can afford to hand over 1.5 million dollars to stop your fiancée from being kidnapped, how much will you be willing to lose to save her life?

The only good that came from Julian's generosity was the massive alteration it caused Castro's plan. He wanted Melody dead, no matter what the cost, until he realized keeping her alive would be far more beneficial to his resurrection than old Russian money. Dimitri was paying him out the eye to keep his daughter alive, and now Castro had a new gold mine to excavate.

It's probably lucky Dimitri stepped in when he did. There are no guarantees Castro would have kept both his ruses running. The kidnap game is already messy, but when it involves a kid, it's a whole other kettle of fish.

I'm drawn from my thoughts when I spot Melody eyeballing me

for the fifth time. "Will you quit staring at me like that, you're giving me a complex." The chuckle my words come out with ensures her there's no malice in my tone. I'm not feeling myself, but that doesn't mean I need to take my unease out on her.

"I can't help it," she replies, smiling. "I never saw you as a sports car type of guy, BJ. Dad would be rolling in his grave if he knew what you were getting around in."

Although confident his unrest has nothing to do with my choice of vehicle, I keep that snippet of information to myself. "What's wrong with my ride? She's—"

"Flashy, pretentious, and nothing like her owner."

She has me there. I was one of those suckers car salesmen see coming from a mile out. She didn't sell me on style and sophistication. I got caught on its safety features and good mileage, which, in case you're wondering, aren't as good as the salesman made out. What can I say? I'm a sucker for dirty blondes with big brown eyes.

"What kind of car should I be driving?" I could let our conversation end, but since it's the first we've had that doesn't involve canceled weddings and rapist siblings, I'm going to run with it.

Melody taps on her lips that are super glossy thanks to the high-hanging sun. "Something classic with a fit body that heats up when it's revved with excitement." Like an a-grade fucking loser, my cheeks inflame during her last comment. "Yes," she mutters, looking pleased, "Just like that."

When I reach a T-intersection, I indicate to turn left. We've been holed up at the hotel the gala was held at for the past three days. We only ventured out today so Melody could give an official statement to the Special Victims Unit at Saugerties PD. Although she could have done that at a precinct closer to our hotel, Melody is hopeful keeping things local will slow the rumor mill. She's not ashamed about what happened to her, but she'd rather tell her boss in person than have him discover it from someone else.

I peer at Melody when she says, "You should take a right."

"Yeah?" I sound hesitant. Justly so. Right only leads one way.

Back to our family ranches.

"Yeah," she copies, nodding. "I'm sure Socks would appreciate a visit."

Her smile turns blinding when I argue, "Socks doesn't give a shit about anyone—"

"As long as he's getting fed," she fills in, laughing.

After settling my unexpected laughter, I switch my turn signal from left to right. "Are you sure you're up for this, Melody?" Only three days ago, she asked Grayson to gather the evidence from her house. I thought it was because she couldn't face going there. Only now am I wondering if it's because she didn't want any holes in her defense. It would be mighty suspicious if the victim and the accused's brother handed in the evidence. Grayson's involvement made it official. He followed the correct procedures and conducted his search along with two deputies from Saugerties PD.

When Melody murmurs, "I'm sure. It's time to stop letting my past haunt me," I slowly apply pressure to the gas pedal. I won't lie, this will be hard for both of us.

———

TWENTY MINUTES later when I pull down a familiar street, Melody's eyes stray to two faded white crosses tacked to a power pole on the corner where her parents lost their lives.

"They're not there, you know." I take my hand off the gearshift and place it high on Melody's chest. "They're in here. They have *always* been in here."

Nodding, she places her hand over mine. It makes it hard to pull into her family ranch without downshifting the gears, but I manage. I'd rather stall and look like an idiot than take away her comfort when she needs it the most.

"Richie!" Melody shouts at a man entering the barn Socks is housed in. "I thought you weren't due back until Friday?"

When she throws off her seat belt and tosses open my door,

Richie peers back at her. As tunnel-vision forms, my lungs stop sucking in air. Even with his bald head covered by waves of black locks and a wide-brimmed cowboy hat, I recognize Richie's face. I scanned it into the FBI's database too often the past two weeks to act oblivious.

After grabbing my gun from under my seat, the frantic stomps of my boots overtake the shrill of my pulse in my ears. "Melody, seek shelter now." Out of habit, I stomp out her name as well as saying it.

As Melody spins around to face me, her face as white as a ghost, I take aim at the crease between Kwan's dark brows. "BJ... what are you doing?" Melody asks, her voice fretful. "He's a ranch hand. He isn't dangerous."

When Melody fails to take coverage as directed, I place myself between Kwan and her before tugging her behind me. Ignoring her numerous pleas that I'm mistaken, I demand Kwan to put down the bucket he's holding and raise his hands in the air.

"It's just animal feed. I'm not armed," Kwan assures as he lowers a bucket full of horse pellets to the ground.

"Hands up!" I fire a warning shot over Kwan's left shoulder, pissed he thought I wouldn't see him moving for the gun strapped to his ankle. The bulge on his left ankle was the first thing I noticed during my approach. "If you make one more move for a gun, a coroner will spend his night digging a bullet out of your head."

With a dangerous smirk, Kwan raises his hands into the air. "Henry won't be happy."

"I don't give a fuck what Henry thinks." I motion my head to the barn he was walking toward before Melody called out his alias. "Hands against the wall, then spread your legs wide."

"I'm not getting frisked outside of a barn by you—" His words stop when the bullet I pop into his kneecap buckles his legs out from beneath him.

"Inside now," I shout to Melody when Kwan's stumble knocks off his disguise, exposing his infamous neck tattoo.

As Melody races up the front stairs of her family ranch, I kick the gun Kwan is stretching for out of his reach before attempting to knock him out as I did Col's goon months ago.

Regretfully, Kwan's neck is too thick for my move to be effective. So, instead, I keep him down by scolding the skin on his temple with the heat of a recently fired gun. "Why are you here?"

A bullet shattered his kneecap, and he's being threatened to have one burrowed into his brain, yet Kwan still finds the time to smile. He must be certifiably insane. "I was feeding Socks… as I have every day for almost seven years."

"Who sent you here?" I don't believe a word he said, but the fact he's talking keeps me talking.

With his white teeth gleaming in the sunlight, he answers, "Why not ask him yourself? He's standing right behind you."

I've barely cranked my neck halfway back when the butt of a gun strikes my temple, knocking me out.

BRANDON

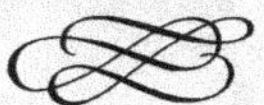

When I wake up groggy and confused, trained survival techniques kick in. I grab the first person I sense, having no clue I'm clutching the arm of the woman I love firm enough to snap her bone until she frailly whispers my name. She isn't panicked I'm about to hurt her, I dropped my hand the instant she muttered my name. She's worried about the cool metal material brushing my temple.

This time around, Kwan has his gun butted against my head.

Doesn't mean I'll go down without a fight, though.

Even with my head still murky, I disarm him so fast, Wren would have baked me enough peanut butter and chocolate chip cookies to last me a month if she were still alive.

When I turn Kwan's weapon back on him, four are focused on me. Henry's goons are as big as Kwan, and their guns are just as powerful.

There are many ways to get out of a gun battle alive, but they don't usually involve a second hostage. Since I can't risk Melody catching a wayward bullet, I don't take down the threat as I've been taught. Instead, I unload the magazine from Kwan's gun onto the dining table I'm waking up on, then remove the spare out of the chamber.

After skidding the gun across the floor, putting a good six or so feet between it and its owner, Henry signals for his men to stand down. He's seated at the end of the table, acting as regal as a king.

I guess he can gloat since years of investigations haven't slanted his crown.

"What do you want?" When Henry drifts his desolate, yet oddly possessive eyes to Melody, I shake my head. "She's not up for negotiation."

"I'm not here to negotiate." Melody forcefully swallows when Henry stands to his feet, exposing I wasn't out long enough for him to disclose they're related. She isn't acting as if her blood is standing across from her. "I want to know why you haven't told her who I am."

Melody's eyes snap to mine when I answer, "The timing hasn't been right." I can see a million questions in her eyes, but since she's fearful about what my answers will be, she remains quiet. "I'll tell her… just not yet."

Henry slants his head, his brow cocking. "Does the ill-timing have anything to do with her visit to Saugerties PD earlier today?"

My lips twitch, preparing to answer, but before I can, Melody beats me to it. "I'm standing right here, so if you have something you want to know about me, why don't you ask me?"

When Henry smiles, so do his goons. "Such spark. You're very much like your mother."

Red dots line my chest when he attempts to touch Melody's face. I grabbed his wrist before his hand could get anywhere near Melody's cheek, soundlessly warning him I'd rather die than have her touched without permission again.

Although frustrated by my protectiveness of Melody, Henry also seems pleased by it. "If only you had gotten more of your father's blood, then perhaps we could have put your skills to good use. Alas…" as he twists his lips, he shrugs, "… you prefer playing on the wrong side of the law." He once again signals for his men to stand down before he takes a step back from Melody, thinning the solidified blood coursing through my veins. "The ranch will not be sold. It will remain in the Gottle name as it was meant to be." After clicking his fingers two times, a blond man on his left hands Kwan a briefcase. "This should cover expenses until I'm long gone. If it doesn't, you know where to find me."

"Boss?" Kwan interrupts, his voice barely a squeak.

Henry blows air out of his nose. "Kwan would like to continue feeding Socks each evening. He has a weird fondness for him." He drifts his eyes to me. "His daily visits will also ensure no *unexpected* ones occur."

I nod, hearing his unvoiced words the clearest. If people believe this is Gottle turf, they won't dare come here without Henry's permission. Although I'd rather leave Melody's protection up to me, I've done a piss-poor job of it in the past, so a little help wouldn't go astray, even if it comes from the wrong side of the law.

Mistaking my head bob as me agreeing to his terms, Kwan snaps open the suitcase. Melody's gasp fans my nape when bundles upon bundles of hundred-dollar bills are exposed. There would have to be over two million dollars stuffed into the case.

After slamming the case shut and placing it onto the dining table, Henry hands me a USB stick. "This will set it straight on what happened to your brother. Once you've watched it, destroy it." The threat in his eyes turns deadly when he mutters, "Don't make me come back here and tie up more loose ends."

He glances at Melody for the quickest second before he spins on his heels and leaves. His men follow closely behind him, Kwan a little slower since he's sporting a bullet.

Melody and I stand in silence for the next several minutes, only speaking once the sound of tires rolling over untouched land no longer fills our ears.

"What the fuck was that?" Melody's voice reveals she's on the verge of another terrifying panic attack. "That's blood money." She thrusts her hand at the suitcase Henry left as her chest heaves. "I can't take that money. I'm an assistant district attorney for crying out loud, I can't accept money from the head of the Mafia." As she begins pacing, the color drains from her cheeks. "Do you know how that looks? It will make it seem as if I'm corrupt."

"If you don't accept it, no one will think you're corrupt."

She stops frozen to glare at me. "Exactly how do I reject his offer, BJ? Thanks for the bundle of cash, Mr. Gottle, mob boss of New York, but I don't want your money. Here, take it back."

I'm an ass for smiling, but I can't help it. I forgot how cute she is when she's angry.

"BJ... don't... this isn't funny." With each word she speaks, her anger lessens. She must put her frustration into her fists because when she whacks me in the stomach, the air in my lungs evicts from the strength of her punch. "You shot a goon, got knocked out by another, then threatened to kill a mob boss if he so much as ran the back of his hand down my cheek. Now is *not* the time for laughter."

My smile grows, loving that she heard my unvoiced threat, but when our eyes collide for the quickest second, the seriousness of our situation smacks back into me. "There are many ways we can handle this. But first, I need to disclose some things to you."

"I don't like the way you said *disclosed*. That didn't sound like a good *disclosed*."

As I guide her into the living room, I ask, "Do you remember the first night we slept together? When I said I needed to rock my hips up for just a second, and that it will hurt, but it won't last long." Melody looks as uncomfortable as I feel when she nods. "That's kind of like this. It will hurt, but the pain won't last long."

While guiding her to the couch, I ponder on how to tell her the news. Should I rip it off like a band-aid, so it's quick and fast or gently ease her into it.

I lose the chance to do either of those things when our trek to the sofa covered with a sheet has me veering Melody past the last family portrait taken of her family. Even without deducting the aura of arrogance that forever pumps out of Henry, the similarities between him and Liam are uncanny in this photo. If you added a decade of wariness onto Liam's face, you could pretend he was Henry.

Even a woman bogged down with grief can't deny their likeness. "He's my *actual* uncle." Melody shifts on her feet to face me. "Henry Gottle is my uncle."

MELODY

As I stare at my family portrait for the umpteenth time the past three days, unease melds through my veins. I don't know how I missed it. Even with him being a mob boss, Henry's face is well known to all levels of society. I've perused it many times the past ten years—in papers, on reports, during depositions. I've seen him a hundred times, if not more, yet, I failed to notice how his nose is the exact shape my dad's was. How his top lip is slightly bigger than his bottom one, and that his eyes can share a lifetime of secrets without his mouth opening.

I'm shocked, but in all honesty, my dad's overbearing parenting style now makes sense. He left that lifestyle for my mom, he did everything to protect her from being hurt by it. However, it didn't work. She was still brutalized by his family's enemies.

Although my adult nightmare slowly overtook the one from my childhood, I still recall how my mom's nails dragged across the floorboards when she was pulled away from me and the vibrations of her screams hitting my chest.

I also remember how the pleas in my dad's eyes shifted to anarchy when they refused his numerous requests for clemency. It was the same look Brandon's eyes held when he played the video on the USB stick Henry gave him.

Joey didn't kill himself. He was murdered. Brandon's CIA friend, Phillipa, identified two of the men in the footage. The third is still under investigation. They're hoping he's one of the men killed during the Castro raid last week, but until their faces are digitally reconstructed, we won't know for sure. A shotgun wound to the face makes identification a little hard.

We could have asked Castro, but that avenue was lost when Henry finished tying up the loose ends as he mentioned earlier this week. Castro was found hanging in his cell the same way Crombie was. Neither Phillipa nor Brandon believe it was suicide.

Those who didn't know Brandon would believe his quietness the past few days is because he's determined to get justice for his brother. I know that isn't the case. He's angry at himself, confident he is to blame for Joey's death… and perhaps my assault.

There's no truth behind either of his theories.

The footage Henry gave Brandon clearly shows Joey knew the men were trouble the instant his eyes landed on them. When they asked him if he was Brandon, he simply replied, "If I am, who's asking?"

His cocky attitude usually worked in his favor.

That night, it didn't.

Mercifully, the footage stopped before we reached the outcome of their exchange. It was for the best. We all know how things ended that night, we didn't need to witness it again.

Both good and bad came from learning the real cause of Joey's death. I can one hundred percent testify that he died as an honorable man. He was kind and sweet and put himself in danger to ensure his baby brother was safe.

But it also bombarded me with additional guilt.

I knew the type of man Joey was, so why didn't I look deeper into the doubts festering in my gut the past seven years? Why didn't I give my intuition the chance to speak? If I hadn't run, I could have stopped Madden from hurting the woman Nichole discussed during my statement.

Unfortunately, Gemma Calderon-Levesque's rape can't be mentioned during my hearing. Because her charges were dismissed and she filed a civil suit against Madden, my case will be tried as if hers never occurred.

That makes me angry. If Madden used his trust fund to pay off Gemma, doesn't that show culpability? The non-lawyer side of my head wants to say yes. Alas, not even ADAs can alter the law to suit themselves.

I'm drawn from my thoughts when soft voices project from the laptop Brandon is seated behind. After placing down my nighttime mug of hot chocolate, I float to his side of the living room. Instead of going back to the hotel three days ago, we stayed at the ranch. Only last week, it felt odd being here. With Brandon, it feels normal. I can almost forget the past seven years has happened.

Brandon's eyes lift to mine when I ask, "What are you watching?"

For the first time in days, his voice sounds happy when he answers, "Grayson asked for an extra set of eyes on a case before he went back undercover. With everything going on, I put it on the backburner." My heart does a weird flutter when he signs. *It is not a case. It is us.*

"Us?"

His smile when he nods—*Kill. Me. Now.* My engagement was only dissolved seven days ago, yet here I am getting flutters in a damp place several inches lower than my heart over a smile. It's not even a straight smile, but it is damn near perfect.

"Look." When Brandon swivels his laptop around to face me, my cheeks groan in protest about how fast they incline into a smile. "How old were we there? Around eight or nine."

"Seven." I point to the tiniest little slither of red across Brandon's forehead in the footage of us playing a board game on the floor of my childhood bedroom. "Remember when I pushed Tania Rich off the swing, and her seat accidentally smacked you in the head?"

Brandon laughs. "I do recall that. I was certain you were seconds from kissing the bump better—"

"But before I could, Mrs. Foster arrived out of nowhere to take care of your boo-boo." I'm laughing so hard recalling how Brandon's head got lost between Mrs. Foster's gigantic bosoms when she carried him to the nurse's office. My words are barely understandable, so I switch to signing instead. *"I was certain you would never be a breast man."*

He keeps his hands low, however, I don't miss his reply, *"If yours didn't blossom as they did, I wouldn't have been."* The heat bristling between us turns roasting when he playfully growls. I've felt his growls before, but this is the first time I've heard them.

"BJ..." There's a need in my voice I can't explain. It hasn't been there in years, and in all honesty, I didn't think it would ever come back.

After floating his eyes up my body, taking in my peaked nipples, thrusting chest, and taut neck on his way, Brandon's eyes land on my face. "Yeah?"

I want to beg him to kiss me, I want to tell him I love him and that he doesn't need to be sad, but more than anything, I want him to know what happened to Joey and me isn't his fault, but instead of doing any of those things, I bump the two-seater dining table out of my way with my hip before straddling his lap. The old wooden chair I sat on every morning for almost eighteen years creaks in protests about our combined weight. It won't collapse, though. Life couldn't be so cruel to the same man continuously. He eventually has to catch a break, doesn't he?

Hopefully, I am that for him.

Although Brandon hardens beneath me in an instant, hesitation still fires in his eyes, "Melo—"

I steal the unease from his throat with my tongue by kissing him with everything I have. It goes above and beyond our kiss at the gala and fills my heart with both sentimental muckiness and an urge to wipe the slate clean. He smells different, yet the same. His jaw is holding the beloved prickles it always had when we weren't at school, and the living room is fully lit.

I feel safe and protected even with my heart racing a million miles an hour.

This is a huge step for me, but I can imagine it's even more massive for Brandon. This is all so fresh and new to him, he still thinks my rape occurred last week. I'm not fairing much better, but unlike Brandon, I've had years of counseling and the care of a supporting man to see me through it.

He has no one but me.

The knowledge has me deepening our embrace.

Mercifully, Brandon kisses me back, forever an equal participant in each exchange we've shared. It isn't a hurried kiss or a messy one. He doesn't demand anything more than I'm willing to give and follows the prompts of my lips and tongue when I require more. It's perfect, just like him.

"Please," I murmur over his mouth when he stops the slither of my hand to the waistband of his pants.

He locks his eyes with mine. They're wide and brimming with lust. His lips are well kissed, and his cheeks are heated. He wants this, he's just afraid to answer the many pleas filtering through his head. He's always been so logical-thinking. Even when we were kids, he was forever looking two steps ahead.

Hoping I can get him over the line, I remove myself from his lap, gather his hand in mine, then guide him to my room. It's not my childhood bedroom. I had trouble sleeping there our first night here, so Brandon agreed to switch rooms with me, so I could have the guest bedroom. It didn't aid in getting more sleep, but it was a little less awkward.

Brandon doesn't utter a sound the entire trip to my room, but he does gasp out a breath when I push him onto the bed before balancing my knee between his splayed thighs. My aggressiveness in the bedroom is nothing new to him. It's the unbuttoning of my shirt that has his lungs fighting for air.

I send thanks to my mom for good genes when Brandon's hand moves to cup my breasts after I fan open my shirt. It's like he's acting on instincts. He's here, but he isn't really here if that makes any sense.

The nervousness knotted in my stomach slackens when his index finger creeps into the space between the lace of my bra and my heated skin. Excitement bundles low in my stomach, loving the roughness of his finger on my silky-smooth nipple.

While peering up at me, he tugs down the cups of my bra, fully exposing my breasts to his avid eyes before he sucks one of my nipples into his warm and inviting mouth. I call out, the sensation overwhelming. When we were teens, I thought I had sensitive nipples. Numerous attempts to self-please myself the past seven years prove I don't. Brandon just has the knack for knowing the exact amount of suction to use and the perfect pressure of his teeth.

"*More*," I beg, signing, my mind too spiraling to talk.

"Guide me," Brandon murmurs against my breasts, heightening my senses even more. "Tell me what to do." His voice is still as stiff as his movements, but my mind is too hazed by lust to look further into it.

I need this as much as my lungs desire their next breath.

"Take my shirt off, then my bra." He does both things in a calm, precise way that has my emotions teetering in a good way. "Now my skirt." My hair fans against the bedding when he gently guides me onto the bed so he can slide down the zipper of my skintight pencil skirt before shimmering the rigid material down my thighs.

When he drags his eyes up from my feet to my face, my legs scissor together. Yearning is in his eyes, but I need to get it past the doubt.

"Now?"

"Kiss me…" I swallow to soothe my dry throat with some of the spit pooling in the corner of my mouth before finalizing my demand. "Everywhere."

He starts at my neck, then drops to my collarbone before

moving to my breasts. Once he has my nipples stiff enough to cut glass, he shifts his focus to my stomach. I squirm uncontrollably when his lips stop within an inch of the waistband of my panties. I can feel his breaths heavy against me, feel his eyes on me, but something is holding him back.

I discover what when his eyes lift to my face.

It's me.

"I can't," he mutters, shaking his head. "I'm sorry, I just can't."

I grab for the blanket to cover myself when he makes a beeline for the door. Madden's assault violated me. He took something I was unwilling to give and made me feel broken and used, but Brandon's rejection feels even more defiling than that.

Madden abused me, but Brandon may have very well broken me.

BRANDON

"*Yes, Brandon. Keep going.*"

I shake my head, freeing it of the image of Mr. Gregg prancing with me around the boxing ring while I throw a left-right-left combination at a frail boxing bag hanging next to the ring. It's four in the morning, and I can't sleep, so instead of wasting the time, I'm getting in a quick workout.

I doubt I'll sleep for a month after my piss-poor performance last night.

Could you imagine having the girl of your dreams right there, splayed out in front of you while play by play of her rape flashed before your eyes.

I couldn't get it out of my head. I could feel the heat of Melody's skin under my hands, taste her on the tip of my tongue, but no matter how many times I yelled at my fucked-up head to get with the program, it didn't listen. Madden kept flashing before my eyes—his sleezy grin and the gleam his eyes got any time he got away with something.

Then the images worsened.

Grayson was right. I shouldn't have read the report on what had happened to Melody. I thought if I knew the exact recollection of events, I could ensure I stayed away from them if Melody and I ever reached the intimacy stage in our relationship again.

All it did was fuck with my head more.

Just like Mr. Gregg taunts me the longer I dispel the anger tearing me in two.

"Focus, Brandon. Get your head in the game."

Sweat rolls down my back as I punish the bag as I wish I could myself. I'm so angry. *So fucking angry.* I hurt Melody. Me, the man who swore he wouldn't, the man who pledged to save her from pain.

I work the bag harder, not the least bit concerned at the blistering of my knuckles. I deserve the pain. I deserve the punishment.

I also deserve Mr. Gregg's taunts.

"Protect, honor, obey, and serve. It isn't that hard."

As my teeth grit, I kick and punch the bag acting as if the salty blobs sliding down my cheeks are sweat.

"If you are making gaga eyes at her, you're not monitoring the area. You're not watching her back. You are not doing any of the things I trained you to do."

I told him he was wrong.

I said I'd never let anything happen to her.

I fucking failed.

"They made me pick. They made me pick between Wren and Melody. They either raped my wife or my daughter. She was five, Brandon. Five! Do you have any idea how much that question fucked with my head?"

I thought I did.

I thought I understood his pain.

I didn't.

I had no clue how much that would have torn him up until now.

Now, I understand. The pain is unlike anything I've ever felt. He was right. I couldn't love and protect his daughter. I got slack, I got complacent, and Melody got hurt.

As if that isn't bad enough, she was hurt by my brother, a man who has the same blood as me while our other brother was being murdered.

A roar works up from my gut to my throat as I continue working the bag. I throw punch after punch after punch until exhaustion eventually knocks me on my ass.

The howl that escapes my mouth isn't from the hard impact of my backside hitting the ground, it's from the sob it arrived with. I'm broken. Fucking wrecked, certain I don't deserve to live, even more so when Liam's last words to me ring through my ears.

"I trusted you with her. I don't anymore."

"I fucked up. I'm sorry! I didn't protect her as I said I would." I scream at the pitch-black sky. "I didn't keep her safe. It's my fault. I'm to blame."

Dust kicks up around me when my fist lands on the ground dotted with my tears. I punch the rock-hard dirt on repeat until the pain ripping through my chest radiates through my hand, then I collapse, giving in as I should have when Liam advised me to.

I'm done. So fucking done.

BRANDON

I don't know how much time passes before I wake up groggy and confused. Since my head is pounding as much as my knuckles, I doubt I've been out for long.

I scrub a red dirt-stained hand across my tired eyes before pricking my ears. A car engine is breaking through the chirps of birds enjoying the early morning sun. My muscles scream in disgust when I head in the direction the noise is coming from. I'm aching all over, but it has nothing on the pain that rockets through me when I discover the reason for the early morning visitor. A cab is in the driveway. The driver is loading Melody's suitcases we gathered from the hotel into the trunk.

I can tell the exact moment Melody spots my gawk. Her breathing slows as her hands dart down to fiddle with the hem of her skirt. After exhaling a chest-deflating breath, she hands the driver a bundle of cash, then moves to the back-passenger side door. Her eyes only lift to mine once she has one foot inside the cab. She stares at me for several long seconds, begging for me to run, to fight for her like I did when we were kids.

She swipes at the tears falling from her eyes when my feet remain planted on the ground before she signs, "*Goodbye, BJ.*"

When the closure of her door is quickly followed by the taxi rolling down the driveway of her family ranch, my heart screams for me to chase her down, to fight, not to let Madden win, but no matter how loud it yells, my feet refuse to budge. I saw the pain that flashed in Melody's eyes last night. I can't be responsible for that level of hurt again. I love her too much to gut her like I did when I bolted out of her room like a coward. So, as much as this will kill me, I have to let her go.

She deserves a level of happiness I can no longer give her.

I stand halfway between Melody's family ranch and the old shed her father and I worked out in every day he wasn't on assignment for the next twenty minutes. I'm shirtless and shoeless, and my sleeping pants aren't capable of keeping out the cold winds whipping in from the west. With my determination building, I don't feel cold.

I can't feel anything.

I'm dead on the inside.

Needing to distract myself before I put my mother through the pain of losing another child, I sprint into the house as fast as I fled it last night. Within ten minutes, I've showered, dressed, and brushed my teeth. I don't touch the stubble on my chin. The smell of Melody's perfume in the fine hairs is the only reminder I have that last night did occur. Even if I can't have her, the knowledge that she *wanted* me will keep the fire in my gut blazing when I bury myself in the trenches.

As I make my way to my BMW, the quickest flash of silver slows my steps. The morning winds weren't just freezing, they were brutal enough to whip off half of the car cover keeping the 1969 Hellcat Mr. Gregg and I restored before his death hidden.

This time, I listen to the pleas of my heart instead of ignoring them. After tossing the keys for my BMW onto the driver's seat, I hotfoot it to the Hellcat. Its battery will most likely be dead, and its fuel will be old, but I can't help but check. If Kwan is in love with classic cars as much as he is with old horses, there's a possibility she'll have enough spark to get me to town. Any half-decent mechanic will get me the rest of the way.

The hollow feeling in my chest fills in by a microdot when I pull off the rest of the car cover. The effort Mr. Gregg and I put into the Hellcat's rebuild is undeniable. Every detail of her restoration has been meticulously done. Just peering at her, you wouldn't know she's spent the last seven years in storage. She's a real beauty.

When I slide into the driver's seat, it feels like I'm going home. This is exactly how I felt last night when I cupped Melody's breast in my hand. The blood pumping through my body was scorching hot, but it wasn't the reason for the warmth of my veins. It was the person I was caressing and how she still responded to my touch even after years of absence.

After shaking my head, endeavoring to keep my focus on track, I peer up at the sky, praying Mr. Gregg will grant me one final wish. It appears as if not all my luck has run out when the engine cranks to life on the first turn of the keys.

As I roll down the window to suffocate the stuffy conditions with fresh air, I glide my cell phone out of my pocket. The number I dial isn't one I anticipated calling anytime soon, but it will be good for me.

"Hey, BJ," Phillipa greets, her voice both shocked and pleased. "I thought you had lost my number."

After licking my dry lips, I ask, "Where do you need me?"

She cups her phone to advise the people I hear mingling in the background that she'll be back in a minute before she devotes all her attention to me. "You want to join forces?" She sounds shocked. Justly so. I was less than polite when I found out she was a CIA officer.

I scrub at my jaw, shocked by its rough feeling. I usually shave before every mission. "I can't technically join forces since I'm not with the Bureau anymore, but that frees up plenty of time for me to be a consultant."

Phillipa waits a beat before asking, "Is Melody okay with that?"

She can't see me, but I nod my head, words above me.

Seemingly having a direct link to my inner psyche, Phillipa asks, "And you, Brandon? Are you ready for this?"

I nod again. "I want justice for Joey." When Phillipa remains quiet, knowing there's more, I push out, "Then perhaps I can lose the guilt I feel for what happened to Melody."

She sighs. It sounds as antagonized as the pain stretched across my chest. "What happened wasn't your fault."

"If Joey wasn't dealing with the people looking for me, he could have stopped Madden."

"You don't know that, Brandon."

"I do," I argue with the utmost certainty. "Joey was good like that. He would have protected Melody." I stop just before I say, *unlike me.*

Phillipa sighs again. This one is more from her struggle not to get in an argument with me over the phone. She'd rather save her drilling until we're face to face. "Where are you?"

"At Saugerties, but I can be anywhere you need me to be within hours."

My interests overtake my heartache when she mutters, "Even Ravenshoe?"

"Even Ravenshoe," I reply after forcefully swallowing.

I was hoping since Phillipa is based in New York, she'd keep me a little closer to Melody, but I guess I can't add stipulations to a game I have no control over.

"Once you're back, reach out. I have a few leads I need you to chase up."

Stealing my chance to reply, she disconnects our call, freeing me to commence my long journey back to the town that switched me from being a morally upstanding citizen to that of a vigilante.

MELODY

"Believe me, you're not the only one who wants that prick sent away for life, but we need to do this right. We can't have any holes in our evidence." After standing from my seat, I roam my eyes over my colleagues gathered around the boardroom table at the District Attorney's Office in New York. "Have a second forensic team run over the results. If the defense discredits our first expert, we'll hit them with a second and third."

"Great," Leo jumps in, clapping his hands together. "Let's get the evidence in this case wrapped up tight."

Smiling to thank him for his backup, I commence packing away the stacks of evidence I've trawled over for sixteen plus hours a day for the past week. This is my version of heartbreak—work and more work. To others, it seems like a pathetic way to ease the heartache, but it works well for me. My father's training ensured I'd never be an ice-cream-and-sappy-movies type of girl. If my hurt can help someone else, why not put it to good use?

"Before you go, Melody," Leo mutters, stopping my brisk exit. "Can I have a quick word?"

My throat works hard to swallow when he asks a newly appointed intern to close the conference room door on his way out. I'm not scared to be alone with Leo, he's a gentle giant. It's seeing the cause of his meeting request in his eyes that has my heart stuttering.

Think of the worst conversation you've ever had. Now double the awkwardness. That will give you an idea of how my conversation went with Leo when my presence popped back onto his radar late last week.

Nichole had kept her word, she didn't pass on news of my case to anyone outside of her division, but Leo knew there was more to my absence than my run-in with Mr. McGee the week earlier.

I never said I hid my heartache well. I just put it to good use.

I don't know who Leo was pissed with more, Madden for what he had done or Mr. McGee for dusting off his old defense lawyer skills to represent his son.

I kind of hate them both the same.

After propping his hip on the glass desk separating us, Leo folds his arms in front of his broad chest. "I was talking to Julian earlier—"

"How is he?" I ask before I can stop myself. We haven't had contact since he left two weeks ago.

The unease in Leo's eyes softens when he nods. "He's good. Enjoying the weather in California."

"It has to be better than here."

"Anywhere is better than here," he replies with a laugh.

Once his chuckles settle, he gets to the point of our conversation. "He told me you two aren't together anymore. Is that true?"

My mouth falls open, then I close it again. Leo has been friends with Julian for years, so I'm shocked he doesn't believe his recollection of events.

I'm reminded of Leo's mindreading powers when he says, "I'm not discrediting him. I'm just stunned. That man was head over heels in love with you. I didn't think he'd let you go for anything or anyone."

His words are like a knife to the chest, but I pull through his maiming—regretfully. "I know." I restack the files in my briefcase like they fell as well as Leo's words dropped my heart from my chest. "But sometimes that isn't enough."

My failed attempt to seduce Brandon is proof of this.

Once I have the folders in order as they were before I started fussing, I ask, "Is that all? I've got a ton of backdated work to catch up on."

"Just one last thing." He rounds the desk to join me on the other side. "He also told me you repaid the 1.5 million-dollar ransom he paid Rimi Castro."

Lying will never be my forte, but I give it a whirl. "It was returned from evidence—"

My eyes snap up to Leo's when he interrupts, "The sequence numbers didn't match. They weren't close to the ones they recorded before the drop."

"They?" I interrogate, unsure about the possessiveness in his reply.

A dash of hesitation flares through his eyes when he says, "The CIA coordinated the drop with Julian. That's why he couldn't accompany you to the fundraising gala straight away. He was waiting for confirmation the drop had taken place, and that the sting it instigated went ahead."

My heart drops from my stomach to my shoes when all the evidence slots into place. I kissed Brandon while Julian was paying an arm and a leg to keep me safe.

My God, could I be any worse of a person?

Sickened at the evil woman I've become, I confess my sins. "The money didn't come from the sting. It was given to me by Henry Gottle."

Leo tries to tuck away the shock my confession slapped him

with, but he isn't quite quick enough for me to miss it. "Why would Henry Gottle give you 1.5 million dollars?"

"He gave me 2.4 million dollars. I figured it would look a little suspicious if Julian received back more than he had put in, so I removed nine hundred thousand from the suitcase before handing it to Fetu." Thinking back, it was pretty reckless of me to entrust so much money to a no-longer employed security detail, but Fetu hasn't given me any reason to distrust him, so I don't. "I donated the remaining nine hundred thousand to numerous charity organizations."

"Please tell me you were given a receipt for each donation?" When I shake my head, Leo curses under his breath. "You do realize you could be prosecuted for bribery?"

"I didn't take any of the money for myself. Furthermore, I would have given it back to Henry, but he refused to take it."

Leo's words fan my cheeks with coffee-scented air when he shouts, "So you not only accepted over two million dollars from a mafia kingpin, you visited him as well?"

I forcefully swallow, my mouth suddenly dry. "My visit wasn't witnessed."

"Of course it was, Melody. Henry has more law enforcement personnel on him than any other man in the country." As he rakes his fingers through his dark locks, his eyes lift to the ceiling. He thought we were going to have a simple conversation about me coming into a small windfall. He had no inkling how murky the waters I've been swimming in are.

After several deep breaths, Leo's head drops back into place. "Okay, first things first, was the money for anything illegal?"

I shake my head.

"Do you believe it has anything to do with your case?" His tone is lower this time around, more compassionate.

"No. Henry isn't aware of what happened." I stop talking before I add, *Madden would be dead if he did.*

I've mused over that outcome multiple times the past two weeks, and more times than not, I've been in favor of it. The only reason I haven't taken the easy way out is because Grayson was right when he stopped Brandon from killing Madden. Mrs. McGee has been through enough. She doesn't deserve more pain.

"Then why did he give you so much money, Melody?"

Needing to be honest, I say, "He's my uncle."

Leo's head slants to the side as his brow cocks. "Henry Gottle is your uncle?"

It still sounds shocking to my ears. "Uh-huh. He found out I was selling the ranch, didn't want it sold, so he gave me the funds to maintain its upkeep."

"And that's it? That's all that happened." When I hesitate, Leo grunts my name in a growly groan.

"There was an altercation at the ranch. BJ..." I stop before correcting, "Brandon fired at one of his goons."

My eyes snap to Leo when he mumbles in anger, "So Julian's assumptions were right. You were holed up at your ranch with Brandon the past week."

"It wasn't like that." *Not by my choice*, but I keep that snippet of information to myself. My ego is already knocked. It doesn't need another sting. "He's my friend."

My brows furrow in confusion when Leo asks, "When was the last time you heard from him?"

"Earlier this morning. Why?" Brandon's contact was nothing more than a transfer of assets for his BMW since he took the Hellcat as offered, but I'm so curious to see where Leo is going with this, I can't help but play along.

Leo scrubs his hair-free chin before asking, "Sorry, let me rephrase my question. When was the last time you contacted Brandon?"

It takes me a little longer to answer this time around. Guilt does that to you. "I haven't returned any of his messages."

"But he's your friend... *right?*"

Forgetting he's my boss, I hand some of his snappy attitude back to him. "Don't judge me. You don't know what it's like for me."

"I think I can take a guess. Do you clam up at the thought of being touched? Choose years of abstinence over forcing a connection?" The wetness in my eyes leaps into his when he mutters, "Did you agree not to sleep with someone until you're married because the fear of being touched isn't just coming from your fiancée's side of the fence? You're just as scared as her." My guards crumble when he asks, "Why do you think he was so patient with you, Melody? Why did you think he never pushed you? A victim knows a victim, right?" When I nod, agreeing with him, he says, "Then why did you never notice Julian's pain as you did mine?"

I've barely absorbed his first hit when he smacks me with another. "I need to place you on paid leave until we can work out if there will be any backlash to the office for the funds you disbursed. I appreciate the hard work you've given our office the past year, but I suggest you use the time of your suspension for personal endeavors instead of work-related ones."

"Okay." *That's it? Seven years of hard work reduced to one lousy word.* "I'll clean out my desk now."

I'm halfway to the door when my steps are slowed by a low, panicked tone. "If Julian ever finds out what I told you—"

"He won't find out," I assure him before standing up for myself as I should have years ago. "But the next time you go on a friend-bashing rant, perhaps you should view *all* the evidence first. I've texted Julian multiple times the past two weeks. He has never messaged me back."

Apologies brim in Leo's eyes when he says, "I'm sorry. He never mentioned that."

"When do victims ever accept culpability? We're taught not to, unaware the leeway we're given to cope isn't supposed to extend to all aspects of our lives."

When Leo remains quiet, having no defense, I dip my chin in

farewell before exiting the conference room. The buzz throughout our office usually keeps me enthralled for hours, so I suck in as much of it as I can while heading to my office at the back of the bustling space.

Although most of my belongings technically belong to the state, I still have a handful of things to pack. Mainly photographs of my parents, the Donald Duck Pez collectible Julian gifted me when he proposed, and a newspaper write-up of our engagement party. My laptop is mine, so I place that into my briefcase after removing the files I updated the team on earlier. Then I'm done. My entire career packed into one tiny box in less than twenty minutes.

My lonesome walk to the elevator should be somber, but I'm accustomed to being alone. I've never been surrounded by a bunch of people, so solidarity is more comforting to me than it would be an extrovert. I doubt that will still be the case when I don't have work to keep me occupied, but I can't say I blame Leo. I did compromise his office's integrity. It just occurred long before he realized. I should have never accepted a position anywhere the McGee name was known. That was just asking for trouble.

I smile at the security officer at the door before pushing through the rotating entryway door. It's mid-morning, but you wouldn't know it when I break outside. It's dreary and miserable, not that the sun can ever be seen through the tall buildings surrounding me.

When I gallop down the stairs of my office building, my heart rate kicks into a cantor. A familiar black SUV is idling at the curb. Its tags are recognizable.

"Julian, what are you doing here?"

The pop of orange coloring on the top of Julian's head makes the day not seem so dreary. "I had an inkling you needed me." His eyes lower to the box in my hands. "If that's anything to go by, I'm glad I listened." The sun isn't needed to brighten the miserable day when he nudges his head to the open back passenger door of his car and says, "Come on. I'll give you a ride home."

I should jump into his car. Instead, I leap straight into his arms.

BRANDON

I pull pods from my ears when Harlow kicks my boots with her shoe. She's balancing a stack of dirty dishes in one hand while the other is gripping a coffee pot. "Did you say something?"

She takes my snarly tone in stride. "I was asking if you'd like a refill."

Shaking my head, I place my hand over my empty mug. "I'm good. Thanks."

I wait for her to leave before dropping my eyes back to Tobias's newer-looking laptop. Grayson shit his pants when I said I refurbished it. It was only after I assured him the shell was the only thing I changed did he stop threatening to punch me into next week. The last time I saw him that worked up was when I told him I let Melody leave me for the second time without putting up a fight.

He called me every derogative name known under the sun, his rant only ending when I confessed the real reason I was struggling. No one can predict how they'll handle something until they face the dilemma head-on. Am I handling this one right? Probably not. But

I'm hoping to keep my head so buried with work, I won't have to come up for air anytime soon.

For now, it's working. Phillipa is a slave driver. Her work ethics are paying off, though. Not only have we discovered Isaac isn't just making payments to the Popovs, he's been dipping his toes into the Petretti conglomerate as well. We have statements going back years. Although the recipient's surname isn't Petretti, she has clear ties with them.

As does Alex, Grayson's brother, and my once supervisor.

I close the screen of Tobias's laptop and replace it with my own when Harlow floats my way again. I get her bakery is a little quiet, but I'd rather her focus not be on me. "Have you heard from Izzy at all today?"

"No. Why would I hear from Izzy?" *It's not like she has time for anyone not named Isaac.*

I grow panicked I said my last comment out loud when Harlow kicks me again. This time, she aims for my shin instead of my boots. "Okay, Snappy McWhappy. No need to get nasty. Anyone would swear you're on your period."

I wish it were that simple.

Even knowing I shouldn't nibble at the bait Harlow is throwing out, I can't help myself. I told Tobias I'd keep Isabelle safe. You're probably not surprised to hear I've done a shit job of it. "Sorry. Long night. What's up with Izzy? Is she okay?"

"Yeah…" Harlow screws up her nose. "… I think so." I almost whine when she slots into the seat across from me. That indicates she's settling in for the long haul. "We went clubbing last night." Her comment both shocks and surprises me. Cormack isn't as bad as Isaac when it comes to alpha-male possessiveness, but he's a close second. "Isaac found out." See? What more proof do you need. "My source isn't reliable, but I heard Izzy went home with him."

"Is that unusual? They're practically living together." My intel is as unfounded as Harlow's, but I'm running with it.

Harlow pulls a face. I don't know her well enough to tell you which one. "They kind of were… until the gala."

"What happened at the gala?" If it's anything like the set of circumstances I faced, I'm a worse friend than I realized.

To make sure her news isn't shared with anyone but Isabelle's supposed 'closest friends,' Harlow leans to my side of the table. "Clara made assumptions Isaac couldn't deny. It's been rough."

"Isaac cheated on Isabelle?" When Harlow halfheartedly shrugs, I snap, "This isn't an accusation you should be throwing around without facts, Harlow. Shit like this can really fuck up a man, so you need to be sure."

Her face goes stonewalled in an instant. "I'm not making assumptions. Other than talking to you, *Izzy's friend*, I haven't murmured a peep to anyone. I wouldn't even be talking to you if I wasn't worried about her."

"Have you tried ringing her?"

She slaps me up the side of the head with a tea towel. "I've tried numerous times this morning. I've not yet had any luck." She does a weird head-bobbing thing while glaring at me. "Why do you think I came to you?" After sliding out of the booth, she adds a threat to her glare. "Keep this between us, dickwad, or I'll cut yours off."

Not only does her quick departure stop me from voicing a comeback, so does the buzz of my cell phone. I assume it's another message from Grayson telling me to pull my head out of my ass, so you can imagine my surprise when I notice it's from the private investigator I still have following Melody.

My already pissy attitude drops even further when I open his message. There's no text. Just an image. *A gut-wrenching image.* It shows Melody and Julian hugging outside of her office building. They look super friendly like they've never been apart.

As I tighten my grip on my phone, I glare at the smidge of Julian's face not buried in Melody's neck. I want to hate the guy, but no matter how hard I try, I can't. He helped Melody like I couldn't and loved her enough to take a 1.5-million-dollar hit, so maybe he's more suited for her than me?

With my mood too low to handle more of Grayson's antics, I hit the end call button on my cell when his face pops up on the screen of my phone two seconds later.

He tries another three times before I finally succumb to his annoying nature. "Have you ever heard of a day off?" I chide down the line, frustrated.

"Not when it comes to eradicating scum," he replies coolly, not the least bit turned off by the scold in my tone. "I need your help."

The desperateness in his final sentence has me throwing a twenty onto the table. After storing my laptop into my soft leather briefcase next to Tobias's, I slide out of the booth. "What do you need?"

"Remember how you were chasing proof Isaac is working with Vladimir?" Even though he's asking a question, he doesn't wait for me to answer him. "He's meeting with him. Now. At Tastes. Like *right* fucking now."

The chime above Harlow's bakery door rings in my ear before all of 'Tastes' leaves his mouth. After adjusting my briefcase, I hustle through the foot traffic, weaving and darting as much as Grayson's sprint bellows down the line.

"Do we know what they're meeting is about?"

Grayson huffs out a frustrated laugh. "Not a fucking clue. We're hoping it's about the order he placed. Rumors are it has been shipped, but it headed Melody's way instead of yours."

"Thanks for the reminder that we're in different states," I grumble under my breath.

Air whizzes out of his nose before words convey his displeasure. "Anytime you need a reminder about how you fucked-up, punk, I'm your man."

"I didn't fuck up. I'm giving her time—"

"To find another man. Yep, I got that."

"Grayson..."

My growl doesn't ruffle his feathers in the slightest. "Don't growl at me, punk. You weren't the one who was raped, so you don't get to act sensitive."

"I failed her," I reply, speaking truthfully for the first time in days.

"Now? Yep, I got that, too." Ignoring the hostess at Tastes asking if I'd like to dine inside or out, I enter the main part of the restaurant to scan my eyes over the crowd, acting as if I didn't hear Grayson grumble, "She gave you a free pass for what happened to her seven years ago, but you had to stuff it up by letting that weasel prickface of a brother get into your head."

When I don't find the men I'm hunting, I signal to the hostess that I'd like a table for one inside before directing my focus back to Grayson. "Unless you want me to put a bullet in my head, shut the fuck up with your assumptions. You don't know what I'm going through."

"That's not funny, punk. You might be facing a hard time right now, but saying shit like that isn't funny," he immediately snaps back.

For the first time since I've known him, he's left speechless when I say, "Who said I was joking?"

Before he can get the jump on me for the second time today, I hang up before shadowing the waiter to my seat. Grayson isn't the only one taken aback by my comment. I'm just as stunned. I've never felt like this before, but still, comments like the one I just made aren't kosher for me.

Needing to get my head into game mode before I convince myself I need to have it examined by a shrink, I take a seat at my assigned table before grabbing a copy of *Ravenshoe News*.

I've barely cracked open the newspaper to conceal my face from Isaac when it's snatched out from in front of me. "Fool me once, shame on you. Fool me twice, shame on me. But there's no fucking chance you'll fool me a third time."

I balk as startled as the person badgering me. "Regan, what are you doing here? Is Izzy with you?" I rescan the restaurant, wondering if my eagerness to seek Isaac had me skimming past Isabelle.

My eyes snap back to Regan when she snatches Tobias's laptop out of my briefcase. If she destroys it, Grayson will destroy me. Although it isn't technically his, half the videos on it most certainly are. There's a lot of undercover surveillance of Katie on there. It was taken during a failed attempt to purchase her. Kirill wanted her no matter the cost, and his means far exceeded the Bureau's.

I realize I have Regan's motives mixed up when she snarls. "Let's see how you like having your privacy invaded."

When she unlocks Tobias's laptop without asking for the passcode, I stare at her like she's Superwoman. *How the fuck did she know the password?*

The truth smacks into me when I see the jealous possessiveness beaming out of her. Isaac trained his staff well. Even when he isn't around, they make sure there's no chance another man will be moseying in on his turf. I had wondered how many of his staff viewed the video of Isabelle and me kissing. I'm now sitting at five.

When Regan's growl vibrates through my chest, my eyes snap to an invoice on the screen. "That's not what it looks like." I slam down the laptop screen, unsure how I can explain that Grayson's computer is linked to this laptop without breaking his cover. Grayson and Regan have met previously. It was brief, but enough for Grayson to know Regan is as quick-witted as she is attractive. "I was researching business opportunities. Those files are assessable to anyone with the knowledge of how to find them."

Regan glares at me, her lips twisted. "True... but I wonder what Isabelle's take on it will be?"

When she hightails it out of the restaurant, I'm nipping at her heels two seconds later. "I'm trying to protect her." *Unlike you.*

Regan is as blind to Isaac's shadiness as Isabelle. Or perhaps she knows all his secrets, and that's why he pays her so well. It's not every day you hear about an acquisition lawyer being on a two-million-dollar-a-year retainer.

"She has no clue who Isaac really is. He's keeping things from her." Before she can slide into an idling cab outside of the restaurant, I block her entrance while digging a wire transfer transaction list out of my briefcase. "Look, I'll prove it. He's been making secret payments to a woman in Arlington the past six years." When Regan snatches the document out of my hand, I point out the payments. "See, one hundred thousand dollars a month for over six years."

I watch Regan closely when she works the payee's name through her head a few times. It appears as if the name is familiar to her, but she can't work out why.

My assumptions are proven accurate when she snatches Tobias's laptop from under my arm, tosses it onto the taxi's hood, then logs back in. Her throat works hard to swallow when she types Kristin Liberman's name into the search bar. The view isn't pretty. The screen is full of new articles on the suicide death of Dane Liberman, Kristin's husband.

The usually ball-clutching pitch of Regan's voice is reduced to a whisper when she asks, "When was he killed?"

She looks like I ran over her cat when I point to the date of death in Dane's obituary. She takes a few moments drinking in images of men with the same name as Dane, only stopping when she stumbles upon one that includes Alex, Grayson's brother. It's a photograph of Dane and Alex when their college team claimed victory on the lacrosse field. I'm reasonably sure I've never seen Alex smile the way he is in this picture.

Come to think of it, I don't think I've ever seen Grayson smile like that either.

I guess I'm not the only one who has a fucked-up past.

After brushing a rogue tear off her cheek, Regan's eyes drift to mine. "How did he die?"

I inwardly curse when it dawns on me why Grayson reacted to my earlier comment so negatively. Dane was Alex's best friend, which means he would have known Grayson. Dane killed himself, so I don't think Grayson will ever find my morbid sense of humor entertaining.

Fuck, I'm an asshole.

While rubbing a kink from the back of my neck, I answer the question Regan is desperately seeking from my eyes. "He killed himself."

"Why?" She sounds as shocked as I feel guilty. "He had a beautiful wife, an illustrious career, and two gorgeous daughters. Why would he leave that?"

I shrug. "Maybe he was depressed?" *I most certainly am.*

I don't get time to dwell on my unexpected inner monologue when Regan's squeal pierces my eardrums. "But why, Brandon?"

As curious as Regan, I take control of my laptop before logging into the Bureau mainframe. Shock horror, I still have access even with my resignation officially being handed in over two weeks ago.

Regan appears impressed when I bring up the official reports on Dane's death, but she keeps her excitement on the down-low. She doesn't trust me any more than I trust her.

For the length of time it takes for Regan to read the main report, it's clear she needed more than a quick once-over to absorb all the information in front of her. Dane's file doesn't just disclose his cause of death, it reveals how he was paralyzed from the waist down after being shot during a raid six years ago. Alex saved him by carrying him down a meadow on his back, but Dane's life was irreverently changed.

Is that why Isaac is paying Kristin a substantial chunk of money each month?

Was he responsible for Dane's injuries?

Before I can seek answers to my questions in the reports in front of me, Regan closes the laptop screen, then hands it back to me. I grow worried my surly mood is contagious when her eyes lift and lock with mine. She looks like a woman on the edge of a cliff—not an orgasmic one.

"Thank you for showing me that."

I dip my chin before voicing the only question in my head she can answer. "Are you going to tell Izzy about today?"

I'm hoping she says yes, but I'm left short-changed when she replies, "I won't have anything to tell her if you tell her first."

I almost say, 'I doubt Isabelle will believe me,' but before I can, she slides into the back of the taxi, leaving me defenseless to the bullets flying over my head on the corner of Tivot and St. Thomas Street.

BRANDON

While signaling for the diners eating outside to get down, I dump my briefcase in a hidey-hole before unclipping the revolver harnessed to my waist. After doing a quick scope of the area, it's obvious which direction the bullets are coming from. A large, brute of a man is hanging out the passenger side window of a heavily-tinted white Range Rover. His gun is pointed at Hugo, who's chasing the vehicle on foot.

"Fuck. Get down," Hugo shouts before barging an elderly lady waiting on the bus out of the firing zone.

Just as the lady's backside lands on the steel bench seat of the bus shelter, Hugo's left shoulder is hit with a bullet. As he struggles to get back on his feet, I fire at the Range Rover. I take out the passenger's side mirror and rear windshield, but the assailant goes around the corner too quickly for me to fire at the driver.

"My name is Brandon James. I'm an FBI Field Agent. My number is 443567. I need an ambulance sent to the corner of Tivot and Welsh."

"Blondie?" Hugo coughs up a good chunk of blood when he

peers up at me. His pupils are massive, and blood is squirting out of his wound, but the fact he can greet me is a good sign.

When Hugo commences convulsing a short time later, the urgency of the situation dawns on me. "A bullet appears to have nicked an artery," I relay to the operator on the other end of the line. "How far out are first responders?"

My teeth grit when she answers, "Ten, fifteen minutes."

"He'll bleed out by then." I search the area, seeking any instruments that will help me save Hugo's life. "Bring me the bucket of ice," I shout to a couple enjoying a Sunday morning mimosa with their brunch. The middle-aged gentleman is unsure how ice will help a man who's been shot, but he brings me the goods as requested. "Take your shirt off and wrap the ice cubes in it. The coolness of the ice will constrict his blood vessels, giving me some time to hunt for the nicked artery."

Nodding, the gray-haired man tugs off his expensive-looking polo shirt before dumping the full bucket of ice into it. Once I show him how to compress the makeshift dressing to Hugo's chest, I dig two fingers into Hugo's bullet wound, seeking the vein responsible for the puddle of blood I'm kneeling in. With most arteries pumping around one hundred milliliters of blood per heartbeat, I don't have minutes to save Hugo.

I have seconds.

Certain the gush against my fingers is from a severed artery, I lift my eyes to the bystander caught in the middle of a turf war. "Pass me your money clip."

The urgency of my tone doesn't give the stranger time to question how I know he has a money clip. His expensive loafers, three-hundred-dollar jeans, and thick gold chain gave away the fact he'd never place his money into a wallet like a normal person. He can't show off his large bundle of cash if he keeps it hidden.

"Ahh... should you be doing that?" The man talks through the lump in his throat, sickened by me inching his money clip into Hugo's wound.

"We need to clamp the artery. Unless you have a set of sterile surgical clamps, I'll work with what we have." Once I'm happy the money clip is slowing the flow of blood pumping out of Hugo's heart, I check his pulse. It's there, but it is weak as hell.

Hugo's blood smears on my cheek when I lift my phone to my ear. "Do you have an update on an ETA?" My pulse overtakes the operator's voice when I lose Hugo's pulse. "If you don't get them here now, he's dead!" I scream down the line before throwing my cell back onto the asphalt to commence CPR.

"Come on, Hugo." I thump on his tattooed chest to shock his heart before commencing compressions. "Don't give up! Do you hear me? You're *not* allowed to die."

Ignoring the fact I screamed the same words to Joey, I compress Hugo's chest until first responders arrive to overtake the legwork. As they attach an oxygen mask to Hugo's face, I scuttle backward, praying the outcome this time around won't end with a white sheet being draped. I've seen that image too many times in my life. I don't want to see it again.

I breathe for the first time in what feels like minutes when the transportable heart monitor picks up a faint, yet there, heartbeat. "You did good," the paramedic praises, stunned he didn't arrive to a DOA.

"Well done," my assistant commends, patting me on the shoulder. He looks like he wants to hug me, but considering my shirt is covered with vibrant red blood, he holds back.

I shift on my feet to face an elderly lady with a face full of wrinkles when she asks, "What happened to the woman in the Range Rover? Did your team get her?"

"Woman? What woman?" I ask, shocked.

Her pupils widen to the size of saucers as the color drains from her face. "That's why he was chasing them. They pulled a female into the back of a Range Rover at the bottom of St. Thomas Hill." She clutches her chest as her bottom lip shakes. "Oh dear, I hope she's okay?"

"What did she look like? Can you give me a brief description?" I say 'brief' as this lady looks like she could talk my ear off.

"About this tall." She holds her hand a foot taller than her height, which I'd guess to be around four-eight or so. "Chestnut hair. Was wearing jogging clothes and running with him." She nudges her head to Hugo who's being placed onto a gurney by four first responders.

"Was it her?" My hand shakes when I scroll through the images on my phone, seeking one of Isabelle. I scanned many of her into the Bureau mainframe the past few months, but these are from my private collection. "She's a couple of years older than this photo now."

When I spin my phone around to face the lady, she nods.

Fuck!

As I strive to keep my head in game mode, I ponder what to do. I could have the operator busying up my phone to dispatch Ravenshoe PD, but they'll take minutes to get here. Furthermore, just like the New York PD doesn't run New York, neither does Ravenshoe PD.

Isaac all but owns this town.

When I spot Hugo's cell phone sitting just left of a puddle of blood, I jump into action. "Wait." The first responders stop pushing Hugo toward the ambulance, startled by my shout. "I need his thumbprint." Hugo's phone isn't your standard cell phone. I haven't seen this brand before, leading me to believe it's a private network Isaac's team uses.

"Where are you taking him?"

As a dark-haired responder replies, I scroll through Hugo's recently called list to locate the last number he dialed. Although the area code is foreign, Isaac answers two seconds later. The worry in his tone advises me he's aware of the critical situation unfolding. I'm not surprised. He seems to know what's going to happen in Ravenshoe before it occurs.

"Hugo."

"It's Brandon," I correct, my greeting somewhat curt. "Hugo has been shot. They're taking him to Mercer Hospital."

Isaac's exhale is rigid enough to be felt from here. "Instruct them to take him to Ravenshoe Private. Tell them it's at the request of Isaac Holt. I'll call the head of surgery there and advise her of his impending arrival."

"Okay." After muzzling the phone, I pass on my instructions. The unnamed first responder looks surprised by my request, but he nods his head, nonetheless.

Once they have Hugo loaded into the back of the ambulance, I shift my focus back to Isaac. "Isaac…"

"Yes…"

The desperateness in his voice has me switching tactics. I was planning to tell him to be cautious, his every move is being monitored. Instead, I disclose just how closely he's being scrutinized. "Ask Regan to call the head of the FBI division in our county. Alex will help if he knows it's for Izzy." When silence resonates down the line, I give credit to my advice. "He has a higher clearance than Hunter does on the police database. It may be your only chance of finding her before it's too late. If this is Col, he won't keep Isabelle alive for long."

The heaviness on my chest eases when Isaac replies, "Regan is here. I'll call him." His clipped tone advises my suggestion won't be easy for him to swallow, but he's willing to do anything to keep Isabelle safe.

If that's the case, why is he working with the Popovs? It truly makes no sense.

I stop debating his strangeness when Isaac calls my name.

"Yes."

A bout of restlessness smacks into me when he mutters, "Thank you for your help. Please keep me updated on Hugo."

"I will." With shock stealing my words, I disconnect our call before shifting on my feet to face the first responders. "Give me a sec to grab my belongings so I can ride with you."

When he attempts to cite an objection to my request, I fan open my coat. I don't know whether the gun stuffed down the front of my pants convinces him or my credentials. Whatever it is, he agrees to my suggestion remarkably quick.

After dipping my chin in thanks, I hightail it to the spot I left my briefcase.

I could have sworn I hid it between the outside tables, but I can't see it anywhere. There are no bags on the ground at all.

"Did you see a soft leather briefcase sitting here?" I ask a shaken waiter gathering up the dishes left by the diners who went running when bullets were sprayed. "I left it right here."

"No, sorry," she answers with a shake of her head.

"It was right there!" I scream at her, frustrated. "It couldn't have just vanished."

"Maybe someone took it?"

"Yeah, maybe someone did." My voice is more sarcastic than hers, and ten times more furious. "And when I find out who they are, maybe I'll remove their fingers." When she swallows harshly, I realize I'm projecting my anger at the wrong person. "Sorry…" After another big exhale, I add, "If anyone hands it in, can you please contact me?"

Her cheeks bloom when I hand her my business card. Grayson said flashing your credentials works well with the ladies. I've never had an opportunity to test his theory until now.

"I will, *Agent James*." She purrs my name like my no-longer accurate title made me instantly cuter.

Ignoring my intuition warning me she's planning to use my private cell number for more than to contact me about my briefcase, I race back to the ambulance mounted on the curb. As they race Hugo to Ravenshoe Private, I send a quick message to Phillipa to update her on the current events occurring in Ravenshoe. Although Isaac isn't a direct target of hers, three of the bodies located at the Shroud family ranch were from Ravenshoe, so the CIA is paying close attention to this region.

Once my email whizzes off to Phillipa's secure inbox, I dial Grayson's number then squash my phone to my ear. "Tell them to take a right on Webster. The emergency lane on the interstate has a minivan with a flat. Even with sirens, they won't get through traffic," he says, not bothering to issue a greeting.

After passing his instructions onto the driver, and watching him turn right, I ask, "You've got eyes on me?"

"Yep." The 'P' pops from his mouth. "I'm piggybacking on Isaac's hacker's feed. It's about time that fucker paid me back. He's been riding my ass all year." Keys being stroked sound down the line before Grayson's gruff moan. "I don't think Alex will appreciate his morning visitor. Isaac is heading straight for his office building."

Guilt dangles off my vocal cords when I confess, "I told Isaac to reach out to him."

"I know. I heard. Good move."

"Good?" That wasn't close to the response I was anticipating.

"If Isaac is desperate enough, he'll make a mistake—"

"That could result in Isabelle's death," I interrupt, shouting. "Jesus, Grayson. Have a fucking heart."

Grayson doesn't understand the words 'back down.' "Two of the females found at Shrouds' lived in an apartment building owned by Isaac."

"So? He owns half the damn town." Even the ambulance officer conducting a range of tests on Hugo hums out an agreement.

My attitude takes a seat when Grayson continues speaking as if I never interrupted him. "And the third victim's identity was discovered earlier today. Who was she last seen with?" Although he's asking a question, he doesn't wait for me to answer him. "Isaac Holt. Reid has images of him picking her up from her apartment the night he returned from The Hamptons."

His disclosure is shocking, but there are too many loose threads for me to ignore. "The Shrouds' ranch was a baby-making facility's dumping site. Isaac's trip to The Hamptons was only months ago, the date range doesn't add up."

"Does in an industry where babies cut both production and profit margins."

It takes me a few seconds to read between the lines, but when I do, it smacks me in the gut. "Isaac's date was a prostitute?"

"Uh-huh. Had her tubes tied a few years back at her gigolo's request. He didn't want to get her shacked up with a baby when she was bringing in over eight G a night."

Now her death makes sense. The Castros wouldn't have kept her alive long after finding out she was worthless to them. They weren't working the prostitution conglomerate. It also discloses why Phillipa's team is looking so closely at Ravenshoe. The Castros have been bunkered down for over a year, so why are some of the victims' deaths so fresh?

Before I can answer my question, the ambulance arrives at Ravenshoe Private.

"We've arrived at the hospital. I've got to go."

Grayson calls my name before I fully lower my phone from my ear. "Alex and Isaac are on the move. I'll keep you updated."

"Thanks," I reply, genuinely grateful.

Even more so when he adds, "I'll also find your briefcase. You're not the only one who likes wasting Sundays immersing himself in times gone by. I've got the files backed up, but nothing replicates seeing decade-old footage on an ancient screen."

I stare down at my phone's screen when he disconnects our call. If he only piggybacked the CTC feed when Isaac's hacker logged in, how did he know I was watching videos of Melody and me before he called me? His mainframe is linked to Tobias's laptop, but I used a private proxy, aware he's a creep who has no qualms stepping over lines deemed as acceptable for friends.

Clearly, I need to start watching Grayson as closely as he's watching me.

MELODY

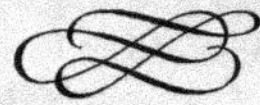

"Are you sure you don't want to come in and clean up before your flight?"

Julian's smile competes with the low-hanging sun. "Thank you for the offer, but I'm good. I don't want to be late for my flight."

"It's a private jet, Julian. I'm sure it can wait." I rib him with my elbow, ensuring he knows there's no malice to my tone.

The past twenty-nine hours have been good for us. Although Julian didn't expand on the disclosure Leo made yesterday morning, he was more open and honest than he had been the three years of our relationship. We talked as we should have the morning he left and ended things more amicably.

Heartache is associated with any breakup, especially one as long as ours, but when both parties agree it's for the best, it can also be encouraging. For years, I relied on Brandon. When I didn't have him, I felt lost and alone, which had me leaning on Julian more than I should have. It wasn't fair of me to do. However, I'm taking steps to fix that now.

That's why I'm back here at the ranch. I lost who I was here, so it's only right for me to re-find myself here. Then, once that's achieved, I can shift my focus to fixing all the mistakes I made. Brandon included.

Not wanting Julian to see the wetness dwelling in my eyes, I move our exchange onto the dreaded farewell stage. "Thank you for the ride. I much appreciate it."

Julian waits for me to press a kiss to his cheek before replying, "You're very welcome." After raking his eyes over my family ranch standing proud in the distance, he shifts them back to me. "Are you sure you don't want Tiny to stay with you?"

"I'm sure." I nudge my head to the tinted SUV that followed us here. It doesn't belong to Julian's convoy of vehicles, however, I know who's inside. "I'm safe here. Kwan will make sure of it."

It's amazing how the shredding of someone's shield has you seeing them in a new light. Kwan isn't a man to be messed with, but that only applies if you're hurting the people he classes as family. Since I have Gottle blood running through my veins, I've been given that title from him.

After dragging my purse from the back of Julian's car into my lap, I pull out a small wrapped box. "Will you please give this to your mom for me? She was eyeing it earlier this year during our weekend in Santa Barbara, and I really want her to have it."

When Julian dips his chin, agreeing to my request, I throw open the door of his flashy sports car. After climbing out and straightening my clothes, I pop my head back in. "There's also a gift for you in the trunk. Don't eat them all at once like you did last year, or you'll get an upset stomach." He laughs, fully aware as to what I'm referencing.

I wait for his laughter to die down before saying, "Goodbye, Julian."

A touch of sentiment is added to our exchange when he signs, *"Goodbye, Mel."*

Once the taillights of his vehicle fade into the distance, I shift on my feet to face the lonely SUV parked at the fence line of my property. "Are you coming inside? Julian's cook stowed some mouthwatering pastries into my bags."

Kwan slips out of his car quicker than I can snap my fingers. "You won't tell the boss, will ya?"

"It will be our little secret." He freezes mid-stride when I barter, "On one condition." I wait until he's sweating before spelling out my terms. "You have to clean Socks' stall in the morning. I don't do poop."

"Deal." His smile would have you convinced I said he could have Socks. "I'll get to that as soon as I've fixed the thermostat in the water boiler. Damn near froze my nuts off last month when I snuck in for a quick shower."

I laugh for the first time in over a week. I'm not laughing at Kwan's confession. It's recalling Brandon griping about the same thing two weeks ago when the water temperature barely rose past freezing.

"She loved it, Mel. Thank you."

I nurse my hot chocolate into my chest before snuggling deeper under the blanket. "You're very welcome. I'm glad she liked it. It's not expensive, but sent—"

"Sentimental value far exceeds the highest price tag," Julian fills in, smiling. "Is that why you've decided not to sell the ranch?"

After adjusting my phone so he can see me better, I shrug. "Yes and no. It's cheap to stay here, and since I'm not technically working right now, affordability must be considered." When Julian grumbles, annoyed I won't accept his many offers of help, I talk faster. "But I also like it here. It's…" I stop talking, unable to find the right word.

Julian doesn't face the same dilemma. "Home."

Smiling, I nod. "Yeah, it is."

A stretch of silence spans between us. It isn't awkward. More comforting than anything.

The same can't be said when Julian asks, "Have you heard from Nichole?"

"Yes." For how short my reply is, it shouldn't seem as affirmative as it is. "Proceedings will commence February twenty-third."

Julian's sigh is so strong I feel it on the other side of the country. "Can I ask you something, Mel?"

"Anything."

"It could be hurtful."

I smirk, appreciating his honesty. "I'm okay with that. I'm a big girl. I can handle it." That's one of the biggest steps I've taken the past week. I had to learn that it's okay to stumble as long as you get back up. Today is Christmas Day. I should be feeling lonely and isolated, especially since Kwan left to spend the day with his family, however, I don't. I'm finally growing comfortable with my own skin. "Come on, Julian, out with it before you're dragged away for brunch."

His chest deflates when he exhales. "You were raped by the Governor's son... so why isn't the media blasting the story? It would usually be front-page news."

It dawns on me that I know Julian better than I realized when I unearth the hidden agenda of his message. As much as he appreciates my name not being splashed across the tabloids, he's also curious if this is the norm. His family is uber-rich. Their wealth and stature already have them targeted by the media, so you can only imagine how bad the scrutiny would be if Leo's disclosure had been to anyone but me.

"In all honesty, I had wondered the same thing. Then I remembered what Vincent McGee is like. He's unscrupulous, Julian. He doesn't care who he has to steamroll to get his point across. Not even his own blood is safe." I take a quick breather before adding, "I also asked for the charges not to be publicly acknowledged. Although I was technically an adult when the assault occurred, so there was no reason for Nichole to grant my request, I'm glad she did. The people I count on know what happened to me. I don't need anyone else's sympathies." I stare straight at him while saying, "If you're not getting the support you need from the ones you love, you need to get a new support network, Julian."

He only nods, but I feel like I'm getting through to him. "Can I call you later?" He nudges his head to the party-like atmosphere happening behind him. "When that dies down."

"Of course, you can. I'm not going anywhere." My response has a double meaning. I have no plans to leave the ranch any time soon, but even if I did, I can still be there for Julian as he was for me for years.

Julian mouths his thanks before he shuts down our chat window. I'm still smiling about our friendly conversation when my phone receives a text message. I am hoping it's from Brandon but am left disappointed when I realize it's from the shipping company I used to return Brandon's BMW to him. It was supposed to take two weeks for delivery, giving me plenty of time to work up the courage to tell Brandon his generosity wasn't necessary. The Hellcat was his, so no payment was required, but the company's text message advises they're in the process of dropping his car off now. Christmas Day of all days. Even the Grinch knows that's poor form. Brandon won't see it as me saying payment for the Hellcat isn't required. He'll think I'm cutting him off and being ungrateful.

God, I need to fix this.

After returning a text to the shipping company, I leave a message on their voicemail begging for them not to drop off Brandon's car today.

When another three attempts to contact them fails, I dial Brandon's number. It rings and rings and rings, remaining unanswered until the sun is no longer visible in the sky, and my hopes are dashed.

I thought returning his car would shine a little bit of light into the darkness surrounding us. Now I'm worried it may have shrouded us even more.

BRANDON

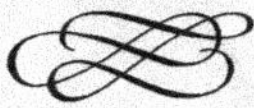

After silencing Melody's fifth call for this morning, I slide my cell phone into the pocket of my jeans before stuffing my arms into my winter coat. It doesn't get as chilly here the day after Christmas as it does in Saugerties, but the iciness of my veins makes it seem much cooler than it is.

Ignoring the keys of my BMW sitting on the entryway table, I snatch up my house keys before hotfooting it outside. My legs are a little wobbly when I gallop down the stairs. Alcohol is known for step impediments, and I've had more than my fair share the past few days. Isabelle was found safely. Isaac was touted as being her hero, and I was informed by Phillipa I had failed the mandatory psych evaluation to be officially signed on as a consultant with her team.

Me.

I failed.

Part of me thinks Phillipa is making out I didn't pass so I'll be forced to attend the counseling sessions she suggested after Hugo's shooting. She made out I was a part of a 'traumatic incident,' but I have an inkling Grayson told her about my quip about being suicidal.

I'm not suicidal. If I were, would I be looking into the death of a man who took the easy way out? Bar the handful of times Alex and Grayson have mentioned him, I don't know Dane Liberman, but I couldn't stop playing Regan's response to his death through my head while I laid in bed, doing nothing. Instead of wasting time, I either went on an eight-mile run or combed through Dane's file.

While I pop down to the shop to grab some supplies, my computer is downloading the many video logs I found on Dane's personal computer when I hacked in via an open banking app. I doubt it will lead to anything, but I've got nothing better to do, so it's worth a shot.

When I reach the footpath at the front of my apartment block, I raise the collar of my trench coat, effectively blocking out both the wind whipping off the ocean and the view of my BMW parked in my assigned bay. With my Hellcat being impounded yesterday for being illegally parked, I'll have to walk to the store for supplies—*regretfully.*

FORTY MINUTES LATER, I stuff a half-pint bottle of whiskey I was sneakily consuming on my trek back to my apartment deep into my bag of groceries. I'm not ashamed I am drinking in the middle of the day. I'm just so stunned by my unexpected visitor, alcohol isn't needed to give me the buzz life is supposed to give me.

Isabelle jumps out of her skin when I greet her with a back-the-front hug. With one arm juggling a bag of groceries, and the other clutching a six-pack of beer, I had to use my shoulder.

After gathering her heart from the ground, Isabelle slaps my shoulder. "Jesus, Brandon, you scared the shit out of me."

"Sorry, Izzy." I slant my head like a dog getting whacked over the head with a newspaper, feeling bad I scared her. "What are you doing here?"

An array of emotions hit me at once when she replies, "I just left Alex's office."

I was hoping it was a personal visit.

Clearly, we're not that close.

Nodding, I place the security code into the door Isabelle is standing next to before gesturing for her to enter the foyer before me. I follow her inside after doing a quick scope of the area. Not only am I suspicious Isaac has someone tailing Isabelle, I'm also wary about Grayson's uncanny knack for knowing more than he should.

Confident we're alone, I head for the elevator. I'm not willing to risk the stairs with how unstable my footing is. My aftershave can mask the scent of whiskey on my breath, but what excuse would I have for stumbling up steps?

"Does Isaac know you're here?"

Isabelle freezes before she shakes her head. "He's in a meeting. I left him a note."

While calculating how long it will take for Isaac to have one of his security details kick down my door, I suggest for Isabelle to enter the elevator before me. With the space confined, I don't voice any of the questions in my head for our fourteen-floor climb. I can taste the whiskey on my lips. I don't want Isabelle to smell it.

Isabelle takes advantage of my unusual quietness when she shadows my walk to my apartment. She takes in the high-end features and masculine feel of the space while I place the perishables into the fridge and hide my half-consumed bottle of whiskey in the cutlery drawer.

Just as she spins around to face me, I place the beers onto the counter. When she stares at them for several long seconds, I offer her one. She shakes her head while saying, "Beer has never been my liquor of choice."

"What about a glass of red, then?"

Eager to get her as sloshed as me, I snag a wine glass from a frosted overhead cupboard before pouring her a generous helping of merlot. She eyes me with suspicion when I hand it to her but remains quiet, unsure if she knows me well enough to notice my change in temperament.

As I enter the living room, I give thanks to my insomnia of late. If I weren't up all night removing the perp boards from my walls, Isabelle would have realized just how crooked Isaac is. In a way, I kind of wished they were still there. Perhaps that's what Isabelle needs—a hard wake-up call.

When I plonk onto my rock-hard sofa, Isabelle fills in the spot next to me. After folding her legs under her bottom to lessen the stiffness of the material, she tilts closer to me. "What happened?"

Even with a woozy head, I still know who her question is referencing. She wears her heart on her sleeve, and for some stupid-ass reason, she's worried about me.

After swishing my tongue around my mouth, I say, "We had opposing opinions on a matter."

I'm hoping my all-encompassing reply will subdue Isabelle's inquisitiveness. Regretfully, she's more clued in than I give her credit for. "We've all had that with Alex, but nothing bad enough to warrant him letting us go—"

"It doesn't matter. I'm not concerned about my position."

I snap my mouth closed, pissed at the curtness of my tone. My mother would be slapping me up the side of my head if she could hear me now.

"What's going on, Brandon?" When Isabelle dips her chin to force eye contact, my mood worsens. Phillipa's shrink did the same thing when she probed into my past more than I liked. "Something is bothering you. You seem off, upset even."

I gulp down half my beer before placing it onto the coffee table. While staring at nothing, I think about all the things I want to say. How the number of blows I've been hit with in my life isn't fair. How I worked so fucking hard for nothing. I don't have a job or a stable family environment. I have nothing.

I don't even have my girl anymore.

All the while, men like Isaac have everything—money, looks, cars, multiple business opportunities. They even get love, and for what, for them to piss it to the wall when it no longer suits them? Isaac was seen on surveillance with a prostitute. Isabelle saw the photos herself, yet, she stands at his side, supporting him as no one has *ever* supported me.

You've just got to keep moving, Brandon.

You've just got to keep putting one foot in front of the other.

You've just got to accept what life has to give you and be grateful for what you get.

But what happens when you don't want to accept the same shit over and over again? Do you become like them? Like Isaac and my father. Do you take the law into your own hands and pray for understanding when it backfires in your face?

Or do you just give up?

"If you knew something would hurt your friend, but you also knew they'd never forgive you if you didn't tell them, would you tell them?" I don't recognize my voice. It's like I'm here, but I'm not. Kind of similar to how I've been feeling the past week and a half.

"Yes," Isabelle replies, reminding me I'm not as alone as I feel. "I'd want to know."

"Are you sure, Izzy? Because once you know, it can't be undone." Believe me, I know that better than anyone. I can't unread the reports I read. I can't rewind the video in my head. It's there, stuck, never to be gone, never to be erased.

When Isabelle nods, I move to the leather briefcase hanging over my dining room chair—the leather briefcase Phillipa replaced for me when mine was never found.

"Alex told me about the payment between Isaac and Vladimir today," Isabelle advises, wrongly believing the FBI folder I dug out corresponds with the payments Isaac made to her father last month.

It isn't that.

It's way worse than that.

"This isn't regarding that." Almost robotic-like, I return to the couch, pull out a six-by-ten-inch photograph from my folder, then hand it to Isabelle.

"No." Her one word is like a punch to the stomach. It's equally remorseful and heart-wrenching. "It can't be."

"I'm sorry, Izzy," I murmur through the pain tearing at my chest. "It's true. Ophelia is alive."

After a painstaking thirty seconds, instead of letting me help her as I wish someone would help me, Isabelle leaps to her feet before seeking the closest exit. "Is there a back entrance to this building? Somewhere I can leave without Roger seeing me?"

"You should stay. We should discuss this."

She shakes her head so fiercely, strands of dark brown hair fall in front of her eye. "No. I need a minute to digest this." She's quick to wipe away the solemn tear trekking down her cheek, but I still see it. "I can't do that here. I'm sorry, Brandon. I just can't."

With her words being oddly familiar, I move to the front door of my apartment. "If you take a right at the end of the stairwell, it will direct you to the back entrance. You'll need to input a security code to stop the fire alarm from sounding."

I grab a pen off the desk to write the four digits of Melody's birthday onto her palm. I'm shaking so much, my handwriting is barely legible. I want to say it's the alcohol I guzzled the past week slowly seeping out of my body, but that would be a lie. It's knowing I hurt someone just with the hope of easing my pain.

How fucked up am I?

Who thrives on other people's unhappiness? I know misery loves company, but this is ridiculous. I'm better than this.

Or so I thought.

I wait for the familiar bell of the elevator advising its doors are closing before I take my frustration out on the entryway table. When I send it flying across the room, it knocks my laptop off the dining room table before it smashes the protective glass barrier around the fireplace. It feels good freeing some of the anger tearing me up inside, I'm tempted to see how sturdy my dining table is by taking a baseball bat to it, but before I can, an unfamiliar voice sounds through my ears.

"I would have never guessed she was the reason for my missing files..."

I move closer to my laptop, certain that's where the voice is projecting from.

"I don't know how long this has been going on, but from what I've unearthed so far this week, it appears to have been occurring for a few years."

When I flip my laptop over to face me, the man reflecting back at me doesn't match the strength of his voice. He has a deep, gravelly tone that belongs to a fit, early thirties man. This face is gaunt, white, and has more similarities to mine than I care to share.

My heart pains for Dane when he says, "Then the rest of the money... God, I don't even know where it's gone. Our mortgage is above our means, and Kristin is driving my old sedan." Determination sparks in his eyes when he stares down the lens. "But I *will* find out. Put your money on it—"

"Jesus," I mutter under my breath when a second person joins the frame. I can't see much of the face of the person who snuck up on Dane unaware, but it doesn't take away from the sickening act occurring. She has wrapped an extension cord around his neck. It isn't in a loving way.

When the blonde pulls Dane's mobility chair out from beneath him, I drop my eyes to the ground. The sound of his struggle is more than I can handle. I don't want to watch it. His gurgles as he fights to fill his lungs with air thrusts images of the last time I saw Joey into my head, but instead of letting it knock me down as many other things have the past few weeks, I recall how much lighter my shoulders felt when I was given closure.

I want Grayson and Alex to experience the same relief, so instead of continuing to dispel my rage, I do what I was trained to do. I protect, I serve, I honor, and I obey.

It just isn't to the person I thought it would be.

BRANDON

I scrub a hand over my eyes when my phone commences hollering. I fell asleep on my sofa—*again*—even with it being designed to discourage couch sleepers. Even someone without a dime to their name would choose a cardboard box in a cold alleyway over my couch. It has my back out of whack as well as my mood.

Aware no one would call this early unless it were urgent, I snag up my cell phone, slide my finger across the screen, then squish it to my ear. My caller breaks into a panicked script before I have the chance to issue a greeting. "How did you hack into Dane's bank accounts? He didn't leave his shit open for anyone to see. He was pedantic about security."

My surly mood is heard in my reply. "Good morning to you, too, Alex."

Not that Alex cares how I'm feeling. He's as bad as Isaac. Unless it directly affects him, he doesn't give a fuck about anything or anyone. "You hacked in like you did Regan's laptop, didn't you? Hung around until you got what you needed?"

"No. I had a search warrant for a *very* valid reason—"

"Dane wasn't rogue!" he interrupts, having no clue he's once again shifting his anger onto the wrong person. I've spent the last sixteen hours combing through evidence on a case that has nothing to do with me for *him,* so the least he could do is give me some fucking respect.

After giving him a moment to calm down, and perhaps myself, I say, "I never said he was."

The pause must have done Alex some good. He's thinking more rationally now, albeit a little hesitant. "The warrant was for Kristin?" I barely pop out a halfhearted sigh when he demands, "Tell me everything you know, Brandon."

"I don't know anything." I do, but I'm sure as fuck not giving him *all* the details. My first search was illegal, so if news of it gets out, my career will nosedive even more than it already has.

"Tell me everything you fucking know, Brandon!" Confident shouted words won't rattle me, Alex low-balls with a tasteless threat. "Or I'll make sure every agency from New York to Burbank knows the real reason you go by an alias."

Does that mean what I think it does? Is he aware Melody was raped by my brother? If so, it's fucked he's using that against me. If I had it my way, I'd drag Madden's name through the mud. The only reason I've kept quiet is because Melody doesn't want her name associated with a political scandal. She wants to give it the merit it deserves. I owe her that much to see her request through. It's the least I can do after I failed her so badly.

Although I'm pissed about Alex's demanding ways, I hit him with a fact that will knock his attitude down a peg or two. "Kristin made a $30,000 payment to Gabriele Francesco two weeks before the FBI's raid on Substanz." I give him a second to absorb my first disclosure before hitting him with another. "It was refunded in full the day following Dane's accident."

He clicks on rather quickly. "Because the hitman didn't get his mark?"

An agreeing hum has barely left my lips when someone's fist pounding into a steering wheel sounds down the line.

"Alex…" I pull my phone away from my ear to check our call is still connected before squashing it back up against it. "Are you there?"

When my question is answered with nothing but silence, I realize Alex wasn't beating the steering wheel with his fists. He used his cell phone.

Cursing, I disconnect our call before trying Alex's work number. He didn't let me finish, so he isn't just working off half-truths. If he's going home as suspected, he could potentially walk straight into a death trap.

When the phone in Alex's office rings out two times in a row, I resort to a new low.

With my number being unknown, I didn't anticipate for Isaac to answer as quickly as he does. "Unless your calling to tell me what got Isabelle so worked up after seeing you yesterday morning, I don't have time for you." His tone is thicker than usual, incapable of hiding his anguish.

"I need Regan's cell phone number."

He's quick to deny any knowledge of her existence, but before he can hang up on me, I aim to sway his opinion on the matter. "I could have hacked into her laptop, but this was quicker and more respectful. Which would you prefer me to do?" When nothing but his burly breaths come down the line, I add, "Please. It's urgent."

I don't know what gets me over the line, the desperateness in my tone or Isaac's eagerness to keep me out of his records, but he hands over Regan's details with only the slightest threat. "If I find out this wasn't critical, my reputation *will* live up to your expectations."

While murmuring out a halfhearted agreement, I scratch pen to paper, farewell Isaac with a grunt, then punch Regan's cell phone number into a device tracker I designed during my time with the analyst division of the Bureau. It's faster than the old version, and it brings up Regan's location immediately.

It's worse than I thought.

Alex isn't just heading straight into the line of fire.

So is his girlfriend.

After punching an alert into the Bureau's mainframe, announcing gunfire at the Bureau-owned apartment block Alex lives in, I dial Regan's number while hightailing it to my car. I could get in shit if it's a false alarm, but I'd rather be cautious than sorry. Some mistakes you can't undo.

I learned that the hard way.

It takes Regan a few seconds to answer, but when she does, I'm confident Isaac gave me the wrong number. "Hello." She only speaks one word, but her tone is so brittle, I'm confident she's on the verge of crying. That's not like Regan at all. Not in the slightest.

"Regan?" The unease in my voice is understandable. I feel like I'm about to be snagged in a trap. When a *whoosh* sounds down the line, I take that as confirmation I have the right person. "Is Alex with you?"

"No, he's in his apartment..." I hear her forcefully swallow before she mutters, "... with Kristin." The brutal slam of my car door drowns out what she says next.

After pressing the start button on the dashboard, I pull my seat belt across my torso. "He's with Kristin?"

The whoosh from earlier returns. "I think?"

"You think or you know?" I don't mean to snap at her, but I've had enough assumptions the past few weeks to last me a lifetime. It's time for me to start working off facts.

As I throw my gearshift into reverse, then tear out of my parking bay, Regan replies, "I don't know. He cuffed me in his car." When I curse under my breath, her panic doubles. "Why does it bother you if he's with Kristin?"

"Because he didn't let me finish." I push my car to its absolute limit. I'm not going to lie, I need the hit of adrenaline that comes from a sting. I've missed it more than I realized the past year and a half. "Kristin didn't just organize the hit on Dane, she killed him, Regan. She was brought in for questioning this afternoon."

"Is she still under arrest?"

Air leaves my lungs in a hurry when I shake my head. "No. She was released two hours ago."

When I hear Regan throw open a car door, I shout, "Authorities are on their way," before giving my car the thrashing of its life.

I race through the streets of Ravenshoe feeling more alive than I have the past year. Only one moment in time has trumped it. When I kissed a trail from Melody's neck to the waistband of her panties. The taste of her skin on my tongue should have been enough. I should have appreciated what I had.

Instead, I fucked it up.

I *always* fuck it up.

As I skid to a stop next to Alex's old sedan, I shake my head, ridding it of the negativity bombarding it. My already brisk strides double when the ricochet of a gun being fired bellows down the stairwell I'm climbing. It's a quick *pop, pop, pop* noise that's closely followed by a fourth *bang*. The final shot appears to be a higher caliber than its predecessor.

With the firing of multiple guns waking them from their sleep, several agents leave the safety of their apartments. Mercifully, none of them mistake me as the intruder. I may not be a part of their team anymore, but they know I'm not a baddie.

"FBI agents. Put down your weapon," I shout before pushing open Alex's partially cracked open door and storming into his living room.

The scene is one I've entered many times before, but for once, the good guys won. Two small blonde girls are clutching Regan's thighs. Alex has been shot in the shoulder but appears stable, and Kristin is lying lifeless on the floor with three bullet wounds to her torso and one to her head.

I should be pleased by the outcome, it could have ended much worse, but for some reason, I can't find joy in it. I guess my mom's old saying is true:

> *Every thought is a battle*
> *Every breath is a war*
> *But once you give up*
> *You can't win anymore.*

BRANDON

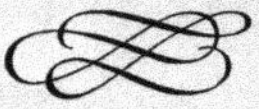

"Did you catch up on any sleep today? You look like shit."

I roll my eyes at Phillipa before accepting the towel she's holding out for me. I'm in the bathroom in my apartment, and she has no respect for privacy.

While wrapping the towel around my waist and grabbing another from under the vanity to dry my shaggy hair, I ask, "Did Kristin pull through?"

Phillipa waits for me to get myself into some sort of order before she shakes her head, acting ignorant to the liquor she smells leeching from my pores. "Her daughters will stay with Alex until their next of kin arrive."

My lips twist. "I thought Alex was their guardian?"

Phillipa sighs. "So did I. Turns out Kristin changed that part of her will when Dane's insurance fell through. She couldn't suck him dry anymore, so she went after his parents."

A *pfft* vibrates off my lips. "From the reports I read, that's the equivalent of seeking blood out of a stone. They don't have any money."

I can only work off what I've seen, but it appears as if Kristin was accepting payments from Isaac without Dane's knowledge. Was it for illegal purposes? I don't know. That's something Grayson's team will look at when they endeavor to unearth how all the storylines surrounding this town are merging into one.

When Phillipa lifts her chin, agreeing with me, I gesture mine to my open bedroom door, requesting a minute to get dressed. A half-hearted grin tugs at my lips when she rolls her eyes. She hasn't flirted with me since the gala. I assumed her lack of interest was because her cover was blown. I've been thinking differently the past few days.

I can't one hundred percent testify to this, but I'm reasonably sure her focus was on something else—or should I say, *someone* else. You can't continue crushing on someone when a new crush shows up. Only fools who believe they can reignite old flames give that notion a run for its money.

After yanking on a pair of sweatpants and tugging a shirt over my head, I join Phillipa in my living room. "How did you get past my security?"

She pulls a *'duh'* face. "You mean the digital lock with Melody's date of birth as the pin?"

Not needing further explanation, I pace into the kitchen, eager to get back to the commiserating I was doing before sweaty pits demanded an intermission.

"Did you want a drink?"

Phillipa's eyes drop to the almost-empty bottle of whiskey in my hand before they return to my face "I thought you were more a margarita type of man?"

"I'll down anything if it takes the edge off," I mutter before I can stop myself. "Don't," I plea when the humor in Phillipa's eyes switches to worry. "I had my ass chewed out by Grayson before I entered the shower and was eyed like a freak by Alex earlier today. I'm at my quota for explaining myself today, so either drink with me or leave me to drink alone. *Please.*"

After a few seconds of uncomfortable silence, she mutters, "I'll drink with you." The tension depriving the air of oxygen eases when she mutters under her breath, "Just don't blame me if I ram my tongue down your throat after a scotch or two. It was proven without a doubt two weeks ago that I get randy when drunk." When my brow cocks, wordlessly demanding an explanation, she gives as good as she's getting. "Don't go picking locks you don't want open, BJ. Because if we unlock this vault of craziness, we'll move straight onto yours."

More than happy to miss that shitshow, I pour us a generous serving of whiskey before nudging my head to the living room, wordlessly inviting for her to join me in there.

When she follows me with only the slightest groan, I ask, "What's the reason for your visit?" I shut down the lie I see in her eyes before she can deliver it. "Don't act like you flew down here for no reason, Phillipa. You like me, but you don't like me *that* much."

She scoffs. "I like you a lot, thank you very much. I just found out the hard way that my feelings would never be reciprocated." After snatching one of the whiskeys out of my hand, she throws down the double shot in one hit, then slams the empty glass onto the coffee table. "I saw you kiss Melody. It sucked." If I thought her first confession was shocking, it has nothing on her second one, "Then I kissed Julian. It didn't mean anything. We were both drunk, and we had no clue who the other was until you invited me to Melody's ranch a few days later."

"You said you handled the ransom Julian paid to Castro."

"No," she corrects, her voice fierce. "My *team* did. I was too busy…"

When her words trail off to silence, I fill in the quiet. "Pretending to be an FBI agent. Got it."

She rolls her eyes before locking them with mine. There's something in them I haven't seen before. "I kind of like him, but I shouldn't because I don't really know him." If she were a cartoon, love hearts would be bouncing out of her eyes right now. "But I do. I do like him."

Although nothing but honesty is heard in her voice, I'm still lost. "And you're telling me this because..." I understand I have the boy-next-door, best-friend persona down pat, but still, this seems odd.

My eyes snap to Phillipa when she mumbles, "Because there's a possible conflict of interest."

I stare at her, begging for her to fill in the blanks.

When she leaves me hanging, I squawk, "How?"

"Do you remember how we theorized about Melody possibly being sold?" When I nod, her big exhale fans my face with whiskey. "I'm reasonably sure Julian was sold."

The thrashing of my heart juts up my words. "Reasonably sure? Or *sure* sure? I can't accept half-assed assumptions, Phillipa. I'm way beyond that."

My throat works hard to swallow when she mutters, "He *was* sold. He could have quite possibly been the first..."

"The first..." I gulp when I read the truth from her eyes. "The first baby sold by the Castros' baby-making syndicate?"

She screws up her face before nodding. She isn't apprehensive. She's cringing over the high pitch of my voice. "It gets worse."

"I don't know how, but hit me with it."

Phillipa waits for me to finish my whiskey before spilling her guts. "You also have an undisclosed conflict of interest."

I'm about to say, 'No shit, Sherlock.' Melody was Julian's fiancée —if not still—so that automatically links me to Julian's case, but I realize I'm way off the money when I see the worry in Phillipa's eyes.

"Who?"

I'm desperate for another shot of whiskey when she mutters, "Olivia Wilde. Previously known as Ophelia—"

"Petretti," I interrupt. "How is she involved?"

After snagging her briefcase off the ground where my entryway table once stood and detouring past the kitchen to snatch up the half-consumed bottle of whiskey, she retakes her seat next to me. "If you were manufacturing babies for well-to-do clients who either were infertile or didn't want to ruin years of plastic surgery by growing their own baby, what services would be on your speed-dial list?"

A normal person would automatically say an obstetrician. I'm not close to ordinary. Mr. Gregg taught me to think outside of the box, which is precisely what I do in this situation.

"A pharmacist?" I suggest a few seconds later. "They have access to fertility drugs without needing a prescription, meaning there won't be a messy paper trail for authorities to find."

"Exactly." The whiskey burns my throat for a second time when Phillipa places an employee identification card next to our empty glasses. Although I only spent twelve hours with the woman smiling up at me from on the card, I'll never forget her face. She's one of a handful of people I blame for ruining my life.

I want to believe the evidence Phillipa is presenting, but with my trust low, I have to remain cautious. "Olivia…" I stop, then correct, "*Ophelia* has only been 'deceased' for six years. Julian is a decade older than her. Your dates don't add up, Phillipa. You're missing a huge chunk of the timeline."

She smiles, pleased with herself. "I would say you're smarter than you look, BJ, but you rock the smart, cutie vibe as well, so I won't mess with your head." She places a second ID card onto the first. This one is from many decades ago.

"Ophelia's mom was a pharmacist." Since I'm not asking a question, it doesn't sound like one. "Do you believe she was running the same scheme as Oli… Ophelia?"

"I don't think. I know." She hands me a bunch of autopsy reports. "Drugs found in the older victims' autopsies were matched to prescriptions filled at the drug store Lana worked at." When she locks her eyes with mine, the confidence in them is nearly enough to put me on my ass. "The Petrettis were working with the Castros. I'm confident of it."

When I take a moment to work the facts through my head, the pause in time awards me more confusion.

"There's something we're missing. Dimitri would *never* work with the Castros." I don't disclose how I know he hates them with every fiber of his being, but I do disclose we've had private conversations. "He's also unaware Ophelia is alive. If your beliefs are true, Dimitri is in the dark about it all." I am shocked I'm standing up for a criminal, but at the end of the day, Dimitri isn't in the wrong—this time.

"I guess time will tell." Phillipa balances on the edge of my couch before digging her hand into her briefcase. "We have surveillance in place for Ophelia."

"When were these taken?" I ask when she dumps a file full of still images onto the coffee table.

As she pours us another generous serving of whiskey, I rummage through the photographs. "My guy has been there since dawn…" Her words trail off when I curse under my breath. "What?"

"That's Isabelle." I point to a photograph in the middle of the stack, cursing for the second time when I recall Isabelle's sudden desire for a trip to Tiburon. "I told Izzy Ophelia was alive. I gave her a photo from Tobias's folders."

Phillipa looks a cross between wanting to strangle me and hug me. "Brandon, why would you do that?"

"I had no clue she'd seek her out." That's a lie. I knew the instant I showed Isabelle the picture, she'd do everything in her power to locate Ophelia as it's exactly what I would have done if I were in the same situation. "I've got to go. Can you show yourself out?" Not waiting for her to answer me, I race to my front door.

"Where are you going?" Phillipa shouts as I jab my finger into the elevator call button.

As I dash into the awaiting cart, I answer, "To fix a fuck-up."

One of many I've made the past two weeks.

THIRTY MINUTES LATER, I pull my BMW into the driveway of Isaac's private residence. No one had knowledge this property existed until Alex tailed Isaac and Isabelle home from his penthouse apartment a couple of months ago. I was in awe of the architect when I arrived to catalog evidence following the execution of a search warrant, but the inside of his palatial palace required a creative imagination. I don't know who conducted Alex's search warrant, but they spent more time destroying Isaac's property than hunting for evidence.

When several presses on the buzzer go unanswered, I pull my car to the side of Isaac's estate so I can check for any incoming flights to Ravenshoe's private airstrip. Isaac wasn't seen in any of Phillipa's surveillance images, but that doesn't mean he wasn't with Isabelle in Tiburon. He never lets her out of his sight.

I stop punching in the flight manifest for a private jet that arrived back earlier this evening when the headlights of a car shine into the cab of my BMW. Although I can't see any features of the person seated behind the driver's seat, I'm confident it is Isaac. His arrogance is felt from here, although it's a little light tonight compared to normal.

After a few minutes of psyching myself up for World War III, I curl my hand around my door latch, prepared to confront Isaac for the second time in under twenty-four hours. I've only just cracked open my door when another set of headlights beam into my car. These aren't sleek and curved like most sports cars. They're round and classic, convincing me they don't belong to any of the cars in Isaac's fleet. If its price tag is under one hundred thousand dollars, he won't touch it with a ten-foot pole.

My teeth grit when Hugo spots me as quickly as I spot him, then they're crunched down to nubs when he conducts an illegal U-turn to pull in behind me. He's got issues with me, and in all honesty, I understand why. I just wish he'd take his frustration out on my brother instead of me.

I'm carrying more than my load. I don't know if I can take another ounce.

"What are you doing here, Blondie?" Hugo snarls, strutting my way. "You sniffing around hoping Isaac left out a bone?"

A wish to ram Grayson's suggestion for me to rile Isaac slams into me. Ever since I kissed Isabelle, I've taken hit after hit after hit.

I guess that's what happens when you mess with a taken girl.

When Hugo stops in front of me, he puffs out his chest, ensuring I'm aware he has a good six to eight inches on me in height. Although his cocky stance would have most men running, some things Mr. Gregg taught me will never be forgotten.

"I just want to make sure Izzy is all right," I reply, fighting to hide my smile about how intimidated he is of me. He wouldn't be parading around like a peacock if he thought he had one over me. The fact he's constantly on alert assures me he knows I can give as good as I get.

"Then why not go knock on the door like a real man?"

An unexpected chuckle rumbles in my chest. "Been there. Done that." *More than once.* When Hugo glares at me, confused, I relieve his confusion. "I've tried numerous times to see Izzy since she left the hospital. My attempts were always denied by Isaac."

He hates giving me any leeway, but the honesty in my reply doesn't give him much choice. "Izzy is fine. She's with Isaac… where she belongs."

Hugo's brisk strides to his classic ride halts when my curiosity gets the better of me. "Even with Ophelia being alive?" I didn't mean to voice my question out loud. I was just too shocked to hold it back.

Hugo pivots around to face me, his brow cocking. "How do you know about that?"

My throat works hard to swallow when it dawns on me that I blew my cover. I'll blame my woozy head for my mistake.

"You gave Izzy the photo, didn't you? You thought it was your way in, the key to breaking up Isaac and Izzy."

I shake my head, both stunned by his suggestion and agitated by it. I may be an agent, but that doesn't automatically place me on the opposition's team. I've helped Isaac many times the past few months. I let his team into Megan's ranch before authorities, and I got Isabelle out of Theresa's clutch before the damage of her claws was irreversible. I've helped.

Not that anyone ever notices.

Hugo's reply ensures I can't be mistaken about this. "Bullshit. You weaseled your way into Izzy's life by pretending you're her friend, *all* so you could undermine her relationship with Isaac. I've got news for you… you can't fight fate, so I suggest you give up while you're ahead."

"I'm her friend," I retaliate, my anger rising. "Everything I've done is because I'm trying to protect her," I continue to shout, unaware I'm projecting my fears for Melody onto Isabelle.

"She doesn't need your protection!" Hugo's roar is as violent as the bomb ticking deep in my gut. It's indestructible and seconds from detonation. "She has Isaac. She has me." He bangs his chest during his last confirmation. "She doesn't need you, so go jump on your white horse and find another damsel in distress to save because Izzy doesn't need saving."

When he stalks back to his car, I fight to control my anger. I remind myself time and time again that I've done nothing wrong, and that he's just taking his anger out on the wrong person. But no matter how hard I fight, no matter how much I try to be the bigger person, I can't.

I'm done playing nice.

"Are you going to protect her like you did Gemma?"

Hugo's spin this time around is faster than his previous. With his steps fortified with anger, he storms my way looking as if he wants to kill me.

I could only be so lucky.

After fisting my shirt, he drags me to within an inch of his face. He stares at me for what feels like minutes but is barely seconds. I can see the hate in his eyes, the anger. It mimics the hurt in mine to a T.

"Who are you?" he asks, shuddering through the shivers wreaking havoc with every inch of his body.

Pissed by my lack of response, he repeats, "Who are you?"

Needing the pain to end, I mutter, "My name is Brandon James..." He grips my shirt tighter, his fury uncontained. "McGee."

Shock fills his face as he scans mine, seeking similarities only brothers have. When he finds them, he takes a stumbling step back. "You're Grabby McGee's brother?"

Grabby McGee? I wish that were the worst of it.

When I nod, answering the unvoiced questions in his eyes, he yanks me forward before ramming me back. The brutal crunch of my body into my car is sickening, however, it fills me with calm. Pain is good. Pain reminds me of how I failed.

"Do you know who I am?" Hugo growls in my face, his spit sizzling on my cheeks.

"Yes," I reply, ashamed. I know every sordid detail, and I did *nothing* about it. Kind of similar to how I responded to Melody's injustice as well. Madden is sitting in jail, awaiting his trial, but if I were a real man, he'd be dead. There'd be no question about that.

I recall the reason for my shift in focus when Hugo asks, "Do you know what they did?" An array of emotions flares through his eyes—anger, hurt, frustration, they're all there—even more so when he repeats his question. "Do you know what they did to me?"

"Yes." The simplicity of my reply doesn't lessen Hugo's annoyance. The redness on his cheeks doubles as he fights to maintain a cool head. I wish he wouldn't. "But I'm nothing like them," I assure, even with my confidence not as high as it once was. "I didn't change my name because I didn't want people to know who my father is. I changed it because I'm ashamed of it. I'm ashamed of them." Him. My brother. The man who raped my girlfriend.

I want Hugo to crack. I want him to break. I want him to hurt me until my outsides match my hideously ugly insides, but instead of doing any of those things, Hugo proves what I've always known.

He isn't a monster like Madden. He's merely a broken man—*just like me*.

After a final stare and an ashamed shake of his head, he stalks to his car, leaving me alone.

Again.

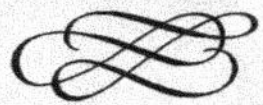

My steps falter halfway up the stairs leading to my apartment building. A man is in the foyer, a man who shouldn't be here. He's undercover miles and miles from here. Usually, I'd be pleased to see him. That isn't the case today.

Grayson isn't here because he needs my help. He's here to help me. The worried expression on his face is very telling, much less the lady standing behind him, backing up his campaign.

"Phillipa was supposed to show herself out, not let in strays."

Grayson doesn't scoff at my low, woeful tone. He uses it to fortify his campaign. "You need help, BJ."

"Leave it alone," I warn him, stepping past him and Phillipa. I jab my finger into the elevator call button in rhythm to the stabbing punctuation of my words. "I'm tired, restless, and I need to fucking sleep. That's what *I* need."

"You *need* to admit that you're hurting. You *need* to admit your brother did you wrong. You do *not* need to take the blame for him. *He* hurt Melody, Brandon. *He—*"

"Raped her!" I interrupt, screaming. "That's way beyond hurt,

Grayson." I step closer to him with my fists clenched and my nostrils flaring. "If *you* hadn't stopped me, he'd be dead, and justice would have been served." I get up in his face as Hugo did mine forty minutes ago. "Just like if *you* hadn't forced Tobias to intervene, she would have *never* been hurt. This is as much on your shoulders as it is mine, Grayson. You deserve just as much of the blame."

"Yeah, it is, punk. It's on my shoulders. I feel the weight. I feel your pain. But I'm not going to let that prick eat at my conscience until I don't recognize myself anymore." His eyes bounce between mine. They're shimmering with tears. "I'm not going to let him win… unlike you."

He slaps my chest before taking a step back, having no clue the thread I'm clutching is extremely thin. If the desperateness to see Madden punished for his crimes wasn't keeping me motivated, I would have let go by now.

That's how much it hurts.

That's how ashamed I am.

I work my jaw side to side when Phillipa mutters, "We're worried about you, BJ. You're not yourself."

"I'm fine." I grit my teeth when my lie doesn't come out as strong as I'm hoping. "I just need to keep my head busy."

"And what happens when the busyness stops?" she asks, stepping forward, taking over the Brandon-is-a-wimp baton. "What happens then?"

I won't answer her question because, in all honesty, I don't know how. I'm barely holding on. I can feel the cracks deepening, they're seconds from being exposed.

Since I don't want that to occur in front of witnesses, I spin on my heels and dart up the stairwell. I've barely climbed half a floor when Phillipa shouts my name. She sounds worried about me. Or even worse, sorry for me. Both are as bad as the other.

"I'm fine!" As a big chunk of the wall around my heart comes away with a brutal sob, I race up fourteen floors like my fitness hasn't gone to shit the past two months. "I'm fucking fine."

When I burst through the front door of my apartment, I think I'm in the clear.

I think I am safe from additional pain.

I'm an idiot.

This hurt is different than the agitated restlessness Grayson and Phillipa's exchange instigated. It is sore, remorseful, and catastrophic. It's bigger than me—not in stature, we stand at almost the same height—but in sorrow, deep, anguish-filled sorrow.

Well played, Grayson, well played. You just utterly annihilated me.

As I stand in the middle of my entryway, the girl from my dreams spins around to face me. She must have arrived in a hurry. Her dirty-blonde hair is kinked from letting it dry naturally, and her face is free of makeup. Even with her eyes full of tears, she's even more breathtaking than she is when she graces my dreams. You can't beat perfection unless your name is Melody Gregg.

"Hi, BJ," Melody signs as her eyes float over my face.

When gut-wrenching heartache beams out of me in invisible waves, she bridges the gap between us before throwing her arms around my neck. I try to be brave when she whispers in my ear that I'm not to blame for what happened to her. I try to be strong like I've been taught both as a child and an adult. I try to represent those men who never cry, not even when they're attending the funerals of their mothers.

But then I remember I'm not one of those men.

I am Brandon James McGee.

Peanut butter lover, baseball loather, and Melody Gregg's best friend.

I can fall because Melody will catch me.

I can break because Melody will fix me.

And I can say I'm sorry because only after I forgive myself for the mistakes I've made will I be able to accept Melody's forgiveness.

Furthermore, I'll never grip love if I don't let go of the pain. It's not possible to keep them both. So, instead of continuing to hold onto that teeny tiny thread I've been clutching the past month, I let it go.

The fall is brutal, and it hurts, but as predicted, Melody catches me.

I can only hope she never lets me go.

MELODY

Have you ever sat in a dark room and just let your mind drift? I never had until Grayson called me out of the blue last night. I wouldn't necessarily say it was an eye-opening experience for me personally, but it was epiphanic to the person I was once.

As I sat in the dark, hoping to clear the gunk from my head, I kept hearing the same six words over and over again.

"A victim knows a victim, right?"

Leo's words were for Julian, but the more they played through my head, the more they resonated with Brandon. A victim doesn't have to be physically scarred from an assault. Emotional abuse is just as detrimental, especially to a gentle soul like Brandon.

As I struggled to work through the debilitating weight Grayson's call had placed on my chest, truth after truth smacked into me.

I lost my parents.

So did Brandon.

They weren't his biological parents, but they were his family.

I was forced to attend a college I didn't want to attend.

So was Brandon.

Browns was our first pick, but he didn't want to go without me. I forced him to.

I was victimized by Madden.

So was Brandon.

He trusted his brother. He believed I was safe around him.

Can you blame him?

He could have never predicted what would happen. I was cautious of Madden, yet I still struggle comprehending why he took it as far as he did.

Brandon lost his brother.

So did I.

Once again, blood isn't thicker than water.

There's only one thing we didn't experience together.

Brandon lost me.

I never lost him.

I tried to replace him. I tried to live without him, but I never truly lost him. He was always there, protecting my six as he'd been taught, but while he was doing that, who was protecting him?

Could you imagine going through everything Brandon has been through the past eight years and not having anyone there to support and comfort you? I tried, but in all honesty, I only ever saw things from my side.

That was wrong of me. So very wrong.

Brandon pledged to protect me. He vowed to keep me safe, but he wasn't the only one who made that pledge.

So did I.

It was before the crazy butterflies started taking flight in my stomach. Before friends' prolonged gawks made my skin green with jealousy. And long before we made things official in a way that was remarkably mature for how young we were.

We were only eight when we said our vows, but the words I spoke that day were the most honest I've ever spoken. Brandon was my friend, my light, *my everything* before he was *ever* my boyfriend. So, although my ego was bruised and my confidence faltered, for once in my life in that dark, cold room, I remembered the pledges I had made to Brandon instead of the ones he'd made to me.

He needs me. There's no doubt about that. If that's only as a friend, I'm okay with that. Our relationship was perfect before we became boyfriend and girlfriend, and it will be perfect years after.

I'll make sure of it because my parents didn't just teach me how to be strong, they showed me what love really looks like. It is ugly, it is messy, and it can be cruel, but if it is given to the right person, it can be the most fulfilling thing you'll ever do in your life.

MELODY

I prick my ears to ensure Brandon is still in the shower before pacing to the front door of his apartment to see who's knocking. I won't lie, my steps are sluggish and weighed down even with our intervention being staged a little over five weeks ago. The first night was the hardest. It was rough pushing Brandon over the edge instead of guiding him off the ledge, but Grayson and I didn't have much choice. If we didn't force Brandon to crack, we may have lost the chance to piece him back together.

I was never going to let that happen.

Not in a million years.

I had wondered during our days at the ranch if Brandon was depressed. He was more reserved than usual and somewhat withdrawn. Since he was an adult instead of the teen I once knew, I blamed the seven-year gap in our friendship for not being able to read him as I once could. In reality, I was scared. Scared of pushing him away, scared of being alone, and scared to face the truth that I still loved the man whose brother raped me.

The last revelation was the hardest for me to overcome. I took

Brandon's rejection personally instead of assessing what it was really about. He wasn't rejecting me, his head wasn't even in the room with us that night. He was rejecting the pain eating him whole, swallowing it down as he had been taught.

My dad was a brilliant, protective man, but he had his faults. Teaching Brandon and me to bottle up our emotions was one of his downfalls. He taught us it's okay to be brave, to fight for what we believe in, and never give up no matter how bad the odds, but he didn't tell us it's okay to cry, to ask for help, and to admit when you're drowning.

Thank God the love my mother showered my father with ensured I learned those things without extensive training. My father believed he had hurt her, he took blame for what had happened to her, yet she loved him with everything she had. She never blamed him, not once. She loved him unconditionally as I do Brandon. That's why it wouldn't have mattered how rough it got, I bunkered down for the long haul, and I'll continue being here for as long as Brandon needs me.

When I peek through the peephole in Brandon's front door, my heart flutters out an extra beat. Grayson is standing on the other side. His visits have been scarce the past five weeks. He hasn't gone back undercover. I just asked him and Phillipa to steer clear of Brandon's apartment until I could work my magic. I didn't know at the time exactly what my magic would entail. I just knew Brandon well enough to know he'd rather it occur without an audience.

We've done pretty much nothing the past five weeks. We ate in every night, watched movies, we even recommenced our Monopoly championship. It still caused us to snicker at each other as we did in the footage my dad captured of us when we were seven. It wouldn't be so bad if Brandon didn't always buy-up Boardwalk and Park Place. Without fail, I land on the damn things every time I circle the board.

When we were kids, our game always ended with me tossing up

the board and storming off to sulk. Although my dramatics weren't quite as bad this time around, I'm ashamed to admit the sulk-fest still occurred.

It wasn't all bad. That night was the first time Brandon laughed in almost a week. It wasn't his full-hearted laugh, and it was quickly killed by Dr. Avery, Brandon's counselor, doing a house call to check up on him, but it was perfect.

I don't know if it was the words Dr. Avery spoke during their forty-five-minute session, or the fact Brandon accepted my offer to stop sleeping on the couch by sharing his humongous bed, but whatever it was, things changed for us that night. We still act as if the other has cooties when we stuff pillows between us, but the tension that was there the first night all but eradicated last night.

This morning, I woke up with my leg hooked around Brandon's waist and his fingers knitted in my hair. It honestly killed me untangling myself from the web we had weaved throughout the night, but I did it. Barely.

I didn't have much choice. I can't issue Brandon a no-intimacy clause to our friendship then hump his leg in the middle of the night. That's just asking for trouble.

For me, not Brandon. He was a remarkable boy, but he's an even more remarkable man. I can see why Phillipa has developed a crush on him. He's impossible not to love.

I stop listening to the voice in my head telling me a true friend would give Phillipa her blessing when Grayson waves his hand in front of my face, drawing me from my somber thoughts. "You with me, Melody? You seem to have spaced out."

"Sorry, I'm here. Long night." When Grayson purses his lips, I backhand him in the chest. "Not like that." I'm tempted to hit him for the second time when his smile grows at the disappointment in my tone. "Are you here for a reason, Grayson? Or just to stir me?"

"I had come for a purpose, but I'm kinda thinking I should stick to teasing. I thought BJ was the only one whose face lit up like a

Christmas tree when he was embarrassed." After tracking his fingers down my bloomed cheek, he mutters, "My bad."

I whack him in the stomach for the second time before dragging him into the entryway. I'm in a nightie, so I don't want Brandon's neighbors seeing me in a state of undress.

With Brandon's fireplace keeping his apartment super cozy, Grayson slips out of his jacket before tossing it over one of the chairs in the dining room. His face reveals he wants the details on why we're keeping things super warm, but with the removal of his coat announcing why he's arrived here at eight in the morning, he's interrogation will have to wait.

"You found it?" I pace closer to the silver box Grayson placed onto the dining room table a second after removing his coat. It's the time capsule Brandon and I buried years ago. It's covered with red dirt and has rusted a little, but the initials my dad engraved on the top ensures it will never be mistaken.

"Yep." The 'P' pops from Grayson's mouth. "It was exactly where you said it would be. Right under the tree you got married in front of."

As I lift one of my mom's old jewelry boxes into my hand, tears well in my eyes. "Did you open it?"

A *pfft* noise vibrates Grayson's lips. "Do I look like a nosy-body?" When I arch my brow, he rolls his eyes. "Whatever. I didn't snoop." A smile stretches across my face when he mumbles under his breath, "The damn thing is locked."

His reply is as humorous as it is disappointing. "I forgot it was locked. I don't have the key here."

Grayson offers to jimmy the lock at the same time a third person joins our conversation. "I do."

When Brandon walks out of his room, drying his soaking-wet hair with a towel, my eyes drop to take in the generous ridges of his body not covered by his sweatpants. This is the exact reason my steps are sluggish and slow. It has nothing to do with the minimal sleep schedule we've been working the past five weeks, and everything to do with how many times I've pressed my thighs together. Just like when he was a teen, Brandon's body is divine. No amount of ogling will *ever* have me grow tired of eyeballing it.

Furthermore, the last time his abs contracted and released while he paced my way was the first night we slept together. That night was painful, but it was also beautiful. It has highlighted my dreams many times the past eight years.

While lifting my jaw back to its rightful spot, Grayson lets out a chuckle. "Now I understand why the fire is over-stacked." I pout like a child when he tosses his coat to Brandon. "Put a shirt on, punk. Your girl is about to get drool on my shoes."

I'm about to lay into him for the third time in the past five minutes, but Brandon's laugh stops me. It's an exquisite thing to hear even with the appreciation of its arrival being shared between Grayson and me. However, the fact he doesn't deny that I'm his girl may be even more beautiful.

Once Brandon's laughter settles down, he dumps Grayson's jacket onto the dining room table, presses his lips to my temple, then paces to a safe hidden behind a torn painting. I don't know what happened to his pricy artwork and the glass that once wrapped around his fireplace. My emotions have been too high to ask—even more so when he removes a shoebox from inside his safe. It's *our* shoebox. The one we stored all the precious things we refused to bury in the ground in case they got lost.

When Grayson spots the tears welling in my eyes, he takes them as his queue to leave. "I'm out." He throws his arm around Brandon's shoulders to give him a quick man-hug before he makes a beeline for the door. "Call me when you're ready to dive back in, punk. I've got a few cases lined up for you."

He's out the door before Brandon can reply. It's for the best. Brandon's mindset isn't ready for the slaughtering the Bureau will hit it with. I'm sure he'll get there one day, just not today.

When Brandon stuffs the bent key from the bottom of our shoebox of treasures into the time capsule's lock, I curl my hand over his. "Breakfast first. You haven't eaten since dinner." He almost argues with me, but my quick, snapped comment stops him. "Peanut butter directly out of the jar doesn't count as a meal, BJ."

My steps into the kitchen wobble when he mumbles, "That's not what you said that night in your dorm," but I pretend not to hear him because as much as this sucks to admit, he's not ready for that stage of our friendship yet either.

"What do you want? Pancakes, eggs…" I roll my eyes when his light up. "Peanut butter on toast it is."

SEVERAL HOURS LATER, I snuggle into Brandon's side before burrowing my head into his neck. I have my consumed Ring Pop candy ring on the finger where a real engagement ring once sat, my favorite scrunchie wrapped around my wrist, and the love letter I wrote Brandon is resting on his coffee table next to our 'marriage certificate.'

Brandon read my love letter, smiled, then read it again. It's the biggest fluff piece you could possibly imagine, but give me a break, I was ten and convinced Brandon was going to divorce me so he could marry my mom. I would have said anything to convince him to stay married to me. I even agreed to ride Socks, who, in case you're wondering, is still at the ranch.

It wasn't just Kwan's dropped lip when Socks was loaded in his new owners' horse trailer that caused my change of heart, it was remembering how Brandon pledged to help me clean the horse stall every weekend when I begged my parents to buy me a horse. I was in love with the *Saddle Club* and convinced I was set to compete in dressage at the Olympics.

By the time my parents agreed to buy me a horse, I fell out of love with the *Saddle Club* and realized horses' backs aren't as close to the ground as I thought. Brandon kept his promise, though. He was in Socks' stall every Saturday morning at dawn. He's never forgotten a promise he's given, not even the one we put in writing when we thought we were more grown-up than we were.

When Samara from *The Ring* commences crawling out of the well in the misty woods, I burrow my face even deeper into Brandon's neck. We're supposed to be watching the horror movies our parents wouldn't let us watch back in the day. However, I've spent the majority of our day with my head buried in some region of Brandon's body.

It could be worse. He could discourage my closeness instead of encouraging it. Every time I get frightened, he tightens his grip around my waist. One more scare, and I'll be sitting on his lap.

"Is it over?" The rich tomato paste on the chicken parmigiana I made from scratch for dinner bounces off Brandon's neck before filtering into my nose.

He pulls me in closer. "Not yet."

I take the quickest peek at the flat-screen television, feigning bravery. When I spot Noah bleeding as he crawls across glass to get away from Samara, I return to counting out the beeps of the vein in Brandon's neck. "I can't believe we wrote this list. What was wrong with us?"

"It's almost over," Brandon assures me, tightening his grip some more.

When Naomi Watts, who's playing Rachel in the movie, screams, I jump out of my skin.

Mercifully, the terrifying film ends only a few short minutes later.

"That's it? She's going to pass on the tape to another poor, unsuspecting victim?" Would you listen to me criticizing a movie I barely watched. I'm the worst critic.

"It was either help her son make a copy, or Samara would have killed him. She chose her son over anyone." The blanket curled around our waist falls to the floor when Brandon stands to his feet. It's not an easy task since I'm all up in his business. "It's kind of commendable when you think about it." Just like him holding out his hand to help me up. "We still have another two movies on our list, but I'm kinda beat."

"Me too," I admit, shadowing his walk to his room. "I'm also a little scared, so please don't push me away if I end up on your side of the mattress tonight. I don't want Samara, or Freddy, or Jason to pull me under the bed, so I better sleep in the middle of the mattress."

Brandon's chuckle has me forgetting the reason my veins are hot. "Any excuse to hog the bed."

"I'm not a hog."

"Yeah, you are," Brandon argues, folding down the bedding. "You have been for as long as I've known you. For someone with a teeny tiny body, you certainly need a lot of space for sleeping."

"I like to stretch out." I poke out my tongue to add some playfulness to the intimacy firing in the air. If I don't, I might misconstrue the looks he's been giving me all evening as lusty ones. He was just protecting me. It's naturally ingrained in him. His pulse was spiking because of the scary movies we were watching, not my closeness. Right?

Ignoring the voice in my head screaming out a resounding 'no,' I snatch up my retro alarm clock from the bedside table, then spin around to face Brandon. "What time is your appointment with Dr. Avery tomorrow? I don't want you being late again." When he remains quiet, confusion twists in my stomach. "You do have an appointment, right? It is Wednesday."

I stop seeking an invisible wall planner when Brandon confesses, "I canceled my appointment."

"BJ—"

He cuts me off with a confident tone. "I don't need to go anymore. I'm good. I've got my head screwed back on."

Although I want to believe him, I know depression isn't something that's cured in a matter of weeks. It may never leave him.

"I agree you're doing better, but I still think you should attend your sessions. Talking helps, and Dr. Avery has a weird knack for getting people to open up." I've been in therapy for years, yet I've never been as open and honest as I have been with Dr. Avery during my joint sessions with Brandon.

Brandon dumps the spare pillows off his bed onto the floor before slipping between the sheets. Since he's so worked up, he's forgotten about the pillow barrier he usually places between us each evening. "Can't I just talk to you?"

"You wouldn't open up to me, BJ. Not for what you need to get off your chest." When he scoffs like I'm lying, I hit him with straight-up honesty. "Okay, then tell me why you read the report about my rape?"

His eyes snap to mine in an instant, and just as quickly, they fill with remorse. "Because I... I thought..." He drags a hand over his head as his eyes float down to his sleeping pants. "I thought if I knew what he did to you, I could make sure I didn't hurt you the same way."

Wow. That wasn't what I was anticipating for him to say. I assumed he'd close up on me again, or that he'd lie to ensure he didn't hurt me. I'm pleased he didn't, but I'm still shocked.

After joining him in bed, I scoot across the mattress until our thighs are nearly touching. "Did you ever think to ask me if I had any triggers instead of reading the report? You know what those documents are like, BJ. They're so cut and dry and de—"

"Demoralizing," he fills in, peering back at me. "The entire time I was reading it, I couldn't see you. The way you spoke and what you said, none of it made it seem as if it were you. It was just another report on yet another victim."

When I see the words he can't speak in his eyes, I voice them for him. "Until that night in my room?"

I think I'm on the money until Brandon shakes his head. "I wasn't seeing you then either. I was seeing him. I was seeing Madden." When his eyes drift over my face, the pain in his eyes softens to regret. "Then I wondered if he was who you were seeing, too."

"Oh, BJ." I inch across the mattress until there's no doubt our thighs are touching. "He wasn't on my mind. He has *never* been on my mind anytime I've been with you." Even knowing this will hurt him, I have to be honest. "It was quick, the assault barely lasted a few minutes. It doesn't take away from what happened, or how wrong he was, but it means I only have to squeeze a few minutes of horror between years and years of happiness."

After tugging back the sheet, I straddle Brandon's lap like I disastrously did all those weeks ago. I'm not going to kiss him or beg for him to let me take away his pain. I just don't want the odd angle of our heads to have him missing the absolute honesty in my eyes when I say, "Madden tried to take away my worth, my self-respect, my confidence, and my voice. To begin with, he won. I was silenced by Joey's death."

My eyes bounce between his when I say, "But he's learning differently now. I'm not a victim of his. I am a survivor. That makes me stronger than him. It makes me more powerful. He won't win, BJ. He'll *never* win... *if* you don't let him." Confusion blisters through his eyes as his brows join. "You're as much of a survivor of Madden's as I am. When he hurt me, he hurt you, too, but at the moment, he's winning the battle against you."

Brandon vehemently shakes his head. "No. I'm not letting him win. I hurt him. I was going to kill him. I would have if Grayson hadn't stopped me."

The anger burning him from the inside out cools when I mutter, "Not physically, BJ. Emotionally. This isn't a game of skill for him. It's a mindfuck. But that's also why I know in the long term, he won't win. He's no match for you. He'll *never* have your level of skillset and intellect. Just like he'll never win against *us*."

"Us?" Brandon asks, his tone low.

"Yes, BJ. *Us*. It's always been us." I scoot up his legs like a raging river is dividing us. It doubles the tension between us, but since it's a good tension, I work with it. "It was wrong of me to leave the way I did. If I hadn't, we may have found out what happened to Joey sooner, and I could have stopped Madden from hurting other women." When he tries to interrupt me, I talk faster, "But everything happens for a reason. You've done so many wonderful things the past seven years, BJ. You've broke cases that would have never been broken. You saved hundreds and hundreds of children from horrible situations, and you grew as a person. I'm so incredibly proud of the man you have become, and I know my dad would be too."

Brandon shakes his head. "He warned me that I couldn't protect *and* love you. He told me you would get hurt. He knew I was going to make a mistake. That's why he didn't trust me with you."

"That's not true, BJ. If he had any idea Madden would grow into the man he is, he would have removed me from that situation immediately. He was as blinded by the evil skating through Madden's veins as you were."

Having no plausible defense, Brandon remains quiet. Although I could leave our conversation there, I don't. The words we're speaking now should have been spoken years ago. "Have you ever wondered why I wasn't in the car with my parents the day they were murdered? Dad was adamant we weren't to be together, so why would he leave me home alone only days after finding me in your sex-scented room?"

Brandon's brows join as a hopeful mask slips over his face. "He knew he was fighting a battle he'd never win."

I nod. "But he would have *never* admitted that. He would have preferred us to sneak around behind his back than admit he was wrong trying to keep us apart."

An unexpected chuckle vibrates my chest when Brandon murmurs under his breath, "Stubborn bastard."

"A stubborn bastard who loved you like a son." When Brandon's eyes float up to mine, I give him the assurance he deserves. "He didn't mean what he said, BJ. He was scared, that's all. I promise you that. He was never ashamed of you. He loved you." The heavy sentiment in the air crackles when I murmur, "Not as much as me, but it was still there."

I nuzzle into Brandon's palm when he lifts his hand to cup my cheek. His thumb isn't as rough as it usually is since it hasn't gripped a gun the past five weeks, but it doesn't weaken the zap that roars through me when he tracks it across my lips. He doesn't speak, he just lets me see how much my words positively impacted him. I'll need a ton more to fix the cracks Grayson and I forced onto him when we made him break, but tonight's conversation was a great lead-up for future ones.

After a few minutes of heart-fixing comfort, I remove Brandon's hand from my jaw, kiss his palm, then slip off his lap. In quicker than I can snap my fingers, panic overtakes the crackling of sexual energy in the air. "Where are you going?"

My bare feet squeak on the polished floorboards when I twist around to face Brandon. I'm not heated-up with the guilt I've felt more times than I can count the past five weeks. I'm warm from the flare igniting between us. I'd give anything to act on it, but since that could possibly shove Brandon's recovery back a few spots, I must wait.

"I don't know about you, but dinner was over three hours ago, so I need a midnight snack to keep my energy up. Did you want something?" My last two words quiver when Brandon's eyes stray to the jar of peanut butter on his nightstand. "I'll bring you back a spoon," I mutter before I make a beeline for the fridge. It's winter, however, I'm going to stand in front of the fridge until the heat roaring through my body cools a few degrees.

Tonight is the first in-depth conversation we've had.

It's *not* the time for me to get horny.

That logic would be easier to follow if Brandon didn't add a request to his wordless demand for a spoon. "Can you bring our horror movie list in with the spoon? I forgot about the TV in my room."

Does he want to watch scary movies because he's craving gore and violence? Or is he wanting me plastered to him as I have been most of the day?

I guess there's only one way to find out. "Should I bring an extra jar of peanut butter with me as well? The one you have is half empty?"

My breathing all but stops when he replies, "Perhaps you should bring two."

MELODY

I roll over with a groan when the annoying rattle of someone's knuckles on a door trickles into my ears. My mouth is bone-dry, my head is throbbing, and even with Brandon's bed being big enough for ten, I'm confident I am waking up alone for the first time in weeks.

This sucks.

The annoyance thickening my blood eases when I spot a note from Brandon on the bedside table he specially purchased for me my first week here. He went to see Dr. Avery as he has twice a week for the past five weeks. I'm glad I convinced him to continue with their sessions. Stepping back from counseling just as it's beginning to work is the worst thing any patient can do. I did it years ago, and it back-fired in my face.

I'd rather save Brandon the pain.

When a second rattle taps through my ears, I groan out that I'm coming before tossing back the sheets and dragging my sorry ass out of bed. I don't usually sleep with my implants in, so my head isn't just throbbing from a couple of hours sleep, my ears are aching as well.

Brandon and I watched the final two movies on our list last night. We didn't go to bed until a little after four this morning. Since I fell asleep with my head buried in Brandon's lap, no nightmares occurred. I wouldn't have minded if they did. Brandon was trained to protect, so there's nothing more he loves than saving a damsel in distress. Although the movies were the cause of my frightened state, I'm reasonably sure he gobbled up every ounce of need beaming out of me. We were even more touchy-feely under the blanket last night than we were when we were teens.

"Jeez, I said I'm coming. Hold your horses," I grunt when the visitor racks their knuckles on the door for a third time.

In my eagerness to teach them some manners, I swing open the door without peeking out of the peephole. It was silly of me to do. I'm not in any danger, but my heart sure is when I identify the person stumbling forward at a pace so fast, I have to catch her.

After helping my guest back to her feet, I greet her. "Phillipa, hi."

Nothing against Phillipa. From what Brandon has told me, when she's not lying about what she does for a living, she is kind and helpful. I'm just finding it difficult to get past the fact she kissed my fiancé while crushing on my high school sweetheart.

Brandon didn't tell me about Phillipa and Julian's kiss. I'm not even sure if he knows about it. Julian did. He was so remorseful, he confessed as if their kiss wasn't the result of his heart being torn out of his chest from watching me kiss Brandon in a room full of witnesses.

Their kiss happened two hours after ours. The knowledge should weaken the knot in my stomach, but for some reason, it doesn't. I can see Phillipa cares for Brandon. It may not be as much as I do, but it's still very much there.

If I really want the best for Brandon, I should have let Phillipa step up to the plate as she tried when I arrived weeks ago. Alas, sometimes I'm as selfish as I am sorrow-filled.

A honeysuckle scent fills my nostrils when Phillipa steps into the alcove to glance over my shoulder. "Melody, hi. Is BJ... ah... Brandon here?"

"No. He's with Dr. Avery." I'm not sharing guarded secrets. Phillipa is aware of Brandon's counseling sessions as she was the one who organized them for him. The first visit was under the guise he needed a psych workup to become a consultant with the CIA.

I nod when Phillipa mumbles, "I thought you went with him to his sessions?"

"Usually, I do. I must have slept through my alarm." After opening the door wider, I gesture for Phillipa to come in. "He left me a note. He should be back in around thirty minutes or so. You can wait for him inside if you'd like."

"Ah..." She looks more uncomfortable now than she did when her eyes landed on my bare legs sticking out the bottom of one of Brandon's shirts. "It isn't really a pop-in visit. I just... ah... needed to borrow a cup of sugar."

Her stumbling words already have my suspicions rising, much less the way she keeps blinking. And don't get me started on her piss-poor excuse for her visit, or we'll be here all morning. She's not only lying, her silence adds to the controversy of her visit. Her high-pitch isn't the only voice my implants are picking up.

"It isn't as it seems," Phillipa garbles out when I tug out a listening device from her right ear.

When I press it to my ear, I hear Grayson curse before he produces his own pathetic excuse for the invasion of privacy. "I swear to you, we're trying to save him unnecessary worry, Melody. That's it."

I don't want to believe him, but I do. "Then you better get your ass up here and tell me what's going on before BJ gets home."

After handing Phillipa back the bead-like device, I head to the kitchen, conscious I'll need an IV of coffee to get me through the reason for the unease in Grayson's voice. He sounded more concerned now than he did when he called me out of the blue weeks ago.

"How confident are you that Bobby isn't Ophelia's husband's son?"

As Grayson's eyes stray over the mess known as Ophelia Petretti's life, he shrugs. "The dates add up—"

"I know that. I scoured the reports from BJ's case for hours when he reached out for my help, even after passing on the details for a defense lawyer who specialized in these types of cases. But that means *nothing.* For all we know, Ophelia could have moved onto her next target the instant she realized BJ wasn't going to fall for her ruse." I'm shouting, and it's unacceptable, but I can't help it. I'm truly panicked.

I don't care if Brandon has a child with someone else. In some warped way, it will be good for him to have someone new to protect. I just don't trust Ophelia. I don't care who you are, if you falsely accuse a man of rape, you're a piece of shit. Your lie undoes all the good victims of assault have fought decades to achieve. You steal the voice of rape victims even more than their rapists attempted to do, and you stop victims from coming forward because they're convinced no one will believe them.

One lie casts a shadow of doubt on hundreds of real cases, so I wish people would remember that when they're angry their Tinder date didn't return their call the next day. You have the right to say no. It's your body, so you're free to do with it as you wish, but I beg for you not to pretend you were assaulted because your feelings were hurt. That isn't fair. Not to rape victims like me nor the men who have been wrongly accused and convicted.

Air leaves my lungs in a hurry when Grayson places down a photo of a little boy I'd guess to be around the age of five or six. His hair is as dark as his mother's, but the shape of his face and the determined twinkle in his eyes aren't from Ophelia. I've seen them many times in my lifetime. All he needs is snow-white hair, and I'd be convinced I'm looking at a portrait of Brandon.

Grayson pushes out a halfhearted chuckle when I mutter, "Is a DNA test even needed?"

Mistaking the tears in my eyes as sadness, he curls his arm around my shoulders and squeezes me tight. I am sad, it just isn't in the way you're anticipating. I'm not upset Brandon has a child, I'm sad for him. He's missed so many years of Bobby's life, and if anything Grayson and Phillipa are saying is true, he's set to miss so many more.

As my eyes bounce between Phillipa and Grayson, I ask, "Is there any way we can gain access to Bobby's DNA without Ophelia's permission?"

I know the answer to my question. I studied law for years. I just don't like the answers that knowledge gains me, so I'm willing to act stupid if it increases the possibility of finding a way around our dilemma.

When Phillipa peers at me through lowered lashes, I try to have her looking at me as more of a friend than a once assistant district attorney. She cares for Brandon. Is it enough for her to tiptoe onto the wrong side of the law? I don't know, but I'm determined to find out.

"You said Ophelia agreed to Isaac's request for a DNA test, so why is she refusing this one?"

"Because she knows the results won't swing in her favor this time around," Grayson answers on Phillipa's behalf. "She has her ex-husband on a knife's edge. If he doesn't do exactly what she wants when she wants, he won't see his son."

"Bobby isn't his son," I argue, shouting.

Phillipa's dark, stormy eyes dance between mine. "We know that, Melody, but Louis doesn't." Her tone reveals she feels truly sorry for another victim of Ophelia's.

"Can he be turned? Surely, he'd consider siding with us if his son's livelihood was on the line. If any of this is true…" I scan the documents showing numerous payments between the Castros, the Petrettis, and Louis's many bank accounts. "He and Ophelia are looking at over twenty years. Who will support their son then? Has anyone asked him that?"

Grayson shrugs. "The hierarchies in IA aren't willing to test that angle just yet. They're still gathering intel."

"They're always gathering intel," Phillipa and I say at the same time.

I don't want to smile, but I can't help it. If you can change the color of her hair and exclude her Mediterranean skin coloring, we have a lot of similarities. She'd be a good pick for Brandon *if* I were willing to give him up.

It's a pity for Phillipa I will *never* do that.

"What about the DNA company used to conduct Isaac's test? Would they still have Bobby's DNA on file?" What I'm asking is illegal and somewhat imprudent considering the two people seated across from me are government officials, but I'm so desperate to get answers for Brandon, I am willing to risk it. My daddy always said I could tiptoe onto the wrong side of the law as long as I found my way back. I've never been tempted before, but I'd do anything for Brandon.

My spine straightens when reality dawns. "Is that why you were attempting to break in? You were going to secure BJ's DNA without his permission." I can't tell if I'm angry or pleased with my assumption. It could be a combination of them both. I hate that they were planning to take away Brandon's God-given rights, but I also understand their desperateness for answers.

I realize I'm way off the mark when Phillipa shakes her head. "I came for his shoebox of photos. We wanted to do a facial comparison of Brandon and Bobby at the same age. We needed to make sure our theory had credit before bringing our findings to Brandon." The edginess on her face softens when she mutters, "Your confirmation made facial profiling unnecessary."

After a few moments of silent ruminating, I get desperate. "If I could get you a sample of BJ's DNA, would you be able to compare it to Bobby's sample on file?"

I'm hit with a second brutal blow today when Grayson shakes his head. "Most companies retain samples for six months. That wasn't the case this time around."

"Isaac asked them to be destroyed earlier?" I say, filling in the words Grayson didn't articulate. When he nods, my chest deflates. "Then, we need to convince Ophelia to do the right thing."

Phillipa's scoff is louder than Grayson's. "You're talking about a woman who allegedly distributed fertility drugs, scalpels, and medical equipment to a cartel organization without asking a single question. All she sees is money signs, Melody. She isn't a good person."

"Then, we'll use that to convince her." When unease flares through both Phillipa and Grayson's eyes, I talk faster, "If Bobby is BJ's biological son, he has a fundamental right to see him. Family law won't allow Ophelia to repress his rights."

My eyes snap to Grayson when he grumbles, "They can if Ophelia proves Brandon is unstable."

"He's depressed, Grayson," I snap back, even though I'm confident the old Brandon is emerging quicker than anyone could have predicted. "That doesn't make him incapable of being a parent. He just needs some extra help and understanding. That's why we're here, isn't it?"

"Grayson wasn't referencing Brandon's stability now. He's talking about the charges Ophelia ignored once she had a new target hooked." Phillipa opens a case file I haven't seen in years before spinning it around to face me. "If we push too hard to prove what we *all* believe is true, Ophelia will shove back harder."

"He's his son, Phillipa. You can't expect him to give him up because he's being threatened with false charges. If you are, you clearly don't know who BJ *really* is." I push the file back to her side of the desk before dropping my eyes to my watch. "You need to leave. BJ is due home at any moment."

Phillipa is reluctant to leave, but Grayson jumps straight up to his feet. "What are you going to tell him?"

I want to say nothing. I want to pretend this is a problem for another day, but since that will make me just as bad as Ophelia, I shrug instead. "Give me a second to catch my breath before asking again."

For the first time since I've known him, a serious mask slips over Grayson's face. "Do you want me to be here when you tell him?"

"No," I answer without pause for thought. "But, can you leave that?" I nudge my head to the file Phillipa is in the process of putting away. "If we want to beat Ophelia at her game, we need to get one step ahead of her. BJ is the best agent to do that."

Grayson nods, fully agreeing with me. "All right." He shifts on his feet to face Phillipa when a disbelieving huff leaves her mouth. "Come on, Pip. It's the least you can give the guy after how much he helped you." He yanks her the rest of the way over the fence when he adds, "If it weren't for him, you would have never gotten Castro."

Phillipa folds her arms in front of her chest. "Castro is dead."

"Now," Grayson fires back with a chuckle. "Henry waited for you to pry a lifetime of secrets out of him before he tied off the loose end."

Having no plausible defense, Phillipa huffs out, "Fine," before dumping the file onto the dining table and hightailing it out of Brandon's apartment. Grayson is nipping at her heels two seconds later. I can't hear what he riles her about during their fourteen-floor descent, but I'm grateful that their cars disappear from Brandon's street just as his Hellcat pulls into his assigned parking bay.

Needing a few minutes to get my headspace right, I slot Ophelia's file between two magazines in the rack in the living room before heading for the shower. A relieved breath vibrates my lips when I remove the sound processors from behind my ears. You know the pain you get when sunglasses dig into the back of your ears from prolonged usage? It's the same for cochlear implants, just more painful.

When I first got them done, I asked Julian to place me onto a candidate list to trial the new fully implantable implants. That's how much I hated the feeling of constant heaviness behind my ears. Mercifully, the processors shrunk each time they were updated, so I declined the trial when I was approved.

Although I'm reconsidering my decision now. Not because I'm too lazy to remove the processors before swimming, showering, and going to bed, but because the conference for the trial is being held in San Francisco. That's only miles from the pharmacy Ophelia is running her black-market drug scheme from, making it the ideal location for a long weekend visit.

———

TWENTY MINUTES LATER, a grin tugs on my lips when the stomp of my name tickles the bottom of my bare feet. With the shower being recently switched off, Brandon is aware I can't hear him, but instead of startling me, he reverted to an old method of communicating.

I kind of love it.

"Hey," I sign when I spot him leaning on the doorjamb of his room. I don't talk when I don't have my implants on. I hate my voice in general, so I don't want to consider how cringeworthy it is when I have no idea of the depth and pitch of my tone. *"How was your session with Dr. Avery?"*

After dragging his eyes up my legs barely covered by a teeny pair of shorts, they land on my face. The heat in them makes me squirm in a good way. *"It was good. She is..."* I smile when he pauses, incapable of describing Dr. Avery's uncanny knack for getting people to open up. *"I told her what you said last night. How I am Madden's victim as well."*

"And?" I beg, hating that he's leaving me hanging. I'm not a suspense type of girl. I like to know the news as it's happening.

His smile has me craving another shower. I'm hot and sticky all over. *"She asked if you wanted a job."*

I throw my head back and laugh. *"Let us hope she was serious because if I stay cooped up in this apartment for much longer, I will go crazy."* I could smack myself for sliding our conversation into uncomfortable territory remarkably quick. *"Not that I want to be anywhere else."*

Brandon steps closer to me, his eyes nurturing. *"You should accept Leo's offer. It is not at the District Attorney's Office, but it will keep you in the know until their investigation is finalized."*

"No." I shake my head to authenticate my short reply while moving for the tube of moisturizer on the bedside table. It's next to Brandon's jar of consumed peanut butter like it's always belonged there. *"Leo's offer is in New York. You are nowhere near New York, so I am not interested."*

I stop rubbing moisturizer into my legs when Brandon signs, *"I will come to New York with you."*

"You want to go to New York?"

The honesty in his eyes when he replies makes my heart flutter extra fast. *"It is not my favorite city, but I am sure I will enjoy it with you."*

I take a few minutes to consider his objective before asking, *"Is this a ploy to get out of counseling sessions? Because if it is, I hate to tell you, Dr. Avery does phone consultations."*

Brandon smiles like I am joking. I'm not, but I can still admire his grin. *"This has nothing to do with that."* His lips twists as his eyes brighten. *"Dr. Avery agrees a change in location could be good for us."*

I wish I had my hearing aids connected so I could have heard the way he expressed 'us.' If it sounded anything like the way he signed it, my hopes would be skyrocketing. It was possessive and protective—very much on par with the Brandon I used to know.

"Us?"

As he bridges the gap between us, my heart breaks out a new tune. *"Yes, us. I cannot do this without you, Melody. I would have never made it this far without you."* His shirt gathers the moisture sliding down my face I'm pretending is leftover residue from the shower when he pulls me into his chest. It wouldn't matter if we were standing in the middle of a snowfield, his hugs forever warm me up.

After giving me a few moments to relish the healthy vibrations of his heart, Brandon kisses my temple, my cheek, then my mouth before inching back. It's the simplest gesture, but it has the biggest impact on my heart.

As does what he signs next, *"Will you come on this new adventure with me, Mellowy? Test the limits of our relationship in a place that is both exciting and scary."*

"Are you sure this is what you want, BJ?" I can see the confirmation in his eyes, smell it on his skin, but I still need vocal confirmation. This is a huge step for both of us. New York is the only city we don't control. There are ghosts there, but there are also good memories— many of them.

When Brandon nods without pause for thought, my skin mists with sweat like I didn't dry off after my shower. *"Then I guess we better get packing."* I'd give anything to be able to kiss the living hell out of him when he grins a smile I haven't seen in weeks, but since I'm seconds away from killing his happiness, I can't. *"After we have talked. There is something really important I need to tell you."*

BRANDON

Several long months later…

"What time did she say she was coming again?" Brandon's nervous voice is cute as hell, but I'd rather him not be worried. I'm not in any danger. Over a dozen FBI agents are in the room next to ours, and he's in the bedroom of our master suite watching my every move. I'm safer than I've ever been. "I still can't believe I agreed to let you do this. Clearly, I need my head re-examined."

"Do you want to see your son, BJ?" I hate that we're required to have this conversation with Brandon's work colleagues listening in, but I don't have much choice. With my ears clogged up with implants, I can't wear the standard earpieces most Honey Pots use during a sting, so Brandon's voice has to be relayed to me via the speakers in the ceiling of the New York hotel we're luring Ophelia to.

Brandon took the news he may be a father better than I

expected. He cursed, ranted, and called Ophelia more than a few names, but within minutes, his focus shifted to me. He was worried I'd be upset, and that I wouldn't be able to forgive him for having a child without me. It was only when we reached a mutual understanding of our dislikes did he calm down.

I wanted to hurt Ophelia. I wanted her to suffer for the anguish she had and was about to put Brandon through, but then I realized anything I did to her, I did to Bobby. That wasn't fair. He's an innocent child. I couldn't hurt him any more than I wanted Mrs. McGee punished for what Madden had done to me.

When I explained that to Brandon, it was like a lightbulb switched on inside of his head. He finally understood why Grayson stopped him from killing Madden all those months ago. As much as Madden hurt us, killing him would have hurt Mrs. McGee even more. Neither Brandon nor I wanted that. So, instead of plotting ways to take Madden down illegally, Brandon transfixed his attention on serving justice to both Madden and Ophelia legally.

We worked side by side for months, filing motions and scouring through stacks of evidence for hours at a time.

Some days we had wins.

Others, we didn't.

Our bid to make Madden serve time for his crimes failed. I was railroaded on the witness stand by Mr. McGee. He based his entire defense on the fact I never said 'no.' He made out that I had a fascination with his family and used my friendship with his 'less attributed child' to get closer to his 'astute son.' My financial records were splashed across the tabloids, and my sex life was scrutinized. Not even Brandon pretending to side with the defense in the hope of turning the knife on his father worked.

Mr. McGee did what he had done his entire life. He used his charm to have the jury side with him. In all honesty, I was pissed. When the verdict was handed down, I almost spiraled as deeply as Brandon did months earlier. But, out of nowhere, little rays of sunshine broke through the dark clouds swarming us.

My courage to fight for justice saw other women step forward. The first person was Gemma Calderon-Levesque. After Brandon reached out to her, she risked a multi-million- dollar settlement with the McGees to speak out with me. Then, one by one, more women came forward. Some were from Madden's past, and others were as recent as last year.

While Leo and I sorted through a sickening number of victim accounts to have Madden charged with multiple counts of rape, sexual harassment, and workplace bullying, Brandon returned to his position in the Bureau under Grayson's branch. For the most part, it was both healing and painful for him. He lived for the adrenaline a hard and seemingly impossible race to win gave him, but every contest has speedbumps.

Isaac Holt is Brandon's.

How was Brandon to know the payments Isaac set up for Bobby weren't as Ophelia stated. She made out the money Isaac was placing in her account every month was to help her fight Brandon's bid for custody of Bobby.

Could you imagine how much that hurt Brandon to hear? He'd been fighting Ophelia in the courts for months just to get proof Bobby was his son, then when he finally had DNA evidence he was, Ophelia not only reopened the rape case she had 'forgotten' she'd instigated when it wasn't of use to her, she also supposedly sought help from a man she knew didn't like Brandon.

Her accusation switched Brandon's custody agreement from being every second weekend to one supervised hourly visit a month. As you can imagine, that made Brandon agitated, and unfortunately, he sometimes took it out on the wrong people.

Brandon didn't tell me exactly what he said to Isabelle the day he wired her up to be interviewed by Kirill Bobrov, but I could tell it was harsh. His eyes were tainted with as much remorse as they held the day Madden's verdict was returned not guilty for my rape.

Although we've yet to achieve justice for me, with every day bringing us closer to achieving our combined goals, the weight on

Brandon's shoulders grows weaker as the months move on, and our relationship is blossoming.

We still spend a majority of our weekends holed up in my loft, eating takeaway and watching corny 90s movies, but instead of our time together being doused by awkward unease, it's fueled by mutual passion, heart-soaring murmurs, and faint brushes of fingertips under a blanket. We've even managed to sneak in the occasional heated kiss.

We're not close to the level of intimacy we had before Madden tried to snuff it, but since our friendship is more important than anything, I'm not worried. We're closer than we've ever been, so I'm confident even if the intimacy side never returns, we'll still be okay. Brandon is my best friend, and I'd pick for him to have that title over lover any day of the week.

Brandon loses the chance to answer my question when a gruff voice over the speaker advises me Ophelia is on her way up. I never thought this meeting would occur. Why would a known mafia princess meet with a previously-appointed ADA in another state? She wouldn't, and that's why Ophelia has no idea about my job descriptions, former or current.

To her, I'm Melody Gottle, wannabee founder of the baby-making ring the Castros and Petrettis let fold when Col Petretti was killed during a sting days before I arrived in Ravenshoe many months ago.

I'll give it to Ophelia, she's smarter than she looks. She didn't take my claims of being mafia royalty at face value. She researched my family and me. Fortunately for the Bureau, Henry was willing to play along. He sees no shame in his name, so he was more than happy for me to use it however I saw fit. It is, after all, my real name.

When a heavy knock sounds at the door of my suite, I spin to face the entryway mirror. *"I am fine,"* I sign into my reflection, knowing only one man on the other end of the surveillance is capable of deciphering what I say. *"It is time to get your son back."*

THE FRANTIC BEAT of my heart drops several inches lower when Brandon's eyes swing my way. They're full of pride, although it's barely seen through the lust clouding them. He's hardly taken his eyes off me since our joint FBI-CIA sting.

Our ruse worked. It wasn't easy. It took me living up to my namesake to have Ophelia convinced I had what it would take to harvest children as if they're cobs of corn, but I did it. I played the role, and I played it well.

We have enough evidence to put Ophelia away for life and to have her husband charged with criminal conspiracy, larceny, and attempted murder. Neither he nor Ophelia killed the women found at the Shroud's ranch, but they knew what was happening, and they didn't alert authorities. That's a convictable offense.

My inflated chest sinks a little when Brandon asks, "What about Bobby? What happens to him?"

"At the moment, he's under the care of the couple from the pharmacy." When Phillipa's reply fills Brandon's eyes with panic, she talks faster, "They had no idea what Ophelia and Louis were doing. They're innocent in this." She waits for him to absorb the truth in her eyes before adding, "I've also requested an emergency hearing with the judge who presided over your family court hearings." The happiness stretching across her face burns my eyes with tears, much less what she says next, "With Ophelia willing to cooperate for a reduced sentence, and Dr. Avery giving your mental stability a glowing review, you could be taking Bobby home as early as next week."

"Next week?" I squeeze Brandon's hand so hard, I'm afraid I am about to break it. This is everything we've been working toward for months.

Laughing at our shocked silence, Phillipa nods before she stands to her feet to gather her belongings. While Brandon walks her to the door, I breathe out the excited butterflies in my stomach.

I only got to meet Bobby once before Brandon's visits were switched to supervised, but now there's a high possibility he'll get to live with us in New York. Jesus. This turned out better than we were hoping.

"We need a bigger apartment," I jest with a laugh when Brandon closes the door with Phillipa on the other side. "And another bed. You know how much I love to hog. Poor Bobby will get squashed—"

My words stop when my eyes collide with Brandon's across the room. His eyes are holding the same amount of excitement as mine. It just isn't giddy, kiddy-like enthusiasm brightening his. He's in awe, and every inch of his admiration is directed at me.

"Grayson…" I don't know what Grayson replies in the earpiece in Brandon's ear, but I hear cords being yanked out through the speakers above our heads before the room falls into resolute silence. A few seconds after that, Brandon says, "Thank you. I will."

After a smile that curves my knees inward, Brandon removes the wireless device from his ear, switches it off, then dumps it in the drawer in the entryway table. My heart patters in rhythm to his polished shoes when he bridges the gap between us, then it breaks into a dangerous cantor when he signs, *"You are so fucking brave, so strong, and so damn pretty. I have never been more impressed in my life…"* his pause almost kills me, *"… or turned on. Jesus, Melody, when you put Ophelia in her place, even Grayson got hard."*

I laugh. I can't help it. *"Grayson gets horny when the wind blows."*

"He does, but I don't," Brandon argues, stepping closer. *"I thought I was broken."* He pauses again. This one is more to reflect than tease me. *"I was broken. You fixed me. You resuscitated me and breathed life back into my lungs… and then you gave me back my son. I don't know how I can ever thank you."*

The sob his praise lodged into the back of my throat rattles my vocal cords when I say, *"You did it, too, BJ. You fought for this as fiercely as I did. I am so incredibly proud of you as well."*

His hands shake when he cups my jaw. He's not scared. I've never met a man as strong as him. There are just too many emotions firing between us for a nonchalant response. "I want to kiss you."

My tongue instinctively darts out to moisten my lips before they raise into a smile. "Then kiss me."

An excited zap darts down my spine when he mutters, "I don't think I'll be able to stop if I start."

"Then don't stop," I reply without an ounce of hesitation, caught up in the sentiment fueling our exchange. Our adrenaline is high from our successful sting, but it has nothing on the mutual respect, admiration, and love we have for each other. The past few months were tough, but we were tougher, and we came out of it stronger.

As Brandon's eyes bounce between mine, he replies, "I don't want to hurt you, Mellowy."

I trace my index finger across the jaw of a man I'll never stop loving. It's stronger than it was when we were kids, more determined, but it's still very much him. It still belongs to my Brandon. "You don't know how to hurt me, BJ. You're incapable of hurting me."

When I step back, pulling out of his embrace, the euphoric gleam in his eyes fades to vulnerability. He has nothing to be worried about, nothing at all. I'm not going anywhere.

Not now.

Not ever.

Brandon's chest rises and falls in rhythm with mine when I commence unbuttoning my shirt. He watches each pearl button pierce between the shimmery fabric before stalking the material soundlessly float to the floor. I'm still wearing a pleated business skirt, thigh-high stockings and a bra that's more frumpy than sexy, but the way Brandon looks at me makes it appear as if I am naked.

Mercifully, it's a heated stare.

After giving him time to absorb the tiny imperfections on my body he knows by heart, I sign, *"Your turn."*

I wait and wait and wait, praying my wish to fall back in time works in my favor.

It's answered brilliantly three heart-thrashing seconds later. After tugging his dress shirt out of his black trousers, Brandon undoes the top three buttons of his shirt before pulling it over his head. His impatience to get undressed forces a ghost-like grin onto my mouth.

It doesn't last long.

It vanishes when I realize he's wearing an undershirt.

While smiling at my childish stomp of disappointment, Brandon rips off his white t-shirt like it's made out of tissue paper before signing, *"Better?"*

"Much."

While chewing on his bottom lip, hiding his smile, Brandon's eyes roam over my body as he signs, *"Your turn."*

With my eyes on the crotch of his trousers that grows bigger with every millimeter my zipper descends, I release the clasp on my skirt, then shimmy it down my thighs. Hoping to give the impression of a mafia princess with money to burn, I brought lace-top stockings and a sexy boy-leg suspender package at a lingerie store earlier today while picking my powerhouse outfit.

Well, that's what I'm planning to tell the IRS when I claim its two-hundred-dollar price tag on my expenses this tax season.

Brandon doesn't have a chance in hell of hiding his smile when I kick my skirt to the side while signing, *"I am really hoping you have grown averse to boxer shorts the past eight years."* I know he hasn't, but it's fun to tease him. His flaming red cheeks were one of the first things I noticed about him.

My eyes bulge out of my head when the lowering of Brandon's zipper gives me a tiny preview of the cropped blond curls spread across his groin. Before excitement can take hold of every sense I own, his thumb releases the waistband of his Calvin Klein boxers, snapping them back into place.

I pout like a baby. *"You are no fun."*

I'm lying. I've seen snippets of Brandon's playful side the past few months, but it's never had this depth, so I'm going to relish it as long as possible. He could never be accused of being cocky, but as he stands across from me without a care in the world, there's no denying his confidence.

Can you blame him for standing proud? His face is gorgeous, his body is divine, and his smile, although slightly crooked, is perfect. He should be strutting like a peacock. He just doesn't know how because it was never taught to him.

I fell in love with a courageous, handsome, and lively boy when I was only a child, and I get to stand across from that same courageous, handsome, and lively man twenty-three years later.

How lucky am I?

Even if he doesn't touch me, this moment will stay with me forever. We're stripped, naked and raw, and completely free. It's just us. Me and the boy who piggybacked me across a sloshy field because it didn't matter how impossible the task, he never let me down.

Just like he doesn't this time, either.

When the emotions teaming between us become too much to bear, Brandon's fingers weave through my hair, his lips land on my neck, and his arm bands around my back to pull me in close to his fit body. "Tell me your triggers?"

Although I'd prefer to keep my assault out of our exchange, Dr. Avery is adamant this is a step we need to take to move our relationship past the friends' zone. We need to be open and honest, both inside and outside of the bedroom.

As my hand drops to stroke Brandon's cock through his boxer shorts, which I'm pleased to report is virile and thick despite the uncomfortable subject matter we're discussing, I say, "Don't flip me over or pin my arms behind my back."

"Okay," Brandon agrees softly, kissing my neck in a way that makes me want to purr like a kitten. "Anything else?"

While using the precum pooled on the tip of his cock as lubricant to quicken my strokes, I mutter, "Don't fully shave beforehand. Keep the stubble you had when we were kids, and you were too lazy to shave. I like the roughness." He acknowledges he heard me by dragging his stubble-covered chin across my collarbone and over the mounds of my breasts. "Yesss…" I hiss out on a moan, "… just like that."

After tugging his boxer shorts the rest of the way down his thighs, he guides me onto the bed like he did all those months ago. Strands of blonde hair fall into his hazel eyes that are a little greener today when he commences sliding my lace-topped stockings down my quivering thighs. "Anything else?"

"One thing," I say, breathing heavily. Can you blame me for my gasping response? The person I've loved for two decades is perched above me, naked, thick, and staring at me like he loves me. I'd be insane to act coolly right now. I'm on the verge of climaxing. Everything is beyond me right now—including acting.

"What is it?" Brandon's breaths are as vocal as mine, his excitement just as palpable.

As my eyes dance between his, I mutter, "Be you. That's all I need. *You.*"

He doesn't formulate a response. He just smiles, dumps my stockings onto the floor next to the bed, then drags his tongue down my jittering stomach. He's not anywhere near my aching sex, but the sensation it roars through my body is heavenly. He's cherishing me as only he can, loving and supporting me with both touch and emotions.

When the travels of his tongue stop within an inch from my aching sex, panic sets in. "I swear to God, if you leave me hanging this time around, BJ, I'll kill—"

My threat is cut off in the most delicious way. After tugging my panties to the side, Brandon spears his tongue between the folds of my pussy before he slithers it up to suckle my clit into his mouth. With months of sexual tension feeling more like foreplay, it only takes a few flicks of his tongue on my aching bud to send me freefalling into ecstasy.

As I shudder through an orgasmic wave, my thighs clamp Brandon's head, saving his ears from being pierced with moans I'm certain were never this loud. I also don't think I've ever orgasmed this hard. I'm drenched front to back, the silky wetness of my skin aiding in Brandon's quest to slip two fingers inside of me.

Fire burns through me as a shuddering groan leaves my mouth. I'm full, aroused, and on the verge of coming again. As he pumps his thick fingers in and out of me in a slow, yet mind-hazing way, Brandon applies the perfect amount of pressure to my clit with his tongue.

"BJ…" My voice is scratchy, almost ragged. I'd cringe at how husky it is if the moan of his name didn't have Brandon eating me more expertly. He moves faster, taking me deeper, cherishing every inch of me. "It feels *sooo* good. You feel so good."

I writhe underneath him, incapable of breathing or speaking when he hums my name into my pussy. The vibration it shudders my sex with is catastrophic to my insanity. I shimmer and shake and shout his name on repeat, loving the sensation roaring through every inch of me. The rush is frantic like fireworks in the sky or slow kisses on a rainy day.

When I return from the haze back-to-back climaxes cause, I mindlessly beg him, lost to him, but forever needing more. "Please, BJ."

He answers my plea in an instant. While crawling up my body, he licks, kisses, and sucks the skin burning with need before he stops an inch from my face. He stares straight at me, beautiful yet reserved.

"*I love you,*" I sign, caught up in the emotions about a time I thought would never happen again. "*I love you so much.*" The last of the tautness on his face disappears when I add, "*But if you do not take your socks off this instant, I will finish this in the shower… alone.*"

Brandon stills for the quickest second before the rumbles of his laughter almost have me falling into ecstasy for the third time. He laughs until his eyes can't hold the wetness of his chuckles, and his cheeks are the color of beets. He laughs until he remembers the number of times we laughed when we were kids, and the happiness of those memories overtake the horrid ones he's struggling to forget. Then he laughs until the intimate way our bodies are joined becomes too much for either of us to bear.

After gripping his sock-covered feet into the mattress and getting final permission from my eyes, he thrusts his hips forward, entering me for the first time in almost eight years with one precisely-timed lunge. The pain is intense, but it has nothing on the admiration beaming out of Brandon's eyes. It's even more passionate than the gleam they held when we gave each other our virginity.

As he stills, giving me time to adjust to his girth, he pushes back the strands of dirty blonde locks clinging to my sweaty temples.

Even after giving him permission to move, he keeps his hand on my face. He strokes my cheek with his thumb while occasionally dragging it over my blistered lips from the number of times I put my teeth over them as he ate me.

In no time at all, he finds a gentle yet sexual pace to rock in and out of me.

We're not fucking.

We aren't close to that.

We're making love.

Consuming each other.

Intimately joining as only we ever have.

The slowness of his pumps doesn't weaken their intensity in the slightest. I'm hot all over, my core clenching as it begs for release.

When I clutch Brandon's ass, digging in my nails, he purrs my name in a virile, hot groan. It has my back arching off the mattress as I struggle to match the perfection of his grinds stroke for stroke.

"God, BJ... it shouldn't feel this good... making love isn't supposed to feel this good."

As his cock thickens more, he rocks into me faster. The pain from earlier is no longer in existence, and nothing but orgasmic tingles are felt.

As our lips lock, lust tears through me like a wildfire. His kiss is as sweet as the rock of his hips but heart blistering. It sends my mind into a tailspin. It feels so good. Almost too good. I may not survive it. You can't shatter this well and expect to be put back together without hideous scars. It isn't possible.

Yet, Brandon did it without a single crack to be seen.

As admiration snatches up the last morsel of my sanity, I shudder without control. "Oh God, BJ, oh God. I'm going to come."

Groaning, he spreads me wider with his sweaty hips, giving me another inch. I feel like I'm on fire. My skin is burning with desire. I expect negative images to pop into my head at any moment. I anticipate to be sickened with regret. I don't feel either of those things. I feel loved and desired. Cherished. Wanted. *So very wanted.*

My moans turn into screams when I'm blinded by an earth-shattering climax. I convulse around Brandon's thick cock as I quiver his name on repeat. The sucks of my pussy as I ride the intense wave entices Brandon to climax along with me. He thrusts in deep before his eyes drop to mine. While staring at me like I'm his world, he brutally comes, filling me with his seed as well as the admiration shining from his eyes fills my heart with love.

BRANDON

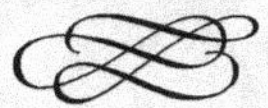

"Good morning, punk. Late night? I haven't heard your voice this groggy since..." Grayson pauses, lost on an excuse. "... since ever. How's your girl? Did I remove all surveillance for the right reasons?" Don't misconstrue his words as being caring. You can't hear his pitch. He's in full shit-stirring mode.

"Melody is good. She's sleeping." As my eyes stray to the master bedroom of our suite, my dick twitches. Even with last night being months in the making, it went above and beyond anything I could have anticipated.

I won't lie. There was a snippet of hesitation in the minutes leading to penetration, but that had more to do with the fact Melody hadn't slept with anyone since her assault. I didn't want to hurt her as much as I didn't want her recalling what Madden had done to her.

Mercifully, her jest about me wearing socks soon reminded me there was no one in the room with me except the girl I've loved for twenty-three years. Her smile when I laughed faded the world away. It was just us—as it should have *always* been.

I recall Grayson asked me a question when he growls down the line. "I swear to God, punk, if you moan one more time, you'll have to book me in for an appointment with Dr. Avery. She might help me work through my hardness... and I don't mean with punk-assed words either."

When the last half of his response comes out with a grunt, my suspicions jump. "Is someone there with you?"

"No one important." Grayson grunts again before cupping his phone to tell the person beating him that he's joking. He whispers a few more words after that, but since my dick has just come out of a very long hiatus, I'm not going to repeat them.

The squeak of Grayson's office chair sounds down the line before its closely followed by his gravelly tone. "I did call for a reason."

"I'm listening," I assure when he pauses for dramatics.

I hear him scrub at his jaw before he sighs. "Do you recall that time I piggybacked off Isaac's hacker's server?"

"The same server you infiltrated when Alex granted me access to Regan's laptop?" When he hums out an agreement, my jaw firms. "Grayson... things are just working out for those two. Don't fuck it up for them. Alex will kill you if you put Regan on the opposing team again."

"I'm not putting her on the opposing team. I'm using her connections to put *you* on the opposing team."

"Huh?"

I realize I voiced my confusion out loud when Grayson responds to it. "Or should I say, 'your father on the opposite team.'" His chair pops back into place before fingers stroking a keyboard boom down the line. "We've got enough evidence to take down your father, we just don't have any fucker with big enough gonads to go after him." I almost correct him until he adds, "*Legally.* If we weren't agents, we would have gotten the job done months ago."

He's not lying. If you thought Madden was a sick fuck, there won't be enough derogative words in your vocabulary to describe my father. Do you recall all those years ago when Grayson called me to tell me Melody was at the airport? Can you remember the name on one of the legitimate-looking invoices I pushed across my father's desk while hunting for clues he had bribed the admission clerk at Browns?

No, me neither. I had completely forgotten about my dad's business dealing with Kirill Bobrov until my mom asked for my help to locate numerous hidden assets she was certain my father was hiding from her divorce attorney.

The warehouses the Bobrovs and Castros distributed their drugs from weren't owned by them. They were in my mother's name. Their 'rent' went toward my father's campaign for office. Even with their monthly rental agreement being thirty percent lower than comparable warehouses in the same location, not once the past fifteen-plus years did my father seek an increase in rent. He was happy with the agreement he'd made with the Castros, so why stir the pot when its contents aren't close to burning. It's not every day a married father of four gets first pick of any girl in an under-age sex-trafficking ring.

There are times I want to blame Madden's issues on our father, but then I realize that's a cop-out. Joey and I were raised in the same household, and we turned out okay. Even Phoenix has gotten on the straight and narrow. Some people are just born evil. Madden is one of those people.

Tired and somewhat uneased I haven't had an update from Phillipa about Bobby yet, my restlessness gets the better of me. "What *exactly* are you getting at, Grayson? You're kind of talking in riddles."

My huff is barely heard over the shower switching on in the main room when Grayson replies, "Isaac has a beef with you."

"That's the understatement of the century."

Grayson acts as if I never spoke. "So it's only right if he can't get you, he'd go after your family, right?"

I take a second to contemplate what he's saying before jerking up my chin. I don't see Isaac targeting Bobby, especially after I discovered he was telling the truth when he said the payments he was making to Ophelia were for Bobby's trust fund, but I'm confident he'd have no issues pursuing other members of my family. His security team has been investigating Madden as well as I have the past eight months.

Grayson must hear my non-verbal reply. "So why don't we help him along. Give him some info even someone with their head shoved so far up their own ass couldn't miss."

"You want to leak my father's reports to Isaac Holt?" Surely, I'm missing something. This is a far stretch from how Grayson usually operates. It has me wondering if it's even his idea.

"Think about it, punk. Isaac is friendly with Henry. Henry *owns* New York. If you want your dad to do time for his crime, this is an angle we should be looking at."

He has a point, but it doesn't make it any easier to swallow, though. One of my biggest downfalls when I spiraled headfirst into depression was believing nothing I did was ever recognized. I worked hard for years, yet I had nothing to show for it—no job, no family, and no Melody.

It took Melody weeks to show me differently, and Dr. Avery months to have me believing what Melody was saying was true. Will this have me taking a step back in my recovery? If I couldn't hear Melody humming in the shower, unaware she talks more when she's not wearing her implants than she does when they're on, I would have said yes. Now, I'm man enough to admit I don't give a fuck what Isaac Holt thinks. He isn't anyone I'm out to impress, so why not let him think he has one over me, where, in reality, he's helping me?

"All right. Release the info."

"Yeah?" Grayson double-checks, stunned I agreed with his idea.

"Yeah." As a grin tugs on my lips, I add, "Can you just give me a few hours. I've got plans today I don't want ruined when the news breaks."

Grayson sounds pleased when he replies, "I'll keep everything on the burner until you give me the green light." With the tension keeping his back straight slackened, he slouches low into his chair. How do I know this if we're talking over the phone? I heard his chair creak. "I think this will work well for us, punk. It isn't kosher, but when has anything we've ever done been kosher?"

His reply has a double meaning, but you won't unearth what it is until *after* I've ensured every inch of Melody is clean. I'm the one who made her all sticky, so shouldn't I be the one who ensures she's thoroughly cleaned?

"Call me in a couple of hours, then we'll go over the best way to have Isaac unknowingly working for us."

I hear Grayson's cheeks incline into a smile. "Will a couple of hours be long enough, punk?"

My lips crack into a true and genuine smile. They're more and more often these days. "Probably not, but since I've got a lifetime of hours at the ready, I'll take what I can get."

Pride projects in Grayson's voice. It's barely heard over his chuckles. "Tell your girl I said hello... maybe not while cleaning her insides with your sausage, though. Don't want her accidentally shouting my name."

"Grayson..."

His chuckles pick up, loving that I fell straight into his trap. "I'm joking, punk. Have fun."

His laughter rings in my ears long after he disconnects our call, only weakening when the beat of my heart overtakes it. Fear isn't responsible for the spike in my pulse, it's realizing happiness is guiding my motives this morning instead of worry.

"*Melody*," I say with a stomp before pushing open the partially cracked bathroom door. The mirror is foggy from how hot she likes her showers, but no amount of steam has me missing her smile when our eyes collide. "*Can I come in?*"

When she nods without hesitation, I enter the bathroom, removing my shirt as I go. My chest swells with smugness when Melody drags her hand across the misty glass to improve her view.

As I remove my sleeping pants, she stares at me with hungry eyes, hardening my cock to the point it's painful.

Once my boxer shorts are kicked to the side, she opens the door, welcoming me into the steamy space with a blistering smile. Upon noticing an open shampoo bottle on the bathroom shelf, I gather up the conditioner before squirting a generous amount into my palm. For years I thought I was trained to protect, honor, obey, and serve Melody, but only the past few months have I realized I had planned to do those things long before I pinkie promised her father.

When Melody galloped down the stairs of her family ranch with a mouth full of toothpaste and a foamy smile, I didn't even know her name, but I knew I'd love her for eternity. That's why I trained so hard and never gave up. And that is why I'll condition her hair even with my erect cock keeping a good distance between us.

Intimacy isn't purely physical, it's about being open, honest, and free. Seeing someone's bad flaws and still loving them despite them, and being so deeply connected to someone that you feel like you see their soul in their eyes any time you look at them, confirms those intimate feelings.

That's what Melody and I have. We're best friends, lovers, and soul mates. And once all is said and done, I'm also hoping she'll be my wife.

BRANDON

"Looky here, looky here, the goody-two-shoes son came to pay his evil brother a visit." Madden's tone is way too cocky for my liking. He's shackled, wearing an orange jumpsuit and being guided down the hall by a man with biceps as big as his head, yet he still thinks he has the world at his feet. What can I say? You can't change arrogance.

"What's up, BJ? Daddy's tenancies finally rubbing off on you." Since his hands are cuffed at his front, he has no issues grabbing his cock to get across his point. "I've got a list of names longer than my arm. What's your preference? Do you want a screamer? Or a woman who's as quiet as a mouse…" He slants his head as his smirk doubles, "… just like your girl was. Didn't murmur one motherfucking peep when I flipped her over and rode her hard from behind."

He thinks he's safe from prosecution because he was found not guilty of raping Melody.

He's dead fucking wrong.

A nervous twitch impinges Madden's jaw when I swing my eyes to the guard standing at his side. "That will be all, Kwan. I don't want you caught in the middle of this."

"What the fuck are you doing, Brandon?" Madden mutters in panic when Kwan tosses a set of keys into my chest before he spins on his heels and stalks to the door.

I wait for the locks of an old county house jail to clang into place before I disperse some of the anger thickening my veins onto Madden's jaw. The crack my fist makes with his chin is lyrical gold to my ears as is the thud his head makes with the concrete when he drops like a bag of shit.

After laying my boot into his stomach three times, I stand over a man not worthy of my time. When I take in his bloody chin and already swelling nose, a sense of calm washes over me. I can still smell Melody's heated skin on mine, even with us making love in the shower, and taste her toothpaste on my lips. I've got this. I've got it so fucking good Madden won't know what hit him.

"Why didn't you plead guilty last month, Madden? Thirty-three women came forward to accuse you of rape, yet you're still pleading innocence." My words are growls when I recite how many victims he's amassed the past ten years, sickened we share an ounce of the same blood.

When Madden attempts to prop himself on his elbows, I pin him to the ground by squishing my 'pretty-boy' shoes against his face. I bet he's not thinking they're 'gay man's' shoes now. "Why... didn't you plead... guilty... last month, Madden?" I talk extra slow, ensuring the twists of my foot are felt by Madden's cheek for every word I articulate. It's like his face is a campfire in the middle of a dead bush, and I'm attempting to stub it out.

With Madden's face as screwed up as his morals, his words don't come out as clear as he's hoping. "Why would I plead guilty, fuck-face? I'm *not* guilty, so why pretend I am?"

You'd think his reply would spike my agitation. It has somewhat of the opposite effect. "I figured you'd say that. You've never been one to take responsibility for your fuck-ups, so why would you let thirty-three women say otherwise?"

He coughs and garbles when I remove my shoe from his face, then he grunts when I help him to his feet. His unsteady movements aren't to blame for his breathy response. The opening of the switchblade on my trusty utility knife is what has him panicked.

"How long have you been here again, Madden? Two, three months?"

He doesn't answer me because he knows I've been tracking his whereabouts even more closely than my father has been watching me. My father knows I'm onto him, but since I'm always one step ahead of him, he can't catch me.

"Do you know some prisoners have been here for decades? Some real sick fucks too." As I step closer to Madden, I test the sharpness of the blade on my knife. "Some have been here so long, they no longer care if you've got boy parts or girl parts." His Adam's apple bobs up and down when I mutter, "As long as you're pretty, they'll take you any way they can get you."

As I stand an inch from his face, I drag my blade down his cheek. I don't apply enough pressure to make him bleed. I just tease him with a scratch, making him hopeful I've marked him enough the men getting rowdy in the cell next to us won't find him attractive.

"That's how you like them, isn't it, Madden? Really pretty?"

Not giving him the chance to answer, I drop my hands to the crotch of his jumpsuit to cut a large hole in the material. Once his dick and balls are exposed, it's the fight of my life not to cut them off. The only reason I don't is because I know my plans will hurt Madden more than losing his appendage.

When I walk Madden closer to the cell grunted moans are coming from, he stutters, "BJ... I'm your brother. You can't do this to me—"

"Melody was my girlfriend! She was the love of my life! Yet, that didn't stop you from raping her, did it? You brutalized her to hurt me, so now I get to hurt you." The shackles around his ankles jingle on the floor when I spin him around so I can make his back as accessible as his front. I forgot his cellmates will be eager to have access to both sides of him. "You think rape is a game. That it's your right to take what you want, from who you want, whenever you want?" I press my lips to his ear before whispering, "I wonder if you'll feel the same way once you've been sodomized by men twice your weight and strength."

"Brandon, no, please, I'm begging you, please don't do this," Madden begs on repeat when I drag him to a cell full of the roughest and meanest prisoners Henry could find.

After smashing Madden's face to the cool metal material, I slot a key into the cell's lock, then pull open the heavy-weighted door. Although there's a metal bar jail door separating us from prisoners serving life sentences, they circle the cage door like vultures eager for a fresh piece of meat.

They taunt Madden when his dick shrivels at the sight of them before telling him he has nothing to be afraid of. Big Papa will look after him. He's the giant in the corner of the space, stroking his cock through his half-removed jumpsuit while licking his lips. He's clearly the alpha in the room, and if rumors are true, he gets first dibs even with his compadres being just as big and violent as him.

When I hunt for the key needed to open the bar door separating Madden from his bevy of wannabe lovers, Madden's pleas turn frantic. "Please, BJ. I'll do anything. *Anything* at all. I'll give you my car, my inheritance. I'll take you to fucking Paris." He's crying— *actual* tears, full-on snot bubble blubbering. "Please!" he screams, shattering my eardrums when I find the right key. "I can't go in there. I won't survive."

"Don't be dramatic. You'll survive. Big Papa is a giant teddy bear. He loves his little ones so much, he *never* lets them go." The innuendo in my tone ensures he can't mistake my reply. I'm not implying Big Papa will go easy on him. It's quite the opposite, actually. Rumors are once you've been claimed by Big Papa, you remain his property, only being loaned out when he wants another 'little bird' to lay in his nest.

When I slot the key into the lock, the words I've been dying to hear Madden say for months roar through my ears, "I'll admit to raping Melody. I will plead guilty. I'll do anything you want me to do as long as you don't make me go in there." He snaps his eyes to mine, his chin quivering. "Please, Brandon. I'm begging you." He falls to his knees to authenticate his claims. It makes the men inside the cage more desperate for me to ignore his begs. His mouth is now directly lined up with their cocks. "Why won't you believe me?" he wails when I twist the key.

"Why would I believe you, Madden? You've done nothing but lie to me my entire life, so you don't deserve my trust."

His eyes float up and to the left when he endeavors to find a way to convince me I can believe him. "I'll tell you where I hid the drugs I slipped into their drinks. It's not even an hour from here. You can test the canister for my prints."

I breathe out slowly, acting pissed about him wasting my time. "It's not enough. I need more."

"Umm..." After drifting his eyes to Big Papa for the quickest second, he returns them to me. "I kept trophies. I have Melody's earring. The one with the opals in them. They're in a jewelry pouch in the hollow of the tree you and Melody got married under when you were kids."

A combined hiss comes out of the holding cell when I grip Madden's sweat-slicked hair in my hand before slamming his head into the steel bar. I've kept my cool long enough. I'm beyond being reasonable now.

"Change your plea to guilty at your trial next month for *all* charges, and publicly apologize to Melody, Gemma, and our mother, then, if I'm satisfied with the judge's ruling, I won't come back here and watch Big Papa make you his bitch." When I yank Madden's head back, blood trickles down his nose and over his lips. "Have I made myself clear, Madden? Or are you still seeing this as a game?"

"You made yourself clear. I-I-I'll plead guilty. I-I-I'll say I'm sorry."

Although it's hard for me to do, I slide the key out of the lock, slip it into my pocket, then stalk down the corridor leaving my rapist brother withering on the floor and crying like a baby.

BRANDON

One month later...

$\mathcal{I}$ slip into the back row of the court chambers just as the bailiff announces Madden's docket is the next to be heard. I haven't seen Madden since the morning I had planned to make him experience what he put Melody and another thirty-two women through. I didn't need to see him again to know he'd follow my demand. Kwan told me it wasn't fear I was smelling when I left Madden kneeling across from men ready to brutalize him. He pissed his pants twice that night.

Even if Madden wanted to deny our exchange ever occurred, evidence doesn't lie. I found the trophies he kept from each rape where he said they'd be. They were positively matched by his victims, and his fingerprints were lifted off seventeen articles of jewelry and clothing. He's going down. I'm just hoping it's sooner than Melody believes.

A smile touches my lips when Melody stands to greet the judge before starting proceedings. Although she's not officially an ADA anymore, her position in the Justice Department is vital. She works closely with detectives of Special Victims Units to ensure evidence is gathered from victims correctly and with dignity before she aids in the prosecution of the criminals responsible for the heinous acts.

In under a year, she's helped place nineteen sexual offenders behind bars and has been the support person for many more victims. I'm sure she finds her work tiring, but the understanding she gives the victims of sexual assault can't be matched by anyone else.

A victim knows a victim.

Before Melody can commence proceedings, Madden's attorney requests to speak on behalf of his client. Since my father is currently indicted to face his own arm-long list of felonies, Madden's lawyer is a fat, balding man with crumbs of potato chips stuck in his knitted vest. "Your Honor, my client has had a change of heart. He wishes to plead guilty to *all* charges."

Melody's gasp is almost drowned out by the many supporters seated behind her. With this being the largest multi-victim rape trial in the country, the chamber is full to the brim with supporters. Even my mom is here, sitting on the prosecution's side of the galley.

I didn't tell Melody about Madden's plan to plead guilty because, in all honesty, I couldn't trust Madden would do the right thing. I'm glad he kept his word, but I still don't trust him. Even from a distance, I can feel arrogance beaming out of him.

"Is that correct, young man? Are you changing your plea to guilty?" the judge asks Madden, his tone shocked. When Madden dips his chin, the judge scoots closer to his podium. "You do understand what that means, don't you? You could be looking at life behind bars."

While licking his cracked lips, Madden nods again. "Yes, Your Honor. I'm aware of my decision. What I did was wrong, and I can only hope you'll show mercy for my admission of guilt."

My jaw tightens when an admired flare darts through the judge's eyes. Even with Madden admitting guilt, he's using his boyish good looks to his advantage. That pisses me the fuck off and proves he still hasn't learned his lesson.

"Very well." The judge sits low in his leather chair before making a tee-pee with his index fingers. "I extensively read the reports drafted by both Ms. Gregg and the District Attorney's Office over the weekend, so I feel confident in issuing a sentence now if neither party objects."

"We're happy with that, Your Honor," assures Madden's lawyer.

After popping his glasses onto his face, the judge shifts his eyes to Melody. "And what says the prosecution, Ms. Gregg?"

"We're also happy for sentencing to occur now, Your Honor," Melody replies, her tone equally shocked and pleased.

"Good." The judge's glasses notch down his nose when he glares at Madden. "I must say, your crimes are both extensive and sickening, Mr. McGee. You lack humility, and you treated your victims as worthless commodities. Not once in my thirty-nine years of office have I read such demoralizing, heartless, and downright nauseating claims. You used your privileged life to escape conviction and seek new victims at every turn without *once* showing remorse."

He peers down at a stack of papers in front of him to check the extent of Madden's charges before continuing, "Your crimes are too broad to offer you the mercy you're seeking, Mr. McGee. So, in saying that, I sentence Madden Vincent McGee to ninety-nine consecutive years behind bars with parole not eligible for the first sixty. Three years for each victim." After banging down his gavel to quieten the sobs of joy breaking across the chambers, the judge says, "You'll be ninety before parole will be considered. Hopefully, by then, you would have matured enough to reflect true sorrow for what you have done."

"All rise," the bailiff requests when the judge stands to his feet.

When the judge breaks through the mahogany stained door at the back of the podium, it's the fight of my life not to throw my fist into the air. I wouldn't hesitate if the faintest buzz of my cell phone in my pocket wasn't stealing my focus. I told Grayson I'd update him as soon as the verdict was handed down. Even he must be growing impatient.

"He got ninety-nine years," I laugh down the line, my words choked by a sob.

"About fucking time," Grayson replies, breathing out in relief. "You did it, punk. You brought the bad guy to justice. How does it feel?"

"It feels good." It takes me a little longer to reply than I care to admit. I'm glad justice has been finally served, but I also understand the judge's stern ruling. Madden pled guilty, but he's yet to express an ounce of remorse for what he has done. He truly doesn't understand what his victims went through because he's never been victimized.

"Hey, Grayson, can I call you back? There's someone I need to talk to."

He makes kissy noises. "Give your girl a kiss for me."

I hang up before his laughter hackles half my nerves. I wasn't referencing Melody when I said there was someone I needed to speak with. It's the man seated in the back of an almost tank-like SUV. It's the same SUV I approached weeks ago when I realized the only way I could get Madden to take blame for what he had done was by scaring him as he had scared his victims.

The Mob has arrived in Saugerties.

As I gallop down the stairs of the courthouse, Henry slides down the heavily-tinted window of his bulletproof ride. He doesn't ask what the verdict was. His face shows he already knows. "Are you happy?"

I shrug, truly unsure how I feel.

I do know one thing, though. I have more power than Madden has ever had, and that is thanks to both Liam and his daughter.

Henry's gleaming smile competes with the midday sun when I ask, "You wouldn't happen to have any influence on who inmates are housed with, would you?"

"Perhaps. Why? Do you have a request?"

As Mr. Gregg's words ring in my head on repeat, I mutter, "Big Papa seemed a little lonely last month. Perhaps Madden could keep him entertained during his transition from citizen to inmate. It may be the only way he'll truly learn from his mistakes."

Henry's smile is as evil as the man he wants you to believe he is. "I'll have Kwan collect earbuds on the way home from his shift this evening. He'll need them by tomorrow afternoon." When the quickest flare of hesitation darts through my eyes, he adds, "It's okay to tiptoe onto the wrong side of the law as long—"

"As I find my way back," I interrupt. Feeling lighter and freer than I've ever felt, I get cheeky. "Have you ever considered taking your brother's advice, Henry?"

His chuckles are as dark as his hair coloring. "Are you sure I haven't already, Brandon James McGee?" After nudging his head behind my shoulder, he commences winding up his window. "Look after her. I don't want to be forced to tie up more loose ends."

I discover who Henry is referencing when Melody's reflection beams off the tinted window of his SUV. She's racing down the stairs as quickly as I did earlier, her face glowing with excitement.

I assume her eagerness to reach me stems from Madden's sentencing, so you can imagine my surprise when she asks, "Why don't you ever answer your phone? Bobby is on his way. He's coming here tonight."

I take a step back, shocked. "Tonight?"

"Yes! Tonight. He's at the airport with Phillipa. She's been calling you nonstop." With my mind shut down, Melody slips her hand around mine before stepping onto the curb to hail a taxi. Our cars are both here, but her eagerness to get to Bobby is too high to contain.

We've been waiting for this day for weeks. Although Ophelia played nice with authorities, she wasn't as amicable with me. She knew Bobby was her only bargaining chip, so she extorted him for all his worth. I doubt any of the child support I've paid the past year has gone toward Bobby's well-being, but when nothing but the care for your child is on your mind, you hand over any amount requested.

"What changed between now and last week?"

Melody shrugs. "I don't know. I was so eager to find you, I hung up on Phillipa." Her grimace is cute as hell. She and Phillipa are friends, but they'll never be best friends. Melody thinks they're too alike for that ever to happen. I kind of agree with her. "Should I call her back?"

When I nod, Melody slides her cell phone out of her pocket and hits the last call on her recently called list, then activates the speaker mode.

Phillipa answers two seconds later. "Did you find him?"

"I'm here. How did you achieve this? I thought custody was months away?"

We have a bad line, but nothing can take away from what Phillipa says next, "Ophelia is being extradited to Italy on undisclosed charges. Bobby is a US citizen. She can't take him with her. We made an agreement that she'd award full custody of Bobby to you on the condition she conducts the handover. She doesn't want Bobby to know she's being arrested."

My gut gurgles more in unease than happiness. "That doesn't sound right, Phillipa. She's being too reasonable. You can't trust her."

"I know, BJ." Her tone isn't as harsh as mine, somewhat understanding. "But I also know what I'm doing. Bobby will *never* leave my sight, and he'll *never* be in any danger. I promise you that."

Her response all but confirms my worries.

They're hoping to use Bobby for a sting.

"I'm not okay with this, Phillipa. I will *not* have my son used more than he already has been."

"BJ—"

"No, Phillipa," I interrupt, shouting. "I will not change my mind about this. If you want to know who Ophelia is working with, you'll have to find a way to do that without using an innocent child as bait."

With Phillipa and me at a stalemate, Melody jumps into the conversation. "Can you change the location of the drop? Henry's men have full coverage of the Upper West Side. Even if Ophelia has arrangements in place, they'll never get through Henry's men." Feeling my unease, Melody drifts her eyes to mine. "Henry values family ties. Bobby is like a son to me, so Henry will keep him safe." She grips my balled hand with the one not clutching her phone. "This may be our only way to free Bobby from his mother's clutches, BJ, so we have to consider all possibilities. If she flees the country with him, we may never get him back."

My knee bobs out my agitation as I contemplate. I don't want Bobby close to harm, but I guess, just like what happened to Melody, I'm too late. He's already in danger.

That doesn't mean I can't protect him from hereon out, though.

A sigh vibrates Phillipa's lips when I say, "We do this my way or not at all."

"Okay," she agrees rather quickly, relieved.

FOUR HOURS and fifty-five minutes later, I'm standing on a cold and windy corner, praying my good fortune of late doesn't come tumbling down. I've worked hard for this. I've put in years of dedicated service, decades of training, and just as many hours of love. You'll never call me cocky, and you'll never see me fanning out peacock feathers and strutting, but I hope you think I'm deserving of happiness.

Bobby is the final piece of the puzzle I've been striving to complete the past year. If today's sting backfires, my life will never be complete. I missed the first five years of Bobby's life, but that doesn't mean I love him any less. Our connection was as immediate as it was when my eyes locked on Melody for the first time. He was weary standing across from the stranger claiming to be his father, but like all five-year-olds, curiosity soon overtook his anxiety.

He asked if I had any other children, if I had ever been to Disney World, and if I lived in a house or an apartment. He was disappointed when I answered no to his first two questions, but his curiosity piqued when I told him about the ranch I grew up on. Unlike Melody, he has a fondness for horses. Although I hadn't lived on the ranch for many years, hours flew by as we talked about all the different adventures he could have on a farm.

Then, out of the blue, he asked if he could visit the ranch one day. I told him I'd love nothing more than for him to visit Saugerties with me. Tonight, I might be able to keep the promise we made that day.

"Breathe out those nerves, punk. You're going to be this boy's hero, so show him that," Grayson mutters in my ear when my nerves almost have me wanting to bend in two.

After breathing out my nerves as suggested, I ask, "Any visual?"

"They've left the hotel on foot. ETA is five minutes."

I lift my chin, aware Grayson would have eyes on me as well. "What about the Sicilian's Henry's men contained earlier today."

"Still holed up in Customs." An ill-timed grin raises my cheeks when he adds, "Those fuckers will be walking funny by the time they're released, Ophelia will be on her way to Milan, and your boy will be heading home with you and your girl." Keys being stroked sound down the line before Grayson mutters, "What the fuck is he doing here?"

"Who?"

Grayson waits a beat before answering, "No one for you to worry about. Focus on your boy. They're moving faster than anticipated, ETA is less than two minutes."

As the click of him changing radio frequency dongs into my ear, I discover the cause for his worry. Isaac and Isabelle Holt are briskly walking down the sidewalk. This is the first time I've seen either of them since they paired with Grayson's team to take down Kirill's

Hopeton operation. Half of me believes they deserve an apology for the things I said in anger that day, but the other half thinks Isaac deserved my wrath.

Bobby isn't his son, but if he were, imagine what his reaction would have been to me placing money into his son's trust fund every month? Even if he were being helpful, he stepped over a line he would have decimated any other men for.

If that isn't a sign of a narcissistic personality, I don't know what is.

My eyes drift from Isaac and Isabelle when Grayson's gruff tone rumbles down the line. "Expect visual in five… four… three… two…" Just as my eyes lock with Bobby's on the other side of the street, Grayson announces to the agents on the end of our feed to prepare for evacuation. Just because members of the Sicilian mob are holed up at Customs doesn't mean we can get sloppy. Tobias taught us better than that.

When Bobby spots my inconspicuous wave for him to run to me, he slips his hand out of Ophelia's grasp and dashes my way. "Daddy!" he shouts at the same time Grayson mutters in my ear, "Move in to secure target, mark removed. Do it quietly."

"Daddy! Daddy! Daddy!" Bobby continues to shout as overwhelmed as me. We haven't been in the same room for months, and I've missed him so much, I'm not ashamed to say tears are burning my eyes.

While Bobby sidesteps a frozen and stunned Isaac and Isabelle halfway down the sidewalk, Phillipa and Harvey slap a piece of duct tape over Ophelia's mouth, throw cuffs on her wrists, then toss a black hood over her head.

"Hey, buddy. Come here. Good job." I pull Bobby in close to my chest before twisting him away from the direction he sprinted to ensure he doesn't witness his mother being placed into the back of a white van mounted at the curb.

As I walk Bobby in the direction of the hotel Melody is waiting for us at, Grayson's deep tone vibrates my eardrum. "Target contained, commencing direct route to LaGuardia." The familiar click of him switching radio signals is heard before he says, "Enjoy your vacation, punk. I'll see you when you get back."

Stealing my chance to thank him for his help, he disconnects our feed just as the white van holding Ophelia darts by us. I can't see anything through the super dark tint, but I can imagine Phillipa's smile. It's as big as mine.

"Mellowy." Bobby breaks away from me when we enter the hotel lobby, eager to reach Melody who's nervously pacing the marble tiles. I'm pleased to say Bobby can't pronounce his D's any better than I did when I was his age.

"*Hi, Bobby,*" Melody signs and speaks at the same time before she bobs down to return his friendly greeting with a big hug. They've only met once and FaceTimed a handful of times, but I'm confident Bobby is as smitten with Melody as I am. "*I can't believe you have finally come to live with us.*"

I run my fingers through Bobby's dark locks when he curls his arm around my thigh before taking in the elaborate foyer. "Is this where you live?" he stutters out with a lisp.

"*No,*" Melody answers on our behalf. "*When your daddy told me you love animals, we moved into a house with lots of paddocks.*" Bobby's pupils expand to the size of saucers when Melody discloses, "*We have pigs, horses, cows, and a dozen chickens. Would you like to go see them?*"

Bobby nods so quickly, I'm certain his brain is rattled. "*Please, Mellowy.*"

Melody's heart melts when he purposely mispronounces her name while signing it as taught, then it completely stops when I join her at Bobby's level. I'm not squatting, though. I'm down on one knee, proposing to a woman who loves my son simply because he's mine.

Furthermore, the ring box has been burning a hole in my pocket all day. I can't wait a second longer.

Bobby slaps a hand over his mouth to hide his smile when I ask, "*Mellowy, will you please do me the honor of becoming my wife?*"

Then he full-heartedly laughs when Melody lifts her hand in the air to wiggle her eaten candy pop ring around. "*Too late.*" After tickling Bobby's belly, making him chuckle more, she cups my scruff-covered jaw in her hands, lowers her mouth to mine, then whispers against my lips, "But I'd love to make it official."

PROLOGUE

Brandon

One year later…

"**W**hat do you think, B? Peanut butter makes it so much better, doesn't it?"

Bobby drags a hand over his peanut-butter-chocolate-milkshake stained lips before nodding. "Mommy was right. It's good to try new things."

Melody is quick to wipe away the tear Bobby's reply dribbled down her cheek, but she isn't quick enough for me to miss it. The first two weeks Bobby was with us flew by without a single hiccup. Regretfully, he started missing his mother shortly after that. He couldn't understand why he couldn't ring her or why she never accepted his invitations to visit when he wrote to her like Melody suggested.

Although dislike never flared through his eyes when he took his anger out on the wrong person, I felt Melody's struggles when he told her she wasn't his mother and that he never wanted her to be.

Mercifully, that stage of his anguish only lasted a few weeks. Melody was kind, open, and honest with Bobby. She never lied to him when he asked her questions, and she said she understood his pain. She had lost her parents, so she truly knew what he was going through.

Around three months after we moved Bobby into Melody's old childhood bedroom, Bobby asked Melody if they could paint his room. A fresh coat of paint soon turned into a mini-renovation. His bunk bed now resembles a jungle-gym, and the hand-painted decals Melody and Bobby painted on the walls glow in the dark when you switch off the light.

Although things were still a little awkward the weeks following the makeover, Melody never gave up on Bobby. She showed him how to mount Socks even with her being scared shitless to do it herself, and they've been witnessed many times having bounce competitions on Bobby's springless trampoline he got from Santa. She's even taught him how to sign.

Her efforts have paid off. Today wasn't the first time Bobby has called her mommy. He's dropped it a handful of times the past month like he's testing out how it feels in preparation for when his sister joins our family in just over three months time.

Melody is beautiful as she is, but the glow of her face during pregnancy is better than I could have ever imagined. She truly is brave and so very *very* pretty.

I stop halfway down the sidewalk of Mary's Café when Bobby's hand suddenly slips out of my hold. When he darts down the cracked concrete as quickly as he did a year ago, he sends my mind into a tailspin.

I have no reason to panic. He's not sprinting for his mother, he's racing for a tiny stuffed rabbit that looks in bad need of repair.

"Here, you dropped it," he says to a little girl with raven hair and big blue eyes. When he thrusts the grubby toy toward the girl, she doubles the clutch on her mother's thigh before cowering away from him. "It's okay," he tells her with a stutter. "I won't hurt you."

My eyes drift to Melody when Bobby's simple reassurance causes the girl to slowly move out of her hiding spot. Her hand rattles when she accepts her beloved rabbit from Bobby's clutch before she signs the quickest, *"Thank you."*

Melody's smile is as large as Bobby's when he replies, *"You are welcome."*

He waits for the girl I'd guess to be around five or six to continue walking down the sidewalk with her mother before he returns to my side. I'm so shocked by his naturally engrained protective instincts, I'm lost for words, so instead of prompting him about it, I guide him to our car parked a few spots down, smiling.

BOBBY'S EXCHANGE with the unnamed girl is still in the forefront of my mind a few weeks later when he joins me in the derelict gym in the back shed of the Greggs' family ranch. With my position at the Bureau being more of a consultant role than an agent, I don't need to keep my fitness at the peak physical condition I once did, but for some reason, I do.

Melody likes the bumps in my midsection, so who am I to take them away from her? Furthermore, her insatiable needs grew tenfold when we found out she was pregnant. I've got to keep my energy up.

I'm not surprised we can't keep our hands off each other. We had eight years of lost time to make up. If Grayson's teases are close to being true, we fixed the injustice within the first six months. Doesn't mean we need to slow down, though. Our daughter is due in two months, so we'll lose more time then, not that Melody will ever agree with that. She's adamant nothing will stop her from having her way with me. I love that about her. She's always been so determined and headstrong.

When I spot a confused crinkle pop between Bobby's brows, my curiosity gets the better of me. "Hey, buddy, what's up? Do you want to go a few rounds with me in the ring?"

My brow cocks when he nods. He's more a video-game-console type of kid than the outdoorsy type.

After suiting him up with my old gear, I pull apart the ropes of the frayed ring Mr. Gregg taught me how to fight in before gesturing for Bobby to enter before me.

I teach him the basics before we go a couple of rounds. All fathers say their kids have natural talent, but I'm not lying when I say Bobby does. He's only seven, but he has enough power behind his swings for me to consider adding extra cushioning to the pads on my hands before our next session.

As sweat dribbles from Bobby's temples to his chin, he lifts his big eyes from his gloves to me. "Can I ask you something?"

While smiling at the cute way he stumbles over his words, I jerk up my chin. His stutter is why Melody taught him how to sign. Now he can express himself any way he likes without being worried he'll be picked on for having a speech impediment. You can talk in many ways—vocalized words are just one of them.

"You can ask me anything, buddy. You know that."

He swishes his tongue around his mouth to loosen up his words before asking, "Can you teach me how to fight?"

"Isn't that what we're doing?" I keep my tone playful, hoping it will ease the tension riddling his adorable face. He didn't look this worried when I told him his mother wouldn't be able to visit him for a very long time. Ophelia was sentenced to fifteen years earlier this year.

Bobby nods, then shrugs. "Kinda, but I want to know how to fight *properly*." I stop prancing around the ring when he mumbles, "Then I can punch Jye Langer in the face."

After stooping down to his level as Melody always does any time they talk, I ask, "Is Jye bullying you?"

"No," he answers immediately with a shake of his head. "But he's mean to Cassidy all the time."

"Who's Cassidy?" When a protective flare darts through his eyes, the truth smacks into me. "She was the little girl with the bunny."

Although I'm not asking a question, Bobby nods as if I am.

"Do you want to protect her, B?"

He nods again. "Yeah. I don't like it when she cries. It makes me sad."

I rustle his sweat-slicked hair, loving the empathy in his eyes. It proves what I've always known—your DNA has nothing to do with your ability to have a caring, loving soul.

After removing a pad from my hand, I quickly clear away a tear sitting high on Bobby's cheek, then ask, "Do you know what's making her upset?"

He fights with all his might to hold in his tears when he answers, "No, but I think I can help her if I know how to fight."

Since there's some truth in his reply, I say, "Okay. I'll teach you how to fight…" His bright smile sags a little when I add, "… but I can't teach you how to properly protect Cassidy if I don't also show you how to take care of yourself. If you're willing to fight for her, B, you've also got to be willing to fight for yourself. Do you think you can handle that?"

He nods his head extremely quick.

"All right, then let's get started." After removing the second protective pad from my hand, I tug off Bobby's gloves before pulling him into my chest. My hug breaks his little heart, but I know better than anyone that it's for the best. "It's okay to cry if you're sad. Just like it's okay to get mad. Don't hold them in, B, or one day you'll crack." He laughs through the tiny sobs breaking free from his throat. "Even when you are protecting, honoring, obeying, and serving, you're still you. Don't ever forget that."

"I won't, Daddy," he replies, hugging me tighter. "I won't ever forget."

As the wetness of his tears soaks my shirt, I remember the words Mr. Gregg spoke to my father many moons ago.

Don't wait until your son is a man to make him great.
Make him great as a boy.

MR. GREGG HAD to take up the challenge for me. Mercifully, Bobby will never face that burden. He's my son, and I'll protect, honor, obey, and serve him as well as I will his mother, his baby sister, and his grandmother. I will love him until the end of time, even on the days it hurts because that's precisely what I've done the past twenty-four years.

The End!

Are alpha males your thing? The Russian Mob Chronicles is a super hot Alpha male series with Nikolai, who was introduced in Rico's book. You can find his first book here: <u>Nikolai: A Mafia Prince Romance</u>

Facebook: facebook.com/authorshandi

Instagram: instagram.com/authorshandi

Email: authorshandi@gmail.com

Reader's Group: bit.ly/ShandiBookBabes

Website: authorshandi.com

Newsletter: https://www.subscribepage.com/AuthorShandi

Rico, Asher, Isaac, Hugo, Hawke, Ryan, Cormack, Enrique & Brax stories have already been released, but Grayson, Julian, Phillipa, and all the other great characters of Ravenshoe will be getting their own stories at some point during 2019/2020.

If you enjoyed this book please leave a review.

MESSAGE FROM THE AUTHOR

Jesus, that was book twenty in the Enigma Series. TWENTY! Like, WTF. I'm so sad this series is now done. We still have many great side characters to explore, but because they're not essentially attached to Isaac and Isabelle, they will not be part of the Enigma Series. That makes me sad, but in a way, I'm also proud.

If you made it this far, you read all twenty of the books in this series. That makes me damn proud of myself. To have people read that many books and not grow bored feels phenomenal. And let's not get me started on if you've read all 42 of my titles or my head might not fit through the door anymore.

I am so humbled by your support. It has been an awesomely crazy four years.

I can't see what the next four years brings.

Talk soon,

Shandi xx

ABOUT THE AUTHOR

Shandi Boyes is a *USA Today* Bestselling Author who was an avid reader for many years before she discovered the love of writing in February 2016. Her first penned novel 'Perception of Life' is a new adult rockstar romance that will have you sitting on the edge of your seat until the very last word. In September 2016, her focus shifted to hot alpha men in steamy contemporary reads that sizzle off the pages.

Shandi's novel 'Enigma' is an award-winning story on an FBI agent and the subject she was assigned to investigate. Her men are swoon-worthy, devoted, and alpha; and her heroines are strong-willed, determined, and loveable. You should start her stories first thing in the morning, or you may not sleep.

You will laugh and you will cry, but Shandi's characters will stay with you for a lifetime!

ALSO BY SHANDI BOYES

Perception Series

Saving Noah (Noah & Emily)

Fighting Jacob (Jacob & Lola)

Taming Nick (Nick & Jenni)

Redeeming Slater (Slater and Kylie)

Saving Emily (Noah & Emily - Novella)

Wrapped Up with Rise Up (Perception Novella - should be read after the Bound Series)

Enigma

Enigma (Isaac & Isabelle #1)

Unraveling an Enigma (Isaac & Isabelle #2)

Enigma The Mystery Unmasked (Isaac & Isabelle #3)

Enigma: The Final Chapter (Isaac & Isabelle #4)

Beneath The Secrets (Hugo & Ava #1)

Beneath The Sheets (Hugo & Ava #2)

Spy Thy Neighbor (Hunter & Paige)

The Opposite Effect (Brax & Clara)

I Married a Mob Boss (Rico & Blaire)

Second Shot (Hawke & Gemma)

The Way We Are (Ryan & Savannah #1)

The Way We Were (Ryan & Savannah #2)

Sugar and Spice (Cormack & Harlow)

Lady In Waiting (Regan & Alex #1)

Man in Queue (Regan & Alex #2)

Couple on Hold(Regan & Alex #3)

Enigma: The Wedding (Isaac and Isabelle)

Silent Vigilante (Brandon and Melody #1)

Hushed Guardian (Brandon & Melody #2)

Quiet Protector (Brandon & Melody #3)

Bound Series

Chains (Marcus & Cleo #1)

Links(Marcus & Cleo #2)

Bound(Marcus & Cleo #3)

Restrain(Marcus & Cleo #4)

Psycho (Dexter & ??)

Russian Mob Chronicles

Nikolai: A Mafia Prince Romance (Nikolai & Justine #1)

Nikolai: Taking Back What's Mine (Nikolai & Justine #2)

Nikolai: What's Left of Me(Nikolai & Justine #3)

Nikolai: Mine to Protect(Nikolai & Justine #4)

Asher: My Russian Revenge (Asher & Zariah)

Nikolai: Through the Devil's Eyes(Nikolai & Justine #5)

Trey (Trey & K)

K: A Trey Sequel

The Italian Cartel

Dimitri

Roxanne

Reign

Mafia Ties (Novella)

Maddox

Demi

Rocco

Clover

Smith

<u>RomCom Standalones</u>

Just Playin' (Elvis & Willow)

<u>Ain't Happenin'</u> (Lorenzo & Skylar)

<u>The Drop Zone</u> (Colby & Jamie)

Very Unlikely (Brand New Couple)

<u>Short Stories</u>

Christmas Trio (Wesley, Andrew & Mallory -- short story)

Falling For A Stranger (Short Story)

<u>Coming Soon</u>

Skitzo

www.ingramcontent.com/pod-product-compliance
Lightning Source LLC
Chambersburg PA
CBHW062310200726

48292CB00006BA/1926